The ADVENTURES IN LITERATURE Program

ADVENTURES FOR READERS: BOOK ONE

Annotated Teacher's Edition
Teacher's Manual
Tests

ADVENTURES FOR READERS: BOOK TWO

Annotated Teacher's Edition
Teacher's Manual
Tests

ADVENTURES IN READING

Annotated Teacher's Edition
Teacher's Manual
Tests

ADVENTURES IN APPRECIATION

Annotated Teacher's Edition
Teacher's Manual
Tests

ADVENTURES IN AMERICAN LITERATURE

Annotated Teacher's Edition
Teacher's Manual
Tests

ADVENTURES IN ENGLISH LITERATURE

Annotated Teacher's Edition
Teacher's Manual
Tests

CURRICULUM AND WRITING

Fannie Safier
Secondary English Editorial Staff
Harcourt Brace Jovanovich, Publishers

Katherine H. Simmons
Formerly Bay High School
Panama City, Florida

Special Adviser
Jerome Smiley
Chairperson Elmont Memorial High School
Coordinator of English for
Sewanhaka Central High School District
New York

ADVENTURES
for Readers Book One

PEGASUS EDITION

HBJ **Harcourt Brace Jovanovich, Publishers**
Orlando San Diego Chicago Dallas

X 38583

ACKNOWLEDGMENTS

For permission to reprint copyrighted material, grateful acknowledgment is made to the following sources:

Andrews and McMeel: From *River Notes: The Dance of Herons* by Barry Holstun Lopez. Copyright © 1979 by Barry Holstun Lopez. All rights reserved.

Elizabeth Barnett: "The Courage That My Mother Had" from *Collected Poems* by Edna St. Vincent Millay. Copyright © 1954 by Norma Millay Ellis. Published by Harper & Row, Publishers, Inc.

T. O. Beachcroft: "The Erne from the Coast" by T. O. Beachcroft. Copyright © 1930; renewed 1966 by T. O. Beachcroft.

Gwendolyn Brooks: "Home" from *The World of Gwendolyn Brooks* by Gwendolyn Brooks. Copyright 1953 by Gwendolyn Brooks Blakely.

Joseph Bruchac III: "Birdfoot's Grampa" by Joseph Bruchac III.

Don Congdon Associates, Inc.: "Luke Baldwin's Vow" by Morley Callaghan from *The Saturday Evening Post*. Copyright © 1947 by Saturday Evening Post; renewed 1974 by Morley Callaghan.

Crown Publishers, Inc.: "When I Was a Boy on the Ranch" by J. Frank Dobie from *Treasury of Best-Loved Stories, Poems, Games, and Riddles from St. Nicholas Magazine,* edited by Henry Steele Commager. Copyright © MCML, © MCMLXVIII by Henry Steele Commager.

The Devin-Adair Company, Inc.: "The Wild Duck's Nest" from *The Game Cock and Other Stories* by Michael McLaverty. Copyright © 1947, 1975 by The Devin-Adair Company.

Dodd, Mead & Company, Inc.: "A School for Foxes" (Retitled: "Animals Go to School") from *The Lost Woods* by Edwin Way Teale. Copyright 1945, 1973 by Edwin Way Teale.

Doubleday & Company, Inc.: "The Reward of Baucis and Philemon" from *The Stories of the Gods and Heroes* by Sally Benson. Copyright 1940 by Sally Benson. "Dogs That Have Known Me" from *Please Don't Eat the Daisies* by Jean Kerr. Copyright © 1957 by Conde Nast Publications, Inc.

Esquire Associates: "The Tiger's Heart" by Jim Kjelgaard from *Esquire,* April 1951. Copyright © 1951 by Esquire Associates.

Farrar, Straus & Giroux, Inc.: From "A Walk to the Jetty" in *Annie John* by Jamaica Kincaid. Copyright © 1983, 1984, 1985 by Jamaica Kincaid. Originally published in *The New Yorker.* "Bad Characters" from *The Collected Stories of Jean Stafford* by Jean Stafford. Copyright © 1934, 1969 by Jean Stafford. Originally published in *The New Yorker.*

Samuel French, Inc.: From Act II, Scene 2 in *The Boy David* by James M. Barrie. Copyright 1936 by James Barrie; copyright (Acting Edition) 1948 by Samuel French, Ltd. "A Sunny Morning" by Serafín and Joaquín Alvarez Quintero, translated by Lucretia Xavier Floyd, arranged by John Garrett Underhill. Copyright 1920 by Lucretia Xavier Floyd; copyright renewed 1947 by Mrs. Geneva Floyd. *CAUTION:* Professionals and amateurs are hereby warned that "A Sunny Morning," being fully protected under the copyright laws of the United States of America, the British Commonwealth countries, including Canada, and the other countries of the Copyright Union, is subject to a royalty. All rights, including professional, amateur, motion picture, recitation, public reading, radio, television and cablevision broadcasting, and the rights of translation into foreign languages, are strictly reserved. Amateurs may produce this play upon payment of a royalty of $15 for the first performance and $10 for each repeat performance, payable one week before the play is to be given, to Samuel French, Inc., 45 West 25th Street, New York, NY 10010 or at 7623 Sunset

Cover: *Knight on Horseback.* English stained glass from the nineteenth century.
Photo: Hans Halberstadt

Back Cover: Greek silver coin from fourth century B.C. Collection of Athena Blackorby
Photo: Benn Mitchell

CRITICAL READERS AND CONTRIBUTORS

Martha Arnold
Indianapolis Public Schools
Indianapolis, Indiana

Craig Bowman
Alameda Junior High School
Denver, Colorado

Todd Church
Walker Middle School
Salem, Oregon

Robert Emerson
Westwood Junior High School
Minneapolis, Minnesota

David England
Louisiana State University
Baton Rouge, Louisiana

Clyde Harrelson
McKinley Middle Magnet School
Baton Rouge, Louisiana

Billy Joe Jacob
Hartman Middle School
Houston, Texas

Grace N. Lomba
Lawless High School
New Orleans, Louisiana

Victoria M. Meister
Sycamore Junior High School
Cincinnati, Ohio

Michael Michelozzi
Millwood Junior High School
Kalamazoo, Michigan

Sherry Nabors
Richardson, Texas

Florence Schoenfeld
Division of Curriculum and Instruction
Brooklyn, New York

Kathleen Seaburg
Cherokee Middle School
Scottsdale, Arizona

Thomas C. Shea
Middle Island Junior High School
Middle Island, New York

CONTENTS

Part One THEMES IN LITERATURE

REFLECTIONS

FAMILY ALBUM

THE NATURAL WORLD

Part Two FORMS OF LITERATURE

SHORT STORIES

DRAMA

NONFICTION

POETRY

Part Three LITERARY HERITAGE

NORSE MYTHOLOGY

FABLES

WRITING ABOUT LITERATURE

PART I

THEMES IN LITERATURE

CLOSE READING
OF A SELECTION

Developing Skills in Critical Thinking

When you read a chapter in a social studies or science textbook, you read primarily to get the facts. Your purpose may be to find out how a bill proposed in Congress becomes a law or to understand how bats capture their prey by using sonar. You read chiefly to gather information that is stated *directly* on the page.

Reading literature calls for more than understanding what all the words mean and getting the facts straight. Much of the meaning of a work may be stated *indirectly*. For example, a writer may not *tell* you directly that a character has courage. However, by having that character face up to some difficult or dangerous situation the writer may *show* you that the character is brave. In other words, when you read literature, you depend a good deal on *inference,* drawing conclusions from different kinds of evidence. To read literature critically and grasp its meaning, you have to be an active reader, aware of *what* the author is doing, *how* the author is doing it, and *why.*

A skillful reader cooperates with an author, following the development of characters and ideas, predicting actions, drawing connections between events, responding to language, and seeking to understand the author's purpose. The skillful reader also judges literature, determining whether characters are believable and whether their actions are consistent, or whether the ending of a story follows logically from everything that has gone before.

In the following selection a well-known American writer tells about one of the experiences that helped to shape her imagination. As you read, ask yourself how Eudora Welty transforms a commonplace event—a ride on a train—into a vivid and interesting narrative. Use the notes alongside the selection to guide you in your reading. Then turn to the analysis on page 6.

FROM
One Writer's Beginnings

EUDORA WELTY

I had the window seat. Beside me, my father checked the progress of our train by moving his finger down the timetable and springing open his pocket watch. He explained to me what the position of the arms of the semaphore[1] meant; before we were to pass through a switch we would watch the signal lights change. Along our track, the mileposts could be read; he read them. Right on time by Daddy's watch, the next town sprang into view, and just as quickly was gone.

Side by side and separately, we each lost ourselves in the experience of not missing anything, of seeing everything, of knowing each time what the blows of the whistle meant. But of course it was not the same experience: what was new to me, not older than ten, was a landmark to him. My father knew our way mile by mile; by day or by night, he knew where we were. Everything that changed under our eyes, in the flying countryside, was the known world to him, the imagination to me. Each in our own way, we hungered for all of this: my father and I were in no other respect or situation so congenial.[2]

In Daddy's leather grip was his traveler's drinking cup, collapsible; a lid to fit over it had a ring to carry it by; it traveled in a round leather box. This treasure would be brought out at my request, for me to bear to the water cooler at the end of the Pullman

What is the importance of this contrast?

1. **semaphore** (sĕm′ə-fôr′, -fōr′): a signaling apparatus with mechanically moving arms.
2. **congenial** (kən-jēn′yəl): agreeable; compatible.

car, fill to the brim, and bear back to my seat, to drink water over its smooth lip. The taste of silver could almost be relied on to shock your teeth.

`After dinner in the sparkling dining car, my father and I walked back to the open-air observation platform at the end of the train and sat on the folding chairs placed at the railing. We watched the sparks we made fly behind us into the night. Fast as our speed was, it gave us time enough to see the rose-red cinders turn to ash, each one, and disappear from sight. Sometimes a house far back in the empty hills showed a light no bigger than a star. The sleeping countryside seemed itself to open a way through for our passage, then close again behind us.

The swaying porter would be making ready our berths for the night, pulling the shade down just so, drawing the green fish-net hammock across the window so the clothes you took off could ride along beside you, turning down the tight-made bed, standing up the two snowy pillows as high as they were wide, switching on the eye of the reading lamp, starting the tiny electric fan—you suddenly saw its blades turn into gauze and heard its insect murmur; and drawing across it all the pair of thick green theaterlike curtains—billowing, smelling of cigar smoke—between which you would crawl or dive headfirst to button them together with yourself inside, to be seen no more that night.

When you lay enclosed and enwrapped, your head on a pillow parallel to the track, the rhythm of the rail clicks pressed closer to your body as if it might be your heart beating, but the sound of the engine seemed to come from farther away than when it carried you in daylight. The whistle was almost too far away to be heard, its sound wavering back from the engine over the roofs of the

What precise details make this memory vivid? How many senses does Welty appeal to?

Which words give exact descriptions of sights, smells, and sounds? What imaginative comparisons does Welty use?

How is she surrounded by sounds during the night?

cars. What you listened for was the different sound that ran under you when your own car crossed on a trestle, then another sound on an iron bridge; a low or a high bridge— each had its pitch, or drumbeat, for your car.

Riding in the sleeper rhythmically lulled me and waked me. From time to time, waked suddenly, I raised my window shade and looked out at my own strip of the night. Sometimes there was unexpected moonlight out there. Sometimes the perfect shadow of our train, with our car, with me invisibly included, ran deep below, crossing a river with us by the light of the moon. Sometimes the encroaching[3] walls of mountains woke me by clapping at my ears. The tunnels made the train's passage resound like the "loud" pedal of a piano, a roar that seemed to last as long as a giant's temper tantrum.

What comparisons does Welty use to convey the force and intensity of these sounds?

But my father put it all into the frame of regularity, predictability, that was his fatherly gift in the course of our journey. I saw it going by, the outside world, in a flash. I dreamed over what I could see as it passed, as well as over what I couldn't. Part of the dream was what lay beyond, where the path wandered off through the pasture, the red clay road climbed and went over the hill or made a turn and was hidden in trees, or toward a river whose bridge I could see but whose name I'd never know. A house back at its distance at night showing a light from an open doorway, the morning faces of the children who stopped still in what they were doing, perhaps picking blackberries or wild plums, and watched us go by—I never saw with the thought of their continuing to be there just the same after we were out of sight. For now, and for a long while to come, I was proceeding in fantasy.

How was her imagination stimulated by the journey?

3. **encroaching** (ĕn-krōch′əng): advancing.

Analysis

Writers often draw upon their personal experiences in both fictional and nonfictional works. In this narrative from a book of memoirs, Eudora Welty recalls a journey she took when she was ten years old. For her, as a child, the train journey was a voyage of the imagination, and as she sets down her memories of the trip, we can see how the writer absorbs experience and then re-creates it.

Welty conveys her childhood thoughts and sensations convincingly; we share the sense of newness and wonder she experienced on her first train ride. She recalls her fascination with a collapsible drinking cup, a "treasure" that she can still visualize clearly, even to the detail of its traveling case. Similarly, she can recall precisely what her sleeping berth looked like: the color of the hammock, the "eye" of the reading lamp, the snowy pillows. She remembers the whirring sound of the fan, like an "insect murmur," and the smell of the curtains. She re-creates the child's experience of sounds, using comparisons that would occur to a child. As the train passes through tunnels, the sound reverberates like the "loud" piano pedal and lasts "as long as a giant's temper tantrum."

Unlike her father, who took comfort in what was familiar and predictable, Welty, as a child, needed to proceed "in fantasy," to dream about what she could see and what lay beyond. Her narrative shows that writers do not need extraordinary experiences to stimulate their imaginations—there is ample material in everyday, ordinary events.

With practice you can develop skill in reading and analyzing a literary work. Here are some guidelines to follow.

Guidelines for Close Reading

1. *Read for pleasure and for meaning.* Part of the enjoyment of reading good literature is thinking about it and sharing your thoughts with others.

2. *Read at a comfortable pace.* Gather in and appreciate details of narrative and style.

3. *Look up unfamiliar words and phrases.* Try to get the meaning of unfamiliar words and expressions from context, and then check the meaning in a dictionary.

4. *Read poetry aloud.* Your pleasure in poetry will be enhanced by listening to its sound.

5. *Take note of any interesting comparisons or unusual associations.* Be aware of language that appeals to your senses and comparisons that suggest imaginative relationships.

6. *Read actively, asking questions as you read.* Respond to clues and draw inferences from them. At the opening of her narrative, Welty contrasts her father's reactions to the countryside with her own reactions. This contrast is important and serves as a signal to the reader.

7. *Determine the author's overall purpose or the underlying meaning of the selection.* Try to phrase this idea in a sentence or two, in this fashion: *In this narrative, Eudora Welty shows how her imagination was fed by the ordinary experiences of a train ride.*

In the first section of this anthology, you will find that selections have been grouped according to certain thematic ideas. In the first unit, *Reflections*, each selection deals with a different aspect of growing up. These selections show young people in a variety of roles, both serious and comic, as they face up to challenges and decisions. In the second unit, *Family Album*, the selections include portraits of family members and stories about family relationships. In the third unit, *The Natural World*, all selections deal with the ways human beings have reacted to other living things and to the earth.

In reading a group of selections dealing with a similar theme, you have opportunity to explore an idea in depth and to compare and contrast characters and situations. Instead of a single point of view, you have many different perspectives that allow you to draw your own conclusions about a subject.

REFLECTIONS

It is natural for you to respond to the characters in a story as you would to real people. As you read, you gather impressions and form opinions of them. You may decide you like certain characters and dislike others. You may find yourself judging the characters' actions, approving or disapproving of what they do.

All the selections in this unit are about young people who are forming an idea of themselves as individuals. Sometimes the characters are moody and confused, and uncertain of how to handle their problems. At other times they show insight into themselves and others, and act with courage and determination.

Some of the experiences you read about in this unit may be familiar to you. You may even recognize yourself in some of the characters you meet.

Mrs. Chase in Prospect Park by William Merritt Chase. Oil on panel.
The Metropolitan Museum of Art, The Chester Dale Collection

FROM
A Walk to the Jetty

JAMAICA KINCAID

In this selection the narrator is about to leave her island home in the West Indies. She shares with us her thoughts about growing up. Note how she passes through the years of her life, carefully selecting specific incidents and recalling people and places in precise detail. What impression do you get of the narrator from her recollections?

My mother had arranged with a stevedore to take my trunk to the jetty ahead of me. At ten o'clock on the dot, I was dressed, and we set off for the jetty. An hour after that, I would board a launch that would take me out to sea, where I then would board the ship. Starting out, as if for old time's sake and without giving it a thought, we lined up in the old way: I walking

between my mother and my father. I loomed way above my father and could see the top of his head. We must have made a strange sight: a grown girl all dressed up in the middle of a morning, in the middle of the week, walking in step in the middle between her two parents, for people we didn't know stared at us. It was all of half an hour's walk from our house to the jetty, but I was passing through most of the years of my life. We passed by the house where Miss Dulcie, the seamstress that I had been apprenticed to for a time, lived, and just as I was passing by, a wave of bad feeling for her came over me, because I suddenly remembered that the months I spent with her all she had me do was sweep the floor, which was always full of threads and pins and needles, and I never seemed to sweep it clean enough to please her. Then she would send me to the store to buy buttons or thread, though I was only allowed to do this if I was given a sample of the button or thread, and then she would find fault even though they were an exact match of the samples she had given me. And all the while she said to me, "A girl like you will never learn to sew properly, you know." At the time, I don't suppose I minded it, because it was customary to treat the first-year apprentice with such scorn, but now I placed on the dustheap of my life Miss Dulcie and everything that I had had to do with her.

We were soon on the road that I had taken to school, to church, to Sunday school, to choir practice, to Brownie meetings, to Girl Guide meetings, to meet a friend. I was five years old when I first walked on this road unaccompanied by someone to hold my hand. My mother had placed three pennies in my little basket, which was a duplicate of her bigger basket, and sent me to the chemist's shop[1] to buy a pennyworth of senna leaves, a pennyworth of eucalyptus leaves, and a pennyworth of camphor. She then instructed me on what side of the road to walk, where to make a turn, where to cross, how to look carefully before I crossed, and if I met anyone that I knew to politely pass greetings and keep on my way. I was wearing a freshly ironed yellow dress that had printed on it scenes of acrobats flying through the air and

___
1. **chemist's shop:** a pharmacy.

swinging on a trapeze. I had just had a bath, and after it, instead of powdering me with my baby-smelling talcum powder, my mother had, as a special favor, let me use her own talcum powder, which smelled quite perfumy and came in a can that had painted on it people going out to dinner in nineteenth-century London and was called Mazie. How it pleased me to walk out the door and bend my head down to sniff at myself and see that I smelled just like my mother. I went to the chemist's shop, and he had to come from behind the counter and bend down to hear what it was that I wanted to buy, my voice was so little and timid then. I went back just the way I had come, and when I walked into the yard and presented my basket with its three packages to my mother, her eyes filled with tears and she swooped me up and held me high in the air and said that I was wonderful and good and that there would never be anybody better. If I had just conquered Persia, she couldn't have been more proud of me.

We passed by our church—the church in which I had been christened and received and had sung in the junior choir. We passed by a house in which a girl I used to like and was sure I couldn't live without had lived. Once, when she had mumps, I went to visit her against my mother's wishes, and we sat on her bed and ate the cure of roasted, buttered sweet potatoes that had been placed on her swollen jaws, held there by a piece of white cloth. I don't know how, but my mother found out about it, and I don't know how, but she put an end to our friendship. Shortly after, the girl moved with her family across the sea to somewhere else. We passed the doll store, where I would go with my mother when I was little and point out the doll I wanted that year for Christmas. We passed the store where I bought the much-fought-over shoes I wore to church to be received in. We passed the bank. On my sixth birthday, I was given, among other things, the present of a sixpence.[2] My mother and I then went to this bank, and with the sixpence I opened my own savings account. I was given a little gray book with my name in big letters on it, and in the balance column it said "6d."[3] Every Saturday morning after that, I was given a sixpence—later a shilling, and later a two-and-sixpence piece—and I would take it to the bank for deposit. I had never been allowed to withdraw even a farthing[4] from my bank account until just a few weeks before I was to leave; then the whole account was closed out, and I received from the bank the sum of six pounds ten shillings and two and a half pence.

2. **sixpence:** in British money, a former coin worth six pennies. The basic unit of money is the pound, now equal to 100 new pence. The shilling was worth one-twentieth of the pound.
3. **6d:** the letter *d* stands for "penny."
4. **farthing:** a former British coin worth one-fourth of a penny.

We passed the office of the doctor who told my mother three times that I did not need glasses, that if my eyes were feeling weak a glass of carrot juice a day would make them strong again. This happened when I was eight. And so every day at recess I would run to my school gate and meet my mother, who was waiting for me with a glass of juice from carrots she had just grated and then squeezed, and I would drink it and then run back to meet my chums. I knew there was nothing at all wrong with my eyes, but I had recently read a story in *The Schoolgirl's Own Annual* in which the heroine, a girl a few years older than I was then, cut such a figure to my mind with the way she was always adjusting her small, round, horn-rimmed glasses that I felt I must have a pair exactly like them. When it became clear that I didn't need glasses, I began to complain about the glare of the sun being too much for my eyes, and I walked around with my hands shielding them—especially in my mother's

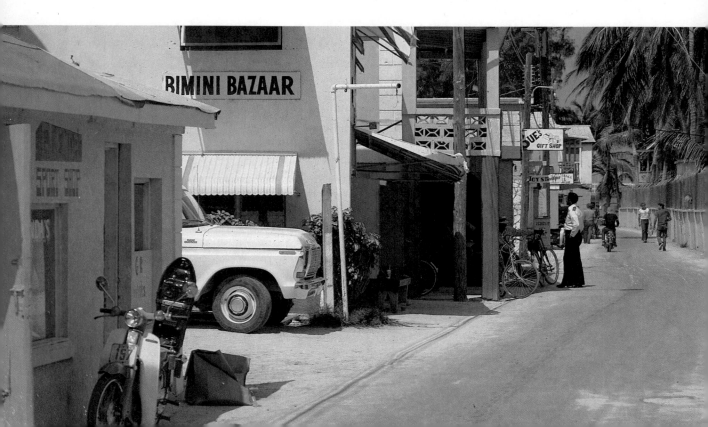

presence. My mother then bought for me a pair of sunglasses with the exact horn-rimmed frames I wanted, and how I enjoyed the gestures of blowing on the lenses, wiping them with the hem of my uniform, adjusting the glasses when they slipped down my nose, and just removing them from their case and putting them on. In three weeks, I grew tired of them and they found a nice resting place in a drawer, along with some other things that at one time or another I couldn't live without.

We passed the store that sold only grooming aids, all imported from England. This store had in it a large porcelain dog—white, with black spots all over and a red ribbon of satin tied around its neck. The dog sat in front of a white porcelain bowl that was always filled with fresh water, and it sat in such a way that it looked as if it had just taken a long drink. When I was a small child, I would ask my mother, if ever we were near this store, to please take me to see the dog, and I would stand in front of it, bent over slightly, my hands resting on my knees, and stare at it and stare at it. I thought this dog more beautiful and more real than any actual dog I had ever seen or any actual dog I would ever see. I must have outgrown my interest in the dog, for when it disappeared I never asked what became of it. We passed the library, and if there was anything on this walk that I might have wept over leaving, this most surely would have been the thing. My mother had been a member of the library long before I was born. And since she took me everywhere with her when I was quite little, when she went to the library she took me along there, too. I would sit in her lap very quietly as she read books that she did not want to take home with her. I could not read the words yet, but just the way they looked on the page was interesting to me. Once, a book she was reading had a large pic-

ture of a man in it, and when I asked her who he was she told me that he was Louis Pasteur and that the book was about his life. It stuck in my mind, because she said it was because of him that she boiled my milk to purify it before I was allowed to drink it, that it was his idea, and that that was why the process was called pasteurization. One of the things I had put away in my mother's old trunk in which she kept all my childhood things was my library card. At that moment, I owed sevenpence in overdue fees.

As I passed by all these places, it was as if I were in a dream, for I didn't notice the people coming and going in and out of them, I didn't feel my feet touch ground, I didn't even feel my own body—I just saw these places as if they were hanging in the air, not having top or bottom, and as if I had gone in and out of them all in the same moment. The sun was bright; the sky was blue and just above my head. We then arrived at the jetty.

My heart now beat fast, and no matter how hard I tried, I couldn't keep my mouth from falling open and my nostrils from spreading to the ends of my face. My old fear of slipping between the boards of the jetty and falling into the dark-green water where the dark-green eels lived came over me. When my father's stomach started to go bad, the doctor had recommended a walk every evening right after he ate his dinner. Sometimes he would take me with him. When he took me with him, we usually went to the jetty, and there he would sit and talk to the night watchman about cricket[5] or some other thing that didn't interest me, because it was not personal; they didn't talk about their wives, or their children, or their parents, or about any of their likes and dislikes.

5. **cricket:** a game played with ball, bats, and wire arches called *wickets*.

They talked about things in such a strange way, and I didn't see what they found funny, but sometimes they made each other laugh so much that their guffaws would bound out to sea and send back an echo. I was always sorry when we got to the jetty and saw that the night watchman on duty was the one he enjoyed speaking to; it was like being locked up in a book filled with numbers and diagrams and what-ifs. For the thing about not being able to understand and enjoy what they were saying was I had nothing to take my mind off my fear of slipping in between the boards of the jetty.

Now, too, I had nothing to take my mind off what was happening to me. My mother and my father—I was leaving them forever. My home on an island—I was leaving it forever. What to make of everything? I felt a familiar hollow space inside. I felt I was being held down against my will. I felt I was burning up from head to toe. I felt that someone was tearing me

up into little pieces and soon I would be able to see all the little pieces as they floated out into nothing in the deep blue sea. I didn't know whether to laugh or cry. I could see that it would be better not to think too clearly about any one thing. The launch was being made ready to take me, along with some other passengers, out to the ship that was anchored in the sea. My father paid our fares, and we joined a line of people waiting to board. My mother checked my bag to make sure that I had my passport, the money she had given me, and a sheet of paper placed between some pages in my Bible on which were written the names of the relatives—people I had not known existed—with whom I would live in England. Across from the jetty was a wharf, and some stevedores were loading and unloading barges. I don't know why seeing that struck me so, but suddenly a wave of strong feeling came over me, and my heart swelled with a great gladness as the words "I shall never see this again" spilled out inside me. But then, just as quickly, my heart shriveled up and the words "I shall never see this again" stabbed at me. I don't know what stopped me from falling in a heap at my parents' feet.

When we were all on board, the launch headed out to sea. Away from the jetty, the water became the customary blue, and the launch left a wide path in it that looked like a road. I passed by sounds and smells that were so familiar that I had long ago stopped paying any attention to them. But now here they were, and the ever-present "I shall never see this again" bobbed up and down inside me. There was the sound of the seagull diving down into the water and coming up with something silverish in its mouth. There was the smell of the sea and the sight of small pieces of rubbish floating around in it. There were boats filled with fishermen coming in early. There was the sound of their voices as they shouted greetings to each other. There was the hot sun, there was the blue sea, there was the blue sky. Not very far away, there was the white sand of the shore, with the run-down houses all crowded in next to each other, for in some places only poor people lived near the shore. I was seated in the launch between my parents, and when I realized that I was gripping their hands tightly I glanced quickly to see if they were looking at me with scorn, for I felt sure that they must have known of my never-see-this-again feelings. But instead my father kissed me on the forehead and my mother kissed me on the mouth, and they both gave over their hands to me, so that I could grip them as much as I wanted. I was on the verge of feeling that it had all been a mistake, but I remembered that I wasn't a child anymore, and that now when I made up my mind about something I had to see it through. At that moment, we came to the ship, and that was that.

Reading Check

1. Why is the narrator leaving her home?
2. What kind of work did she do for Miss Dulcie, the seamstress?
3. Which of the places she passes does the narrator most regret leaving?
4. What old fear does the narrator experience when she reaches the jetty?

For Study and Discussion

Analyzing and Interpreting the Selection

1. During the walk from her home to the jetty, the narrator passes a number of places associated with pleasant and unpleasant childhood memories. **a.** What does she mean when she says she places Miss Dulcie on the "dustheap" of her life? **b.** What particularly happy memory is associated with the chemist's shop?

2. The narrator recalls some things she once believed she could not live without. Why did she insist on having glasses that she did not need?

3. The narrator says that the one place on her walk that she regrets leaving is the library. What happy memories does she associate with books?

4. What indications are there that the narrator's parents were extremely affectionate and attentive?

5a. What are the narrator's reactions to leaving the island? **b.** How does she finally resolve her conflict?

6a. Do the narrator's recollections of growing up remind you of your own experiences? **b.** At what point in the narrative did you most identify with her?

Literary Elements

Recognizing Unity

A piece of writing is unified when all its parts help to develop a single idea. Any sentence or paragraph that doesn't deal with this idea weakens the unity of the piece.

The selection by Jamaica Kincaid is made up of a series of short recollections. All the memories she chooses to tell are about growing up on her island home. Each separate incident reveals something of the narrator's own feelings and perceptions as a child.

Where does she illustrate the child's limited understanding of the adult world? How does she show us that as a child she was close to her parents? Where does she show herself developing an identity and will of her own?

Language and Vocabulary

Determining Exact Meanings

A *jetty* is a wall-like structure built out into the water, usually to protect a harbor. Consider the following words, which are related in meaning:

wharf
pier
quay (kē)

Are these words exact synonyms for *jetty*? Use a dictionary to determine similarities and differences in meaning.

Descriptive Writing

Using Sensory Details

Through description a writer helps you to use your senses—to see, hear, smell, taste, and feel in your mind. Note how Jamaica Kincaid appeals to the senses in this passage:

I passed by sounds and smells that were so familiar that I had long ago stopped paying any attention to them. . . . There was the sound of the seagull diving down into the water and coming up with something silverish in its mouth. There was the smell of the sea and the sight of small pieces of rubbish floating around in it. There were boats filled with fishermen coming in early. There was the sound of their voices as they shouted greetings to each other. There was the hot sun, there was the blue sea, there was the blue sky. Not very far away, there was the white sand of the shore, with the run-down houses all crowded in next to each other . . .

In a paragraph, describe a setting with which you are familiar.

Prewriting Suggestion: Make a list of the most significant details. Think of effective verbs and modifiers that will appeal to your reader's senses.

For assistance in planning and writing your paper, see the section called *Practice in Reading and Writing* on page 89.

About the Author

Jamaica Kincaid (1949–   )

Jamaica Kincaid was born in St. John's, Antigua, in the West Indies, and she has written many stories about her childhood in the Caribbean. Her stories have appeared in *The New Yorker, Rolling Stone,* and *The Paris Review.* "A Walk to the Jetty" is from the collection of stories called *Annie John.*

The King of Mazy May

JACK LONDON

On August 16, 1896, gold was discovered on Bonanza Creek in the Klondike, a region in the Yukon Territory, Canada, close to Alaska. This discovery led to a gold rush, and in 1897 Jack London went to seek his fortune in the Far North. How does London use his knowledge of the Yukon to make this exciting adventure story believable?

Walt was born a thousand m<u>ile</u>s or so down the Yukon, in a trading post below the Ramparts. After his mother died, his father and he came on up the river, step by step, from camp to camp, till they settled down on the Mazy May Creek in the Klondike country. They and several others had spent much toil and time on the Mazy May, and endured great hardships; the creek, in turn, was just beginning to show up its richness and to reward them for their heavy labor. But with the news of their discoveries, strange men began to come and go through the short days and long nights, and many unjust things they did to the men who had worked so long upon the creek.

Si Hartman had gone away on a moose hunt,

to return and find new stakes driven and his claim jumped. George Lukens and his brother had lost their claims in a like manner, having delayed too long on the way to Dawson[1] to record them. In short, it was an old story, and quite a number of the earnest, industrious prospectors had suffered similar losses.

But Walt Master's father had recorded his claim at the start, so Walt had nothing to fear, now that his father had gone on a short trip up the White River prospecting for quartz. Walt was well able to stay by himself in the cabin, cook his three meals a day, and look after things. Not only did he look after his father's claim, but he had agreed to keep an eye on the adjoining one of Loren Hall, who had started for Dawson to record it.

Loren Hall was an old man, and he had no dogs, so he had to travel very slowly. After he had been gone some time, word came up the river that he had broken through the ice at Rosebud Creek, and frozen his feet so badly that he would not be able to travel for a couple of weeks. Then Walt Masters received the news that old Loren was nearly all right again, and about to move on afoot for Dawson, as fast as a weakened man could.

Walt was worried, however; the claim was liable to be jumped at any moment because of this delay, and a fresh stampede had started in on the Mazy May. He did not like the looks of the newcomers, and one day, when five of them came by with crack dog teams and the lightest of camping outfits, he could see that they were prepared to make speed, and resolved to keep an eye on them. So he locked up the cabin and followed them, being at the same time careful to remain hidden.

He had not watched them long before he was sure that they were professional stampeders, bent on jumping all the claims in

1. **Dawson** (dô′sən): city which became the center of the Klondike mining region.

sight. Walt crept along the snow at the rim of the creek and saw them change many stakes, destroy old ones, and set up new ones.

In the afternoon, with Walt always trailing on their heels, they came back down the creek, unharnessed their dogs, and went into camp within two claims of his cabin. When he saw them make preparations to cook, he hurried home to get something to eat himself, and then hurried back. He crept so close that he could hear them talking quite plainly, and by pushing the underbrush aside he could catch occasional glimpses of them. They had finished eating and were smoking around the fire.

"The creek is all right, boys," a large, black-bearded man, evidently the leader, said, "and I think the best thing we can do is to pull out tonight. The dogs can follow the trail; besides, it's going to be moonlight. What say you?"

"But it's going to be beastly cold," objected one of the party. "It's forty below zero now."

The leader said, "If we can get to Dawson and record, we're rich men; and there is no telling who's been sneaking along in our tracks, watching us, and perhaps now off to give the alarm. The thing for us to do is to rest the dogs a bit, and then hit the trail as hard as we can. What do you say?"

Evidently the men had agreed with their leader, for Walt Masters could hear nothing but the rattle of the tin dishes which were being washed. Peering out cautiously, he could see the leader studying a piece of paper. Walt knew what it was at a glance—a list of all the unrecorded claims on Mazy May. Any man could get these lists by applying to the gold commissioner at Dawson.

"Thirty-two," the leader said, lifting his face to the men. "Thirty-two isn't recorded, and this is thirty-three. Come on; let's take a look at it. I saw somebody had been working on it when we came up this morning."

Three of the men went with him, leaving

one to remain in camp. Walt crept carefully after them till they came to Loren Hall's shaft. One of the men went down and built a fire on the bottom to thaw out the frozen gravel, while the others built another fire on the dump and melted water in a couple of gold pans. This they poured into a piece of canvas stretched between two logs, used by Loren Hall in which to wash his gold.

In a short time a couple of buckets of dirt were sent up by the man in the shaft, and Walt could see the others grouped anxiously about their leader as he proceeded to wash it. When this was finished, they stared at the broad streak of black sand and yellow gold grains on the bottom of the pan, and one of them called excitedly for the man who had remained in camp to come. Loren Hall had struck it rich, and his claim was not yet recorded. It was plain that they were going to jump it.

Walt lay in the snow, thinking rapidly. He was only a boy, but in the face of the threatened injustice against old lame Loren Hall he felt that he must do something. He waited and watched, with his mind made up, till he saw the men begin to square up new stakes. Then he crawled away till out of hearing, and broke into a run for the camp of the stampeders. Walt's father had taken their own dogs with him prospecting, and the boy knew how impossible it

Miners weighing gold during the gold rush of 1898.

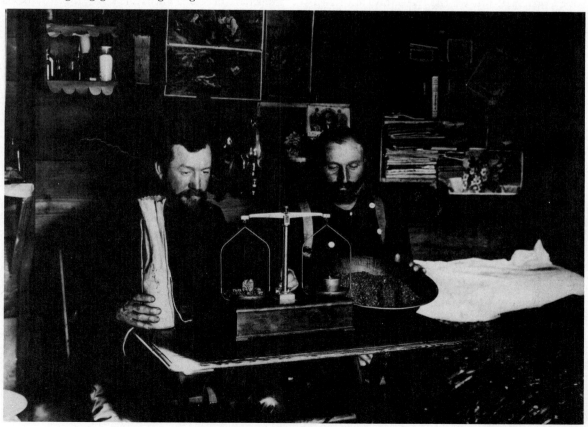

was for him to undertake the seventy miles to Dawson without the aid of dogs.

Gaining the camp, he picked out, with an experienced eye, the easiest running sled and started to harness up the stampeders' dogs. There were three teams of six each, and from these he chose ten of the best. Realizing how necessary it was to have a good head dog, he strove to discover a leader amongst them; but he had little time in which to do it, for he could hear the voices of the returning men. By the time the team was in shape and everything ready, the claim jumpers came into sight in an open place not more than a hundred yards from the trail, which ran down the bed of the creek. They cried out to him, but he gave no heed, grabbing up one of their fur sleeping robes which lay loosely in the snow, and leaping upon the sled.

"Mush! Hi! Mush on!" he cried to the animals, snapping the keen-lashed whip among them.

The dogs sprang against the yoke straps, and the sled jerked under way so suddenly as to almost throw him off. Then it curved into the creek, poising perilously on one runner. He was almost breathless with suspense, when it finally righted with a bound and sprang ahead again. The creek bank was high and he could not see, although he could hear the cries of the men and knew they were running to cut him off. He did not dare to think what would happen if they caught him; he only clung to the sled, his heart beating wildly, and watched the snow rim of the bank above him.

Suddenly, over this snow rim came the flying body of one of the men, who had leaped straight for the sled in a desperate attempt to capture it; but he was an instant too late. Striking on the very rear of it, he was thrown from his feet, backward, into the snow. Yet, with the quickness of a cat, he had clutched the end of the sled with one hand, turned over, and was

dragging behind on his breast, swearing at the boy and threatening all kinds of terrible things if he did not stop the dogs; but Walt cracked him sharply across the knuckles with the butt of the dog whip till he let go.

It was eight miles from Walt's claim to the Yukon—eight very crooked miles, for the creek wound back and forth like a snake, "tying knots in itself," as George Lukens said. And because it was so crooked, the dogs could not get up their best speed, while the sled ground heavily on its side against the curves, now to the right, now to the left.

Travelers who had come up and down the Mazy May on foot, with packs on their backs, had declined to go around all the bends, and instead had made short cuts across the narrow necks of creek bottom. Two of his pursuers had gone back to harness the remaining dogs, but the others took advantage of these short-cuts, running on foot, and before he knew it they had almost overtaken him.

"Halt!" they cried after him. "Stop, or we'll shoot!"

But Walt only yelled the harder at the dogs, and dashed round the bend with a couple of revolver bullets singing after him. At the next bend they had drawn up closer still, and the bullets struck uncomfortably near to him; but at this point the Mazy May straightened out and ran for half a mile as the crow flies. Here the dogs stretched out in their long wolf swing, and the stampeders, quickly winded, slowed down and waited for their own sled to come up.

Looking over his shoulder, Walt reasoned that they had not given up the chase for good, and that they would soon be after him again. So he wrapped the fur robe about him to shut out the stinging air, and lay flat on the empty sled, encouraging the dogs, as he well knew how.

At last, twisting abruptly between two river

Dawson City at the height of the gold rush in 1898.

islands, he came upon the mighty Yukon sweeping grandly to the north. He could not see from bank to bank, and in the quick-falling twilight it loomed a great white sea of frozen stillness. There was not a sound, save the breathing of the dogs, and the churn of the steel-shod sled.

No snow had fallen for several weeks, and the traffic had packed the main-river trail till it was hard and glassy as glare ice.[2] Over this the sled flew along, and the dogs kept the trail fairly well, although Walt quickly discovered that he had made a mistake in choosing the leader. As they were driven in single file, with-

out reins, he had to guide them by his voice, and it was evident the head dog had never learned the meaning of "gee" and "haw."[3] He hugged the inside of the curves too closely, often forcing his comrades behind him into the soft snow, while several times he thus capsized the sled.

There was no wind, but the speed at which he traveled created a bitter blast, and with the thermometer down to forty below, this bit through fur and flesh to the very bones. Aware that if he remained constantly upon the sled he would freeze to death, and knowing the practice of Arctic travelers, Walt shortened up one

2. **glare ice:** ice with a smooth, slippery surface.

3. **gee** (jē): a command to turn to the right or to move ahead; **haw** (hô): a command to turn to the left.

of the lashing thongs, and whenever he felt chilled, seized hold of it, jumped off, and ran behind till warmth was restored. Then he would climb on and rest till the process had to be repeated. Looking back he could see the sled of his pursuers, drawn by eight dogs, rising and falling over the ice hummocks like a boat in a seaway.

Night fell, and in the blackness of the first hour or so, Walt toiled desperately with his dogs. On account of the poor lead dog, they were constantly floundering off the beaten track into the soft snow, and the sled was as often riding on its side or top as it was in the proper way. This work and strain tried his strength sorely. Had he not been in such haste he could have avoided much of it, but he feared the stampeders would creep up in the darkness and overtake him. However, he could hear them occasionally yelling to their dogs, and knew from the sounds that they were coming up very slowly.

When the moon rose he was off Sixty Mile, and Dawson was only fifty miles away. He was almost exhausted, and breathed a sigh of relief as he climbed on the sled again. Looking back, he saw his enemies had crawled up within four hundred yards. At this space they remained, a black speck of motion on the white river breast. Strive as they would, they could not shorten this distance, and strive as he would he could not increase it.

He had now discovered the proper lead dog, and he knew he could easily run away from them if he could only change the bad leader for the good one. But this was impossible, for a moment's delay, at the speed they were running, would bring the men behind upon him.

When he got off the mouth of Rosebud Creek, just as he was topping a rise, the ping of a bullet on the ice beside him, and the report of a gun, told him that they were this time shooting at him with a rifle. And from then on,

as he cleared the summit of each ice jam, he stretched flat on the leaping sled till the rifle shot from the rear warned him that he was safe till the next ice jam.

Now it is very hard to lie on a moving sled, jumping and plunging and yawning like a boat before the wind, and to shoot through the deceiving moonlight at an object four hundred yards away on another moving sled performing equally wild antics. So it is not to be wondered at that the black-bearded leader did not hit him.

After several hours of this, during which, perhaps, a score of bullets had struck about him, their ammunition began to give out and their fire slackened. They took greater care, and only whipped a shot at him at the most favorable opportunities. He was also beginning to leave them behind; the distance slowly increasing to six hundred yards.

Lifting clear on the crest of a great jam off Indian River, Walt Masters met his first accident. A bullet sang past his ears, and struck the bad lead dog.

The poor brute plunged in a heap, with the rest of the team on top of him.

Like a flash, Walt was by the leader. Cutting the traces with his hunting knife, he dragged the dying animal to one side and straightened out the team.

He glanced back. The other sled was coming up like an express train. With half the dogs still over their traces, he cried, "Mush on!" and leaped upon the sled just as the pursuing team dashed abreast of him.

One of the men was just preparing to spring for him—they were so sure they had him that they did not shoot—when Walt turned fiercely upon them with his whip.

He struck at their faces, and men must save their faces with their hands. So there was no shooting just then. Before they could recover from the hot rain of blows, Walt reached out from his sled, catching their wheel dog by the forelegs in midspring, and throwing him heavily. This brought the whole team into a snarl, capsizing the sled and tangling his enemies up beautifully.

Away Walt flew, the runners of his sled fairly screaming as they bounded over the frozen surface. And what had seemed an accident, proved to be a blessing in disguise. The proper lead dog was now to the fore, and he stretched low to the trail and whined with joy as he jerked his comrades along.

By the time he reached Ainslie's Creek, seventeen miles from Dawson, Walt had left his pursuers, a tiny speck, far behind. At Monte Cristo Island he could no longer see them. And at Swede Creek, just as daylight was silvering the pines, he ran plump into the camp of old Loren Hall.

Almost as quick as it takes to tell it, Loren had his sleeping furs rolled up, and had joined Walt on the sled. They permitted the dogs to travel more slowly, as there was no sign of the chase in the rear, and just as they pulled up at the gold commissioner's office in Dawson, Walt, who had kept his eyes open to the last, fell asleep.

And because of what Walt Masters did on this night, the men of the Yukon have become very proud of him, and always speak of him now as the King of Mazy May.

Reading Check

1. Where has Walt Master's father gone?
2. Why is Loren Hall's claim not safe?
3. What are professional stampeders?
4. Why does Walt jump off the sled periodically?
5. What is the only weapon Walt uses?

Analyzing and Interpreting the Story

1a. Why is Walt at first suspicious of the newcomers at Mazy May Creek? **b.** How are his suspicions confirmed?

2. How do the claim jumpers test Loren Hall's mine?

3. How does Walt plan to stop the stampeders from jumping Loren Hall's claim?

4. The chase is the most exciting part of the story. **a.** What difficulties does Walt have in trying to outrace his pursuers? **b.** How do they nearly stop him? **c.** What accident saves him?

5. What details of life in the Yukon does London use to make his story convincing?

Language and Vocabulary

Using the Glossary

At the back of this book, you will find a list of words, together with their pronunciations and meanings, called a *glossary*. The words in this glossary are found in the selections that appear throughout the book. You can use this glossary as you would a dictionary—to find the pronunciations and meanings of words that are unfamiliar to you.

For example, take the word *poising* in this sentence from London's story:

Then it curved into the creek, *poising* perilously on one runner.

If you consult the glossary, you will find this entry for the word *poise*:

poise (poiz) *v.* To balance or steady.—**poised** *adj.*

The abbreviation *v.* tells you that the word *poise*, as used here, is a verb. You probably know that the ending *-ing* represents ongoing action. To get the meaning of *poising,* change the definition to "balancing."

To show how a word is pronounced, a dictionary uses special marks called *diacritical marks.* Accent marks show you which syllables are stressed. Other marks show how vowels are pronounced. In the glossary, the pronunciation of a word is given in parentheses. You can use the pronunciation key at the bottom of each right-hand page to determine which sounds the marks stand for.

Use the glossary to find the pronunciation and meaning of each italicized word in the following sentences from the story.

> Not only did he look after his father's claim, but he had agreed to keep an eye on the *adjoining* one of Loren Hall, who had started for Dawson to record it.

> At last, twisting *abruptly* between two river islands, he came upon the mighty Yukon sweeping grandly to the north.

> On account of the poor lead dog, they were constantly *floundering* off the beaten track into the soft snow, and the sled was as often riding on its side or top as it was in the proper way.

> After several hours of this, during which, perhaps, a score of bullets had struck about him, their ammunition began to give out and their fire *slackened.*

For more information about the words in the glossary, consult a dictionary.

Descriptive Writing

Using Precise Details

Note how this description is made vivid through the use of precise details:

> Before they could recover from the hot rain of blows, Walt reached out from his sled, catching their wheel dog by the forelegs in midspring, and throwing him heavily. This brought the whole team into a snarl, capsizing the sled and tangling his enemies up beautifully.

In one or two sentences describe a moment in an exciting race or contest you have seen. Choose your details and verbs carefully.

About the Author

Jack London   (1876–1916)

Jack London, who became one of the most successful and popular writers in the world, was born in grim poverty in San Francisco. He never received much formal education. He educated himself by studying for hours at a time in public libraries.

In his teens he was a longshoreman, an oyster pirate, a seaman, and a hobo. When he was nineteen, he decided to finish high school. He condensed a four-year course into one year and was able to pass the entrance examination at the University of California in the following year. In 1897 he left college to seek gold in the Klondike. He found no gold and returned to San Francisco, sailing 1,900 miles (about 3,060 kilometers) in an open boat. His experiences in the Arctic gave him the material for many short stories and for his famous novels *The Call of the Wild* and *White Fang.*

London worked hard at being a writer. In seventeen years he produced fifty books. His popularity grew until he became the highest-paid writer in the United States. When he died at the age of forty, he had either spent or given away all his money. London's tales of rough adventure are widely read today. His books and short stories have been translated into many languages.

Stolen Day

SHERWOOD ANDERSON

In order for a character in a story to be believable, there must be a purpose, or motivation, *for the character's actions. What motivates the narrator in this story to "steal" a day?*

It must be that all children are actors. The whole thing started with a boy on our street named Walter, who had inflammatory rheumatism.[1] That's what they called it. He didn't have to go to school.

Still he could walk about. He could go fishing in the creek or the waterworks pond. There was a place up at the pond where in the spring the water came tumbling over the dam and formed a deep pool. It was a good place. Sometimes you could get some good big ones there.

I went down that way on my way to school one spring morning. It was out of my way but I wanted to see if Walter was there.

He was, inflammatory rheumatism and all. There he was, sitting with a fish pole in his hand. He had been able to walk down there all right.

It was then that my own legs began to hurt. My back too. I went on to school but, at the recess time, I began to cry. I did it when the teacher, Sarah Suggett, had come out into the schoolhouse yard.

She came right over to me.

"I ache all over," I said. I did, too.

I kept on crying and it worked all right.

1. **inflammatory rheumatism** (rōō′mə-tĭz′əm): a painful disease affecting the joints and muscles.

"You'd better go on home," she said.

So I went. I limped painfully away. I kept on limping until I got out of the schoolhouse street.

Then I felt better. I still had inflammatory rheumatism pretty bad but I could get along better.

I must have done some thinking on the way home.

"I'd better not say I have inflammatory rheumatism," I decided. "Maybe if you've got that you swell up."

I thought I'd better go around to where Walter was and ask him about that, so I did—but he wasn't there.

"They must not be biting today," I thought.

I had a feeling that, if I said I had inflammatory rheumatism, Mother or my brothers and my sister Stella might laugh. They did laugh at me pretty often and I didn't like it at all.

"Just the same," I said to myself, "I have got it." I began to hurt and ache again.

I went home and sat on the front steps of our house. I sat there a long time. There wasn't anyone at home but Mother and the two little ones. Ray would have been four or five then and Earl might have been three.

It was Earl who saw me there. I had got tired

sitting and was lying on the porch. Earl was always a quiet, solemn little fellow.

He must have said something to Mother for presently she came.

"What's the matter with you? Why aren't you in school?" she asked.

I came pretty near telling her right out that I had inflammatory rheumatism but I thought I'd better not. Mother and Father had been speaking of Walter's case at the table just the day before. "It affects the heart," Father had said. That frightened me when I thought of it. "I might die," I thought. "I might just suddenly die right here; my heart might stop beating."

On the day before I had been running a race with my brother Irve. We were up at the fairgrounds after school and there was a half-mile track.

"I'll bet you can't run a half-mile," he said. "I bet you I could beat you running clear around the track."

And so we did it and I beat him, but afterwards my heart did seem to beat pretty hard. I remembered that lying there on the porch. "It's a wonder, with my inflammatory rheumatism and all, I didn't just drop down dead," I thought. The thought frightened me a lot. I ached worse than ever.

"I ache, Ma," I said. "I just ache."

She made me go in the house and upstairs and get into bed.

It wasn't so good. It was spring. I was up there for perhaps an hour, maybe two, and then I felt better.

I got up and went downstairs. "I feel better, Ma," I said.

Mother said she was glad. She was pretty

busy that day and hadn't paid much attention to me. She had made me get into bed upstairs and then hadn't even come up to see how I was.

I didn't think much of that when I was up there but when I got downstairs where she was, and when, after I had said I felt better and she only said she was glad and went right on with her work, I began to ache again.

I thought, "I'll bet I die of it. I bet I do."

I went out to the front porch and sat down. I was pretty sore at Mother.

"If she really knew the truth, that I have the inflammatory rheumatism and I may just drop down dead any time, I'll bet she wouldn't care about that either," I thought.

I was getting more and more angry the more thinking I did.

"I know what I'm going to do," I thought; "I'm going to go fishing."

I thought that, feeling the way I did, I might be sitting on the high bank just above the deep pool where the water went over the dam, and suddenly my heart would stop beating.

And then, of course, I'd pitch forward, over the bank into the pool and, if I wasn't dead when I hit the water, I'd drown sure.

They would all come home to supper and they'd miss me.

"But where is he?"

Then Mother would remember that I'd come home from school aching.

She'd go upstairs and I wouldn't be there. One day during the year before, there was a child got drowned in a spring. It was one of the Wyatt children.

Right down at the end of the street there was a spring under a birch tree and there had been a barrel sunk in the ground.

Everyone had always been saying the spring ought to be kept covered, but it wasn't.

So the Wyatt child went down there, played around alone, and fell in and got drowned.

Mother was the one who had found the drowned child. She had gone to get a pail of water and there the child was, drowned and dead.

This had been in the evening when we were all at home, and Mother had come running up the street with the dead, dripping child in her arms. She was making for the Wyatt house as hard as she could run, and she was pale.

She had a terrible look on her face, I remembered then.

"So," I thought, "they'll miss me and there'll be a search made. Very likely there'll be someone who has seen me sitting by the pond fishing, and there'll be a big alarm and all the town will turn out and they'll drag the pond."

I was having a grand time, having died. Maybe, after they found me and had got me out of the deep pool, Mother would grab me up in her arms and run home with me as she had run with the Wyatt child.

I got up from the porch and went around the house. I got my fishing pole and lit out for the pool below the dam. Mother was busy—she always was—and didn't see me go. When I got there I thought I'd better not sit too near the edge of the high bank.

By this time I didn't ache hardly at all, but I thought.

"With inflammatory rheumatism you can't tell," I thought.

"It probably comes and goes," I thought.

"Walter has it and he goes fishing," I thought.

I had got my line into the pool and suddenly I got a bite. It was a regular whopper. I knew that. I'd never had a bite like that.

I knew what it was. It was one of Mr. Fenn's big carp.

Mr. Fenn was a man who had a big pond of his own. He sold ice in the summer and the pond was to make the ice. He had bought some big carp and put them into his pond and then, earlier in the spring when there was a freshet,[2] his dam had gone out.

So the carp had got into our creek and one or two big ones had been caught—but none of them by a boy like me.

The carp was pulling and I was pulling and I was afraid he'd break my line, so I just tumbled down the high bank, holding onto the line and got right into the pool. We had it out, there in the pool. We struggled. We wrestled. Then I got a hand under his gills and got him out.

He was a big one all right. He was nearly half as big as I was myself. I had him on the bank and I kept one hand under his gills and I ran.

I never ran so hard in my life. He was slippery, and now and then he wriggled out of my arms; once I stumbled and fell on him, but I got him home.

So there it was. I was a big hero that day. Mother got a washtub and filled it with water. She put the fish in it and all the neighbors came to look. I got into dry clothes and went down to supper—and then I made a break that spoiled my day.

There we were, all of us, at the table, and suddenly Father asked what had been the matter with me at school. He had met the teacher, Sarah Suggett, on the street and she had told him how I had become ill.

"What was the matter with you?" Father asked, and before I thought what I was saying I let it out.

"I had the inflammatory rheumatism," I said—and a shout went up. It made me sick to hear them, the way they all laughed.

It brought back all the aching again, and like a fool I began to cry.

"Well, I *have* got it—I *have*, I *have*," I cried, and I got up from the table and ran upstairs.

---

2. **freshet:** a sudden overflowing of a stream from a heavy rain or thaw.

I stayed there until Mother came up. I knew it would be a long time before I heard the last of the inflammatory rheumatism. I was sick all right, but the aching I now had wasn't in my legs or in my back.

Reading Check

1. During what season does this story take place?
2. What was the narrator's favorite fishing spot?
3. How did the narrator get himself sent home from school?
4. How did the narrator capture the carp?
5. What happened to spoil the narrator's day?

For Study and Discussion

Analyzing and Interpreting the Story

1. Why do you suppose the narrator's "symptoms" develop after he sees Walter fishing at the pond?

2. How do you know that the narrator wants his mother to pay more attention to him?

3. Why does he insist that he had "the inflammatory rheumatism"?

4. Explain the title of the story.

Literary Elements

Recognizing and Understanding Flashback

A writer usually tells the events of a story in the order in which they happen. However, sometimes the writer will interrupt the action to tell of something that happened in the past. In "Stolen Day," the narrator interrupts his own fantasy about dying to tell about a drowning accident the year before.

This interruption of action to tell something that happened in the past is called a **flashback.** A flashback is often used to clarify something that is happening in the present. How does the flashback help you to understand the narrator's feelings?

Language and Vocabulary

Recognizing Informal Language

In order for characters to be believable, they must act and speak appropriately. Anderson tells his story in a conversational style, using language that is natural to his character.

The narrator uses some informal, or **colloquial,** (kə-lō′kwē-əl) expressions. He says that he became "sore" at his mother. Used in this way, the word *sore* means "angry" or "resentful." He tells us that he got his fishing pole and "lit out" for the pool. The phrase *light out* is a colloquial expression meaning "to leave suddenly."

What is the meaning of *whopper*? Check your answer in a dictionary.

Writing About Literature

Explaining the Narrator's Actions

In the opening sentence of the story, the narrator, looking back on his childhood, says, "It must be that all children are actors." Did the narrator, as a boy, realize that he was acting? What evidence can you find in the story to support your answer? Write a short paragraph in which you state your opinion and give your reasons.

For assistance in developing your essay, see the section called *Writing About Literature* at the back of this textbook.

Creative Writing

Telling About a Stolen Day

Invent a story about a stolen day of your own. Did you go to the beach, watch the ball game on television, or go to the movies when you were supposed to be attending to something else? Make your account interesting by revealing your thoughts and feelings, as Sherwood Anderson does in "A Stolen Day."

About the Author

Sherwood Anderson   (1876–1941)

Sherwood Anderson was born in Camden, Ohio, and spent much of his youth in Clyde. He left school when he was fourteen and worked at a variety of odd jobs. He became successful as a businessman and organized a paint-manufacturing company. He was not happy, however, and gave up his business in order to devote himself to writing. Anderson is best known for his stories of small-town life in America. His stories, like "Stolen Day," are often told by a narrator who is recalling some incident from the past. Anderson developed a style based on the spoken American language. His style and subject matter have strongly influenced other twentieth-century writers.

The Medicine Bag

VIRGINIA DRIVING HAWK SNEVE

Characters are believable when they behave consistently. The reader must be prepared for any dramatic change in a character's actions or beliefs. How does the author of this story make the change in her narrator convincing?

My kid sister Cheryl and I always bragged about our Sioux grandpa, Joe Iron Shell. Our friends, who had always lived in the city and only knew about Indians from movies and TV, were impressed by our stories. Maybe we exaggerated and made Grandpa and the reservation sound glamorous, but when we'd return home to Iowa after our yearly summer visit to Grandpa we always had some exciting tale to tell.

We always had some authentic Sioux article to show our listeners. One year Cheryl had new moccasins that Grandpa had made. On another visit he gave me a small, round, flat, rawhide drum which was decorated with a painting of a warrior riding a horse. He taught me a real Sioux chant to sing while I beat the drum with a leather-covered stick that had a feather on the end. Man, that really made an impression.

We never showed our friends Grandpa's picture. Not that we were ashamed of him, but because we knew that the glamorous tales we told didn't go with the real thing. Our friends would have laughed at the picture, because

Grandpa wasn't tall and stately like TV Indians. His hair wasn't in braids, but hung in stringy, gray strands on his neck and he was old. He was our great-grandfather, and he didn't live in a tepee, but all by himself in a part log, part tar-paper shack on the Rosebud Reservation in South Dakota. So when Grandpa came to visit us, I was so ashamed and embarrassed I could've died.

There are a lot of yippy poodles and other fancy little dogs in our neighborhood, but they usually barked singly at the mailman from the safety of their own yards. Now it sounded as if a whole pack of mutts were barking together in one place.

I got up and walked to the curb to see what the commotion was. About a block away I saw a crowd of little kids yelling, with the dogs yipping and growling around someone who was walking down the middle of the street.

I watched the group as it slowly came closer and saw that in the center of the strange procession was a man wearing a tall black hat. He'd pause now and then to peer at something in his hand and then at the houses on either

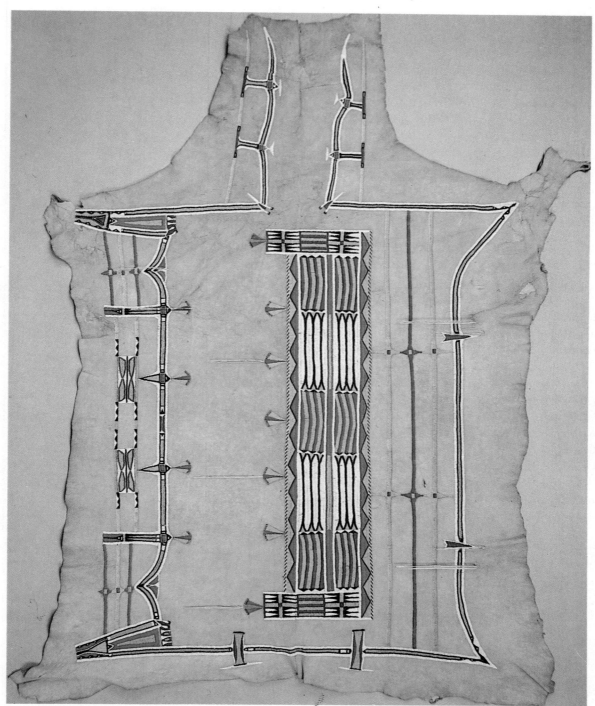

Sioux beaded buffalo robe.

side of the street. I felt cold and hot at the same time as I recognized the man. "Oh, no!" I whispered. "It's Grandpa!"

I stood on the curb, unable to move even though I wanted to run and hide. Then I got mad when I saw how the yippy dogs were growling and nipping at the old man's baggy pant legs and how wearily he poked them away with his cane. "Stupid mutts," I said as I ran to rescue Grandpa.

When I kicked and hollered at the dogs to get away, they put their tails between their legs and scattered. The kids ran to the curb where they watched me and the old man.

"Grandpa," I said and felt pretty dumb when my voice cracked. I reached for his beat-up old tin suitcase, which was tied shut with a rope. But he set it down right in the street and shook my hand.

"*Hau, Takoza,* Grandchild," he greeted me formally in Sioux.

All I could do was stand there with the whole neighborhood watching and shake the hand of the leather-brown old man. I saw how his gray hair straggled from under his big black hat, which had a drooping feather in its crown. His rumpled black suit hung like a sack over his stooped frame. As he shook my hand, his coat fell open to expose a bright-red, satin shirt with a beaded bolo tie[1] under the collar. His get-up wasn't out of place on the reservation, but it sure was here, and I wanted to sink right through the pavement.

"Hi," I muttered with my head down. I tried to pull my hand away when I felt his bony hand trembling, and looked up to see fatigue in his face. I felt like crying. I couldn't think of anything to say so I picked up Grandpa's suitcase, took his arm, and guided him up the driveway to our house.

Mom was standing on the steps. I don't know

1. **bolo tie:** a string tie held together by a sliding device.

Hear Crow Dog of the Sioux.

how long she'd been watching, but her hand was over her mouth and she looked as if she couldn't believe what she saw. Then she ran to us.

"Grandpa," she gasped. "How in the world did you get here?"

She checked her move to embrace Grandpa and I remembered that such a display of affection is unseemly to the Sioux and would embarrass him.

"*Hau*, Marie," he said as he shook Mom's hand. She smiled and took his other arm.

As we supported him up the steps the door banged open and Cheryl came bursting out of the house. She was all smiles and was so obviously glad to see Grandpa that I was ashamed of how I felt.

"Grandpa!" she yelled happily. "You came to see us!"

Grandpa smiled and Mom and I let go of him as he stretched out his arms to my ten-year-old sister, who was still young enough to be hugged.

"*Wicincala*, little girl," he greeted her and then collapsed.

He had fainted. Mom and I carried him into her sewing room, where we had a spare bed.

After we had Grandpa on the bed Mom stood there helplessly patting his shoulder.

"Shouldn't we call the doctor, Mom?" I suggested, since she didn't seem to know what to do.

"Yes," she agreed with a sigh. "You make Grandpa comfortable, Martin."

I reluctantly moved to the bed. I knew Grandpa wouldn't want to have Mom undress him, but I didn't want to, either. He was so skinny and frail that his coat slipped off easily. When I loosened his tie and opened his shirt collar, I felt a small leather pouch that hung from a thong around his neck. I left it alone and moved to remove his boots. The scuffed old cowboy boots were tight and he moaned as I put pressure on his legs to jerk them off.

I put the boots on the floor and saw why they fit so tight. Each one was stuffed with money. I looked at the bills that lined the boots and started to ask about them, but Grandpa's eyes were closed again.

Mom came back with a basin of water. "The doctor thinks Grandpa is suffering from heat exhaustion," she explained as she bathed Grandpa's face. Mom gave a big sigh, "*Oh hinh*, Martin. How do you suppose he got here?"

We found out after the doctor's visit. Grandpa was angrily sitting up in bed while Mom tried to feed him some soup.

"Tonight you let Marie feed you, Grandpa," spoke my dad, who had gotten home from work just as the doctor was leaving. "You're not really sick," he said as he gently pushed Grandpa back against the pillows. "The doctor said you just got too tired and hot after your long trip."

Grandpa relaxed, and between sips of soup he told us of his journey. Soon after our visit to him Grandpa decided that he would like to see where his only living descendants lived and what our home was like. Besides, he admitted sheepishly, he was lonesome after we left.

I knew everybody felt as guilty as I did—especially Mom. Mom was all Grandpa had left. So even after she married my dad, who's a white man and teaches in the college in our city, and after Cheryl and I were born, Mom made sure that every summer we spent a week with Grandpa.

I never thought that Grandpa would be lonely after our visits, and none of us noticed how old and weak he had become. But Grandpa knew and so he came to us. He had ridden on buses for two and a half days. When he arrived in the city, tired and stiff from sitting for so long, he set out, walking, to find us.

He had stopped to rest on the steps of some building downtown and a policeman found him. The cop, according to Grandpa, was a good man who took him to the bus stop and waited until the bus came and told the driver to let Grandpa out at Bell View Drive. After Grandpa got off the bus, he started walking again. But he couldn't see the house numbers on the other side when he walked on the sidewalk so he walked in the middle of the street.

That's when all the little kids and dogs followed him.

I knew everybody felt as bad as I did. Yet I was proud of this eighty-six-year-old man, who had never been away from the reservation, having the courage to travel so far alone.

"You found the money in my boots?" he asked Mom.

"Martin did," she answered, and roused herself to scold. "Grandpa, you shouldn't have carried so much money. What if someone had stolen it from you?"

Grandpa laughed. "I would've known if anyone tried to take the boots off my feet. The money is what I've saved for a long time—a hundred dollars—for my funeral. But you take it now to buy groceries so that I won't be a burden to you while I am here."

"That won't be necessary, Grandpa," Dad said. "We are honored to have you with us and you will never be a burden. I am only sorry that we never thought to bring you home with us this summer and spare you the discomfort of a long trip."

Grandpa was pleased. "Thank you," he answered. "But do not feel bad that you didn't bring me with you, for I would not have come then. It was not time." He said this in such a way that no one could argue with him. To Grandpa and the Sioux, he once told me, a thing would be done when it was the right time to do it and that's the way it was.

"Also," Grandpa went on, looking at me, "I have come because it is soon time for Martin to have the medicine bag."

We all knew what that meant. Grandpa thought he was going to die and he had to follow the tradition of his family to pass the medicine bag, along with its history, to the oldest male child.

"Even though the boy," he said still looking at me, "bears a white man's name, the medicine bag will be his."

I didn't know what to say. I had the same hot and cold feeling that I had when I first saw Grandpa in the street. The medicine bag was the dirty leather pouch I had found around his neck. "I could never wear such a thing," I almost said aloud. I thought of having my friends see it in gym class, at the swimming pool, and could imagine the smart things they would say. But I just swallowed hard and took a step toward the bed. I knew I would have to take it.

But Grandpa was tired. "Not now, Martin," he said, waving his hand in dismissal, "it is not time. Now I will sleep."

So that's how Grandpa came to be with us for two months. My friends kept asking to come see the old man, but I put them off. I told myself that I didn't want them laughing at Grandpa. But even as I made excuses I knew it wasn't Grandpa that I was afraid they'd laugh at.

Nothing bothered Cheryl about bringing her friends to see Grandpa. Every day after school started there'd be a crew of giggling little girls or round-eyed little boys crowded around the old man on the patio, where he'd gotten in the habit of sitting every afternoon.

Grandpa would smile in his gentle way and patiently answer their questions, or he'd tell them stories of brave warriors, ghosts, animals, and the kids listened in awed silence. Those little guys thought Grandpa was great.

Finally, one day after school, my friends came home with me because nothing I said stopped them. "We're going to see the great Indian of Bell View Drive," said Hank, who was supposed to be my best friend. "My brother has seen him three times so he oughta be well enough to see us."

When we got to my house Grandpa was sitting on the patio. He had on his red shirt, but today he also wore a fringed leather vest that was decorated with beads. Instead of his usual cowboy boots he had solidly beaded moccasins on his feet that stuck out of his black trousers. Of course, he had his old black hat on—he was seldom without it. But it had been brushed and the feather in the beaded headband was proudly erect, its tip a brighter white. His hair lay in silver strands over the red shirt collar.

I started just as my friends did and I heard one of them murmur, "Wow!"

Grandpa looked up and when his eyes met mine they twinkled as if he were laughing inside. He nodded to me and my face got all hot. I could tell that he had known all along I was afraid he'd embarrass me in front of my friends.

"*Hau, hoksilas,* boys," he greeted and held out his hand.

My buddies passed in a single file and shook his hand as I introduced them. They were so polite I almost laughed. "How, there, Grandpa," and even a "How-do-you-do, sir."

"You look fine, Grandpa," I said as the guys sat on the lawn chairs or on the patio floor.

"*Hanh,* yes," he agreed. "When I woke up this morning it seemed the right time to dress in the good clothes. I knew that my grandson would be bringing his friends."

"You guys want some lemonade or something?" I offered. No one answered. They were listening to Grandpa as he started telling how he'd killed the deer from which his vest was made.

Grandpa did most of the talking while my friends were there. I was so proud of him and amazed at how respectfully quiet my buddies were. Mom had to chase them home at suppertime. As they left they shook Grandpa's hand again and said to me:

"Martin, he's really great!"

"Yeah, man! Don't blame you for keeping him to yourself."

"Can we come back?"

But after they left, Mom said, "No more visi-

Bandolier bag, worn across the chest. Sioux.

American Museum of Natural History

The Medicine Bag **35**

tors for a while, Martin. Grandpa won't admit it, but his strength hasn't returned. He likes having company, but it tires him."

That evening Grandpa called me to his room before he went to sleep. "Tomorrow," he said, "when you come home, it will be time to give you the medicine bag."

I felt a hard squeeze from where my heart is supposed to be and was scared, but I answered, "OK, Grandpa."

All night I had weird dreams about thunder and lightning on a high hill. From a distance I heard the slow beat of a drum. When I woke up in the morning I felt as if I hadn't slept at all. At school it seemed as if the day would never end and, when it finally did, I ran home.

Grandpa was in his room, sitting on the bed. The shades were down and the place was dim and cool. I sat on the floor in front of Grandpa, but he didn't even look at me. After what seemed a long time he spoke.

"I sent your mother and sister away. What you will hear today is only for a man's ears. What you will receive is only for a man's hands." He fell silent and I felt shivers down my back.

"My father in his early manhood," Grandpa began, "made a vision quest to find a spirit guide for his life. You cannot understand how it was in that time, when the great Teton Sioux were first made to stay on the reservation. There was a strong need for guidance from *Wakantanka,* the Great Spirit. But too many of the young men were filled with despair and hatred. They thought it was hopeless to search for a vision when the glorious life was gone and only the hated confines of a reservation lay ahead. But my father held to the old ways.

"He carefully prepared for his quest with a purifying sweat bath and then he went alone to a high butte top to fast and pray. After three days he received his sacred dream—in which he found, after long searching, the white man's iron. He did not understand his vision of finding something belonging to the white people, for in that time they were the enemy. When he came down from the butte to cleanse himself at the stream below, he found the remains of a campfire and the broken shell of an iron kettle. This was a sign which reinforced his dream. He took a piece of the iron for his medicine bag, which he had made of elk skin years before, to prepare for his quest.

"He returned to his village, where he told his dream to the wise old men of the tribe. They gave him the name Iron Shell, but neither did they understand the meaning of the dream. This first Iron Shell kept the piece of iron with him at all times and believed it gave him protection from the evils of those unhappy days.

"Then a terrible thing happened to Iron Shell. He and several other young men were taken from their homes by the soldiers and sent far away to a white man's boarding school. He was angry and lonesome for his parents and the young girl he had wed before he was taken away. At first Iron Shell resisted the teachers' attempts to change him and he did not try to learn. One day it was his turn to work in the school's blacksmith shop. As he walked into the place he knew that his medicine had brought him there to learn and work with the white man's iron.

"Iron Shell became a blacksmith and worked at the trade when he returned to the reservation. All of his life he treasured the medicine bag. When he was old, and I was a man, he gave it to me, for no one made the vision quest anymore."

Grandpa quit talking and I stared in disbelief as he covered his face with his hands. His shoulders were shaking with quiet sobs and I looked away until he began to speak again.

"I kept the bag until my son, your mother's father, was a man and had to leave us to fight in the war across the ocean. I gave him the bag, for I believed it would protect him in battle, but he did not take it with him. He was afraid that he would lose it. He died in a faraway place."

Again Grandpa was still and I felt his grief around me.

"My son," he went on after clearing his throat, "had only a daughter and it is not proper for her to know of these things."

He unbuttoned his shirt, pulled out the leather pouch, and lifted it over his head. He held it in his hand, turning it over and over as if memorizing how it looked.

"In the bag," he said as he opened it and removed two objects, "is the broken shell of the iron kettle, a pebble from the butte, and a piece of the sacred sage."[2] He held the pouch upside down and dust drifted down.

"After the bag is yours you must put a piece of prairie sage within and never open it again until you pass it on to your son." He replaced the pebble and the piece of iron, and tied the bag.

I stood up, somehow knowing I should. Grandpa slowly rose from the bed and stood upright in front of me, holding the bag before my face. I closed my eyes and waited for him to slip it over my head. But he spoke.

"No, you need not wear it." He placed the soft leather bag in my right hand and closed my other hand over it. "It would not be right to wear it in this time and place where no one will understand. Put it safely away until you are again on the reservation. Wear it then, when you replace the sacred sage."

Grandpa turned and sat again on the bed. Wearily he leaned his head against the pillow. "Go," he said, "I will sleep now."

"Thank you, Grandpa," I said softly and left with the bag in my hands.

That night Mom and Dad took Grandpa to

2. **sage:** a plant with aromatic leaves, believed to have healing powers.

the hospital. Two weeks later I stood alone on the lonely prairie of the reservation and put the sacred sage in my medicine bag.

Reading Check

1. How are Joe Iron Shell and the narrator related?
2. What does Grandpa have in his boots?
3. What does the medicine bag contain?
4. How does Grandpa entertain Cheryl's friends?
5. Who was the first person to wear the medicine bag?

For Study and Discussion

Analyzing and Interpreting the Story

1. Martin says that he and his sister always bragged about Grandpa. Why, then, is Martin embarrassed when Grandpa arrives?

2. Grandpa explains that the purpose of his visit is to pass along the medicine bag and its history to Martin. Why is Martin miserable at the thought of wearing the medicine bag?

3. Martin is concerned about how his friends will react to Grandpa. What actually happens when they come to visit Grandpa?

4. When he feels it is time, Grandpa tells Martin the history of the medicine bag. Why does Grandpa treasure it?

5. Martin's feelings toward Grandpa begin to change after he sees how much his friends admire the old man. **a.** When do his feelings about the medicine bag change? **b.** How do you know at the end of the story that he understands and respects the tradition it represents?

Language and Vocabulary

Recognizing Words of American Indian Origin

Many words in our language are **loan words,** or words that have been borrowed from other languages. For example, the word *butte* comes from French, the word *patio* from Spanish, and the word *Indian* from Latin.

A number of words in English have been borrowed from American Indian languages. The word *moccasin* comes from a family of languages called Algonquian. The word *tepee* comes from a word in the Siouan language family.

Many place names come from Indian words. The state names Iowa and South Dakota, both mentioned in the story, are Indian names. What other state names can you think of that are American Indian names? What cities and rivers carry Indian names?

All the words in the following list come from American Indian languages. Give the meaning of each word, using a dictionary if necessary.

hogan	manitou	succotash
kayak	pemmican	terrapin
mackinaw	sagamore	totem

Descriptive Writing

Using Specific Details

When Martin and his friends come home from school, they find Grandpa sitting on the patio. The author uses specific details to give the reader a clear picture of Grandpa.

> He had on his red shirt, but today he also wore a fringed leather vest that was decorated with beads. Instead of his usual cowboy boots he had solidly beaded moccasins on his feet that stuck out of his black trousers. Of course, he had his old black hat on—he was seldom without it. But it had been brushed and the feather in the beaded head-band was proudly erect, its tip a brighter white. His hair lay in silver strands over the red shirt collar.

What details help you visualize Grandpa's vest? His hat?

Write a short description telling what some person looks like. If you wish, you may choose someone whose picture appears in a book, newspaper, or magazine. Use specific details in your description.

About the Author

Virginia Driving Hawk Sneve   (1933–   )

Virginia Driving Hawk Sneve, who grew up on the Rosebud Sioux reservation in South Dakota, draws upon her personal experiences in creating the people and situations in her stories. In addition to her career as a writer, she has worked as a teacher and guidance counselor. Her books about Indian life include *Jimmy Yellow Hawk, High Elk's Treasure,* and *When Thunders Spoke.*

Guinea Pig

RUTH McKENNEY

A guinea pig is something or someone used in an experiment or a test of some kind. How does the narrator turn her experiences as a "guinea pig" into a hilarious story?

I was nearly drowned, in my youth, by a Red Cross Lifesaving Examiner, and I once suffered, in the noble cause of saving human life from a watery grave, a black eye which was a perfect daisy and embarrassed me for days. Looking back on my agonies, I feel that none of my sacrifices, especially the black eye, were in the least worthwhile. Indeed, to be brutally frank about it, I feel that the whole modern school of scientific lifesaving is a lot of hogwash.

Of course, I've had rather bad luck with lifesavers, right from the beginning. Long before I ever had any dealings with professional lifesavers my sister nearly drowned me, quite by mistake. My father once took us to a northern Michigan fishing camp, where we found the life very dull. He used to go trolling for bass on our little lake all day long, and at night come home to our lodge, dead beat and minus any bass. In the meantime Eileen and I, who were nine and ten at the time, used to take an old rowboat out to a shallow section of the lake and, sitting in the hot sun, feed worms to an unexciting variety of small, undernourished

fish called gillies. We hated the whole business.

Father, however, loved to fish, even if he didn't catch a single fish in three weeks, which on this trip he didn't. One night, however, he carried his enthusiasm beyond a decent pitch. He decided to go bass fishing after dark, and rather than leave us alone in the lodge and up to heaven knows what, he ordered us to take our boat and row along after him.

Eileen and I were very bored rowing around in the dark, and finally, in desperation, we began to stand up and rock the boat, which resulted, at last, in my falling into the lake with a mighty splash.

When I came up, choking and mad as anything, Eileen saw me struggling, and, as she always says with a catch in her voice, she only meant to help me. Good intentions, however, are of little importance in a situation like that. For she grabbed an oar out of the lock, and with an uncertain gesture hit me square on the chin.

I went down with a howl of pain. Eileen, who could not see much in the darkness, was now

really frightened. The cold water revived me after the blow and I came up to the surface, considerably weakened but still able to swim over to the boat. Whereupon Eileen, in a noble attempt to give me the oar to grab, raised it once again, and socked me square on the top of the head. I went down again, this time without a murmur, and my last thought was a vague wonder that my own sister should want to murder me with a rowboat oar.

As for Eileen, she heard the dull impact of the oar on my head and saw the shadowy figure of her sister disappear. So she jumped in the lake, screeching furiously, and began to flail around in the water, howling for help and

looking for me. At this point I came to the surface and swam over to the boat, with the intention of killing Eileen.

Father, rowing hard, arrived just in time to pull us both out of the water and prevent me from attacking Eileen with the rowboat anchor. The worst part about the whole thing, as far as I was concerned, was that Eileen was considered a heroine and Father told everybody in the lake community that she had saved my life. The postmaster put her name in for a medal.

After what I suffered from amateur lifesaving, I should have known enough to avoid even the merest contact with the professional variety of water mercy. I learned too late that being socked with an oar is as nothing compared to what the Red Cross can think up.

From the very beginning of that awful lifesaving course I took the last season I went to a girls' camp, I was a marked woman. The rest of the embryo[1] lifesavers were little, slender maidens, but I am a peasant type, and I was monstrously big for my fourteen years. I approximated, in poundage anyway, the theoretical adult we energetic young lifesavers were scheduled to rescue, and so I was, for the teacher's purpose, the perfect guinea pig.

The first few days of the course were unpleasant for me, but not terribly dangerous. The elementary lifesaving hold, in case you haven't seen some hapless victim being rescued by our brave beach guardians, is a snakelike arrangement for supporting the drowning citizen with one hand while you paddle him in to shore with the other. You are supposed to wrap your arm around his neck and shoulders, and keep his head well above water by resting it on your collarbone.

This is all very well in theory, of course, but the trick that none of Miss Folgil's little pupils could master was keeping the victim's nose and mouth above the waterline. Time and again I was held in a viselike[2] grip by one of the earnest students with my whole face an inch or two under the billowing waves.

"No, no, Betsy," Miss Folgil would scream through her megaphone, as I felt the water rush into my lungs. "No, no, you must keep the head a little higher." At this point I would begin to kick and struggle, and generally the pupil would have to let go while I came up for air. Miss Folgil was always very stern with me.

"Ruth," she would shriek from her boat, "I insist! You must allow Betsy to tow you all the

way in. We come to Struggling in Lesson 6."

This was but the mere beginning, however. A few lessons later we came to the section of the course where we learned how to undress under water in forty seconds. Perhaps I should say we came to the point where the *rest* of the pupils learned how to get rid of shoes and such while holding their breaths. I never did.

There was quite a little ceremony connected with this part of the course. Miss Folgil, and some lucky creature named as timekeeper and armed with a stopwatch, rowed the prospective victim out to deep water. The pupil, dressed in high, laced tennis shoes, long stockings, heavy bloomers, and a middy blouse, then stood poised at the end of the boat. When the timekeeper yelled "Go!" the future boon to mankind dived into the water and, while holding her breath under the surface, unlaced her shoes and stripped down to her bathing suit. Miss Folgil never explained what connection, if any, this curious rite had with saving human lives.

I had no middy of my own, so I borrowed one of my sister's. My sister was a slender little thing and I was, as I said, robust, which puts it politely. Eileen had some trouble wedging me into that middy, and once in it I looked like a stuffed sausage. It never occurred to me how hard it was going to be to get that middy off, especially when it was wet and slippery.

As we rowed out for my ordeal by undressing, Miss Folgil was snappish and bored.

"Hurry up," she said, looking irritated. "Let's get this over with quick. I don't think you're ready to pass the test, anyway."

I was good and mad when I jumped off the boat, and determined to Make Good and show that old Miss Folgil, whom I was beginning to dislike thoroughly. As soon as I was under water, I got my shoes off, and I had no trouble with the bloomers or stockings. I was just beginning to run out of breath when I held up

1. **embryo** (ĕm′brē-ō): here, beginning.
2. **viselike** (vīs′līk′): like a vise, or clamping device.

my arms and started to pull off the middy.

Now, the middy, in the event you don't understand the principle of this girl-child garment, is made with a small head opening, long sleeves, and no front opening. You pull it on and off over your head. You do if you are lucky, that is. I got the middy just past my neck, so that my face was covered with heavy linen cloth, when it stuck.

I pulled frantically and my lungs started to burst. Finally I thought the heck with the test, the heck with saving other people's lives, anyway. I came to the surface, a curious sight, my head enfolded in a water-soaked middy blouse. I made a brief sound, a desperate glub-glub, a call for help. My arms were stuck in the middy and I couldn't swim. I went down. I breathed in large quantities of water and linen cloth.

I came up again, making final frantic appeals. Four feet away sat a professional lifesaver, paying absolutely no attention to somebody drowning right under her nose. I went down again, struggling with last panic-stricken feverishness, fighting water and a middy blouse for my life. At this point the timekeeper pointed out to Miss Folgil that I had been under water for eighty-five seconds, which was quite a time for anybody. Miss Folgil was very annoyed, as she hated to get her bathing suit wet, but, a thoughtful teacher, she picked up her megaphone, shouted to the rest of the class on the beach to watch, and dived in after me.

If I say so myself, I gave her quite a time rescuing me. I presented a new and different problem, and probably am written up in textbooks now under the heading "What to Do When the Victim Is Entangled in a Tight Middy Blouse." Miss Folgil finally towed my still-breathing body over to the boat, reached for her bowie knife, which she carried on a ring with her whistle, and cut Eileen's middy

straight up the front. Then she towed me with Hold No. 2 right in to the shore and delivered me up to the class for artificial respiration. I will never forgive the Red Cross for that terrible trip through the water, when I might have been hoisted into the boat and rowed in except for Miss Folgil's overdeveloped sense of drama and pedagogy.

I tried to quit the lifesaving class after that, but the head counselor at the camp said I must keep on, to show that I was the kind of girl who always finished what she planned to do. Otherwise, she assured me, I would be a weak character and never amount to anything when I grew up.

So I stayed for Lesson 6: "Struggling." After that I didn't care if I never amounted to anything when I grew up. In fact, I hoped I wouldn't. It would serve everybody right, especially Miss Folgil. I came a little late to the class session that day and missed the discussion of theory, always held on the beach before the actual practice in the lake. That was just my hard luck. I was always a child of misfortune. I wonder that I survived my youth at all.

"We were waiting for you, Ruth," Miss Folgil chirped cheerily to me as I arrived, sullen and downcast, at the little group of earnest students sitting on the sand.

"What for?" I said warily. I was determined not to be a guinea pig any more. The last wave had washed over my helpless face.

"You swim out," Miss Folgil went on, ignoring my bad temper, "until you are in deep water—about twelve feet will do. Then you begin to flail around and shout for help. One of the students will swim out to you."

All of this sounded familiar and terrible. I had been doing that for days, and getting water in my nose for my pains.

"But when the student arrives," Miss Folgil went on, "you must not allow her to simply tow you away. You must struggle, just as hard as you can. You must try to clutch her by the head, you must try to twine your legs about her, and otherwise hamper her in trying to save you."

Now, *this* sounded something like.[3] I was foolishly fired by the attractive thought of getting back at some of the fiends who had been ducking me in the name of science for the past two weeks. Unfortunately, I hadn't studied Chapter 9, entitled "How to Break Holds the Drowning Swimmer Uses." Worse, I hadn't heard Miss Folgil's lecture on "Be Firm with the Panic-Stricken Swimmer—Better a Few Bruises Than a Watery Grave." This last was Miss Folgil's own opinion, of course.

So I swam out to my doom, happy as a lark. Maybelle Anne Pettijohn, a tall, lean girl who ordinarily wore horn-rimmed spectacles, was Miss Folgil's choice to rescue Exhibit A, the panic-stricken swimmer.

I laughed when I saw her coming. I thought I could clean up Maybelle Anne easily enough, but alas, I hadn't counted on Maybelle Anne's methodical approach to life. She had read Chapter 9 in our textbook, and she had listened carefully to Miss Folgil's inspiring words. Besides, Maybelle Anne was just naturally the kind of girl who ran around doing people dirty for their own good. "This may hurt your feelings," she used to say mournfully, "but I feel I have to tell you . . ."

When Maybelle Anne got near me, I enthusiastically lunged for her neck and hung on with both hands while getting her around her waist with my legs. Maybelle Anne thereupon dug her fingernails into my hands with ferocious force, and I let go and swam away, hurt

3. **something like:** the way it should be.

and surprised. This was distinctly not playing fair.

"What's the idea?" I called out.

"It says to do that in the book," Maybelle Anne replied, treading water.

"Well, you lay off of that stuff," I said, angered, book or no book. Maybelle Anne was a Girl Scout, too, and I was shocked to think she'd go around using her fingernails in a fair fight.

"Come on, struggle," Maybelle Anne said, getting winded from treading water. I swam over, pretty reluctant and much more wary. Believe it or not, this time Maybelle Anne, who was two medals from being a Beaver or whatever it is Girl Scouts with a lot of medals get to be, bit me.

In addition to biting me, Maybelle Anne swung her arm around my neck, with the intention of towing me in to the shore. But I still had plenty of fight left and I had never been so mad in my life. I got Maybelle Anne underwater two or three times, and I almost thought I had her when suddenly, to my earnest surprise, she hauled off and hit me as hard as she could, right in the eye. Then she towed me in, triumphant as anything.

Maybelle Anne afterward claimed it was all in the book, and she wouldn't even apologize for my black eye. Eileen and I fixed her, though. We put a little garter snake in her bed and scared the daylights out of her. Maybelle Anne was easy to scare anyway, and really a very disagreeable girl. I used to hope that she would come to a bad end, which, from my point of view, at least, she did. Maybelle Anne grew up to be a Regional Red Cross Lifesaving Examiner.

I'll bet she just loves her work.

Reading Check

1. What caused Ruth to fall out of the rowboat?
2. Why did Eileen jump into the lake?
3. In the elementary lifesaving hold, what trick were the pupils unable to master?
4. How did Miss Folgil remove the middy Ruth was wearing?
5. How did Maybelle Anne subdue Ruth during their struggle?

For Study and Discussion

Analyzing and Interpreting the Story

1. What two surprising events revealed in the first sentence tell you that this is a humorous story?

2. Ruth tells you that her sister once nearly drowned her. Which details of the "rescue" are particularly funny?

3. Why does Miss Folgil consider Ruth to be the perfect guinea pig for the lifesaving course?

4. Reread Ruth's description of being helped into Eileen's middy blouse (page 41). How does this passage prepare you for Ruth's underwater struggle with the middy?

5. Why does Ruth agree to be the guinea pig for the lesson on struggling?

6. Ruth expects a "fair fight" from Maybelle Anne. **a.** What kind of fight do you think she considers "fair"? **b.** What is "unfair" about Maybelle Anne's methods?

7a. Although Ruth says that she was nearly drowned on several occasions, how do you know that she is a good swimmer? **b.** How does this knowledge make the story even funnier?

Literary Elements

Recognizing Humor in Situations

"Guinea Pig" begins like a serious story about a near-fatal accident: "I was nearly drowned, in my youth. . . ." Before you are midway through the first sentence, however, you realize that the author is going to treat the subject humorously. After all, who ever heard of being drowned by a Lifesaving Examiner, an expert in saving lives? And what a reward for serving a noble cause—a black eye! These unlikely events are surprising and funny.

Some of the funniest situations in the story occur when people's intentions misfire. Instead of helping, a character ends up hindering. Instead of winning, a character winds up losing. How is this humor shown when Eileen attempts to help Ruth back into the rowboat? How do Ruth's plans for Maybelle Anne misfire?

Some of the situations in the story are funny because they are exaggerated. Reread the description of the underwater test on page 41. Which details in this test are particularly silly?

You often enjoy a comic situation more if you know that it is coming. Before Ruth appears for the test, you know that she will have trouble with the middy blouse. How do you know that Maybelle Anne has some surprises in store for Ruth?

Language and Vocabulary

Analyzing Words with *dis-*

Many words in our language are made up of individual elements or parts. For example, the word **disagreeable** has three parts. The **root,** or main part of the word, is *agree*. The part that follows the root, *-able*, is a **suffix** that means "capable of" or "tending to." The part that stands in front of the root, *dis-*, is a **prefix** meaning "not" or "the lack of" or "the opposite of." When you put these meanings together, you get the definition of *disagreeable:* "not tending to agree." Ruth thinks Maybelle Anne is disagreeable because she is hard to get along with.

You can sometimes figure out the meaning of an unfamiliar word by analyzing its structure. Using the definitions of the prefix *dis-* given above, work out the meanings of the following words. Then check your answers in a dictionary.

discontent	displease	disservice
disorder	disregard	disunion

Creative Writing

Relating a Humorous Experience

Perhaps you once played the victim in a lifesaving course, allowed yourself to be hypnotized, or volunteered to be the subject of an experiment. If you like, imagine yourself in such a situation. Write an account of the experience. Use strong action verbs and specific details. You may use exaggeration for added humor. Keep the reader guessing about the outcome of the story until the very end.

About the Author

Ruth McKenney (1911–1972)

Ruth McKenney was an American writer, best known for the humorous family sketches she wrote for *The New Yorker,* collected and published in 1938 as *My Sister Eileen.* This book was the source for a hit play, a musical, and a movie. It was followed by *The McKenneys Carry On* (1940), *Loud Red Patrick* (1947), and *All About Eileen* (1952). "Guinea Pig" is one of the most popular selections from *My Sister Eileen.*

The Cat and the Pain Killer

MARK TWAIN

Mark Twain is generally thought to be one of the greatest humorists this country has produced. Note how he uses comic exaggeration in this excerpt from The Adventures of Tom Sawyer.

One of the reasons why Tom's mind had drifted away from its secret troubles was that it had found a new and weighty matter to interest itself about. Becky Thatcher had stopped coming to school. Tom had struggled with his pride a few days and tried to "whistle her down the wind,"[1] but failed. He began to find himself hanging around her father's house, nights, and feeling very miserable. She was ill. What if she should die! There was distraction in the thought. He no longer took an interest in war, nor even in piracy. The charm of life was gone; there was nothing but dreariness left. He put his hoop away, and his bat; there was no joy in them any more. His aunt was concerned. She began to try all manner of remedies on him. She was one of those people who are infatuated with patent medicines and all newfangled methods of producing health or mending it. She was an inveterate[2] experimenter in these things. When something fresh in this line came out she was in a fever, right away, to try it, not on herself, for she was never ailing, but on anybody else that came handy. She was a subscriber for all the "Health" periodicals and phrenological frauds;[3] and the solemn ignorance they were inflated with was breath to her nostrils. All the "rot" they contained about ventilation, and how to go to bed, and how to get up, and what to eat, and what to drink, and how much exercise to take, and what frame of mind to keep one's self in, and what sort of clothing to wear, was all gospel to her, and she never observed that her health journals of the current month customarily upset everything they had recommended the month before. She was as simple-hearted and honest as the day was long, and so she was an easy victim. She gathered together her quack periodicals and her quack medicines, and thus armed with death, went about on her pale horse, metaphorically speaking,[4] with "hell following after." But she never suspected that she was

1. **"whistle . . . wind":** forget about her.
2. **inveterate** (ĭn-vĕt′ər-ĭt): habitual.
3. **phrenological** (frĕn′ə-lŏj′ĭk-əl) **frauds:** claims that studying the bumps on a person's skull could reveal character, intelligence, and temperament.
4. **metaphorically** (mĕt′ə-fôr′ĭk-lē) **speaking:** to use a comparison. Twain humorously compares Aunt Polly to Death, who traditionally rides a pale horse. He is referring to a passage in the Bible (Revelation 6:8).

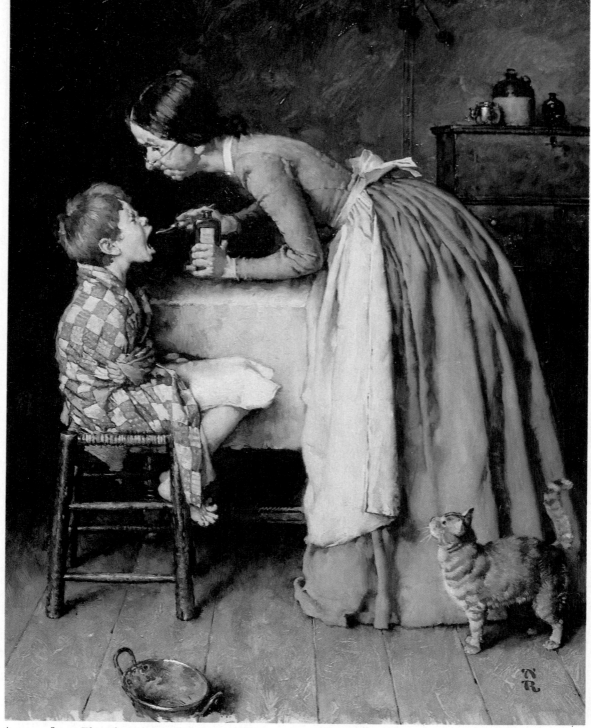

A scene from *The Adventures of Tom Sawyer*, illustrated around 1936 by Norman Rockwell (1894–1978).

not an angel of healing and the balm of Gilead[5] in disguise, to the suffering neighbors.

The water treatment was new, now, and Tom's low condition was a windfall to her. She had him out at daylight every morning, stood him up in the woodshed and drowned him with a deluge of cold water; then she scrubbed him down with a towel like a file, and so brought him to; then she rolled him up in a wet sheet and put him away under blankets till she sweated his soul clean and "the yellow stains of it came through his pores"—as Tom said.

Yet notwithstanding all this, the boy grew more and more melancholy and pale and dejected. She added hot baths, sitz baths,[6] shower baths, and plunges. The boy remained as dismal as a hearse. She began to assist the water with a slim oatmeal diet and blister plasters. She calculated his capacity as she would a jug's, and filled him up every day with quack cure-alls.

Tom had become indifferent to persecution by this time. This phase filled the old lady's heart with consternation.[7] This indifference must be broken up at any cost. Now she heard of Pain Killer for the first time. She ordered a lot at once. She tasted it and was filled with gratitude. It was simply fire in a liquid form. She dropped the water treatment and everything else and pinned her faith to Pain Killer. She gave Tom a teaspoonful and watched with the deepest anxiety for the result. Her troubles were instantly at rest, her soul at peace again, for the "indifference" was broken up. The boy could not have shown a wilder, heartier interest if she had built a fire under him.

Tom felt that it was time to wake up; this sort of life might be romantic enough, in his blighted condition, but it was getting to have too little sentiment and too much distracting variety about it. So he thought over various plans for relief and finally hit upon that of professing to be fond of Pain Killer. He asked for it so often that he became a nuisance, and his aunt ended by telling him to help himself and quit bothering her. If it had been Sid, she would have had no misgivings to alloy her delight, but since it was Tom, she watched the bottle clandestinely.[8] She found that the medicine did really diminish, but it did not occur to her that the boy was mending the health of a crack in the sitting-room floor with it.

One day Tom was in the act of dosing the crack when his aunt's yellow cat came along, purring, eyeing the teaspoon avariciously, and begging for a taste. Tom said:

"Don't ask for it unless you want it, Peter."

But Peter signified that he did want it.

"You better make sure."

Peter was sure.

"Now you've asked for it, and I'll give it to you, because there ain't anything mean about *me*; but if you find you don't like it, you mustn't blame anybody but your own self."

Peter was agreeable. So Tom pried his mouth open and poured down the Pain Killer. Peter sprang a couple of yards in the air and then delivered a war whoop and set off round and round the room, banging against furniture, upsetting flowerpots, and making general havoc. Next he rose on his hind feet and pranced around, in a frenzy of enjoyment, with his head over his shoulder and his voice proclaiming his unappeasable[9] happiness. Then he went tearing around the house again spreading chaos and destruction in his path.

5. **balm** (bäm) **of Gilead** (gĭl′ē-əd): a reference to a passage in Jeremiah 8:22. In ancient times, the people of Gilead, a region in what is now Jordan, produced balm, an ointment used for healing.
6. **sitz** (sĭts) **baths:** baths taken sitting in shallow water.
7. **consternation** (kŏn′stər-nā′shən): alarm.

8. **clandestinely** (klăn-dĕs′tən-lē): secretly.
9. **unappeasable** (ŭn′ə-pēz′əb-əl): not capable of being reduced or quieted.

Aunt Polly entered in time to see him throw a few double somersaults, deliver a final mighty hurrah, and sail through the open window, carrying the rest of the flowerpots with him. The old lady stood petrified with astonishment, peering over her glasses; Tom lay on the floor expiring with laughter.

"Tom, what on earth ails that cat?"

"*I* don't know, Aunt," gasped the boy.

"Why, I never see anything like it. What *did* make him act so?"

"'Deed I don't know, Aunt Polly; cats always act so when they're having a good time."

"They do, do they?" There was something in the tone that made Tom apprehensive.

"Yes'm. That is, I believe they do."

"You *do*?"

"Yes'm."

The old lady was bending down, Tom watching, with interest emphasized by anxiety. Too late he divined her "drift." The handle of the telltale teaspoon was visible under the bed valance.[10] Aunt Polly took it, held it up. Tom winced and dropped his eyes. Aunt Polly raised him by the usual handle—his ear—and cracked his head soundly with her thimble.

"Now, sir, what did you want to treat that poor dumb beast so for?"

"I done it out of pity for him—because he hadn't any aunt."

"Hadn't any aunt!—you numskull. What has that got to do with it?"

"Heaps. Because if he'd 'a' had one she'd 'a' burnt him out herself! She'd 'a' roasted his bowels out of him 'thout any more feeling than if he was a human!"

Aunt Polly felt a sudden pang of remorse. This was putting the thing in a new light; what was cruelty to a cat *might* be cruelty to a boy, too. She began to soften; she felt sorry. Her eyes watered a little, and she put her hand on Tom's head and said gently:

"I was meaning for the best, Tom. And, Tom, it *did* do you good."

Tom looked up in her face with just a perceptible twinkle peeping through his gravity:[11]

"I know you was meaning for the best, Auntie, and so was I with Peter. It done *him* good, too. I never see him get around so since——"

"Oh, go 'long with you, Tom, before you aggravate me again. And you try and see if you can't be a good boy, for once, and you needn't take any more medicine."

Tom reached school ahead of time. It was noticed that this strange thing had been occurring every day latterly. And now, as usual of late, he hung about the gate of the schoolyard instead of playing with his comrades. He was sick, he said, and he looked it. He tried to seem to be looking everywhere but whither he really was looking—down the road. Presently Jeff Thatcher hove in sight,[12] and Tom's face lighted; he gazed a moment, and then turned sorrowfully away. When Jeff arrived, Tom accosted him and "led up" warily to opportunities for remarks about Becky, but the giddy lad never could see the bait. Tom watched and watched, hoping whenever a frisking frock came in sight, and hating the owner of it as soon as he saw she was not the right one. At last frocks ceased to appear, and he dropped hopelessly into the dumps; he entered the empty schoolhouse and sat down to suffer. Then one more frock passed in at the gate, and Tom's heart gave a great bound. The next instant he was out and "going on," like an Indian; yelling, laughing, chasing boys, jumping over the fence at risk of life and limb, throwing

10. **valance** (văl'əns): drapery hanging from the edge of the bed.

11. **gravity:** here, seriousness.
12. **hove in sight:** came into view, like a ship on the horizon.

handsprings, standing on his head—doing all the heroic things he could conceive of, and keeping a furtive eye out, all the while, to see if Becky Thatcher was noticing. But she seemed to be unconscious of it all; she never looked. Could it be possible that she was not aware that he was there? He carried his exploits to her immediate vicinity, came war-whooping around, snatched a boy's cap, hurled it to the roof of the schoolhouse, broke through a group of boys, tumbling them in every direction, and fell sprawling, himself, under Becky's nose, almost upsetting her—and she turned, with her nose in the air, and he heard her say: "Mf! Some people think they're mighty smart—always showing off!"

Tom's cheeks burned. He gathered himself up and sneaked off, crushed and crestfallen.

Reading Check

1. Why does Tom's aunt become concerned about him?
2. What is the "water treatment"?
3. How does Tom secretly get rid of the medicine?
4. How does Aunt Polly find out that Tom has given the cat his medicine?
5. What finally cures Tom of his melancholy?

For Study and Discussion

Analyzing and Interpreting the Selection

1. Tom's condition might be described as "lovesickness." What are his symptoms?

2. A pain killer is supposed to relieve pain. a. What is unusual about the Pain Killer in this story? b. In what way is it "good" for Tom?

3. Tom's explanation of his treatment of Peter makes Aunt Polly see her own treatment of Tom in a "new light." Why does Aunt Polly suddenly become gentle with Tom?

4. Tom recovers as soon as Becky Thatcher returns to school. How does he show that he is cured?

5a. Why do you suppose Tom doesn't tell Becky that he is glad to see her? b. Do you believe Becky is really annoyed by Tom's behavior? Give reasons to support your answers.

Language and Vocabulary

Getting Meaning from Context

When you come across an unfamiliar word in your reading, you may be able to work out its meaning by looking at the **context**, that is, the sentence or paragraph in which the word appears. You can probably guess the meaning of *avariciously* from its use in this sentence:

> One day Tom was in the act of dosing the crack when his aunt's yellow cat came along, purring, eyeing the teaspoon *avariciously*, and begging for a taste.

The word *avariciously* means "greedily." What other words in the sentence give clues to this meaning?

Look at the passage on page 48 in which Twain describes Peter's reaction to Pain Killer. Can you guess the meaning of the words *havoc* and *chaos* from the context? Check your answers in the glossary. How close did you come to the precise meanings of these words? What is the difference in meaning between them?

Descriptive Writing

Describing Action

Here is the passage describing Peter's reaction to Pain Killer. Twain makes his description vivid by using lively action words.

> Peter *sprang* a couple of yards in the air and then delivered a war whoop and set off round and round the room, *banging* against furniture, *upsetting* flowerpots, and making general havoc. Next he rose on his hind feet and *pranced* around, in a frenzy of enjoyment, with his head over his shoulder and his voice proclaiming his unappeasable happiness. Then he went *tearing* around the house again spreading chaos and destruction in his path. Aunt Polly entered in time to see him *throw* a few double somersaults, deliver a final mighty hurrah, and *sail* through the open window, carrying the rest of the flowerpots with him.

Write a paragraph describing an action-filled event that you have seen or taken part in recently. You may use a sports event, such as a track race, a basketball game, or a swimming contest. Use words that help the reader see and hear the action.

About the Author

Mark Twain (1835–1910)

You may know that Mark Twain was the pen name of Samuel Langhorne Clemens. He began using the name Mark Twain after working as a steamboat pilot on the Mississippi River. He took the name from a cry of the riverboatmen, "By the mark, twain!" This cry meant that the depth of the river was two fathoms (twelve feet or about four meters), a depth that was safe for the riverboats.

Twain grew up in Hannibal, Missouri, a small town on the Mississippi River. Many of his own experiences as a boy are re-created in *The Adventures of Tom Sawyer* and *Adventures of Huckleberry Finn,* two of the best-known and best-loved books in American literature. When Twain was twelve, his father died. He had to leave school and go to work. After working for five years as a printer's apprentice, he left Missouri to see the world. He spent the next four years as an apprentice to a steamboat pilot. He later wrote about his experiences as a cub pilot in *Life on the Mississippi.*

When the Civil War broke out, he headed west and supported himself by writing for newspapers. Much of Twain's writing grew out of his experiences in the West. Some of his best stories are tall tales of the frontier, such as "The Notorious Jumping Frog of Calaveras County." A number of humorous sketches about life in mining camps are contained in *Roughing It,* an autobiographical account of his years in the West. As his writing became well known, he began to give lecture tours throughout America and abroad, entertaining audiences with his wonderful stories.

Bad Characters

JEAN STAFFORD

A writer often gives you clues to character early in a story in order to prepare you for what is going to happen. As you read, look for these clues. What do you learn about Emily at the beginning of the story that prepares you for her actions later on?

Up until I learned my lesson in a very bitter way, I never had more than one friend at a time, and my friendships, though ardent, were short. When they ended and I was sent packing in unforgetting indignation, it was always my fault; I would swear vilely in front of a girl I knew to be pious and prim (by the time I was eight, the most grandiloquent[1] gangster could have added nothing to my vocabulary—I had an awful tongue), or I would call a Tenderfoot Scout a sissy or make fun of athletics to the daughter of the high school coach. These outbursts came without plan; I would simply one day, in the middle of a game of Russian bank[2] or a hike or a conversation, be possessed with a passion to be by myself, and my lips instantly and without warning would accommodate me. My friend was never more surprised than I was when this irrevocable slander, this terrible, talented invective, came boiling out of my mouth.

Afterward, when I had got the solitude I had wanted, I was dismayed, for I did not like it. Then I would sadly finish the game of cards as if someone were still across the table from me; I would sit down on the mesa and through a glaze of tears would watch my friend departing with outraged strides; mournfully, I would talk to myself. Because I had already alienated everyone I knew, I then had nowhere to turn, so a famine set in and I would have no companion but Muff, the cat, who loathed all human beings except, significantly, me—truly. She bit and scratched the hands that fed her, she arched her back like a Halloween cat if someone kindly tried to pet her, she hissed, laid her ears flat to her skull, growled, fluffed up her tail into a great bush and flailed it like a bullwhack.[3] But she purred for me, she patted me with her paws, keeping her claws in their velvet scabbards. She was not only an ill-natured cat, she was also badly dressed. She was a calico, and the distribution of her colors was a mess; she looked as if she had been left out in the rain and her paint had run. She had

1. **grandiloquent** (grăn-dĭl′ə-kwənt): speaking in a grand and highflown manner (here used sarcastically).
2. **Russian bank:** a card game for two players.

3. **bullwhack:** a long whip used to drive a team of animals.

a Roman nose[4] as the result of some early injury, her tail was skinny, she had a perfectly venomous look in her eye. My family said—my family discriminated against me—that I was much closer kin to Muff than I was to any of them. To tease me into a tantrum, my brother Jack and my sister Stella often called me Kitty instead of Emily. Little Tess did not dare, because she knew I'd chloroform her if she did. Jack, the meanest boy I have ever known in my life, called me Polecat and talked about my mania for fish, which, it so happened, I despised. The name would have been far more appropriate for *him*, since he trapped skunks up in the foothills—we lived in Adams, Colorado—and quite often, because he was careless and foolhardy, his clothes had to be buried, and even when that was done, he sometimes was sent home from school on the complaint of girls sitting next to him.

Along about Christmastime when I was eleven, I was making a snowman with Virgil Meade in his backyard, and all of a sudden, just as we had got around to the right arm, I had to be alone. So I called him a son of a sea cook, said it was common knowledge that his mother had bedbugs and that his father, a dentist and the deputy marshal, was a bootlegger on the side. For a moment, Virgil was too aghast to speak—a little earlier we had agreed to marry someday and become millionaires—and then, with a bellow of fury, he knocked me down and washed my face in snow. I saw stars, and black balls bounced before my eyes. When finally he let me up, we were both crying, and he hollered that if I didn't get off his property that instant, his father would arrest me and send me to Canon City. I trudged slowly home, half frozen, critically sick at heart. So it was old Muff again for me for quite some time. Old Muff, that is, until I met Lottie Jump, although

"met" is a euphemism[5] for the way I first encountered her.

I saw Lottie for the first time one afternoon in our own kitchen, stealing a chocolate cake. Stella and Jack had not come home from school yet—not having my difficult disposition, they were popular, and they were at their

---

4. **Roman nose:** a nose with a high, curved bridge.

5. **euphemism** (yōo′fə-mĭz′əm): a mild word substituted for a harsher word.

friends' houses, pulling taffy, I suppose, making popcorn balls, playing cassino,[6] having fun—and my mother had taken Tess with her to visit a friend in one of the TB sanitariums. I was alone in the house, and making a funny-looking Christmas card, although I had no one to send it to. When I heard someone in the kitchen, I thought it was Mother home early, and I went out to ask her why the green pine tree I had pasted on a square of red paper looked as if it were falling down. And there, instead of Mother and my baby sister, was this pale, conspicuous child in the act of lifting the glass cover from the devil's-food my mother had taken out of the oven an hour before and set on the plant shelf by the window. The child had her back to me, and when she heard my footfall, she wheeled with an amazing look of fear and hatred on her pinched and pasty face. Simultaneously, she put the cover over the cake again, and then she stood motionless as if she were under a spell.

I was scared, for I was not sure what was happening, and anyhow it gives you a turn to find a stranger in the kitchen in the middle of the afternoon, even if the stranger is only a skinny child in a moldy coat and sopping-wet basketball shoes. Between us there was a lengthy silence, but there was a great deal of noise in the room: the alarm clock ticked smugly; the teakettle simmered patiently on the back of the stove; Muff, cross at having been waked up, thumped her tail against the side of the terrarium in the window where she had been sleeping—contrary to orders—among the geraniums. This went on, it seemed to me, for hours and hours while that tall, sickly girl and I confronted each other. When, after a long time, she did open her mouth, it was to tell a prodigious[7] lie. "I came to see if

you'd like to play with me," she said. I think she sighed and stole a sidelong and regretful glance at the cake.

Beggars cannot be choosers, and I had been missing Virgil so sorely, as well as all those other dear friends forever lost to me, that in spite of her flagrance[8] (she had never clapped eyes on me before, she had had no way of knowing there was a creature of my age in the house—she had come in like a hobo to steal my mother's cake), I was flattered and consoled. I asked her name and, learning it, believed my ears no better than my eyes: Lottie Jump. What on earth! What on earth—you surely will agree with me—and yet when I told her mine, Emily Vanderpool, she laughed until she coughed and gasped. "Beg pardon," she said. "Names like them always hit my funny bone. There was this towhead boy in school named Delbert Saxonfield." I saw no connection and I was insulted (what's so funny about Vanderpool, I'd like to know), but Lottie Jump was, technically, my guest and I *was* lonesome, so I asked her, since she had spoken of playing with me, if she knew how to play Andy-I-Over.[9] She said "Naw." It turned out that she did not know how to play any games at all; she couldn't do anything and didn't want to do anything; her only recreation and her only gift was, and always had been, stealing. But this I did not know at the time.

As it happened, it was too cold and snowy to play outdoors that day anyhow, and after I had run through my list of indoor games and Lottie had shaken her head at all of them (when I spoke of Parcheesi, she went "Ugh!" and pretended to be sick), she suggested that we look through my mother's bureau drawers.

8. **flagrance** (flā′grəns): shocking behavior (here referring to the girl's glaring lie).
9. **Andy-I-Over:** a game in which a ball is tossed over a building or bounced against its side.

6. **cassino:** a card game.
7. **prodigious** (prə-dĭj′əs): enormous.

This did not strike me as strange at all, for it was one of my favorite things to do, and I led the way to Mother's bedroom without a moment's hesitation. I loved the smell of the lavender she kept in gauze bags among her chamois gloves and linen handkerchiefs and filmy scarves; there was a pink fascinator[10] knitted of something as fine as spider's thread, and it made me go quite soft—I wasn't soft as a rule, I was as hard as nails and I gave my mother a rough time—to think of her wearing it around her head as she waltzed on the ice in the bygone days. We examined stockings, nightgowns, camisoles, strings of beads and mosaic pins, keepsake buttons from dresses worn on memorial occasions, tortoiseshell combs, and a transformation[11] made from Aunt Joey's hair when she had racily had it bobbed.[12] Lottie admired particularly a blue cloisonné[13] perfume flask with ferns and peacocks on it. "Hey," she said, "this sure is cute. I like thing-daddies like this here." But very abruptly she got bored and said. "Let's talk instead. In the front room." I agreed, a little perplexed this time, because I had been about to show her a remarkable powder box that played "The Blue Danube."[14] We went into the parlor, where Lottie looked at her image in the pier glass[15] for quite a while and with great absorption, as if she had never seen herself before. Then she moved over to the window seat and knelt on it, looking out at the front walk. She kept her hands in the pockets of her thin dark-red coat; once she took out one of her dirty paws to rub her nose for a minute and I saw a bulge in that pocket, like a bunch of jackstones. I know now that it wasn't jackstones, it was my mother's perfume flask; I thought at the time her hands were cold and that that was why she kept them put away, for I had noticed that she had no mittens.

Lottie did most of the talking, and while she talked, she never once looked at me but kept her eyes fixed on the approach to our house. She told me that her family had come to Adams a month before from Muskogee,[16] Oklahoma, where her father, before he got tuberculosis, had been a brakeman on the Frisco.[17] Now they lived down by Arapahoe[18] Creek, on the west side of town, in one of the cottages of a wretched settlement made up of people so poor and so sick—for in nearly every ramshackle house someone was coughing himself to death—that each time I went past I blushed with guilt because my shoes were sound and my coat was warm and I was well. I wished that Lottie had not told me where she lived, but she was not aware of any pathos[19] in her family's situation, and, indeed, it was with a certain boastfulness that she told me her mother was the short-order[20] cook at the Comanche Café (she pronounced this word in one syllable), which I knew was the dirtiest, darkest, smelliest place in town, patronized by coal miners who never washed their faces and sometimes had such dangerous fights that the sheriff had to come. Laughing, Lottie said that her brother didn't have any brains and had never been to school. She herself was eleven years old, but she was only in the third grade, because teachers had always had it in for her—making her go to the blackboard and all like that when she was tired. She hated school—she

10. **fascinator:** a woman's scarf.
11. **transformation:** a hairpiece.
12. **bobbed:** cut short.
13. **cloisonné** (kloi′zə-nā′): decorative enamelware.
14. **"The Blue Danube":** a waltz by Johann Strauss.
15. **pier glass:** a tall mirror set between windows.

16. **Muskogee** (mŭs-kō′gē).
17. **Frisco:** a railroad line.
18. **Arapahoe** (ə-răp′ə-hō).
19. **pathos** (pā′thŏs′): something that moves people to feel pity.
20. **short-order:** food that is prepared and served quickly.

went to Ashton, on North Hill, and that was why I had never seen her, for I went to Carlyle Hill—and she especially hated the teacher, Miss Cudahy, who had a head shaped like a pine cone and who had killed several people with her ruler. Lottie loved the movies ("Not them Western ones or the ones with apes in," she said. "Ones about hugging and kissing. I love it when they die in that big old soft bed with the curtains up top, and he comes in and says 'Don't leave me, Marguerite de la Mar' "), and she loved to ride in cars. She loved Mr. Goodbars, and if there was one thing she despised worse than another it was tapioca. ("Pa calls it fish eyes. He calls floating island[21] horse spit. He's a big piece of cheese.") She did not like cats (Muff was now sitting on the mantelpiece, glaring like an owl); she kind of liked snakes—except cottonmouths and rattlers—because she found them kind of funny; she had once seen a goat eat a tin can. She said that one of these days she would take me downtown—it was a slowpoke town, she said, a one-horse burg (I had never heard such gaudy, cynical talk and was trying to memorize it all)—if I would get some money for the trolley fare; she hated to walk, and I ought to be proud that she had walked all the way from Arapahoe Creek today for the sole solitary purpose of seeing me.

Seeing our freshly baked dessert in the window was a more likely story, but I did not care, for I was deeply impressed by this bold, sassy girl from Oklahoma and greatly admired the poise with which she aired her prejudices. Lottie Jump was certainly nothing to look at. She was tall and made of skin and bones; she was evilly ugly, and her clothes were a disgrace, not just ill-fitting and old and ragged but dirty, unmentionably so; clearly she did not wash much or brush her teeth, which were

21. **floating island:** a custard dessert.

notched like a saw, and small and brown (it crossed my mind that perhaps she chewed tobacco); her long, lank hair looked as if it might have nits. But she had personality. She made me think of one of those self-contained dogs whose home is where his handout is and who travels alone but, if it suits him to, will become the leader of a pack. She was aloof, never looking at me, but amiable in the way she kept calling me "kid." I liked her enormously, and presently I told her so.

At this, she turned around and smiled at me. Her smile was the smile of a jack-o'-lantern—high, wide, and handsome. When it was over, no trace of it remained. "Well, that's keen, kid, and I like you, too," she said in her downright Muskogee accent. She gave me a long, appraising look. Her eyes were the color of mud. "Listen, kid, how much do you like me?"

"I like you loads, Lottie," I said. "Better than anybody else, and I'm not kidding."

"You want to be pals?"

"Do I!" I cried. So *there*, Virgil Meade, you big fat hootenanny, I thought.

"All right, kid, we'll be pals." And she held out her hand for me to shake. I had to go and get it, for she did not alter her position on the window seat. It was a dry, cold hand, and the grip was severe, with more a feeling of bones in it than friendliness.

Lottie turned and scanned our path and scanned the sidewalk beyond, and then she said, in a lower voice, "Do you know how to lift?"

"Lift?" I wondered if she meant to lift *her*. I was sure I could do it, since she was so skinny, but I couldn't imagine why she would want me to.

"Shoplift, I mean. Like in the five-and-dime."

I did not know the term, and Lottie scowled at my stupidity.

"*Steal*, for crying in the beer!" she said impatiently. This she said so loudly that Muff jumped down from the mantel and left the room in contempt.

I was thrilled to death and shocked to pieces. "Stealing is a sin," I said. "You get put in jail for it."

"Ish ka bibble! I should worry if it's a sin or not," said Lottie, with a shrug. "And they'll never put a smart old whatsis like *me* in jail. It's fun, stealing is—it's a picnic. I'll teach you if you want to learn, kid." Shamelessly she winked at me and grinned again. (That grin! She could have taken it off her face and put it on the table.) And she added, "If you don't, we can't be pals, because lifting is the only kind of playing I like. I hate those dumb games like Statues. Kick-the-Can—phooey!"

I was torn between agitation (I went to Sunday school and knew already about morality; Judge Bay, a crabby old man who loved to punish sinners, was a friend of my father's and once had given Jack a lecture on the criminal mind when he came to call and found Jack looking up an answer in his arithmetic book) and excitement over the daring invitation to misconduct myself in so perilous a way. My life, on reflection, looked deadly prim; all I'd ever done to vary the monotony of it was to swear. I knew that Lottie Jump meant what she said—that I could have her friendship only on her terms (plainly, she had gone it alone for a long time and could go it alone for the rest of her life)—and although I trembled like an aspen[22] and my heart went pitapat, I said, "I want to be pals with you, Lottie."

"All right, Vanderpool," said Lottie, and got off the window seat. "I wouldn't go braggin' about it if I was you. I wouldn't go telling my ma and pa and the next-door neighbor that you and Lottie Jump are going down to the five-and-dime next Saturday aft[23] and lift us some nice rings and garters and things like that. I mean it, kid." And she drew the back of her forefinger across her throat and made a dire face.

"I won't, I promise, I won't. My *gosh*, why would I?"

"That's the ticket," said Lottie, with a grin. "I'll meet you at the trolley shelter at two o'clock. You have the money. For both down and up. I ain't going to climb up that ornery hill after I've had my fun."

"Yes, Lottie," I said. Where was I going to get twenty cents? I was going to have to start stealing before she even taught me how. Lottie was facing the center of the room, but she had eyes in the back of her head, and she whirled around back to the window; my mother and Tess were turning in our front path.

"Back way," I whispered, and in a moment Lottie was gone; the swinging door that usually squeaked did not make a sound as she vanished through it. I listened and I never heard the back door open and close. Nor did I hear her, in a split second, lift the glass cover and remove that cake designed to feed six people.

I was restless and snappish between Wednesday afternoon and Saturday. When Mother found the cake was gone, she scolded me for not keeping my ears cocked. She assumed, naturally, that a tramp had taken it, for she knew I hadn't eaten it; I never ate anything if I could help it (except for raw potatoes, which I loved) and had been known as a problem feeder from the beginning of my life. At first it occurred to me to have a tantrum and bring her around to my point of view: my tantrums scared the living daylights out of her because my veins stood out and I turned blue and couldn't get my breath. But I rejected this for a more sensible

---

22. **aspen:** a tree whose leaves flutter in the slightest breeze.

23. **aft:** afternoon.

plan. I said, "It just so happens I didn't hear anything. But if I had, I suppose you wish I had gone out in the kitchen and let the robber cut me up into a million little tiny pieces with his sword. You wouldn't even bury me. You'd just put me on the dump. *I* know who's wanted in this family and who isn't." Tears of sorrow, not of anger, came in powerful tides and I groped blindly to the bedroom I shared with Stella, where I lay on my bed and shook with big, silent *weltschmerzlich*[24] sobs. Mother followed me immediately, and so did Tess, and both of them comforted me and told me how much they loved me. I said they didn't; they said they did. Presently, I got a headache, as I always did when I cried, so I got to have an aspirin and a cold cloth on my head, and when Jack and Stella came home, they had to be quiet. I heard Jack say, "Emily Vanderpool is the biggest polecat in the U.S.A. Whyn't she go in the kitchen and say, 'Hands up'? He woulda lit out." And Mother said, "Sh-h-h! You don't want your sister to be sick, do you?" Muff, not realizing that Lottie had replaced her, came in and curled up at my thigh, purring lustily; I found myself glad that she had left the room before Lottie Jump made her proposition to me, and in gratitude I stroked her unattractive head.

Other things happened. Mother discovered the loss of her perfume flask and talked about nothing else at meals for two whole days. Luckily, it did not occur to her that it had been stolen—she simply thought she had mislaid it—but her monomania[25] got on my father's nerves and he lashed out at her and at the rest of us. And because I was the cause of it all and my conscience was after me with red-hot pokers, I finally *had* to have a tantrum. I slammed my fork down in the middle of supper on the second day and yelled, "If you don't stop fighting, I'm going to kill myself. Yammer, yammer, nag, nag!" And I put my fingers in my ears and squeezed my eyes tight shut and screamed so the whole country could hear, "Shut *up!*" And then I lost my breath and began to turn blue. Daddy hastily apologized to everyone, and Mother said she was sorry for carrying on so about a trinket that had nothing but sentimental value—she was just vexed with herself for being careless, that was all, and she wasn't going to say another word about it.

I never heard so many references to stealing and cake, and even to Oklahoma (ordinarily no one mentioned Oklahoma once in a month of Sundays) and the ten-cent store as I did throughout those next days. I myself once made a ghastly slip and said something to Stella about "the five-and-dime." "The five-and-*dime!*" she exclaimed. "Where'd you get *that* kind of talk? Do you by any chance have reference to the *ten-cent store?*"

The worst of all was Friday night—the very night before I was to meet Lottie Jump—when Judge Bay came to play two-handed pinochle[26] with Daddy. The Judge, a giant in intimidating haberdashery[27]—for some reason, the white piping on his vest bespoke, for me, handcuffs and prison bars—and with an aura of disapproval for almost everything on earth except what pertained directly to himself, was telling Daddy, before they began their game, about the infamous vandalism that had been going on among the college students. "I have reason to believe that there are girls in this gang as well as boys," he said. "They ransack vacant houses and take everything. In one house on Pleasant Street, up there by the Catholic

---

24. *weltschmerzlich* (vēlt′shměrts′lǐкн): a German word meaning "sorrowful over the state of the world."
25. **monomania** (mŏn′ō-mā′nē-ə): exaggerated interest in one thing.

26. **pinochle** (pē′nŭk′əl): a card game for two to four players.
27. **haberdashery** (hăb′ər-dăsh′ə-rē): men's clothing. The judge's appearance filled Emily with fear.

church, there wasn't anything to take, so they took the kitchen sink. Wasn't a question of taking everything *but*—they took the kitchen sink."

"Whatever would they want with a kitchen sink?" asked my mother.

"Mischief," replied the Judge. "If we ever catch them and if they come within my jurisdiction,[28] I can tell you I will give them no quarter. A thief, in my opinion, is the lowest of the low."

Mother told about the chocolate cake. By now, the fiction was so factual in my mind that each time I thought of it I saw a funny-paper bum in baggy pants held up by rope, a hat with holes through which tufts of hair stuck up, shoes from which his toes protruded, a disreputable stubble on his face; he came up beneath the open window where the devil's-food was cooling, and he stole it and hotfooted it for the woods, where his companion was frying a small fish in a beat-up skillet. It never crossed my mind any longer that Lottie Jump had hooked that delicious cake.

Judge Bay was properly impressed. "If you will steal a chocolate cake, if you will steal a kitchen sink, you will steal diamonds and money. The small child who pilfers a penny from his mother's pocketbook has started down a path that may lead him to holding up a bank."

It was a good thing I had no homework that night, for I could not possibly have concentrated. We were all sent to our rooms, because the pinochle players had to have absolute quiet. I spent the evening doing cross-stitch. I was making a bureau runner for a Christmas present; as in the case of the Christmas card, I had no one to give it to, but now I decided to give it to Lottie Jump's mother. Stella was

reading *Black Beauty*,[29] crying. It was an interminable evening. Stella went to bed first; I saw to that, because I didn't want her lying there awake listening to me talking in my sleep. Besides, I didn't want her to see me tearing open the cardboard box—the one in the shape of a church, which held my Christmas Sunday-school offering. Over the door of the church was this shaming legend: "My mite[30] for the poor widow." When Stella had begun to grind her teeth in her first deep sleep, I took twenty cents away from the poor widow, whoever she was (the owner of the kitchen sink, no doubt), for the trolley fare, and secreted it and the remaining three pennies in the pocket of my middy. I wrapped the money well in a handkerchief and buttoned the pocket and hung my skirt over the middy. And then I tore the paper church into bits—the heavens opened and Judge Bay came toward me with a double-barreled shotgun—and hid the bits under a pile of pajamas. I did not sleep one wink. Except that I must have, because of the stupendous nightmares that kept wrenching the flesh off my skeleton and caused me to come close to perishing of thirst; once I fell out of bed and hit my head on Stella's ice skates. I would have waked her up and given her a piece of my mind for leaving them in such a lousy place, but then I remembered: I wanted *no* commotion of any kind.

I couldn't eat breakfast and I couldn't eat lunch. Old Johnny-on-the-spot Jack kept saying "*Poor* Polecat. Polecat wants her fish for dinner." Mother made an abortive[31] attempt to take my temperature. And when all that hullabaloo subsided, I was nearly in the soup because Mother asked me to mind Tess while she

28. **jurisdiction** (joor'əs-dĭk'shən): authority or legal power.

29. ***Black Beauty:*** a well-known story about a horse by Anna Sewell.
30. **mite:** a small sum of money. The reference to the widow is from Mark 12:42–44.
31. **abortive** (ə-bôr'tĭv): unsuccessful.

went to the sanitarium to see Mrs. Rogers, who, all of a sudden, was too sick to have anyone but grown-ups near her. Stella couldn't stay with the baby, because she had to go to ballet, and Jack couldn't, because he had to go up to the mesa and empty his traps. ("No, they *can't* wait. You want my skins to rot in this hot-one-day-cold-the-next weather?") I was arguing and whining when the telephone rang. Mother went to answer it and came back with a look of great sadness; Mrs. Rogers, she had learned, had had another hemorrhage. So Mother would not be going to the sanitarium after all and I needn't stay with Tess.

By the time I left the house, I was as cross as a bear. I felt awful about the widow's mite and I felt awful for being mean about staying with Tess, for Mrs. Rogers was a kind old lady, in a cozy blue hug-me-tight[32] and an oldfangled boudoir cap,[33] dying here all alone; she was a friend of Grandma's and had lived just down the street from her in Missouri, and all in the world Mrs. Rogers wanted to do was go back home and lie down in her own big bedroom in her own big, high-ceilinged house and have Grandma and other members of the Eastern Star[34] come in from time to time to say hello. But they wouldn't let her go home; they were going to kill or cure her. I could not help feeling that my hardness of heart and evil of intention had had a good deal to do with her new crisis; right at the very same minute I had been saying "Does that old Mrs. Methuselah[35] *always* have to spoil my fun?" the poor wasted thing was probably coughing up her blood and saying to the nurse, "Tell Emily Vanderpool not to mind me, she can run and play."

I had a bad character, I know that, but my badness never gave me half the enjoyment Jack and Stella thought it did. A good deal of the time I wanted to eat lye. I was certainly having no fun now, thinking of Mrs. Rogers and of depriving that poor widow of bread and milk; what if this penniless woman without a husband had a dog to feed, too? Or a baby? And besides, I didn't want to go downtown to steal anything from the ten-cent store; I didn't want to see Lottie Jump again—not really, for I knew in my bones that that girl was trouble with a capital *T*. And still, in our short meeting she had mesmerized[36] me; I would think about her style of talking and the expert way she had made off with the perfume flask and the cake (how had she carried the cake through the streets without being noticed?) and be bowled over, for the part of me that did not love God was a black-hearted villain. And apart from these considerations, I had some sort of idea that if I did not keep my appointment with Lottie Jump, she would somehow get revenge; she had seemed a girl of purpose. So, revolted and fascinated, brave and lily-livered, I plodded along through the snow in my flopping galoshes up toward the Chautauqua,[37] where the trolley stop was. On my way, I passed Virgil Meade's house; there was not just a snowman, there was a whole snow family in the backyard, and Virgil himself was throwing a stick for his dog. I was delighted to see that he was alone.

Lottie, who was sitting on a bench in the shelter eating a Mr. Goodbar, looked the same as she had the other time except that she was wearing an amazing hat. I think I had expected her to have a black handkerchief over the lower part of her face or to be wearing a

---

32. **hug-me-tight:** a short wraparound jacket worn by a woman.
33. **boudoir** (bōō′dwär′) **cap:** a woman's nightcap.
34. **Eastern Star:** a Masonic order for women.
35. **Mrs. Methuselah** (mĕ-thōō′zə-lə): According to Genesis 5:27, Methuselah lived 969 years.

36. **mesmerized** (mĕz′mə-rīzd′): fascinated.
37. **Chautauqua** (shə-tô′kwə): an annual program of educational assemblies, which flourished during the late nineteenth and early twentieth centuries; here applied to the meetinghouse.

Jesse James waistcoat. But I had never thought of a hat. It was felt; it was the color of cooked meat; it had some flowers appliquéd[38] on the front of it; it had no brim, but rose straight up to a very considerable height, like a monument. It sat so low on her forehead and it was so tight that it looked, in a way, like part of her.

"How's every little thing, bub?" she said, licking her candy wrapper.

"Fine, Lottie," I said, freshly awed.

A silence fell. I drank some water from the drinking fountain, sat down, fastened my galoshes, and unfastened them again.

"My mother's teeth grow wrong way too," said Lottie, and showed me what she meant: the lower teeth were in front of the upper ones. "That so-called trolley car takes its own sweet time. This town is blah."

To save the honor of my hometown, the trolley came scraping and groaning up the hill just then, its bell clanging with an idiotic frenzy, and ground to a stop. Its broad, proud cowcatcher[39] was filled with dirty snow, in the middle of which rested a tomato can, put there, probably, by somebody who was bored to death and couldn't think of anything else to do—I did a lot of pointless things like that on lonesome Saturday afternoons. It was the custom of this trolley car, a rather mysterious one, to pause at the shelter for five minutes while the conductor, who was either Mr. Jansen or Mr. Peck, depending on whether it was the A.M. run or the P.M., got out and stretched and smoked and spit. Sometimes the passengers got out, too, acting like sightseers whose destination was this sturdy stucco gazebo instead of, as it really was, the Piggly Wiggly or the Nelson Dry. You expected them to take snapshots of the drinking fountain or of the Chautauqua meetinghouse up on the hill. And when they all got back in the car, you expected them to exchange intelligent observations on the aborigines[40] and the ruins they had seen.

Today there were no passengers, and as soon as Mr. Peck got out and began staring at the mountains as if he had never seen them before while he made himself a cigarette, Lottie, in her tall hat (was it something like the Inspector's hat in the Katzenjammer Kids?),[41] got into the car, motioning me to follow. I put our nickels in the empty box and joined her on the very last double seat. It was only then that she mapped out the plan for the afternoon, in a low but still insouciant[42] voice. The hat—she did not apologize for it, she simply referred to it as "my hat"—was to be the repository[43] of whatever we stole. In the future, it would be advisable for me to have one like it. (How? Surely it was unique. The flowers, I saw on closer examination, were tulips, but they were blue, and a very unsettling shade of blue.) I was to engage a clerk on one side of the counter, asking her the price of, let's say, a tube of Daggett & Ramsdell vanishing cream, while Lottie would lift a round comb or a barrette or a hair net or whatever on the other side. Then, at a signal, I would decide against the vanishing cream and would move on to the next counter that she indicated. The signal was interesting; it was to be the raising of her hat from the rear—"like I've got the itch and gotta scratch," she said. I was relieved that I was to have no part in the actual stealing, and I was touched that Lottie, who was going to do all the work, said we would "go halvers" on the take. She asked me if there was anything in particular I wanted—she herself had nothing special in mind and was going to shop around

38. **appliquéd** (ap'lə-kād'): attached as a decoration.
39. **cowcatcher:** a metal frame on the front of a streetcar used to clear the tracks.
40. **aborigines** (ăb'ə-rĭj'ə-nēz): the earliest inhabitants of a region.
41. **Katzenjammer Kids:** the name of a comic strip.
42. **insouciant** (ĭn-sōō'sē-ənt): carefree.
43. **repository** (rĭ-pŏz'ə-tôr'ē): place used for storage.

first—and I said I would like some rubber gloves. This request was entirely spontaneous; I had never before in my life thought of rubber gloves in one way or another, but a psychologist—or Judge Bay—might have said that this was most significant and that I was planning at that moment to go on from petty larceny to bigger game, armed with a weapon on which I wished to leave no fingerprints.

On the way downtown, quite a few people got on the trolley, and they all gave us such peculiar looks that I was chickenhearted until I realized it must be Lottie's hat they were looking at. No wonder. I kept looking at it myself out of the corner of my eye; it was like a watermelon standing on end. No, it was like a tremendous test tube. On this trip—a slow one, for the trolley pottered through that part of town in a desultory,[44] neighborly way, even going into areas where no one lived—Lottie told me some of the things she had stolen in Muskogee and here in Adams. They included a white satin prayer book (think of it!), Mr. Goodbars by the thousands (she had probably never paid for a Mr. Goodbar in her life), a dinner ring valued at two dollars, a strawberry emery, several cans of corn, some shoelaces, a set of poker chips, countless pencils, four spark plugs ("Pa had this old car, see, and it was broke, so we took 'er to get fixed; I'll build me a radio with 'em sometime—you know? Listen in on them earmuffs to Tulsa?"), a Boy Scout knife, and a Girl Scout folding cup. She made a regular practice of going through the pockets of the coats in the cloakroom every day at recess, but she had never found anything there worth a red cent and was about to give that up. Once, she had taken a gold pencil from a teacher's desk and had got caught—she was sure that this was one of the reasons she was only in the third grade. Of this unjust ex-

perience, she said, "The old hoot owl! If I was drivin' in a car on a lonesome stretch and she was settin' beside me, I'd wait till we got to a pile of gravel and then I'd stop and say, 'Git out, Miss Priss.' She'd git out, all right."

Since Lottie was so frank, I was emboldened at last to ask her what she had done with the cake. She faced me with her grin; this grin, in combination with the hat, gave me a surprise from which I have never recovered. "I ate it up," she said. "I went in your garage and sat on your daddy's old tires and ate it. It was pretty good."

There were two ten-cent stores side by side in our town. Kresge's and Woolworth's, and as we walked down the main street toward them, Lottie played with a yo-yo. Since the street was thronged with Christmas shoppers and farmers in for Saturday, this was no ordinary accomplishment; all in all, Lottie Jump was someone to be reckoned with. I cannot say that I was proud to be seen with her; the fact is that I hoped I would not meet anyone I knew, and I thanked my lucky stars that Jack was up in the hills with his dead skunks, because if he had seen her with that lid and that yo-yo, I would never have heard the last of it. But in another way I *was* proud to be with her; in a smaller hemisphere, in one that included only her and me, I was swaggering—I felt like Somebody, marching along beside this lofty Somebody from Oklahoma who was going to hold up the dime store.

There is nothing like Woolworth's at Christmastime. It smells of peanut brittle and terrible chocolate candy, Djer-Kiss talcum powder and Ben Hur perfume—smells sourly of tinsel and waxily of artificial poinsettias.[45] The crowds are made up largely of children and women, with here and there a delibera-

44. **desultory** (dĕs′əl-tôr′ē): aimless.

45. **poinsettias** (poin-sĕt′ē-əz): yellow flowers surrounded by red leaves.

tive[46] old man; the women are buying ribbons and wrappings and Christmas cards, and the children are buying asbestos pot holders for their mothers and, for their fathers, suede bookmarks with a burnt-in design that says "A good book is a good friend" or "Souvenir from the Garden of the Gods." It is very noisy. The salesgirls are forever ringing their bells and asking the floorwalker to bring them change for a five; babies in go-carts are screaming as parcels fall on their heads; the women, waving rolls of red tissue paper, try to attract the attention of the harried girl behind the counter. ("Miss! All I want is this one batch of the red. Can't I just give you the dime?" And the girl, beside herself, mottled with vexation, cries back, "Has to be rung up, Moddom, that's the rule.") There is pandemonium[47] at the toy counter, where things are being tested by the customers—wound up, set off, tooted, pounded, made to say "Maaaah-Maaaah!" There is very little gaiety in the scene and, in fact, those baffled old men look as if they were walking over their own dead bodies, but there is an atmosphere of carnival, nevertheless, and as soon as Lottie and I entered the doors of Woolworth's golden-and-vermilion bedlam,[48] I grew giddy and hot—not pleasantly so. The feeling, indeed, was distinctly disagreeable, like the beginning of a stomach upset.

Lottie gave me a nudge and said softly, "Go look at the envelopes. I want some rubber bands."

This counter was relatively uncrowded (the seasonal stationery supplies—the Christmas cards and wrapping paper and stickers—were at a separate counter), and I went around to examine some very beautiful letter paper; it was pale pink and it had a border of roses all

46. **deliberative** (dĭ-lĭb′ə-rā′tĭv): deep in thought.
47. **pandemonium** (păn′də-mō′nē-əm): disorder.

48. **bedlam** (bĕd′ləm): noise and confusion.

around it. The clerk here was a cheerful middle-aged woman wearing an apron, and she was giving all her attention to a seedy old man who could not make up his mind between mucilage and paste. "Take your time, Dad," she said. "Compared to the rest of the girls, I'm on my vacation." The old man, holding a tube in one hand and a bottle in the other, looked at her vaguely and said, "I want it for stamps. Sometimes I write a letter and stamp it and then don't mail it and steam the stamp off. Must have ninety cents' worth of stamps like that." The woman laughed. "I know what you mean," she said. "I get mad and write a letter and then I tear it up." The old man gave her a condescending look[49] and said, "That so? But I don't suppose yours are of a political nature." He bent his gaze again to the choice of adhesives.

This first undertaking was duck soup for Lottie. I did not even have to exchange a word with the woman; I saw Miss Fagin[50] lift up *that hat* and give me the high sign, and we moved away, she down one aisle and I down the other, now and again catching a glimpse of each other through the throngs. We met at the foot of the second counter, where notions were sold.

"Fun, huh?" said Lottie, and I nodded, although I felt wholly dreary. "I want some crochet hooks," she said. "Price the rickrack."

This time the clerk was adding up her receipts and did not even look at me or at a woman who was angrily and in vain trying to buy a paper of pins. Out went Lottie's scrawny hand, up went her domed chimney. In this way for some time she bagged sitting birds: a tea strainer (there was no one at all at that counter), a box of Mrs. Carpenter's All-Purpose Nails, the rubber gloves I had said I wanted, and four packages of mixed seeds. Now you have some idea of the size of Lottie Jump's hat.

I was nervous, not from being her accomplice but from being in this crowd on an empty stomach, and I was getting tired—we had been in the store for at least an hour—and the whole enterprise seemed pointless. There wasn't a thing in her hat I wanted—not even the rubber gloves. But in exact proportion as my spirits descended, Lottie's rose; clearly she had only been target-practicing and now she was moving in for the kill.

We met beside the books of paper dolls, for reconnaissance.[51] "I'm gonna get me a pair of pearl beads," said Lottie. "You go fuss with the hairpins, hear?"

Luck, combined with her skill, would have stayed with Lottie, and her hat would have been a cornucopia[52] by the end of the afternoon if, at the very moment her hand went out for the string of beads, that idiosyncrasy[53] of mine had not struck me full force. I had never known it to come with so few preliminaries; probably this was so because I was oppressed by all the masses of bodies poking and pushing me, and all the open mouths breathing in my face. Anyhow, right then, at the crucial time, I *had to be alone*.

I stood staring down at the bone hairpins for a moment, and when the girl behind the counter said, "What kind does Mother want, hon? What color is Mother's hair?" I looked past her and across at Lottie and I said, "Your brother isn't the only one in your family that doesn't have any brains." The clerk, aston-

49. **condescending** (kŏn′dĭ-sĕnd′ĭng) **look:** a look suggesting a low opinion of another person.
50. **Miss Fagin** (fā′gən): Fagin is a character who runs a school for thieves in Charles Dickens' novel *Oliver Twist*. Like Fagin, Lottie gives lessons in stealing.
51. **reconnaissance** (rĭ-kŏn′ə-səns): a survey made in preparation for an attack.
52. **cornucopia** (kôr′nə-kō′pē-ə): a container overflowing with abundance.
53. **idiosyncrasy** (ĭd′ē-ō-sĭng′krə-sē): a personal peculiarity.

of shoulder and jaw, was instantly standing beside Lottie, holding her arm with one hand while with the other he removed her hat to reveal to the overjoyed audience that incredible array of merchandise. Her hair all wild, her face a mask of innocent bewilderment, Lottie Jump, the scurvy thing, pretended to be deaf and dumb. She pointed at the rubber gloves and then she pointed at me, and Mr. Bellamy, able at last to prove his mettle, said "Aha!" and, still holding Lottie, moved around the counter to me and grabbed *my* arm. He gave the hat to the clerk and asked her kindly to accompany him and his red-handed catch to the manager's office.

I don't know where Lottie is now—whether she is on the stage or in jail. If her performance after our arrest meant anything, the first is quite as likely as the second. (I never saw her again, and for all I know she lit out of town that night on a freight train. Or perhaps her whole family decamped as suddenly as they had arrived; ours was the most transient population. You can be sure I made no attempt to find her again, and for months I avoided going anywhere near Arapahoe Creek or North Hill.) She never said a word but kept making signs with her fingers, ad-libbing[54] the whole thing. They tested her hearing by shooting off a popgun right in her ear and she never batted an eyelid.

They called up my father, and he came over from the Safeway on the double. I heard very little of what he said because I was crying so hard, but one thing I did hear him say was "Well, young lady, I guess you've seen to it that I'll have to part company with my good friend Judge Bay." I tried to defend myself, but it was useless. The manager, Mr. Bellamy, the clerk, and my father patted Lottie on the shoulder,

ished, turned to look where I was looking and caught Lottie in the act of lifting up her hat to put the pearls inside. She had unwisely chosen a long strand and was having a little trouble; I had the nasty thought that it looked as if her brains were leaking out.

The clerk, not able to deal with this emergency herself, frantically punched her bell and cried, "Floorwalker! Mr. Bellamy! I've caught a thief!"

Momentarily there was a violent hush—then such a clamor as you have never heard. Bells rang, babies howled, crockery crashed to the floor as people stumbled in their rush to the arena.

Mr. Bellamy, nineteen years old but broad

---

54. **ad-libbing** (ăd-lĭb′ĭng): making up on the spot.

and the clerk said, "Poor, afflicted child." For being a poor, afflicted child, they gave her a bag of hard candy, and she gave them the most fraudulent smile of gratitude, and slobbered a little, and shuffled out, holding her empty hat in front of her like a beggarman. I hate Lottie Jump to this day, but I have to hand it to her—she was a genius.

The floorwalker would have liked to see me sentenced to the reform school for life, I am sure, but the manager said that considering this was my first offense, he would let my father attend to my punishment. The clerk, who looked precisely like Emmy Schmalz, clucked her tongue and shook her head at me. My father hustled me out of the office and out of the store and into the car and home, muttering the entire time; now and again I'd hear the words *morals* and *nowadays*.

What's the use of telling the rest? You know what happened. Daddy on second thoughts decided not to hang his head in front of Judge Bay but to make use of his friendship in this time of need, and he took me to see the scary old curmudgeon[55] at his house. All I remember of that long declamation, during which the Judge sat behind his desk never taking his eyes off me, was the warning "I want you to give this a great deal of thought, Miss. I want you to search and seek in the innermost corners of your conscience and root out every bit of badness." Oh, *him*! Why, listen, if I'd rooted out all the badness in me, there wouldn't have been anything left of me. My mother cried for days

because she had nurtured an outlaw and was ashamed to show her face at the neighborhood store; my father was silent, and he often looked at me. Stella, who was a prig, said, "And to think you did it at *Christmas*time!" As for Jack—well, Jack a couple of times did not know how close he came to seeing glory when I had a butcher knife in my hand. It was Polecat this and Polecat that until I nearly went off my rocker. Tess, of course, didn't know what was going on, and asked so many questions that finally I told her to go to Helen Hunt Jackson[56] in a savage tone of voice.

Good old Muff.

It is not true that you don't learn by experience. At any rate, I did that time. I began immediately to have two or three friends at a time—to be sure, because of the stigma on me, they were by no means the elite[57] of Carlyle Hill Grade—and never again when that terrible need to be alone arose did I let fly. I would say, instead, "I've got a headache. I'll have to go home and take an aspirin," or "Gosh all hemlocks, I forgot—I've got to go to the dentist."

After the scandal died down, I got into the Campfire Girls. It was through pull, of course, since Stella had been a respected member for two years and my mother was a friend of the leader. But it turned out all right. Even Muff did not miss our periods of companionship, because about that time she grew up and started having literally millions of kittens.

55. **curmudgeon** (kər-mŭj′ən): a bad-tempered person.

56. **Helen Hunt Jackson:** the author of *Ramona*, a love story.
57. **elite** (ĭ-lēt′): the most distinguished social group.

Reading Check

1. At the opening of the story, why is Emily without any friends?
2. What does Lottie steal from Emily's house?
3. How does Emily get fare for the trolley?
4. How does Lottie use her hat?
5. Why isn't Lottie punished?

For Study and Discussion

Analyzing and Interpreting the Story

1. This story tells of the brief but eventful relationship of two girls who turn out to be the "bad characters" of the title. Are Lottie and Emily "bad" in the same way? Tell how their characters are different.

2. Emily surprises Lottie Jump in the act of stealing a cake. However, when Lottie explains her presence with a lie, Emily accepts the explanation. Why?

3. Although Lottie is "nothing to look at," Emily is drawn to her. What does she find attractive in Lottie's personality?

4. Emily says she knows about *morality*, that is, the difference between right and wrong. **a.** Why, then, does she come under Lottie's harmful influence so easily? **b.** Why does she agree to help Lottie steal?

5. As Saturday afternoon draws near, Emily's conscience is troubled. What events occur on Friday night that increase her sense of guilt?

6. When she is standing at the counter in Woolworth's, Emily suddenly gets the urge to be alone. Do you think she wants to be caught? Explain your answer.

7. Lottie has the stolen merchandise in her hat, but it is Emily who is punished for stealing. **a.** How does Lottie manage to outwit everyone? **b.** Why do you think Emily is unable to defend herself?

8. How does Emily reform at the end of the story?

Literary Elements

Recognizing Clues to Later Actions

Very often a writer establishes the way a character behaves early in a story to prepare the reader for what that character will do later on. What you learn about Emily in the first few paragraphs prepares you for her actions later in the story. For example, you are told that Emily sometimes has a powerful need to be alone, a need that leads her to insult her friends. In what way does the incident with Virgil Meade prepare you for what happens later in Woolworth's? You also learn that Emily's brother and sister often tease her into a tantrum. How does this information prepare you for the scene that takes place later at the dinner table (page 58)?

When you first meet Lottie, you learn certain things about her that signal what is to come. When she is caught stealing the cake, she makes up a monstrous lie. She then manages to steal a perfume flask under Emily's very nose. At the end of the story, how does Lottie use her talent for deceiving people?

Language and Vocabulary

Learning Words That Come from Names

You probably know that the word *pasteurize* comes from the name of Louis Pasteur, the French bacteriologist who found a way of destroying harmful bacteria in milk and other liquids. A number of words in our language come from the names of persons and places.

The word *mesmerize* means "to hypnotize" or "to fascinate." It comes from the name of Franz Anton Mesmer, an Austrian physician who practiced hypnotism in connection with certain of his theories. When Emily says that she is *mesmerized* by Lottie, she means that she is unable to resist Lottie's influence.

Emily speaks of entering the *bedlam* of Woolworth's. The word *bedlam* now means any place of confusion. Use a dictionary to find the origin of this word.

Each of these words comes from the name of a person or place. Use a dictionary to find the origin of the word, what it means today, and how it came to have its modern meaning.

badminton	gerrymander	maverick
boycott	hamburger	tuxedo
derrick	macadam	watt

Descriptive Writing

Describing an Unusual Object

Reread the humorous description of Lottie Jump's hat on page 61, noting the author's use of detail. Choose an unusual object (or create one) and write a description, using specific details and vivid modifiers. Here are some suggestions:

An original Halloween costume
A super burger
A one-of-a-kind dessert
A coin (stamp) collection

About the Author

Jean Stafford (1915–1979)

Jean Stafford once said that her roots were in the semifictitious town of Adams, Colorado, where her stories about Emily Vanderpool are set. Her short stories and articles appeared in *The New Yorker*, *Vogue, Harper's,* and other magazines. Among her novels are *Boston Adventure, The Mountain Lion,* and *The Catherine Wheel.* She also wrote a children's book with the intriguing title *Elephi, the Cat with the High IQ.* Elephi can turn on electric lights, drink from a faucet, and play games. Jean Stafford was awarded the Pulitzer Prize in 1970 for her book *Collected Stories.*

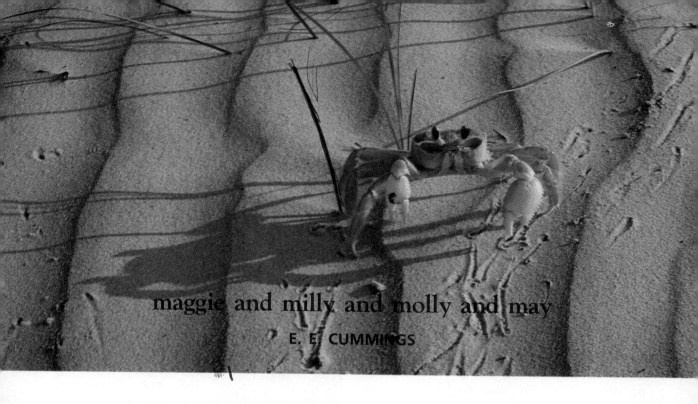

maggie and milly and molly and may

E. E. CUMMINGS

What makes this poem look unusual? Can you suggest the poet's reason for not using capitalization and standard punctuation?

maggie and milly and molly and may
went down to the beach(to play one day)

and maggie discovered a shell that sang
so sweetly she couldn't remember her troubles,and

milly befriended a stranded star   5
whose rays five languid fingers were;

and molly was chased by a horrible thing
which raced sideways while blowing bubbles:and

may came home with a smooth round stone
as small as a world and as large as alone.   10

For whatever we lose(like a you or a me)
it's always ourselves we find in the sea

Analyzing and Interpreting the Poem

1. The poet tells us that *maggie* "discovered a shell that sang." **a.** What kind of music does a seashell make? **b.** How do you know that *maggie* tends to daydream?

2a. How do you know that the "star" in line 5 is a starfish? (What clues does the poet give you?) **b.** What does *milly*'s discovery tell you about her?

3a. What is the "horrible thing" that races with a sidewise motion? **b.** What does *molly*'s reaction reveal about her?

4a. In what way can a stone be both small and large? Explain the meaning of line 10. **b.** Do you think *may* is imaginative?

5. The poet says in the last line that we always find ourselves in the sea. How does each girl's personality determine what she sees?

6. E. E. Cummings' poetry looks unusual on the page. He experiments with capitalization and punctuation. His purpose, in part, is to make readers approach his poems as original and fresh works. **a.** Can you suggest a reason for *not* capitalizing the names in this poem? **b.** What do you think is the purpose of closing up spaces before parenthetical expressions? **c.** How do these visual devices add a sense of fun?

For Oral Recitation

Preparing a Reading of the Poem

Practice reading Cummings' poem aloud, paying attention to meaning as well as to sound. Where will you pause in your reading? Does Cummings give you any clues in the way he punctuates the poem?

About the Author

E. E. Cummings (1894–1962)

E. E. Cummings, whose full name was Edward Estlin Cummings, was born in Cambridge, Massachusetts, and educated at Harvard University. He went to France during World War I to serve as an ambulance driver, but because of a censor's mistake, he spent three months in a French detention camp. He later wrote about this experience in *The Enormous Room*.

Cummings is known for his highly individual poetic technique, particularly his unusual arrangement of words on the page and his minimal use of capital letters and punctuation. However, the subject matter of his poems is often traditional. Many of his poems are about the beauty and joy of nature.

The Circuit

FRANCISCO JIMÉNEZ°

Chicano literature is literature written by Americans of Mexican descent. A number of Chicano stories, like this one, deal with the hard lives of migrant workers and the hopes and dreams of their children.

It was that time of year again. Ito, the strawberry sharecropper,[1] did not smile. It was natural. The peak of the strawberry season was over and the last few days the workers, most of them braceros,[2] were not picking as many boxes as they had during the months of June and July.

As the last days of August disappeared, so did the number of braceros. Sunday, only one—the best picker—came to work. I liked him. Sometimes we talked during our half-hour lunch break. That is how I found out he was from Jalisco,[3] the same state in Mexico my family was from. That Sunday was the last time I saw him.

When the sun had tired and sunk behind the mountains, Ito signaled us that it was time to

° **Jiménez** (hē-měn'ĕz).
1. **sharecropper:** one who farms land belonging to someone else and who pays rent by giving part of his crop to the owner.
2. **braceros** (brä-sâr'ōs): farm laborers.

3. **Jalisco** (hä-lēs'kō): a state in west-central Mexico.

go home. "Ya esora,"[4] he yelled in his broken Spanish. Those were the words I waited for twelve hours a day, every day, seven days a week, week after week. And the thought of not hearing them again saddened me.

As we drove home Papá did not say a word. With both hands on the wheel, he stared at the dirt road. My older brother, Roberto, was also silent. He leaned his head back and closed his eyes. Once in a while he cleared from his throat the dust that blew in from outside.

Yes, it was that time of year. When I opened the front door to the shack, I stopped. Everything we owned was neatly packed in cardboard boxes. Suddenly I felt even more the weight of hours, days, weeks, and months of work. I sat down on a box. The thought of having to move to Fresno and knowing what was in store for me there brought tears to my eyes.

That night I could not sleep. I lay in bed thinking about how much I hated this move.

A little before five o'clock in the morning, Papá woke everyone up. A few minutes later, the yelling and screaming of my little brothers and sisters, for whom the move was a great adventure, broke the silence of dawn. Shortly, the barking of the dogs accompanied them.

While we packed the breakfast dishes, Papá went outside to start the "Carcanchita."[5] That was the name Papá gave his old '38 black Plymouth. He bought it in a used-car lot in Santa Rosa in the winter of 1949. Papá was very proud of his little jalopy. He had a right to be proud of it. He spent a lot of time looking at other cars before buying this one. When he finally chose the "Carcanchita," he checked it thoroughly before driving it out of the car lot. He examined every inch of the car. He listened to the motor, tilting his head from side to side like a parrot, trying to detect any noises that

spelled car trouble. After being satisfied with the looks and sounds of the car, Papá then insisted on knowing who the original owner was. He never did find out from the car salesman, but he bought the car anyway. Papá figured the original owner must have been an important man because behind the rear seat of the car he found a blue necktie.

Papá parked the car out in front and left the motor running. "Listo," he yelled. Without saying a word, Roberto and I began to carry the boxes out to the car. Roberto carried the two big boxes and I carried the two smaller ones. Papá then threw the mattress on top of the car roof and tied it with ropes to the front and rear bumpers.

Everything was packed except Mamá's pot. It was an old large galvanized[6] pot she had picked up at an army surplus store in Santa María the year I was born. The pot had many dents and nicks, and the more dents and nicks it acquired the more Mamá liked it. "Mi olla,"[7] she used to say proudly.

I held the front door open as Mamá carefully carried out her pot by both handles, making sure not to spill the cooked beans. When she got to the car, Papá reached out to help her with it. Roberto opened the rear car door and Papá gently placed it on the floor behind the front seat. All of us then climbed in. Papá sighed, wiped the sweat off his forehead with his sleeve, and said wearily: "Es todo."[8]

As we drove away, I felt a lump in my throat. I turned around and looked at our little shack for the last time.

At sunset we drove into a labor camp near Fresno. Since Papá did not speak English, Mamá asked the camp foreman if he needed any more workers. "We don't need no more,"

4. **Ya esora** (ĕs ô′rä): *es hora* (It's time).
5. **"Carcanchita"** (kär-kän-chē′tä).

6. **galvanized** (găl′və-nīzd′): coated with zinc to resist rust.
7. **Mi olla** (mē ô′yä): My pot.
8. **Es todo** (ĕs tō′*thō*): That's all.

said the foreman, scratching his head. "Check with Sullivan down the road. Can't miss him. He lives in a big white house with a fence around it."

When we got there, Mamá walked up to the house. She went through a white gate, past a row of rose bushes, up the stairs to the front door. She rang the doorbell. The porch light went on and a tall husky man came out. They exchanged a few words. After the man went in, Mamá clasped her hands and hurried back to the car. "We have work! Mr. Sullivan said we can stay there the whole season," she said, gasping and pointing to an old garage near the stables.

The garage was worn out by the years. It had no windows. The walls, eaten by termites, strained to support the roof full of holes. The dirt floor, populated by earthworms, looked like a gray road map.

That night, by the light of a kerosene lamp, we unpacked and cleaned our new home. Roberto swept away the loose dirt, leaving the hard ground. Papá plugged the holes in the walls with old newspapers and tin can tops. Mamá fed my little brothers and sisters. Papá and Roberto then brought in the mattress and placed it on the far corner of the garage. "Mamá, you and the little ones sleep on the mattress. Roberto, Panchito, and I will sleep outside under the trees," Papá said.

Early next morning Mr. Sullivan showed us where his crop was, and after breakfast, Papá, Roberto, and I headed for the vineyard to pick.

Around nine o'clock the temperature had risen to almost one hundred degrees. I was completely soaked in sweat and my mouth felt as if I had been chewing on a handkerchief. I walked over to the end of the row, picked up the jug of water we had brought, and began drinking. "Don't drink too much; you'll get sick," Roberto shouted. No sooner had he said that than I felt sick to my stomach. I dropped to my knees and let the jug roll off my hands. I remained motionless with my eyes glued on the hot sandy ground. All I could hear was the drone of insects. Slowly I began to recover. I poured water over my face and neck and watched the dirty water run down my arms to the ground.

I still felt a little dizzy when we took a break to eat lunch. It was past two o'clock and we sat underneath a large walnut tree that was on the side of the road. While we ate, Papá jotted down the number of boxes we had picked. Roberto drew designs on the ground with a stick. Suddenly I noticed Papá's face turn pale as he looked down the road. "Here comes the school bus," he whispered loudly in alarm. Instinctively, Roberto and I ran and hid in the vineyards. We did not want to get in trouble for not going to school. The neatly dressed boys about my age got off. They carried books under their arms. After they crossed the street, the bus drove away. Roberto and I came out from hiding and joined Papá. "Tienen que tener cuidado,"[9] he warned us.

After lunch we went back to work. The sun kept beating down. The buzzing insects, the wet sweat, and the hot dry dust made the afternoon seem to last forever. Finally the mountains around the valley reached out and swallowed the sun. Within an hour it was too dark to continue picking. The vines blanketed the grapes, making it difficult to see the bunches. "Vámonos,"[10] said Papá, signaling to us that it was time to quit work. Papá then took out a pencil and began to figure out how much we had earned our first day. He wrote down numbers, crossed some out, wrote down some more. "Quince,"[11] he murmured.

9. **Tienen que tener cuidado** (tyĕ′nĕn kĕ tĕ-nĕr′ kwē-thä′thō): You have to be careful.
10. **Vámonos** (vä′mä-nōs′): Let's go.
11. **Quince** (kēn′sĕ): Fifteen.

When we arrived home, we took a cold shower underneath a waterhose. We then sat down to eat dinner around some wooden crates that served as a table. Mamá had cooked a special meal for us. We had rice and tortillas with "carne con chile,"[12] my favorite dish.

The next morning I could hardly move. My body ached all over. I felt little control over my arms and legs. This feeling went on every morning for days until my muscles finally got used to the work.

It was Monday, the first week of November. The grape season was over and I could now go to school. I woke up early that morning and lay in bed, looking at the stars and savoring the thought of not going to work and of starting sixth grade for the first time that year. Since I could not sleep, I decided to get up and join Papá and Roberto at breakfast. I sat at the table across from Roberto, but I kept my head down. I did not want to look up and face him.

12. **carne con chile** (kär′nĕ kōn chēl′ĕ): a dish made of meat, beans, and red peppers.

I knew he was sad. He was not going to school today. He was not going tomorrow, or next week, or next month. He would not go until the cotton season was over, and that was sometime in February. I rubbed my hands together and watched the dry, acid stained skin fall to the floor in little rolls.

When Papá and Roberto left for work, I felt relief. I walked to the top of a small grade next to the shack and watched the "Carcanchita" disappear in the distance in a cloud of dust.

Two hours later, around eight o'clock, I stood by the side of the road waiting for school bus number twenty. When it arrived I climbed in. Everyone was busy either talking or yelling. I sat in an empty seat in the back.

When the bus stopped in front of the school, I felt very nervous. I looked out the bus window and saw boys and girls carrying books under their arms. I put my hands in my pant pockets and walked to the principal's office. When I entered I heard a woman's voice say: "May I help you?" I was startled. I had not

125. My mouth was dry. My eyes began to water. I could not begin. "You can read later," Mr. Lema said understandingly.

For the rest of the reading period I kept getting angrier and angrier with myself. I should have read, I thought to myself.

During recess I went into the restroom and opened my English book to page 125. I began to read in a low voice, pretending I was in class. There were many words I did not know. I closed the book and headed back to the classroom.

Mr. Lema was sitting at his desk correcting papers. When I entered he looked up at me and smiled. I felt better. I walked up to him and asked if he could help me with the new words. "Gladly," he said.

The rest of the month I spent my lunch hours working on English with Mr. Lema, my best friend at school.

One Friday during lunch hour Mr. Lema asked me to take a walk with him to the music room. "Do you like music?" he asked me as we entered the building.

"Yes, I like corridos,"[13] I answered. He then picked up a trumpet, blew on it and handed it to me. The sound gave me goose bumps. I knew that sound. I had heard it in many corridos. "How would you like to learn how to play it?" he asked. He must have read my face because before I could answer, he added: "I'll teach you how to play it during our lunch hours."

That day I could hardly wait to get home to tell Papá and Mamá the great news. As I got off the bus, my little brothers and sisters ran up to meet me. They were yelling and screaming. I thought they were happy to see me, but when I opened the door to our shack, I saw that everything we owned was neatly packed in cardboard boxes.

heard English for months. For a few seconds I remained speechless. I looked at the lady who waited for an answer. My first instinct was to answer her in Spanish, but I held back. Finally, after struggling for English words, I managed to tell her that I wanted to enroll in the sixth grade. After answering many questions, I was led to the classroom.

Mr. Lema, the sixth-grade teacher, greeted me and assigned me a desk. He then introduced me to the class. I was so nervous and scared at that moment when everyone's eyes were on me that I wished I were with Papá and Roberto picking cotton. After taking roll, Mr. Lema gave the class the assignment for the first hour. "The first thing we have to do this morning is finish reading the story we began yesterday," he said enthusiastically. He walked up to me, handed me an English book, and asked me to read. "We are on page 125," he said politely. When I heard this, I felt my blood rush to my head; I felt dizzy. "Would you like to read?" he asked hesitantly. I opened the book to page

13. **corridos** (kô-rē′thōs): ballads.

Reading Check

1. At the opening of the story, why is it necessary for the narrator and his family to move?
2. In Fresno where does the narrator's family live?
3. When is the narrator able to start going to school?
4. Why is his brother unable to go to school?
5. How does the narrator spend his lunch hours at school?

For Study and Discussion

Analyzing and Interpreting the Selection

1. The people in this story are migrant workers who move from one region to another in order to harvest crops. What does this story reveal about the hardships of their lives?

2. Despite the difficult lives they lead, how do the father and mother give their children a sense of being a family and having a home?

3a. How does the narrator show that he wants a better life for himself? **b.** In what ways does his teacher try to help him?

4. A *circuit* is any regular path or journey that someone makes. The person following such a course always returns to the starting point. **a.** In what way is the narrator's life a circuit? **b.** How does the ending of the story bring him back to the starting point?

Language and Vocabulary

Recognizing Special Uses of a Word

The word *circuit* in the title of Jiménez's story refers to the pattern of the characters' lives. They are always breaking up their home to move to some other place where there is work. *Circuit* has several special uses in our language. You have probably heard the word used for the path of electric current. You may also have heard the phrase "circuit breaker" used for a device that interrupts the flow of an electric current.

In a college dictionary, find out what the word *circuit* means in each of the following phrases:

> circuit court of appeals
> circuit preacher
> closed circuit telecast
> lecturer's circuit

What other uses can you add to this list?

About the Author

Francisco Jiménez (1943–   )

Like the narrator of his story, Francisco Jiménez was born in Jalisco, a state in west-central Mexico. He is a professor of Spanish and teaches at the University of Santa Clara. Jiménez has edited books about Chicano literature and has written articles and textbooks. One of his collections, in Spanish, is devoted completely to the prose of Hispanic women writers.

Luke Baldwin's Vow

MORLEY CALLAGHAN

*This story opens and closes with Luke making a solemn promise. What does he
learn about his uncle and what does he find out about himself?*

That summer when twelve-year-old Luke
Baldwin came to live with his Uncle Henry in
the house on the stream by the sawmill, he did
not forget that he had promised his dying father he would try to learn things from his
uncle; so he used to watch him very carefully.

Uncle Henry, who was the manager of the
sawmill, was a big, burly man weighing more
than two hundred and thirty pounds, and he
had a rough-skinned, brick-colored face. He
looked like a powerful man, but his health was
not good. He had aches and pains in his back
and shoulders which puzzled the doctor. The
first thing Luke learned about Uncle Henry
was that everybody had great respect for him.
The four men he employed in the sawmill
were always polite and attentive when he spoke
to them. His wife, Luke's Aunt Helen, a kindly,
plump, straightforward woman, never argued
with him. "You should try and be like your
Uncle Henry," she would say to Luke. "He's so
wonderfully practical. He takes care of everything in a sensible, easy way."

Luke used to trail around the sawmill after
Uncle Henry not only because he liked the

fresh clean smell of the newly cut wood and
the big piles of sawdust, but because he was impressed by his uncle's precise, firm tone when
he spoke to the men.

Sometimes Uncle Henry would stop and explain to Luke something about a piece of lumber. "Always try and learn the essential facts,
son," he would say. "If you've got the facts, you
know what's useful and what isn't useful, and
no one can fool you."

He showed Luke that nothing of value was
ever wasted around the mill. Luke used to listen, and wonder if there was another man in
the world who knew so well what was needed
and what ought to be thrown away. Uncle
Henry had known at once that Luke needed a
bicycle to ride to his school, which was two
miles away in town, and he bought him a good
one. He knew that Luke needed good, serviceable clothes. He also knew exactly how much
Aunt Helen needed to run the house, the price
of everything, and how much a woman should
be paid for doing the family washing. In the
evenings Luke used to sit in the living room
watching his uncle making notations in a black
notebook which he always carried in his vest

pocket, and he knew that he was assessing the value of the smallest transaction that had taken place during the day.

Luke promised himself that when he grew up he, too, would be admired for his good, sound judgment. But, of course, he couldn't always be watching and learning from his Uncle Henry, for too often when he watched him he thought of his own father; then he was lonely. So he began to build in another secret life for himself around the sawmill, and his companion was the eleven-year-old collie, Dan, a dog blind in one eye and with a slight limp in his left hind leg. Dan was a fat, slow-moving old dog. He was very affectionate and his eye was the color of amber. His fur was amber too. When Luke left for school in the morning, the old dog followed him for half a mile down the road, and when he returned in the afternoon, there was Dan waiting at the gate.

Sometimes they would play around the millpond or by the dam, or go down the stream to the lake. Luke was never lonely when the dog was with him. There was an old rowboat that they used as a pirate ship in the stream, and they would be pirates together, with Luke shouting instructions to Captain Dan and with the dog seeming to understand and wagging his tail enthusiastically. Its amber eye was alert, intelligent, and approving. Then they would plunge into the brush on the other side of the stream, pretending they were hunting tigers. Of course, the old dog was no longer much good for hunting; he was too slow and too lazy. Uncle Henry no longer used him for hunting rabbits or anything else.

When they came out of the brush, they would lie together on the cool, grassy bank being affectionate with each other, with Luke talking earnestly, while the collie, as Luke believed, smiled with the good eye. Lying in the grass, Luke would say things to Dan he could not say to his uncle or his aunt. Not that what

he said was important; it was just stuff about himself that he might have told to his own father or mother if they had been alive. Then they would go back to the house for dinner, and after dinner Dan would follow him down the road to Mr. Kemp's house, where they would ask old Mr. Kemp if they could go with him to round up his four cows. The old man was always glad to see them. He seemed to like watching Luke and the collie running around the cows, pretending they were riding on a vast range in the foothills of the Rockies.

Uncle Henry no longer paid much attention to the collie, though once when he tripped over him on the veranda he shook his head and said thoughtfully, "Poor old fellow, he's through. Can't use him for anything. He just eats and sleeps and gets in the way."

One Sunday during Luke's summer holidays, when they had returned from church and had had their lunch, they had all moved out to the veranda where the collie was sleeping. Luke sat down on the steps, his back against the veranda post, Uncle Henry took the rocking chair, and Aunt Helen stretched herself out in the hammock, sighing contentedly. Then Luke, eyeing the collie, tapped the step with the palm of his hand, giving three little taps like a signal, and the old collie, lifting his head, got up stiffly with a slow wagging of the tail as an acknowledgment that the signal had been heard, and began to cross the veranda to Luke. But the dog was sleepy; his bad eye was turned to the rocking chair; in passing his left front paw went under the rocker. With a frantic yelp, the dog went bounding down the steps and hobbled around the corner of the house, where he stopped, hearing Luke coming after him. All he needed was the touch of Luke's hand. Then he began to lick the hand methodically, as if apologizing.

"Luke," Uncle Henry called sharply, "bring that dog here."

When Luke led the collie back to the veranda, Uncle Henry nodded and said, "Thanks, Luke." Then he took out a cigar, lit it, put his big hands on his knees, and began to rock in the chair while he frowned and eyed the dog steadily. Obviously he was making some kind of an important decision about the collie.

"What's the matter, Uncle Henry?" Luke asked nervously.

"That dog can't see any more," Uncle Henry said.

"Oh, yes, he can," Luke said quickly. "His bad eye got turned to the chair, that's all, Uncle Henry."

"And his teeth are gone, too," Uncle Henry went on, paying no attention to what Luke had said. Turning to the hammock, he called, "Helen, sit up a minute, will you?"

When she got up and stood beside him, he went on, "I was thinking about this old dog the other day, Helen. It's not only that he's about blind, but did you notice that when we drove up after church he didn't even bark?"

"It's a fact he didn't, Henry."

"No, not much good even as a watchdog now."

"Poor old fellow. It's a pity, isn't it?"

"And no good for hunting either. And he eats a lot, I suppose."

"About as much as he ever did, Henry."

"The plain fact is the old dog isn't worth his keep any more. It's time we got rid of him."

"It's always so hard to know how to get rid of a dog, Henry."

"I was thinking about it the other day. Some people think it's best to shoot a dog. I haven't had any shells for that shotgun for over a year. Poisoning is a hard death for a dog. Maybe drowning is the easiest and quickest way. Well, I'll speak to one of the mill hands and have him look after it."

Crouching on the ground, his arms around

the old collie's neck, Luke cried out, "Uncle Henry, Dan's a wonderful dog! You don't know how wonderful he is!"

"He's just a very old dog, son," Uncle Henry said calmly. "The time comes when you have to get rid of any old dog. We've got to be practical about it. I'll get you a pup, son. A smart little dog that'll be worth its keep. A pup that will grow up with you."

"I don't want a pup!" Luke cried, turning his face away. Circling around him, the dog began to bark, then flick his long pink tongue at the back of Luke's neck.

Aunt Helen, catching her husband's eye, put her finger on her lips, warning him not to go on talking in front of the boy. "An old dog like that often wanders off into the brush and sort of picks a place to die when the time comes. Isn't that so, Henry?"

"Oh, sure," he agreed quickly. "In fact, when Dan didn't show up yesterday, I was sure that was what had happened." Then he yawned and seemed to forget about the dog.

But Luke was frightened, for he knew what his uncle was like. He knew that if his uncle had decided that the dog was useless and that it was sane and sensible to get rid of it, he would be ashamed of himself if he were diverted by any sentimental consideration. Luke knew in his heart that he couldn't move his uncle. All he could do, he thought, was keep the dog away from his uncle, keep him out of the house, feed him when Uncle Henry wasn't around.

Next day at noontime Luke saw his uncle walking from the mill toward the house with old Sam Carter, a mill hand. Sam Carter was a dull, stooped, slow-witted man of sixty with an iron-gray beard, who was wearing blue overalls and a blue shirt. He hardly ever spoke to anybody. Watching from the veranda, Luke noticed that his uncle suddenly gave Sam Carter a cigar, which Sam put in his pocket. Luke had never seen his uncle give Sam a cigar or pay much attention to him.

Then, after lunch, Uncle Henry said lazily that he would like Luke to take his bicycle and go into town and get him some cigars.

"I'll take Dan," Luke said.

"Better not, son," Uncle Henry said. "It'll take you all afternoon. I want those cigars. Get going, Luke."

His uncle's tone was so casual that Luke tried to believe they were not merely getting rid of him. Of course he had to do what he was told. He had never dared to refuse to obey an order from his uncle. But when he had taken his bicycle and had ridden down the path that followed the stream to the town road and had got about a quarter of a mile along the road, he found that all he could think of was his uncle handing old Sam Carter the cigar.

Slowing down, sick with worry now, he got off the bike and stood uncertainly on the sunlit road. Sam Carter was a gruff, aloof old man who would have no feeling for a dog. Then suddenly Luke could go no farther without getting some assurance that the collie would not be harmed while he was away. Across the fields he could see the house.

Leaving the bike in the ditch, he started to cross the field, intending to get close enough to the house so Dan could hear him if he whistled softly. He got about fifty yards away from the house and whistled and waited, but there was

no sign of the dog, which might be asleep at the front of the house, he knew, or over at the sawmill. With the saws whining, the dog couldn't hear the soft whistle. For a few minutes Luke couldn't make up his mind what to do, then he decided to go back to the road, get on his bike, and go back the way he had come until he got to the place where the river path joined the road. There he could leave his bike, go up the path, then into the tall grass and get close to the front of the house and the sawmill without being seen.

He had followed the river path for about a hundred yards, and when he came to the place where the river began to bend sharply toward the house his heart fluttered and his legs felt paralyzed, for he saw the old rowboat in the one place where the river was deep, and in the rowboat was Sam Carter with the collie.

The bearded man in the blue overalls was smoking the cigar; the dog, with a rope around its neck, sat contentedly beside him, its tongue going out in a friendly lick at the hand holding the rope. It was all like a crazy dream picture to Luke; all wrong because it looked so lazy and friendly, even the curling smoke from Sam Carter's cigar. But as Luke cried out, "Dan! Dan! Come on, boy!" and the dog jumped at the water, he saw that Sam Carter's left hand was hanging deep in the water, holding a foot of rope with a heavy stone at the end. As Luke cried out wildly, "Don't! Please don't!" Carter dropped the stone, for the cry came too late; it was blurred by the screech of the big saws at the mill. But Carter was startled, and he stared stupidly at the riverbank, then he ducked his head and began to row quickly to the bank.

But Luke was watching the collie take what looked like a long, shallow dive, except that the hind legs suddenly kicked up above the surface, then shot down, and while he watched, Luke sobbed and trembled, for it was as if the happy secret part of his life around the sawmill was being torn away from him. But even while he watched, he seemed to be following a plan without knowing it, for he was already fumbling in his pocket for his jackknife, jerking the blade open, pulling off his pants, kicking his shoes off, while he muttered fiercely and prayed that Sam Carter would get out of sight.

It hardly took the mill hand a minute to reach the bank and go slinking furtively around the bend as if he felt that the boy was following him. But Luke hadn't taken his eyes off the exact spot in the water where Dan had disappeared. As soon as the mill hand was out of sight, Luke slid down the bank and took a leap at the water, the sun glistening on his slender body, his eyes wild with eagerness as he ran out to the deep place, then arched his back and dived, swimming under water, his open eyes getting used to the greenish-gray haze of the water, the sandy bottom, and the imbedded rocks.

His lungs began to ache, then he saw the shadow of the collie floating at the end of the taut rope, rock-held in the sand. He slashed at the rope with his knife. He couldn't get much strength in his arm because of the resistance of the water. He grabbed the rope with his left hand, hacking with his knife. The collie suddenly drifted up slowly, like a water-soaked log. Then his own head shot above the surface, and, while he was sucking in the air, he was drawing in the rope, pulling the collie toward him and treading water. In a few strokes he was away from the deep place and his feet touched the bottom.

Hoisting the collie out of the water, he scrambled toward the bank, lurching and stumbling in fright because the collie felt like a dead weight.

He went on up the bank and across the path to the tall grass, where he fell flat, hugging the dog and trying to warm him with his own body. But the collie didn't stir; the good amber eye remained closed. Then suddenly Luke wanted to act like a resourceful, competent man. Getting up on his knees, he stretched the dog out on its belly, drew him between his knees, felt with trembling hands for the soft places on the flanks just above the hipbones, and rocked back and forth, pressing with all his weight, then relaxing the pressure as he straightened up. He hoped that he was working the dog's lungs like a bellows. He had read that men who had been thought drowned had been saved in this way.

"Come on, Dan. Come on, old boy," he pleaded softly. As a little water came from the collie's mouth, Luke's heart jumped, and he muttered over and over, "You can't be dead, Dan! You can't, you can't! I won't let you die, Dan!" He rocked back and forth tirelessly, applying the pressure to the flanks. More water dribbled from the mouth. In the collie's body he felt a faint tremor. "Oh, gee, Dan, you're alive," he whispered. "Come on, boy. Keep it up."

With a cough the collie suddenly jerked his head back, the amber eye opened, and there they were looking at each other. Then the collie, thrusting his legs out stiffly, tried to hoist himself up, staggered, tried again, then stood there in a stupor. Then he shook himself like any other wet dog, turned his head, eyed Luke, and the red tongue came out in a weak flick at Luke's cheek.

"Lie down, Dan," Luke said. As the dog lay down beside him, Luke closed his eyes, buried his head in the wet fur, and wondered why all the muscles of his arms and legs began to jerk in a nervous reaction, now that it was all over. "Stay there, Dan," he said softly, and he went back to the path, got his clothes, and came back beside Dan and put them on. "I think we'd better get away from this spot, Dan," he said. "Keep down, boy. Come on." And he crawled on through the tall grass till they were about seventy-five yards from the place where he had undressed. There they lay down together.

In a little while he heard his aunt's voice calling, "Luke. Oh, Luke! Come here, Luke!"

"Quiet, Dan," Luke whispered. A few minutes passed, and then Uncle Henry called, "Luke, Luke!" and he began to come down the path. They could see him standing there, massive and imposing, his hands on his hips as he looked down the path; then he turned and went back to the house.

As he watched the sunlight shine on the back of his uncle's neck, the exultation Luke had felt at knowing the collie was safe beside him turned to bewildered despair, for he knew that even if he should be forgiven for saving the dog when he saw it drowning, the fact was that his uncle had been thwarted.[1] His mind was made up to get rid of Dan, and in a few days' time, in another way, he would get rid of him, as he got rid of anything around the mill that he believed to be useless or a waste of money.

As he lay back and looked up at the hardly moving clouds, he began to grow frightened. He couldn't go back to the house, nor could he take the collie into the woods and hide him and feed him there unless he tied him up. If he didn't tie him up, Dan would wander back to the house.

"I guess there's just no place to go, Dan," he whispered sadly. "Even if we start off along the road, somebody is sure to see us."

But Dan was watching a butterfly that was circling crazily above them. Raising himself a little, Luke looked through the grass at the corner of the house, then he turned and looked the other way to the wide blue lake. With a sigh he lay down again, and for hours they lay there together, until there was no sound from the saws in the mill and the sun moved low in the western sky.

"Well, we can't stay here any longer, Dan," he said at last. "We'll just have to get as far away as we can. Keep down, old boy," and he began to crawl through the grass, going farther away from the house. When he could no longer be seen, he got up and began to trot across the field toward the gravel road leading to town.

On the road, the collie would turn from time to time as if wondering why Luke shuffled along, dragging his feet wearily, head down. "I'm stumped, that's all, Dan," Luke explained. "I can't seem to think of a place to take you."

When they were passing the Kemp place, they saw the old man sitting on the veranda, and Luke stopped. All he could think of was that Mr. Kemp had liked them both and it had been a pleasure to help him get the cows in the evening. Dan had always been with them. Staring at the figure of the old man on the veranda, he said in a worried tone, "I wish I could be sure of him, Dan. I wish he was a dumb, stupid man who wouldn't know or care whether you were worth anything. . . . Well, come on." He opened the gate bravely, but he felt shy and unimportant.

"Hello, son. What's on your mind?" Mr. Kemp called from the veranda. He was a thin, wiry man in a tan-colored shirt. He had a gray, untidy mustache, his skin was wrinkled and leathery, but his eyes were always friendly and amused.

"Could I speak to you, Mr. Kemp?" Luke asked when they were close to the veranda.

"Sure. Go ahead."

"It's about Dan. He's a great dog, but I guess you know that as well as I do. I was wondering if you could keep him here for me."

"Why should I keep Dan here, son?"

"Well, it's like this," Luke said, fumbling the words awkwardly. "My uncle won't let me keep

---

1. **thwarted** (thwôrt′ĭd): prevented from carrying out his plans.

him any more . . . says he's too old." His mouth began to tremble, then he blurted out the story.

"I see, I see," Mr. Kemp said slowly, and he got up and came over to the steps and sat down and began to stroke the collie's head. "Of course, Dan's an old dog, son," he said quietly. "And sooner or later you've got to get rid of an old dog. Your uncle knows that. Maybe it's true that Dan isn't worth his keep."

"He doesn't eat much, Mr. Kemp. Just one meal a day."

"I wouldn't want you to think your uncle was cruel and unfeeling, Luke," Mr. Kemp went on. "He's a fine man . . . maybe just a little bit too practical and straightforward."

"I guess that's right," Luke agreed, but he was really waiting and trusting the expression in the old man's eyes.

"Maybe you should make him a practical proposition."

"I—I don't know what you mean."

"Well, I sort of like the way you get the cows for me in the evenings," Mr. Kemp said, smiling to himself. "In fact, I don't think you need me to go along with you at all. Now, supposing I gave you seventy-five cents a week. Would you get the cows for me every night?"

"Sure I would, Mr. Kemp. I like doing it, anyway."

"All right, son. It's a deal. Now I'll tell you what to do. You go back to your uncle, and before he has a chance to open up on you, you say right out that you've come to him with a business proposition. Say it like a man, just like that. Offer to pay him the seventy-five cents a week for the dog's keep."

"But my uncle doesn't need seventy-five cents, Mr. Kemp," Luke said uneasily.

"Of course not," Mr. Kemp agreed. "It's the principle of the thing. Be confident. Remember that he's got nothing against the dog. Go to it, son. Let me know how you do," he added,

with an amused smile. "If I know your uncle at all, I think it'll work."

"I'll try it, Mr. Kemp," Luke said. "Thanks very much." But he didn't have any confidence, for even though he knew that Mr. Kemp was a wise old man who would not deceive him, he couldn't believe that seventy-five cents a week would stop his uncle, who was an important man. "Come on, Dan," he called, and he went slowly and apprehensively[2] back to the house.

When they were going up the path, his aunt cried from the open window, "Henry, Henry, in heaven's name, it's Luke with the dog!"

Ten paces from the veranda, Luke stopped and waited nervously for his uncle to come out. Uncle Henry came out in a rush, but when he saw the collie and Luke standing there, he stopped stiffly, turned pale, and his mouth hung open loosely.

"Luke," he whispered, "that dog had a stone around his neck."

"I fished him out of the stream," Luke said uneasily.

"Oh, oh, I see," Uncle Henry said, and gradually the color came back to his face. "You fished him out, eh?" he asked, still looking at the dog uneasily. "Well, you shouldn't have done that. I told Sam Carter to get rid of the dog, you know."

"Just a minute, Uncle Henry," Luke said, trying not to falter. He gained confidence as Aunt Helen came out and stood beside her husband, for her eyes seemed to be gentle, and he went on bravely, "I want to make you a practical proposition, Uncle Henry."

"A what?" Uncle Henry asked, still feeling insecure, and wishing the boy and the dog weren't confronting him.

"A practical proposition," Luke blurted out quickly. "I know Dan isn't worth his keep to

2. **apprehensively** (ăp′rĭ-hĕn′sĭv-lē): fearfully.

you. I guess he isn't worth anything to anybody but me. So I'll pay you seventy-five cents a week for his keep."

"What's this?" Uncle Henry asked, looking bewildered. "Where would you get seventy-five cents a week, Luke?"

"I'm going to get the cows every night for Mr. Kemp."

"Oh, for heaven's sake, Henry," Aunt Helen pleaded, looking distressed, "let him keep the dog!" and she fled into the house.

"None of that kind of talk!" Uncle Henry called after her. "We've got to be sensible about this!" But he was shaken himself, and overwhelmed with a distress that destroyed all his confidence. As he sat down slowly in the rocking chair and stroked the side of his big face, he wanted to say weakly, "All right, keep the dog," but he was ashamed of being so weak and sentimental. He stubbornly refused to yield to this emotion; he was trying desperately to turn his emotion into a bit of good, useful common sense, so he could justify his distress. So he rocked and pondered. At last he smiled. "You're a smart little shaver, Luke," he said slowly. "Imagine you working it out like this. I'm tempted to accept your proposition."

"Gee, thanks, Uncle Henry."

"I'm accepting it because I think you'll learn something out of this," he went on ponderously.

"Yes, Uncle Henry."

"You'll learn that useless luxuries cost the smartest men hard-earned money."

"I don't mind."

"Well, it's a thing you'll have to learn sometime. I think you'll learn, too, because you certainly seem to have a practical streak in you. It's a streak I like to see in a boy. OK, son," he said, and he smiled with relief and went into the house.

Turning to Dan, Luke whispered softly, "Well, what do you know about that?"

As he sat down on the step with the collie beside him and listened to Uncle Henry talking to his wife, he began to glow with exultation. Then gradually his exultation began to change to a vast wonder that Mr. Kemp should have had such a perfect understanding of Uncle Henry. He began to dream of someday being as wise as old Mr. Kemp and knowing exactly how to handle people. It was possible, too, that he had already learned some of the things about his uncle that his father had wanted him to learn.

Putting his head down on the dog's neck, he vowed to himself fervently that he would always have some money on hand, no matter what became of him, so that he would be able to protect all that was truly valuable from the practical people in the world.

Reading Check

1. Why does Luke live with his Uncle Henry and Aunt Helen?
2. What kind of business is Uncle Henry in?
3. How does Luke become friendly with Mr. Kemp?
4. How does Luke save his dog's life?

For Study and Discussion

Analyzing and Interpreting the Story

1. At the beginning of the story, Luke Baldwin wants to be like his Uncle Henry. Why does Luke admire his uncle?

2a. Why does Uncle Henry believe that Luke's collie is worthless? b. What does the dog mean to Luke?

3. When his uncle sends him into town on an errand, Luke becomes worried about Dan.

Why does he suspect that the collie will come to harm?

4. Mr. Kemp tells Luke that his uncle is not "cruel or unfeeling" but "maybe just a little bit too practical" (page 84). Do you agree with Mr. Kemp's judgment of Uncle Henry? Give evidence from the story to support your answer.

5a. What is the "practical proposition" that Luke offers Uncle Henry? **b.** Why is Uncle Henry upset by the offer?

6. At the end of the story, Uncle Henry accepts Luke's proposition, claiming that it will teach Luke to be practical. Luke does learn an important lesson. How is it different from the lesson Uncle Henry intended to teach him?

7a. A *vow* is a solemn promise. What is Luke's vow? **b.** Is money always the answer to a problem such as the one Luke faced?

Literary Elements

Drawing Conclusions

Very often, after completing a story, the reader is left with certain thoughts or questions about the meaning of the story—those ideas that reach beyond the individual characters and events. "Luke Baldwin's Vow" tells how a boy manages to save his dog's life by appealing to his uncle's practical nature. The meaning of the story lies in what it tells about *values,* or the things or qualities that are important to people.

The story presents the reader with two very different sets of values. What is most important to Uncle Henry? By contrast, what is most important to Luke? How do these values clash during the course of the story?

Which of these statements do you think best describes the outcome of the story? Explain your answer.

Luke learns that only his own values matter.
Luke learns that he must have regard for his uncle's values even if he does not agree with them.
Luke convinces Uncle Henry to change his values.

Language and Vocabulary

Forming Modifiers with *-ly*

The suffix *-ly* is used to form both adjectives and adverbs. When used to form an adjective, it has the meaning "like" or "characteristic of." When added to the noun *brother,* it forms the word *brotherly,* which means "like a brother."

Used as an adverb-forming suffix, *-ly* means "in the manner of" or "to the extent of." When added to the adjective *nervous,* it forms the adverb *nervously,* which can be defined as "in a nervous manner."

Here is a list of words from the story. Some of the words are adjectives that modify nouns. Other words are adverbs modifying verbs or adjectives. Determine which words are adjectives and which are adverbs. Give the definition of each word.

carefully (page 77)
kindly (page 77)
wonderfully (page 77)
newly (page 77)
lonely (page 78)
enthusiastically (page 78)
earnestly (page 78)
thoughtfully (page 79)
contentedly (page 79)
friendly (page 81)
fiercely (page 82)
fervently (page 85)

Descriptive Writing

Combining Details in Description

A good writer often combines two or more closely related ideas into a single longer sentence.

> Uncle Henry, who was the manager of the saw-mill, was a big, burly man weighing more than two hundred and thirty pounds, and he had a rough-skinned, brick-colored face.

In this sentence, Morley Callaghan tells the reader what Uncle Henry does and what he looks like. What characteristics of Uncle Henry's physical appearance are emphasized?

Compare the picture you have of Uncle Henry with this picture of Mr. Kemp:

> He was a thin, wiry man in a tan-colored shirt. He had a gray, untidy mustache, his skin was wrinkled and leathery, but his eyes were always friendly and amused.

What details have been combined in the second sentence?

You can picture both characters clearly because the author uses specific details in describing them.

Observe people in a crowd—on a bus, in a store, or at a sports event. Write a description of one person, combining specific details into one or two sentences.

About the Author

Morley Callaghan (1903–   )

Morley Callaghan is one of Canada's most distinguished novelists and short-story writers. He was born in Toronto and educated at the University of Toronto and at the Osgoode Hall Law School. While he was working as a reporter on the Toronto *Daily Star,* he met Ernest Hemingway, who took an interest in Callaghan's work and encouraged him to write. In a number of his stories, like "Luke Baldwin's Vow," Callaghan shows a keen understanding of young people and their problems. Some of his well-known stories are "The Snob," "A Cap for Steve," and "All the Years of Her Life."

DEVELOPING SKILLS IN CRITICAL THINKING

Drawing Inferences

When you draw an inference, you arrive at a conclusion from certain facts or evidence. In "The Cat and the Pain Killer" (page 49), Tom's Aunt Polly sees the handle of a teaspoon under the bed valence. Using this clue she draws the correct inference—that Tom has given Peter, the cat, a dose of Pain Killer.

When you read, you are constantly making inferences on the basis of different kinds of evidence. Some inferences are relatively simple; they depend on drawing a conclusion from a single detail or statement. Other inferences are more complex; they require putting together scattered clues in order to arrive at a logical conclusion.

The following passage is the opening paragraph of a well-known story by Robert Louis Stevenson, "The Sire de Malétroit's Door." The passage is rich in clues about the setting of the story and the character of its hero. Read the passage several times. What can you infer about the time and place of the action? What impression do you form of Denis de Beaulieu? What kind of action is hinted at? Cite evidence to support your inferences.

Denis de Beaulieu was not yet two-and-twenty, but he counted himself a grown man, and a very accomplished cavalier into the bargain. Lads were early formed in that rough, war-faring epoch; and when one has been in a pitched battle and a dozen raids, has killed one's man in an honorable fashion, and knows a thing or two of strategy and mankind, a certain swagger in the gait is surely to be pardoned. He had put up his horse with due care, and supped with due deliberation; and then, in a very agreeable frame of mind, went out to pay a visit in the gray of the evening. It was not a very wise proceeding on the young man's part. He would have done better to remain beside the fire or go decently to bed. For the town was full of the troops of Burgundy and England under a mixed command; and though Denis was there on safe-conduct, his safe-conduct was like to serve him little on a chance encounter.

PRACTICE IN READING AND WRITING

The Writing Process

The word *process* refers to a series of actions or some method of doing something in a number of steps. The writing process consists of several important stages or phases: *prewriting, writing a first draft, evaluating, revising, proofreading,* and *writing the final version.* Much of the work that goes into a paper actually precedes the writing. In the prewriting stage, writers make decisions about what to say and how to say it. Prewriting activities include choosing and limiting a topic, identifying purpose and audience, gathering ideas, organizing ideas, and arriving at a controlling idea for the paper. Some people do most of the planning in their heads; other people like to jot down their ideas on note cards or on a sheet of paper. During the prewriting stage some people find it helpful to make an outline. In the next stage, the writer uses notes or an outline to prepare a first draft of the paper. The writer then evaluates, or judges, the work and considers how it might be improved. In the revising stage, the writer rewrites the draft, often several times, adding or deleting ideas, rearranging sentences, rephrasing for clarity. The writer then proofreads the paper for errors in spelling, punctuation, and grammar. After the final corrections are made, the writer produces a clean copy of the paper and proofreads it once more.

The steps in this process are interdependent. Writers often find that even after they have rewritten a paper more than once, they want to make changes in its organization or to add new ideas.

Descriptive Writing

Through description, a writer helps you to use your senses—to see, hear, smell, taste, and feel as you read. By selecting details with care, a writer can communicate a single strong impression about a character or setting. A writer need not describe every aspect of a person or a scene. Effective description includes only significant details.

In this passage from "The King of Mazy May," how does London help you to see and feel what his character experiences?

> There was no wind, but the speed at which he traveled created a bitter blast, and with the thermometer down to forty below, this bit through fur and flesh to the very bones. Aware that if he remained constantly upon the sled he would freeze to death, and knowing the practice of Arctic travelers, Walt shortened up one of the lashing thongs, and whenever he felt chilled, seized hold of it, jumped off, and ran behind till warmth was restored. Then he would climb on and rest till the process had to be repeated. Looking back he could see the sled of his pursuers, drawn by eight dogs, rising and falling over the ice hummocks like a boat in a seaway.

A writer selects details that develop a single strong impression of a character. In the following paragraph from "Luke Baldwin's Vow," Callaghan describes Uncle Henry. Notice that every sentence in the paragraph supports the idea that Uncle Henry is a practical man.

He showed Luke that nothing of value was ever wasted around the mill. Luke used to listen, and wonder if there was another man in the world who knew so well what was needed and what ought to be thrown away. Uncle Henry had known at once that Luke needed a bicycle to ride to his school, which was two miles away in town, and he bought him a good one. He knew that Luke needed good, serviceable clothes. He also knew exactly how much Aunt Helen needed to run the house, the price of everything, and how much a woman should be paid for doing the family washing. In the evenings Luke used to sit in the living room watching his uncle making notations in a black notebook which he always carried in his vest pocket, and he knew that he was assessing the value of the smallest transaction that had taken place during the day.

1. How many specific details are used to emphasize Uncle Henry's concern with the price and value of things?

2. What words are associated with money or business?

Suggestions for Writing

Select one of the following sentences to open a paragraph of description, or write an opening sentence of your own. Then provide a paragraph to support the ideas in the sentence.

What I like about holiday dinners is the variety of smells that come from the kitchen.

One look told me that the shopper was completely exhausted.

The home of the future will be very different from the home of today.

Here are some guidelines to help you plan and write your paper.

Prewriting

- Be sure you are familiar with what you are describing.
- Select specific details that will create a picture in your reader's mind.
- Choose precise nouns, verbs, adjectives, and adverbs that will appeal to the reader's senses.
- Arrange the details in some logical sequence, in order of time, space, or some other order.
- If you write your own opening sentence, be sure it gives the main impression you want your reader to get.

Evaluating and Revising

- Does your opening sentence convey a main impression of the character or scene?
- Does every sentence support the main impression?
- Are there enough details to develop the idea in the opening sentence?
- Do the details follow some logical order?
- Are there transitions—words like *first, then, here, however*—to connect the ideas in your paper?
- Have you used precise details?

Proofreading

- Reread your revised version and correct mistakes in grammar, usage, spelling, capitalization, and punctuation.
- Ask a classmate to check your revision for accuracy, and then prepare a final copy.

For Further Reading

Bagnold, Enid, *National Velvet* (several editions)
Velvet Brown, a fourteen-year-old English girl, wins a horse in a village lottery and decides to race it in the Grand National Steeplechase.

Burch, Robert, *Queenie Peavy* (Viking, 1966)
An imaginative, rebellious, and likable girl, growing up in Georgia during the 1930s, discovers her own values.

Byars, Betsy, *Summer of the Swans* (Viking, 1970)
Fourteen-year-old Sara Godfrey forgets her own feelings of unhappiness in her frantic search for her ten-year-old retarded brother, who is lost.

Hamilton, Virginia, *M. C. Higgins, the Great* (Macmillan, 1974; paperback, Dell, 1986)
While both his parents work, M. C. (which stands for Mayo Cornelius) takes care of his younger brothers and sisters on Sarah Mountain. Two strangers who come to the mountain—a wandering girl and a folk-song collector—make important changes in M. C.'s life.

Harris, Marilyn, *The Runaway's Diary* (paperback, Archway, 1983)
A sensitive fifteen-year-old keeps a diary of her adventures as she journeys from her home in Pennsylvania to the Canadian wilderness, accompanied by an adopted German shepherd puppy.

L'Engle, Madeleine, *The Young Unicorns* (Farrar, Straus & Giroux, 1968)
A gang called the Alphabats spell trouble and danger for Dave, a former member, who resists returning to the gang.

Mazer, Harry, *Snow Bound* (paperback, Dell, 1986)
Cindy and Tom, running away from home for different reasons, find their lives in danger when they are lost in a blizzard.

McKenney, Ruth, *My Sister Eileen* (Harcourt Brace Jovanovich, 1968)
The author recalls hilarious adventures with her younger sister in a small town in Ohio and later in New York City.

Neville, Emily, *It's Like This, Cat* (Harper & Row, 1963; paperback, 1985)
Fourteen-year-old Dave tells about his life in New York City, his family, his friends, and the new people he comes to know—including his first girlfriend—when he adopts a stray cat.

Rawlings, Marjorie Kinnan, *The Yearling* (Scribner, 1961; paperback, 1982)
Jody Baxter grows up quickly when he must make a painful decision about his pet fawn, which has been destroying his parents' crops.

Twain, Mark, *The Adventures of Tom Sawyer* (many editions)
This famous novel is set in a small town in Missouri in the nineteenth century. Tom's adventures include witnessing a murder, falling in love with Becky Thatcher, attending his own funeral, and being rescued from a cave.

West, Jessamyn, *Cress Delahanty* (Harcourt Brace Jovanovich, 1954; paperback, Avon)
Cress is an amiable teen-ager growing up on a California ranch. The stories in the book cover her life from twelve to sixteen.

Wojciechowska, Maia, *Shadow of a Bull* (Macmillan, 1964; paperback)
Manolo does not wish to become a bullfighter like his father, but he is expected to face his first bull in the ring when he is twelve.

HOMER '78

FAMILY ALBUM

Every family has its own stories to tell—of shared experiences—of special joys and sorrows. Each selection in this unit might be considered a page or a chapter from a different family album—a collection of memories about family members and home. Some selections are told from the point of view of a young person; others are told from the point of view of an adult looking back on childhood. What you will find are different attitudes, values, and judgments about family relationships.

Detail from *The Pumpkin Patch* by Winslow Homer (1836–1910). Watercolor.
The Mead Art Museum, Amherst College

The Miraculous Phonograph Record

WILLIAM SAROYAN

Many of William Saroyan's stories tell about his growing up in an Armenian neighborhood in the San Joaquin Valley in California. In this story the narrator recalls his mother with humorous affection. As you read, ask yourself what is "miraculous" about the phonograph record.

Sometime soon after I was thirteen years old in 1921 I rode home from the heart of Fresno with a wind-up Victor phonograph under my arm, hitched above my hipbone, and one Victor record. On a bicycle, that is.

The bicycle went to pieces from the use I gave it as a Postal Telegraph messenger.

The phonograph developed motor trouble soon after my first book was published; and while I was traveling in Europe for the first time, in 1935, it was given to the Salvation Army.

But I still have the record, and I have a special fondness for it.

The reason I have a special fondness for it is that whenever I listen to it, I remember what happened when I reached home with the phonograph and the record.

The phonograph had cost ten dollars and the record seventy-five cents, both brand new. I had earned the money as a messenger in my first week of work, plus four dollars and twenty-five cents not spent.

My mother had just got home from Guggenheim's, where, judging from the expression on her face, she had been packing figs in eight-ounce packs, which I knew was the weight and size that was least desired by the packers, because a full day of hard work doing eight-ounce packs, at so much per pack, meant only about a dollar and a half, or at the most two dollars, whereas, if they were packing

Sheet music for "Song of India."

four-ounce packs, they could earn three and sometimes even four dollars which in those days was good money, and welcome, especially as the work at Guggenheim's, or at any of the other dried-fruit packinghouses such as Rosenberg's or Inderrieden's, was seasonal, and the season was never long.

When I walked into the house, all excited, with the phonograph hitched to my hip, my mother gave me a look that suggested an eight-ounce day. She said nothing, however, and I said nothing, as I placed the phonograph on the round table in the parlor, checked it for any accidents to exposed parts that might have happened in transit, found none, lifted the record from the turntable where the girl in the store had fixed it with two big rubber bands, examined both sides of it, and noticed that my mother was watching. While I was still cranking the machine, she spoke at last, softly and

politely, which I knew meant she didn't like the looks of what was going on. She spoke in Armenian.

"Willie, what is that you have there?"

"This is called a phonograph."

"Where did you get this phonograph?"

"I got it from Sherman, Clay, on Broadway."

"The people at Sherman, Clay—did they *give* you this phonograph?"

"No, I paid for it."

"How much did you pay, Willie?"

"Ten dollars."

"Ten dollars is a lot of money in this family. Did you *find* the ten dollars in the street perhaps?"

"No, I got the ten dollars from my first week's pay as a Postal Telegraph messenger. And seventy-five cents for the record."

"And how much money have you brought

home for the whole family—for rent and food and clothing—out of your first week's pay?"

"Four dollars and twenty-five cents. My pay is fifteen dollars a week."

Now, the record is on the machine, and I am about to put the needle to the revolving disc when I suddenly notice that I had better forget it and get out of there, which I do, and just in time too. The screen door of the back porch slams once for me, and then once for my mother.

As I race around the house, I become aware of two things: (1) that it's a beautiful evening, and (2) that Levon Kemalyan's father, who is a very dignified man, is standing in front of his house across the street with his mouth a little open, watching. Well, he's an elder at the First Armenian Presbyterian Church; he isn't from Bitlis,[1] as we are; he's not a Saroyan, and this sort of thing comes as a surprise to him. Surely Takoohi Saroyan and her son are not racing around their house for exercise, or in an athletic contest of some kind, so why are they running?

In a spirit of neighborliness I salute Mr. Kemalyan as I race to the front porch and back into the parlor, where I quickly put needle to disc, and hurry to the dining room, from whence I can both witness the effect of the music on my mother, and, if necessary, escape to the back porch, and out into the yard again.

The music of the record begins to come from the machine just as my mother gets back into the parlor.

For a moment it looks as if she is going to ignore the music and continue the chase, and then suddenly it happens—the thing that makes the record something to cherish forever.

My mother comes to a halt, perhaps only to catch her breath, perhaps to listen to the music—there's still no way of telling for sure.

As the music moves along, I can't help noticing that my mother either is too tired to run anymore or is actually listening. And then I notice that she is very *definitely* listening. I watch her turn from the chase to the machine. I watch her take one of the six cane chairs that have remained in the family from the time of my father, from 1911, and move it to the round table. I watch her sit down. I notice now that her expression no longer suggests that she is tired and angry. I remember the man in the Bible who was mad and was comforted by somebody playing a harp.[2] I stand in the doorway to the parlor, and when the record ends I go to the machine, lift the needle from the disc and stop the motor.

Without looking at me, my mother says, this time in English, "All right, we keep this." And then in softly spoken Armenian, "Play it again, I beg of you."

I quickly give the crank a few spins and put needle to disc again.

This time when the needle comes to the end of the record my mother says, "Show me how it's done." I show her, and she starts the record a third time for herself.

Well, of course the music *is* beautiful, but only a moment ago she had been awfully mad at me for what she had felt had been the throwing-away of most of my week's wages for some kind of ridiculous piece of junk. And then she had heard the music; she had got the message, and the message had informed her that not only had the money *not* been thrown away, it had been wisely invested.

She played the record six times while I sat at the table in the dining room looking through a small catalogue of records given to me free of charge by the girl at Sherman, Clay, and then

---

1. **Bitlis** (bĭt-lēs′): a province in eastern Turkey.

2. **man . . . a harp:** In I Samuel 16:23, the "evil spirit" leaves King Saul when David plays on his lyre.

she said, "You have brought home only the one record?"

"Well, there's another song on the other side."

I went back to the machine, turned the record over, and put it in place.

Sheet music showing Paul Whiteman and his orchestra.

"What is this other one?"

"Well, it's called 'Song of India.' I've never heard it. At the store I listened only to the first one, which is called 'Cho-Cho-San.'"[3]

"What is the meaning of *that*—'Cho-Cho-San'?"

"It's just the name of the song, I guess. Would you like to hear the other one, 'Song of India'?"

3. **Cho-Cho-San:** the heroine of an opera called *Madama Butterfly* by Giacomo Puccini (1858–1924). She is a Japanese girl who marries an American naval lieutenant and then is deserted by him.

by N. RIMSKY-KORSAKOW

ARRANGED by FERDIE GROFÉ

AS PLAYED by PAUL WHITEMAN AND HIS ORCHESTRA

VICTOR RECORD 18777

"I beg of you."

Now, as the other members of the family came home, they heard music coming from the parlor, and when they went in they saw the brand-new phonograph and my mother sitting on the cane chair, directly in front of it, listening.

Why wouldn't that record be something I would want to keep as long as possible, and something I deeply cherish? Almost instantly it had won over my mother to art, and for all I know marked the point at which she began to suspect that her son rightfully valued some things higher than he valued money, and possibly even higher than he valued food, drink, shelter and clothing.

A week later she remarked to everybody during supper that the time had come to put some of the family money into a second record, and she wanted to know what was available. I got out the catalogue and went over the names, but they meant nothing to her, so she told me to just go to the store and pick out something *hrashali*, the Armenian word for miraculous, which I was happy to do.

Now, as I listen to the record again, forty-two years later, and try to guess what happened, I think it was the banjo beat that got my mother, that spoke directly to her as if to one long known, deeply understood, and totally loved; the banjo chords just back of the clarinet that remembered everything gone, accepted everything present, and waited for anything more still to come, echoing in and out of the story of the Japanese girl betrayed by the American sailor, the oboe saying words and the saxophone choking on swallowed emotion: "Fox Trot (On Melodies by G. Puccini, arranged by Hugo Frey) Paul Whiteman and His Orchestra. 18777-A."

After that, whenever other members of the family attacked me for some seeming eccentricity, my mother always patiently defended me until she lost her temper, whereupon she shouted, "He is not a businessman, thank God."

Reading Check

1. How does the narrator earn the money for the phonograph and record?
2. What is his weekly salary?
3. What kind of work does his mother do?
4. Why does his mother become angry?
5. When does she decide that her son has made a wise investment?

For Study and Discussion

Analyzing and Interpreting the Story

1. The narrator never tells us directly why he spent most of his first week's salary for the phonograph and record. What sentence in the story gives the best explanation for his action?

2a. How does the narrator's mother react to his purchases at first? b. What causes her to change her attitude toward the phonograph and toward her son?

3. Why does the grown man have such a fondness for the old record?

4. What elements of humor does Saroyan introduce into his narrative?

5. What is meant by the mother's statement in the last paragraph when she defends Willie by saying, "He is not a businessman, thank God"?

6. In what way is the phonograph record "miraculous"?

Learning Word Origins

The narrator tells us at the end of the story that members of his family sometimes attacked him for some *eccentricity*. In this context the word means "some oddness" or "some eccentric or unusual behavior." The words *eccentric* and *eccentricity* can be traced back to a Greek prefix, *ek-*, meaning "out of," and a root, *kentron*, meaning "center." Literally, that which is *eccentric* is "out of the center." You can see how the word would come to have the meaning of "odd" or "unconventional."

In a dictionary look up the word *eccentric* and find out what is meant by an *eccentric wheel*. What antonyms can you find for *eccentric*?

Narrative Writing

Relating an Anecdote

Saroyan's story is an **anecdote**—a short humorous incident drawn from the author's personal experience. Think of a brief entertaining incident of your own as the subject of a short narrative. For assistance in planning and writing your paper, see *Practice in Reading and Writing,* page 139.

About the Author

William Saroyan   (1908–1981)

Saroyan was born in Fresno, California, and grew up in the San Joaquin Valley. Before he turned to writing as a full-time career, he earned his living at many different jobs—selling newspapers, working in his uncle's vineyards, and delivering telegrams. When he was twenty-six, he published his first collection of stories, *The Daring Young Man on the Flying Trapeze,* which was an immediate success. During his lifetime he published more than five hundred short stories.

Many of Saroyan's stories are about his own childhood. Many of his characters are Armenian immigrants, like the members of his own family. Some of Saroyan's best-known books are *My Name Is Aram, The Human Comedy,* and *The Assyrian and Other Stories.*

Saroyan also wrote plays. His best-known play, *The Time of Your Life,* won the Pulitzer Prize in 1939.

The Courage That My Mother Had

EDNA ST. VINCENT MILLAY

The courage that my mother had
Went with her, and is with her still:
Rock from New England quarried;°
Now granite in a granite hill.

The golden brooch my mother wore   5
She left behind for me to wear;
I have no thing I treasure more:
Yet, it is something I could spare.

Oh, if instead she'd left to me
The thing she took into the grave!—   10
That courage like a rock, which she
Has no more need of, and I have.

3. **quarried:** dug from a pit.

For Study and Discussion

Analyzing and Interpreting the Poem

1a. In what way is courage like a rock?
b. What does this comparison suggest about the mother's character?

2. Which line suggests that the mother's character was formed by the land where she was born? Explain your answer.

3. The word *granite* appears twice in line 4. What is the granite that is now buried in a "granite hill"?

4. Why does the poet feel that her mother's courage would have been a greater gift than the golden brooch?

About the Author

Edna St. Vincent Millay   (1892–1950)

Edna St. Vincent Millay began writing poetry in her childhood. She published "Renascence," a long poem that expressed delight in the world of nature, when she was only nineteen. Her first volume of poetry came out in 1917, the year she graduated from Vassar College. Readers were attracted to the intensity of feeling and highly personal tone in her work. By the 1920s she was recognized as a major American poet. Her volume *The Harp-Weaver and Other Poems* won the Pulitzer Prize in 1923.

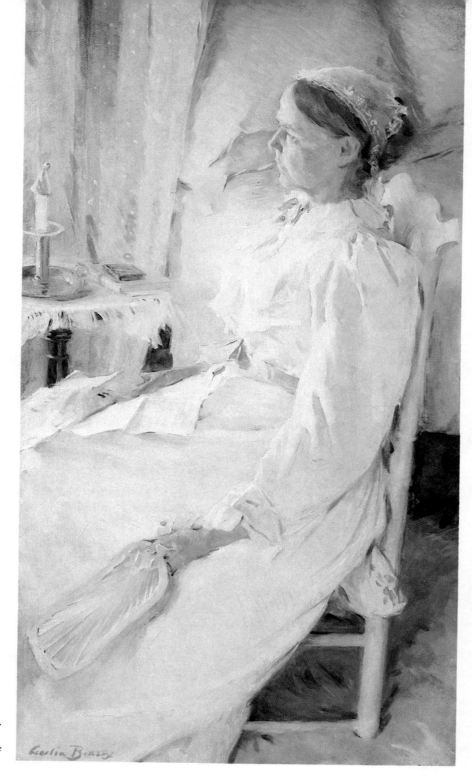

New England Woman
(1895) by Cecilia Beaux.
Oil on canvas.
Pennsylvania Academy of Fine
Arts, Temple Fund Purchase

One-Shot Finch

HARPER LEE

The selection you are about to read is a chapter from a novel called To Kill a Mockingbird. *"Scout" Finch, the girl who tells the story, and her brother, Jem, think they know all there is to know about their father, Atticus. What do they discover about him that other people have known all along?*

Atticus was feeble: he was nearly fifty. When Jem and I asked him why he was so old, he said he got started late, which we felt reflected upon his abilities and manliness. He was much older than the parents of our school contemporaries, and there was nothing Jem or I could say about him when our classmates said, "*My father——*"

Jem was football-crazy. Atticus was never too tired to play keep-away, but when Jem wanted to tackle him Atticus would say, "I'm too old for that, son."

Our father didn't do anything. He worked in an office, not in a drugstore. Atticus did not drive a dump truck for the county, he was not the sheriff, he did not farm, work in a garage, or do anything that could possibly arouse the admiration of anyone.

Besides that, he wore glasses. He was nearly blind in his left eye, and said left eyes were the tribal curse of the Finches. Whenever he wanted to see something well, he turned his head and looked from his right eye.

He did not do the things our schoolmates' fathers did: he never went hunting, he did not play poker or fish or drink or smoke. He sat in the living room and read.

With these attributes, however, he would not remain as inconspicuous as we wished him to: that year, the school buzzed with talk about him defending Tom Robinson,[1] none of which was complimentary. After my bout with Cecil Jacobs,[2] when I committed myself to a policy of cowardice, word got around that Scout Finch wouldn't fight any more, her daddy wouldn't let her. This was not entirely correct: I wouldn't fight publicly for Atticus, but the family was private ground. I would fight anyone from a third cousin upwards tooth and nail. Francis Hancock, for example, knew that.

When he gave us our air rifles Atticus wouldn't teach us to shoot. Uncle Jack instructed us in the rudiments thereof; he said Atticus wasn't interested in guns. Atticus said to Jem one day, "I'd rather you shot at tin cans

---

1. **Tom Robinson:** Atticus is a lawyer.
2. **Cecil Jacobs:** a boy who teased Scout about her father's defense of Tom Robinson. Scout fought him.

Scenes on pages 103 and 106 from a film version of *To Kill a Mockingbird*.

in the backyard, but I know you'll go after birds. Shoot all the bluejays you want, if you can hit 'em, but remember it's a sin to kill a mockingbird."

That was the only time I ever heard Atticus say it was a sin to do something, and I asked Miss Maudie[3] about it.

"Your father's right," she said. "Mockingbirds don't do one thing but make music for us to enjoy. They don't eat up people's gardens, don't nest in corncribs, they don't do one thing but sing their hearts out for us. That's why it's a sin to kill a mockingbird."

"Miss Maudie, this is an old neighborhood, ain't it?"

"Been here longer than the town."

"Nome, I mean the folks on our street are old. Jem and me's the only children around here. Mrs. Dubose is close on to a hundred and

Miss Rachel's old and so are you and Atticus."

"I don't call fifty very old," said Miss Maudie tartly. "Not being wheeled around yet, am I? Neither's your father. But I must say Providence was kind enough to burn down that old mausoleum of mine, I'm too old to keep it up—maybe you're right, Jean Louise,[4] this is a settled neighborhood. You've never been around young folks much, have you?"

"Yessum, at school."

"I mean young grown-ups. You're lucky, you know. You and Jem have the benefit of your father's age. If your father was thirty you'd find life quite different."

"I sure would. Atticus can't do anything. . . ."

"You'd be surprised," said Miss Maudie. "There's life in him yet."

"What can he do?"

3. **Miss Maudie:** Maudie Atkinson, the family's neighbor.

4. **Jean Louise:** Scout's real name.

"Well, he can make somebody's will so air-tight can't anybody meddle with it."

"Shoot. . . ."

"Well, did you know he's the best checker player in this town? Why, down at the Landing when we were coming up, Atticus Finch could beat everybody on both sides of the river."

"Good Lord, Miss Maudie, Jem and me beat him all the time."

"It's about time you found out it's because he lets you. Did you know he can play a jew's-harp?"[5]

This modest accomplishment served to make me even more ashamed of him.

"*Well . . .*" she said.

"Well what, Miss Maudie?"

"Well nothing. Nothing—it seems with all that you'd be proud of him. Can't everybody play a jew's-harp. Now keep out of the way of the carpenters. You'd better go home, I'll be in my azaleas and can't watch you. Plank might hit you."

I went to the backyard and found Jem plugging away at a tin can, which seemed stupid with all the bluejays around. I returned to the front yard and busied myself for two hours erecting a complicated breastworks at the side of the porch, consisting of a tire, an orange crate, the laundry hamper, the porch chairs, and a small U.S. flag Jem gave me from a popcorn box.

When Atticus came home to dinner he found me crouched down aiming across the street. "What are you shooting at?"

"Miss Maudie's rear end."

Atticus turned and saw my generous target bending over her bushes. He pushed his hat to the back of his head and crossed the street. "Maudie," he called, "I thought I'd better warn you. You're in considerable peril."

Miss Maudie straightened up and looked toward me. She said, "Atticus, you are a devil from hell."

When Atticus returned he told me to break camp. "Don't you ever let me catch you pointing that gun at anybody again," he said.

I wished my father was a devil from hell. I sounded out Calpurnia[6] on the subject. "Mr. Finch? Why, he can do lots of things."

"Like what?" I asked.

Calpurnia scratched her head. "Well, I don't rightly know," she said.

Jem underlined it when he asked Atticus if he was going out for the Methodists and Atticus said he'd break his neck if he did, he was just too old for that sort of thing. The Methodists were trying to pay off their church mortgage, and had challenged the Baptists to a game of touch football. Everybody in town's father was playing, it seemed, except Atticus. Jem said he didn't even want to go, but he was unable to resist football in any form, and he stood gloomily on the sidelines with Atticus and me watching Cecil Jacobs' father make touchdowns for the Baptists.

One Saturday Jem and I decided to go exploring with our air rifles to see if we could find a rabbit or a squirrel. We had gone about five hundred yards beyond the Radley Place when I noticed Jem squinting at something down the street. He had turned his head to one side and was looking out of the corners of his eyes.

"Whatcha looking at?"

"That old dog down yonder," he said.

"That's old Tim Johnson, ain't it?"

"Yeah."

Tim Johnson was the property of Mr. Harry Johnson, who drove the Mobile bus and lived on the southern edge of town. Tim was a liver-colored bird dog, the pet of Maycomb.

"What's he doing?"

5. **jew's-harp:** a musical instrument held between the teeth and plucked with a finger.

6. **Calpurnia:** the family's housekeeper. The children's mother is dead.

"I don't know, Scout. We better go home."

"Aw Jem, it's February."

"I don't care, I'm gonna tell Cal."

We raced home and ran to the kitchen.

"Cal," said Jem, "can you come down the sidewalk a minute?"

"What for, Jem? I can't come down the sidewalk every time you want me."

"There's somethin' wrong with an old dog down yonder."

Calpurnia sighed. "I can't wrap up any dog's foot now. There's some gauze in the bathroom, go get it and do it yourself."

Jem shook his head. "He's sick, Cal. Something's wrong with him."

"What's he doin', trying to catch his tail?"

"No, he's doin' like this."

Jem gulped like a goldfish, hunched his shoulders and twitched his torso. "He's goin' like that, only not like he means to."

"Are you telling me a story, Jem Finch?" Calpurnia's voice hardened.

"No Cal, I swear I'm not."

"Was he runnin'?"

"No, he's just moseyin' along, so slow you can't hardly tell it. He's comin' this way."

Calpurnia rinsed her hands and followed Jem into the yard. "I don't see any dog," she said.

She followed us beyond the Radley Place and looked where Jem pointed. Tim Johnson was not much more than a speck in the distance, but he was closer to us. He walked erratically, as if his right legs were shorter than his left legs. He reminded me of a car stuck in a sand bed.

"He's gone lopsided," said Jem.

Calpurnia stared, then grabbed us by the shoulders and ran us home. She shut the wood door behind us, went to the telephone and shouted, "Gimme Mr. Finch's office!"

"Mr. Finch!" she shouted. "This is Cal. I swear . . . there's a mad dog down the street a

piece—he's comin' this way, yes sir, he's—Mr. Finch, I declare he is—old Tim Johnson, yes sir . . . yessir . . . yes——"

She hung up and shook her head when we tried to ask her what Atticus had said. She rattled the telephone hook and said, "Miss Eula May—now ma'am, I'm through talkin' to Mr. Finch, please don't connect me no more—listen, Miss Eula May, can you call Miss Rachel and Miss Stephanie Crawford and whoever's got a phone on this street and tell 'em a mad dog's comin'? Please ma'am!"

Calpurnia listened. "I know it's February, Miss Eula May, but I know a mad dog when I see one. Please ma'am hurry!"

Calpurnia asked Jem, "Radleys got a phone?"

Jem looked in the book and said no. "They won't come out anyway, Cal."

"I don't care, I'm gonna tell 'em."

She ran to the front porch, Jem and I at her heels. "You stay in that house!" she yelled.

Calpurnia's message had been received by the neighborhood. Every wood door within our range of vision was closed tight. We saw no trace of Tim Johnson. We watched Calpurnia running toward the Radley Place, holding her skirt and apron above her knees. She went up to the front steps and banged on the door. She got no answer, and she shouted, "Mr. Nathan, Mr. Arthur, mad dog's comin'! Mad dog's comin'!"

"She's supposed to go around in back," I said.

Jem shook his head. "Don't make any difference now," he said.

Calpurnia pounded on the door in vain. No one acknowledged her warning; no one seemed to have heard it.

As Calpurnia sprinted to the back porch a black Ford swung into the driveway. Atticus and Mr. Heck Tate got out.

Mr. Heck Tate was the sheriff of Maycomb

County. He was as tall as Atticus, but thinner. He was long-nosed, wore boots with shiny metal eyeholes, boot pants and a lumber jacket. His belt had a row of bullets sticking in it. He carried a heavy rifle. When he and Atticus reached the porch, Jem opened the door.

"Stay inside, son," said Atticus. "Where is he, Cal?"

"He oughta be here by now," said Calpurnia, pointing down the street.

"Not runnin', is he?" asked Mr. Tate.

"Naw sir, he's in the twitchin' stage, Mr. Heck."

"Should we go after him, Heck?" asked Atticus.

"We better wait, Mr. Finch. They usually go in a straight line, but you never can tell. He

might follow the curve—hope he does or he'll go straight in the Radley backyard. Let's wait a minute."

"Don't think he'll get in the Radley yard," said Atticus. "Fence'll stop him. He'll probably follow the road. . . ."

I thought mad dogs foamed at the mouth, galloped, leaped and lunged at throats, and I thought they did it in August. Had Tim Johnson behaved thus, I would have been less frightened.

Nothing is more deadly than a deserted, waiting street. The trees were still, the mockingbirds were silent, the carpenters at Miss Maudie's house had vanished. I heard Mr. Tate sniff, then blow his nose. I saw him shift his gun to the crook of his arm. I saw Miss Stephanie Crawford's face framed in the glass window of her front door. Miss Maudie appeared and stood beside her. Atticus put his foot on the rung of a chair and rubbed his hand slowly down the side of his thigh.

"There he is," he said softly.

Tim Johnson came into sight, walking dazedly in the inner rim of the curve parallel to the Radley house.

"Look at him," whispered Jem. "Mr. Heck said they walked in a straight line. He can't even stay in the road."

"He looks more sick than anything," I said.

"Let anything get in front of him and he'll come straight at it."

Mr. Tate put his hand to his forehead and leaned forward. "He's got it all right, Mr. Finch."

Tim Johnson was advancing at a snail's pace, but he was not playing or sniffing at foliage: he seemed dedicated to one course and motivated by an invisible force that was inching him toward us. We could see him shiver like a horse shedding flies; his jaw opened and shut; he was alist, but he was being pulled gradually toward us.

"He's lookin' for a place to die," said Jem.

Mr. Tate turned around. "He's far from dead, Jem, he hasn't got started yet."

Tim Johnson reached the side street that ran in front of the Radley Place, and what remained of his poor mind made him pause and seem to consider which road he would take. He made a few hesitant steps and stopped in front of the Radley gate; then he tried to turn around, but was having difficulty.

Atticus said, "He's within range, Heck. You better get him now before he goes down the side street—Lord knows who's around the corner. Go inside, Cal."

Calpurnia opened the screen door, latched it behind her, then unlatched it and held onto the hook. She tried to block Jem and me with her body, but we looked out from beneath her arms.

"Take him, Mr. Finch." Mr. Tate handed the rifle to Atticus; Jem and I nearly fainted.

"Don't waste time, Heck," said Atticus. "Go on."

"Mr. Finch, this is a one-shot job."

Atticus shook his head vehemently: "Don't just stand there, Heck! He won't wait all day for you——"

". . . Mr. Finch, look where he is! Miss and you'll go straight into the Radley house! I can't shoot that well and you know it!"

"I haven't shot a gun in thirty years——"

Mr. Tate almost threw the rifle at Atticus. "I'd feel mighty comfortable if you did now," he said.

In a fog, Jem and I watched our father take the gun and walk out into the middle of the street. He walked quickly, but I thought he moved like an underwater swimmer: time had slowed to a nauseating crawl.

When Atticus raised his glasses Calpurnia murmured, "Sweet Jesus help him," and put her hands to her cheeks.

Atticus pushed his glasses to his forehead;

they slipped down, and he dropped them in the street. In the silence, I heard them crack. Atticus rubbed his eyes and chin; we saw him blink hard.

In front of the Radley gate, Tim Johnson had made up what was left of his mind. He had finally turned himself around, to pursue his original course up our street. He made two steps forward, then stopped and raised his head. We saw his body go rigid.

With movements so swift they seemed simultaneous, Atticus' hand yanked a ball-tipped lever as he brought the gun to his shoulder.

The rifle cracked. Tim Johnson leaped, flopped over and crumpled on the sidewalk in a brown-and-white heap. He didn't know what hit him.

Mr. Tate jumped off the porch and ran to the Radley Place. He stopped in front of the dog, squatted, turned around and tapped his finger on his forehead above his left eye. "You were a little to the right, Mr. Finch," he called.

"Always was," answered Atticus. "If I had my 'druthers I'd take a shotgun."

He stooped and picked up his glasses, ground the broken lenses to powder under his heel, and went to Mr. Tate and stood looking down at Tim Johnson.

Doors opened one by one, and the neighborhood slowly came alive. Miss Maudie walked along the steps with Miss Stephanie Crawford.

Jem was paralyzed. I pinched him to get him moving, but when Atticus saw us coming he called, "Stay where you are."

When Mr. Tate and Atticus returned to the yard, Mr. Tate was smiling. "I'll have Zeebo collect him," he said. "You haven't forgot much, Mr. Finch. They say it never leaves you."

Atticus was silent.

"Atticus?" said Jem.

"Yes?"

"Nothin'."

"I saw that, One-Shot Finch!"

Atticus wheeled around and faced Miss Maudie. They looked at one another without saying anything, and Atticus got into the sheriff's car. "Come here," he said to Jem. "Don't you go near that dog, you understand? Don't go near him, he's just as dangerous dead as alive."

"Yes, sir," said Jem. "Atticus——"

"What, son?"

"Nothing."

"What's the matter with you, boy, can't you talk?" said Mr. Tate, grinning at Jem. "Didn't you know your daddy's——"

"Hush, Heck," said Atticus, "let's go back to town."

When they drove away, Jem and I went to Miss Stephanie's front steps. We sat waiting for Zeebo to arrive in the garbage truck.

Jem sat in numb confusion, and Miss Stephanie said, "Uh, uh, uh, who'da thought of a mad dog in February? Maybe he wadn't mad, maybe he was just crazy. I'd hate to see Harry Johnson's face when he gets in from the Mobile run and finds Atticus Finch's shot his dog. Bet he was just full of fleas from somewhere——"

Miss Maudie said Miss Stephanie'd be singing a different tune if Tim Johnson was still coming up the street, that they'd find out soon enough, they'd send his head to Montgomery.

Jem became vaguely articulate: "'d you see him, Scout? 'd you see him just standin' there? . . . 'n' all of a sudden he just relaxed all over, an' it looked like that gun was a part of him . . . an' he did so quick, like . . . I hafta aim for ten minutes 'fore I can hit somethin'. . . ."

Miss Maudie grinned wickedly. "Well now,

Miss Jean Louise," she said, "still think your father can't do anything? Still ashamed of him?"

"Nome," I said meekly.

"Forgot to tell you the other day that besides playing the jew's-harp, Atticus Finch was the deadest shot in Maycomb County in his time."

"Dead shot . . ." echoed Jem.

"That's what I said, Jem Finch. Guess you'll change *your* tune now. The very idea, didn't you know his nickname was Ol' One-Shot when he was a boy? Why, down at the Landing when he was coming up, if he shot fifteen times and hit fourteen doves he'd complain about wasting ammunition."

"He never said anything about that," Jem muttered.

"Never said anything about it, did he?"

"No ma'am."

"Wonder why he never goes huntin' now," I said.

"Maybe I can tell you," said Miss Maudie. "If your father's anything, he's civilized in his heart. Marksmanship's a gift of God, a talent—oh, you have to practice to make it perfect, but shootin's different from playing the piano or the like. I think maybe he put his gun down when he realized that God had given him an unfair advantage over most living things. I guess he decided he wouldn't shoot till he had to, and he had to today."

"Looks like he'd be proud of it," I said.

"People in their right minds never take pride in their talents," said Miss Maudie.

We saw Zeebo drive up. He took a pitchfork from the back of the garbage truck and gingerly lifted Tim Johnson. He pitched the dog onto the truck, then poured something from a gallon jug on and around the spot where Tim fell. "Don't yawl come over here for a while," he called.

When we went home I told Jem we'd really have something to talk about at school on Monday. Jem turned on me.

"Don't say anything about it, Scout," he said.

"What? I certainly am. Ain't everybody's daddy the deadest shot in Maycomb County."

Jem said, "I reckon if he'd wanted us to know it, he'da told us. If he was proud of it, he'da told us."

"Maybe it just slipped his mind," I said.

"Naw, Scout, it's something you wouldn't understand. Atticus is real old, but I wouldn't care if he couldn't do anything—I wouldn't care if he couldn't do a blessed thing."

Jem picked up a rock and threw it jubilantly at the carhouse. Running after it, he called back: "Atticus is a gentleman, just like me!"

Reading Check

1. What is the "tribal curse" of the Finches?
2. According to Miss Maudie, why is it a sin to kill a mockingbird?
3. Who is the first one to spot the mad dog?
4. What happens to Atticus' glasses when he raises them to take aim?
5. Why does Atticus warn Scout and Jem to stay away from the dead dog?

For Study and Discussion

Analyzing and Interpreting the Selection

1. At the opening of the selection, Scout and Jem are disappointed that their father, Atticus, isn't more like their schoolmates' fathers. What are some of the things they wish their father could do?

2a. Why are Scout and Jem surprised when they see Heck Tate, the sheriff, hand his rifle to Atticus? **b.** Why does the sheriff tell Atticus that this is a "one-shot job"?

3. How did Atticus get the nickname "Ol' One-Shot"?

4. After Atticus shoots the mad dog, Scout and Jem see their father in a new light. Scout wants to brag about Atticus' talent, but Jem has a different reaction. **a.** Why does he tell Scout not to mention the shooting? **b.** What has he learned to admire in Atticus?

5. Why do you think Atticus never told his children about his skill as a marksman? Consider what you have learned about his attitude toward guns throughout the selection.

Literary Elements

Noting Details That Reveal Character

At the opening of the story, you know what Scout and her brother think of their father. They believe that Atticus is "feeble" and has no accomplishments they can be proud of. By the end of the selection, however, you know how wrong they have been. You have been able to form a different opinion of Atticus from what he says and does and from what other characters say about him.

Atticus is not a "feeble" man, as Scout believes at first, but a *gentle* man who dislikes violence. How is this characteristic revealed through Atticus' speech and actions? How is it revealed by what other characters say about him? What does Atticus do that shows that he is brave? How do you learn that Atticus is modest about his accomplishments?

Language and Vocabulary

Adding Different Meanings with *in-*

Scout says that she and her brother wanted Atticus to remain *inconspicuous*. Because they were not proud of Atticus' accomplishments, they did not want him to draw attention to himself.

Conspicuous people attract attention. People who are *inconspicuous* are just the opposite—they do not attract attention. Adding the negative prefix *in-* reverses the meaning of the word *conspicuous*.

See how the addition of *in-* changes the meaning of the following words.

activity	correct	secure
inactivity	incorrect	insecure

In these words, the prefix *in-* means "not" or "without." What pairs can you add to the list?

The prefix *in-* does not always add the meaning "not" or "without" to a word. The prefix *in-* can also mean "in." Decide which meaning the prefix has in each of these words:

inability	input	intake
incomplete	insane	invisible

Narrative Writing

Narrating Events in Order

Narrative is another word for *story*. A narrative relates a series of events. In most narratives, the events are presented in *chronological order,* or the order in which they happen. Scout tells the events that lead up to the shooting of the dog in chronological order. Notice how she builds up to the most exciting part of the narrative by reporting every detail she witnesses from the moment Atticus takes the gun until he raises it to shoot.

In a fog, Jem and I watched our father take the gun and walk out into the middle of the street. He walked quickly, but I thought he moved like an underwater swimmer: time had slowed to a nauseating crawl.

When Atticus raised his glasses Calpurnia murmured, "Sweet Jesus help him," and put her hands to her cheeks.

Atticus pushed his glasses to his forehead; they slipped down, and he dropped them in the street. In the silence, I heard them crack. Atticus rubbed his eyes and chin; we saw him blink hard.

In front of the Radley gate, Tim Johnson had made up what was left of his mind. He had finally turned himself around, to pursue his original course up our street. He made two steps forward, then stopped and raised his head. We saw his body go rigid.

With movements so swift they seemed simultaneous, Atticus' hand yanked a ball-tipped lever as he brought the gun to his shoulder.

Write a narrative based on a series of events you have witnessed or heard about. Narrate the events in chronological order.

About the Author

Harper Lee (1926–   )

Harper Lee, whose family is related to Robert E. Lee, lived in Alabama as a child. Her novel *To Kill a Mockingbird* was one of the most widely acclaimed books of the 1960s. It won many awards, including the 1961 Pulitzer Prize. The action of the book covers three years in the life of Scout Finch and her older brother, Jem, who live in a small Alabama town during the Depression of the 1930s. Scout's experiences are based on Harper Lee's recollections of life in the South.

Those Winter Sundays

ROBERT HAYDEN

Sundays too my father got up early
and put his clothes on in the blueblack cold,
then with cracked hands that ached
from labor in the weekday weather made
banked fires° blaze. No one ever thanked him.　　　5

I'd wake and hear the cold splintering, breaking.
When the rooms were warm, he'd call,
and slowly I would rise and dress,
fearing the chronic angers of that house,

Speaking indifferently to him,　　　10
who had driven out the cold
and polished my good shoes as well.
What did I know, what did I know
of love's austere and lonely offices?

5. **banked fires:** fires kept burning low.

For Study and Discussion

Analyzing and Interpreting the Poem

1. Which lines tell you the father worked hard on weekdays?

2. As a child, the poet feared "the chronic angers" in his house. *Chronic* means "constant" or "recurring." What do you think the phrase "chronic angers" refers to?

3. The word *austere* in line 14 means "requiring sacrifice or self-denial." **a.** Which details in the poem explain why the father's "offices," or duties, could be called "austere"? **b.** Which details explain why they could be called "lonely"?

4. In the last two lines, the poet indicates that as a child he failed to understand his father's expressions of love. What might have happened in the course of time to make him understand and appreciate his father's sacrifices?

Literary Elements

Responding to Images in Poetry

In line 2 of "Those Winter Sundays," Hayden uses the phrase "blueblack cold." What does this phrase suggest to you about winter mornings?

The phrase "blueblack cold" is an **image.** An image represents something that you can experience through your senses. The image "blueblack cold" summons up dark, chilling winter mornings. You can *see* and even *feel* what such mornings are like. An image may also help you *smell, taste,* or *hear* something—in your imagination, of course.

In contrast to the image of "blueblack cold," Hayden uses an image of heat in line 5. We are told that the father made "banked fires blaze." What do you see happening to the low-burning fires?

Love is often described as "warmth," and lack of love or indifference as "coldness." In what way does the contrast between *warm* and *cold* also apply to the feelings of people in the poem?

About the Author

Robert Hayden (1913–1980)

Robert Hayden, a prizewinning poet and a teacher, grew up in Detroit. One summer when he was in high school, he began reading the works of the poets Edna St. Vincent Millay and Countee Cullen. It was then that he began applying himself seriously to writing poetry, spending hours struggling to get his own thoughts down on paper.

Hayden once said this about his poem "Those Winter Sundays": "It is a sad poem, and one that I had to write. . . . The last stanza—oh, it's full of regret. Many people have told me this poem expresses their own feelings exactly. . . . It seems to speak to all people, as I certainly want my poems to do."

Sled

THOMAS E. ADAMS

This short story focuses on the relationship between a brother and sister. As you read, ask yourself how the author makes Joey a convincing character. What makes the change in Joey's attitude toward his sister believable?

All the adventure of the night and snow lay before him: if only he could get out of the house.

"You can't go out," his mother said, "until you learn how to act like a gentleman. Now apologize to your sister."

He stared across the table at his sister.

"Go on," his mother said.

His sister was watching her plate. He could detect the trace of a smile at the corners of her mouth.

"I won't! She's laughing at me!" He saw the smile grow more pronounced. "Besides, she *is* a liar!"

His sister did not even bother to look up, and he felt from looking at her that he had said exactly what she had wanted him to say. He grew irritated at his stupidity.

"That settles it," his mother said calmly, without turning from the stove. "No outs for you."

He stared at his hands, his mind in a panic. He could feel the smile on his sister's face. His hand fumbled with the fork on his plate. "No," he said meekly, prodding a piece of meat with the fork. "I'll apologize."

His sister looked up at him innocently.

"Well?" said his mother. "Go on."

He took a deep breath. "I'm . . ." He met his sister's gaze. "I'm sorry!" But it came out too loudly, he knew.

"He is not," his sister said.

He clenched his teeth and pinched his legs with his fingers. "I am too," he said. It sounded good, he knew; and it was half over. He had control now, and he relaxed a bit and even said further: "I'm sorry I called you a liar."

"That's better," his mother said. "You two should love each other. Not always be fighting."

He paused strategically for a long moment. "Can I go out now?"

"Yes," his mother said.

He rose from the table glaring at his sister with a broad grin, calling her a liar with his eyes.

His hand plucked his jacket from the couch and swirled it around his back. The buttons refused to fit through the holes, so he let them go in despair. He sat down just long enough to pull on his shiny black rubbers. Finally he put on his gloves. Then with four proud strides he arrived at the door and reached for the knob.

"Put your hat on," his mother said without looking at him.

His face toward the door, screwed and tightened with disgust. "Aw, Ma."

"Put it on."

"Aw, Ma, it's not that cold."

"Put it on."

"Honest, Ma, it's not that cold out."

"Are you going to put your hat on, or are you going to stay and help with the dishes?"

He sighed. "All right," he said. "I'll put it on."

The door to the kitchen closed on his back and he was alone in the cold gloom of the shed. Pale light streamed through the frosted window and fell against the wall where the sled stood. The dark cold room was silent, and he was free. He moved into the shaft of light and stopped, when from the kitchen he heard the muffled murmur of his mother's voice, as if she were far away. He listened. The murmuring hushed, and he was alone again.

The sled. It was leaning against the wall, its varnished wood glistening in the moonlight. He moved closer to it and saw his shadow block the light, and he heard the cold cracking of the loose linoleum beneath his feet.

He picked it up. He felt the smooth wood slippery in his gloved hands. The thin steel runners shone blue in the light as he moved one finger along the polished surface to erase any dust. He shifted the sled in his hands and stood getting the feel of its weight the way he had seen his brother hold a rifle. He gripped the sled tightly, aware of the strength in his arms; and he felt proud to be strong and alone and far away with the sled in the dark cold silent room.

The sled was small and light. But strong. And when he ran with it, he ran very quickly, quicker than anyone, because it was very light and small and not bulky like other sleds. And when he ran with it, he carried it as if it were part of him, as if he carried nothing in his arms. He set the rear end on the floor, now, and let the sled lean against him, his hands on the steering bar. He pushed down on the bar and the thin runners curved gracefully because they were made of shiny blue flexible steel; and with them he could turn sharply in the snow, sharper than anyone. It was the best sled. It was his.

He felt a slight chill in the cold room, and in the moonlight he saw his breath in vapor rising like cigarette smoke before his eyes. His body shivered with excitement as he moved hurriedly but noiselessly to the door. He flung it open; and the snow blue and sparkling, and the shadows deep and mysterious, the air silent and cold, all awaited him.

"Joey!" From the kitchen came his mother's voice. He turned toward the kitchen door and refused to answer.

"Joseph!"

"What!" His tone was arrogant, and a chill of fear rushed through his mind.

There was a long awful silence.

"Don't you forget to be home by seven o'clock." She hadn't noticed, and his fear was gone.

"All right!" He answered, ashamed of his fear. He stepped across the threshold and closed the door. Then he removed the hat and dropped it in the snow beside the porch.

He plodded down the alley, thrilling in the cold white silence—the snow was thick. The gate creaked as he pushed it open, holding and guiding the sled through the portal. The street was white, and shiny were the icy tracks of automobiles in the lamplight above. While between him and the light the black branches of trees ticked softly, in the slight wind. In the gutters stood enormous heaps of snow, pale dark in the shadows, stretching away from him like a string of mountains. He moved out of the shadows, between two piles of snow, and into the center of the street, where he stood for a moment gazing down the white road that gradually grew darker until it melted into the gloom at the far end.

Then he started to trot slowly down the street. Slowly, slowly gaining speed without losing balance. Faster he went now, watching the snow glide beneath his shiny black rubbers. Faster and faster, but stiffly, don't slip. Don't fall, don't fall: now! And his body plunged downward, and the sled whacked in the quiet, and the white close to his eyes was flying be-

neath him as he felt the thrill of gliding alone along a shadowy street, with only the ski-sound of the sled in the packed snow. Then before his eyes the moving snow gradually slowed. And stopped. And he heard only the low sound of the wind and his breath.

Up again and start the trot. He moved to the beating sound of his feet along the ground. His breath came heavily and quickly, and matched the rhythm of his pumping legs, straining to carry the weight of his body without the balance of his arms. He reached a wild dangerous breakneck speed, and his leg muscles swelled

and ached from the tension, and the fear of falling too early filled his mind: and down he let his body go. The white road rushed to meet him; he was off again, guiding the sled obliquely across the street toward a huge pile of snow near a driveway.

Squinting his eyes into the biting wind, he calculated when he would turn to avoid crashing. The pile, framed against the darkness of the sky, glistened white and shiny. It loomed larger and larger before him. He steered the sled sharply, bending the bar; and the snow flew as the sled churned sideways, and he heard suddenly a cold metallic snap. He and the sled went tumbling over in the hard wet snow. He rolled with it and the steering bar jarred his forehead. Then the dark sky and snow stopped turning, and all he felt was the cold air stinging the bump on his forehead.

The runner had snapped; the sled was broken. He stared at the shiny smooth runner and touched the jagged edge with his fingers. He sat in the middle of the driveway, the sled cradled in his lap, running his fingers up and down the thin runner until he came to the jagged edge where it had broken.

With his fingers he took the two broken edges and fitted them back into place. They stuck together with only a thin crooked line to indicate the split. But it was like putting a broken cup together. He stared at it, and wished it would be all right and felt like crying.

He got up and walked slowly back down to the street to his house. He sat down between the back bumper of a parked car and a pile of snow. Through his wet eyelids he saw the lamplight shimmering brightly against them. He felt a thickness in his throat, and he swallowed hard to remove it, but it did not go away.

He leaned back, resting his head against the snowpile. Through his wet eyelids he saw the lamplight shimmering brightly against the sky. He closed his eyes and saw again the shiny graceful curve of the runner. But it was broken now. He had bent it too far; too far. With his hand he rubbed his neck, then his eyes, then his neck again. He felt the snow coming wet through his pants. As he shifted to a new position, he heard the creaking of a gate. He turned toward the sound.

His sister was walking away from his house. He watched her move slowly across the street and into the grocery store. Through the plate-glass window he saw her talking with the storekeeper. He stared down at the runner. With his gloves off, he ran his fingers along the cold smooth surface and felt the thin breakline. He got up, brushed the snow off the seat of his pants, and walked to the gate to wait for his sister.

He saw her take a package from the man and come out of the store. She walked carefully on the smooth white, her figure dark in its own shadow as she passed beneath the streetlight, the package in her arm. When she reached the curb on his side, he rested his arms on the nose of the sled and exhaled a deep breath nervously. He pretended to be staring in the opposite direction.

When he heard her feet crunching softly in the snow, he turned: "Hi," he said.

"Hi," she said and she paused for a moment. "Good sledding?"

"Uh-huh," he said. "Just right. Snow's packed nice and hard. Hardly any slush at all." He paused. "I'm just resting a bit now."

She nodded. "I just went for some milk."

His fingers moved slowly down the runner and touched the joined edges.

"Well . . ." she said, about to leave.

His fingers trembled slightly, and he felt his heart begin to beat rapidly: "Do you want to take a flop?" In the still night air he heard with surprise the calm sound of his voice.

Her face came suddenly alive. "Can I? I mean, will you let me? Really?"

"Sure," he said. "Go ahead." And he handed her the sled very carefully. She gave him the package.

He put the bag under his arm and watched her move out of the shadows of the trees and into the light. She started to trot slowly, awkwardly, bearing the sled. She passed directly beneath the light and then she slipped and slowed to regain her balance. The sled looked large and heavy in her arms, and seeing her awkwardness, he realized she would be hurt badly in the fall. She was moving away again, out of the reach of the streetlight, and into the gray haze farther down the road.

He moved to the curb, holding the bag tightly under his arm, hearing his heart pounding in his ears. He wanted to stop her, and he opened his mouth as if to call to her; but no sound came. It was too late: her dark figure was already starting the fall, putting the sled beneath her. Whack! And her head dipped with the front end jutting the ground, and the back of the sled and her legs rose like a seesaw and down they came with another muffled sound. The street was quiet, except for a low whimper that filled his ears.

He saw her figure rise slowly and move toward him. He walked out to meet her beneath the light. She held the sled loosely in one hand, the broken runner dangling, reflecting light as she moved.

She sobbed, and looking up he saw bright tears falling down her cheeks and a thin line of blood trickling down her chin. In the corner of her mouth near the red swelling of her lip, a little bubble of spit shone with the blood in the light.

He felt that he should say something, but he did not speak.

"I'm . . . I'm sorry," she said, and the bubble broke. "I'm sorry I . . . your sled." She looked down at the sled. "It'll never be the same."

"It'll be all right," he said. He felt that he ought to do something, but he did not move. "I can get it soldered. Don't worry about it." But he saw from her expression that she thought he was only trying to make her feel better.

"No," she said, shaking her head emphatically. "No, it won't! It'll always have that weak spot now." She began to cry very hard. "I'm sorry."

He made an awkward gesture of forgiveness with his hand. "Don't cry," he said.

She kept crying.

"It wasn't your fault," he said.

"Yes, it was," she said. "Oh, yes, it was."

"No!" he said. "No, it wasn't!" But she didn't seem to hear him, and he felt his words were useless. He sighed wearily with defeat, not knowing what to say next. He saw her glance up at him as if to see whether he were still watching her, then she quickly lowered her gaze and said with despair and anguish: "Oh . . . girls are so stupid!"

There was no sound. She was no longer crying. She was looking at the ground: waiting. His ears heard nothing; they felt only the cold silent air.

"No, they aren't," he said halfheartedly. And

he heard her breathing again. He felt he had been forced to say that. In her shining eyes he saw an expression he did not understand. He wished she would go in the house. But seeing the tears on her cheeks and the blood on her chin, he immediately regretted the thought.

She wiped her chin with her sleeve, and he winced, feeling rough cloth on an open cut. "Don't do that." His hand moved to his back pocket. "Use my handkerchief."

She waited.

The pocket was empty. "I haven't got one," he said.

Staring directly at him, she patted gingerly the swollen part of her lip with the tips of her fingers.

He moved closer to her. "Let me see," he said. With his hands he grasped her head and tilted it so that the light fell directly on the cut.

"It's not too bad," she said calmly. And as she said it she looked straight into his eyes, and he felt she was perfectly at ease; while standing that close to her, he felt clumsy and out of place.

In his hands her head was small and fragile, and her hair was soft and warm; he felt the rapid pulsing of the vein in her temple: his ears grew hot with shame.

"Maybe I better go inside and wash it off?" she asked.

With his finger he wiped the blood from her chin. "Yes," he said, feeling relieved. "You go inside and wash it off." He took the sled and gave her the package.

He stared at the ground as they walked to the gate in silence. When they reached the curb he became aware that she was watching him.

"You've got a nasty bump on your forehead," she said.

"Yes," he said. "I fell."

"Let me put some snow on it," she said, reaching to the ground.

He caught her wrist and held it gently. "No," he said.

He saw her about to object: "It's all right. You go inside and take care of your lip." He said it softly, but with his grip and his eyes he told her more firmly.

"All right," she said after a moment, and he released his hold. "But don't forget to put your hat on."

He stared at her.

"I mean, *before* you go back in the house."

They both smiled.

"Thanks for reminding me," he said, and he dropped the sled in the snow and hurried to hold the gate open for her.

She hesitated, then smiled proudly as he beckoned her into the alley.

He watched her walk away from him down the dark alley in the gray snow. Her small figure swayed awkwardly as she stepped carefully in the deep snow, so as not to get her feet too wet. Her head was bowed, and her shoulders hunched, and he humbly felt her weakness. And he felt her cold. And he felt the snow running cold down her boots around her ankles. And though she wasn't crying now, he could still hear her low sobbing, and he saw her shining eyes and the tears falling and her trying to stop them and them falling even faster. And he wished he had never gone sledding. He wished that he had never even come out of the house tonight.

The back door closed. He turned and moved about nervously kicking at the ground. At the edge of the curb he dug his hands deep into the cold wet snow. He came up with a handful and absently began shaping and smoothing it. He stopped abruptly and dropped it at his feet.

He did not hear it fall. He was looking up at the dark sky, but he did not see it. He put his cold hands in his back pockets, but he did not feel them. He was wishing that he were some time a long time away from now and somewhere a long way away from here.

In the corner of his eye something suddenly dimmed. Across the street in the grocery store the light was out: it was seven o'clock.

Reading Check

1. Why have Joey and his sister been fighting at the dinner table?
2. Why does the runner on Joey's sled snap?
3. How does Joey hurt his head?
4. Why does Joey's sister come out of the house?
5. How is she hurt by her fall?

For Study and Discussion

Analyzing and Interpreting the Story

1. At the opening of the story, Joey does not want to apologize to his sister. **a.** Why not? **b.** Why does he force himself to apologize?

2a. Why does Joey feel that his sled is so special? **b.** After the runner breaks, Joey feels he is to blame. Why?

3. Why do you think Joey offers his sister a ride on the broken sled?

4. Joey's sister, believing she has broken the sled, wants her brother to forgive her. **a.** How does she apologize to Joey? **b.** Why does her behavior make her brother uncomfortable?

5. Early in the story, Joey's mother says, "You two should love each other. Not always be fighting." How do Joey and his sister show that they do care about each other after the accident with the sled? Find passages that support your answer.

Inferring Character from Thoughts and Feelings

In addition to learning about Joey from what he says and does, you learn about him from his thoughts and feelings.

At the beginning of the story, you can tell that Joey feels humiliated. He has been forced to apologize to his sister, and he sees that she is laughing at him.

What passages reveal that the sled makes Joey feel strong and important?

When Joey breaks the sled, he feels miserable. What passage reveals his deep hurt?

At what point does Joey realize how seriously his sister might be hurt?

Where do you learn that Joey feels ashamed of tricking his sister?

How do you know that he understands his sister's feelings and sympathizes with her?

Language and Vocabulary

Using Context Clues

While Joey was in the shed, "he heard the muffled *murmur* of his mother's voice, as if she were far away." If you were not familiar with the word *murmur,* you could use clues within the sentence to determine what it means. Other words in the sentence tell you that here the word *murmur* refers to a voice, that it is "muffled," and that it seems "far away." A *murmur* is a sound that is low and unclear.

Use context clues to figure out the meanings of the italicized words in these sentences from the story. Check your answers in a dictionary.

The gate creaked as he pushed it open, holding and guiding the sled through the *portal.*

Through his wet eyelids he saw the lamplight *shimmering* brightly against the sky.

She wiped her chin with her sleeve, and he *winced,* feeling rough cloth on an open cut.

Narrative Writing

Using Descriptive Details in Narration

If you have sledded downhill, you may have experienced the excitement Joey feels as he builds up to the plunge. Reread the passage on page 116 beginning "Up again and start the trot" and ending "pile of snow near a driveway." Which words or phrases help you *see* Joey's movements? Which words or phrases help you *hear* the sounds Joey makes? Which words or phrases help you *feel* what Joey feels?

Write a paragraph describing a person in action: running, swimming, cycling, skateboarding, surfing, or pole-vaulting. Re-create the action in detail. Choose words that will help your readers experience the action as directly as possible.

FROM
Nisei Daughter

MONICA SONE

Monica Sone grew up in Seattle's Japanese community. Her parents were immigrants, known as Issei, *"first generation." She herself was a* Nisei, *the name given to second-generation Japanese Americans. Here she tells how her family celebrated New Year's.*

New Year's, as my family observed it, was a mixture of pleasure and agony. I enjoyed New Year's Eve which we spent together, waiting for midnight. On New Year's Eve, no one argued when Mother marched us into the bathtub, one by one. We understood that something as important as a new year required a special sacrifice on our part. Mother said the bath was a symbolic act, that we must scrub off the old year and greet the new year clean and refreshed in body and spirit.

The rest of the evening we spent crowded around the table in the living room playing *Karuta,* an ancient Japanese game. It consisted of one hundred old classic poems beautifully brushed upon one hundred cards, about the size of a deck of cards. There was one set of cards on which were written the *shimo no ku,* the second half of the poems. These were laid out on the table before the players. A reader presided over a master set of one hundred cards which contained the *kami no ku,* the first half of the poem as well as the *shimo no ku.* As the reader read from the key cards, the players were to try to pick up the card on the table before anyone else could claim it. The player or the team who picked up the greatest number of cards was the winner. An expert player

knew the entire one hundred poems by heart so that when the reader had uttered the first few words, he knew instantly which card was being called out. When several experts competed the game was exciting and stimulating. But in our family only Mother and Father knew the poems, and they slowed their paces to match ours.

Mother was always the reader, chanting out the poems melodically. Sumiko, being the baby of the family, was allowed to stand on a chair at Mother's elbow and get a preview of the card being read. Sumiko would look, jump off the chair, and scurry around the table to find the card while we waited impatiently for Mother to get to the second half of the poem. I howled with indignation, "Mama, make Sumiko stop cheating! It's not fair . . . I'll never find a card as long as she peeks at the *kami no ku!*"

Mother laughed indulgently, "Now, don't get so excited. Sumichan's just a little girl. She has to have some fun, too."

The evening progressed noisily as we fluttered about like anxious little moths, eyes riveted on the table. Anyone who found a card would triumphantly shout *"Hai!"* and slam down on it with a force that would have flattened an opponent's fingers. Promptly at midnight we stopped. Out in the harbor, hundreds of boats sounded their foghorns to herald the New Year. Automobiles raced by under our windows, their horns blowing raucously. Guns exploded, cowbells clanged, the factory whistle shrilled. Henry swept the cards off the table, leaped into the air in his billowing night-shirt and shouted "Happy New Year, every-body! Happy New Year!" We turned on the radio full blast so we could hear the rest of the city cheer and sing "Auld Lang Syne." Horri-fied, Father implored us, "Ohhh the guests, the guests. Lower that radio. We'll wake our guests."[1]

Then Father and Mother slipped quietly down the hallway to the kitchen to prepare re-freshments. Although the black-painted steampipe, running alongside one wall in the room, made energetic knocking noises which meant that it was piping hot, the parlor was chilly. I turned the tiny gas heater higher and Sumiko and I sat in front of it, pulling our vo-luminous flannel gowns over our knees and cold toes. We sat with our chins resting com-

1. **guests:** hotel guests. The family owned the Carrollton Hotel, which was close to the waterfront.

fortably on our knees and huddled so close to the heater that our faces began to tighten and glow beet-red. I was floating in half sleep when I heard Mother and Father's voices murmur-ing gently. "*Sah,* who gets the smallest piece of pie?"

"Not me!" Sumiko jumped up defensively. Then she saw Father's eyes smiling.

Father had carried in a pot of hot coffee and fresh, honey-crusted apple pie with its golden juice bubbled through the slits. Mother brought in thick hot chocolate, with plump soft marshmallow floating on top, for us.

It was customary for the Japanese to eat buckwheat noodles on New Year's Eve, but every year whenever Mother wondered aloud whether she should make some, we voted it down. Father said, "No noodles for me either, Mama. A good hot cup of coffee is what will please me most."

Father sliced the pie and as we let the flaky, butter-flavored crust melt in our mouths, we did not envy anyone eating noodles.

The next morning when we were breakfast-ing on fruit juice, ham and eggs, toast and milk, Mother said, "We really should be eating *ozoni* and *mochi* on New Year's morning."

We gagged, "Oh, no, not in the morning!"

"Well now, don't turn your nose up like that. It's a perfectly respectable tradition."

Ozoni was a sort of thick chicken stew with solid chunks of carrots, bamboo sprouts, giant white radishes and taro roots. Into this piping hot mixture, one dipped freshly toasted rice dumplings, puffed into white airy plumpness, in the same way one dunked doughnuts into coffee. But the rice dumpling had an annoying way of sticking to everything like glue . . . to the chopsticks, to the side of the bowl, and on the palate. It was enough to cause a panic when the thick, doughy dumpling fastened itself in the throat and refused to march on down to the stomach.

Father backed us up once more, "*Ozoni* is good, I admit, but I don't like to battle with my food so early in the morning. Let's have some more coffee, Mama."

"Well, having a whimsical family like this certainly saves me a lot of work."

Up to that moment the family was in perfect harmony about whether we would celebrate New Year's in the Japanese or the American way. But a few hours later our peace was shattered when Mother said, "*Sah*, now we must pay our respects to the Matsuis."

"Not again," Henry shuddered.

"Yes again, and I don't want to hear any arguments."

"But why must *we* go? Why can't you and Papa go by yourselves this time?"

"We are all going together for the New Year's call," Mother said firmly. "I don't want to hear another word. Put your clothes on."

We sighed loudly as we dressed ourselves. We would have to sit silently like little Buddhas[2] and listen while our elders dredged up the past and gave it the annual overhaul. Even the prospect of Mrs. Matsui's magnificent holiday feast was dampened by the fact that we knew we would have to eat quietly like meek little ghosts and politely refuse all second helpings.

"Mama . . . " Henry shouted from his room. "What was that now, that New Year's greeting we have to say to the Matsuis? I've forgotten how it goes. '*Ake-mashite omede toh gozai masu. Konen mo, ahhh, konen mo . . .* ' What comes after that? I can't remember."

Mother said, "*Soh, soh . . .* I want you all to say it properly when we arrive at the Matsui-san's[3] home. It goes like this . . . *ake-mashite omede toh gozai masu,* which means 'This New Year is indeed a happy occasion.' Then you say *konen mo yoroshiku onegai itashi-masu.* 'I hope that the coming year will find us close friends as ever.' "

As we climbed up Yesler Hill to the Matsuis, we repeated the greeting over and over again. We raised our voices so we could hear ourselves better whenever a chunky bright orange cable car lurched up the hill like a lassoed bronco, inching its way furiously to the top.

The Matsui residence was a large yellow frame house which squatted grandly on an elevated corner lot. At the front door, Father and Mother and Mr. and Mrs. Matsui bowed and murmured, bowed and murmured. Standing behind our parents, we bowed vigorously, too. Then Mrs. Matsui looked at us expectantly and Mother pushed us forward. We bowed again, then started out in unison. "*Ake-mashite omede toh gozai masu.*" A long pause followed. We forgot the rest. Then Henry recalled a fragment, "*Konen mo . . . konen mo . . . ahhh,* something about *onegai shimasu.*"

The adults burst into laughter, bringing the affair to a merciful end.

2. **Buddha** (boōʹdə, bŏōdʹə): an Indian philosopher who founded Buddhism, a religion of eastern and central Asia. Statues of Buddha shown him meditating.

3. **Matsui-san:** The suffix *san* added to a name is a title of respect.

In the living room, we waited patiently while Mrs. Matsui offered the best chairs to Father and Mother who politely refused them. Mrs. Matsui insisted and they declined. When at last we were all seated as Mrs. Matsui wanted— Father and Mother on the overstuffed brown mohair chairs and the four of us primly lined up on the huge davenport, our polished shoes placed neatly together and hands in our laps— she brought in tea and thin, crisp, rice cookies. As she poured the tea, she said, "Perhaps the little folks would rather have 'sodawata' instead?"

Henry and Kenji smirked at each other while Sumiko and I hung our heads, trying not to look eager, but Mother said quickly, "Oh, no, please, Mrs. Matsui, don't trouble yourself. My children love tea." So we sipped scalding tea out of tiny, burning teacups without handles and nibbled at brittle rice wafers.

While the Matsuis and our parents reminisced about the good old days, we thumbed through the worn photograph albums and old Japanese tourist magazines. Finally Mrs. Matsui excused herself and bustled feverishly around the dining room. Then she invited us in. "*Sah,* I have nothing much to offer you, but please eat your fill."

"*Mah, mah,* such a wonderful assortment of *ogochi-soh,*" Mother bubbled.

Balding Mr. Matsui snorted deprecatingly. Mrs. Matsui walked around the table with an enormous platter of *osushi,* rice cakes rolled in seaweed. We each took one and nibbled at it daintily, sipping tea. Presently she sailed out of the kitchen bearing a magnificent black and silver lacquered tray loaded with carmine lacquer bowls filled with fragrant *nishime.* In pearly iridescent china bowls, Mrs. Matsui served us hot chocolatey *oshiruko,* a sweetened bean soup dotted with tender white *mochi,* puffed up like oversized marshmallows.

Father and Mother murmured over the su-

perb flavoring of each dish, while Mr. Matsui guffawed politely, "*Nani,* this woman isn't much of a cook at all."

I was fascinated with the *yaki-zakana,* barbecued perch, which, its head and tail raised saucily, looked as if it were about to flip out of the oval platter. Surrounding this centerpiece were lacquer boxes of desserts, neatly lined rows of red and green oblong slices of sweet bean cakes, a mound of crushed lima beans, tinted red and green, called *kinton.* There was a vegetable dish called *kimpira* which looked like a mass of brown twigs. It turned out to be burdock,[4] hotly seasoned with red pepper.

Every now and then Mrs. Matsui urged us from the side line, "Please help yourself to more food."

And each time, we were careful to say, "*Arigato,* I have plenty, thank you," although I could have counted the grains of rice I had so far consumed. I felt that a person could starve amidst this feast if he carried politeness too far. Fortunately, Mrs. Matsui ignored our refusals. She replenished our half-empty dishes and kept our teacups filled so that without breaking the illusion that we were all dainty eaters, we finally reached a semiconscious state of satiation.

We moved heavily to the parlor to relax. Mrs. Matsui pursued us there with more green, pickled radishes and *kazunoko,* fish eggs, and a bowl of fresh fruit. She brought out fresh tea and *yokan.* To turn down Mrs. Matsui's offer so often was very rude, so we accepted with a wan smile and firmly closed our mouths over the cake and chewed.

When Father and Mother finally came to their senses and decided it was time to go home, we nearly tore the door off its hinges in our rush to get out into the hallway for our wraps.

---

4. **burdock:** a plant that is native to Europe and Asia.

I staggered out at last into the frosty night, feeling tight as a drum and emotionally shaken from being too polite for too long. I hoped on our next call our hostess would worry less about being hospitable and more about her guests' comfort, but that was an impudent thought for a Japanese girl.

Reading Check

1. In the game of *Karuta,* what are the players expected to match?
2. What was the customary Japanese food on New Year's Eve?
3. What problem did the children have with rice dumplings?
4. How did the children entertain themselves at the Matsuis' home?

For Study and Discussion

Analyzing and Interpreting the Selection

1. The narrator says that observing New Year's was a mixture of pleasure and agony. **a.** Which activities did she consider pleasurable? **b.** Which did she dislike?

2. In what way did the family observe both Japanese and American customs?

3a. How were the children expected to behave when they visited the Matsuis? **b.** What does this scene reveal about traditional Japanese customs of hospitality? **c.** About the attitude of children toward their elders?

4. At the end of the selection, the narrator tells us that her thought was "impudent." What does this remark reveal about the traditional roles of Japanese women?

Language and Vocabulary

Getting Meaning from Context

In her autobiography Monica Sone frequently uses Japanese words and phrases. She makes their meaning clear by providing a translation or by giving us sufficient context clues to derive their meaning for ourselves.

Locate the following words and, using context clues, tell what you think they mean:

mochi (pages 123–124)
Arigato (page 125)
yokan (page 125)

Narrative Writing

Telling About a Holiday Celebration

All people have special ways of celebrating holidays. In Latin American countries, for example, it is traditional on certain festivals to hang a candy-filled container called a piñata from the ceiling. Children are blindfolded and then try to break the piñata open with a stick.

Think about a holiday custom that is observed by the members of your own family or by some group of people. In a short narrative, tell how the custom is observed.

About the Author

Monica Sone (1919–   )

In *Nisei Daughter,* Monica Sone tells about growing up in Seattle's Japanese community, and she describes the intermingling of Japanese and American cultures. After the outbreak of World War II, her family was evacuated to an internment camp. When she left the camp, she went to the Midwest and eventually enrolled at college in Indiana. She now lives in Canton, Ohio, where she works as a clinical psychologist.

Home

GWENDOLYN BROOKS

In this story a family faces a crisis. How does each member of the family react?
What are the special things Maud Martha fears losing?

What had been wanted was this always, this always to last, the talking softly on this porch, with the snake plant in the jardiniere[1] in the southwest corner, and the obstinate slip from Aunt Eppie's magnificent Michigan fern at the left side of the friendly door. Mama, Maud Martha, and Helen rocked slowly in their rocking chairs, and looked at the late afternoon light on the lawn and at the emphatic iron of the fence and at the poplar tree. These things might soon be theirs no longer. Those shafts and pools of light, the tree, the graceful iron, might soon be viewed possessively by different eyes.

1. **jardiniere** (järd′n-îr′): an ornamental pot for plants.

Papa was to have gone that noon, during his lunch hour, to the office of the Home Owners' Loan. If he had not succeeded in getting another extension, they would be leaving this house in which they had lived for more than fourteen years. There was little hope. The Home Owners' Loan was hard. They sat, making their plans.

"We'll be moving into a nice flat[2] somewhere," said Mama. "Somewhere on South Park, or Michigan, or in Washington Park Court." Those flats, as the girls and Mama knew well, were burdens on wages twice the size of Papa's. This was not mentioned now.

"They're much prettier than this old house," said Helen. "I have friends I'd just as soon not bring here. And I have other friends that wouldn't come down this far for anything, unless they were in a taxi."

Yesterday, Maud Martha would have attacked her. Tomorrow she might. Today she said nothing. She merely gazed at a little hopping robin in the tree, her tree, and tried to keep the fronts of her eyes dry.

"Well, I do know," said Mama, turning her hands over and over, "that I've been getting tireder and tireder of doing that firing.[3] From October to April, there's firing to be done."

"But lately we've been helping, Harry and I," said Maud Martha. "And sometimes in March and April and in October, and even in November, we could build a little fire in the fireplace. Sometimes the weather was just right for that."

She knew, from the way they looked at her, that this had been a mistake. They did not want to cry.

But she felt that the little line of white, sometimes ridged with smoked purple, and all that cream-shot saffron[4] would never drift across any western sky except that in back of this house. The rain would drum with as sweet a dullness nowhere but here. The birds on South Park were mechanical birds, no better than the poor caught canaries in those "rich" women's sun parlors.

"It's just going to kill Papa!" burst out Maud Martha. "He loves this house! He *lives* for this house!"

"He lives for us," said Helen. "It's us he loves. He wouldn't want the house, except for us."

"And he'll have us," added Mama, "wherever."

"You know," Helen sighed, "if you want to know the truth, this is a relief. If this hadn't come up, we would have gone on, just dragged on, hanging out here forever."

"It might," allowed Mama, "be an act of God. God may just have reached down and picked up the reins."

"Yes," Maud Martha cracked in, "that's what you always say—that God knows best."

Her mother looked at her quickly, decided the statement was not suspect, looked away.

Helen saw Papa coming. "There's Papa," said Helen.

They could not tell a thing from the way Papa was walking. It was that same dear little staccato walk,[5] one shoulder down, then the other, then repeat, and repeat. They watched his progress. He passed the Kennedys', he passed the vacant lot, he passed Mrs. Blakemore's. They wanted to hurl themselves over the fence, into the street, and shake the truth out of his collar. He opened his gate— the gate—and still his stride and face told them nothing.

"Hello," he said.

Mama got up and followed him through the

2. **flat:** an apartment.
3. **firing:** starting a coal fire.
4. **saffron:** a yellow-orange color.

5. **staccato** (stə-kä′tō) **walk:** a walk of short, abrupt steps.

front door. The girls knew better than to go in too.

Presently Mama's head emerged. Her eyes were lamps turned on.

"It's all right," she exclaimed. "He got it. It's all over. Everything is all right."

The door slammed shut. Mama's footsteps hurried away.

"I think," said Helen, rocking rapidly, "I think I'll give a party. I haven't given a party since I was eleven. I'd like some of my friends to just casually see that we're homeowners."

Reading Check

1. What news is the family awaiting?
2. What plans does Mama make for moving?
3. What news does Papa bring?
4. Why does Helen plan to give a party?

For Study and Discussion

Analyzing and Interpreting the Selection

1. Why do the members of the family feel they are in danger of losing their home?

2a. What reasons do Mama and Helen give for wanting to move? b. Are they telling the truth, or are they trying to prepare themselves for disappointment? Support your answer with passages from the selection.

3. When Mama returns from speaking to Papa, her eyes are described as "lamps turned on." What emotion do you think Mama is feeling?

Literary Elements

Drawing Conclusions

Gwendolyn Brooks never tells you directly that Maud Martha values the beauties of the natural world. However, you can draw this conclusion from what she tells you about Maud Martha's responses to nature. You are told of the pleasure Maud Martha takes in looking at the late afternoon light on the lawn, in watching a sunset, and in listening to the rain drumming on the roof. You also learn that she feels sorry for "mechanical" birds that are kept in cages.

To understand what an author tells you about characters, you often must read below the surface and draw your own conclusions. Read the following statements about the characters in the story. Do you agree with all of them? Support your answers with passages from the selection.

Maud Martha and Helen value different things in life.
Their home is in a wealthy neighborhood.
Maud Martha is not afraid to be honest about her feelings.
Papa has lost his job.

Language and Vocabulary

Finding the Appropriate Meaning

Often the meaning and pronunciation of a word depend on how it is used in a sentence. The word *progress,* for example, may be used as a noun or a verb. Find the word in a dictionary and note the meaning and pronunciation for each part of speech. Look at the word *progress* in this sentence from "Home":

They watched his *progress.*

How is *progress* used here? How is it pronounced? Give its meaning.

The word *suspect* may be used as a noun, a

verb, or an adjective. Find the meaning and pronunciation for each part of speech. How is *suspect* used in this sentence?

> Her mother looked at her quickly, decided the statement was not *suspect,* looked away.

What does the word mean? How is it pronounced?

Look up the following words in a dictionary. In how many different ways can each word be used? Give the meaning and pronunciation for each part of speech.

excuse   perfect   record

Descriptive Writing

Describing a Room or Place

Write a one-paragraph description of a favorite room or place. Follow some logical order in your description: for example, spatial order—from left to right or from top to bottom; general to specific—from overall impression to individual items; order of importance—from minor to major features (or vice versa). Concentrate on creating a strong impression through specific details and well-chosen modifiers.

About the Author

Gwendolyn Brooks (1917–   )

Gwendolyn Brooks recalls that as a child she was writing all the time: "My mother says I began rhyming at seven—but my notebooks date back to my eleventh year only."

In 1950 she won the Pulitzer Prize for *Annie Allen,* a collection of poems about a black girl growing up in Chicago. She returned to the same subject in her novel *Maud Martha,* from which "Home" is taken. Of that work, she has written: "My one novel is not autobiographical in the usual sense. . . . But it is true that much in the 'story' was taken out of my own life, and twisted, highlighted or dulled, dressed up or down. . . . 'Home' is indeed fact-bound. The Home Owners' Loan Corporation was a sickening reality."

In 1968, Gwendolyn Brooks succeeded Carl Sandburg as the poet laureate of Illinois.

My Grandmother Would Rock Quietly and Hum

LEONARD ADAMÉ

Although the sentences in this poem do not begin with capital letters and end with periods, you will find that every stanza contains one or more complete thoughts.

in her house
she would rock quietly and hum
until her swelled hands
calmed

in summer   5
she wore thick stockings
sweaters
and gray braids

(when el cheque° came
we went to Payless°   10
and I laughed greedily
when given a quarter)

mornings,
sunlight barely lit
the kitchen   15
and where
there were shadows
it was not cold

she quietly rolled
flour tortillas—   20
the papas°
cracking in hot lard
would wake me

---

9. **el cheque** (ĕl chĕ′kā): the check.   10. **Payless:** a chain of food stores.   21. **papas** (pä′päs): potatoes.

she had lost her teeth
and when we ate   25
she had bread
soaked in café°

always her eyes
were clear
and she could see   30
as I cannot yet see—
through her eyes
she gave me herself

she would sit
and talk   35
of her girlhood—
of things strange to me:
    México°
    epidemics
    relatives shot   40
    her father's hopes
    of this country—
how they sank
with cement dust
to his insides   45

now
when I go
to the old house
the worn spots
by the stove   50
echo of her shuffling
and
México
still hangs in her
fading   55
calendar pictures

27. **café** (kä-fā′).   38. **México** (mě′hē-kō).

For Study and Discussion

Analyzing and Interpreting the Poem

1. What images of his grandmother does the poet recall?

2. In what ways did his grandmother enrich his life?

Language and Vocabulary

Recognizing Words of Spanish Origin

The word *tortilla*, which appears in line 20 of Adamé's poem, is a Spanish word that has entered the English language. The word *cheque* in line 9 is an example of an English word that has entered Spanish. Many Spanish words have come into English, just as many English words have found their way into Spanish.

Here are several Spanish words that have become part of the English language. Tell what each one means. Use a dictionary to find the meanings of any unfamiliar words.

adios	fiesta	siesta
adobe	rodeo	sombrero

About the Author

Leonard Adamé (1947–   )

Leonard Adamé was born in Fresno, California. He says that he began writing "because I had feelings that needed to be expressed." His work has been published in *The American Poetry Review* and *The Greenfield Review*. He has also written *Cantos Pa' la Memoria,* which has been published as part of the Chicano Chapbook Series.

The Night the Bed Fell

JAMES THURBER

Some of the most hilarious stories in American literature are those that James Thurber has told about his family. Here is the story of one memorable night in the Thurber household.

I suppose that the high-water mark of my youth in Columbus, Ohio, was the night the bed fell on my father. It makes a better recitation (unless, as some friends of mine have said, one has heard it five or six times) than it does a piece of writing, for it is almost necessary to throw furniture around, shake doors, and bark like a dog, to lend the proper atmosphere and verisimilitude[1] to what is admittedly a somewhat incredible tale. Still, it did take place.

It happened, then, that my father had decided to sleep in the attic one night, to be away where he could think. My mother opposed the notion strongly because, she said, the old wooden bed up there was unsafe; it was wobbly, and the heavy headboard would crash down on Father's head in case the bed fell, and kill him. There was no dissuading him, however, and at a quarter past ten he closed the attic door behind him and went up the narrow twisting stairs. We later heard ominous creakings as he crawled into bed. Grandfather, who usually slept in the attic bed when he was with us, had disappeared some days before. (On these occasions he was usually gone six or eight days and returned growling and out of temper, with the news that the Federal Union was run by a passel of blockheads and that the Army of the Potomac didn't have a chance.[2])

We had visiting us at this time a nervous first cousin of mine named Briggs Beall, who believed that he was likely to cease breathing when he was asleep. It was his feeling that if he were not awakened every hour during the night, he might die of suffocation. He had been accustomed to setting an alarm clock to ring at intervals until morning, but I persuaded him to abandon this. He slept in my room and I told him that I was such a light sleeper that if anybody quit breathing in the same room with me, I would wake instantly. He tested me the first night—which I had suspected he would—by holding his breath after my regular breathing had convinced him I was asleep. I was not asleep, however, and called to

---

1. **verisimilitude** (vĕr′ə-sĭm-ĭl′ə-tōōd′): the appearance of truth.

2. **the Federal . . . chance:** Grandfather, who lives in the past, thinks the Civil War is still going on.

He Came to the Conclusion That He Was Suffocating
©1933, 1961 by James Thurber. From *My Life and Hard Times*, Harper & Row

him. This seemed to allay his fears a little, but he took the precaution of putting a glass of spirits of camphor on a little table at the head of his bed. In case I didn't arouse him until he was almost gone, he said, he would sniff the camphor, a powerful reviver.

Briggs was not the only member of his family who had his crotchets.[3] Old Aunt Melissa Beall (who could whistle like a man, with two fingers in her mouth) suffered under the premonition that she was destined to die on South High Street because she had been born on South High Street and married on South High Street. Then there was Aunt Sarah Shoaf, who never went to bed at night without the fear that a burglar was going to get in and blow chloroform under her door through a tube. To avert this calamity—for she was in greater dread of

anesthetics than of losing her household goods—she always piled her money, silverware, and other valuables in a neat stack just outside her bedroom, with a note reading "This is all I have. Please take it and do not use your chloroform, as this is all I have." Aunt Gracie Shoaf also had a burglar phobia, but she met it with more fortitude. She was confident that burglars had been getting into her house every night for forty years. The fact that she never missed anything was to her no proof to the contrary. She always claimed that she scared them off before they could take anything, by throwing shoes down the hallway. When she went to bed, she piled, where she could get at them handily, all the shoes there were about her house. Five minutes after she had turned off the light, she would sit up in bed and say "Hark!" Her husband, who had learned to ignore the whole situation as long

3. **crotchets** (krŏch′ĭts): odd or fantastic ideas.

ago as 1903, would either be sound asleep or pretend to be sound asleep. In either case he would not respond to her tugging and pulling, so that presently she would arise, tiptoe to the door, open it slightly, and heave a shoe down the hall in one direction and its mate down the hall in the other direction. Some nights she threw them all, some nights only a couple of pairs.

But I am straying from the remarkable incidents that took place during the night that the bed fell on Father. By midnight we were all in bed. The layout of the rooms and the disposition of their occupants is important to an

Some Nights She Threw Them All
©1933, 1961 by James Thurber. From *My Life and Hard Times*, Harper & Row

understanding of what later occurred. In the front room upstairs (just under Father's attic bedroom) were my mother and my brother Herman, who sometimes sang in his sleep, usually "Marching Through Georgia" or "Onward, Christian Soldiers." Briggs Beall and myself were in a room adjoining this one. My brother Roy was in a room across the hall from ours. Our bull terrier, Rex, slept in the hall.

My bed was an army cot, one of those affairs which are made wide enough to sleep on comfortably only by putting up, flat with the middle section, the two sides which ordinarily hang down like the sideboards of a dropleaf table. When these sides are up, it is perilous to roll too far toward the edge, for then the cot is likely to tip completely over, bringing the whole bed down on top of one, with a tremendous banging crash. This, in fact, is precisely what happened about two o'clock in the morning. (It was my mother who, in recalling the scene later, first referred to it as "the night the bed fell on your father.")

Always a deep sleeper, slow to arouse (I had lied to Briggs), I was at first unconscious of what had happened when the iron cot rolled me onto the floor and toppled over on me. It left me still warmly bundled up and unhurt, for the bed rested above me like a canopy. Hence I did not wake up, only reached the edge of consciousness and went back. The racket, however, instantly awakened my mother, in the next room, who came to the immediate conclusion that her worst dread was realized: the big wooden bed upstairs had fallen on Father. She therefore screamed, "Let's go to your poor father!" It was this shout, rather than the noise of my cot falling, that awakened Herman, in the same room with her. He thought that Mother had become, for no apparent reason, hysterical. "You're all right, Mamma!" he shouted, trying to calm her. They exchanged shout for shout for per-

haps ten seconds: "Let's go to your poor father!" and "You're all right!" That woke up Briggs. By this time I was conscious of what was going on, in a vague way, but did not yet realize that I was under my bed instead of on it. Briggs, awakening in the midst of loud shouts of fear and apprehension, came to the quick conclusion that he was suffocating and that we were all trying to "bring him out." With a low moan, he grasped the glass of camphor at the head of his bed and instead of sniffing it poured it over himself. The room reeked of camphor. "Ugf, ahfg," choked Briggs, like a drowning man, for he had almost succeeded in stopping his breath under the deluge of pungent spirits. He leaped out of bed and groped toward the open window, but he came up against one that was closed. With his hand, he beat out the glass, and I could hear it crash and tinkle on the alleyway below. It was at this juncture that I, in trying to get up, had the uncanny sensation of feeling my bed above me! Foggy with sleep, I now suspected, in my turn, that the whole uproar was being made in a frantic endeavor to extricate me from what must be an unheard-of and perilous situation. "Get me out of this!" I bawled. "Get me out!" I think I had the nightmarish belief that I was entombed in a mine. "Gugh," gasped Briggs, floundering in his camphor.

By this time my mother, still shouting, pursued by Herman, still shouting, was trying to open the door to the attic, in order to go up and get my father's body out of the wreckage. The door was stuck, however, and wouldn't yield. Her frantic pulls on it only added to the general banging and confusion. Roy and the dog were now up, the one shouting questions, the other barking.

Father, farthest away and soundest sleeper of all, had by this time been awakened by the battering on the attic door. He decided that the house was on fire. "I'm coming, I'm coming!"

he wailed in a slow, sleepy voice—it took him many minutes to regain full consciousness. My mother, still believing he was caught under the bed, detected in his "I'm coming!" the mournful, resigned note of one who is preparing to meet his Maker. "He's dying!" she shouted.

"I'm all right!" Briggs yelled to reassure her. "I'm all right!" He still believed that it was his own closeness to death that was worrying Mother. I found at last the light switch in my room, unlocked the door, and Briggs and I joined the others at the attic door. The dog, who never did like Briggs, jumped for him—assuming that he was the culprit in whatever was going on—and Roy had to throw Rex and hold him. We could hear Father crawling out of bed upstairs. Roy pulled the attic door open with a mighty jerk, and Father came down the stairs, sleepy and irritable but safe and sound. My mother began to weep when she saw him. Rex began to howl. "What in the name of heaven is going on here?" asked Father.

The situation was finally put together like a gigantic jigsaw puzzle. Father caught a cold from prowling around in his bare feet, but there were no other bad results. "I'm glad," said Mother, who always looked on the bright side of things, "that your grandfather wasn't here."

Reading Check

1. Why did Thurber's father decide to sleep in the attic?
2. What was Briggs Beall's greatest fear?
3. How did Briggs test Thurber's claim that he was a light sleeper?
4. What was Father's conclusion when he heard the commotion?
5. Why did Rex attack Briggs?

For Study and Discussion

Analyzing and Interpreting the Selection

1. In his opening paragraph Thurber says that the story he is about to tell is a "somewhat incredible tale." After getting to know the members of his family, do you believe that the hilarious events he describes could have taken place? Why or why not?

2. "Crotchets" seem to run in Thurber's family. **a.** Which of the crotchets did you find most amusing? **b.** In what way did Rex, the bull terrier, have his crotchets?

3. During the night, Thurber's cot tipped over and fell on him with a loud crash. How did each member of the household interpret what he or she heard?

4. What do you think might have happened if Grandfather had been there? Why?

Language and Vocabulary

Analyzing Words with -phobia and philo-

Thurber tells us that his Aunt Gracie Shoaf had a "burglar phobia." A *phobia* is an unreasonable fear. It comes from the Greek word *phobos,* meaning "fear." Cousin Briggs also had a phobia, and so did Aunt Melissa Beall.

The word *phobia* can be used alone, as Thurber uses it, or it can be combined with other roots to name particular fears. Look up *hydrophobia* and *claustrophobia* in a dictionary. What specific fears do they name?

The root *philo-* (or *phil-*) comes from the Greek word *philos,* which means "loving." The Greek word *sophia* means "wisdom." What does *philosophy* mean? In Greek the word *adelphos* means "brother." What does the name *Philadelphia* mean?

How is *Anglophobia* different from *Anglophilia*? Use a dictionary to find the answer.

Reciting the Story

Thurber claims that the story "makes a better recitation . . . than it does a piece of writing" (page 133). Prepare to read the story aloud. How will you lend it "proper atmosphere?" Rehearse your reading before presenting it to your audience.

Narrative Writing

Using Exaggeration in a Humorous Story

Thurber makes his narrative funny by exaggerating the humorous characteristics of his family. For example, he says that his cousin Briggs Beall is afraid he will stop breathing in his sleep. Since there is no reason to believe that Briggs is physically ill, this peculiar fear is amusing. Thurber makes it even funnier by showing us what measures Briggs takes to keep from suffocating. He sets an alarm clock to ring at different times during the night. He keeps camphor on his night table to revive himself if he stops breathing. He even holds his breath in order to test whether Thurber is a light enough sleeper to hear him suffocating. These details exaggerate Briggs's "crotchets."

Write a humorous story of your own that is based on an actual event. Start with people and a setting that you know well. You may want to include an animal that has unusual habits. Consider inventing names for your characters. Then let your imagination go. Exaggerate as much as you want to.

About the Author

James Thurber   (1894–1961)

James Thurber is widely considered to be the finest American humorist since Mark Twain. Despite a childhood accident which resulted in the loss of one eye and the gradual weakening of the other, Thurber had a long and successful writing career. Over a period of thirty years, he contributed hundreds of stories, essays, and articles to *The New Yorker* magazine. Thurber was also a masterful cartoonist.

Thurber used material from his childhood in Columbus, Ohio, to create his most famous collection of stories, *My Life and Hard Times*. "The Night the Bed Fell" is taken from this collection.

PRACTICE IN READING AND WRITING

Narrative Writing

A narrative relates a story or a series of events. To make a narrative clear, a writer must arrange the events in some kind of logical order—usually the order in which they occur. A good narrative also has unity—all the events deal with one main action.

The following passage from "Home" illustrates several characteristics basic to good narrative writing. You will recall that when this passage begins, the family is waiting nervously for Papa to return with the answer from the Home Owners' Loan.

Helen saw Papa coming. "There's Papa," said Helen.

They could not tell a thing from the way Papa was walking. It was that same dear little staccato walk, one shoulder down, then the other, then repeat, and repeat. They watched his progress. He passed the Kennedys', he passed the vacant lot, he passed Mrs. Blakemore's. They wanted to hurl themselves over the fence, into the street, and shake the truth out of his collar. He opened his gate—the gate—and still his stride and face told them nothing.

"Hello," he said.

Mama got up and followed him through the front door. The girls knew better than to go in too.

Presently Mama's head emerged. Her eyes were lamps turned on.

"It's all right," she exclaimed. "He got it. It's all over. Everything is all right."

The door slammed shut. Mama's footsteps hurried away.

1. What are the events that make up this narrative passage?
2. What order is used for the events in the model passage?
3. What is the main action of this passage?

Suggestions for Writing

Write a narrative, using one of these topics or a topic of your own:

What happened during vacation
A trip to the circus
An episode at camp
One night in the life of a baby sitter

Here are some guidelines to help you plan and write your paper.

Prewriting
- Choose an anecdote or incident from personal or imaginary experience that will be of interest to your reader.
- If there is a main character, arrange in order the details your reader will need to know about the character.
- Make a list of the actions you will include in your narrative. Use the *5W-How?* questions (*Who? What? When? Where? Why?* and *How?*)
- Plan an opening sentence that will capture your reader's attention.

- Provide your narrative with a beginning, a middle, and an end.

Writing

- Tell the story, including only those events that deal with the main action.
- Use variety in sentence structure so that not all sentences begin the same way.

Evaluating and Revising

- Does the opening sentence catch the reader's attention?
- Are there sufficient details for clarity?
- Are there any unnecessary or repetitive details?
- Have the events been arranged in logical order?
- Are there transitions to connect ideas?
- Have you used vivid nouns, verbs, and modifiers?

Proofreading

- Check your revised paper for errors in grammar, usage, and mechanics.
- Prepare a final copy and check it for accuracy.

Writing Dialogue

Dialogue is often an important part of narrative writing. Remember these points:

- Begin a new paragraph for each speaker.
- Use quotation marks to enclose each speaker's exact words.
- Begin each quotation with a capital letter. If the sentence is divided into two parts, begin the second part with a small letter.
- Use commas to separate a quotation from the rest of the sentence.
- Do not use quotation marks unless you are quoting a person's exact words.

Choose a passage of narrative from one of the selections in this unit, and rewrite it as dialogue.

For Further Reading

Alcott, Louisa May, *Little Women* (many editions)
This famous novel is about the four March sisters—Jo, Meg, Amy, and Beth—who grow up in New England at the time of the Civil War.

Armstrong, William, *Sounder* (Harper & Row, 1969; paperback, Harper 1972)
A Southern family struggles to survive after the father is sent to prison for stealing food. This is a moving story about a mother's dignity, and the love between a boy and his dog.

Benary-Isbert, Margot, *The Ark* (Harcourt Brace Jovanovich, 1953)
A refugee family in postwar Germany rebuild their lives.

Cleaver, Vera, and Bill Cleaver, *Where the Lilies Bloom* (Lippincott, 1969; paperback, New American Library, 1974)
When her father dies, fourteen-year-old Mary Call Luther becomes the head of the family, assuming responsibility for a ten-year-old brother and an older sister. The story takes place in the Appalachian hill country.

Forbes, Kathryn, *Mama's Bank Account* (Harcourt Brace Jovanovich, 1968; paperback)
The oldest daughter of a Norwegian-American family describes her family's experiences in turn-of-the-century San Francisco.

Gilbreth, Frank B., and Ernestine Gilbreth Carey, *Cheaper by the Dozen* (Thomas Y. Crowell, 1963; paperback, Bantam)
The authors write humorously of growing up in a family of twelve children, with a remarkable mother and an efficiency expert for a father.

Lindsay, Howard, and Russell Crouse, *Life with Father* and *Life with Mother* (Alfred A. Knopf, 1953)
These plays are based on Clarence Day's entertaining stories about his family.

Nash, Ogden, *Parents Keep Out: Elderly Poems for Youngerly Readers* (Little, Brown, 1951)
Here is a collection of humorous poems about family life.

Peck, Robert Newton, *A Day No Pigs Would Die* (Alfred A. Knopf, 1972; paperback, Dell, 1986)
Thirteen-year-old Rob raises a prizewinning pig on a Vermont farm during the 1920s. Rob's parents help him accept a painful decision.

Ruark, Robert, *The Old Man and the Boy* (Holt, Rinehart & Winston, 1957; paperback, Fawcett)
The author is the boy and his understanding grandfather is the old man in this memoir of a happy boyhood spent along the North Carolina seacoast.

Sone, Monica, *Nisei Daughter* (University of Washington Press, rpt. 1984)
A Japanese-American woman tells of growing up in Seattle in the 1920s and 30s, and her experiences after the outbreak of war between Japan and the United States.

Taylor, Sydney, *All-of-a-Kind Family* (Follett Publishing, 1951; paperback, Dell)
Five sisters grow up on New York's Lower East Side in the early 1900s.

Trapp, Maria August, *The Story of the Trapp Family Singers* (Lippincott, 1949; paperback, Doubleday, 1957)
The author tells how her family fled from Austria during World War II and settled in Vermont. *The Sound of Music*, a Broadway musical and also a film, was based on this book.

Wyss, Johann David, *Swiss Family Robinson* (many editions)
A family, shipwrecked on an island in the South Seas, survive by working together.

THE NATURAL WORLD

About three thousand years ago, in Biblical times, a poet named David composed sacred songs called *psalms* in praise of God. In these lines from Psalm 8, David celebrates the splendor of the universe. He also tells how humble he feels in the presence of such wonders.

When I consider thy heavens, the work of thy fingers, the moon and the stars, which thou hast ordained;
What is man, that thou art mindful of him?

From earliest times people have responded to the beauty and wonder of the natural world. Like the psalmist David, they have questioned their relationship to the universe. They have sought answers to such questions as these: What responsibilities do human beings have to the natural world? How can they live in harmony with the earth and the different forms of life on it? In this unit you will find different expressions of the relationship between human beings and the earth, which is their home.

Sunset on the Sea (1872) by John Frederick Kensett. Oil on canvas.
The Metropolitan Museum of Art, gift of Thomas Kensett

143

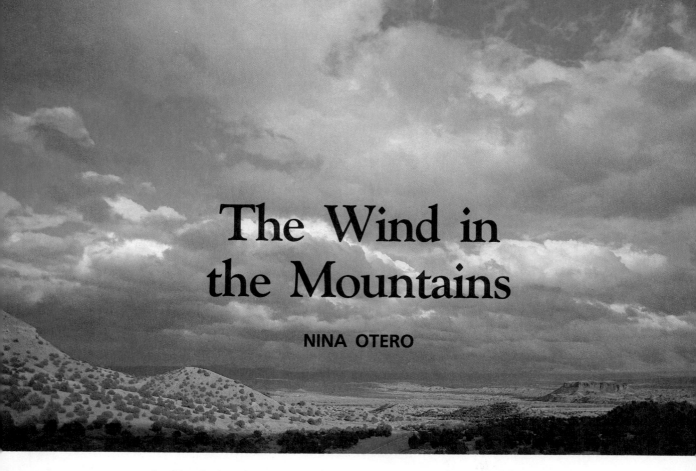

The Wind in the Mountains

NINA OTERO

In this selection the writer refers to the country around Santa Fé as a "region of struggles." What does she mean?

A storm was coming over the country around Santa Fé, the ancient City of the Holy Faith. This southwestern country, explored and settled nearly four hundred years ago by a people who loved nature, worshiped God and feared no evil, is still a region of struggles.

I spent this night on my homestead in a small adobe house in the midst of cedars on the top of a hill. We face the great *Sangre de Cristo*[1] range as we look to the rising sun: a beauty too great for human beings to have had a hand in creating. Cedars and piñones,[2] twisted, knotted, dwarfed by the wind, were all around me. Arroyos[3] were cut in the ground, innocent looking in dry weather, but terrible in storms, for the water rushing through them can fell trees and roll boulders as easily as children roll marbles.

I watched the sun sink gloomily behind a yellow light. The hills looked gray and solemn. At a distance we heard a dog bark, a coyote

1. *Sangre de Cristo* (săng′grē də krĭs′tō): a range of the Rocky Mountains extending from central Colorado to northern New Mexico. The name means "Blood of Christ."

2. **piñones** (pĭn-yō′nēz): pine trees.
3. **Arroyos** (ə-roi′ōs): dry gulches formed by running streams.

howl. A shepherd was calling to his dog. The shepherd and his dog, taking warning of the coming storm, were herding the sheep to protect them better. Here and there the shepherd picked up a stray lamb and carried it in his arms. He made a fire quickly and soon the fragrance of coffee and burning cedar filled the air. Smoke rose above the trees, a signal in olden times of hospitality, perhaps, or hostility, for the Indians have not always been friendly. Soon the herder laid a sheep pelt, thick with "wool in the grease" and gray with sand, on the most level stretch. He threw his only blanket over his shoulders and lay down on the extemporized bed. A look at the fire, a glance at the sky, the exclamation, "God help us!", and he dropped asleep to the sound of his sheep bleating.

In the only room of my house, a melancholy candle was flickering as if gasping for breath. As the darkness came down like a curtain, I lit the fire to try to make the room more cheerful. I had a feeling of vastness, of solitude, but never of loneliness. Crickets and myriads of other insects were incessantly buzzing. The night was alive with sounds of creatures less fearful than humans, speaking a language I couldn't understand, but could feel with every sense.

In the night the storm broke, wild and dismal. The wind hissed like a rattler, and as it struck the branches of the trees, it made a weird sound like a musical instrument out of tune. Trees were bowing as if in obeisance to their Master. An unmuffled candle alone illuminated the small room. It kept vigil through the stormy night.

At dawn, the clouds parted as if a curtain were raised, revealing the outline of the mountains. The hush following the storm was tremendous. Again I heard a voice in the canyon. The shepherd was kindling his fire and rolling up his sheep pelt.

"Ah, me," he said to himself, "we must get out of this wild canyon. Here we must leave four of our little lambs dead. Bad luck! But . . . then . . . here comes the light, the sun, and, after all, *this* is another day."

As the shepherd was extinguishing the camp fire, there appeared on the top of the hill a form with arms stretched to heaven as though offering himself to the sun. The shepherd from his camp and I from my window watched this half-clad figure that seemed to have come from the earth to greet the light. A chant, a hymn—the Indian was offering his prayer to the rising sun. The shepherd, accustomed to his Indian neighbors, went his way slowly, guiding his sheep out of the canyon. The Indian finished his offering of prayer. I, alone, seemed not in complete tune with the instruments of God. I felt a sense of loss that they were closer to nature than I, more understanding of the storm. I had shuddered at the wind as it came through the cracks of my little house; now I had to cover my eyes from the bright rays of the sun, while my neighbors, fearing nothing, welcomed with joy "another day."

Reading Check

1. What makes the arroyos dangerous in bad weather?
2. Where is the narrator during the storm?
3. What does she use for light?
4. What two people does she observe from her window?

For Study and Discussion

Analyzing and Interpreting the Selection

1. The author says that during the storm she had a feeling of solitude but not of loneliness. What companionship did she have?

2a. How does the shepherd prepare for the storm? **b.** How does he react to the loss of some of his flock?

3a. How is the author affected by both the shepherd and the Indian who prays to the sun? **b.** Why do you suppose she is "not in complete tune with the instruments of God"?

4. How does this selection show both the benevolent and destructive aspects of nature?

Language and Vocabulary

Learning Word Origins

We are told that the shepherd prepared an "extemporized bed" with a sheep pelt. In other words, he made a temporary or makeshift bed out of what was available. To *extemporize* is to do something without preparation or to improvise.

Extemporize is related in meaning to *extemporaneous* (ĕk-stĕm′pə-rā′nē-əs), an adjective meaning "offhand," "without preparation," or "impromptu." What is an extemporaneous speech?

Both *extemporize* and *extemporaneous* are derived from Latin. The Latin prefix *ex-* means "from" or "out of." The Latin word *tempore* is a form of *tempus*, meaning "time." What connection is there between the Latin source and the present meaning of the words?

Descriptive Writing

Describing the Two Faces of Nature

Nina Otero shows us the beauty and magnificence of nature as well as its destructiveness. Think of a time when you encountered both aspects of nature. Write a description of the scene, evoking both moods as Otero does. To review the elements of descriptive writing, see pages 89–90.

Desert Creatures

EDWARD ABBEY

Through his powers of observation and finely tuned senses, Edward Abbey shares with us his experience of the Sonoran Desert in northwest Mexico. As you read, note how carefully he describes the desert creatures and their environment.

Into the backlands, the back of beyond, the original and primitive Mexico. For the next three days we would see few human beings and not a motor vehicle of any kind, nor a gas station, nor a telephone pole. The inevitable vultures soaring overhead reminded us, though, that somewhere in this brushy wilderness was life, sentient[1] creation, living meat. Hard to see, of course, during the day, for most desert animals keep themselves concealed in the bush or in burrows under the surface of the ground. But you could see their tracks: birds, lizards,

1. **sentient** (sĕn′chĭ-ənt): having sensations and feelings.

rodents, now and then a coyote, here and there the handlike footprints of raccoon, the long claws of badger, the prints of ring-tailed cat, the heart-shaped hoof marks of deer and javelina,[2] the rounded pads of bobcat, the long narrow tracks of the coatimundi,[3] or *chulu,* as the Mexicans call it.

I have barely begun to name the immense variety of mammals, large and small, that inhabit this area. There are, for example, dozens of species of little rodents—rock squirrels, pocket gophers, pocket mice, grasshopper mice, cactus mice, kangaroo rats, wood rats, prairie dogs—and a large assortment of skunks, cottontail rabbits, jackrabbits, porcupines, kit foxes and gray foxes.

Some of these animals, especially the rodents and other smaller mammals, may never drink free water in their entire lives. Instead they get by on what moisture they can obtain from plant food and through the internal manufacture of what is called "metabolic water."[4] Particularly distinguished in this regard is the kangaroo rat, which subsists on a diet of dried seeds, bathes itself in sand, ignores green and succulent plants, and shuns water even when it is available.

But of all these Sonoran beasts surely the most curious is *Nasua narica,* the chulu, or coatimundi. Generally chulus travel in bands of a dozen or more, sometimes as many as two hundred, according to report. But the first one I ever saw was a loner—the older males are often solitary—prowling in a garbage dump near the town of Nogales.[5] Preoccupied with its search for something to eat, the chulu ignored me, or perhaps did not perceive me, and I had ample opportunity to observe it closely.

It was an old one, a grandfather no doubt, unable to keep up with its band, which would also explain why it had been reduced to scavenging in a dump for survival. It was about four feet long, including the two-foot tail, which in the chulu is held upright, at a right angle to the body. The fur was rusty brown, the tail marked with light and dark rings like that of a raccoon, which the chulu somewhat resembles. But it looked a little like a small bear, too, with long hind legs and shambling gait. In fact it looked like a mixture of several mammals, with the tail of a raccoon, the gait of a bear, the nose of a pig, a face masked like that of a badger, long wolflike canine teeth and the lean slab-sided body of a fox or coyote.

As I watched this chulu, I saw it turn over rocks, tin cans, boards and other junk with its front paws, exhibiting the manual dexterity of a human. It was probably searching for insects,

5. **Nogales** (nō-gäl′əs): in Sonora, in northwest Mexico, adjacent to Nogales, Arizona.

2. **javelina** (hä′və-lē′nə): wild swine resembling small pigs.
3. **coatimundi** (kō-ä′tē mŭn′dē): mammals also called *coati* (kō-ä′tē).
4. **metabolic** (mĕt′ə-bŏl′ĭk) **water:** water produced within the creature's own body.

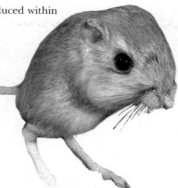

grubs, arachnids[6] and snakes, as it spent a great deal of time rooting about underneath things with its long and flexible snout. I have learned since that chulus, like coyotes and javelinas, will eat most anything they can find or catch; like us, they are omnivorous.

To see what it would do, I walked toward the chulu, whistled and held out one hand. It looked at me with soft brown eyes, seemingly full of trust, but a snarling grin that exposed long yellow fangs conveyed a different impression. I would not have cared to tangle with this animal bare-handed, but before I got close enough to risk attack it turned tail and scurried as nimbly as a tomcat up the trunk of a big juniper.

My favorite desert animal, I think, after such obvious choices as coyote, vulture, cougar, ring-tailed cat, Gila monster and gopher snake, is the whimsical, cockeyed, half-mad, always eccentric, more or less lovable *Pecari angulatus sonoriensis*, otherwise known as javelina or peccary.[7] A herd of them scampered across the road in front of us as we bounced over the backlands toward the sea. We stopped and watched them go up a hillside and over the crest, the dust flying from their busy hoofs.

What are javelinas? Well, they are piglike animals, but they are not true pigs. They look more like razorback hogs, but they are not true razorbacks either. Someone has likened them to a child's notion of what a pig should look like. They are comical, myopic,[8] vicious and excitable. They have sharp little hoofs, pointed ears, small square bodies and huge heads mounted on massive necks; neck and head appear to take up nearly half the total body volume. The tail is so small as to be ridiculous, but the teeth are sharp. Javelinas are capable (it is said) of inflicting severe—even fatal—damage upon anyone unlucky enough to find himself between a charging javelina and an immovable wall.

I remembered my first encounter with javelinas. I was blundering about in the Sonoran hills, daydreaming as usual, when I gradually became aware of a snorting, snuffling sound ahead, accompanied by the shuffle of many active hoofs. The terrain was brushy, the lilac twilight falling about me, so that I

---

6. **arachnids** (ə-răk′nĭdz): a class of invertebrates having four pairs of legs, such as the spider and the scorpion.

7. **peccary** (pĕk′ə-rē): See footnote 2.
8. **myopic** (mī-ŏp′ĭk, -ō′pĭk): nearsighted.

could not see much, and besides I was listening primarily to the melancholy chorus of red-spotted toads in the canyon below. I crashed on through the thickets. The nearsighted javelinas did not notice my approach until I almost stumbled over them. At that point the herd exploded in all directions at once, two of them stampeding past me so close on either side that I felt the friction of their bristles. They must have been even more startled than I was. A moment later I stood alone in a now-quiet clearing, among uprooted roots and overturned stones, and sniffed at the curious musky odor in the air. Off in the distance, at sixteen different compass points, I could still hear the panicked scramble, the outraged snorts, squeals and grunts, of the shattered herd of javelinas. It must have taken them hours to get properly reassembled and back to their evening feed.

As with humans and chulus, javelinas will eat anything—snails, locusts, roots, berries, clams, truffles, mushrooms, garlic, bugs, birds, eggs, general assorted garbage. This is reputed to be an indication of intelligence. Living in the Sonoran Desert, however, the javelina specializes in the consumption of cactus—spines, barbs, hooks, needles, thorns, hair and all; its favorite cactus is the succulent pad of the prickly pear.

The javelina also fancies the barrel cactus—that bloated monster of a vegetable that rises up like an overgrown green fireplug, leaning south over the sunny sides of hills. But the barrel cactus, armored by an intricate network of rosy claws, cannot easily be approached, except for the yellowish fruit on top, which the javelina and other creatures will extricate and consume in due season. The only way a javelina can get at the tender insides of a barrel cactus is from the base, which is sometimes exposed when excessive growth or a storm or a weakened root system causes the plant to keel over. Then the javelina, seizing its chance, drops to its knees and burrows headfirst into the bottom of the now-defenseless plant. I have never actually seen this performance but I have seen barrel cactus fallen over and hollowed out, surrounded by the scuffle marks and scat of the javelina.

Reading Check

1. According to the author, why is it hard to see the desert creatures during the day?
2. Which desert creatures mentioned in the selection "may never drink free water in their entire lives"?
3. The chulu looks "like a mixture of several mammals." Name two and tell how the chulu resembles each one.
4. Though javelinas will eat anything, what is their favorite food?
5. How many days did the trip into the backlands last?

For Study and Discussion

Analyzing and Interpreting the Selection

1a. Although the desert creatures are unseen during the day, what details reveal that they are nearby? **b.** What do these details reveal about Edward Abbey's powers of observation?

2. Abbey describes the chulu as the "most curious" of the Sonoran creatures. **a.** What is so strange about this animal's appearance? **b.** What conclusion does the author come to when he sees a solitary chulu scavenging? **c.** Briefly describe the encounter between the author and the chulu.

3. Abbey states that "as with humans and chulus, javelinas will eat anything," and "this is reputed to be an indication of intelligence." What does he mean?

4. Many forms of wildlife have special features or abilities that help them survive even the harshest conditions. The ability to stay hidden is only one of the survival skills of desert creatures. **a.** What are some other protective means discussed in the selection? **b.** In your opinion, what is a human being's most important asset or ability?

5. At the opening of the selection, Abbey talks about the backlands of Mexico as "the back of beyond." **a.** What does he mean? **b.** In what specific ways are the backlands different from your living environment?

Language and Vocabulary

Recognizing Sensory Details

Abbey's style reveals his sharp powers of observation. Sensory details—those that appeal to our senses—enable us to see the vultures "soaring overhead"; we hear the "shuffle" of the javelina hoofs.

List at least five other examples of sensory details in the selection. Try to find one to illustrate each of the five senses.

Expository Writing

Writing an Explanation

Exposition is the kind of writing used to give information or to explain something. Whenever you write a report or give directions, you are using exposition.

Reread the last paragraph of the selection (page 151), in which Abbey explains how the javelina eats the barrel cactus. What parts of the plant are edible? What problems are there in getting to the tender insides of the cactus? What is the javelina's method of burrowing into the base of the plant? What does the cactus look like after the javelina is through with it?

Write a paragraph in which you explain how a particular animal gets its food. If you wish, choose one of the desert creatures mentioned in the selection. Use an encyclopedia or other reference work for your facts.

About the Author

Edward Abbey (1927–)

A well-known writer with twelve books to his credit, Edward Abbey conveys his love for the wilderness and his impatience with people who spoil the land. Pulitzer Prizewinning nature writer Edwin Way Teale once stated: "Abbey writes with a deep undercurrent of bitterness. But . . . the bitter man may be the one who cares enough to be bitter and he often is the one who says things that need to be said."

Abbey makes his home in Wolf Hole, Arizona. He is comfortable in the forest and the desert with the Indians, or with the aborigines in the Australian outback. His past experiences include degrees from the University of New Mexico, service in the United States Army, and a coveted Fulbright fellowship. He has worked as a park ranger and fire lookout for the National Park Service in the Southwest. Currently he is working on a collection of essays and a novel.

Last Cover

PAUL ANNIXTER

In this story the narrator helps us understand the background of events by using flashbacks. *As you read, note how carefully the passage of time is indicated.*

I'm not sure I can tell you what you want to know about my brother; but everything about the pet fox is important, so I'll tell all that from the beginning.

It goes back to a winter afternoon after I'd hunted the woods all day for a sign of our lost pet. I remember the way my mother looked up as I came into the kitchen. Without my speaking, she knew what had happened. For six hours I had walked, reading signs, looking for a delicate print in the damp soil or even a hair that might have told of a red fox passing that way—but I had found nothing.

"Did you go up in the foothills?" Mom asked.

I nodded. My face was stiff from held-back tears. My brother, Colin, who was going on twelve, got it all from one look at me and went into a heartbroken, almost silent, crying.

Three weeks before, Bandit, the pet fox Colin and I had raised from a tiny kit, had disappeared, and not even a rumor had been heard of him since.

"He'd have had to go off soon anyway," Mom comforted. "A big, lolloping fellow like him, he's got to live his life same as us. But he may come back. That fox set a lot of store by you boys in spite of his wild ways."

"He set a lot of store by our food, anyway," Father said. He sat in a chair by the kitchen window mending a piece of harness. "We'll be seeing a lot more of that fellow, never fear. That fox learned to pine for table scraps and young chickens. He was getting to be an egg thief, too, and he's not likely to forget that."

"That was only pranking when he was little," Colin said desperately.

From the first, the tame fox had made tension in the family. It was Father who said we'd better name him Bandit, after he'd made away with his first young chicken.

"Maybe you know," Father said shortly. "But when an animal turns to egg sucking he's usually incurable. He'd better not come pranking around my chicken run again."

It was late February, and I remember the bleak, dead cold that had set in, cold that was a rare thing for our Carolina hills. Flocks of sparrows and snowbirds had appeared to peck hungrily at all that the pigs and chickens didn't eat.

"This one's a killer," Father would say of a morning, looking out at the whitened barn roof. "This one will make the shoats[1] squeal."

A fire snapped all day in our cookstove and another in the stone fireplace in the living room, but still the farmhouse was never warm. The leafless woods were bleak and empty, and I spoke of that to Father when I came back from my search.

"It's always a sad time in the woods when the seven sleepers are under cover," he said.

"What sleepers are they?" I asked. Father was full of woods lore.

"Why, all the animals that have got sense enough to hole up and stay hid in weather like this. Let's see, how was it the old rhyme named them?

Surly bear and sooty bat,
Brown chuck and masked coon,
Chippy-munk and sly skunk,
And all the mouses
'Cept in men's houses.

"And man would have joined them and made it eight, Granther Yeary always said, if he'd had a little more sense."

"I was wondering if the red fox mightn't make it eight," Mom said.

Father shook his head. "Late winter's a high time for foxes. Time when they're out deviling, not sleeping."

My chest felt hollow. I wanted to cry like Colin over our lost fox, but at fourteen a boy doesn't cry. Colin had squatted down on the floor and got out his small hammer and nails to start another new frame for a new picture. Maybe then he'd make a drawing for the frame and be able to forget his misery. It had been that way with him since he was five.

I thought of the new dress Mom had brought home a few days before in a heavy cardboard box. That box cover would be fine for Colin to draw on. I spoke of it, and Mom's glance thanked me as she went to get it. She and I worried a lot about Colin. He was small for his age, delicate and blond, his hair much lighter and softer than mine, his eyes deep and wide and blue. He was often sick, and I knew the fear Mom had that he might be predestined.[2] I'm just ordinary, like Father. I'm the sort of stuff that can take it—tough and strong—but Colin was always sort of special.

Mom lighted the lamp. Colin began cutting his white cardboard carefully, fitting it into his frame. Father's sharp glance turned on him now and again.

"There goes the boy making another frame

---

1. **shoats:** young hogs.

2. **predestined** (prē-dĕs'tĭnd): here, fated to die young.

before there's a picture for it," he said. "It's too much like cutting out a man's suit for a fellow that's, say, twelve years old. Who knows whether he'll grow into it?"

Mom was into him then, quick. "Not a single frame of Colin's has ever gone to waste. The boy has real talent, Sumter, and it's time you realized it."

"Of course he has," Father said. "All kids have 'em. But they get over 'em."

"It isn't the pox[3] we're talking of," Mom sniffed.

"In a way it is. Ever since you started talking up Colin's art, I've had an invalid for help around the place."

Father wasn't as hard as he made out, I knew, but he had to hold a balance against all Mom's frothing. For him the thing was the land and all that pertained to it. I was following in Father's footsteps, true to form, but Colin threatened to break the family tradition with his leaning toward art, with Mom "aiding and abetting him," as Father liked to put it. For the past two years she had had dreams of my brother becoming a real artist and going away to the city to study.

It wasn't that Father had no understanding of such things. I could remember, through the years, Colin lying on his stomach in the front room making pencil sketches, and how a good drawing would catch Father's eyes halfway across the room, and how he would sometimes gather up two or three of them to study, frowning and muttering, one hand in his beard, while a great pride rose in Colin, and in me too. Most of Colin's drawings were of the woods and wild things, and there Father was a master critic. He made out to scorn what seemed to him a passive "white-livered" interpretation of nature through brush and pencil instead of rod and rifle.

3. **the pox:** chicken pox.

At supper that night Colin could scarcely eat. Ever since he'd been able to walk, my brother had had a growing love of wild things, but Bandit had been like his very own, a gift of the woods. One afternoon a year and a half before, Father and Laban Small had been running a vixen through the hills with their dogs. With the last of her strength the she-fox had made for her den, not far from our house. The dogs had overtaken her and killed her just before she reached it. When Father and Laban came up, they'd found Colin crouched nearby holding her cub in his arms.

Father had been for killing the cub, which was still too young to shift for itself, but Colin's grief had brought Mom into it. We'd taken the young fox into the kitchen, all of us, except Father, gone a bit silly over the little thing. Colin had held it in his arms and fed it warm milk from a spoon.

"Watch out with all your soft ways," Father had warned, standing in the doorway. "You'll make too much of him. Remember, you can't make a dog out of a fox. Half of that little critter has to love, but the other half is a wild hunter. You boys will mean a whole lot to him while he's kit, but there'll come a day when you won't mean a thing to him and he'll leave you shorn."

For two weeks after that Colin had nursed the cub, weaning it from milk to bits of meat. For a year they were always together. The cub grew fast. It was soon following Colin and me about the barnyard. It turned out to be a patch fox, with a saddle of darker fur across its shoulders.

I haven't the words to tell you what the fox meant to us. It was far more wonderful owning him than owning any dog. There was something rare and secret like the spirit of the woods about him, and back of his calm, straw-gold eyes was the sense of a brain the equal to a man's. The fox became Colin's whole life.

Each day, going and coming from school, Colin and I took long side trips through the woods, looking for Bandit. Wild things' memories were short, we knew; we'd have to find him soon or the old bond would be broken.

Ever since I was ten I'd been allowed to hunt with Father, so I was good at reading signs. But, in a way, Colin knew more about the woods and wild things than Father or me. What came to me from long observation, Colin seemed to know by instinct.

It was Colin who felt out, like an Indian, the stretch of woods where Bandit had his den, who found the first slim, small fox-print in the damp earth. And then, on an afternoon in March, we saw him. I remember the day well,

the racing clouds, the wind rattling the tops of the pine trees and swaying the Spanish moss. Bandit had just come out of a clump of laurel; in the maze of leaves behind him we caught a glimpse of a slim red vixen, so we knew he had found a mate. She melted from sight like a shadow, but Bandit turned to watch us, his mouth open, his tongue lolling as he smiled his old foxy smile. On his thin chops, I saw a tell-tale chicken feather.

Colin moved silently forward, his movements so quiet and casual he seemed to be standing still. He called Bandit's name, and the fox held his ground, drawn to us with all his senses. For a few moments he let Colin actually put an arm about him. It was then I knew that he loved us still, for all of Father's warnings. He really loved us back, with a fierce, secret love no tame thing ever gave. But the urge of his life just then was toward his new mate. Suddenly, he whirled about and disappeared in the laurels.

Colin looked at me with glowing eyes. "We haven't really lost him, Stan. When he gets through with his spring sparking[4] he may come back. But we've got to show ourselves to him a lot, so he won't forget."

"It's a go," I said.

"Promise not to say a word to Father," Colin said, and I agreed. For I knew by the chicken feather that Bandit had been up to no good.

A week later the woods were budding and the thickets were rustling with all manner of wild things scurrying on the love scent. Colin managed to get a glimpse of Bandit every few days. He couldn't get close though, for the spring running was a lot more important to a fox than any human beings were.

Every now and then Colin got out his framed box cover and looked at it, but he never drew anything on it; he never even picked up his pencil. I remember wondering if what Father had said about framing a picture before you had one had spoiled something for him.

I was helping Father with the planting now, but Colin managed to be in the woods every day. By degrees he learned Bandit's range, where he drank and rested and where he was likely to be according to the time of day. One day he told me how he had petted Bandit again, and how they had walked together a long way in the woods. All this time we had kept his secret from Father.

As summer came on, Bandit began to live up to the prediction Father had made. Accustomed to human beings he moved without fear about the scattered farms of the region, raiding barns and hen runs that other foxes wouldn't have dared go near. And he taught his wild mate to do the same. Almost every night they got into some poultry house, and by late June Bandit was not only killing chickens and ducks but feeding on eggs and young chicks whenever he got the chance.

Stories of his doings came to us from many sources, for he was still easily recognized by the dark patch on his shoulders. Many a farmer took a shot at him as he fled and some of them set out on his trail with dogs, but they always returned home without even sighting him. Bandit was familiar with all the dogs in

4. **sparking:** courting.

the region, and he knew a hundred tricks to confound them. He got a reputation that year beyond that of any fox our hills had known. His confidence grew, and he gave up wild hunting altogether and lived entirely off the poultry farmers. By late September the hill farmers banded together to hunt him down.

It was Father who brought home that news one night. All time-honored rules of the fox chase were to be broken in this hunt; if the dogs couldn't bring Bandit down, he was to be shot on sight. I was stricken and furious. I remember the misery of Colin's face in the lamplight. Father, who took pride in all the ritual of the hunt, had refused to be a party to such an affair, though in justice he could do nothing but sanction any sort of hunt, for Bandit, as old Sam Wetherwax put it, had been "purely getting in the Lord's hair."

The hunt began next morning, and it was the biggest turnout our hills had known. There were at least twenty mounted men in the party and as many dogs. Father and I were working in the lower field as they passed along the river road. Most of the hunters carried rifles, and they looked ugly.

Twice during the morning I went up to the house to find Colin, but he was nowhere around. As we worked, Father and I could follow the progress of the hunt by the distant hound music on the breeze. We could tell just where the hunters first caught sight of the fox and where Bandit was leading the dogs during the first hour. We knew as well as if we'd seen it how Bandit roused another fox along Turkey Branch and forced it to run for him, and how the dogs swept after it for twenty minutes before they sensed their mistake.

Noon came, and Colin had not come in to eat. After dinner Father didn't go back to the field. He moped about, listening to the hound talk. He didn't like what was on any more than

I did, and now and again I caught his smile of satisfaction when we heard the broken, angry notes of the hunting horn, telling that the dogs had lost the trail or had run another fox.

I was restless, and I went up into the hills in midafternoon. I ranged the woods for miles, thinking all the time of Colin. Time lost all meaning for me, and the short day was nearing an end, when I heard the horn talking again, telling that the fox had put over another trick. All day he had deviled the dogs and mocked the hunters. This new trick and the coming night would work to save him. I was wildly glad, as I moved down toward Turkey Branch and stood listening for a time by the deep, shaded pool where for years we boys had gone swimming, sailed boats, and dreamed summer dreams.

Suddenly, out of the corner of my eye, I saw the sharp ears and thin, pointed mask of a fox—in the water almost beneath me. It was Bandit, craftily submerged there, all but his head, resting in the cool water of the pool and the shadow of the two big beeches that spread above it. He must have run forty miles or more since morning. And he must have hidden in this place before. His knowing, crafty mask blended perfectly with the shadows and a mass of drift and branches that had collected by the bank of the pool. He was so still that a pair of thrushes flew up from the spot as I came up, not knowing he was there.

Bandit's bright, harried eyes were looking right at me. But I did not look at him direct. Some woods instinct, swifter than thought, kept me from it. So he and I met as in another world, indirectly, with feeling but without sign or greeting.

Suddenly I saw that Colin was standing almost beside me. Silently as a water snake, he had come out of the bushes and stood there. Our eyes met, and a quick and secret smile passed between us. It was a rare moment in which I really "met" my brother, when something of his essence flowed into me and I knew all of him. I've never lost it since.

My eyes still turned from the fox, my heart pounding. I moved quietly away, and Colin moved with me. We whistled softly as we went, pretending to busy ourselves along the bank of the stream. There was magic in it, as if by will we wove a web of protection about the fox, a ring-pass-not that none might penetrate. It was so, too, we felt, in the brain of Bandit, and that doubled the charm. To us he was still our little pet that we had carried about in our arms on countless summer afternoons.

Two hundred yards upstream, we stopped beside slim, fresh tracks in the mud where Bandit had entered the branch. The tracks angled upstream. But in the water the wily creature had turned down.

We climbed the far bank to wait, and Colin told me how Bandit's secret had been his secret ever since an afternoon three months before, when he'd watched the fox swim downstream to hide in the deep pool. Today he'd waited on the bank, feeling that Bandit, hard pressed by the dogs, might again seek the pool for sanctuary.

We looked back once as we turned homeward. He still had not moved. We didn't know until later that he was killed that same night by a chance hunter, as he crept out from his hiding place.

That evening Colin worked a long time on his framed box cover that had lain about the house untouched all summer. He kept at it all the next day too. I had never seen him work so hard. I seemed to sense in the air the feeling he was putting into it, how he was *believing* his picture into being. It was evening before he finished it. Without a word he handed it to Father. Mom and I went and looked over his shoulder.

It was a delicate and intricate pencil drawing of the deep branch pool, and there was Bandit's head and watching, fear-filled eyes hiding there amid the leaves and shadows, woven craftily into the maze of twigs and branches, as if by nature's art itself. Hardly a fox there at all, but the place where he was—or should have been. I recognized it instantly, but Mom gave a sort of incredulous sniff.

"I'll declare," she said, "It's mazy as a puzzle. It just looks like a lot of sticks and leaves to me."

Long minutes of study passed before Father's eye picked out the picture's secret, as few men's could have done. I laid that to Father's being a born hunter. That was a picture that might have been done especially for him. In fact, I guess it was.

Finally he turned to Colin with his deep, slow smile. "So that's how Bandit fooled them all," he said. He sat holding the picture with a sort of tenderness for a long time, while we glowed in the warmth of the shared secret. That was Colin's moment. Colin's art stopped being a pox[5] to Father right there. And later, when the time came for Colin to go to art school, it was Father who was his solid backer.

5. **pox:** here, an annoyance.

Reading Check

1. Why is the pet fox named Bandit?
2. What prediction does Father make when Bandit runs away?
3. Why does Father refuse to join the hunt for the fox?
4. What secret does Colin discover?
5. What changes Father's mind about Colin's art?

Analyzing and Interpreting the Story

1. Both Colin and his father love the woods and wild things, but their responses to the pet fox are different. **a.** How is this difference shown when Colin finds the cub? **b.** When Bandit runs away?

2. Father refers to Colin's drawings as a "passive 'white-livered' interpretation of nature." What does he believe is a more appropriate response to nature?

3. You learn from Stan that Father is full of woods *lore,* or knowledge. How do Father's predictions about Bandit show that this statement is true?

4. How does Colin show that he knows even more about the woods and wild things than his father and his brother know?

5. At the beginning of the story, Father does not take a serious interest in Colin's art. How does he come to respect and appreciate Colin's talent?

6. At first, the pet fox creates tension in the family. How does Bandit's secret finally bring the family closer together?

Literary Elements

Following the Order of Events

The events in this story cover a period of about six months, from late winter, after Bandit disappears, until September, when he is hunted down and killed. The storyteller carefully notes the passage of time for the reader:

. . . on an afternoon in March . . .
                (page 156, column 1)
A week later . . .   (page 157, column 1)
As summer came on . . .
                (page 157, column 1)

. . . by late June . . .   (page 157, column 2)
By late September . . .   (page 158, column 1)

The storyteller also interrupts the action of his story twice to relate events that have already occurred. These interruptions, which are called **flashbacks,** fill in the background of the story. The first of these flashbacks, which begins on page 154, takes the action back about a year. Stan recalls, "From the first, the tame fox had made tension in the family." We learn how Bandit got his name. We also learn that Father had tried to warn the boys that Bandit would become a chicken thief.

Locate the second flashback, which tells how Bandit was found. How long was Bandit with the family before he ran away?

Reread the passages of the story that relate the events on the day of the hunt (page 158). Identify the words and phrases that specify the time of each action.

Language and Vocabulary

Identifying Animal Names

The word *vixen* is the name of a particular animal—a female fox. The words *cub* and *kit* have a more general meaning. The young of many mammals, such as wolves and foxes, are known as *cubs.* The word *kit* is short for *kitten,* but it may be used for any fur-bearing animal.

See if you can identify each of the animal names in the following list. Tell whether the name refers to the male or female, the adult or young of the species. Tell whether the name is used for one or more species of animals. Use a dictionary to check your answers.

boar	drake	mare
buck	ewe	pup
bull	gander	sow
cow	gosling	stag
doe	kid	tom

Using Examples to Develop a Topic

When he is pursued by the farmers and their dogs, Bandit takes cover in the branch pool, where he blends into the background. The color pattern of Bandit's "mask," or face, helps to camouflage him. His mask cannot be distinguished from the shadows and the driftwood around the branch pool.

Many animals conceal themselves from their enemies by *protective coloration,* which allows them to blend into their environment. Think about the natural coloration of animals that are familiar to you. How is a grasshopper protected by its color? A frog? What disguise does a sparrow have? A fawn?

Write a paragraph in which you use several examples to show that animals are protected by their coloration. If you wish, you may concentrate on a particular group—birds, fish, insects, reptiles, cats, and so on. Open your paragraph with a sentence that states the central idea. You may use this sentence if you like: Natural coloration helps animals conceal themselves from their enemies.

About the Author

Paul Annixter (1894–   )

Paul Annixter, whose real name is Howard Sturtzel, was born in Minneapolis, Minnesota. He began writing stories when he was nineteen. At that time he lived alone in the woods of northern Minnesota, working on a timber claim. During the next thirty-seven years he published more than five hundred short stories. One of his best-known books, *Swiftwater,* is about a boy growing up in the Maine woods. In 1955 he and his wife, Jane Annixter, began collaborating on novels for young people. Among them are the adventure stories *Windigo* and *Horns of Plenty.*

In Time of Silver Rain

LANGSTON HUGHES

In time of silver rain
The earth
Puts forth new life again,
Green grasses grow
And flowers lift their heads,   5
And over all the plain
The wonder spreads
    Of life,
    Of life,
    Of life!   10

In time of silver rain
The butterflies
Lift silken wings
To catch a rainbow cry,
And trees put forth   15
New leaves to sing
In joy beneath the sky
As down the roadway
Passing boys and girls
Go singing, too,   20
In time of silver rain
    When spring
    And life
    Are new.

About the Author

Langston Hughes (1902–1967)

Langston Hughes was born in Joplin, Missouri. He went to sea in 1922 and worked at a variety of odd jobs around the world before returning to the United States. While he was working in a hotel in Washington, D.C., he came to the attention of the well-known poet Vachel Lindsay. Lindsay read some of Hughes's work at a poetry recital he was giving in the hotel auditorium. The next day newspapers acclaimed Lindsay's discovery of the young poet. *The Weary Blues,* Hughes's first volume of poems, appeared in 1926. Although Hughes is remembered chiefly as a poet, he also wrote short stories, plays, movie scripts, and children's books. In addition, he edited several anthologies of prose and poetry by black writers.

For Study and Discussion

Analyzing and Interpreting the Poem

1. In this poem Langston Hughes expresses a joyous attitude toward the natural world. **a.** What does the phrase "silver rain" suggest? **b.** What is the "time of silver rain"?

2. In the second stanza Hughes describes the colorful wings of butterflies in an imaginative way. **a.** What does the word *silken* suggest about the wings? **b.** What is the meaning of line 14?

3. A line or phrase that is repeated at intervals in a poem is called a **refrain**. **a.** What is the refrain in this poem? **b.** What does the poet emphasize by repeating these words? **c.** What other repetition does the poet use? **d.** What is its effect?

The Wreck (1939) by Morris Kantor. Oil on linen.
National Museum of American Art, Smithsonian Institution

The Wreck of the *Hesperus*

HENRY WADSWORTH LONGFELLOW

*The story told in the following poem is based on an actual shipwreck that oc-
curred more than a hundred years ago. How does Longfellow use vivid comparisons to emphasize the terrible destructiveness of the elements?*

164 THE NATURAL WORLD

It was the schooner *Hesperus,*
   That sailed the wintry sea;
And the skipper had taken his little daughter,
   To bear him company.

Blue were her eyes as the fairy flax,   5
   Her cheeks like the dawn of day,
And her bosom white as the hawthorn buds,
   That ope° in the month of May.

The skipper he stood beside the helm,
   His pipe was in his mouth,   10
And he watched how the veering flaw° did blow
   The smoke now West, now South.

Then up and spake an old Sailor,
   Had sailed to the Spanish Main,°
"I pray thee, put into yonder port,   15
   For I fear a hurricane.

"Last night, the moon had a golden ring,
   And tonight no moon we see!"
The skipper, he blew a whiff from his pipe,
   And a scornful laugh laughed he.   20

Colder and louder blew the wind,
   A gale from the Northeast,
The snow fell hissing in the brine,
   And the billows frothed like yeast.

Down came the storm, and smote amain°   25
   The vessel in its strength;
She shuddered and paused, like a frighted steed,
   Then leaped her cable's length.

"Come hither! come hither! my little daughter,
   And do not tremble so;   30
For I can weather the roughest gale
   That ever wind did blow."

8. **ope:** open.

11. **flaw:** a sudden blast of wind.

14. **Spanish Main:** parts of the Caribbean Sea once traveled by Spanish ships.

25. **smote amain:** struck with great force.

He wrapped her warm in his seaman's coat
   Against the stinging blast;
He cut a rope from a broken spar,   35
   And bound her to the mast.

"O father! I hear the church bells ring;
   Oh, say, what may it be?"
"'Tis a fog bell on a rock-bound coast!"
   And he steered for the open sea.   40

"O father! I hear the sound of guns,
   Oh, say, what may it be?"
"Some ship in distress, that cannot live
   In such an angry sea!"

"O father! I see a gleaming light;   45
   Oh, say, what may it be?"
But the father answered never a word,
   A frozen corpse was he.

Lashed to the helm, and stiff and stark,
   With his face turned to the skies,
The lantern gleamed through the gleaming snow   50
   On his fixed and glassy eyes.

Then the maiden clasped her hands and prayed
   That savèd she might be;
And she thought of Christ, who stilled the wave   55
   On the Lake of Galilee.°

And fast through the midnight dark and drear,
   Through the whistling sleet and snow,
Like a sheeted ghost, the vessel swept
   Towards the reef of Norman's Woe.°   60

And ever the fitful gusts between,
   A sound came from the land;
It was the sound of the trampling surf
   On the rocks and the hard sea sand.

55–56. Christ . . . Galilee: This story is told in Matthew 8: 23–27.

60. Norman's Woe: a chain of rocks near Gloucester, Massachusetts.

The breakers were right beneath her bows,
   She drifted a dreary wreck,
And a whooping billow swept the crew
   Like icicles from her deck.

65

She struck where the white and fleecy waves
   Looked soft as carded° wool,
But the cruel rocks, they gored her side
   Like the horns of an angry bull.

70   **70. carded:** combed.

Her rattling shrouds,° all sheathed in ice,
   With the masts went by the board;
Like a vessel of glass, she stove° and sank;
   Ho! ho! the breakers roared!

73. shrouds: ropes hanging from the mast.

75   **75. stove:** smashed.

The Wreck of the *Hesperus*   **167**

At daybreak, on the black sea beach,
    A fisherman stood aghast,
To see the form of a maiden fair,
    Lashed close to a drifting mast.   80

The salt sea was frozen on her breast,
    The salt tears in her eyes;
And he saw her hair, like the brown seaweed,
    On the billows fall and rise.

Such was the wreck of the *Hesperus,*   85
    In the midnight and the snow!
Christ save us all from a death like this,
    On the reef of Norman's Woe!

For Study and Discussion

Analyzing and Interpreting the Poem

1a. What signs are there of the approaching storm? **b.** Why is the skipper confident that he can ride out the storm?

2. Why does the skipper bind his daughter to the mast?

3a. What is the first warning from the people on land? **b.** How does the skipper react to this warning?

4. Two other warnings are sent to the ship. **a.** What do you think is the meaning of the guns in line 41? **b.** The gleaming light in line 45?

5a. What is the fate of the skipper and his crew? **b.** Of the skipper's daughter?

6. In which lines does Longfellow emphasize the strength and cruelty of the storm?

Literary Elements

Understanding Similes

Longfellow gives this description of the ship's movement when the storm strikes:

> She shuddered and paused, like a frighted
>   steed,
> Then leaped her cable's length.

The ship is compared here to a frightened horse that trembles, then springs from the ground. What can you picture happening to the ship?

Longfellow is here using a special kind of comparison known as a **simile.** A simile is a comparison between two unlike things which uses a word such as *like* or *as* to express the comparison.

In which lines does the poet compare the rocks to the horns of a bull? How does this simile emphasize the violence of the storm?

How do the similes in lines 5–8 stress the girl's delicate beauty? Compare this picture with the one in lines 81–84.

Tell in your own words what the similes in the following lines suggest to you.

And the billows frothed like yeast.

(line 24)

Like a sheeted ghost, the vessel swept
  Towards the reef of Norman's Woe.

(lines 59–60)

And a whooping billow swept the crew
  Like icicles from her deck.

(lines 67–68)

She struck where the white and fleecy waves
  Looked soft as carded wool,

(lines 69–70)

Like a vessel of glass, she stove and sank;

(line 75)

For Oral Reading

Preparing a Presentation

Imagine that you are to deliver Longfellow's poem in a public reading. How will you prepare your presentation so that it is dramatic and effective? How should the lines in each stanza be spoken? Where, for example, should you pause? Where should you raise or lower your voice? How will you indicate the change of speakers by your tone? Practice with a classmate and then, if you wish, tape your reading and listen to it before your performance.

About the Author

Henry Wadsworth Longfellow (1807–1882)

For many years, Longfellow was one of the best-loved and most widely read of all American poets. He was one of a group of New England poets who became known as the "Fireside Poets." Their poetry had a large family audience. The members of a family would gather together, often before the fireside, and read poems aloud.

For a number of years, Longfellow combined a literary career with teaching. He was a professor of modern languages at Bowdoin College and later at Harvard University. Eventually he was able to leave teaching and devote himself to writing poetry full time. "The Wreck of the *Hesperus*" is one of his best-known poems.

The Tiger's Heart

JIM KJELGAARD°

This story takes you to a jungle in tropical America. How is the natural world depicted? What do you think the title refers to?

The approaching jungle night was, in itself, a threat. As it deepened, an eerie silence enveloped the thatched village. People were silent. Tethered cattle stood quietly. Roosting chickens did not stir and wise goats made no noise. Thus it had been for countless centuries and thus it would continue to be. The brown-skinned inhabitants of the village knew the jungle. They had trodden its dim paths, forded its sulky rivers, borne its steaming heat, and were intimately acquainted with its deer, tapir,[1] crocodiles, screaming green parrots and countless other creatures.

° **Kjelgaard** (kĕl′gärd).

1. **tapir** (tā′pər): large jungle animals related to the rhinoceros.

That was the daytime jungle they could see, feel and hear, but at night everything became different. When darkness came, the jungle was alive with strange and horrible things which no man had ever seen and no man could describe. They were shadows that had no substance and one was unaware of them until they struck and killed. Then, with morning, they changed themselves back into the shape of familiar things. Because it was a time of the unknown, night had to be a time of fear.

Except, Pepe Garcia[2] reflected, to the man who owned a rifle. As the night closed in, Pepe reached out to fondle his rifle and make sure that it was close beside him. As long as it was, he was king.

That was only just, for the rifle had cost him dearly. With eleven others from his village, Pepe had gone to help chop a right of way for the new road. They used machetes,[3] the indispensable long knife of all jungle dwellers, and they had worked hard. Unlike the rest, Pepe had saved every peso[4] he didn't have to spend for immediate living expenses. With his savings, and after some haggling, he had bought his muzzle-loading rifle, a supply of powder, lead, and a mold in which he could fashion bullets for his rifle.

Eighty pesos the rifle had cost him. But it was worth the price. Though the jungle at night was fear itself, no man with a rifle had to fear. The others, who had only machetes with which to guard themselves from the terrors that came in the darkness, were willing to pay well for protection. Pepe went peacefully to sleep.

He did not know what awakened him, only that something was about. He listened intently, but there was no change in the jungle's monotonous night sounds. Still, something was not as it should be.

Then he heard it. At the far end of the village, near Juan Aria's[5] hut, a goat bleated uneasily. Silence followed. The goat bleated again, louder and more fearful. There was a pattering rush of small hoofs, a frightened bleat cut short, again silence.

Pepe, who did not need to people the night with fantastic creatures because he owned a rifle, interpreted correctly what he had heard. A tiger, a jaguar,[6] had come in the night, leaped the thorn fence with which the village was surrounded, and made off with one of Juan Aria's goats.

Pepe went peacefully back to sleep. With morning, certainly, Juan Aria would come to him.

He did not awaken until the sun was up. Then he emerged from his hut, breakfasted on a papaya he had gathered the day before, and awaited his expected visitor. They must always come to him; it ill befitted a man with a rifle to seek out anyone at all.

Presently Pepe saw two men, Juan Aria and his brother, coming up one of the paths that wound through the village. Others stared curiously, but nobody else came because their flocks had not been raided. They had no wish to pay, or to help pay, a hunter.

Pepe waited until the two were near, then said, "*Buenos días*."[7]

"*Buenos días*," They replied.

They sat down in the sun, looking at nothing in particular, not afraid any more, because the day was never a time of fear. By daylight, only now and again did a tiger come to raid a flock of goats, or kill a burro or a cow.

2. **Pepe Garcia** (pā′pā gär-sē′ä).
3. **machetes** (mə-shĕt′ēz).
4. **peso** (pā′sō): a monetary unit in several Latin American countries.

5. **Juan Aria** (hwän ä-rē′ä).
6. **jaguar** (jăg′wär′): a large cat of tropical America, similar to the leopard. The word *tiger* is often used for several animals of the cat family; here, for the jaguar.
7. *Buenos días* (bwā′nōs dē′äs): Spanish for "Good day."

After a suitable lapse of time, Juan Aria said, "I brought my goats into the village last night, thinking they would be safe."

"And were they not?"

"They were not. Something came and killed one, a fine white-and-black nanny, my favorite. When the thing left, the goat went too. Never again shall I see her alive."

"What killed your goat?" Pepe inquired.

"A devil, but this morning I saw only the tracks of a tiger."

"Did you hear it come?"

"I heard it."

"Then why did you not defend your flock?"

Juan Aria gestured with eloquent hands. "To attack a devil, or a tiger, with nothing but a machete would be madness."

"That is true," Pepe agreed. "Let us hope that the next time it is hungry, this devil, or tiger, will not come back for another goat."

"But it will!"

Pepe relaxed, for Juan Aria's admission greatly improved Pepe's bargaining position. And it was true that, having had a taste of easy game, the tiger would come again. Only death would end his forays, and since he knew where to find Juan Aria's goats, he would continue to attack them.

Pepe said, "That is bad, for a man may lose many goats to a tiger."

"Unless a hunter kills him," Juan Aria said.

"Unless a hunter kills him," Pepe agreed.

"That is why I have come to you, Pepe," Juan Aria said. A troubled frown overspread his face. "I hope you will follow and kill this tiger, for you are the only man who can do so."

"It would give me pleasure to kill him, but I cannot work for nothing."

"Nor do I expect you to. Even a tiger will not eat an entire goat, and you are sure to find what is left of my favorite nanny. Whatever the

tiger has not eaten, you may have for your pay."

Pepe bristled. "You are saying that I should put myself and my rifle to work for carrion left by a tiger?"

"No, no!" Juan Aria protested. "In addition I will give you one live goat!"

"Three goats."

"I am a poor man!" the other wailed. "You would bankrupt me!"

"No man with twenty-nine goats is poor, though he may be if a tiger raids his flock a sufficient number of times," Pepe said.

"I will give you one goat and two kids."

"Two goats and one kid."

"You drive a hard bargain," Juan Aria said, "but I cannot deny you now. Kill the tiger."

Affecting an air of nonchalance, as befitted the owner of a firearm, Pepe took his rifle from the fine blanket upon which it lay when he was not carrying it. He looked to his powder horn and bullet pouch, strapped his machete on, and sauntered toward Juan Aria's hut. A half-dozen worshipful children followed.

"Begone!" Pepe ordered.

They fell behind, but continued to follow until Pepe came to that place where Juan Aria's flock had passed the night. He glanced at the dust, and saw the tiger's great paw marks imprinted there. It was a huge cat, lame in the right front paw, or it might have been injured in battle with another tiger.

Expertly, Pepe located the place where it had gone back over the thorn fence. Though the tiger had carried the sixty-pound goat in its jaws, only a couple of thorns were disturbed at the place where it had leaped.

Though he did not look around, Pepe was aware of the villagers watching him and he knew that their glances would be very respectful. Most of the men went into the jungle from time to time to work with their machetes, but none would work where tigers were known to be. Not one would dare take a tiger's trail. Only Pepe dared and, because he did, he must be revered.

Still affecting nonchalance, Pepe sauntered through the gate. Behind him, he heard the village's collective sigh of mingled relief and admiration. A raiding tiger was a very real and terrible threat, and goats and cattle were not easily come by. The man with a rifle, the man able to protect them, must necessarily be a hero.

Once in the jungle, and out of the villagers' sight, Pepe underwent a transformation.

He shed his air of indifference and became as alert as the little doe that showed him only her white tail. A rifle might be a symbol of power, but unless a man was also a hunter, a rifle did him no good. Impressing the villagers was one thing; hunting a tiger was quite another.

Pepe knew the great cats were dappled death incarnate. They could move with incredible swiftness and were strong enough to kill an ox. They feared nothing.

Jungle-born, Pepe slipped along as softly as a jungle shadow. His machete slipped a little, and he shifted it to a place where his legs would not be bumped. From time to time he glanced at the ground before him.

To trained eyes, there was a distinct trail. It consisted of an occasional drop of blood from the dead goat, a bent or broken plant, a few hairs where the tiger had squeezed between trees, paw prints in soft places. Within the first quarter-mile Pepe knew many things about this tiger.

He was not an ordinary beast, or he would have gone only far enough from the village so his nostrils could not be assailed by its unwelcome scents and eaten what he wanted there, then covered the remainder of the goat with sticks and leaves. He was not old, for his was not the lagging gait of an old cat, and the ease with which he had leaped the thorn fence with a goat in his jaws was evidence of his strength.

Pepe stopped to look to the loading and priming of his rifle. There seemed to be nothing amiss, and there had better not be. When he saw the tiger, he must shoot straight and true. Warned by some super jungle sense, Pepe slowed his pace. A moment later he found his game.

He came upon it suddenly in a grove of scattered palms. Because he had not expected it there, Pepe did not see it until it was nearer than safety allowed.

The tiger crouched at the base of a palm whose fronds waved at least fifty feet above the roots. Both the beast's front paws were on what remained of the dead goat. It did not snarl or grimace, or even twitch its tail. But there was a lethal quality about the great cat and an extreme tension. The tiger was bursting with raw anger that seemed to swell and grow.

Pepe stopped in his tracks and cold fear crept up his spine. But he did not give way to fear. With deliberate, studied slowness he brought the rifle to his shoulder and took aim. He had only one bullet and there would be no time to reload, but even a tiger could not withstand the smash of that enormous leaden ball right between the eyes. Pepe steadied the rifle.

His finger tightened slowly on the trigger, for he must not let nervousness spoil his aim. When the hammer fell, Pepe's brain and body became momentarily numb.

There was no satisfying roar and no puff of black powder smoke wafting away from the muzzle. Instead there was only a sudden hiss, as though cold water had spilled on a hot stone, and the metallic click of the falling hammer. Pepe himself had loaded the rifle, but he could not have done so correctly. Only the powder in the priming pan flashed.

It was the spark needed to explode the anger in the tiger's lithe and deadly body. He emitted a coughing snarl and launched his charge. Lord of the jungle, he would crush this puny man who dared interfere with him.

Pepe jerked back to reality, but he took time to think of his rifle, leaning it lovingly against a tree and in the same motion jerking his machete from its sheath.

It was now a hopeless fight, to be decided in the tiger's favor, because not within the memory of the village's oldest inhabitant had any man ever killed a tiger with a machete. But it was as well to fight hopelessly, as to turn and run, for if he did that he would surely be killed. No tiger that attacked anything was ever known to turn aside.

Machete in hand, Pepe studied the onrushing cat. He had read the tracks correctly, for from pad to joint the tiger's right front foot was swollen to almost twice the size of the other. It must have stepped on a poisonous thorn or been bitten by a snake.

Even with such a handicap, a tiger was more than a match for a man armed only with a machete—but Pepe watched the right front paw carefully. If he had any advantage, it lay there. Then the tiger, a terrible, pitiless engine of destruction, flung himself at Pepe. Pepe had known from the first that the tiger's initial strike would be exactly this one, and he was ready for it. He swerved, bending his body outward as the great cat brushed past him. With all the strength in his powerful right arm, he swung the machete. He stopped his downward stroke just short of the tiger's silken back, for he knew suddenly that there was just one way to end this fight.

The tiger whirled, and hot spittle from his mouth splashed on the back of Pepe's left hand. Holding the machete before him, like a sword, he took a swift backward step. The tiger sprang, launching himself from the ground as

though his rear legs were made of powerful steel springs, and coming straight up. His flailing left paw flashed at Pepe. It hooked in his shirt, ripping it away from the arm as though it were paper, and burning talons sank into the flesh. Red blood welled out.

Pepe did not try again to slash with the machete, but thrust, as he would have thrust with a knife or sword. The machete's point met the tiger's throat, and Pepe put all his strength and weight behind it. The blade explored its way into living flesh, and the tiger gasped. Blood bubbled over the machete.

With a convulsive effort, the tiger pulled himself away. But blood was rushing from his throat now and he shook his head, then stumbled and fell. He pulled himself erect, looked with glazing eyes at Pepe and dragged himself toward him. There was a throttled snarl. The tiger slumped to the ground. The tip of his tail twitched and was still.

Pepe stared, scarcely seeing the blood that flowed from his lacerated arm. He had done the impossible, he had killed a tiger with a machete. Pepe brushed a hand across his eyes and took a trembling forward step.

He picked up his rifle and looked again to the priming. There seemed to be nothing wrong. Repriming, Pepe clasped the rifle with his elbow and seized the machete's hilt. Bracing one foot against the tiger's head, he drew the machete out.

Then he held his rifle so close to the machete wound that the muzzle caressed silken fur. He pulled the trigger. The wound gaped wider and smoke-blackened fur fringed it. All traces of the machete wound were obliterated. Pepe knew a second's anguished regret, then steeled himself, for this was the way it must be.

Everybody had a machete. In his village, the man who owned a rifle must remain supreme.

Reading Check

1. How did Pepe earn the money for his rifle?
2. How does Juan Aria know that the tiger will come again?
3. What does he offer Pepe in place of money?
4. Why does Pepe's rifle fail to fire?
5. How does Pepe destroy all traces of the machete wound?

For Study and Discussion

Analyzing and Interpreting the Story

1. The opening paragraphs of the story contrast daytime and nighttime in the jungle. How is the imagination of the villagers affected by the darkness?

2a. How does Pepe earn a living? b. How does Pepe take advantage of the villagers' fears?

3. How does Pepe show that he is a shrewd businessman when Juan Aria comes to seek his help?

4. To the people of the village, Pepe acts like a man without fear or concern. How does Pepe's attitude change when he enters the jungle?

5. Pepe knows that unless a man is a hunter, a rifle does him no good. a. How does Pepe's experience as a hunter help him to follow the jaguar's trail? b. How does he show that he is a great hunter when his rifle proves to be useless?

6. You are told that no one in the village had ever killed a tiger with a machete. Instead of boasting about his amazing deed, Pepe chooses to keep the truth from the villagers. Why?

7. The word *heart* is sometimes used as a synonym for *courage*. To be *stouthearted* or *lionhearted* is to be very brave. What do you think the title of the story means?

Literary Elements

Focusing on Details of Background

A writer generally attempts to catch the reader's attention at the beginning of a story. Notice how Kjelgaard arouses interest with the opening sentence of "The Tiger's Heart":

> The approaching jungle night was, in itself, a threat.

This sentence draws you into the world of the story—the jungle—and promises you excitement and danger. Notice how the first two paragraphs carry out both purposes of the opening sentence in developing the physical background of the story. What details in the first paragraph give you a vivid picture of the village life of jungle dwellers? Compare this description with the description in the second paragraph. Why does the author deliberately choose less specific details in the second paragraph? What characteristic of the jungle does he wish to emphasize there?

The writer of a short story seeks to create a world the reader can believe in. One way to get the reader to believe in the characters and events of a story is to present them against a lifelike background. Look back at the story and find additional details that give you a realistic picture of village life.

Language and Vocabulary

Finding the Appropriate Meaning

A dictionary often gives more than one meaning for a word. To determine which of the definitions is appropriate for a particular word, you must decide how the word is being used. You must decide which meaning best fits the context. For example, the word *air* may be used as a noun, an adjective, or a verb. As a noun, it has several different meanings. It may mean the mixture of gases that surrounds the earth. It may also mean a song or tune. It may also mean a person's outward appearance or manner. Which meaning does *air* have in this sentence?

> He shed his *air* of indifference and became as alert as the little doe that showed him only her white tail.

Use a dictionary to find the appropriate meaning of the italicized word in each of these sentences.

> Pepe stopped to look at the loading and *priming* of his rifle.

> Pepe had known from the first that the tiger's *initial* strike would be exactly this one, and he was ready for it.

> *Bracing* one foot against the tiger's head, he drew the machete out.

Creative Writing

Creating Atmosphere

Describe some setting that is richly atmospheric: for example, a carnival at night, a fogbound island, or a deserted house. Convey the mood of the place through specific details and appropriate modifiers. For a carnival scene, you might use modifiers like these: *colorful, glittering, festive;* for a fogbound island, *formless, indistinct, misty;* for a deserted house, *eerie, abandoned, solitary.*

About the Author

Jim Kjelgaard   (1910–1959)

Jim Kjelgaard was born in New York City but grew up in the Pennsylvania mountains. He worked at several different jobs before turning to writing. His first book, *Forest Patrol,* which appeared in 1941, was based on his own experiences and those of his brother, a forest ranger. Kjelgaard is well known for his stories about dogs. Three of his books are about Irish setters: *Big Red, Irish Red,* and *Outlaw Red.* In addition to stories about dogs and other animals, Kjelgaard wrote two books about the American frontier—*Rebel Siege* and *Buckskin Brigade.*

The Runaway

ROBERT FROST

*The horse in this poem is one of an American breed of light horses that origi-
nated in Vermont. As you read, take into account the setting, the onlookers, and
the emotion of the speaker.*

Once when the snow of the year was beginning to fall,
We stopped by a mountain pasture to say, "Whose colt?"
A little Morgan had one forefoot on the wall,
The other curled at his breast. He dipped his head
And snorted at us. And then he had to bolt.   5
We heard the miniature thunder where he fled,
And we saw him, or thought we saw him, dim and gray,
Like a shadow against the curtain of falling flakes.
"I think the little fellow's afraid of the snow.
He isn't winter-broken. It isn't play   10
With the little fellow at all. He's running away.
I doubt if even his mother could tell him, 'Sakes,
It's only weather.' He'd think she didn't know!
Where is his mother? He can't be out alone."
And now he comes again with clatter of stone,   15
And mounts the wall again with whited eyes
And all his tail that isn't hair up straight.
He shudders his coat as if to throw off flies.
"Whoever it is that leaves him out so late,
When other creatures have gone to stall and bin,   20
Ought to be told to come and take him in."

Analyzing and Interpreting the Poem

1. In the poem we are told that some people stop by a mountain pasture to watch a colt. **a.** What does the colt do when he sees them? **b.** The phrase "miniature thunder" in line 6 is a **figure of speech**, an imaginative way of drawing a comparison between two unlike things. What do you think the phrase refers to?

2. One of the onlookers believes that the colt is afraid of the snow because he isn't "winter-broken." What does the speaker mean by this expression?

3. What details in lines 15–18 confirm the onlooker's belief that the colt is afraid?

4. Many readers think that Frost uses this incident of the colt to express his deep concern for nature's creatures. Other readers believe that the poem also touches on the issue of responsibility. What is your interpretation of the poem?

About the Author

Robert Frost   (1874–1963)

Although he was born in the West (San Francisco) and named after a Southerner (Robert E. Lee), Robert Frost has become known as a New England poet. After his father died, his mother brought the family to Lawrence, Massachusetts. There Frost wrote poems while working as a mill hand, a schoolteacher, a baseball coach, a newspaper reporter, and a cobbler.

From 1900 to 1912, while raising chickens on a small farm in Derry, New Hampshire, Frost wrote some of his best-known poems. However, magazine editors rejected them. He had no greater success at farming. In 1912 Frost decided to end his isolation and frustration. He sold the farm and sailed for England with his wife and four children. There he made friends with other struggling poets who were interested in his work. He put together two major collections, *A Boy's Will* (1913) and *North of Boston* (1914). These books brought Frost to the attention of influential critics, including Ezra Pound, who helped Frost build a reputation in America.

By the time he returned to this country in 1915, Frost was already a famous poet. He settled once again on a farm, this time on a hill near Franconia, New Hampshire. For the rest of his life, he was America's unofficial poet laureate. He received many honors, including four Pulitzer Prizes. In 1961 he was asked to participate in the inauguration of John F. Kennedy. At the ceremony, he recited one of his poems, "The Gift Outright."

The Wild Duck's Nest

MICHAEL McLAVERTY

As you read this story, note how the main character responds to nature and how nature itself seems to mirror his shifting moods.

The sun was setting, spilling gold light on the low western hills of Rathlin Island.[1] A small boy walked jauntily along a hoof-printed path

1. **Rathlin Island:** an island a few miles off the northern coast of Ireland.

that wriggled between the folds of these hills and opened out into a craterlike valley on the clifftop. Presently he stopped as if remembering something, then suddenly he left the path, and began running up one of the hills. When

he reached the top he was out of breath and stood watching streaks of light radiating from golden-edged clouds, the scene reminding him of a picture he had seen of the Transfiguration.[2] A short distance below him was the cow standing at the edge of a reedy lake. Colm[3] ran down to meet her waving his stick in the air, and the wind rumbling in his ears made him give an exultant whoop which splashed upon the hills in a shower of echoed sound. A flock of gulls lying on the short grass near the lake rose up languidly, drifting like blown snow-flakes over the rim of the cliff.

2. **the Transfiguration:** an event in the life of Jesus Christ, told in Matthew 17:1–8. A painting of this event would probably show a mountaintop with a shining cloud overhead.
3. **Colm** (kŭl′əm).

The lake faced west and was fed by a stream, the drainings of the semicircling hills. One side was open to the winds from the sea and in winter a little outlet trickled over the cliffs making a black vein in their gray sides. The boy lifted stones and began throwing them into the lake, weaving web after web on its calm surface. Then he skimmed the water with flat stones, some of them jumping the surface and coming to rest on the other side. He was delighted with himself and after listening to his echoing shouts of delight he ran to fetch his cow. Gently he tapped her on the side and reluctantly she went towards the brown-mudded path that led out of the valley. The boy was about to throw a final stone into the lake when a bird flew low over his head, its neck astrain, and its orange-colored legs clear in the soft light. It was a wild duck. It circled the lake twice, thrice, coming lower each time and then with a nervous flapping of wings it skidded along the surface, its legs breaking the water into a series of silvery arcs. Its wings closed, it lit silently, gave a slight shiver, and began pecking indifferently at the water.

Colm with dilated eyes eagerly watched it making for the farther end of the lake. It meandered between tall bulrushes,[4] its body black and solid as stone against the graying water. Then as if it had sunk it was gone. The boy ran stealthily along the bank looking away from the lake, pretending indifference. When he came opposite to where he had last seen the bird he stopped and peered through the sighing reeds whose shadows streaked the water in a maze of black strokes. In front of him was a soddy islet guarded by the spears of sedge[5] and separated from the bank by a narrow channel of water. The water wasn't too deep—he could wade across with care.

4. **bulrushes** (bŏŏl′rŭsh′ĭz): grasslike plants.
5. **sedge:** a grasslike plant with pointed leaves.

Rolling up his short trousers he began to wade, his arms outstretched, and his legs brown and stunted in the mountain water. As he drew near the islet, his feet sank in the cold mud and bubbles winked up at him. He went more carefully and nervously. Then one trouser leg fell and dipped into the water; the boy dropped his hands to roll it up, he unbalanced, made a splashing sound, and the bird arose with a squawk and whirred away over the cliffs. For a moment the boy stood frightened. Then he clambered onto the wet-soaked sod of land, which was spattered with sea gulls' feathers and bits of wind-blown rushes.

Into each hummock[6] he looked, pulling back the long grass. At last he came on the nest, facing seawards. Two flat rocks dimpled the face of the water and between them was a neck of land matted with coarse grass containing the nest. It was untidily built of dried rushes, straw and feathers, and in it lay one solitary egg. Colm was delighted. He looked around and saw no one. The nest was his. He lifted the egg, smooth and green as the sky, with a faint tinge of yellow like the reflected light from a buttercup; and then he felt he had done wrong. He put it back. He knew he shouldn't have touched it and he wondered would the bird forsake the nest. A vague sadness stole over him and he felt in his heart he had sinned. Carefully smoothing out his footprints he hurriedly left the islet and ran after his cow. The sun had now set and the cold shiver of evening enveloped him, chilling his body and saddening his mind.

In the morning he was up and away to school. He took the grass rut that edged the road, for it was softer on the bare feet. His house was the last on the western headland and after a mile or so he was joined by Paddy McFall; both boys dressed in similar hand-knitted blue jerseys and gray trousers carried homemade schoolbags. Colm was full of the nest and as soon as he joined his companion he said eagerly: "Paddy, I've a nest—a wild duck's with one egg."

"And how do you know it's a wild duck's?" asked Paddy, slightly jealous.

"Sure I saw her with my own two eyes, her brown speckled back with a crow's patch on it, and her yellow legs—"

"Where is it?" interrupted Paddy in a challenging tone.

"I'm not going to tell you, for you'd rob it!"

"Aach! I suppose it's a tame duck's you have or maybe an old gull's."

Colm put out his tongue at him. "A lot you know!" he said; "for a gull's egg has spots and this one is greenish-white, for I had it in my hand."

And then the words he didn't want to hear rushed from Paddy in a mocking chant. "You had it in your hand! . . . She'll forsake it! She'll forsake it! She'll forsake it!" he said, skipping along the road before him.

Colm felt as if he would choke or cry with vexation.

His mind told him that Paddy was right, but somehow he couldn't give in to it and he replied: "She'll not forsake it! She'll not! I know she'll not!"

But in school his faith wavered. Through the windows he could see moving sheets of rain—rain that dribbled down the panes filling his mind with thoughts of the lake creased and chilled by wind; the nest sodden and black with wetness; and the egg cold as a cave stone. He shivered from the thoughts and fidgeted with the inkwell cover, sliding it backwards and forwards mechanically. The mischievous look had gone from his eyes and the school day dragged on interminably. But at last they were out in the rain, Colm rushing home as fast as he could.

6. **hummock** (hŭm′ək): a small mound of earth.

He was no time at all at his dinner of potatoes and salted fish until he was out in the valley now smoky with drifts of slanting rain. Opposite the islet he entered the water. The wind was blowing into his face, rustling noisily the rushes heavy with the dust of rain. A moss cheeper,[7] swaying on a reed like a mouse, filled the air with light cries of loneliness.

The boy reached the islet, his heart thumping with excitement, wondering did the bird forsake. He went slowly, quietly, onto the strip of land that led to the nest. He rose on his toes, looking over the ledge to see if he could see her. And then every muscle tautened. She was on, her shoulders hunched up, and her bill lying on her breast as if she were asleep. Colm's heart hammered wildly in his ears. She hadn't forsaken. He was about to turn stealthily away. Something happened. The bird moved, her neck straightened, twitching nervously from side to side. The boy's head swam with lightness. He stood transfixed. The wild duck, with a panicky flapping, rose heavily, and flew off towards the sea. . . . A guilty silence enveloped the boy. . . . He turned to go away, hesitated, and glanced back at the bare nest; it'd be no harm to have a look. Timidly he approached it, standing straight, and gazing over the edge. There in the nest lay two eggs. He drew in his breath with delight, splashed quickly from the island, and ran off whistling in the rain.

7. **moss cheeper:** a songbird.

Reading Check

1. At the opening of the story, why does Colm come to the valley?
2. How does he cause the bird to leave its nest?
3. Why does Colm refuse to tell Paddy where the wild duck has built its nest?
4. Why does Colm return to the nest?

For Study and Discussion

Analyzing and Interpreting the Story

1. At the opening of the story, you learn that Colm enjoys the beauty of the countryside. What details in the first paragraph show his delight in nature?

2. How do Colm's actions show that he suspects the wild duck has built a nest on the islet?

3. Colm does not wish to rob the nest. **a.** Why, then, does he lift the egg? **b.** Why does he feel that he has sinned?

4. What steps does Colm take to protect the nest from further harm?

5a. Why does Colm return to the wild duck's nest? **b.** How is he relieved by what he finds?

6. When Colm first finds the nest, he feels that it is his. Do you think he still feels this way at the end of the story? Explain your answer.

7. Sometimes human beings destroy nature through thoughtlessness or carelessness. What do you think Colm learns from his experience with the wild duck's nest?

Language and Vocabulary

Forming Adverbs from Adjectives

Michael McLaverty uses a great many adverbs as modifiers of verbs. In the first paragraph of the story, you are told that Colm "walked *jauntily*." The gulls, disturbed by his shouting, "rose up *languidly*."

Many adverbs in our language are formed by adding the suffix *-ly* to an adjective. When you add *-ly* to the adjective *languid*, you form the adverb *languidly*. The adverb *jauntily* is formed from the adjective *jaunty*. Notice that the *y* in *jaunty* changes to *i* when *-ly* is added. What happens when you change the adjective *gentle* to an adverb?

How many adverbs ending in *-ly* can you locate in the story? List them and give the adjectives from which they are formed.

Using Vivid Verbs

In the first paragraph of the story, the author says that a path "wriggled" between the hills. *Wriggled* is an effective verb because it makes the reader think of the path weaving in and out like a snake.

There are other good descriptive verbs in the story. Explain why each of the following italicized verbs is a good choice.

Then he *skimmed* the water with flat stones . . . .
. . . his feet sank in the cold mud and bubbles *winked* up at him.
And then every muscle *tautened*.
Colm's heart *hammered* wildly in his ears.

Using vivid verbs will make your own writing more lively and interesting. Think of an effective verb to substitute for each of the italicized verbs in these sentences.

The stealthy cat *moved* across the lawn toward the unsuspecting birds.
The surprised winner of the contest *went* to the stage when her name was called.
The hungry lion *ate* its prey.

Explaining Differences

Paddy accuses Colm of mistaking a sea gull's egg for a wild duck's egg, but Colm indicates that he knows the difference.

> "A lot you know!" he said; "for a gull's egg has spots and this one is greenish-white, for I had it in my hand."

Colm is a close observer of nature. One detail—color—is sufficient to tell him the difference between the two eggs.

Write a paragraph in which you explain the difference between two things that are sometimes confused. You might explain the difference between two animals: a frog and a toad, or a guinea pig and a hamster, for example. You might explain the difference between two musical instruments: a violin and a viola, or a flute and a piccolo. You might explain the difference between two sports: football and soccer, or tennis and badminton.

Before you write your paragraph, you may want to list your ideas, beginning with the most important or obvious difference. Open with a sentence that follows this pattern:

> There are three (four, five) major differences between *x* and *y*.

Michael McLaverty (1904–   )

Irish novelist Michael McLaverty was for many years the headmaster of St. Thomas' Secondary School in Belfast, Northern Ireland. He published his first novel, *Call My Brother Back,* in 1939. Other novels by McLaverty include *The Three Brothers* (1947), *Truth in the Night* (1957), and *The Brightening Day* (1965). "The Wild Duck's Nest" is from a collection called *The Game Cock and Other Stories.*

Birdfoot's Grampa

JOSEPH BRUCHAC III

What information in the title of this poem gives you insight into the characters?

The old man
must have stopped our car
two dozen times to climb out
and gather into his hands
the small toads blinded   5
by our lights and leaping,
live drops of rain.

The rain was falling,
a mist about his white hair
and I kept saying   10
you can't save them all,
accept it, get back in
we've got places to go.

But, leathery hands full
of wet brown life,   15
knee deep in the summer
roadside grass,
he just smiled and said
they have places to go to
too.   20

For Study and Discussion

Analyzing and Interpreting the Poem

1. This poem tells about someone who stops a car during a heavy rainfall in order to save some creatures that would otherwise be run over. **a.** How does the poet create sympathy for the animals? **b.** What is the "wet brown life" referred to in line 15?

2a. Contrast the speaker's attitude toward the events with the old man's. **b.** How does the old man show a deep reverence for the natural world?

About the Author

Joseph Bruchac III (1942–   )

Joseph Bruchac (broo' shăk) III has contributed poetry to more than four hundred periodicals and has won a number of awards and honors for his work. He has said, "My writing is informed by several key sources. One of these is nature, another is native American experience (I'm part Indian). . . . I like to work outside, in the earth mother's soil, with my hands."

Antaeus°

BORDEN DEAL

In a story told by the ancient Greeks, Antaeus was a giant whose strength came from the earth. As long as he remained in contact with the earth, no one could defeat him in combat. To find out how he was overcome, see "The Adventures of Hercules" on page 622. In this story you will read about a modern Antaeus.

This was during the wartime, when lots of people were coming North for jobs in factories and war industries, when people moved around a lot more than they do now, and sometimes kids were thrown into new groups and new lives that were completely different from anything they had ever known before. I remember this one kid, T. J. his name was, from somewhere down South, whose family moved into our building during that time. They'd come North with everything they owned piled into the back seat of an old-model sedan that you wouldn't expect could make the trip, with T. J. and his three younger sisters riding shakily on top of the load of junk.

Our building was just like all the others there, with families crowded into a few rooms, and I guess there were twenty-five or thirty kids about my age in that one building. Of course, there were a few of us who formed a gang and ran together all the time after school, and I was the one who brought T. J. in and started the whole thing.

The building right next door to us was a factory where they made walking dolls. It was a low building with a flat, tarred roof that had a parapet[1] all around it about head-high, and we'd found out a long time before that no one, not even the watchman, paid any attention to the roof because it was higher than any of the other buildings around. So my gang used the roof as a headquarters. We could get up there by crossing over to the fire escape from our own roof on a plank and then going on up. It was a secret place for us, where nobody else could go without our permission.

I remember the day I first took T. J. up there to meet the gang. He was a stocky, robust kid with a shock of white hair, nothing sissy about him except his voice; he talked in this slow, gentle voice like you never heard before. He talked different from any of us and you noticed it right away. But I liked him anyway, so I told him to come on up.

We climbed up over the parapet and dropped down on the roof. The rest of the gang were already there.

"Hi," I said. I jerked my thumb at T. J. "He just moved into the building yesterday."

He just stood there, not scared or anything, just looking, like the first time you see somebody you're not sure you're going to like.

° **Antaeus** (ăn-tē′əs).

1. **parapet** (păr′ə-pĭt): a low protective wall.

"Hi," Blackie said. "Where are you from?"

"Marion County," T. J. said.

We laughed. "Marion County?" I said. "Where's that?"

He looked at me for a moment like I was a stranger, too. "It's in Alabama," he said, like I ought to know where it was.

"What's your name?" Charley said.

"T. J.," he said, looking back at him. He had pale blue eyes that looked washed-out, but he looked directly at Charley, waiting for his reaction. He'll be all right, I thought. No sissy in him, except that voice. Who ever talked like that?

"T. J.," Blackie said. "That's just initials. What's your real name? Nobody in the world has just initials."

"I do," he said. "And they're T. J. That's all the name I got."

His voice was resolute with the knowledge of his rightness, and for a moment no one had anything to say. T. J. looked around at the rooftop and down at the black tar under his feet. "Down yonder where I come from," he said, "we played out in the woods. Don't you-all have no woods around here?"

"Naw," Blackie said. "There's the park a few blocks over, but it's full of kids and cops and old women. You can't do a thing."

T. J. kept looking at the tar under his feet.

"You mean you ain't got no fields to raise nothing in?—no watermelons or nothing?"

"Naw," I said scornfully. "What do you want to grow something for? The folks can buy everything they need at the store."

He looked at me again with that strange, unknowing look. "In Marion County," he said, "I had my own acre of cotton and my own acre of corn. It was mine to plant and make ever' year."

He sounded like it was something to be proud of, and in some obscure way it made the rest of us angry. Blackie said, "Who'd want to have their own acre of cotton and corn? That's just work. What can you do with an acre of cotton and corn?"

T. J. looked at him. "Well, you get part of the bale offen your acre," he said seriously. "And I fed my acre of corn to my calf."

We didn't really know what he was talking about, so we were more puzzled than angry; otherwise, I guess, we'd have chased him off the roof and wouldn't let him be part of our gang. But he was strange and different, and we were all attracted by his stolid sense of rightness and belonging, maybe by the strange softness of his voice contrasting our own tones of speech into harshness.

He moved his foot against the black tar. "We could make our own field right here," he said softly, thoughtfully. "Come spring we could raise us what we want to—watermelons and garden truck[2] and no telling what all."

"You'd have to be a good farmer to make these tar roofs grow any watermelons," I said. We all laughed.

But T. J. looked serious. "We could haul us some dirt up here," he said. "And spread it out even and water it, and before you know it, we'd have us a crop in here." He looked at us intently. "Wouldn't that be fun?"

"They wouldn't let us," Blackie said quickly.

"I thought you said this was you-all's roof," T. J. said to me. "That you-all could do anything you wanted to up here."

"They've never bothered us," I said. I felt the idea beginning to catch fire in me. It was a big idea, and it took a while for it to sink in; but the more I thought about it, the better I liked it. "Say," I said to the gang. "He might have something there. Just make us a regular roof garden, with flowers and grass and trees and everything. And all ours, too," I said. "We wouldn't let anybody up here except the ones we wanted to."

"It'd take a while to grow trees," T. J. said quickly, but we weren't paying any attention to him. They were all talking about it suddenly, all excited with the idea after I'd put it in a way they could catch hold of it. Only rich people had roof gardens, we knew, and the idea of our own private domain excited them.

"We could bring it up in sacks and boxes," Blackie said. "We'd have to do it while the folks weren't paying any attention to us, for we'd have to come up the roof of our building and then cross over with it."

"Where could we get the dirt?" somebody said worriedly.

"Out of those vacant lots over close to school," Blackie said. "Nobody'd notice if we scraped it up."

I slapped T. J. on the shoulder. "Man, you had a wonderful idea," I said, and everybody grinned at him, remembering that he had started it. "Our own private roof garden."

He grinned back. "It'll be ourn," he said. "All ourn." Then he looked thoughtful again. "Maybe I can lay my hands on some cotton seed, too. You think we could raise us some cotton?"

We'd started big projects before at one time or

2. **truck:** here, vegetables grown to be sold.

another, like any gang of kids, but they'd always petered out for lack of organization and direction. But this one didn't; somehow or other T. J. kept it going all through the winter months. He kept talking about the watermelons and the cotton we'd raise, come spring, and when even that wouldn't work, he'd switch around to my idea of flowers and grass and trees, though he was always honest enough to add that it'd take a while to get any trees started. He always had it on his mind and he'd mention it in school, getting them lined up to carry dirt that afternoon, saying in a casual way that he reckoned a few more weeks ought to see the job through.

Our little area of private earth grew slowly. T. J. was smart enough to start in one corner of the building, heaping up the carried earth two or three feet thick so that we had an immediate result to look at, to contemplate with awe. Some of the evenings T. J. alone was carrying earth up to the building, the rest of the gang distracted by other enterprises or interests, but T. J. kept plugging along on his own, and eventually we'd all come back to him again and then our own little acre would grow more rapidly.

He was careful about the kind of dirt he'd let us carry up there, and more than once he dumped a sandy load over the parapet into the areaway below because it wasn't good enough. He found out the kinds of earth in all the vacant lots for blocks around. He'd pick it up and feel it and smell it, frozen though it was sometimes, and then he'd say it was good growing soil or it wasn't worth anything, and we'd have to go on somewhere else.

Thinking about it now, I don't see how he kept us at it. It was hard work, lugging paper sacks and boxes of dirt all the way up the stairs of our own building, keeping out of the way of the grown-ups so they wouldn't catch on to what we were doing. They probably wouldn't have cared, for they didn't pay much attention to us, but we wanted to keep it secret anyway. Then we had to go through the trapdoor to our roof, teeter over a plank to the fire escape, then climb two or three stories to the parapet and drop down onto the roof. All that for a small pile of earth that sometimes didn't seem worth the effort. But T. J. kept the vision bright within us, his words shrewd and calculated toward the fulfillment of his dream; and he worked harder than any of us. He seemed driven toward a goal that we couldn't see, a particular point in time that would be definitely marked by signs and wonders that only he could see.

The laborious earth just lay there during the cold months, inert and lifeless, the clods lumpy and cold under our feet when we walked over it. But one day it rained, and afterward there was a softness in the air, and the earth was live and giving again with moisture and warmth.

That evening T. J. smelled the air, his nostrils dilating with the odor of the earth under his feet. "It's spring," he said, and there was a gladness rising in his voice that filled us all with the same feeling. "It's mighty late for it, but it's spring. I'd just about decided it wasn't never gonna get here at all."

We were all sniffing at the air, too, trying to smell it the way that T. J. did, and I can still remember the sweet odor of the earth under our feet. It was the first time in my life that spring and spring earth had meant anything to me. I looked at T. J. then, knowing in a faint way the hunger within him through the toilsome winter months, knowing the dream that lay behind his plan. He was a new Antaeus, preparing his own bed of strength.

"Planting time," he said. "We'll have to find us some seed."

"What do we do?" Blackie said. "How do we do it?"

"First we'll have to break up the clods," T. J. said. "That won't be hard to do. Then we plant the seeds, and after a while they come up. Then you got you a crop." He frowned. "But you ain't got it raised yet. You got to tend it and hoe it and take care of it, and all the time it's growing and growing, while you're awake and while you're asleep. Then you lay it by when it's growed and let it ripen, and then you got you a crop."

"There's those wholesale seed houses over on Sixth," I said. "We could probably swipe some grass seed over there."

T. J. looked at the earth. "You-all seem mighty set on raising some grass," he said. "I ain't never put no effort into that. I spent all my life trying not to raise grass."

"But it's pretty," Blackie said. "We could play on it and take sunbaths on it. Like having our own lawn. Lots of people got lawns."

"Well," T. J. said. He looked at the rest of us, hesitant for the first time. He kept on looking at us for a moment. "I did have it in mind to raise some corn and vegetables. But we'll plant grass."

He was smart. He knew where to give in. And I don't suppose it made any difference to him, really. He just wanted to grow something, even if it was grass.

"Of course," he said, "I do think we ought to plant a row of watermelons. They'd be mighty nice to eat while we was a-laying on that grass."

We all laughed. "All right," I said. "We'll plant us a row of watermelons."

Things went very quickly then. Perhaps half the roof was covered with the earth, the half that wasn't broken by ventilators, and we swiped pocketfuls of grass seed from the open bins in the wholesale seed house, mingling among the buyers on Saturdays and during the school lunch hour. T. J. showed us how to prepare the earth, breaking up the clods and smoothing it and sowing the grass seed. It looked rich and black now with moisture, receiving of the seed, and it seemed that the grass sprang up overnight, pale green in the early spring.

We couldn't keep from looking at it, unable to believe that we had created this delicate growth. We looked at T. J. with understanding now, knowing the fulfillment of the plan he had carried along within his mind. We had worked without full understanding of the task, but he had known all the time.

We found that we couldn't walk or play on the delicate blades, as we had expected to, but we didn't mind. It was enough just to look at it, to realize that it was the work of our own hands, and each evening the whole gang was there, trying to measure the growth that had been achieved that day.

One time a foot was placed on the plot of ground, one time only, Blackie stepping onto it with sudden bravado. Then he looked at the crushed blades and there was shame in his face. He did not do it again. This was his grass, too, and not to be desecrated.[3] No one said anything, for it was not necessary.

T. J. had reserved a small section for watermelons, and he was still trying to find some seed for it. The wholesale house didn't have any watermelon seeds, and we didn't know where we could lay our hands on them. T. J. shaped the earth into mounds, ready to receive them, three mounds lying in a straight line along the edge of the grass plot.

We had just about decided that we'd have to buy the seeds if we were to get them. It was a violation of our principles, but we were anxious to get the watermelons started. Somewhere or other, T. J. got his hands on a seed catalog and brought it one evening to our roof garden.

---

3. **desecrated** (dĕs ə-krāt′ĭd): treated with disrespect.

"We can order them now," he said, showing us the catalog. "Look!"

We all crowded around, looking at the fat, green watermelons pictured in full color on the pages. Some of them were split open, showing the red, tempting meat, making our mouths water.

"Now we got to scrape up some seed money." T. J. said, looking at us. "I got a quarter. How much you-all got?"

We made up a couple of dollars among us and T. J. nodded his head. "That'll be more than enough. Now we got to decide what kind to get. I think them Kleckley Sweets. What do you-all think?"

He was going into esoteric matters[4] beyond our reach. We hadn't even known there were different kinds of melons. So we just nodded our heads and agreed that yes, we thought the Kleckley Sweets too.

"I'll order them tonight," T. J. said. "We ought to have them in a few days."

"What are you boys doing up here?" an adult voice said behind us.

It startled us, for no one had ever come up here before in all the time we had been using the roof of the factory. We jerked around and saw three men standing near the trap door at the other end of the roof. They weren't policemen or night watchmen, but three men in plump business suits, looking at us. They walked toward us.

"What are you boys doing up here?" the one in the middle said again.

We stood still, guilt heavy among us, levied[5] by the tone of voice, and looked at the three strangers.

The men stared at the grass flourishing behind us. "What's this?" the man said. "How did this get up here?"

"Sure is growing good, ain't it?" T. J. said conversationally. "We planted it."

The men kept looking at the grass as if they didn't believe it. It was a thick carpet over the earth now, a patch of deep greenness startling in the sterile industrial surroundings.

"Yes, sir," T. J. said proudly. "We toted that earth up here and planted that grass." He fluttered the seed catalog. "And we're just fixing to plant us some watermelon."

The man looked at him then, his eyes strange and faraway. "What do you mean, putting this on the roof of my building?" he said. "Do you want to go to jail?"

T. J. looked shaken. The rest of us were silent, frightened by the authority of his voice. We had grown up aware of adult authority, of policemen and night watchmen and teachers, and this man sounded like all the others. But it was a new thing to T. J.

"Well, you wasn't using the roof," T. J. said. He paused a moment and added shrewdly, "So we just thought to pretty it up a little bit."

"And sag it so I'd have to rebuild it," the man said sharply. He started turning away, saying to another man beside him, "See that all that junk is shoveled off by tomorrow."

"Yes, sir," the man said.

T. J. started forward. "You can't do that," he said. "We toted it up here, and it's our earth. We planted it and raised it and toted it up here."

The man stared at him coldly. "But it's my building," he said. "It's to be shoveled off tomorrow."

"It's our earth," T. J. said desperately. "You ain't got no right!"

The men walked on without listening and descended clumsily through the trapdoor. T. J. stood looking after them, his body tense with anger, until they had disappeared. They wouldn't even argue with him, wouldn't let him defend his earth-rights.

He turned to us. "We won't let 'em do it," he

---

4. **esoteric** (ĕs′ə-tĕr′ĭk) **matters:** special knowledge.
5. **levied** (lĕv′ēd): imposed or placed upon. The man's tone of voice makes the boys feel guilty.

said fiercely. "We'll stay up here all day tomorrow and the day after that, and we won't let 'em do it."

We just looked at him. We knew there was no stopping it.

He saw it in our faces, and his face wavered for a moment before he gripped it into determination. "They ain't got no right," he said. "It's our earth. It's our land. Can't nobody touch a man's own land."

We kept looking at him, listening to the words but knowing that it was no use. The adult world had descended on us even in our richest dream, and we knew there was no calculating the adult world, no fighting it, no winning against it.

We started moving slowly toward the parapet and the fire escape, avoiding a last look at the green beauty of the earth that T. J. had planted for us, had planted deeply in our minds as well as in our experience. We filed slowly over the edge and down the steps to the plank, T. J. coming last, and all of us could feel the weight of his grief behind us.

"Wait a minute," he said suddenly, his voice harsh with the effort of calling.

We stopped and turned, held by the tone of his voice, and looked up at him standing above us on the fire escape.

"We can't stop them?" he said, looking down at us, his face strange in the dusky light. "There ain't no way to stop 'em?"

"No," Blackie said with finality. "They own the building."

We stood still for a moment, looking up at T. J., caught into inaction by the decision working in his face. He stared back at us, and his face was pale and mean in the poor light, with a bald nakedness in his skin like cripples have sometimes.

"They ain't gonna touch my earth," he said fiercely. "They ain't gonna lay a hand on it! Come on."

He turned around and started up the fire escape again, almost running against the effort of climbing. We followed more slowly, not knowing what he intended. By the time we reached him, he had seized a board and thrust it into the soil, scooping it up and flinging it over the parapet into the areaway below. He straightened and looked at us.

"They can't touch it." he said. "I won't let 'em lay a dirty hand on it!"

We saw it then. He stooped to his labor again and we followed, the gusts of his anger moving in frenzied labor among us as we scattered along the edge of earth, scooping it and throwing it over the parapet, destroying with anger the growth we had nurtured with such tender care. The soil carried so laboriously upward to the light and the sun cascaded swiftly into the dark areaway, the green blades of grass crumpled and twisted in the falling.

It took less time than you would think; the task of destruction is infinitely easier than that of creation. We stopped at the end, leaving only a scattering of loose soil, and when it was finally over, a stillness stood among the group and over the factory building. We looked down at the bare sterility of black tar, felt the harsh texture of it under the soles of our shoes, and the anger had gone out of us, leaving only a sore aching in our minds like overstretched muscles.

T. J. stood for a moment, his breathing slowing from anger and effort, caught into the same contemplation of destruction as all of us. He stooped slowly, finally, and picked up a lonely blade of grass left trampled under our feet and put it between his teeth, tasting it, sucking the greenness out of it into his mouth. Then he started walking toward the fire escape, moving before any of us were ready to move, and disappeared over the edge.

We followed him, but he was already halfway down to the ground, going on past the board where we crossed over, climbing down into the areaway. We saw the last section swing down with his weight, and then he stood on the concrete below us, looking at the small pile of anonymous earth scattered by our throwing. Then he walked across the place where we could see him and disappeared toward the street without glancing back, without looking up to see us watching him.

They did not find him for two weeks.

Then the Nashville police caught him just outside the Nashville freight yards. He was walking along the railroad track, still heading south, still heading home.

As for us, who had no remembered home to call us, none of us ever again climbed the escapeway to the roof.

Reading Check

1. What do the boys in the narrator's gang use as their headquarters?
2. What does T. J. want the boys to raise?
3. Where do the boys get the soil for their garden?
4. Why does T. J. run away?

For Study and Discussion

Analyzing and Interpreting the Story

1. The boys in the narrator's gang are city boys accustomed to living without trees or grass of their own. Why do they become so excited at the idea of a roof garden?

2. The boys work at the garden without fully understanding what it means to T. J. At what point do they begin to experience the wonder of making things grow? Find the passage that gives the answer.

3. In the ancient story, Antaeus' bond with the earth was broken when he was held in midair and strangled. **a.** How is T. J.'s bond with the earth broken? **b.** In what way is his return to the South an attempt to renew that bond?

4. The narrator says that he avoided "a last look at the green beauty of the earth that T. J. had planted for us, had planted deeply in our minds as well as in our experience." What gift has T. J. given the boys that will last even though the garden is gone?

5. Like the character Antaeus in the Greek story, T. J. seems to gain strength from contact with the earth. Antaeus' strength was physical. How would you describe the kind of strength T. J. draws from the earth?

Language and Vocabulary

Using Context Clues

You can often get the meaning of an unfamiliar word by using clues supplied by the context.

> The laborious earth just lay there during the cold months, *inert* and lifeless, the clods lumpy and cold under our feet when we walked over it.

The word *inert* means "not moving; inactive." What clues in the sentence help give you this meaning?

What context clues help you get the meaning of the word *cascaded* in this sentence?

> The soil carried so laboriously upward to the light and the sun *cascaded* swiftly into the dark areaway, the green blades of grass crumpled and twisted in the falling.

The verb *cascade* means "to fall swiftly from a height, like a waterfall."

Write sentences of your own using the words *inert* and *cascade*.

Use context clues to determine the meaning

of each of these words. Check your answers in the glossary.

domain   (page 189, column 2)
contemplate   (page 190, column 1)
distracted   (page 190, column 1)

Expository Writing

Explaining a Procedure

T. J. shows the boys how to plant a garden on the factory roof. First he helps the boys find good growing soil in vacant lots. Then he shows them how to prepare the earth for planting by breaking up the clods, smoothing the soil, and sowing the grass seed.

When you explain how to do something, it is helpful to present your instructions as a series of separate steps. If you arrange the steps in order carefully, the reader will be able to follow your directions. You can make the order clear by using expressions such as *first, second, as soon as, next, in addition to, now, then,* and *finally.* These expressions are *transitional*—that is, they are used to connect the sentences in your writing and speaking.

Write a paragraph in which you explain, step by step, how to do something. Be sure to include all the materials that will be needed. If you must use any technical words, be sure to explain what they mean.

Here are some topics you might want to use:

How to repot a plant
How to bathe a dog
How to fix a flat tire on a bicycle
How to make a pizza
How to paint a room

About the Author

Borden Deal   (1922–1985)

Borden Deal was born on a cotton farm in Mississippi. Before devoting himself full time to writing, he had a variety of jobs. He worked as a firefighter for the Civilian Conservation Corps, a roustabout for a circus and a showboat, an auditor, a finance collector, and a writer for a radio station. He produced several novels and more than one hundred short stories. His work has been adapted for the stage, the movies, and television, and has been translated into many languages.

PRACTICE IN
READING AND WRITING

Expository Writing

The form of writing we use most frequently is exposition. Exposition is the kind of writing that explains something or gives information. Science and history books, reports, and even directions on how to assemble a piece of furniture all make use of exposition.

The following paragraph from "Desert Creatures" states and supports a certain idea.

Some of these animals, especially the rodents and other smaller mammals, may never drink free water in their entire lives. Instead they get by on what moisture they can obtain from plant food and through the internal manufacture of what is called "metabolic water." Particularly distinguished in this regard is the kangaroo rat, which subsists on a diet of dried seeds, bathes itself in sand, ignores green and succulent plants, and shuns water even when it is available.

1. What is the sentence that states the topic, or main idea?

2. What details or examples support the topic sentence?

Suggestions for Writing

Write an expository paragraph developing one of these topics or a topic of your own:

An amateur photographer's equipment
A beginner's stamp collection
Tuning a guitar
Reading a road map

Here are some guidelines to help you plan and write your paper.

Prewriting
- Be clear as to your purpose. Are you going to supply information, give directions, or tell how something works?
- State the topic clearly in a sentence.
- Make a list of specific details, examples, or reasons that develop your topic.
- Arrange your details in a logical order.

Writing
- Keep a steady focus, including only those details that are relevant.
- As a rule, place the topic sentence at the beginning of the paragraph, unless you feel it would be more effective at the end.
- Make an effort at sentence variety so that your style is not dull and mechanical.
- Use transitional expressions to connect ideas.

Evaluating and Revising
- Is there a topic sentence clearly stated?
- Are there sufficient details to develop the topic adequately?
- Have the details or examples been arranged in a logical order?
- Are there transitional words such as *first, next, later,* and the like to link sentences?

Proofreading
- Check your revised paper for errors in grammar, usage, and mechanics.
- Prepare a final copy and check it.

For Further Reading

Adamson, Joy, *Born Free: A Lioness of Two Worlds* (Pantheon, 1960; paperback, Random House, 1974)

> The author tells how she and her husband raised Elsa, a lion cub, as a pet and then trained her to survive in the jungle. *Living Free* (Harcourt Brace Jovanovich, 1961) is a sequel to this book.

Annixter, Paul, *Swiftwater* (Hill & Wang, 1950; paperback, Starline)

> Young Buck Calloway and his father, trappers who love the endangered wilderness, try to establish a bird sanctuary in northern Maine.

Burnford, Sheila, *The Incredible Journey* (Little, Brown, 1961; paperback, Bantam, 1977)

> Three house pets—a young Labrador retriever, an old bull terrier, and a Siamese cat—travel two hundred miles across the Canadian wilderness to return to their home.

Cousteau, Jacques-Yves, and Frederic Dumas, *The Silent World* (Harper & Row, 1953; paperback, Harper)

> The aqualung, developed during World War II, enables divers to explore far below the ocean surface, to search for ancient treasures, and to gain new knowledge of the inhabitants of the deep.

George, Jean Craighead, *Julie of the Wolves* (Harper & Row, 1972; paperback, Harper)

> A thirteen-year-old Eskimo girl, lost in the Alaskan wilderness, survives by living with a pack of wolves.

Herriot, James, *All Creatures Great and Small* (St. Martin's, 1972; paperback, Bantam, 1975)

> The author recounts his experiences as a veterinarian in Yorkshire, England.

London, Jack, *The Call of the Wild* (many editions)

> The hero is a dog named Buck, stolen from his California home and sold as a sled dog during the Alaskan Gold Rush. Buck serves many masters but loves only one. After his kind master dies, Buck yields to his primitive instincts by joining a wolf pack.

Manley, Seon and Gogo Lewis, editors, *Cat Encounters: A Cat-Lover's Anthology* (Lothrop, Lee & Shepard, 1979)

> This is a collection of stories, essays, and poems about cats.

Maxwell, Gavin, *Ring of Bright Water* (Dutton, 1961; paperback, Ballantine Books)

> Life in a lonely cottage on the northwest coast of Scotland is enlivened by Mijbil and Edal, the author's pet otters.

Mowat, Farley, *Owls in the Family* (Little, Brown, 1961; paperback, Bantam, 1981)

> Pet owls named Wol and Weeps take over the author's household and upset the town of Saskatoon in Saskatchewan, Canada. In *The Dog Who Wouldn't Be* (Atlantic Monthly Press, 1957; paperback, Pyramid), Mowat tells the story of Mutt, who was almost too smart to be a dog.

Murphy, Robert, *The Pond* (Dutton, 1964)

> Fourteen-year-old Joey discovers a pond in the woods outside Richmond, Virginia, where he learns about dogs, fishing, hunting, and life.

North, Sterling, *Rascal: A Memoir of a Better Era* (paperback, Dutton, 1984)

> The author tells about his adventures with a pet raccoon.

O'Dell, Scott, *Island of the Blue Dolphins* (Houghton Mifflin, 1960; paperback, Dell)

> Karana, a young Indian girl, lives alone for eighteen years on a desolate island off the California coast. The novel is based on a true story.

O'Hara, Mary, *My Friend Flicka,* new ed. (Harper & Row, 1973)

> Ken's dream comes true when his father gives him a colt of his own.

Ullman, James Ramsey, *Banner in the Sky* (Lippincott, 1954; paperback, Archway, 1984)

> Rudi, the son of a Swiss mountain-climber, struggles to conquer the mountain where his father lost his life.

PART II

FORMS OF LITERATURE

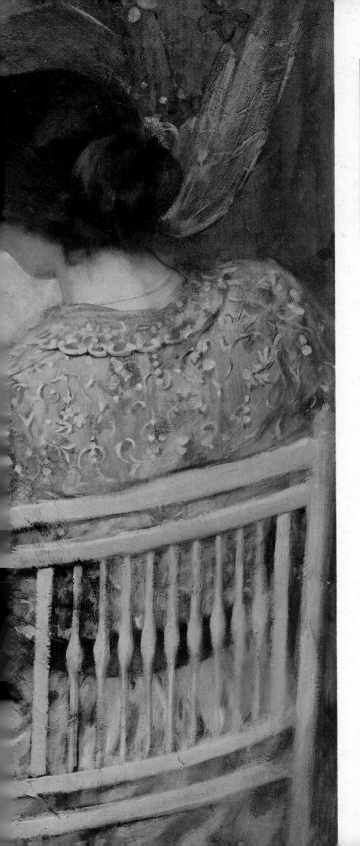

SHORT STORIES

Jungle Tales (Contes de la Jungle) (1895) by James Jebusa Shannon (1862–1923). Oil on canvas.
The Metropolitan Museum of Art, Arthur Hoppock Hearn Fund, 1913

201

CLOSE READING
OF A SHORT STORY

Developing Skills in Critical Thinking

When you examine the stories in this unit closely, you will find that they are made up of similar elements. For example, each story has a *main character*. In "The Erne from the Coast," the main character is a boy of your own age. In "Rikki-tikki-tavi," the central character is an animal. You will find that each story has a *plot,* or sequence of events. "Zlateh the Goat" has a relatively simple plot. "A Christmas Carol" has a more complicated plot, with many threads to the action. Each story has a location in place and time called the *setting.* One of the stories in this unit is set in the Catskill Mountains in New York State in the late 1700s. Another story takes place in nineteenth-century India. Every story is told from a particular *point of view.* In "A Day's Wait," the narrator is a character in the story. In "Rip Van Winkle," the narrator is an observer who knows what each character thinks and feels. In addition to entertaining readers, a short story generally reveals some idea about life or interpretation of experience. This element is called the *theme* of the story. Sometimes the theme is stated directly. Sometimes it is not stated, but may be inferred from the characters and events in the story.

In this unit you will be introduced to these and other basic elements in short stories. The better you understand how these elements work together, the better you will understand and appreciate the storyteller's art.

Here is a brief story that has been read carefully by an experienced reader. The notes in the margin show how this reader thinks in working through a story. Read the story at least twice before proceeding to the analysis on page 205. You may wish to make notes of your own on a separate sheet of paper as you read.

The Dinner Party

MONA GARDNER

Thinking Model

The country is India. A colonial official[1] and his wife are giving a large dinner party. They are seated with their guests—army officers and government attachés[2] and their wives, and a visiting American naturalist[3]—in their spacious dining room, which has a bare marble floor, open rafters and wide glass doors opening onto a veranda.

A spirited discussion springs up between a young girl who insists that women have outgrown the jumping-on-a-chair-at-the-sight-of-a-mouse era and a colonel who says that they haven't.

"A woman's unfailing reaction in any crisis," the colonel says, "is to scream. And while a man may feel like it, he has that ounce more of nerve control than a woman has. And that last ounce is what counts."

The American does not join in the argument but watches the other guests. As he looks, he sees a strange expression come over the face of the hostess. She is staring straight ahead, her muscles contracting slightly. With a slight gesture she summons the native boy standing behind her chair and whispers to him. The boy's eyes widen: he quickly leaves the room.

Of the guests, none except the American notices this or sees the boy place a bowl of milk on the veranda just outside the open doors.

What do I know from the opening paragraph? The setting is India when it was part of the British Empire.

Note the description of the dining room. These details may be important.

A conflict develops between two guests over the subject of self-control.

How is the author going to use this conflict in the story?

What can this expression mean? Why does she look tense?

What would cause the boy's eyes to widen— surprise? alarm? Why does he leave the room quickly? What significance does this action have?

---

1. **colonial official:** When this story was published, in 1942, India was still a British colony.
2. **attachés** (ăt′ə-shāz′, ă-tă′shāz): individuals on the diplomatic staff of an ambassador or a minister to another country.
3. **naturalist:** someone who is a trained observer of animals and plants.

The American comes to with a start. In India, milk in a bowl means only one thing—bait for a snake. He realizes there must be a cobra in the room. He looks up at the rafters—the likeliest place—but they are bare. Three corners of the room are empty, and in the fourth the servants are waiting to serve the next course. There is only one place left—under the table.

His first impulse is to jump back and warn the others, but he knows the commotion would frighten the cobra into striking. He speaks quickly, the tone of his voice so arresting that it sobers everyone.

"I want to know just what control everyone at this table has. I will count to three hundred—that's five minutes—and not one of you is to move a muscle. Those who move will forfeit[4] fifty rupees.[5] Ready!"

The twenty people sit like stone images while he counts. He is saying, ". . . two hundred and eighty . . ." when, out of the corner of his eye, he sees the cobra emerge and make for the bowl of milk. Screams ring out as he jumps to slam the veranda doors safely shut.

"You were right, Colonel!" the host exclaims. "A man has just shown us an example of perfect control."

"Just a minute," the American says, turning to his hostess. "Mrs. Wynnes, how did you know that cobra was in the room?"

A faint smile lights up the woman's face as she replies: "Because it was crawling across my foot."

4. **forfeit** (fôr′fĭt): give up, as a penalty.
5. **rupees** (r$\overline{oo}$-pēz′, r$\overline{oo}$′pēz): The rupee is the basic monetary unit of India, like the dollar in the United States.

As a trained observer, the naturalist would know the habits of snakes.

He logically figures out where the snake must be.
The author heightens the suspense. What will the naturalist do?

What is he going to say?

He invents a game to test their self-control.

Suspense mounts. Will the cobra strike?

Now I know why I needed a clear picture of the scene.

The host interprets the incident as a victory for the colonel's position.

There is one piece of unexplained business.

The ending of the story resolves the conflict in a surprising, yet totally acceptable way. How has the author prepared me for this ending?

Analysis

"The Dinner Party" is clearly a story of plot rather than character. Although two of the characters show remarkable courage and self-control, we are not interested in them as people as much as we are in the situation that confronts them. It is not surprising that only one character is given a name; the author realizes that it is the exciting and suspenseful plot that will hold the reader's interest.

The opening paragraph gives us all the background information we need. The setting is India in the days before independence. The scene is the home of a colonial official. The spacious dining room that opens onto a veranda seems to belong to a large, imposing house. The characters are all, with one exception, associated with the military and the civil service. The exception is an American naturalist. His profession, it turns out, is of great importance to the events of the story.

The action gets under way when two of the guests take opposing positions on the subject of women's reactions to crises. One of the guests, a young girl, argues against the stereotype of female timidity. Her opponent, a colonel, takes the position that a man has superior nerve control. It is this conflict that sets in motion the major action of the story.

At first, the events seem to bear out the truth of the colonel's statement. The American, trained by his profession to be a close observer, notes a strange expression on his hostess' face. He watches her summon the native boy. The communication is obviously significant, for the boy's eyes show concern. When the bowl of milk is placed on the veranda, the naturalist knows that there is a cobra in the room. After looking all over the room, he realizes that it must be under the table.

As the story builds to its climax, the naturalist behaves exactly as the colonel has said a man would behave in a crisis. He maintains masterful control over his own emotions, and he takes command of the situation. He knows that any movement might cause the cobra to strike. To ensure the safety of everyone at the table, he must bring all activity to a dead halt. He achieves this by challenging the others to a test of self-control. For five minutes, no one is to move a muscle. He begins counting to three hundred. Suspense mounts. When the time is almost expired, he sees the cobra moving toward the bowl of milk. Once again he acts quickly, shutting the veranda doors behind the snake.

Just as the reader is on the verge of agreeing with the colonel—that in a crisis men can be counted on to exercise self-control—the tables turn. We learn that quite simply and undramatically, a woman has shown incredible control, maintaining complete composure while a snake was crawling across her foot. Realizing her own danger and the danger of everyone else at the table, she averted a panic by setting bait—a bowl of milk—to draw the cobra toward the open porch.

While the ending comes as a delightful surprise, contrasting with the reader's expectations, the author has planned for it carefully. The earlier events now fall into place: the strange expression on the hostess' face, the contracting of her facial muscles, her whispered instructions to the native boy, his expression of alarm. Because the author has laid these clues, we are prepared to accept the outcome of events. We do not feel that we have been tricked. On the contrary, we find the conclusion wholly satisfying.

This analysis of "The Dinner Party" tells more than the events of the story as they happen. It analyzes the *structure* of the story, making apparent the interconnection between setting, characters, and events. It explains how the major action of the story—the naturalist's demonstration of "perfect control"—is related to the conflict between the guests at the dinner table. It demonstrates how events build toward a point of great intensity—the climax. It shows how the ending of the story resolves the conflict in an unexpected way, by overturning the colonel's prejudice.

The purpose of this exercise has been to demonstrate what is meant by the *close reading* of a story. When you read a story carefully, you read actively, responding to clues, anticipating outcomes, seeking to understand how different elements are related to the overall structure of the story.

With practice you can develop skill in reading and analyzing a literary work. Here are some guidelines for reading a short story.

Guidelines for Reading a Short Story

1. *Read for both enjoyment and understanding.* An imaginative work of fiction can yield pleasure and can also provide us with insight into ourselves and others. Keep both objects in mind as you read.

2. *Look up unfamiliar words and references.* In Mona Gardner's story, the word *naturalist* (which is defined in a footnote) is a key word. It lets the reader know that the American is a trained observer. In this way you are prepared for the American's actions. If you feel uncertain about the meaning of a word and cannot get the meaning from context clues, be sure to check in a standard dictionary or other reference work.

3. *Learn to draw inferences about the characters and events.* Some information may be provided directly, but most often information about characters will be revealed indirectly through thoughts, feelings, actions, and through the reactions of other characters.

4. *Actively question the author's purpose and method.* Ask yourself what significance there might be to details that the author gives you. In the opening paragraph of "The Dinner Party," for example, Mona Gardner gives the reader a clear picture of the dining room, emphasizing details that she will return to later in the story. Very early on, she indicates that the conflict of the story will have something to do with self-control. This alerts you, the reader, to anticipate what is coming.

5. *Probe for the central idea or point.* "The Dinner Party" is an example of literature that is written wholly for entertainment. Other stories that you will read in this unit offer more than an entertaining and clever plot. They also have something to say about life or human nature. This underlying meaning, which is called *theme,* is seldom stated directly. Generally it must be inferred from the characters and their actions.

The Erne from the Coast

T. O. BEACHCROFT

The term plot *refers to the sequence of incidents or actions in a story—whatever the characters do or whatever happens to them. The most important element in a plot is* conflict. *In this story, note how the action builds toward an exciting* climax.

I

"Where's Harry?" Mr. Thorburn came out of the back of the farmhouse. He stood in the middle of the well-kept farmyard. "Here, Harry!" he shouted. "Hi, Harry!"

He stood leaning on a stick and holding a letter in his hand as he looked round the farmyard.

Mr. Thorburn was a red-faced, powerful man; he wore knee breeches and black leather gaiters.[1] His face and well-fleshed body told you at a glance that Thorburn's Farm had not done too badly during the twenty years of his married life.

Harry, a fair-haired boy, came running across the yard.

"Harry," said the farmer to his son, "here's a letter come for old Michael. It will be about this visit he's to pay to his sick brother.

1. **gaiters:** coverings worn over shoes, and sometimes, as here, the calves of the legs.

Nice time of year for this to happen, I must say. You'd better take the letter to him at once."

"Where to?" said Harry.

"He's up on the hill, of course," said the farmer. "In his hut, or with the sheep somewhere. Your own brains could have told you that. Can't you ever use them? Go on, now."

"Right," said Harry. He turned to go.

"Don't take all day," said his father.

Mr. Thorburn stood looking after his son. He leaned heavily on the thorn stick which he always carried. Harry went through the gate in the low gray wall which ran round one side of the yard, where there were no buildings. Directly he left the farmyard, he began to climb. Thorburn's Farm was at the end of a valley. Green fields lay in front of it, and a wide road sloped gently down to the village a mile away; behind, the hill soared up, and high on the ridge of the hill was Michael's hut, three miles off, and climbing all the way.

Harry was thirteen, very yellow-haired and blue-eyed. He was a slip of a boy. It seemed unlikely that he could ever grow into such a stolid, heavy man as his father. Mr. Thorburn was every pound of fourteen stone,[2] as the men on the farm could have told you the day he broke his leg and they had to carry him back to the farmhouse on a hurdle.[3]

Harry started off far too fast, taking the lower slopes almost at a run. His body was loose in its movements, and coltish, and by the time the real work began he was already tiring. However, the April day was fresh and rainy, and the cold of it kept him going. Gray gusts and showers swept over the hillside, and between them, with changing light, came faint gleams of sunshine, so that the shadows of the clouds raced along the hill beside him. Pres-

ently he cleared the gorse and heather[4] and came out on to the open hillside, which was bare except for short, tussocky grass.[5] His home began to look far-off beneath him. He could see his mother walking down towards the village with one of the dogs, and the baker's cart coming up from the village towards her. The fields were brown and green round the farmhouse, and the buildings were gray, with low stone walls.

He stopped several times to look back on the small distant farm. It took him well over an hour to reach the small hut where Michael lived by day and slept during most nights throughout the lambing season. He was not in his hut, but after a few minutes' search Harry found him. Michael was sitting without movement, watching the sheep and talking to his gray-and-white dog. He had a sack across his

2. **stone:** a unit of weight used in Great Britain, equal to 14 pounds (about 6 kilograms).
3. **hurdle:** here, a movable framework of twigs, used to enclose sheep.

4. **gorse and heather** (hĕ*th*′ər): low-growing shrubs found in the highlands of Great Britain.
5. **tussocky** (tŭs′ək-ē) **grass:** grass growing in clumps.

The Erne from the Coast   **209**

shoulders, which made him look rather like a rock with gray lichen on it. He looked up at Harry without moving.

"It's a hildy wildy day," he said, "but there'll be a glent of sunsheen yet."

Harry handed Michael the letter. Michael looked at it, and opened it very slowly, and spread the crackling paper out on his knee with brown hands. Harry watched him for some minutes as he studied the letter in silence.

"Letter'll be aboot my brother," said Michael at length. "I'm to goa and see him." He handed the letter to Harry. "Read it, Harry," he said. Harry read the letter to him twice.

"Tell thy dad," said Michael, "I'll be doon at farm i' the morn. Happen[6] I'll be away three days. And tell him new lamb was born last neet, but it's sickly."

They looked at the small white bundle that lay on the grass beside its mother, hardly moving.

" 'T'll pick up," said Michael. He slowly stood and looked round at the distance.

Michael had rather long hair; it was between gray and white in color, and it blew in the wind. It was about the hue of an old sheep's skull that has lain out on the bare mountain. Michael's clothes and face and hair made Harry feel that he had slowly faded out on the hillside. He was all the color of rain on the stones and last year's bracken.[7]

"It'll make a change," said Michael, "going off and sleeping in a bed."

"Goodbye," said Harry. "You'll be down at the farm tomorrow, then?"

"Aw reet," said Michael.

"Aw reet," said Harry.

Harry went slowly back to the farm. The rain had cleared off, and the evening was sunny, with a watery light, by the time he was home. Michael had been right. Harry gave his father the message, and told him about the lamb.

"It's a funny thing," said Harry, "that old Michael can't even read."

"Don't you be so smart." said Mr. Thorburn. "Michael knows a thing or two you don't. You don't want to go muckering about with[8] an old fellow like Michael—best shepherd I've ever known."

Harry went away feeling somewhat abashed. Lately it seemed his father was always down on him, telling him he showed no sign of sense; telling him he ought to grow up a bit; telling him he was more like seven than thirteen.

He went to the kitchen. This was a big stone-floored room with a huge plain table, where the whole household and several of the farm hands could sit down to dinner or tea at the same time. His mother and his aunt from the village were still lingering over their teacups, but there was no one else in the room except a small tortoise-shell cat, which was pacing

6. **Happen:** perhaps.
7. **bracken:** coarse ferns. "Last year's bracken" would be dried out and therefore brownish in color.

8. **muckering about with:** getting in the way of; hindering.

round them asking for milk in a loud voice. The yellow evening light filled the room. His mother gave him tea and ham and bread and butter, and he ate it in silence, playing with the cat as he did so.

II

Next morning at nine o'clock there was a loud rap with a stick at the kitchen door, and there by the pump, with the hens running round his legs, stood Michael.

"Good morning, Mrs. Thorburn," he said. "Is Measter about?"

"Come on in with you," said Mrs. Thorburn, "and have a good hot cup o' tea. Have you eaten this morning?"

Michael clanked into the kitchen, his hobnails striking the flags,[9] and he sat down at one end of the table.

"Aye," he said, "I've eaten, Missus. I had a good thoom-bit[10] when I rose up, but a cup of tea would be welcome."

As he drank the tea, Mr. Thorburn came in, bringing Harry with him. Michael, thought Harry, always looked rather strange when he was down in the village or in the farmhouse; rather as a pile of bracken or an armful of leaves would look if it were emptied out onto the parlor floor.

Michael talked to Mr. Thorburn about the sheep; about the new lamb; about young Bob, his nephew, who was coming over from another farm to look after the sheep while he was away.

"Tell en to watch new lamb." said Michael; "it's creachy.[11] I've put en in my little hut, and owd sheep is looking roun' t' doorway."

After his cup of tea Michael shook hands all

round. Then he set off down to the village, where he was going to fall in with a lift.

Soon after he had gone, Bob arrived at the farm. He was a tall young man with a freckled face and red hair, big-boned and very gentle in his voice and movements. He listened to all Mr. Thorburn's instructions and then set out for the shepherd's hut.

However, it seemed that Mr. Thorburn's luck with his shepherds was dead out. For the next evening, just as it was turning dark, Bob walked into the farmhouse kitchen. His face was tense with pain, and he was nursing his left arm with his right hand. Harry saw the ugly distorted shape and swelling at the wrist. Bob had fallen and broken the wrist earlier in the day, and by evening the pain had driven him back.

"I'm sorry, Mr. Thorburn," he kept on saying. "I'm a big fule."

The sheep had to be left for that night. Next morning it was again a cold, windy day, and clouds the color of gunmetal raced over the hill. The sun broke through fitfully, filling the valley with a steel-blue light in which the green grass looked vivid. Mr. Thorburn decided to send Harry out to the shepherd's hut for the day and night.

"Happen old Michael will be back sometime tomorrow," he said. "You can look to the sheep, Harry, and see to that sick lamb for us. It's a good chance to make yourself useful."

Harry nodded.

"You can feed the lamb. Bob said it didn't seem to suck enough, and you can let me know if anything else happens. And you can keep an eye on the other lambs and see they don't get over the edges. There's no need to fold them at night; just let the dog round them up and see the flock is near the hut."

"There's blankets and everything in the hut, Harry," said Mrs. Thorburn, "and a spirit lamp to make tea. You can't come to harm."

---

9. **flags:** here, flagstones, which are used in paving.
10. **thoom-bit:** a piece of meat eaten on bread.
11. **creachy:** sick.

Harry set off up the hill and began to climb. Out on the hilltop it was very lonely, and the wind was loud and gusty, with sudden snatches of rain. The sheep kept near the wooden hut most of the time; it was built in the lee[12] of the ridge, and the best shelter was to be found near it. Harry looked after the sick lamb and brewed himself tea. He had Tassie, the gray and white sheep dog, for company. Time did not hang heavy. When evening came he rounded up the sheep and counted them, and, true to advice that Michael had given him, he slept in his boots as a true shepherd does, warmly wrapped up in the rugs.

He was awakened as soon as it was light by the dog barking. He went out in the gray dawn light and found a rustle and agitation among the sheep. Tassie ran to him and back towards the sheep. The sheep were starting up alert, and showed a tendency to scatter. Harry looked round, wondering what the trouble was. Then he saw. A bird was hovering over the flock, and it was this that had attracted the sheep's attention. But what bird was it? It hovered like a hawk, soaring on outstretched wings; yet it was much too big for a hawk. As the bird came nearer Harry was astonished at its size. Once or twice it approached and then went soaring and floating away again. It was larger than any bird he had ever seen before—brownish in color, with a gray head and a hawk's beak.

Suddenly the bird began to drop as a hawk drops. A knot of sheep dashed apart. Tassie rushed towards the bird, his head down and his tail streaming out behind him. Harry followed. This must be an eagle, he thought. He saw it, looking larger still now it was on the ground, standing with outstretched wings over a lamb.

Tassie attacked, snarling in rage. The eagle rose at him. It struck at him with its feet and a flurry of beating wings. The dog was thrown back. He retreated slowly, snarling savagely as he went, his tail between his legs. He was frightened now, and uncertain what to do.

The eagle turned back to the lamb, took it in its talons again, and began to rise. It could not move quickly near the ground, and Harry came up with it. At once the eagle put the lamb on a rock and turned on him. He saw its talons driving towards his face, claws and spurs of steel—a stroke could tear your eyes out. He put up his arms in fear, and he felt the rush of wings round his face. With his arm above his head he sank on one knee.

When he looked up again, the eagle was back on the lamb. It began to fly with long slow wingbeats. At first it scarcely rose, and flew with the lamb almost on the ground.

Harry ran, throwing a stone. He shouted. Tassie gave chase, snapping at the eagle as it went. But the eagle was working towards a chasm, a sheer drop in the hillside where no one could follow it. In another moment it was floating in the air, clear and away. Then it rose higher, and headed towards the coast, which was a few miles away over the hill.

Harry stood and watched it till it was out of sight. When it was gone, he turned and walked slowly back to the hut. There was not a sound to be heard now except the sudden rushes of wind. The hillside was bare and coverless except for the scattered black rocks. Tassie walked beside him. The dog was very subdued and hardly glanced to right or left.

It took some time to round the sheep up, or to find, at least, where the various parts of the flock had scattered themselves. The sick lamb and its mother had been enclosed all this time in a fold near the hut. The ewe[13] was still terrified.

12. **in the lee:** on the protected side.

13. **ewe** (yōō): a female sheep.

An hour later Harry set off down the mountainside to the farm. Tassie looked after him doubtfully. He ran several times after him, but Harry sent him back to the hut.

It was the middle of the morning when Harry came back to the farmyard again. His father was standing in the middle of the yard, leaning on his stick, and giving advice to one of his cowmen. He broke off when he saw Harry come in through the gate and walk towards him across the farmyard.

"Well," he said, "anything wrong, Harry? I thought you were going to stay till Michael came back."

"We've lost a lamb," said Harry, breathlessly. "It's been carried off by an eagle. It must have been an eagle."

"An eagle?" said Mr. Thorburn. He gave a laugh which mocked Harry. "Why didn't you stop it?"

"I tried," said Harry. "But I . . ."

Mr. Thorburn was in a bad mood. He had sold some heifers[14] the day before at a disappointing price. He had had that morning a letter from the builders about repairs to some of the farm buildings, and there was work to be done which he could hardly afford. He was worried about Michael's absence. He felt as if the world were bearing down on him and he had too many burdens to support.

He suddenly shouted at Harry, and his red face turned darker red.

"That's a lie!" he said. "There's been no eagle here in my lifetime. What's happened? Go on—tell me."

Harry stood before him. He looked at his father, but said nothing.

"You've lost that lamb," said Thorburn. "Let it fall down a hole or something. Any child from the village could have watched those sheep for a day. Then you're frightened and

14. **heifers** (hĕf'ərz): young cows.

come back here and lie to me."

Harry still said nothing.

"Come here," said Thorburn suddenly. He caught him by the arm and turned him round. "I'll teach you not to lie to me," he said. He raised his stick and hit Harry as hard as he could; then again and again.

"It's true," began Harry, and then cried out with pain at the blows.

At the third or fourth blow he wrenched himself away. Thorburn let him go. Harry walked away as fast as he could, through the gate and out of the yard without looking round.

"Next time it will be a real beating," his father shouted after him. "Bring the eagle back, and then I'll believe you."

III

As soon as Harry was through the gate, he turned behind one of the barns where he was out of sight from the yard. He stood trembling and clenching his fists. He found there were tears on his face, and he forced himself not to cry. The blows hurt, yet they did not hurt very seriously. He would never have cried for that. But it had been done in front of another man. The other man had looked on, and he and his father had been laughing as he had almost run away. Harry clenched his fists; even now they were still talking about him.

He began to walk and then run up the hillside toward the hut. When he reached it, he was exhausted. He flung himself on the mattress and punched it again and again and clenched his teeth.

The day passed and nobody came from the farm. He began to feel better, and presently a new idea struck him, and with it a new hope. He prayed now that old Michael would not return today; that he would be able to spend another night alone in the hut; and that the eagle would come back next morning and attack the sheep again, and give him one more chance.

Harry went out and scanned the gray sky, and then knelt down on the grass and prayed for the eagle to come. Tassie, the gray and white sheep dog, looked at him questioningly. Soon it was getting dark, and he walked about the hill and rounded up the sheep. He counted the flock, and all was well. Then he looked round for a weapon. There was no gun in the hut, but he found a thick stave[15] tipped with metal, part of some broken tool that had been thrown aside. He poised the stave in his hand and swung it; it was just a good weight to hit with. He would have to go straight at the eagle without hesitation and break its skull. After thinking about this for some time, he made himself tea, and ate some bread and butter and cold meat.

Down at the farm Mr. Thorburn in the evening told his wife what had happened. He was quite sure there had been no eagle. Mrs. Thorburn did not say much, but she said it was an extraordinary thing for Harry to have said. She told her husband that he ought not to have beaten the boy, but should have found out what the trouble really was.

"But I dare say there is no great harm done," she ended, philosophically.

Harry spent a restless night. He slept and lay awake by turns, but, sleeping or waking, he was tortured by the same old images. He saw all the events of the day before. He saw how the eagle had first appeared above him; how it had attacked; how it had driven off Tassie and then him. He remembered his fear, and he planned again just how he could attack the eagle when it came back. Then he thought of himself going down towards the farm, and he saw again the scene with his father.

15. **stave:** a stick of wood.

All night long he saw these pictures and other scenes from his life. In every one of them he had made some mistake; he had made himself look ridiculous, and grown men had laughed at him. He had failed in strength or in common sense; he was always disappointing himself and his father. He was too young for his age. He was still a baby.

So the night passed. Early in the morning he heard Tassie barking.

He jumped up, fully clothed, and ran outside the hut. The cold air made him shiver; but he saw at once that his prayer had been answered. There was the eagle, above him, and already dropping down towards the sheep. It floated, poised on huge wings. The flock stood nervously huddled. Suddenly, as before, the attacker plunged towards them. They scattered, running in every direction. The eagle followed and swooped on one weakly running lamb. At once it tried to rise again, but its heavy wingbeats took it along the earth. Near the ground it seemed cumbersome and awkward. Tassie was after it like a flash; Harry seized his weapon, the stave tipped with iron, and followed. When Tassie caught up with the eagle it turned and faced him, standing over the lamb.

Harry, as he ran, could see blood staining the white wool of the lamb's body; the eagle's wings were half spread out over it and moving slowly. The huge bird was grayish-brown with a white head and tail. The beak was yellow and the legs yellow and scaly.

It lowered its head, and with a fierce movement threatened Tassie; then, as the dog approached, it began to rock and stamp from foot to foot in a menacing dance; then it opened its beak and gave its fierce, yelping cry. Tassie hung back, his ears flattened against his head, snarling, creeping by inches towards the eagle; he was frightened, but he was brave. Then he ran in to attack.

The eagle left the lamb. With a lunging spring it aimed heavily at Tassie. It just cleared the ground and beat about Tassie with its wings, hovering over him. Tassie flattened out his body to the earth and turned his head upwards with snapping jaws. But the eagle was over him and on him, its talons plunged into his side, and a piercing scream rang out. The eagle struck deliberately at the dog's skull three times; the beak's point hammered on his head, striking downwards and sideways. Tassie lay limp on the ground, and, where his head had been, a red mixture of blood and brains flowed on the grass. When Harry took his eyes away from the blood, the eagle was standing on the lamb again.

Harry approached the eagle slowly, step by step. He gripped his stick firmly as he came. The eagle put its head down. It rocked on its feet as if preparing to leap. Behind the terrific beak, sharp as metal, was a shallow head, flat and broad as a snake's, glaring with light yellow un-animal eyes. The head and neck made weaving movements towards him.

At a pace or two from the eagle Harry stood still. In a second he would make a rush. He could break the eagle's skull, he told himself, with one good blow; then he could avenge Tassie and stand up to his father.

But he waited too long. The eagle tried to rise, and with its heavy sweeping beats was beginning to gain speed along the ground. Harry ran, stumbling over the uneven ground, among boulders and outcroppings of rock, trying to strike at the eagle as he went. But as soon as the eagle was in the air it was no longer heavy and clumsy. There was a sudden rush of wings and buffeting about his head as the eagle turned to drive him off. For a second he saw the talons sharp as metal, backed by the metal strength of the legs, striking at his face. He put up his arm. At once it was seared with a red-hot pain, and he could see the blood rush out.

He stepped back, and back again. The eagle, after this one fierce swoop at him, went round in a wide, low circle and returned to the lamb. Harry saw that his coat sleeve was in ribbons, and that blood was running off the ends of his fingers and falling to the ground.

He stood panting; the wind blew across the empty high ground. The sheep had vanished from sight. Tassie lay dead nearby, and he was utterly alone on the hills. There was nobody to watch what he did. The eagle might hurt him, but it could not jeer at him. He attacked it again, but already the eagle with its heavy wingbeats had cleared the ground; this time it took the lamb with it. Harry saw that it meant to fly, as it had flown yesterday, to an edge; and then out into the free air over the chasm, and over the valley far below.

Harry gave chase, stumbling over the broken ground and between the boulders—striking at the eagle as he went, trying to beat it down before it could escape. The eagle was hampered by his attack; and suddenly it swooped onto a projection of rock and turned again to drive him off. Harry was now in a bad position. The eagle stood on a rock at the height of his own shoulders, with the lamb beside it. It struck at his chest with its talons, beating its wings as it did so. Harry felt clothes and flesh being torn; buffeting blows began about his head, but he kept close to the eagle and struck at it again. He did not want simply to frighten it away, but to kill it. The eagle fought at first simply to drive Harry off; then, as he continued to attack, it became ferocious.

Harry saw his only chance was to keep close to the eagle and beat it down; but already it was at the height of his face. It struck at him from above, driving its steel claws at him, beating its wings about him. He was dazed by the buffeting which went on and on all round him; then with an agonizing stab he felt the claws seize and pierce his shoulder and neck. He

struck upwards desperately and blindly. As the eagle drove its beak at his head, his stick just turned the blow aside. The beak struck a glancing blow off the stick and tore away his eyebrow.

Harry found that something was blinding him, and he felt a new sickening fear that already one of his eyes was gone. The outspread beating wings and weight of the eagle dragged him about, and he nearly lost his footing. He had forgotten, now, that he was proving anything to his father; he was fighting for his eyes. Three times he fended off the hammer stroke of the beak, and at these close quarters the blows of his club found their mark. He caught the eagle's head each time, and the bird was half stunned.

Harry, reeling and staggering, felt the grip of the claws gradually loosen, and almost unbelievably the body of his enemy sagged, half fluttering to the ground. With a sudden spurt of new strength, Harry attacked and rained blows on the bird's skull. The eagle struggled, and he followed, beating it down among the rocks. At last the eagle's movements stopped. He saw its skull was broken and that it lay dead.

He stood for many minutes panting and unmoving, filled with a tremendous excitement; then he sat on a boulder. The fight had taken him near a steep edge a long way from the body of Tassie.

His wounds began to ache and burn. The sky and the horizon spun round him, but he forced himself to be firm and collected. After a while he stooped down and hoisted the eagle onto his shoulder. The wings dropped loosely down in front and behind. He set off towards the farm.

IV

When he reached his home, the low gray walls, the plowed fields, and the green pasture fields were swimming before his eyes in a dizzy pattern. It was still the early part of the morning, but there was plenty of life in the farmyard, as usual. Some cows were being driven out. One of the carthorses was standing harnessed to a heavy wagon. Harry's father was talking to the carter and looking at the horse's leg.

When they saw Harry come towards them, they waited, unmoving. They could hardly see at first who or what it was. Harry came up and dropped the bird at his father's feet. His coat was gone. His shirt hung in bloodstained rags about him; one arm was caked in blood; his right eyebrow hung in a loose flap, with the blood still oozing stickily down his cheek.

"Harry!" said Thorburn, catching him by the arm as he reeled.

He led the boy into the kitchen. There they gave him a glass of brandy and sponged him with warm water. There was a deep long wound in his left forearm. His chest was criss-crossed with cuts. The flesh was torn away from his neck where the talons had sunk in.

Presently the doctor came. Harry's wounds began to hurt like fire, but he talked excitedly. He was happier than he had ever been in his life. Everybody on the farm came in to see him and to see the eagle's body.

All day his father hung about him, looking into the kitchen every half-hour. He said very little but asked Harry several times how he felt. "Are you aw reet?" he kept saying. Once he took a cup of tea from his wife and carried it across the kitchen in order to give it to Harry with his own hands.

Later in the day old Michael came back, and Harry told him the whole story. Michael turned the bird over. He said it was an erne, a white-tailed sea eagle from the coast. He measured the wingspan, and it was seven and a half feet. Michael had seen two or three when he was a boy—always near the coast—but this one, he said, was easily the largest.

Three days later Mr. Thorburn took Harry, still stiff and bandaged, down to the village inn. There he set him before a blazing fire all the evening, and in the presence of men from every cottage and farm Thorburn praised his son. He bought him a glass of beer and made Harry tell the story of his fight to everyone.

As he told it, Thorburn sat by him, hearing the story himself each time, making certain that Harry missed nothing about his struggle. Afterwards every man drank Harry's health, and clapped Thorburn on the back and told him he ought to be proud of his son.

Later, in the silent darkness, they walked back to the farm again, and neither of them could find anything to say. Harry wondered if his father might not refer to the beating and apologize. Thorburn moved round the house, raking out fires and locking up. Then he picked up the lamp and, holding it above his head, led the way upstairs.

"Good night, Harry," said his father at last, as he took him to his bedroom door. "Are you aw reet?"

His father held the lamp up and looked into Harry's face. As the lamplight fell on it, he nodded. He said nothing more.

"Aye," said Harry, as he turned into his bedroom door, "I'm aw reet."

Reading Check

1. At what time of year does the story take place?
2. How is Michael employed by Mr. Thorburn?
3. Why does Michael have to leave?
4. Why is Bob unable to look after the flock?
5. Why does Mr. Thorburn beat Harry?
6. Who or what is Tassie?
7. What is unusual about the eagle in this story?
8. Where does Harry's battle with the eagle take place?
9. What weapon does Harry use against the bird?
10. Why is Harry happy at the end of the story?

Analyzing and Interpreting the Story

1. Some characters are the same at the end of a story as they are at the beginning. Other characters change as a result of the experiences they undergo. At the beginning of this story, Harry has no confidence in himself. How do you know at the end of the story that he has changed?

2. Taking care of the sheep is not Harry's responsibility. How does he come to assume that job?

3. From Harry's point of view, "his father was always down on him, telling him he showed no sign of sense; telling him he ought to grow up a bit; telling him he was more like seven than thirteen" (page 210). Find three incidents in the story that confirm Harry's judgment.

4. After Mr. Thorburn beats Harry, you learn that "the blows hurt, yet they did not hurt very seriously. He would never have cried for that." Why, then, are there tears on Harry's face?

5a. Why does Harry pray for the eagle to return? **b.** What does Harry find out about himself during the restless night he spends on the mountain?

6. When Harry and his father return from the village inn, Harry wonders if his father will apologize for beating him. Has Mr. Thorburn already apologized in some way? Explain.

7. Harry wins two victories in this story. What are they?

Literary Elements

Understanding Conflict and Plot

Conflict

In most stories the characters are involved in some sort of problem or struggle called a **con-flict.** Sometimes the characters are involved in more than one conflict.

A conflict with a person, with an animal, or with some force of nature is known as an **external conflict.** What is Harry's conflict with his father? What other external conflict is there in "The Erne from the Coast"?

In addition to these external conflicts, Harry has to overcome his feelings of shame and inadequacy. He also has to struggle against panic when he fights the eagle. Struggles within a character are known as **internal conflicts.**

Plot

The sequence of incidents or actions that make up a story is known as the **plot.** Once the conflict or conflicts of a story have been established, the reader wants to know how things will turn out. The author chooses events that develop the conflict to a peak, or **climax,** and that provide an ending, or **resolution,** to the conflict.

One way to recognize the climax of a story is to look for the moment of most intense, exciting action. Which event is the climax in "The Erne from the Coast"? How does it solve Harry's internal and external conflicts?

Language and Vocabulary

Understanding Dialect

Writers use regional expressions to make the backgrounds and characters of their stories seem authentic. A number of the expressions in Beachcroft's story belong to the **dialect**—the regional variety of English—spoken in the sheep country of Great Britain. The words *thoom-bit* and *creachy* have been defined for you in footnotes. What do you think *hildy-wildy, glent of sunsheen, fule,* and *aw reet* mean?

Writing About Literature

Showing How Conflict Is Developed and Resolved

You have seen that there is more than one conflict in "The Erne from the Coast." Choose one of Harry's conflicts: the conflict with his father, the conflict with the eagle, or his inner conflict. Show how this conflict develops in the story and how it is resolved. Cite specific evidence from the story to support your statements. Plan your essay before writing, and include a *thesis statement,* such as this one:

> Harry's relationship with his father worsens progressively until Harry's courage and determination change his father's attitude.

Descriptive Writing

Describing a Character

A close reading of this paragraph shows that the author has chosen details that create a single impression of Michael. Each descriptive detail shows that Michael blends in with his surroundings:

> Michael had rather long hair; it was between gray and white in color, and it blew in the wind. It was about the hue of an old sheep's skull that has lain out on the bare mountain. Michael's clothes and face and hair made Harry feel that he had slowly faded out on the hillside. He was all the color of rain on the stones and last year's bracken.

Think of someone who might resemble the place where he or she lives or works (perhaps a sea captain, a miner, or safari hunter). List at least three specific ways in which this character resembles his or her surroundings. Write a paragraph describing the character.

To review the elements of good descriptive writing, see *Practice in Reading and Writing,* pages 89–90.

About the Author

T. O. Beachcroft (1902–)

T. O. Beachcroft was born in Clifton, England, and educated at Oxford University. In the 1920s, while he was working for the British Broadcasting Corporation in London, several of his short stories were accepted for publication by literary magazines. This success later prompted him to collect the stories in a book called *A Young Man in a Hurry, and Other Stories* (1934). Since then he has written ten more books, including two studies on the art of the short story.

In *The Modest Art: A Survey of the Short Story in English* (1968), Beachcroft says that a short story often takes very little time to read. "Yet in those few minutes it may enter into the reader's mind, in a way which will never be forgotten. Plainly it must go deep to do this. It is not a trick. It is an encounter between two people—a passage of truth from one mind to another."

The Landlady

ROALD DAHL°

Uncertainty about what will happen next in a story is known as suspense. *To build up suspense, a writer will drop hints about what is to come. This use of clues is called* foreshadowing. *Watch for clues as you read Dahl's story.*

Billy Weaver had traveled down from London on the slow afternoon train, with a change at Reading on the way, and by the time he got to Bath it was about nine o'clock in the evening and the moon was coming up out of a clear starry sky over the houses opposite the station entrance. But the air was deadly cold and the wind was like a flat blade of ice on his cheeks.

"Excuse me," he said, "but is there a fairly cheap hotel not too far away from here?"

"Try The Bell and Dragon," the porter answered, pointing down the road. "They might take you in. It's about a quarter of a mile along on the other side."

Billy thanked him and picked up his suitcase and set out to walk the quarter-mile to The Bell and Dragon. He had never been to Bath before. He didn't know anyone who lived there. But Mr. Greenslade at the Head Office in London had told him it was a splendid town. "Find your own lodgings," he had said, "and then go along and report to the Branch Man-

ager as soon as you've got yourself settled."

Billy was seventeen years old. He was wearing a new navy-blue overcoat, a new brown trilby hat,[1] and a new brown suit, and he was feeling fine. He walked briskly down the street. He was trying to do everything briskly these days. Briskness, he had decided, was *the* one common characteristic of all successful businessmen. The big shots up at Head Office were absolutely fantastically brisk all the time. They were amazing.

There were no shops on this wide street that he was walking along, only a line of tall houses on each side, all of them identical. They had porches and pillars and four or five steps going up to their front doors, and it was obvious that once upon a time they had been very swanky residences. But now, even in the darkness, he could see that the paint was peeling from the woodwork on their doors and windows, and that the handsome white façades were cracked and blotchy from neglect.

Suddenly, in a downstairs window that was

° **Roald Dahl** (rōō′äl däl).

1. **trilby hat:** a soft felt hat.

A view of Bath, England.

brilliantly illuminated by a streetlamp not six yards away, Billy caught sight of a printed notice propped up against the glass in one of the upper panes. It said BED AND BREAKFAST. There was a vase of yellow chrysanthemums, tall and beautiful, standing just underneath the notice.

He stopped walking. He moved a bit closer. Green curtains (some sort of velvety material) were hanging down on either side of the window. The chrysanthemums looked wonderful beside them. He went right up and peered through the glass into the room, and the first thing he saw was a bright fire burning in the hearth. On the carpet in front of the fire, a pretty little dachshund was curled up asleep with its nose tucked into its belly. The room it-self, so far as he could see in the half-darkness, was filled with pleasant furniture. There was a baby-grand piano and a big sofa and several plump armchairs; and in one corner he spotted a large parrot in a cage. Animals were usually a good sign in a place like this, Billy told himself; and all in all, it looked to him as though it would be a pretty decent house to stay in. Certainly it would be more comfortable than The Bell and Dragon.

On the other hand, a pub[2] would be more congenial than a boardinghouse. There would be beer and darts in the evenings, and lots of people to talk to, and it would probably be a good bit cheaper, too. He had stayed a couple

2. **pub:** tavern or inn.

The Landlady **221**

of nights in a pub once before and he had liked it. He had never stayed in any boardinghouses, and, to be perfectly honest, he was a tiny bit frightened of them. The name itself conjured up images of watery cabbage, rapacious[3] land-ladies, and a powerful smell of kippers[4] in the living room.

After dithering about[5] like this in the cold for two or three minutes, Billy decided that he would walk on and take a look at The Bell and Dragon before making up his mind. He turned to go.

And now a queer thing happened to him. He was in the act of stepping back and turning away from the window when all at once his eye was caught and held in the most peculiar man-ner by the small notice that was there. BED AND BREAKFAST, it said. BED AND BREAKFAST, BED AND BREAKFAST, BED AND BREAKFAST. Each word was like a large black eye staring at him through the glass, holding him, compelling him, forcing him to stay where he was and not to walk away from that house, and the next thing he knew, he was actually moving across from the window to the front door of the house, climbing the steps that led up to it, and reaching for the bell.

He pressed the bell. Far away in a back room he heard it ringing, and then *at once*—it must have been at once because he hadn't even had time to take his finger from the bell-button—the door swung open and a woman was stand-ing there.

Normally you ring the bell and you have at least a half-minute's wait before the door opens. But this dame was like a jack-in-the-box. He pressed the bell—and out she popped! It made him jump.

She was about forty-five or fifty years old, and the moment she saw him, she gave him a warm welcoming smile.

"*Please* come in," she said pleasantly. She stepped aside, holding the door wide open, and Billy found himself automatically starting forward. The compulsion or, more accurately, the desire to follow after her into that house was extraordinarily strong.

"I saw the notice in the window," he said, holding himself back.

"Yes, I know."

"I was wondering about a room."

"It's *all* ready for you, my dear," she said. She had a round pink face and very gentle blue eyes.

"I was on my way to The Bell and Dragon." Billy told her. "But the notice in your window just happened to catch my eye."

"My dear boy," she said, "why don't you come in out of the cold?"

"How much do you charge?"

"Five and sixpence[6] a night, including breakfast."

It was fantastically cheap. It was less than half of what he had been willing to pay.

"If that is too much," she added, "then per-haps I can reduce it just a tiny bit. Do you de-sire an egg for breakfast? Eggs are expensive at the moment. It would be sixpence less with-out the egg."

"Five and sixpence is fine," he answered. "I should like very much to stay here."

"I knew you would. Do come in."

She seemed terribly nice. She looked exactly like the mother of one's best school friend wel-coming one into the house to stay for the Christmas holidays. Billy took off his hat, and stepped over the threshold.

"Just hang it there," she said, "and let me help you with your coat."

3. **rapacious** (rə-pā′shəs): greedy; also, living on prey.
4. **kippers:** dried or smoked fish, regularly eaten for breakfast in Great Britain.
5. **dithering about:** hesitating.

6. **Five and sixpence:** about seventy-five cents at the time of the story.

There were no other hats or coats in the hall. There were no umbrellas, no walking sticks—nothing.

"We have it *all* to ourselves," she said, smiling at him over her shoulder as she led the way upstairs. "You see, it isn't very often I have the pleasure of taking a visitor into my little nest."

The old girl is slightly dotty, Billy told himself. But at five and sixpence a night, who gives a hang about that? "I should've thought you'd be simply swamped with applicants," he said politely.

"Oh, I am, my dear, I am, of course I am. But the trouble is that I'm inclined to be just a teeny-weeny bit choosy and particular—if you see what I mean."

"Ah, yes."

"But I'm always ready. Everything is always ready day and night in this house just on the off chance that an acceptable young gentleman will come along. And it is such a pleasure, my dear, such a very great pleasure when now and again I open the door and I see someone standing there who is just *exactly* right." She was halfway up the stairs, and she paused with one hand on the stair rail, turning her head and smiling down at him with pale lips. "Like you," she added, and her blue eyes traveled slowly all the way down the length of Bill's body, to his feet, and then up again.

On the second-floor landing she said to him, "This floor is mine."

They climbed up another flight. "And this one is *all* yours," she said. "Here's your room. I do hope you'll like it." She took him into a small but charming front bedroom, switching on the light as she went in.

"The morning sun comes right in the window, Mr. Perkins. It *is* Mr. Perkins, isn't it?"

"No," he said. "It's Weaver."

"Mr. Weaver. How nice. I've put a water bottle between the sheets to air them out, Mr. Weaver. It's such a comfort to have a hot water bottle in a strange bed with clean sheets, don't you agree? And you may light the gas fire at any time if you feel chilly."

"Thank you," Billy said. "Thank you ever so much." He noticed that the bedspread had been taken off the bed, and that the bedclothes had been neatly turned back on one side, all ready for someone to get in.

"I'm so glad you appeared," she said, looking earnestly into his face. "I was beginning to get worried."

"That's all right," Billy answered brightly. "You mustn't worry about me." He put his suitcase on the chair and started to open it.

"And what about supper, my dear? Did you manage to get anything to eat before you came here?"

"I'm not a bit hungry, thank you," he said. "I think I'll just go to bed as soon as possible because tomorrow I've got to get up rather early and report to the office."

"Very well, then. I'll leave you now so that you can unpack. But before you go to bed, would you be kind enough to pop into the sitting room on the ground floor and sign the book? Everyone has to do that because it's the law of the land, and we don't want to go breaking any laws at *this* stage in the proceedings, do we?" She gave him a little wave of the hand and went quickly out of the room and closed the door.

Now, the fact that his landlady appeared to be slightly off her rocker didn't worry Billy in the least. After all, she not only was harmless—there was no question about that—but she was also quite obviously a kind and generous soul. He guessed that she had probably lost a son in the war, or something like that, and had never gotten over it.

So a few minutes later, after unpacking his suitcase and washing his hands, he trotted downstairs to the ground floor and entered the living room. His landlady wasn't there, but the fire was glowing in the hearth, and the little dachshund was still sleeping soundly in front of it. The room was wonderfully warm and cozy. I'm a lucky fellow, he thought, rubbing his hands. This is a bit of all right.

He found the guest book lying open on the piano, so he took out his pen and wrote down his name and address. There were only two other entries above his on the page, and, as one always does with guest books, he started to read them. One was a Christopher Mulholland from Cardiff. The other was Gregory W. Temple from Bristol.

That's funny, he thought suddenly. Christopher Mulholland. It rings a bell.

Now where on earth had he heard that rather unusual name before?

Was it a boy at school? No. Was it one of his sister's numerous young men, perhaps, or a friend of his father's? No, no, it wasn't any of those. He glanced down again at the book.

Christopher Mulholland
          231 Cathedral Road, Cardiff
Gregory W. Temple
          27 Sycamore Drive, Bristol

As a matter of fact, now he came to think of it, he wasn't at all sure that the second name didn't have almost as much of a familiar ring about it as the first.

"Gregory Temple?" he said aloud, searching his memory. "Christopher Mulholland? . . ."

"Such charming boys," a voice behind him answered, and he turned and saw his landlady sailing into the room with a large silver tea tray in her hands. She was holding it well out in front of her, and rather high up, as though the tray were a pair of reins on a frisky horse.

"They sound somehow familiar," he said.

"They do? How interesting."

"I'm almost positive I've heard those names before somewhere. Isn't that odd? Maybe it was in the newspapers. They weren't famous in any way, were they? I mean famous cricketers[7] or footballers or something like that?"

"Famous," she said, setting the tea tray down on the low table in front of the sofa. "Oh no, I don't think they were famous. But they were incredibly handsome, both of them, I can promise you that. They were tall and young and handsome, my dear, just exactly like you."

Once more, Billy glanced down at the book. "Look here," he said, noticing the dates. "This last entry is over two years old."

"It is?"

"Yes, indeed. And Christopher Mulholland's is nearly a year before that—more than *three years* ago."

"Dear me," she said, shaking her head and heaving a dainty little sigh. "I would never have thought it. How time does fly away from us all, doesn't it, Mr. Wilkins?"

"It's Weaver," Billy said. "*W-e-a-v-e-r.*"

"Oh, of course it is!" she cried, sitting down on the sofa. "How silly of me. I do apologize. In one ear and out the other, that's me, Mr. Weaver."

"You know something?" Billy said. "Something that's really quite extraordinary about all this?"

"No, dear, I don't."

"Well, you see, both of these names—Mulholland and Temple—I not only seem to remember each one of them separately, so to speak, but somehow or other, in some peculiar way, they both appear to be sort of connected together as well. As though they were both famous for the same sort of thing, if you see what I mean—like . . . well . . . like Dempsey and

7. **cricketers:** Cricket is a popular national sport in Great Britain. It is played on a large field with bats, a ball, and wickets.

Tunney,[8] for example, or Churchill and Roosevelt."

"How amusing," she said. "But come over here now, dear, and sit down beside me on the sofa and I'll give you a nice cup of tea and a ginger biscuit before you go to bed."

"You really shouldn't bother," Billy said. "I didn't mean you to do anything like that." He stood by the piano, watching her as she fussed about with the cups and saucers. He noticed that she had small, white, quickly moving hands, and red fingernails.

"I'm almost positive it was in the newspapers I saw them," Billy said. "I'll think of it in a second. I'm sure I will."

There is nothing more tantalizing than a thing like this that lingers just outside the borders of one's memory. He hated to give up.

"Now wait a minute," he said. "Wait just a minute. Mulholland . . . Christopher Mulholland . . . wasn't *that* the name of the Eton schoolboy who was on a walking tour through the West Country, and then all of a sudden . . ."

"Milk?" she said. "And sugar?"

"Yes, please. And then all of a sudden . . ."

"Eton schoolboy?" she said. "Oh no, my dear, that can't possibly be right because *my* Mr. Mulholland was certainly not an Eton schoolboy when he came to me. He was a Cambridge undergraduate. Come over here now and sit next to me and warm yourself in front of this lovely fire. Come on. Your tea's all ready for you." She patted the empty place beside her on the sofa, and she sat there smiling at Billy and waiting for him to come over.

He crossed the room slowly, and sat down on the edge of the sofa. She placed his teacup on the table in front of him.

"*There* we are," she said. "How nice and cozy this is, isn't it?"

Billy started sipping his tea. She did the same. For half a minute or so, neither of them spoke. But Billy knew that she was looking at him. Her body was half turned toward him, and he could feel her eyes resting on his face, watching him over the rim of her teacup. Now and again, he caught a whiff of a peculiar smell that seemed to emanate directly from her person. It was not in the least unpleasant, and it reminded him—well, he wasn't quite sure what it reminded him of. Pickled walnuts? New leather? Or was it the corridors of a hospital?

At length, she said, "Mr. Mulholland was a great one for his tea. Never in my life have I seen anyone drink as much tea as dear, sweet Mr. Mulholland."

"I suppose he left fairly recently," Billy said. He was still puzzling his head about the two names. He was positive now that he had seen them in the newspapers—in the headlines.

"Left?" she said, arching her brows. "But my dear boy, he never left. He's still here. Mr. Temple is also here. They're on the fourth floor, both of them together."

Billy set his cup down slowly on the table and stared at his landlady. She smiled back at him, and then she put out one of her white hands and patted him comfortingly on the knee. "How old are you, my dear?" she asked.

"Seventeen."

"Seventeen!" she cried. "Oh, it's the perfect age! Mr. Mulholland was also seventeen. But I think he was a trifle shorter than you are; in fact I'm sure he was, and his teeth weren't *quite* so white. You have the most beautiful teeth, Mr. Weaver, did you know that?"

"They're not as good as they look," Billy said. "They've got simply masses of fillings in them at the back."

"Mr. Temple, of course, was a little older," she said, ignoring his remark. "He was actually

8. **Dempsey and Tunney:** Jack Dempsey and Gene Tunney, heavyweight boxing champions. Tunney defeated Dempsey in a fight for the world title in 1926, and again in 1927.

twenty-eight. And yet I never would have guessed it if he hadn't told me, never in my whole life. There wasn't a *blemish* on his body."

"A what?" Billy said.

"His skin was *just* like a baby's."

There was a pause. Billy picked up his teacup and took another sip of his tea, then he set it down again gently in its saucer. He waited for her to say something else, but she seemed to have lapsed into another of her silences. He sat there staring straight ahead of him into the far corner of the room, biting his lower lip.

"That parrot," he said at last. "You know something? It had me completely fooled when I first saw it through the window. I could have sworn it was alive."

"Alas, no longer."

"It's most terribly clever the way it's been done," he said. "It doesn't look in the least bit dead. Who did it?"

"I did."

"*You* did?"

"Of course," she said. "And have you met my little Basil as well?" She nodded toward the dachshund curled up so comfortably in front of the fire. Billy looked at it. And suddenly, he realized that this animal had all the time been just as silent and motionless as the parrot. He put out a hand and touched it gently on the top of its back. The back was hard and cold, and when he pushed the hair to one side with his fingers, he could see the skin underneath, grayish-black and dry and perfectly preserved.

"Good gracious me," he said. "How absolutely fascinating." He turned away from the dog and stared with deep admiration at the little woman beside him on the sofa. "It must be most awfully difficult to do a thing like that."

"Not in the least," she said. "I stuff *all* my little pets myself when they pass away. Will you have another cup of tea?"

"No, thank you," Billy said. The tea tasted faintly of bitter almonds, and he didn't much care for it.

"You did sign the book, didn't you?"

"Oh, yes."

"That's good. Because later on, if I happen to forget what you were called, then I could always come down here and look it up. I still do that almost every day with Mr. Mulholland and Mr. . . . Mr. . . ."

"Temple," Billy said. "Gregory Temple. Excuse my asking, but haven't there been *any* other guests here except them in the last two or three years?"

Holding her teacup high in one hand, inclining her head slightly to the left, she looked up at him out of the corners of her eyes and gave him another gentle little smile.

"No, my dear," she said. "Only you."

Reading Check

1. Why has Billy Weaver come to Bath?
2. What is the quality Billy Weaver believes is common to all successful businessmen?
3. What does Billy think will be the advantage of staying at a boarding-house?
4. What does Billy discover about the animals in the living room?
5. Why do the names in the guest book sound familiar to Billy?

For Study and Discussion

Analyzing and Interpreting the Story

1. What you learn about Billy Weaver at the beginning of the story helps explain why he later chooses to stay at the landlady's house. When you first meet Billy, he is looking for a fairly cheap hotel. How does his desire for a bargain drive him into a trap?

2. Billy is obviously impressed by appearances. **a.** What details of the landlady's house first attract him? **b.** Which of these details are not what they appear to be?

3. Billy overlooks dangers that are quite obvious to the reader. What he finds in the landlady's house does not arouse his suspicions. **a.** What clues does Billy ignore? **b.** What explanation does he give for the landlady's odd behavior?

4. The landlady tells Billy, "I was beginning to get worried." **a.** How does Billy interpret this remark? **b.** Considering the number of entries in her guest book, what do you think she was worried about?

5. Potassium cyanide, which is extremely poisonous, is known for its faint, bitter-almond taste. This is what Billy tastes in the landlady's tea. Find as many clues as you can that indicate what Billy's fate is to be.

6. Billy is shown to be quite observant throughout the story. Why does he fail to recognize the danger he is in?

7. Roald Dahl has been called "a master of the macabre and fantastic," and his tales are known for their skillful surprise endings. His stories belong to a tradition of escape literature that is written primarily for entertainment. Such stories may contain no particular moral or lesson or greatly increase our understanding of human nature. The characters (the landlady, for example) may be convincing in the story but would never be mistaken for real human beings. What other stories have you read that you would put in the category of escape literature?

Literary Elements

Understanding Suspense and Foreshadowing

When you read "The Landlady," you find yourself responding to danger signals that Billy Weaver fails to recognize. You can see clearly what is going to happen, but you have no way of warning Billy. You read on, eager to see whether he will connect the clues and act in time to save himself.

This uncertainty about what is going to happen next in a story is known as **suspense.** Roald Dahl creates suspense by placing Billy in danger and keeping you uncertain about whether he will escape or not.

Early in the story, Dahl creates suspense by presenting you with a mystery. When Billy sees the sign in the landlady's window, something strange happens to him.

> Each word was like a large black eye staring at him through the glass, holding him, compelling him, forcing him to stay where he was and not to walk away from that house, and the next thing he knew, he was actually moving across from the window to the front door of the house, climbing the steps that led up to it, and reaching for the bell.

What is this magnetic force that attracts Billy? What will happen when Billy presses the doorbell? Who will be waiting there behind the door? These are the questions that the reader wants answered.

To build up suspense, a writer will drop hints about what is going to come later in the story. This practice is called **foreshadowing.** All the information about Billy's fate is supplied in hints. Dahl never tells what the landlady plans to do to Billy. But we can guess.

Language and Vocabulary

Recognizing Word Origins

Billy finds the mystery of the names in the guest book *tantalizing*. The word *tantalize* has an interesting origin. It comes from the name of a character in Greek mythology, Tantalus. As a punishment for his crimes, Tantalus was made to stand in water that disappeared whenever he tried to drink it and under branches of fruit that he could not reach. Can you see the connection between the myth and the meaning of the word *tantalize*?

Descriptive Writing

Describing a Street Scene

As Billy walks toward The Bell and Dragon, he carefully observes the scene around him.

> There were no shops on this wide street that he was walking along, only a line of tall houses on each side, all of them identical. They had porches and pillars and four or five steps going up to their front doors, and it was obvious that once upon a time they had been very swanky residences. But now, even in the darkness, he could see that the paint was peeling from the woodwork on their doors and windows, and that the handsome white façades were cracked and blotchy from neglect.

The impression you receive through Billy's eyes is one of faded elegance. In a few well-chosen details, the author lets you know that this neighborhood has begun to deteriorate.

Choose a street in your neighborhood and decide what general impression that street makes on you, the observer. Give as many specific details as you can to support that impression.

About the Author

Roald Dahl   (1916–   )

Roald Dahl grew up in the beautiful countryside surrounding Llandaff in South Wales. At sixteen he left school to join an exploratory expedition to Newfoundland. When World War II broke out in 1939, he volunteered for the Royal Air Force as a fighter pilot. Although he was wounded while flying over the Libyan Desert and was hospitalized for four months, he continued to fly until 1942, when he was sent to Washington as an assistant to the British ambassador. He recounts these adventures in his autobiography, *Going Solo*.

Dahl's writing career began when the novelist C. S. Forester asked him to write an account of his most exciting flying experience. The story he wrote was subsequently published in the *Saturday Evening Post*. Dahl has published several collections of short stories. One critic has noted his ability "to steer an unwavering course along the hairline where the gruesome and the comic meet and mingle." "The Landlady" is a good example of the bizarre element in Dahl's work.

Rikki-tikki-tavi

RUDYARD KIPLING

Characters in a short story are revealed in several ways. Writers may tell us about characters by describing them directly. Most often, however, writers prefer to show us what characters are like, through their thoughts, their words, their actions, and the reactions of other characters in the story. As you read this story, note how Kipling uses both direct and indirect methods of characterization.

This is the story of the great war that Rikki-tikki-tavi fought single-handed, through the bathrooms of the big bungalow in Segowlee cantonment.[1] Darzee, the tailorbird, helped him, and Chuchundra,[2] the muskrat, who never comes out into the middle of the floor, but always creeps round by the wall, gave him advice; but Rikki-tikki did the real fighting.

He was a mongoose, rather like a little cat in

1. **Segowlee** (sē-gou′lē) **cantonment:** a British army post in Segowlee, India.

2. **Chuchundra** (chōō-chŭn′drə).

his fur and his tail, but quite like a weasel in his head and his habits. His eyes and the end of his restless nose were pink; he could scratch himself anywhere he pleased with any leg, front or back, that he chose to use; he could fluff up his tail till it looked like a bottlebrush, and his war cry, as he scuttled through the long grass was: "*Rikk-tikk-tikki-tikki-tchk*!"

One day, a high summer flood washed him out of the burrow where he lived with his father and mother, and carried him, kicking and clucking, down a roadside ditch. He found a little wisp of grass floating there, and clung to it till he lost his senses. When he revived, he was lying in the hot sun on the middle of a garden path, very draggled indeed, and a small boy was saying: "Here's a dead mongoose. Let's have a funeral."

"No," said his mother; "let's take him in and dry him. Perhaps he isn't really dead."

They took him into the house, and a big man picked him up between his finger and thumb and said he was not dead but half choked; so they wrapped him in cotton wool and warmed him over a little fire, and he opened his eyes and sneezed.

"Now," said the big man (he was an Englishman who had just moved into the bungalow); "don't frighten him, and we'll see what he'll do."

It is the hardest thing in the world to frighten a mongoose, because he is eaten up from nose to tail with curiosity. The motto of all the mongoose family is "Run and find out"; and Rikki-tikki was a true mongoose. He looked at the cotton wool, decided that it was not good to eat, ran all round the table, sat up and put his fur in order, scratched himself, and jumped on the small boy's shoulder.

"Don't be frightened, Teddy," said his father. "That's his way of making friends."

"Ouch! He's tickling under my chin," said Teddy.

Rikki-tikki looked down between the boy's collar and neck, snuffed at his ear, and climbed down to the floor, where he sat rubbing his nose.

"Good gracious," said Teddy's mother, "and that's a wild creature! I suppose he's so tame because we've been kind to him."

"All mongooses are like that," said her husband. "If Teddy doesn't pick him up by the tail, or try to put him in a cage, he'll run in and out of the house all day long. Let's give him something to eat."

They gave him a little piece of raw meat. Rikki-tikki liked it immensely, and when it was finished he went out into the veranda and sat in the sunshine and fluffed up his fur to make it dry to the roots. Then he felt better.

"There are more things to find out about in this house," he said to himself, "than all my family could find out in all their lives. I shall certainly stay and find out."

He spent all that day roaming over the house. He nearly drowned himself in the bathtubs; put his nose into the ink on a writing table, and burned it on the end of the big man's cigar, for he climbed up in the big man's lap to see how writing was done. At nightfall he ran into Teddy's nursery to watch how kerosene lamps were lighted, and when Teddy went to bed Rikki-tikki climbed up too; but he was a restless companion, because he had to get up and attend to every noise all through the night and find out what made it. Teddy's mother and father came in, the last thing, to look at their boy, and Rikki-tikki was awake on the pillow. "I don't like that," said Teddy's mother; "he may bite the child."

"He'll do no such thing," said the father. "Teddy's safer with that little beast than if he had a bloodhound to watch him. If a snake came into the nursery now——"

But Teddy's mother wouldn't think of anything so awful.

Early in the morning Rikki-tikki came to early breakfast in the veranda, riding on Teddy's shoulder, and they gave him banana and some boiled egg; and he sat on all their laps one after the other, because every well-brought-up mongoose always hopes to be a house mongoose someday and have rooms to run about in; and Rikki-tikki's mother (she used to live in the general's house at Segowlee) had carefully told Rikki what to do if ever he came across Englishmen.

Then Rikki-tikki went out into the garden to see what was to be seen. It was a large garden, only half cultivated, with bushes, as big as summer houses, of roses, lime and orange trees, clumps of bamboos, and thickets of high grass. Rikki-tikki licked his lips. "This is a splendid hunting ground," he said, and his tail grew bottle-brushy at the thought of it, and he scuttled up and down the garden, snuffling here and there till he heard very sorrowful voices in a thornbush. It was Darzee, the tailorbird, and his wife. They had made a beautiful nest by pulling two big leaves together and stitching them up the edges with fibers, and had filled the hollow with cotton and downy fluff. The nest swayed to and fro, as they sat on the rim and cried.

"What is the matter?" asked Rikki-tikki.

"We are very miserable," said Darzee. "One of our babies fell out of the nest yesterday and Nag[3] ate him."

"H'm!" said Rikki-tikki; "that is very sad—but I am a stranger here. Who is Nag?"

Darzee and his wife only cowered down in the nest without answering, for from the thick grass at the foot of the bush came a low hiss—a horrid cold sound that made Rikki-tikki jump back two clear feet. Then inch by inch out of the grass rose up the head and spread hood of Nag, the big black cobra, and he was five feet

3. **Nag** (näg).

long from tongue to tail. When he had lifted one third of himself clear of the ground, he stayed balancing to and fro exactly as a dandelion tuft balances in the wind, and he looked at Rikki-tikki with the wicked snake's eyes that never change their expression, whatever the snake may be thinking of.

"Who is Nag?" he said. "*I* am Nag. The great god Brahm[4] put his mark upon all our people,

4. **Brahm** (bräm): in the Hindu religion, the creator of the universe; usually known as *Brahma*.

when the first cobra spread his hood to keep the sun off Brahm as he slept. Look, and be afraid!"

He spread out his hood more than ever, and Rikki-tikki saw the spectacle mark on the back of it that looks exactly like the eye part of a hook-and-eye fastening. He was afraid for the minute; but it is impossible for a mongoose to stay frightened for any length of time, and though Rikki-tikki had never met a live cobra before, his mother had fed him on dead ones, and he knew that all a grown mongoose's business in life was to fight and eat snakes. Nag knew that too and, at the bottom of his cold heart, he was afraid.

"Well," said Rikki-tikki, and his tail began to fluff up again, "marks or no marks, do you think it is right for you to eat fledglings out of a nest?"

Nag was thinking to himself, and watching the least little movement in the grass behind Rikki-tikki. He knew that mongooses in the garden meant death sooner or later for him and his family; but he wanted to get Rikki-tikki off his guard. So he dropped his head a little, and put it on one side.

"Let us talk," he said. "You eat eggs. Why should not I eat birds?"

"Behind you! Look behind you!" sang Darzee.

Rikki-tikki knew better than to waste time in staring. He jumped up in the air as high as he could go, and just under him whizzed by the head of Nagaina,[5] Nag's wicked wife. She had crept up behind him as he was talking, to make an end of him; and he heard her savage hiss as the stroke missed. He came down almost across her back, and if he had been an old mongoose he would have known that then was the time to break her back with one bite; but he was afraid of the terrible lashing return stroke of the

cobra. He bit, indeed, but did not bite long enough, and he jumped clear of the whisking tail, leaving Nagaina torn and angry.

"Wicked, wicked Darzee!" said Nag, lashing up as high as he could reach toward the nest in the thornbush; but Darzee had built it out of reach of snakes, and it only swayed to and fro.

Rikki-tikki felt his eyes growing red and hot (when a mongoose's eyes grow red, he is angry), and he sat back on his tail and hind legs like a little kangaroo, and looked all around him, and chattered with rage. But Nag and Nagaina had disappeared into the grass. When a snake misses its stroke, it never says anything or gives any sign of what it means to do next. Rikki-tikki did not care to follow them, for he did not feel sure that he could manage two snakes at once. So he trotted off to the gravel path near the house, and sat down to think. It was a serious matter for him. If you read the old books of natural history, you will find they say that when the mongoose fights the snake and happens to get bitten, he runs off and eats some herb that cures him. That is not true. The victory is only a matter of quickness of eye and quickness of foot—snake's blow against the mongoose's jump—and as no eye can follow the motion of a snake's head when it strikes, this makes things much more wonderful than any magic herb. Rikki-tikki knew he was a young mongoose, and it made him all the more pleased to think that he had managed to escape a blow from behind. It gave him confidence in himself, and when Teddy came running down the path, Rikki-tikki was ready to be petted. But just as Teddy was stooping, something wriggled a little in the dust, and a tiny voice said: "Be careful. I am Death!" It was Karait,[6] the dusty brown snakeling that lies for choice on the dusty earth; and his bite is as dangerous as the cobra's. But he is so small that

---

5. **Nagaina** (nə-gī′nə).

6. **Karait** (kə-rīt′).

nobody thinks of him, and so he does the more harm to people.

Rikki-tikki's eyes grew red again, and he danced up to Karait with the peculiar rocking, swaying motion that he had inherited from his family. It looks very funny, but it is so perfectly balanced a gait that you can fly off from it at any angle you please; and in dealing with snakes this is an advantage. If Rikki-tikki had only known, he was doing a much more dangerous thing than fighting Nag, for Karait is so small, and can turn so quickly, that unless Rikki bit him close to the back of the head, he would get the return stroke in his eye or his lip. But Rikki did not know: his eyes were all red, and he rocked back and forth, looking for a good place to hold. Karait struck out, Rikki jumped sideways and tried to run in, but the wicked little dusty gray head lashed within a fraction of his shoulder, and he had to jump over the body, and the head followed his heels close.

Teddy shouted to the house: "Oh, look here! Our mongoose is killing a snake"; and Rikki-tikki heard a scream from Teddy's mother. His father ran out with a stick, but by the time he came up, Karait had lunged out once too far, and Rikki-tikki had sprung, jumped on the snake's back, dropped his head far between his forelegs, bitten as high up the back as he could get hold, and rolled away. That bite paralyzed Karait, and Rikki-tikki was just going to eat him up from the tail, after the custom of his family at dinner, when he remembered that a full meal makes a slow mongoose, and if he wanted all his strength and quickness ready, he must keep himself thin. He went away for a dust bath under the castor-oil bushes, while Teddy's father beat the dead Karait. "What is the use of that?" thought Rikki-tikki; "I have settled it all"; and then Teddy's mother picked him up from the dust and hugged him, crying that he had saved Teddy from death, and Teddy's father said that he was a providence, and Teddy looked on with big scared eyes. Rikki-tikki was rather amused at all the fuss, which, of course, he did not understand. Teddy's mother might just as well have petted Teddy for playing in the dust. Rikki was thoroughly enjoying himself.

That night, at dinner, walking to and fro among the wineglasses on the table, he might have stuffed himself three times over with nice things; but he remembered Nag and Nagaina, and though it was very pleasant to be patted and petted by Teddy's mother, and to sit on Teddy's shoulder, his eyes would get red from time to time, and he would go off into his long war cry of *Rikk-tikk-tikki-tikki-tchk!*

Teddy carried him off to bed, and insisted on Rikki-tikki's sleeping under his chin. Rikki-tikki was too well bred to bite or scratch, but as soon as Teddy was asleep he went off for his nightly walk round the house, and in the dark he ran up against Chuchundra, the muskrat, creeping round by the wall. Chuchundra is a brokenhearted little beast. He whimpers and cheeps all the night, trying to make up his mind to run into the middle of the room; but he never gets there.

"Don't kill me," said Chuchundra, almost weeping. "Rikki-tikki, don't kill me!"

"Do you think a snake-killer kills muskrats?" said Rikki-tikki scornfully.

"Those who kill snakes get killed by snakes," said Chuchundra, more sorrowfully than ever. "And how am I to be sure that Nag won't mistake me for you some dark night?"

"There's not the least danger," said Rikki-tikki; "but Nag is in the garden, and I know you don't go there."

"My cousin Chua, the rat, told me——" said Chuchundra, and then he stopped.

"Told you what?"

"H'sh! Nag is everywhere, Rikki-tikki. You should have talked to Chua in the garden."

"I didn't—so you must tell me. Quick, Chuchundra, or I'll bite you!"

Chuchundra sat down and cried till the tears rolled off his whiskers. "I am a very poor man," he sobbed. "I never had spirit enough to run out into the middle of the room. H'sh! I mustn't tell you anything. Can't you *hear*, Rikki-tikki?"

Rikki-tikki listened. The house was as still as still, but he thought he could just catch the faintest *scratch-scratch* in the world—a noise as faint as that of a wasp walking on a windowpane—the dry scratch of a snake's scales on brickwork.

"That's Nag or Nagaina," he said to himself; "and he is crawling into the bathroom sluice. You're right, Chuchundra; I should have talked to Chua."

He stole off to Teddy's bathroom, but there was nothing there, and then to Teddy's mother's bathroom. At the bottom of the smooth plaster wall there was a brick pulled out to make a sluice for the bath water, and as Rikki-tikki stole in by the masonry curb where the bath is put, he heard Nag and Nagaina whispering together outside in the moonlight.

"When the house is emptied of people," said Nagaina to her husband, "*he* will have to go away, and then the garden will be our own again. Go in quietly, and remember that the big man who killed Karait is the first one to bite. Then come out and tell me, and we will hunt for Rikki-tikki together."

"But are you sure that there is anything to be gained by killing the people?" said Nag.

"Everything. When there were no people in the bungalow, did we have any mongoose in the garden? So long as the bungalow is empty, we are king and queen of the garden; and remember that as soon as our eggs in the melon bed hatch (as they may tomorrow), our children will need room and quiet."

"I had not thought of that," said Nag. "I will go, but there is no need that we should hunt for Rikki-tikki afterward. I will kill the big man and his wife, and the child if I can, and come away quietly. Then the bungalow will be empty, and Rikki-tikki will go."

Rikki-tikki tingled all over with rage and hatred at this, and then Nag's head came through the sluice, and his five feet of cold body followed it. Angry as he was, Rikki-tikki was very frightened as he saw the size of the big cobra. Nag coiled himself up, raised his head, and looked into the bathroom in the dark, and Rikki could see his eyes glitter.

"Now, if I kill him here, Nagaina will know; and if I fight him on the open floor, the odds are in his favor. What am I to do?" said Rikki-tikki-tavi.

Nag waved to and fro, and then Rikki-tikki heard him drinking from the biggest water jar that was used to fill the bath. "That is good," said the snake. "Now, when Karait was killed, the big man had a stick. He may have that stick still, but when he comes in to bathe in the morning he will not have a stick. I shall wait here till he comes. Nagaina—do you hear me? I shall wait here in the cool till daytime."

There was no answer from outside, so Rikki-tikki knew Nagaina had gone away. Nag coiled himself down, coil by coil, round the bulge at the bottom of the water jar, and Rikki-tikki stayed still as death. After an hour he began to move, muscle by muscle, towards the jar. Nag was asleep, and Rikki-tikki looked at his big back, wondering which would be the best place for a good hold. "If I don't break his back at the first jump," said Rikki, "he can still fight; and if he fights—O Rikki!" He looked at the thickness of the neck below the hood, but that was too much for him; and a bite near the tail would only make Nag savage.

"It must be the head," he said at last; "the head above the hood; and when I am once there, I must not let go."

Then he jumped. The head was lying a little clear of the water jar, under the curve of it; and, as his teeth met, Rikki braced his back against the bulge of the red earthenware to hold down the head. This gave him just one second's purchase,[7] and he made the most of it. Then he was battered to and fro as a rat is shaken by a dog—to and fro on the floor, up and down, and round in great circles, but his eyes were red and he held on as the body cartwhipped over the floor, upsetting the tin dipper and the soap dish and the fleshbrush, and banged against the tin side of the bath. As he held he closed his jaws tighter and tighter, for he made sure[8] he would be banged to death, and, for the honor of his family, he preferred to be found with his teeth locked. He was dizzy, aching, and felt shaken to pieces when something went off like a thunderclap just behind him; a hot wind knocked him senseless and red fire singed his fur. The big man had been wakened by the noise, and had fired both barrels of a shotgun into Nag just behind the hood.

Rikki-tikki held on with his eyes shut, for now he was quite sure he was dead; but the head did not move, and the big man picked him up and said: "It's the mongoose again, Alice; the little chap has saved *our* lives now." Then Teddy's mother came in with a very white face, and saw what was left of Nag, and Rikki-tikki dragged himself to Teddy's bedroom and spent half the rest of the night shaking himself tenderly to find out whether he really was broken into forty pieces, as he fancied.

When morning came he was very stiff, but well pleased with his doings. "Now I have Nagaina to settle with, and she will be worse than five Nags, and there's no knowing when the eggs she spoke of will hatch. Goodness! I must go and see Darzee," he said.

Without waiting for breakfast, Rikki-tikki ran to the thornbush where Darzee was singing a song of triumph at the top of his voice. The news of Nag's death was all over the garden, for the sweeper had thrown the body on the rubbish heap.

"Oh, you stupid tuft of feathers!" said Rikki-tikki angrily. "Is this the time to sing?"

---

7. **purchase:** here, advantage.

8. **made sure:** here, felt sure.

"Nag is dead—is dead—is dead!" sang Darzee. "The valiant Rikki-tikki caught him by the head and held fast. The big man brought the bang-stick, and Nag fell in two pieces! He will never eat my babies again."

"All that's true enough; but where's Nagaina?" said Rikki-tikki, looking carefully round him.

"Nagaina came to the bathroom sluice and called for Nag," Darzee went on; "and Nag came out on the end of a stick—the sweeper picked him up on the end of a stick and threw him upon the rubbish heap. Let us sing about the great, the red-eyed Rikki-tikki!" And Darzee filled his throat and sang.

"If I could get up to your nest, I'd roll your babies out!" said Rikki-tikki. "You don't know when to do the right thing at the right time. You're safe enough in your nest there, but it's war for me down here. Stop singing a minute, Darzee."

"For the great, beautiful Rikki-tikki's sake I will stop," said Darzee. "What is it, O Killer of the terrible Nag?"

"Where is Nagaina, for the third time?"

"On the rubbish heap by the stables, mourning for Nag. Great is Rikki-tikki with the white teeth."

"Bother[9] my white teeth! Have you ever heard where she keeps her eggs?"

"In the melon bed, on the end nearest the wall, where the sun strikes nearly all day. She hid them there weeks ago."

"And you never thought it worthwhile to tell me? The end nearest the wall, you said?"

"Rikki-tikki, you are not going to eat her eggs?"

"Not eat exactly; no. Darzee, if you have a grain of sense you will fly off to the stables and pretend that your wing is broken, and let Nagaina chase you away to this bush! I must

9. **Bother:** here, never mind.

get to the melon bed, and if I went there now she'd see me."

Darzee was a featherbrained little fellow who could never hold more than one idea at a time in his head; and just because he knew that Nagaina's children were born in eggs like his own, he didn't think at first that it was fair to kill them. But his wife was a sensible bird, and she knew that cobra's eggs meant young cobras later on; so she flew off from the nest, and left Darzee to keep the babies warm, and continue his song about the death of Nag. Darzee was very like a man in some ways.

She fluttered in front of Nagaina by the rubbish heap and cried out, "Oh, my wing is broken! The boy in the house threw a stone at me and broke it." Then she fluttered more desperately than ever.

Nagaina lifted up her head and hissed, "You warned Rikki-tikki when I would have killed him. Indeed and truly, you've chosen a bad place to be lame in." And she moved toward Darzee's wife, slipping along over the dust.

"The boy broke it with a stone!" shrieked Darzee's wife.

"Well! It may be some consolation to you when you're dead to know that I shall settle accounts with the boy. My husband lies on the rubbish heap this morning, but before night the boy in the house will lie very still. What is the use of running away? I am sure to catch you. Little fool, look at me!"

Darzee's wife knew better than to do *that*, for a bird who looks at a snake's eyes gets so frightened that she cannot move. Darzee's wife fluttered on, piping sorrowfully, and never leaving the ground, and Nagaina quickened her pace.

Rikki-tikki heard them going up the path from the stables, and he raced for the end of the melon patch near the wall. There, in the warm litter about the melons, very cunningly hidden, he found twenty-five eggs, about the size of a bantam's eggs,[10] but with whitish skins instead of shells.

"I was not a day too soon," he said; for he could see the baby cobras curled up inside the skin, and he knew that the minute they were hatched they could each kill a man or a mongoose. He bit off the tops of the eggs as fast as he could, taking care to crush the young cobras, and turned over the litter from time to time to see whether he had missed any. At last there were only three eggs left, and Rikki-tikki began to chuckle to himself, when he heard Darzee's wife screaming:

"Rikki-tikki, I led Nagaina toward the house, and she has gone into the veranda, and—oh, come quickly—she means killing!"

Rikki-tikki smashed two eggs, and tumbled backward down the melon bed with the third egg in his mouth, and scuttled to the veranda as hard as he could put foot to the ground. Teddy and his mother and father were there at early breakfast; but Rikki-tikki saw that they were not eating anything. They sat stone-still, and their faces were white. Nagaina was coiled up on the matting by Teddy's chair, within easy striking distance of Teddy's bare leg, and she was swaying to and fro, singing a song of triumph.

"Son of the big man that killed Nag," she hissed, "stay still. I am not ready yet. Wait a little. Keep very still, all you three! If you move I strike, and if you do not move I strike. Oh, foolish people, who killed my Nag!"

Teddy's eyes were fixed on his father, and all his father could do was to whisper, "Sit still, Teddy. You mustn't move. Teddy, keep still."

Then Rikki-tikki came up and cried: "Turn round, Nagaina; turn and fight!"

"All in good time," said she, without moving her eyes. "I will settle my account with *you*

presently. Look at your friends, Rikki-tikki. They are still and white. They are afraid. They dare not move, and if you come a step nearer I strike."

"Look at your eggs," said Rikki-tikki, "in the melon bed near the wall. Go and look, Nagaina."

The big snake turned half round and saw the egg on the veranda. "Ah-h! Give it to me," she said.

Rikki-tikki put his paws one on each side of the egg, and his eyes were blood-red. "What price for a snake's egg? For a young cobra? For a young king cobra? For the last—the very last of the brood? The ants are eating all the others down by the melon bed."

Nagaina spun clear round, forgetting everything for the sake of the one egg; and Rikki-tikki saw Teddy's father shoot out a big hand, catch Teddy by the shoulder, and drag him across the little table with the teacups, safe and out of reach of Nagaina.

"Tricked! Tricked! Tricked! *Rikk-tck-tck!*" chuckled Rikki-tikki. "The boy is safe, and it was I—I—I that caught Nag by the hood last night in the bathroom." Then he began to jump up and down, all four feet together, his head close to the floor. "He threw me to and fro, but he could not shake me off. He was dead before the big man blew him in two. I did it! *Rikki-tikki-tck-tck!* Come then, Nagaina. Come and fight with me. You shall not be a widow long."

Nagaina saw that she had lost her chance of killing Teddy, and the egg lay between Rikki-tikki's paws. "Give me the egg, Rikki-tikki. Give me the last of my eggs, and I will go away and never come back," she said, lowering her hood.

"Yes, you will go away, and you will never come back; for you will go to the rubbish heap with Nag. Fight, widow! The big man has gone for his gun! Fight!"

10. **bantam's eggs:** small eggs. A bantam is a small chicken.

Rikki-tikki was bounding all round Nagaina, keeping just out of reach of her stroke, his little eyes like hot coals. Nagaina gathered herself together, and flung out at him. Rikki-tikki jumped up and backwards. Again and again and again she struck, and each time her head came with a whack on the matting of the veranda and she gathered herself together like a watchspring. Then Rikki-tikki danced in a circle to get behind her, and Nagaina spun round to keep her head to his head, so that the rustle of her tail on the matting sounded like dry leaves blown along by the wind.

He had forgotten the egg. It still lay on the veranda, and Nagaina came nearer and nearer to it, till at last, while Rikki-tikki was drawing breath, she caught it in her mouth, turned to the veranda steps, and flew like an arrow down the path, with Rikki-tikki behind her. When the cobra runs for her life, she goes like a whiplash flicked across a horse's neck. Rikki-tikki knew that he must catch her, or all the trouble would begin again. She headed straight for the long grass by the thornbush, and as he was running Rikki-tikki heard Darzee still singing his foolish little song of triumph. But Darzee's wife was wiser. She flew off her nest as Nagaina came along, and flapped her wings about Nagaina's head. If Darzee had helped they might have turned her; but Nagaina only lowered her hood and went on. Still, the instant's delay brought Rikki-tikki up to her, and as she plunged into the rathole where she and Nag used to live, his little white teeth were clenched on her tail, and he went down with her—and very few mongooses, however wise and old they may be, care to follow a cobra into its hole. It was dark in the hole; and Rikki-tikki never knew when it might open out and give Nagaina room to turn and strike at him. He held on savagely, and stuck out his feet to act as brakes on the dark slope of the hot, moist earth. Then the grass by the mouth of the hole stopped waving, and Darzee said: "It is all over with Rikki-tikki! We must sing his death song. Valiant Rikki-tikki is dead! For Nagaina will surely kill him underground."

So he sang a very mournful song that he made up all on the spur of the minute, and just as he got to the most touching part the grass quivered again, and Rikki-tikki, covered with dirt, dragged himself out of the hole leg by leg, licking his whiskers. Darzee stopped with a little shout. Rikki-tikki shook some of the dust out of his fur and sneezed. "It is all over," he said. "The widow will never come out again." And the red ants that live between the grass stems heard him, and began to troop down one after another to see if he had spoken the truth.

Rikki-tikki curled himself up in the grass and slept where he was—slept and slept till it was late in the afternoon, for he had done a hard day's work.

"Now," he said, when he awoke, "I will go back to the house. Tell the Coppersmith, Darzee, and he will tell the garden that Nagaina is dead."

The Coppersmith is a bird who makes a noise exactly like the beating of a little hammer on a copper pot; and the reason he is always making it is because he is the town crier to every Indian garden, and tells all the news to everybody who cares to listen. As Rikki-tikki went up the path, he heard his "attention" notes like a tiny dinner gong; and then the steady "Ding-dong-tock! Nag is dead—dong! Nagaina is dead! Ding-dong-tock!" That set all the birds in the garden singing, and the frogs croaking, for Nag and Nagaina used to eat frogs as well as little birds.

When Rikki got to the house, Teddy and Teddy's mother (she looked very white still, for she had been fainting) and Teddy's father came out and almost cried over him; and that night he ate all that was given him till he could eat no more, and went to bed on Teddy's shoulder, where Teddy's mother saw him when she came to look late at night.

"He saved our lives and Teddy's life," she said to her husband. "Just think, he saved all our lives!"

Rikki-tikki woke up with a jump, for the mongooses are light sleepers.

"Oh, it's you," said he. "What are you bothering for? All the cobras are dead; and if they weren't, I'm here."

Rikki-tikki had a right to be proud of himself; but he did not grow too proud, and he kept that garden as a mongoose should keep it, with tooth and jump and spring and bite, till never a cobra dared show its head inside the walls.

Reading Check

1. According to the author, why is it difficult to frighten a mongoose?
2. What is the motto of Rikki-tikki's family?
3. Why is Nag afraid of Rikki-tikki?
4. Who are Rikki-tikki's allies in the war against the cobras?
5. What happens to Rikki-tikki's eyes when he gets angry?
6. Why does Rikki-tikki refrain from eating Karait?
7. Who warns Rikki-tikki that the cobras may come into the house?
8. Why do the cobras want to kill the people in the house?
9. What does Rikki-tikki consider a greater danger than Nag and Nagaina?
10. Where does Rikki-tikki find the cobra's eggs?

For Study and Discussion

Analyzing and Interpreting the Story

1. The major characters in the story are animals that have been given human motives. Identify the major characters in the story that represent the forces of good and those that represent the forces of evil.

2. What conflict, or struggle, does Rikki-tikki face?

3. Kipling says that his story is about "the great war that Rikki-tikki-tavi fought single-handed. . . ." **a.** Identify at least five "battles" in this war. **b.** At what points in the war does Darzee's wife assist Rikki-tikki?

4. Match each character in the left-hand column with one or more of the adjectives in the right-hand column. You may use each adjective as often as you like, but be sure to use each adjective at least once. Support your answers with passages from the story.

Darzee	cold
	cunning
	curious
	featherbrained
Darzee's wife	intelligent
	proud
	quick-witted
	resourceful
Rikki-tikki	sensible
	stupid
	valiant
	wicked
Nagaina	wise

5. Writers frequently treat animals in stories as if they could think, talk, and feel as people do. **a.** Why do you suppose they write about animals in this way? **b.** What other selections have you read in which animals have been given human characteristics?

6. Choose passages of description, conversation, or exciting events that you find appealing. Prepare to read them aloud in classs.

Literary Elements

Understanding Methods of Characterization

The way in which writers let you know what the individuals in a story are like is called **characterization**. When writers *tell* you what characters are like through description, they are using **direct characterization**. For instance, Kipling tells us: "Chuchundra is a broken-hearted little beast. He whimpers and cheeps all the night, trying to make up his mind to run into the middle of the room, but he never gets there."

Writers may also *show* you what characters are like through their thoughts, their speech, their actions, and the reactions of other characters to them. This kind of characterization is called **indirect characterization**. What does Chuchundra say and do (page 234) that confirms Kipling's description of him? What is Rikki-tikki's opinion of Chuchundra? Does his opinion add anything to Kipling's statement?

Show how Kipling develops Rikki-tikki's character through direct and indirect characterization. Be sure to answer the following questions:

Direct Characterization
   What does the author tell you about the character?

Indirect Characterization
   What does the character think, say, and do?
   What do others think and say about the character? How do they treat the character?

Language and Vocabulary

Recognizing Words of Indian Origin

When Rudyard Kipling wrote "Rikki-tikki-tavi," India was part of the British Empire. Many words of Indian origin found their way into the English language. The word *bungalow*, for example, is an *Anglo-Indian* word; it is an English word borrowed from an Indian language. The origin of bungalow is the Hindi word *bānglā*, which means "thatched house."

Here are some other words that are derived from Indian languages. Look them up in a dictionary to find their derivations.

bandanna	jungle	shampoo
dungaree	pajamas	veranda

Writing About Literature

Analyzing Methods of Characterization

You have seen that Kipling develops Rikki-tikki's character through direct and indirect characterization. Choose a character in another story you have read, such as Lottie Jump in "Bad Characters" (page 52) or Harry Thorburn in "The Erne from the Coast" (page 208). Write an essay in which you analyze the author's methods of characterization.

Prewriting Suggestions: Use two columns, one for *direct characterization* and one for *indirect characterization*. As you reread the story, list details in the appropriate categories. You can then edit your lists to select the best details for your essay. For additional help, see *Writing About Literature*.

Creative Writing

Writing About Characters in Action

Rikki-tikki's last fight with Nagaina occurs "offstage," so to speak. Kipling does not describe the battle. He leaves it to the reader's imagination.

Using your knowledge of the characters of Rikki-tikki and Nagaina, write your version of the missing battle. Remember that Nagaina is almost a match for Rikki-tikki and that she is fighting to save her very last egg.

You might open with these sentences taken from the story:

> It was dark in the hole; and Rikki-tikki never knew when it might open out and give Nagaina room to turn and strike at him. He held on savagely, and stuck out his feet to act as brakes on the dark slope of the hot, moist earth.

To review the elements of good narrative writing, see *Practice in Reading and Writing,* pages 139–140.

About the Author

Rudyard Kipling (1865–1936)

When Rudyard Kipling wrote "Rikki-tikki-tavi," he drew on his memories of India, where he was born. Kipling was six when his parents sent him to school in England. He returned to India in 1882 and became a journalist. He soon began to write sketches, short stories, and light verse.

In 1886 his first book, a collection of poems called *Departmental Ditties,* appeared. Between 1887 and 1889 he produced six volumes of short stories. When he returned to England in 1889, he was already considered one of the great writers of his day.

Kipling's short stories, novels, and poems have delighted readers of all ages. Some of his best-known works of fiction are *The Light That Failed, The Jungle Books, Captains Courageous,* and *Kim.* Among his most popular poems are "If," "The Ballad of East and West," and "Danny Deever." Several of Kipling's works have been made into movies. In 1907 he became the first Englishman to win the Nobel Prize for literature.

A Day's Wait

ERNEST HEMINGWAY

Sometimes the narrator of a story is a character who appears in the story. At other times, the narrator tells the story as an outside observer who plays no role in the events. The point of view *from which a writer chooses to have a story told affects your impression of the characters and events. In reading this story, ask yourself why Hemingway has chosen the father as narrator.*

He came into the room to shut the windows while we were still in bed, and I saw he looked ill. He was shivering, his face was white, and he walked slowly as though it ached to move.

"What's the matter, Schatz?"[1]

"I've got a headache."

"You better go back to bed."

"No, I'm all right."

"You go to bed. I'll see you when I'm dressed."

But when I came downstairs he was dressed, sitting by the fire, looking a very sick and miserable boy of nine years. When I put my hand on his forehead I knew he had a fever.

"You go up to bed," I said, "you're sick."

"I'm all right," he said.

When the doctor came he took the boy's temperature.

"What is it?" I asked him.

"One hundred and two."

Downstairs, the doctor left three different medicines in different colored capsules with instructions for giving them. One was to bring down the fever, another a purgative, the third to overcome an acid condition. The germs of influenza can only exist in an acid condition, he explained. He seemed to know all about influenza and said there was nothing to worry about if the fever did not go above one hundred and four degrees. This was a light epidemic of flu and there was no danger if you avoided pneumonia.

Back in the room I wrote the boy's temperature down and made a note of the time to give the various capsules.

"Do you want me to read to you?"

"All right. If you want to," said the boy. His face was very white and there were dark areas under his eyes. He lay still in the bed and seemed very detached from what was going on.

I read aloud from Howard Pyle's *Book of Pirates;* but I could see he was not following what I was reading.

1. **Schatz:** a nickname taken from a German term of affection.

"How do you feel, Schatz?" I asked him.

"Just the same, so far," he said.

I sat at the foot of the bed and read to myself while I waited for it to be time to give another capsule. It would have been natural for him to go to sleep, but when I looked up he was looking at the foot of the bed, looking very strangely.

"Why don't you try to go to sleep? I'll wake you up for the medicine."

"I'd rather stay awake."

After a while he said to me, "You don't have to stay in here with me, Papa, if it bothers you."

"It doesn't bother me."

"No, I mean you don't have to stay if it's going to bother you."

I thought perhaps he was a little lightheaded and after giving him the prescribed capsules at eleven o'clock I went out for a while.

It was a bright, cold day, the ground covered with a sleet that had frozen so that it seemed as if all the bare trees, the bushes, the cut brush and all the grass and the bare ground had been varnished with ice. I took the young Irish setter for a little walk up the road and along a frozen creek, but it was difficult to stand or walk on the glassy surface, and the red dog slipped and slithered and I fell twice, hard, once dropping my gun and having it slide away over the ice.

We flushed a covey of quail under a high clay bank with overhanging brush and I killed two as they went out of sight over the top of the bank. Some of the covey lit in trees, but most of them scattered into brush piles and it was necessary to jump on the ice-coated mounds of brush several times before they would flush. Coming out while you were poised unsteadily on the icy, springy brush they made difficult shooting, and I killed two, missed five, and

started back pleased to have found a covey close to the house and happy there were so many left to find on another day.

At the house they said the boy had refused to let anyone come into the room.

"You can't come in," he said. "You mustn't get what I have."

I went up to him and found him in exactly the position I had left him, white-faced, but with the tops of his cheeks flushed by the fever, staring still, as he had stared, at the foot of the bed.

I took his temperature.

"What is it?"

"Something like a hundred," I said. It was one hundred and two and four tenths.

"It was a hundred and two," he said.

"Who said so?"

"The doctor."

"Your temperature is all right," I said. "It's nothing to worry about."

"I don't worry," he said, "but I can't keep from thinking."

"Don't think," I said. "Just take it easy."

"I'm taking it easy," he said and looked straight ahead. He was evidently holding tight on to himself about something.

"Take this with water."

"Do you think it will do any good?"

"Of course it will."

I sat down and opened the *Pirate* book and commenced to read, but I could see he was not following, so I stopped.

"About what time do you think I'm going to die?" he asked.

"What?"

"About how long will it be before I die?"

"You aren't going to die. What's the matter with you?"

"Oh, yes, I am. I heard him say a hundred and two."

"People don't die with a fever of one hundred and two. That's a silly way to talk."

"I know they do. At school in France the boys told me you can't live with forty-four degrees. I've got a hundred and two."

He had been waiting to die all day, ever since nine o'clock in the morning.

"You poor Schatz," I said. "Poor old Schatz. It's like miles and kilometers. You aren't going to die. That's a different thermometer. On that thermometer thirty-seven is normal. On this kind it's ninety-eight."

"Are you sure?"

"Absolutely," I said. "It's like miles and kilometers. You know, like how many kilometers we make when we do seventy miles in the car?"

"Oh," he said.

But his gaze at the foot of the bed relaxed slowly. The hold over himself relaxed too, finally, and the next day it was very slack and he cried very easily at little things that were of no importance.

Reading Check

1. What is the doctor's diagnosis of the boy's illness?
2. Why does the father keep a record of the boy's temperature?
3. Why does the boy refuse to let anyone come into his room?
4. Why does the father stop reading aloud?

For Study and Discussion

Analyzing and Interpreting the Story

1. The boy in the story assumes that he is going to die before the day is over. What mistake leads him to this conclusion?

2. The father in the story doesn't realize what is going on in his son's mind. What does he assume is troubling the boy?

Ernest Hemingway with his son.

3a. How does the boy show courage in facing what he believes to be his own death? **b.** How does he show concern for his father?

4. People often hold back their emotions when they face a crisis. How does the boy finally show the strain he has been under?

Literary Elements

Understanding the Narrator's Point of View

The person telling this story—the **narrator**—is a character in the story. You see the other characters and events from his point of view. Everything you learn in the story is what the narrator tells you—what he sees, what he hears, what he thinks. What you learn about the boy in the story is what the narrator reveals through direct observation. You have only his impressions of what is happening.

In real life you perceive events the way the narrator in this story does. You cannot read the minds of other people any more than the father in this story can read his son's thoughts.

"A Day's Wait" is an example of a story written from a **first-person point of view.** The term **first person** refers to the form of the pronoun. The narrator is the "I" telling the story.

What the author is able to show through this point of view is how the characters in the story fail to communicate. They talk without making themselves clear to each other. Here, for example, the father and son do not realize that they are talking about different things:

> After a while he said to me, "You don't have to stay here with me, Papa, if it bothers you."
> "It doesn't bother me."
> "No, I mean you don't have to stay if it's going to bother you."
> I thought perhaps he was a little lightheaded and after giving him the prescribed capsules at eleven o'clock I went out for a while.

What does the boy think is going to bother his father? How does the father interpret the boy's words?

Find another passage in the story that shows a similar misunderstanding between father and son.

Language and Vocabulary

Learning Prefixes Used in Measurement

The boy in the story confuses two systems of measurement. He assumes that the doctor is using the Celsius scale of temperature. On this scale, a normal temperature is 37 degrees. The boy doesn't realize that the doctor is using a Fahrenheit thermometer, on which the normal reading is 98.6 degrees.

In order to clear up the boy's confusion, the father uses the example of miles and kilometers, which are two different units of distance. As you probably know, a kilometer is a unit of measurement in the metric system. The *meter* is the basic unit of measurement for length or distance. A kilometer is one thousand meters, which is equal to 0.6214 miles. The prefix *kilo-* comes from a Greek word meaning "a thousand." What is the word for a thousand grams? A thousand liters?

The prefix *milli-* comes from a Latin word meaning "thousand." When it is used in units of measurement, it means "one thousandth." What is the word for a thousandth of a meter? Of a gram? Of a liter?

Here are other prefixes used in the metric system and their meanings:

deca- (*or* deka-)	ten
deci-	one tenth
hecto-	one hundred
centi-	one hundredth

What is the meaning of *decameter*? Of *decagram*? Of *decigram*? Of *deciliter*? What is the difference between a *hectometer* and a *centimeter*?

Creative Writing

Writing a Story from Two Points of View

Write a brief story about a contest or disagreement in which you were involved. Write the story in the first person from your own point of view, including what you thought and felt at the time. Then rewrite part of the story, still using the first person, from your opponent's point of view.

About the Author

Ernest Hemingway (1899–1961)

Ernest Hemingway, who once defined courage as "grace under pressure," admired people who could face their own suffering bravely. The events in "A Day's Wait" are based on an actual incident in Hemingway's life when one of his sons was ill.

Hemingway perfected a simple, spare style that has influenced many other writers. He won the Pulitzer Prize in 1953 for his novel *The Old Man and the Sea,* which has become a favorite with young readers. In 1954 he was awarded the Nobel Prize for literature.

Rip Van Winkle

WASHINGTON IRVING

"Rip Van Winkle" is among the best-known stories in world literature. In the nineteenth century, Joseph Jefferson turned Irving's story into a play, which had a long and successful run on the stage. One of the story's most celebrated aspects is Irving's use of setting to create mood. You may enjoy reading Irving's descriptive passages aloud.

Whoever has made a voyage up the Hudson must remember the Catskill Mountains. They are a branch of the great Appalachian family,[1] and are seen away to the west of the river, swelling up to a noble height, and lording it over the surrounding country. Every change of season, every change of weather, indeed, every hour of the day, produces some change in the magical hues and shapes of these mountains, and they are regarded by all the good wives, far and near, as perfect barometers. When the weather is fair and settled, they are clothed in blue and purple, and print their bold outlines on the clear evening sky; but, sometimes, when the rest of the landscape is cloudless, they will gather a hood of gray vapors about their summits, which, in the last rays of the setting sun, will glow and light up like a crown of glory.

At the foot of these fairy mountains, the voy-

---

1. **Appalachian** (ăp′ə-lā′chē-ən) **family:** a chain of mountains that extends from Quebec in eastern Canada to northern Alabama.

Illustrations for the 1848 edition of *Rip Van Winkle* by Felix O. C. Darley (1822–1888).

ager may have seen the light smoke curling up from a village, whose shingle roofs gleam among the trees, just where the blue tints of the upland melt away into the fresh green of the nearer landscape. It is a little village, of great antiquity, having been founded by some of the Dutch colonists, in the early times of the province. There were some of the houses of the original settlers standing within a few years,[2] built of small yellow bricks brought from Holland, having latticed windows and gable fronts, surmounted with weathercocks.

2. **within a few years:** until a few years ago. This story was written around 1820.

In that same village, and in one of these very houses, which was sadly timeworn and weather-beaten, there lived many years since, while the country was yet a province of Great Britain, a simple, good-natured fellow, of the name of Rip Van Winkle. He was a descendant of the Van Winkles who figured so gallantly in the chivalrous days of Peter Stuyvesant.[3] He inherited, however, but little of the martial character of his ancestors. I have observed that he was a simple, good-natured man; he was,

3. **Peter Stuyvesant** (stī′və-sənt): the last governor (1646–1664) of the Dutch colony of New Netherland, which was renamed New York after the British took control of it in 1664.

moreover, a kind neighbor, and an obedient, henpecked husband. Indeed, to the latter circumstance might be owing that meekness of spirit which gained him such universal popularity; for those men are most apt to be conciliating[4] abroad who are under the discipline of shrews at home. Their tempers, doubtless, are rendered pliant in the fiery furnace of domestic trouble, which is worth all the sermons in the world for teaching the virtues of patience and long-suffering. A quarrelsome wife may, therefore, in some respects, be considered a tolerable blessing; and if so, Rip Van Winkle was thrice blessed.

Certain it is, that he was a great favorite among all the good wives of the village, who took his part in all family squabbles, and never failed, whenever they talked those matters over in their evening gossipings, to lay all the blame on Dame Van Winkle. The children of the village, too, would shout with joy whenever he approached. He assisted at their sports, made their playthings, taught them to fly kites and shoot marbles, and told them long stories of ghosts, witches, and Indians. Whenever he went dodging about the village, he was surrounded by a troop of them, hanging on his coat skirts, clambering on his back, and playing a thousand tricks on him with impunity,[5] and not a dog would bark at him throughout the neighborhood.

The great error in Rip's character was an insuperable dislike of all kinds of profitable labor. It could not be from the want of perseverance; for he would sit on a wet rock, with a rod as long and heavy as a Tartar's lance,[6] and fish all day without a murmur, even though he should not be encouraged by a single nibble. He would carry a fowling piece[7] on his shoulder for hours together, trudging through woods and swamps, and up hill and down dale, to shoot a few squirrels or wild pigeons. He would never refuse to assist a neighbor even in the roughest toil, and was a foremost man at all country frolics for husking Indian corn, or building stone fences. The women of the village, too, used to employ him to run their errands, and to do such little odd jobs as their less obliging husbands would not do for them. In a word, Rip was ready to attend to anybody's business but his own; but as to doing family duty, and keeping his farm in order, he found it impossible.

In fact, he declared it was of no use to work on his farm; it was the most pestilent[8] little piece of ground in the whole country; everything about it went wrong, and would go wrong, in spite of him. His fences were continually falling to pieces; his cow would either go astray or get among the cabbages; weeds were sure to grow quicker in his fields than anywhere else; the rain always made a point of setting in just as he had some outdoor work to do; so that his estate had dwindled away under his management, acre by acre, until there was little more left than a mere patch of Indian corn and potatoes, and was the worst-conditioned farm in the neighborhood.

His children, too, were as ragged and wild as if they belonged to nobody. His son Rip promised to inherit the habits, with the old clothes, of his father. He was generally seen trooping like a colt at his mother's heels, equipped in a pair of his father's castoff galligaskins,[9] which he had to hold up with one hand, as a fine lady does her train in bad weather.

---

4. **conciliating:** friendly; easygoing.
5. **with impunity** (ĭm-pyōō′nə-tē): without fear of punishment.
6. **Tartar's** (tär′tərz) **lance:** The Tartars were Mongolian tribes that invaded Europe in the thirteenth century. The Tartar warriors used lances, or long, heavy spears.
7. **fowling piece:** a light gun, used most often for shooting birds.
8. **pestilent:** here, troublesome.
9. **galligaskins** (găl′ĭ-găs′kĭnz): loose, wide breeches.

Rip Van Winkle, however, was one of those happy mortals, of foolish, well-oiled dispositions, who take the world easy, eat white bread or brown, whichever can be got with least thought or trouble, and would rather starve on a penny than work for a pound.[10] If left to himself, he would have whistled life away in perfect contentment; but his wife kept continually dinning in his ears about his idleness, his carelessness, and the ruin he was bringing on his family. Morning, noon, and night, her tongue was incessantly going, and everything he said or did was sure to produce a torrent of household eloquence. Rip had but one way of replying to all lectures of the kind, and that, by frequent use, had grown into a habit. He shrugged his shoulders, shook his head, cast up his eyes, but said nothing. This, however, always provoked a fresh volley from his wife; so that he would take to the outside of the house—the only side which, in truth, belongs to a henpecked husband.

Rip's sole domestic adherent[11] was his dog Wolf, who was as much henpecked as his master; for Dame Van Winkle regarded them as companions in idleness, and even looked upon Wolf with an evil eye, as the cause of his master's going so often astray. True it is, in all points of spirit befitting an honorable dog, he was as courageous an animal as ever scoured the woods—but what courage can withstand the terrors of a woman's tongue? The moment Wolf entered the house his crest fell, his tail drooped to the ground, or curled between his legs, he sneaked about with a gallows air, casting many a sidelong glance at Dame Van Winkle, and at the least flourish of a broomstick or ladle, he would fly to the door, yelping.

Times grew worse and worse with Rip Van Winkle as years of matrimony rolled on; a tart temper never mellows with age, and a sharp tongue is the only edged tool that grows keener with constant use. For a long while he used to console himself, when driven from home, by frequenting a kind of perpetual club of the sages, philosophers, and other idle personages of the village, which held its sessions on a bench before a small inn, designated by a portrait of His Majesty George the Third. Here they used to sit in the shade through a long, lazy summer's day, talking listlessly over village gossip, or telling endless sleepy stories about nothing. But it would have been worth any statesman's money to have heard the profound discussions that sometimes took place, when by chance an old newspaper fell into their hands from some passing traveler. How

10. **pound:** the basic unit of British money, used in the colonies.
11. **adherent** (ăd-hîr′ənt): follower or supporter.

solemnly they would listen to the contents, as drawled out by Derrick Van Bummel, the schoolmaster, a dapper, learned little man, who was not to be daunted by the most gigantic word in the dictionary; and how sagely they would deliberate upon public events some months after they had taken place.

The opinions of this club were completely controlled by Nicholas Vedder, a patriarch[12] of the village, and landlord of the inn, at the door of which he took his seat from morning till night, just moving sufficiently to avoid the sun and keep in the shade of a large tree; so that the neighbors could tell the hour by his movements as accurately as by a sundial. It is true he was rarely heard to speak, but smoked his pipe incessantly. His adherents, however, perfectly understood him, and knew how to gather his opinions. When anything that was read or related displeased him, he was observed to smoke his pipe vehemently, and to send forth short, frequent, and angry puffs; but when pleased, he would inhale the smoke slowly and tranquilly, and emit it in light and placid clouds; and sometimes, taking the pipe from his mouth, and letting the fragrant vapor curl about his nose, would gravely nod his head in token of perfect approbation.

From even this stronghold the unlucky Rip was at length routed by his wife, who would suddenly break in upon the tranquillity of the assemblage and call the members all to naught; nor was that august[13] personage, Nicholas Vedder himself, sacred from the daring tongue of this terrible shrew, who charged him outright with encouraging her husband in habits of idleness.

Poor Rip was at last reduced almost to despair; and his only alternative, to escape from the labor of the farm and clamor of his wife, was to take gun in hand and stroll away into the woods. Here he would sometimes seat himself at the foot of a tree, and share the contents of his wallet[14] with Wolf, with whom he sympathized as a fellow sufferer in persecution. "Poor Wolf," he would say, "thy mistress leads thee a dog's life of it; but never mind, my lad, whilst I live thou shalt never want a friend to stand by thee!" Wolf would wag his tail, look wistfully in his master's face, and if dogs can feel pity, I believe he returned the sentiment with all his heart.

In a long ramble of the kind on a fine autumnal day, Rip had unconsciously scrambled to one of the highest parts of the Catskill Mountains. He was after his favorite sport of squirrel shooting, and the still solitudes[15] had echoed and reechoed with the reports of his gun. Panting and fatigued, he threw himself, late in the afternoon, on a green knoll, covered with mountain herbage, that crowned the brow of a precipice. From an opening between the trees he could overlook all the lower country for many a mile of rich woodland. He saw at a distance the lordly Hudson, far, far below him, moving on its silent but majestic course, with the reflection of a purple cloud, or the sail of a lagging bark,[16] here and there sleeping on its glassy bosom, and at last losing itself in the blue highlands.

On the other side he looked down into a deep mountain glen, wild, lonely, and shagged, the bottom filled with fragments from the overhanging cliffs, and scarcely lighted by the reflected rays of the setting sun. For some time Rip lay musing on this scene. Evening was gradually advancing. The mountains began to throw their long blue shadows

---

12. **patriarch** (pā'trē-ärk'): a man who is head of a family or a tribe; here, an old man of great dignity and authority.
13. **august** (ô-gŭst'): deserving respect.

14. **wallet:** here, a bag for carrying provisions.
15. **solitudes:** deserted places.
16. **bark:** boat.

over the valleys. He saw that it would be dark before he could reach the village, and he heaved a heavy sigh when he thought of encountering the terrors of Dame Van Winkle.

As he was about to descend, he heard a voice from a distance, hallooing, "Rip Van Winkle! Rip Van Winkle!" He looked round, but could see nothing but a crow winging its solitary flight across the mountain. He thought his fancy[17] must have deceived him, and turned again to descend, when he heard the same cry ring through the still evening air: "Rip Van Winkle! Rip Van Winkle!" At the same time Wolf bristled up his back, and giving a low growl, skulked to his master's side, looking fearfully down into the glen. Rip now felt a vague apprehension[18] stealing over him; he looked anxiously in the same direction, and perceived a strange figure slowly toiling up the rocks, and bending under the weight of something he carried on his back. He was surprised to see any human being in this lonely and unfrequented place, but supposing it to be someone of the neighborhood in need of his assistance, he hastened down to yield it.

On nearer approach he was still more surprised at the singularity of the stranger's appearance. He was a short, square-built old fellow, with thick, bushy hair and a grizzled beard. His dress was of the antique Dutch fashion—a cloth jerkin[19] strapped round the waist—several pairs of breeches, the outer one of ample volume, decorated with rows of buttons down the sides, and bunches at the knees. He bore on his shoulder a stout keg, that seemed full of liquor, and made signs for Rip to approach and assist him with the load. Though rather shy and distrustful of this new acquaintance, Rip complied with his usual readiness; and mutually relieving one another, they clambered up a narrow gully, apparently the dry bed of a mountain torrent. As they ascended, Rip every now and then heard long rolling peals, like distant thunder, that seemed to issue out of a deep ravine, or rather cleft, between lofty rocks, toward which their rugged path conducted. He paused for an instant, but supposing it to be the muttering of one of those transient thundershowers which often take place in mountain heights, he proceeded. Passing through the ravine, they came to a hollow, like a small amphitheater,[20] surrounded by perpendicular precipices, over the brinks of which trees shot their branches, so that you only caught glimpses of the azure sky and the bright evening cloud. During the whole time Rip and his companion had labored on in silence; for though Rip marveled greatly what could be the object of carrying a keg of liquor up this wild mountain, yet there was something strange and incomprehensible about the unknown, that inspired awe and checked familiarity.

On entering the amphitheater, new objects of wonder presented themselves. On a level spot in the center was a company of odd-looking personages playing at ninepins. They were dressed in a quaint, outlandish fashion; some wore short doublets,[21] others jerkins, with long knives in their belts, and most of them had enormous breeches, of style similar to that of the guide's. Their visages,[22] too, were peculiar. One had a large head, broad face, and small, piggish eyes. The face of another seemed to consist entirely of nose, and was surmounted by a white sugar-loaf hat,[23] set off with a little red cock's tail. They all had

---

17. **fancy:** imagination.
18. **apprehension** (ăp'rĭ-hĕn'shən): fear.
19. **jerkin:** a short, fitted jacket.

20. **amphitheater** (ăm'fə-thē'ə-tər): here, a level area surrounded by mountain slopes.
21. **doublets:** close-fitting, elaborate jackets.
22. **visages** (vĭz'ĭj-əz): faces.
23. **sugar-loaf hat:** a cone-shaped hat.

beards, of various shapes and colors. There was one who seemed to be the commander. He was a stout old gentleman, with a weather-beaten countenance; he wore a laced doublet, broad belt and hanger,[24] high-crowned hat and feather, red stockings, and high-heeled shoes, with roses in them. The whole group reminded Rip of the figures in an old Flemish[25] painting, in the parlor of the village parson, which had been brought over from Holland at the time of the settlement.

What seemed particularly odd to Rip was that, though these folks were evidently amusing themselves, yet they maintained the gravest faces, the most mysterious silence, and were the most melancholy party of pleasure he had

ever witnessed. Nothing interrupted the stillness of the scene but the noise of the balls, which, whenever they were rolled, echoed along the mountains like rumbling peals of thunder.

As Rip and his companion approached them, they suddenly stopped their play, and stared at him with such fixed, statuelike gaze, and such strange, lackluster countenances, that his heart turned within him, and his knees smote together. His companion now emptied the contents of the keg into large flagons,[26] and made signs to him to wait upon the company. He obeyed with fear and trembling; they quaffed[27] the liquor in profound silence, and then returned to their game.

By degrees Rip's awe and apprehension sub-

24. **hanger:** here, a short sword.
25. **Flemish:** referring to Flanders, a former country in northwest Europe that included part of modern-day France, all of Belgium, and the southern portion of the Netherlands, or Holland.

26. **flagons** (flăg'ənz): containers with handles and spouts.
27. **quaffed** (kwäft): drank deeply.

sided. He even ventured, when no eye was fixed upon him, to taste the beverage, which he found had much of the flavor of excellent Holland gin. He was naturally a thirsty soul, and was soon tempted to repeat the draft.[28] One taste provoked another; and he repeated his visits to the flagon so often that at length his senses were overpowered, his eyes swam in his head, his head gradually declined, and he fell into a deep sleep.

On waking, he found himself on the green knoll whence he had first seen the old man of the glen. He rubbed his eyes—it was a bright sunny morning. The birds were hopping and twittering among the bushes, and the eagle was wheeling aloft, and breasting the pure mountain breeze. "Surely," thought Rip, "I have not slept here all night." He recalled the occurrences before he fell asleep. The strange man with a keg of liquor—the mountain ravine—the wild retreat among the rocks—the woebegone party at ninepins—the flagon— "Oh! that flagon! that wicked flagon!" thought Rip—"what excuse shall I make to Dame Van Winkle?"

He looked round for his gun, but in place of the clean, well-oiled fowling piece, he found an old firelock lying by him, the barrel incrusted with rust, the lock falling off, and the stock worm-eaten. He now suspected that the grave roisters[29] of the mountain had put a trick upon him, and, having dosed him with liquor, had robbed him of his gun. Wolf, too, had disappeared, but he might have strayed away after a squirrel or partridge. He whistled after him and shouted his name, but all in vain; the echoes repeated his whistle and shout, but no dog was to be seen.

He determined to revisit the scene of the last evening's gambol,[30] and if he met with any of the party, to demand his dog and gun. As he rose to walk, he found himself stiff in the joints. "These mountain beds do not agree with me," thought Rip, "and if this frolic should lay me up with a fit of the rheumatism, I shall have a blessed time with Dame Van Winkle." With some difficulty he got down into the glen. He found the gully up which he and his companion had ascended the preceding evening; but to his astonishment a mountain stream was now foaming down it, leaping from rock to rock, and filling the glen with babbling murmurs. He, however, made shift to scramble up its sides, working his toilsome way through thickets of birch, sassafras, and witch hazel, and sometimes tripped up or entangled by the wild grapevines that twisted their coils or tendrils from tree to tree, and spread a kind of network in his path.

At length he reached to where the ravine had opened through the cliffs to the amphitheater; but no traces of such opening remained. The rocks presented a high wall over which the torrent came tumbling in a sheet of feathery foam, and fell into a broad, deep basin, black from the shadows of the surrounding forest. Here, then, poor Rip was brought to a stand. He again called and whistled after his dog; he was only answered by the cawing of a flock of idle crows, who seemed to look down and scoff at the poor man's perplexities. What was to be done? The morning was passing away, and Rip felt famished for want of his breakfast. He grieved to give up his dog and gun; he dreaded to meet his wife; but it would not do to starve among the mountains. He shook his head, shouldered the rusty firelock, and, with a heart full of trouble and anxiety, turned his steps homeward.

As he approached the village, he met a number of people, but none whom he knew, which somewhat surprised him, for he had thought himself acquainted with everyone in the coun-

28. **draft:** here, a drink.
29. **roisters:** merrymakers; also called *roisterers.*
30. **gambol:** frolic.

try round. Their dress, too, was of a different fashion from that to which he was accustomed. They all stared at him with equal marks of surprise, and whenever they cast their eyes upon him, invariably stroked their chins. The recurrence of this gesture induced Rip to do the same, when, to his astonishment, he found his beard had grown a foot long!

He had now entered the outskirts of the village. A troop of strange children ran at his heels, hooting after him, and pointing at his gray beard. The dogs, too, not one of which he recognized for an old acquaintance, barked at him as he passed. The very village was altered; it was larger and more populous. There were rows of houses which he had never seen before, and those which had been his familiar haunts had disappeared. Strange names were over the doors—strange faces at the windows—everything was strange. His mind now misgave him; he began to doubt whether both he and the world around him were not bewitched. Surely this was his native village, which he had left but the day before. There stood the Catskill Mountains—there ran the silver Hudson at a distance—there was every hill and dale precisely as it had always been— Rip was sorely perplexed. "That flagon last night," thought he, "has addled[31] my poor head sadly!"

31. **addled:** confused.

It was with some difficulty that he found the way to his own house, which he approached with silent awe, expecting every moment to hear the shrill voice of Dame Van Winkle. He found the house gone to decay—the roof fallen in, the windows shattered, and the doors off the hinges. A half-starved dog that looked like Wolf was skulking about it. Rip called him by name, but the cur snarled, showed his teeth, and passed on. This was an unkind cut indeed. "My very dog," sighed poor Rip, "has forgotten me!"

He entered the house, which, to tell the truth, Dame Van Winkle had always kept in neat order. It was empty, forlorn, and apparently abandoned. This desolateness overcame all his fears—he called loudly for his wife and children—the lonely chambers rang for a moment with his voice, and then all again was silence.

He now hurried forth, and hastened to his old resort, the village inn—but it too was gone. A large, rickety wooden building stood in its place, with great gaping windows, some of them broken and mended with old hats and petticoats, and over the door was painted, "The Union Hotel, by Jonathan Doolittle." Instead of the great tree that used to shelter the quiet little Dutch inn of yore, there now was reared a tall naked pole, with something on the top that looked like a red nightcap,[32] and from it was fluttering a flag, on which was a singular assemblage of stars and stripes—all this was strange and incomprehensible. He recognized on the sign, however, the ruby face of King George, under which he had smoked so many a peaceful pipe; but even this was singularly changed. The red coat was changed for one of blue and buff, a sword was held in the hand instead of a scepter, the head was decorated with a cocked hat, and underneath was painted in large characters, GENERAL WASHINGTON.

There was, as usual, a crowd of folk about the door, but none that Rip recollected. The very character of the people seemed changed. There was a busy, bustling tone about it, instead of the accustomed tranquillity. He looked in vain for the sage Nicholas Vedder, with his broad face, double chin, and fair long pipe, uttering clouds of tobacco smoke instead of idle speeches; or Van Bummel, the schoolmaster, doling forth the contents of an ancient

newspaper. In place of these, a lean, bilious-looking[33] fellow, with his pockets full of handbills, was talking vehemently about rights of citizens—elections—members of Congress—liberty—Bunker's Hill—heroes of seventy-six—and other words, which were a perfect Babylonish jargon[34] to the bewildered Van Winkle.

The appearance of Rip, with his long, grizzled beard, his rusty fowling piece, his uncouth dress, and an army of women and children at his heels, soon attracted the attention of the tavern politicians. They crowded round him, eyeing him from head to foot with great curiosity. The orator bustled up to him, and drawing him partly aside, inquired "on which side he voted?" Rip stared in vacant stupidity. Another short but busy little fellow pulled him by the arm, and, rising on tiptoe, inquired in his ear, "whether he was Federal or Democrat?"[35] Rip was equally at a loss to comprehend the question, when a knowing, self-important old gentleman, in a sharp cocked hat, made his way through the crowd, putting them to the right and left with his elbows as he passed, and planting himself before Van Winkle, with one arm akimbo,[36] the other resting on his cane, his keen eyes and sharp hat penetrating, as it were, into his very soul, demanded in an austere tone, "what brought him to the election with a gun on his shoulder, and a mob at his heels; and whether he meant to breed a riot in the village?"

33. **bilious** (bĭl'yəs) **-looking:** having a bad-tempered look.
34. **Babylonish** (băb'ə-lŏn'ĭsh) **jargon:** unintelligible language. According to Genesis 11:1–9, the people of Babel, or Babylon, tried to build a tower that would reach to heaven. They were forced to stop their work when God caused them to speak different languages.
35. **Federal or Democrat:** a member of the Federalist Party or the Democratic-Republican Party. These were the two political parties in the early years of United States history.
36. **akimbo:** holding the hand on the hip with the elbow outward.

32. **red nightcap:** Rip's interpretation of the liberty cap, a symbol of freedom.

"Alas! gentlemen," cried Rip, somewhat dismayed, "I am a poor quiet man, a native of the place, and a loyal subject of the King, God bless him!"

Here a general shout burst from the bystanders—"A Tory![37] a Tory! a spy! a refugee! hustle him! away with him!" It was with great difficulty that the self-important man in the cocked hat restored order; and demanded again of the unknown culprit, what he came there for, and whom he was seeking. The poor man humbly assured him that he meant no harm, but merely came there in search of some of his neighbors, who used to keep about the tavern.

"Well—who are they?—name them."

Rip bethought himself a moment, and inquired, "Where's Nicholas Vedder?"

There was a silence for a little while, when an old man replied, in a thin, piping voice, "Nicholas Vedder! why, he is dead and gone these eighteen years! There was a wooden tombstone in the churchyard that used to tell all about him, but that's rotten and gone too."

"Where's Brom Dutcher?"

"Oh, he went off to the army in the beginning of the war; some say he was killed at the storming of Stony Point[38]—others say he was drowned in a squall at the foot of Antony's Nose.[39] I don't know—he never came back again."

"Where's Van Bummel, the schoolmaster?"

"He went off to the wars too, was a great militia general, and is now in Congress."

Rip's heart died away at hearing of these sad changes in his home and friends, and finding himself thus alone in the world. Every answer puzzled him, too, by treating of such enormous lapses of time, and of matters which he could not understand: war—Congress—Stony Point; he had no courage to ask after any more friends, but cried out in despair, "Does nobody here know Rip Van Winkle?"

"Oh, Rip Van Winkle!" exclaimed two or three; "oh, to be sure! that's Rip Van Winkle yonder, leaning against the tree."

Rip looked, and beheld a precise copy of himself, as he went up the mountain; apparently as lazy, and certainly as ragged. The poor fellow was now completely bewildered. He doubted his own identity, and whether he was himself or another man. In the midst of his bewilderment, the man in the cocked hat demanded who he was, and what was his name.

"God knows," exclaimed he, at his wit's end; "I'm not myself—I'm somebody else—that's me yonder—no—that's somebody else got into my shoes—I was myself last night, but I fell asleep on the mountain, and they've changed my gun, and everything's changed, and I'm changed, and I can't tell what's my name, or who I am!"

The bystanders began now to look at each other, nod, wink significantly, and tap their fingers against their foreheads. There was a whisper, also, about securing the gun, and keeping the old fellow from doing mischief, at the very suggestion of which the self-important man in the cocked hat retired quickly. At this critical moment a fresh, comely[40] woman pressed through the throng to get a peep at the gray-bearded man. She had a chubby child in her arms, which, frightened at his looks, began to cry. "Hush, Rip," cried she, "hush, you little fool; the old man

---

37. **Tory:** someone who sided with the British cause during the American Revolution.
38. **Stony Point:** a town on the Hudson River where American Revolutionary troops under General Anthony Wayne won an important battle against the British in July 1779.
39. **Antony's Nose:** a mountain on the Hudson River. It was called *Antonies Neus* by the Dutch, and changed to *Anthony's Nose* by the British.

40. **comely** (kŭm′lē): beautiful.

won't hurt you." The name of the child, the air of the mother, the tone of her voice, all awakened a train of recollections in his mind. "What is your name, my good woman?" asked he.

"Judith Gardenier."

"And your father's name?"

"Ah, poor man, Rip Van Winkle was his name, but it's twenty years since he went away from home with his gun, and never has been heard of since—his dog came home without him; but whether he shot himself, or was carried away by the Indians, nobody can tell. I was then but a little girl."

Rip had but one question more to ask; but he put it with a faltering voice: "Where's your mother?"

"Oh, she too had died but a short time since; she broke a blood vessel in a fit of passion at a New England peddler."

There was a drop of comfort, at least, in this intelligence.[41] The honest man could contain himself no longer. He caught his daughter and her child in his arms. "I am your father!" cried he—"Young Rip Van Winkle once—old Rip Van Winkle now!—Does nobody know poor Rip Van Winkle?"

All stood amazed, until an old woman, tottering out from among the crowd, put her hand to her brow, and peering under it in his face for a moment, exclaimed, "Sure enough! it is Rip Van Winkle—it is himself! Welcome home again, old neighbor. Why, where have you been these twenty long years?"

Rip's story was soon told, for the whole twenty years had been to him as but one night. The neighbors stared when they heard it; some were seen to wink at each other, and put their tongues in their cheeks; and the self-important man in the cocked hat, who, when the alarm was over, had returned to the field, screwed down the corners of his mouth, and shook his head—upon which there was a general shaking of the head throughout the assemblage.

It was determined, however, to take the opinion of old Peter Vanderdonk, who was seen slowly advancing up the road. He was a descendant of the historian of that name, who wrote one of the earliest accounts of the province. Peter was the most ancient inhabitant of the village, and well versed in all the wonderful events and traditions of the neighborhood. He recollected Rip at once, and corroborated his story in the most satisfactory manner. He assured the company that it was a fact, handed down from his ancestor the historian, that the Catskill Mountains had always been haunted by strange beings. That it was affirmed that the great Henry Hudson, the first discoverer of the river and country,[42] kept a kind of vigil there every twenty years, with his crew of the *Half-Moon;* being permitted in this way to revisit the scenes of his enterprise and keep a guardian eye upon the river and the great city called by his name. That his father had once seen them in their old Dutch dresses playing at ninepins in a hollow of the mountain; and that he himself had heard, one summer afternoon, the sound of their balls, like distant peals of thunder.

To make a long story short, the company broke up, and returned to the more important concerns of the election. Rip's daughter took him home to live with her; she had a snug, well-furnished house, and a stout, cheery farmer for a husband, whom Rip recollected for one of the urchins that used to climb upon his back. As to Rip's son and heir, who was the ditto of himself, seen leaning against the tree, he was employed to work on the farm; but showed an hereditary disposition to attend to anything else but his business.

41. **intelligence:** here, a piece of news.

42. **country:** here, the Catskill area.

Rip now resumed his old walks and habits; he soon found many of his former cronies, though all rather the worse for the wear and tear of time; and preferred making friends among the rising generation, with whom he soon grew into great favor.

Having nothing to do at home, and being arrived at that happy age when a man can be idle with impunity, he took his place once more on the bench at the inn door, and was reverenced as one of the patriarchs of the village, and a chronicle of the old times "before the war." It was some time before he could get into the regular track of gossip, or could be made to comprehend the strange events that had taken place during his sleep. How that there had been a Revolutionary War—that the country had thrown off the yoke of old England—and that, instead of being a subject of His Majesty George the Third, he was now a free citizen of the United States. Rip, in fact, was no politician; the changes of states and empires made but little impression on him; but there was one species of despotism under which he had long groaned, and that was—petticoat government. Happily that was at an end; he had got his neck out of the yoke of matrimony, and could go in and out whenever he pleased, without dreading the tyranny of Dame Van Winkle. Whenever her name was mentioned, however, he shook his head, shrugged his shoulders, and cast up his eyes; which might pass either for an expression of resignation to his fate, or joy at his deliverance.

He used to tell his story to every stranger that arrived at Mr. Doolittle's hotel. He was observed, at first, to vary on some points every time he told it, which was, doubtless, owing to his having so recently awaked. It at last settled down precisely to the tale I have related, and not a man, woman, or child in the neighborhood but knew it by heart. Some always pretended to doubt the reality of it, and insisted that Rip had been out of his head, and that this was one point on which he always remained flighty. The old Dutch inhabitants, however, almost universally gave it full credit. Even to this day they never hear a thunderstorm of a summer afternoon about the Catskills but they say Henry Hudson and his crew are at their game of ninepins; and it is a common wish of all henpecked husbands in the neighborhood, when life hangs heavy on their hands, that they might have a quieting draft out of Rip Van Winkle's flagon.

Reading Check

1. Who were the original colonists of Rip's village?
2. Who is Rip's only follower?
3. What is the "club of the sages"?
4. What is the stranger in the glen carrying?
5. What is the "thunder" Rip hears?
6. Why is Rip asked to follow the stranger?
7. When Rip wakes up, what does he assume has happened to his gun?
8. What does Rip find when he returns to his home?
9. What has happened to Dame Van Winkle?
10. Who finally recognizes Rip Van Winkle?

For Study and Discussion

Analyzing and Interpreting the Selection

1. Although this story is about Rip Van Winkle, Washington Irving doesn't introduce Rip until the third paragraph of the story. In the first two paragraphs, Irving describes the **setting** of the story—the place and the time of the action. How do the phrases "magical hues and shapes" and "fairy mountains" prepare you for the strange events to come?

2. Rip is described as having a "dislike of all kinds of profitable labor." **a.** What kinds of "unprofitable labor" does he enjoy? **b.** What "unprofitable labor" does he find in the mountains?

3a. What contrast is there between Rip's temperament and that of Dame Van Winkle? **b.** How would you describe Rip's conflict? **c.** How is this conflict related to the two places where the action occurs, the village and the mountains?

4. "Rip Van Winkle" opens during the colonial period of American history. By the end of the story, you learn that the colonies have "thrown off the yoke of old England" and become free. **a.** What changes does Rip find in the village when he returns? **b.** In what way is Rip's "history" like the history of his country?

5. The story "Rip Van Winkle" has appealed to generations of readers who have recognized in Rip's experience the fulfillment of their own wishes. Why do you think readers can put themselves in Rip's place so easily?

Literary Elements

Focusing on Setting

Some readers become impatient with descriptions of setting. They are eager to get on with the action and may wonder why the writer interrupts the story with passages describing the physical surroundings.

The setting of "Rip Van Winkle" brings Rip's conflict into sharp focus for the reader. The world of Rip's everyday existence is drawn in realistic detail. Irving describes the houses "built of small yellow bricks brought from Holland," which have "latticed windows and gable fronts, surmounted with weathercocks." He also gives you a detailed and comic picture of Rip's domestic troubles. In this passage he tells you how everything on Rip's farm would go wrong: "His fences were continually falling to pieces; his cow would either go astray or get among the cabbages; weeds were sure to grow quicker in his fields than anywhere else. . . ."

Find the passage that shows you why Rip was a great favorite with the children in the village. What kinds of "unprofitable labor" did Rip perform for the children?

When Irving describes the Catskill Mountains, he dwells on their unreal, magical quality:

> Every change of season, every change of weather, indeed, every hour of the day, produces some change in the magical hues and shapes of these mountains. . . . When the weather is fair and settled, they are clothed in blue and purple, and print their bold outlines on the clear evening sky; but, sometimes, when the rest of the landscape is cloudless, they will gather a hood of gray vapors about their summits, which, in the last rays of the setting sun, will glow and light up like a crown of glory.

The description suggests what the mountains represent for Rip—an escape from the real world and all its problems.

Find the passage on page 251 in which Irving describes evening falling on the mountains. Which words give you an eerie feeling about the mountains? Henry Hudson and his crew are also part of the setting. Which words does Irving use to make the men seem as strange and unusual as the mountains?

Understanding Character Types

Dame Van Winkle's situation is hardly comical. She has a shiftless husband who allows his farm to fall to pieces, who spends more time away from his family than with them, and who leaves his children ill-fed and ill-clothed. Yet Irving treats Dame Van Winkle as a comic character who provides a great deal of humor in the story.

You can laugh at Dame Van Winkle because Irving shows her in only one light. Whenever you see Dame Van Winkle in the story, she is scolding or nagging Rip, his dog Wolf, or his cronies in the village. If you were allowed to see Dame Van Winkle laughing with her children or crying in despair over her hardships, your reaction to her would probably be very different. However, Irving does not show these other qualities in Dame Van Winkle. She is represented only as a *shrew*, a bad-tempered, quarrelsome woman.

You have seen that a writer can use the element of surprise—the contrast between the expected and the unexpected—to produce humor. A writer can also use **exaggeration** for humorous effects. Irving makes Dame Van Winkle laughable by exaggerating one side of her character.

> Morning, noon, and night, her tongue was incessantly going, and everything he said or did was sure to produce a torrent of household eloquence.

The word *torrent* generally refers to a heavy rain. What does Irving mean by the phrase "a torrent of household eloquence"? Find other examples in the story where Dame Van Winkle's bad temper is humorously exaggerated.

Irving also enjoys treating the conflict between Rip and his wife as a series of battles. By shrugging his shoulders, Rip "always provoked a fresh *volley* from his wife." What is a *volley*?

Dame Van Winkle is described as invading the "club of the sages": "From even this stronghold the unlucky Rip was at length *routed* by his wife" (page 251). The word *routed* calls up the image of an army being driven from a fortress in complete disorder and bewilderment. When you realize that this invader uses no weapon but her tongue, the comparison becomes laughable. Rip has as great a fear of his wife's harsh words as a soldier might have of his enemy's firearms.

Irving, of course, is not suggesting that all wives are shrewish any more than he is saying that all husbands are lazy. Irving is showing the reader that there are some qualities in people that provoke laughter if they are carried to excess.

Dame Van Winkle is not presented as a fully rounded individual. She is a **character type**— someone who fits a pattern and who can be recognized by certain typical characteristics. In the case of a shrew, the typical characteristics are nagging and scolding.

Language and Vocabulary

Recognizing Shades of Meaning

Throughout the story Irving stresses the strangeness of Rip's experience. The word *strange* is used on ten separate occasions to describe something unfamiliar. See if you can locate each instance.

Irving also uses words that are closely related in meaning to *strange*:

> On a level spot in the center was a company of *odd*-looking personages playing at ninepins. They were dressed in a *quaint, outlandish* fashion. . . . Their visages, too, were *peculiar*.

The word *odd* has the general meaning "strange," but also carries an additional meaning of being "out of the ordinary":

odd = strange + out of the ordinary

In a dictionary find the words *quaint, outlandish,* and *peculiar*. What shade of meaning does each word have in addition to the meaning of "strange"?

The word *lonely* also appears several times in the story, along with synonyms. Look at the passage where Rip returns to his deserted house (page 256). What words in this passage have the meaning of "lonely"? What additional meaning does each of the words have?

Writing About Literature

Explaining the Function of Setting

Consider the importance of setting in one of the other stories you have read. For example, think about the element of setting in "The Wild Duck's Nest" (page 180). How is the setting in that story a key to the character's thoughts and feelings? How does the change in setting reflect the change in the way Colm feels?

Think about the setting in "Antaeus" (page 187). How is it essential to the plot?

Write a short essay in which you explain the role of setting in one of these stories or another story of your choice.

Creative Writing

Dramatizing the Story

Turn Irving's story into a play of several scenes. Create dialogue and stage directions for your actors. You might choose a narrator to fill in scenes that can't be shown on the stage. Think about ways to make Rip age twenty years while he is asleep. How will you suggest the changes in the village?

If you like, turn the story into a musical. Write your own lyrics to popular tunes. If there is a musician in class, he or she might compose some original music for your play.

For help in writing your play, see pages 377–378.

Extending Your Study

Evaluating Illustrations

The story of Rip Van Winkle has appealed to the imagination of several artists. See if your library contains any early illustrated editions of the story. Bring the books to class and show the illustrations. If you wish, prepare a report comparing the illustrations of different artists. How well does each artist capture the character of Rip? How effective are the illustrations of setting? What details from the story do you recognize in the illustrations?

About the Author

Washington Irving   (1783–1859)

Washington Irving said, "When I first wrote the legend of Rip Van Winkle, my thoughts had been for some time turned toward giving a color of romance and tradition to interesting points of our national scenery." Irving borrowed the idea for his story from an Old German folk tale, but he set it in the Hudson River country of New York. In this way, he glorified an American place as no writer before him had done. Today he is remembered as America's first major literary figure.

As a boy, Irving was adventurous and restless. When he was fourteen, he planned to run away to sea. He prepared for this adventure by eating salt pork and sleeping on the hard floor of his room. He liked to spend his time wandering around New York. "I knew every spot," he said, "where a murder or robbery had been committed, or a ghost seen." He had a lively imagination, and although he studied law, he was quickly drawn to a literary career.

From 1807 to 1808, he contributed humorous essays to *Salmagundi,* a periodical he had helped to create. In 1809 he published the first of his two great books, a comic history of New York with a long title, now known simply as *Knickerbocker's History of New York.* Irving's masterpiece, *The Sketch Book,* appeared ten years later. It was a collection of over thirty pieces, including his two most famous stories, "Rip Van Winkle" and "The Legend of Sleepy Hollow." In his later years, Irving spent a great deal of time in Europe searching for more old tales and anecdotes. After he returned to America, he built himself a remarkable house in Tarrytown, New York, which he called "Sunnyside." There he spent his remaining days writing a five-volume biography of George Washington.

You Can't Take It with You

EVA-LIS WUORIO°

Sometimes in a short story characters' actions bring about an unexpected result. Such a situation, in which things turn out to be different from what characters expect, is called an ironic situation.

What is ironic about the outcome of this story? Is the ending satisfying?

There was no denying two facts. Uncle Basil was rich. Uncle Basil was a miser.

The family were unanimous about that. They had used up all the words as their temper and their need of ready money dictated. Gentle Aunt Clotilda, who wanted a new string of pearls because the one she had was getting old, had merely called him Scrooge[1] Basil. Percival, having again smashed his Aston Martin[2] for which he had not paid, had declared Uncle Basil a skinflint, a miser, tightwad, churl, and usurer with colorful adjectives added. The rest had used up all the other words in the dictionary.

"He doesn't have to be so parsimonious,[3] that's true, with all he has," said Percival's mother. "But you shouldn't use rude words, Percival. They might get back to him."

"He can't take it with him," said Percival's sister Letitia, combing her golden hair. "I need a new fur but he said, 'Why? it's summer.' Well! He's mingy,[4] that's what he is."

3. **parsimonious** (pär′sə-mō′nē-əs): stingy.
4. **mingy** (mĭn′jē): mean and stingy.

° **Eva-Lis Wuorio** (ā′vă-lēs wôr′ē-ō).
1. **Scrooge:** the most famous miser in literature. See Dickens' "A Christmas Carol," page 276.
2. **Aston Martin:** a very expensive sports car.

"He can't take it with him" was a phrase the family used so often it began to slip out in front of Uncle. Basil as well.

"You can't take it with you, Uncle Basil," they said. "Why don't you buy a sensible house out in the country, and we could all come and visit you? Horses. A swimming pool. The lot. Think what fun you'd have, and you can certainly afford it. You can't take it with you, you know."

Uncle Basil had heard all the words they called him because he wasn't as deaf as he made out. He knew he was a mingy, stingy, penny-pinching screw, scrimp, scraper, pinchfist, hoarder, and curmudgeon[5] (just to start with). There were other words, less gentle, he'd also heard himself called. He didn't mind. What galled him was the oft repeated warning, "You can't take it with you." After all, it was all his.

5. **curmudgeon** (kər-mŭj′ən): ill-tempered, disagreeable person.

He'd gone to the Transvaal[6] when there was still gold to be found if one knew where to look. He'd found it. They said he'd come back too old to enjoy his fortune. What did they know? He enjoyed simply having a fortune. He enjoyed also saying no to them all. They were like circus animals, he often thought, behind the bars of their thousand demands of something for nothing.

Only once had he said yes. That was when his sister asked him to take on Verner, her somewhat slow-witted eldest son. "He'll do as your secretary," his sister Maud had said. Verner didn't do at all as a secretary, but since all

6. **Transvaal** (trăns-väl′, trănz-): a province of the Republic of South Africa, formerly known as South African Republic.

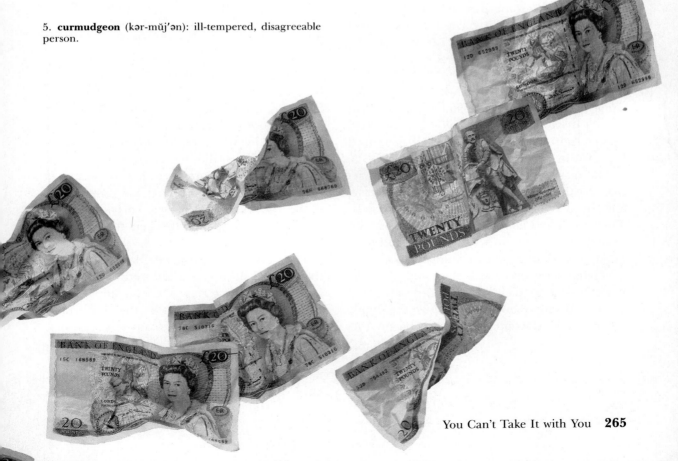

he wanted to be happy was to be told what to do, Uncle Basil let him stick around as an all-around handyman.

Uncle Basil lived neatly in a house very much too small for his money, the family said, in an unfashionable suburb. It was precisely like the house where he had been born. Verner looked after the small garden, fetched the papers from the corner tobacconist, and filed his nails when he had time. He had nice nails. He never said to Uncle Basil, "You can't take it with you," because it didn't occur to him.

Uncle Basil also used Verner to run messages to his man of affairs, the bank, and such, since he didn't believe either in the mails or the telephone. Verner got used to carrying thick envelopes back and forth without ever bothering to question what was in them. Uncle Basil's lawyers, accountants, and bank managers also got used to his somewhat unorthodox[7] business methods. He did have a fortune, and he kept making money with his investments. Rich men have always been allowed their foibles.

Another foible of Uncle Basil's was that, while he still was in excellent health he had Verner drive him out to an old-fashioned carpenter shop where he had himself measured for a coffin. He wanted it roomy, he said.

The master carpenter was a dour countryman of the same generation as Uncle Basil, and he accepted the order matter-of-factly. They consulted about woods and prices, and settled on a medium-price, unlined coffin. A lined one would have cost double.

"I'll line it myself," Uncle Basil said. "Or Verner can. There's plenty of time. I don't intend to pop off tomorrow. It would give the family too much satisfaction. I like enjoying my fortune."

7. **unorthodox** (ŭn'ôr'thə-dŏks'): not customary or traditional.

Then one morning, while in good humor and sound mind, he sent Verner for his lawyer. The family got to hear about this and there were in-fights, out-fights, and general quarreling while they tried to find out to whom Uncle Basil had decided to leave his money. To put them out of their misery, he said, he'd tell them the truth. He didn't like scattering money about. He liked it in a lump sum. Quit bothering him about it.

That happened a good decade before the morning his housekeeper, taking him his tea, found him peacefully asleep forever. It had been a good decade for him. The family hadn't dared to worry him, and his investments had risen steadily.

Only Percival, always pressed for money, had threatened to put arsenic in his tea but when the usual proceedings were gone through Uncle Basil was found to have died a natural death. "A happy death," said the family. "He hadn't suffered."

They began to remember loudly how nice they'd been to him and argued about who had been the nicest. It was true too. They had been attentive, the way families tend to be to rich and stubborn elderly relatives. They didn't know he'd heard all they'd said out of his hearing, as well as the flattering drivel they'd spread like soft butter on hot toast in his hearing. Everyone, recalling his own efforts to be thoroughly nice, was certain that he and only he would be the heir to the Lump Sum.

They rushed to consult the lawyer. He said that he had been instructed by Uncle Basil in sane and precise terms. The cremation was to take place immediately after the death, and they would find the coffin ready in the garden shed. Verner would know where it was.

"Nothing else?"

"Well," said the lawyer in the way lawyers have, "he left instructions for a funeral repast to be sent in from Fortnum and Mason.[8] Everything of the best. Goose and turkey, venison and beef, oysters and lobsters, and wines of good vintage plus plenty of whiskey. He liked to think of a good send-off, curmudgeon though he was, he'd said."

The family was a little shaken by the use of the word "curmudgeon." How did Uncle Basil know about that? But they were relieved to hear that the lawyer also had an envelope, the contents of which he did not know, to read to them at the feast after the cremation.

They all bought expensive black clothes, since black was the color of that season anyway, and whoever inherited would share the wealth. That was only fair.

Only Verner said that couldn't they buy Uncle Basil a smarter coffin? The one in the garden shed was pretty tatty, since the roof leaked. But the family hardly listened to him. After all, it would only be burned, so what did it matter?

So, duly and with proper sorrow, Uncle Basil was cremated.

The family returned to the little house as the housekeeper was leaving. Uncle Basil had given her a generous amount of cash, telling her how to place it so as to have a fair income for life. In gratitude she'd spread out the Fortnum and Mason goodies, but she wasn't prepared to stay to do the dishes.

They were a little surprised, but not dismayed, to hear from Verner that the house was now in his name. Uncle Basil had also given him a small sum of cash and told him how to invest it. The family taxed[9] him about it, but the amount was so nominal they were relieved to know Verner would be off their hands. Verner himself, though mildly missing the old man because he was used to him, was quite content with his lot. He wasn't used to much, so he didn't need much.

The storm broke when the lawyer finally opened the envelope.

There was only one line in Uncle Basil's scrawl.

"I did take it with me."

Of course there was a great to-do. What about the fortune? The millions and millions!

Yes, said the men of affairs, the accountants, and even the bank managers, who finally admitted, yes, there had been a very considerable fortune. Uncle Basil, however, had drawn large sums in cash, steadily and regularly, over the past decade. What had he done with it? That the men of affairs, the accountants, and the bank managers did not know. After all, it had been Uncle Basil's money, ergo,[10] his affair.

Not a trace of the vast fortune ever came to light.

No one thought to ask Verner, and it didn't occur to Verner to volunteer that for quite a long time he had been lining the coffin, at Uncle Basil's behest, with thick envelopes he brought back from the banks. First he'd done a thick layer of these envelopes all around the sides and bottom of the coffin. Then, as Uncle Basil wanted, he'd tacked on blue sailcloth.

He might not be so bright in his head but he was smart with his hands.

He'd done a neat job.

10. **ergo** (ûr′gō, âr′-): therefore.

---

8. **Fortnum and Mason:** a well-known store that supplies food for parties.
9. **taxed:** expressed disapproval of; criticized.

For Study and Discussion

Analyzing and Interpreting the Story

1. How does Uncle Basil manage to take his vast fortune with him when he dies?

2. How do the greed and selfishness of his family assist Uncle Basil in carrying out his plan?

3. Although Uncle Basil is a miser, he provides well for Verner and for his housekeeper. Why does he treat these two people with consideration?

4. You often enjoy a humorous situation more if you know that it is coming.   **a.** How do you know that Uncle Basil has some surprises in store for his family?   **b.** How are you, the reader, prepared for the ending? Find clues that the author supplies throughout the story.

Literary Elements

Recognizing Irony

Throughout the story Uncle Basil's relatives keep reminding him that he can't take his fortune with him when he dies. They expect, of course, that he will leave his money to them. Uncle Basil turns the tables on them so that they don't get a penny. Such a reversal of expectations is **ironic.**

There are other ironic situations in the story. Verner wishes to replace the tatty coffin in the garden shed with a nicer coffin. Because of their greed, the relatives refuse. They don't want to spend any money; ironically, they allow all the money to be destroyed.

An ironic ending is satisfying when it grows out of the events in the story. Think about Uncle Basil's attitude toward money. Think about his attitude toward his family. Consider also his strange business dealings. Are you prepared for the ending?

Language and Vocabulary

Determining Exact Meanings

There are a number of words used in this story to describe a stingy person. Among the nouns are *miser, skinflint, tightwad,* and *churl.* The adjectives include *mingy, penny-pinching,* and *parsimonious.* What other words used in the story can you add to these lists? Which words are slang?

Check the meanings of these words in a college or unabridged dictionary. How many of the words are exact synonyms? What differences are there in shades of meaning?

Writing About Literature

Writing a Plot Summary

Write a plot summary of the story, showing how the pattern of events grows out of a conflict. (For a model, refer to the essay on pages 205–206.)

Discussing Stock Characters

In humorous stories, like "Rip Van Winkle" (page 247) and "You Can't Take It with You," comic characters are frequently **stock characters,** or types, rather than individuals. The characters in Wuorio's story are not intended to be three-dimensional. Uncle Basil is a miser; Letitia is a gold digger; Verner is the slow-witted but good-hearted lackey.

Discuss the stock figures in some of the stories you have read. Who are the stock characters in Westerns? In detective stories?

About the Author

Eva-Lis Wuorio (1918 –   )

Eva-Lis Wuorio was born in Finland. At the age of eleven, she emigrated to Canada. She began her writing career working for newspapers in Toronto. Among her books are two novels about World War II: *Code Polonaise,* set in Poland, and *To Fight in Silence,* about the Dutch underground. She has also written a number of children's books. In 1962 *The Island of Fish in the Trees* was chosen by *The New York Times* as one of the Best Illustrated Children's Books of the Year. "You Can't Take It with You" is from a collection of tales called *Escape If You Can.*

Zlateh the Goat

ISAAC BASHEVIS SINGER

In addition to offering entertainment, a short story often expresses some idea about human nature or interpretation of experience that gives us insight into ourselves and others. This underlying meaning is known as the theme *of the story. As you read, ask yourself what meaning Singer attributes to the events in his story.*

At Hanukkah[1] time the road from the village to the town is usually covered with snow, but this year the winter had been a mild one. Hanukkah had almost come, yet little snow had fallen. The sun shone most of the time. The peasants complained that because of the dry weather there would be a poor harvest of winter grain. New grass sprouted, and the peasants sent their cattle out to pasture.

For Reuven the furrier it was a bad year, and after long hesitation he decided to sell Zlateh the goat. She was old and gave little milk. Feyvel the town butcher had offered eight gulden[2] for her. Such a sum would buy Hanukkah candles, potatoes and oil for pancakes, gifts for the children, and other holiday necessaries for the house. Reuven told his oldest boy, Aaron, to take the goat to town.

Aaron understood what taking the goat to Feyvel meant, but he had to obey his father. Leah, his mother, wiped the tears from her

eyes when she heard the news. Aaron's younger sisters, Anna and Miriam, cried loudly. Aaron put on his quilted jacket and a cap with earmuffs, bound a rope around Zlateh's neck, and took along two slices of bread with cheese to eat on the road. Aaron was supposed to deliver the goat by evening, spend the night at the butcher's, and return the next day with the money.

While the family said goodbye to the goat, and Aaron placed the rope around her neck, Zlateh stood as patiently and good-naturedly as ever. She licked Reuven's hand. She shook her small white beard. Zlateh trusted human beings. She knew that they always fed her and never did her any harm.

When Aaron brought her out on the road to town, she seemed somewhat astonished. She'd never been led in that direction before. She looked back at him questioningly, as if to say, "Where are you taking me?" But after a while she seemed to come to the conclusion that a goat shouldn't ask questions. Still, the road was different. They passed new fields, pastures, and huts with thatched roofs. Here and there a

1. **Hanukkah** (KHä′nōō-kə): a Jewish holiday, usually in December, celebrated for eight days.
2. **gulden** (gōōl′dən): coins used in several European countries; also called *guilders*.

Illustration by Maurice Sendak. © 1987.

dog barked and came running after them, but Aaron chased it away with his stick.

The sun was shining when Aaron left the village. Suddenly the weather changed. A large black cloud with a bluish center appeared in the east and spread itself rapidly over the sky. A cold wind blew in with it. The crows flew low, croaking. At first it looked as if it would rain, but instead it began to hail as in summer. It was early in the day, but it became dark as dusk. After a while the hail turned to snow.

In his twelve years Aaron had seen all kinds of weather, but he had never experienced a snow like this one. It was so dense it shut out the light of the day. In a short time their path was completely covered. The wind became as cold as ice. The road to town was narrow and winding. Aaron no longer knew where he was. He could not see through the snow. The cold soon penetrated his quilted jacket.

At first Zlateh didn't seem to mind the change in weather. She too was twelve years old and knew what winter meant. But when her legs sank deeper and deeper into the snow, she began to turn her head and look at Aaron in wonderment. Her mild eyes seemed to ask, "Why are we out in such a storm?" Aaron hoped that a peasant would come along with his cart, but no one passed by.

The snow grew thicker, falling to the ground in large, whirling flakes. Beneath it Aaron's boots touched the softness of a plowed field. He realized that he was no longer on the road. He had gone astray. He could no longer figure out which was east or west, which way

Zlateh the Goat **271**

was the village, the town. The wind whistled, howled, whirled the snow about in eddies. It looked as if white imps were playing tag on the fields. A white dust rose above the ground. Zlateh stopped. She could walk no longer. Stubbornly she anchored her cleft hooves in the earth and bleated as if pleading to be taken home. Icicles hung from her white beard, and her horns were glazed with frost.

Aaron did not want to admit the danger, but he knew just the same that if they did not find shelter they would freeze to death. This was no ordinary storm. It was a mighty blizzard. The snowfall had reached his knees. His hands were numb, and he could no longer feel his toes. He choked when he breathed. His nose felt like wood, and he rubbed it with snow. Zlateh's bleating began to sound like crying. Those humans in whom she had so much confidence had dragged her into a trap. Aaron began to pray to God for himself and for the innocent animal.

Suddenly he made out the shape of a hill. He wondered what it could be. Who had piled snow into such a huge heap? He moved toward it, dragging Zlateh after him. When he came near it, he realized that it was a large haystack which the snow had blanketed.

Aaron realized immediately that they were saved. With great effort he dug his way through the snow. He was a village boy and knew what to do. When he reached the hay, he hollowed out a nest for himself and the goat. No matter how cold it may be outside, in the hay it is always warm. And hay was food for Zlateh. The moment she smelled it she became contented and began to eat. Outside the snow continued to fall. It quickly covered the passageway Aaron had dug. But a boy and an animal need to breathe, and there was hardly any air in their hideout. Aaron bored a kind of a window through the hay and snow and carefully kept the passage clear.

Zlateh, having eaten her fill, sat down on her hind legs and seemed to have regained her confidence in man. Aaron ate his two slices of bread and cheese, but after the difficult journey he was still hungry. He looked at Zlateh and noticed her udders were full. He lay down next to her, placing himself so that when he milked her he could squirt the milk into his mouth. It was rich and sweet. Zlateh was not accustomed to being milked that way, but she did not resist. On the contrary, she seemed eager to reward Aaron for bringing her to a shelter whose very walls, floor, and ceiling were made of food.

Through the window Aaron could catch a glimpse of the chaos outside. The wind carried before it whole drifts of snow. It was completely dark, and he did not know whether night had already come or whether it was the darkness of the storm. Thank God that in the hay it was not cold. The dried hay, grass, and field flowers exuded the warmth of the summer sun. Zlateh ate frequently; she nibbled from above, below, from the left and right. Her body gave forth an animal warmth, and Aaron cuddled up to her. He had always loved Zlateh, but now she was like a sister. He was alone, cut off from his family, and wanted to talk. He began to talk to Zlateh. "Zlateh, what do you think about what has happened to us?" he asked.

"Maaaa," Zlateh answered.

"If we hadn't found this stack of hay, we would both be frozen stiff by now," Aaron said.

"Maaaa," was the goat's reply.

"If the snow keeps on falling like this, we may have to stay here for days," Aaron explained.

"Maaaa," Zlateh bleated.

"What does 'Maaaa' mean?" Aaron asked. "You'd better speak up clearly."

"Maaaa. Maaaa," Zlateh tried.

"Well, let it be 'Maaaa' then," Aaron said patiently. "You can't speak, but I know you understand. I need you and you need me. Isn't that right?"

"Maaaa."

Aaron became sleepy. He made a pillow out of some hay, leaned his head on it, and dozed off. Zlateh too fell asleep.

When Aaron opened his eyes, he didn't know whether it was morning or night. The snow had blocked up his window. He tried to clear it, but when he had bored through to the length of his arm, he still hadn't reached the outside. Luckily he had his stick with him and was able to break through to the open air. It was still dark outside. The snow continued to fall and the wind wailed, first with one voice and then with many. Sometimes it had the sound of devilish laughter. Zlateh too awoke, and when Aaron greeted her, she answered, "Maaaa." Yes, Zlateh's language consisted of only one word, but it meant many things. Now she was saying, "We must accept all that God gives us—heat, cold, hunger, satisfaction, light, and darkness."

Aaron had awakened hungry. He had eaten up his food, but Zlateh had plenty of milk.

For three days Aaron and Zlateh stayed in the haystack. Aaron had always loved Zlateh, but in these three days he loved her more and more. She fed him with her milk and helped him keep warm. She comforted him with her patience. He told her many stories, and she always cocked her ears and listened. When he patted her, she licked his hand and his face. Then she said, "Maaaa," and he knew it meant, I love you too.

The snow fell for three days, though after the first day it was not as thick and the wind quieted down. Sometimes Aaron felt that there could never have been a summer, that the snow had always fallen, ever since he could remember. He, Aaron, never had a father or mother or sisters. He was a snow child, born of the snow, and so was Zlateh. It was so quiet in the hay that his ears rang in the stillness. Aaron and Zlateh slept all night and a good part of the day. As for Aaron's dreams, they were all about warm weather. He dreamed of green fields, trees covered with blossoms, clear brooks, and singing birds. By the third night the snow had stopped, but Aaron did not dare to find his way home in the darkness. The sky became clear and the moon shone, casting silvery nets on the snow. Aaron dug his way out and looked at the world. It was all white, quiet, dreaming dreams of heavenly splendor. The stars were large and close. The moon swam in the sky as in a sea.

On the morning of the fourth day Aaron heard the ringing of sleigh bells. The haystack was not far from the road. The peasant who drove the sleigh pointed out the way to him—not to the town and Feyvel the butcher, but home to the village. Aaron had decided in the haystack that he would never part with Zlateh.

Aaron's family and their neighbors had searched for the boy and the goat but had found no trace of them during the storm. They feared they were lost. Aaron's mother and sisters cried for him; his father remained silent and gloomy. Suddenly one of the neighbors came running to their house with the news that Aaron and Zlateh were coming up the road.

There was great joy in the family. Aaron told them how he had found the stack of hay and how Zlateh had fed him with her milk. Aaron's sisters kissed and hugged Zlateh and gave her a special treat of chopped carrots and potato peels, which Zlateh gobbled up hungrily.

Nobody ever again thought of selling Zlateh, and now that the cold weather had finally set in, the villagers needed the services of Reuven the furrier once more. When Hanukkah came, Aaron's mother was able to fry pancakes every evening, and Zlateh got her portion too. Even though Zlateh had her own pen, she often came to the kitchen, knocking on the door with her horns to indicate that she was ready to visit, and she was always admitted. In the evening Aaron, Miriam, and Anna played dreidel.[3] Zlateh sat near the stove watching the children and the flickering of the Hanukkah candles.

Once in a while Aaron would ask her, "Zlateh, do you remember the three days we spent together?"

And Zlateh would scratch her neck with a horn, shake her white bearded head and come out with the single sound which expressed all her thoughts, and all her love.

3. **dreidel** (drā′dəl): a game played with a four-sided top; also, the top itself.

Reading Check

1. What kind of work does Reuven do?
2. What does Aaron dream about during the storm?
3. How does Aaron know that the haystack is not far from the road?
4. How does the family celebrate Hanukkah?

For Study and Discussion

Analyzing and Interpreting the Story

1. Nature plays an important role in this story. How does nature bring misery and then happiness to Reuven's family?

2. Why does Reuven decide to sell Zlateh?

3. Just when it seems that Aaron and Zlateh will perish in the storm, Aaron finds the haystack. How does the storm, which threatens their lives, become the means of saving Zlateh?

4. During the three days that Aaron and Zlateh spend in the haystack, they become completely dependent upon each other. What decision does Aaron come to?

5. When Aaron is alone with Zlateh, he begins to acquire wisdom about the meaning of his experience. **a.** What do you think he learns? **b.** What evidence in the story supports your opinion?

Literary Elements

Interpreting Theme

You have seen that a short story is made up of several basic elements. Often, the elements in a short story work together to express a central meaning or idea called the **theme.** Sometimes the theme of a story is stated directly. Sometimes the theme must be inferred from the other elements in a story.

The theme of "Zlateh the Goat" might be stated in this way: The hardships of life often serve to bind us more closely to those we love. Let us see how this statement grows out of the specific events in the story.

The characters in the story are faced with circumstances they cannot control. Reuven is forced through necessity to sell Zlateh. Both Zlateh and Aaron seem headed for tragedy through no fault of their own. They are saved quite unexpectedly when Aaron comes across a haystack. The storm turns out to be a god-send, for the family's circumstances are reversed by the change in weather. The events of the story suggest that the fate of all living creatures is beyond their understanding or control.

However, while the characters have no power to control their circumstances, they are not helpless, for they are sustained by love and trust. This idea becomes clear in the central episode of the story. When Aaron and Zlateh are cut off from the rest of the world, Aaron grows to love Zlateh more and more, and he determines that he will never part with her. When he returns to the village, there is no more talk of selling Zlateh, for the family has learned how much Zlateh means to all of them. We see that the bonds of this family have been strengthened by their ordeal.

Have you a different interpretation of the story? How would you express the theme?

Understanding Point of View

You have seen that a story may be told from the point of view of one of its characters. In "A Day's Wait" (page 242), the narrator is the boy's father. The story is written from a **first-person point of view.**

The narrator in "Zlateh the Goat" stands outside the action as an observer. This narrator tells us not only what the characters say and do, but also what they think and feel. Because the narrator is all-knowing, we refer to this point of view as **omniscient** (ŏm-nĭsh′ənt).

Find passages in the story where you are allowed to share characters' thoughts and feelings. How does the omniscient point of view bring you closer to the characters?

Stories with the omniscient point of view are always written in the third person. Sometimes a writer using the third person will purposely limit the point of view to what one particular character sees, hears, and thinks. "The Landlady" is written in the third person, but the author has chosen to reveal only what Billy knows and feels. This point of view is called **limited third-person point of view.**

Find the passage on page 225 that tells you what Billy is thinking as he sips his tea. Do you know what the landlady is thinking in this pas-sage? If the author had revealed the landlady's thoughts during this scene, would the end of the story have been a surprise?

Writing About Literature

Comparing Treatments of Nature

In Singer's story nature is both destructive and benevolent. In what other literary works have you met this idea? How is it treated in "Last Cover" (page 153), "The Wild Duck's Nest" (page 180), and "Antaeus" (page 187)? Write a short essay in which you compare treatments of nature in two selections.

About the Author

Isaac Bashevis Singer   (1904 –   )

Isaac Bashevis Singer, who writes in Yiddish, is well known for his stories of Jewish family life in eastern Europe. Singer was born in Radzymin, Poland. He received his formal education in Warsaw, the nation's capital, where he worked as a proofreader and editor for several literary magazines. In 1935 he moved to New York City. In 1950 he published *The Family Moskat,* the first of his books to appear in English. Singer says he loves his profession: "When I began to write, I was fifteen . . . I very often met situations which baffled me, and from the moment I knew that there was such a thing as literature, I thought how wonderful it would be to be able to describe such things." He received the Nobel Prize for literature in 1978.

A Christmas Carol

CHARLES DICKENS

Dickens' story has all the elements of a great classic: memorable characters, an intriguing plot, setting that evokes mood, a superb style, and a wonderful, compassionate theme. The tale is ageless, and despite the many adaptations for film, television, and the stage, one never tires of the story.

Dickens wanted to be an actor, and he enjoyed reading his works to the public. Many generations have discovered the pleasure of listening to "A Christmas Carol" read aloud. Share this pleasure with your classmates.

Stave[1] One: Marley's Ghost

Marley was dead, to begin with. There is no doubt whatever about that. The register of his burial was signed by the clergyman, the clerk, the undertaker, and the chief mourner. Scrooge signed it. And Scrooge's name was good upon 'Change[2] for anything he chose to put his hand to.

Old Marley was as dead as a doornail.

Scrooge knew he was dead? Of course he did. How could it be otherwise? Scrooge and he were partners for I don't know how many years. Scrooge was his sole executor, his sole administrator, his sole assign, his sole residuary legatee,[3] his sole friend, his sole mourner.

Scrooge never painted out old Marley's name, however. There it yet stood, years afterward, above the door—SCROOGE AND MARLEY. The firm was known as SCROOGE AND MARLEY. Sometimes people new to the business called Scrooge "Scrooge," and sometimes "Marley." He answered to both names. It was all the same to him.

Oh! But he was a tightfisted hand at the grindstone, was Scrooge! A squeezing, wrenching, grasping, scraping, clutching, covetous old sinner! External heat and cold had little influence on him. No warmth could

---

1. **Stave:** a stanza of a poem or song; here, a section of Dickens' "carol."
2. **'Change:** the Exchange, the place where merchants, brokers, and bankers conduct their business.

3. **executor** (ĕg-zĕk′yə-tər); **administrator; assign; residuary legatee** (rĭ-zĭj′ōō-ĕr′ē lĕg′ə-tē′): legal terms used in a will. Marley had left everything he owned to Scrooge, who handled all the business arrangements after Marley's death.

warm, no cold could chill him. No wind that blew was bitterer than he, no falling snow was more intent upon its purpose, no pelting rain less open to entreaty. Foul weather didn't know where to have him. The heaviest rain and snow and hail and sleet could boast of the advantage over him in only one respect—they often "came down"[4] handsomely, and Scrooge never did.

Nobody ever stopped him in the street to say, with gladsome looks, "My dear Scrooge, how are you? When will you come to see me?" No beggars implored him to bestow a trifle, no children asked him what it was o'clock, no man or woman ever once in all his life inquired the way to such and such a place of Scrooge. Even the blind men's dogs appeared to know him, and when they saw him coming on, would tug their owners into doorways and up courts, and then would wag their tails as though they said, "No eyes at all is better than an evil eye, dark master!"

But what did Scrooge care! It was the very thing he liked. To edge his way along the crowded paths of life, warning all human sympathy to keep its distance, was what the knowing ones call "nuts" to Scrooge.

Once upon a time—of all the good days in the year, upon a Christmas Eve—old Scrooge sat busy in his countinghouse. It was cold, bleak, biting, foggy weather; and the city clocks had only just gone three, but it was quite dark already.

The door of Scrooge's countinghouse was open, that he might keep his eye upon his clerk, who, in a dismal little cell beyond, a sort of tank, was copying letters. Scrooge had a very small fire, but the clerk's fire was so very much smaller that it looked like one coal. But he couldn't replenish it, for Scrooge kept the coalbox in his own room, and so surely as the clerk came in with the shovel, the master predicted that it would be necessary for them to part. Wherefore the clerk put on his white comforter[5] and tried to warm himself at the candle; in which effort, not being a man of a strong imagination, he failed.

"A Merry Christmas, Uncle! God save you!" cried a cheerful voice. It was the voice of Scrooge's nephew, who came upon him so quickly that this was the first intimation Scrooge had of his approach.

"Bah!" said Scrooge. "Humbug!"

"Christmas a humbug, Uncle! You don't mean that, I am sure?"

"I do. Out upon merry Christmas! What's Christmastime to you but a time for paying bills without money; a time for finding yourself a year older, and not an hour richer; a time for balancing your books and having every item in 'em through a round dozen of months presented dead against you? If I had my will, every idiot who goes about with 'Merry Christmas' on his lips should be boiled with his own pudding and buried with a stake of holly through his heart. He should!"

"Uncle!"

"Nephew, keep Christmas in your own way, and let me keep it in mine."

"Keep it! But you don't keep it."

"Let me leave it alone, then. Much good may it do you! Much good it has ever done you!"

"There are many things from which I might have derived good, by which I have not profited, I dare say, Christmas among the rest. But I am sure I have always thought of Christmastime, when it has come round—apart from the veneration due to its sacred origin, if anything belonging to it *can* be apart from that—as a good time; a kind, forgiving, charitable, pleasant time; the only time I know of, in the long calendar of the year, when men and women

---

4. **"came down":** slang for "made a gift or donation."

5. **comforter:** a long scarf.

A Christmas Carol   **277**

seem by one consent to open their shut-up hearts freely and to think of people below them as if they really were fellow travelers to the grave, and not another race of creatures bound on other journeys. And therefore, Uncle, though it has never put a scrap of gold or silver in my pocket, I believe that it *has* done me good, and *will* do me good; and I say, God bless it!"

The clerk in the tank involuntarily applauded.

"Let me hear another sound from *you*," said Scrooge, "and you'll keep your Christmas by losing your situation! You're quite a powerful speaker, sir," he added, turning to his nephew. "I wonder you don't go into Parliament."

"Don't be angry, Uncle. Come! Dine with us tomorrow."

"Good afternoon."

"I want nothing from you; I ask nothing of you; why cannot we be friends?"

"Good afternoon."

"I am sorry, with all my heart, to find you so resolute. We have never had any quarrel to which I have been a party. But I have made the trial in homage to Christmas, and I'll keep my Christmas humor to the last. So a Merry Christmas, Uncle!"

"Good afternoon!"

"And a Happy New Year!"

"Good afternoon!"

His nephew left the room without an angry word, notwithstanding. The clerk, in letting Scrooge's nephew out, had let two other people in. They were portly gentlemen, pleasant to behold, and now stood, with their hats off, in Scrooge's office. They had books and papers in their hands, and bowed to him.

"Scrooge and Marley's, I believe," said one of the gentlemen, referring to his list. "Have I the pleasure of addressing Mr. Scrooge or Mr. Marley?"

"Mr. Marley has been dead these seven years. He died seven years ago this very night."

"At this festive season of the year, Mr. Scrooge," said the gentleman, taking up a pen, "it is more than usually desirable that we should make some slight provision for the poor and destitute, who suffer greatly at the present time. Many thousands are in want of common necessaries; hundreds of thousands are in want of common comforts, sir."

"Are there no prisons?"

"Plenty of prisons. But under the impression that they scarcely furnish Christian cheer of mind or body to the unoffending multitude, a few of us are endeavoring to raise a fund to buy the poor some meat and drink, and means of warmth. We choose this time, because it is a time, of all others, when want is keenly felt, and abundance rejoices. What shall I put you down for?"

"Nothing!"

"You wish to be anonymous?"

"I wish to be left alone. Since you ask me what I wish, gentlemen, that is my answer. I don't make merry myself at Christmas, and I can't afford to make idle people merry. I help to support the prisons and workhouses—they cost enough—and those who are badly off must go there."

"Many can't go there; and many would rather die."

"If they would rather die, they had better do it, and decrease the surplus population."

At length the hour of shutting up the countinghouse arrived. With an ill will Scrooge, dismounting from his stool, tacitly[6] admitted the fact to the expectant clerk in the tank, who instantly snuffed his candle out and put on his hat.

"You want all day tomorrow, I suppose?"

---

6. **tacitly** (tăs′ĭt-lē): without speaking.

"If quite convenient, sir."

"It's not convenient, and it's not fair. If I was to stop half a crown for it, you'd think yourself mightily ill-used, I'll be bound?"

"Yes, sir."

"And yet you don't think *me* ill-used when I pay a day's wages for no work."

"It's only once a year, sir."

"A poor excuse for picking a man's pocket every twenty-fifth of December! But I suppose you must have the whole day. Be here all the earlier *next* morning."

The clerk promised that he would, and Scrooge walked out with a growl. The office was closed in a twinkling, and the clerk, with the long ends of his white comforter dangling below his waist (for he boasted no greatcoat), went down a slide, at the end of a lane of boys, twenty times, in honor of its being Christmas Eve, and then ran home as hard as he could pelt, to play at blindman's buff.

Scrooge took his melancholy dinner in his usual melancholy tavern; and having read all the newspapers and beguiled[7] the rest of the evening with his banker's book, went home to bed. He lived in chambers which had once belonged to his deceased partner. They were a gloomy suite of rooms in a lowering[8] pile of a building up a yard. The building was old enough now, and dreary enough, for nobody lived in it but Scrooge, the other rooms being all let out as offices.

Now it is a fact that there was nothing at all particular about the knocker on the door of his house, except that it was very large; also, that Scrooge had seen it, night and morning, during his whole residence in that place; also, that Scrooge had as little of what is called fancy[9] about him as any man in the city of London.

And yet Scrooge, having his key in the lock of the door, saw in the knocker, without its undergoing any intermediate process of change, not a knocker, but Marley's face.

Marley's face, with a dismal light about it, like a bad lobster in a dark cellar. It was not angry or ferocious, but it looked at Scrooge as Marley used to look—ghostly spectacles turned up upon its ghostly forehead.

As Scrooge looked fixedly at this phenomenon, it was a knocker again. He said, "Pooh, pooh!" and closed the door with a bang.

The sound resounded through the house like thunder. Every room above, and every cask in the wine merchant's cellars below, appeared to have a separate peal of echoes of its own. Scrooge was not a man to be frightened by echoes. He fastened the door and walked across the hall and up the stairs. Slowly, too, trimming his candle as he went.

Up Scrooge went, not caring a button for its being very dark. Darkness is cheap, and Scrooge liked it. But before he shut his heavy door, he walked through his rooms to see that all was right. He had just enough recollection of the face to desire to do that.

Sitting room, bedroom, lumber room,[10] all as they should be. Nobody under the table, nobody under the sofa; a small fire in the grate; spoon and basin ready; and the little saucepan of gruel (Scrooge had a cold in his head) upon the hob.[11] Nobody under the bed; nobody in the closet; nobody in his dressing gown, which was hanging up in a suspicious attitude against the wall. Lumber room as usual. Old fireguards, old shoes, two fish baskets, washing stand on three legs, and a poker.

Quite satisfied, he closed his door and locked himself in; double-locked himself in, which

---

7. **beguiled** (bĭ-gīld′): spent or whiled away.
8. **lowering** (lou′ər-ĭng): dark and threatening.
9. **fancy:** imagination.

10. **lumber room:** storeroom.
11. **hob:** a small shelf at the back or side of a fireplace, used to keep a kettle or a saucepan warm.

was not his custom. Thus secured against surprise, he took off his cravat,[12] put on his dressing gown and slippers and his nightcap, and sat down before the very low fire to take his gruel.

As he threw his head back in the chair, his glance happened to rest upon a bell, a disused bell, that hung in the room and communicated, for some purpose now forgotten, with a chamber in the highest story of the building. It was with great astonishment, and with a strange inexplicable dread, that, as he looked, he saw this bell begin to swing. Soon it rang out loudly, and so did every bell in the house.

This was succeeded by a clanking noise, deep down below, as if some person were dragging a heavy chain over the casks in the wine merchant's cellar.

Then he heard the noise much louder on the floors below; then coming up the stairs; then coming straight toward his door.

It came on through the heavy door, and a specter passed into the room before his eyes. And upon its coming in, the dying flame leaped up, as though it cried, "I know him! Marley's ghost!"

The same face, the very same. Marley in his pigtail, usual waistcoat, tights, and boots. His body was transparent; so that Scrooge, observing him, and looking through his waistcoat, could see the two buttons on his coat behind.

Scrooge had often heard it said that Marley had no bowels,[13] but he had never believed it until now.

No, nor did he believe it even now. Though he looked the phantom through and through and saw it standing before him—though he felt the chilling influence of its death-cold eyes and

Marley's Ghost.
Illustrations by John Leech are from the 1846 edition of *A Christmas Carol.*

noticed the very texture of the folded kerchief bound about its head and chin—he was still incredulous.

"How now!" said Scrooge, caustic and cold as ever. "What do you want with me?"

"Much!"—Marley's voice, no doubt about it.

"Who are you?"

"Ask me who I *was.*"

"Who *were* you then?"

"In life I was your partner, Jacob Marley."

"Can you—can you sit down?"

"I can."

"Do it, then."

Scrooge asked the question because he didn't know whether a ghost so transparent might find himself in a condition to take a chair, and felt that, in the event of its being im-

---

12. **cravat** (krə-văt′): a necktie, or a scarf resembling a necktie.

13. **bowels:** the intestines, which used to be regarded as the source of pity and mercy. When people said Marley had no bowels, they meant that he was cruel.

possible, it might involve the necessity of an embarrassing explanation. But the ghost sat down on the opposite side of the fireplace, as if he were quite used to it.

"You don't believe in me."

"I don't."

"What evidence would you have of my reality beyond that of your senses?"

"I don't know."

"Why do you doubt your senses?"

"Because a little thing affects them. A slight disorder of the stomach makes them cheats. You may be an undigested bit of beef, a blot of mustard, a crumb of cheese, a fragment of an underdone potato. There's more of gravy than of grave about you, whatever you are!"

Scrooge was not much in the habit of cracking jokes, nor did he feel in his heart by any means waggish then. The truth is that he tried to be smart, as a means of distracting his own attention and keeping down his horror.

But how much greater was his horror when, the phantom taking off the bandage round its head, as if it were too warm to wear indoors, its lower jaw dropped down upon its breast!

"Mercy! Dreadful apparition, why do you trouble me? Why do spirits walk the earth, and why do they come to me?"

"It is required of every man that the spirit within him should walk abroad among his fellowmen and travel far and wide; and if that spirit goes not forth in life, it is condemned to do so after death. I cannot tell you all I would. A very little more is permitted to me. I cannot rest, I cannot stay, I cannot linger anywhere. My spirit never walked beyond our countinghouse—mark me!—in life my spirit never roved beyond the narrow limits of our money-changing hole; and weary journeys lie before me!"

"Seven years dead. And traveling all the time? You travel fast?"

"On the wings of the wind."

"You might have got over a great quantity of ground in seven years."

"O blind man, blind man! not to know that ages of incessant labor by immortal creatures for this earth must pass into eternity before the good of which it is susceptible is all developed.[14] Not to know that any Christian spirit working kindly in its little sphere, whatever it may be, will find its mortal life too short for its vast means of usefulness. Not to know that no space of regret can make amends for one life's opportunities misused! Yet I was like this man; I once was like this man!"

"But you were always a good man of business, Jacob," faltered Scrooge, who now began to apply this to himself.

"Business!" cried the ghost, wringing its hands again. "Mankind was my business. The common welfare was my business; charity, mercy, forbearance, benevolence, were all my business. The dealings of my trade were but a drop of water in the comprehensive ocean of my business!"

Scrooge was very much dismayed to hear the specter going on at this rate, and began to quake exceedingly.

"Hear me! My time is nearly gone."

"I will. But don't be hard upon me! Don't be flowery, Jacob! Pray!"

"I am here tonight to warn you that you have yet a chance and hope of escaping my fate. A chance and hope of my procuring,[15] Ebenezer."

"You were always a good friend to me," said Scrooge. "Thank'ee!"

"You will be haunted by three spirits."

"Is that the chance and hope you mentioned, Jacob? I—I think I'd rather not."

"Without their visits, you cannot hope to

14. **ages . . . developed:** In other words, heavenly spirits must work for countless years before the goodness that is possible in the world can come into being.
15. **of my procuring:** that I got for you.

shun the path I tread. Expect the first tomorrow night, when the bell tolls one. Expect the second on the next night at the same hour. The third, upon the next night, when the last stroke of twelve has ceased to vibrate. Look to see me no more; and look that, for your own sake, you remember what has passed between us!"

It walked backward from him; and at every step it took, the window raised itself a little, so that, when the apparition reached it, it was wide open.

Scrooge closed the window, and examined the door by which the ghost had entered. It was double-locked, as he had locked it with his own hands, and the bolts were undisturbed. Scrooge tried to say, "Humbug!" but stopped at the first syllable. And being, from the emotion he had undergone, or the fatigues of the day, or his glimpse of the invisible world, or the dull[16] conversation of the ghost, or the lateness of the hour, much in need of repose, he went straight to bed, without undressing, and fell asleep on the instant.

Stave Two:
The First of the Three Spirits

When Scrooge awoke, it was so dark that, looking out of bed, he could scarcely distinguish the transparent window from the opaque walls of his chamber, until suddenly the church clock tolled a deep, dull, hollow, melancholy ONE.

Light flashed up in the room upon the instant, and the curtains of his bed were drawn aside by a strange figure—like a child; yet not so like a child as like an old man, viewed through some supernatural medium, which gave him the appearance of having receded from the view and being diminished to a child's proportions. Its hair, which hung about

16. **dull:** here, gloomy.

its neck and down its back, was white as if with age; and yet the face had not a wrinkle in it, and the tenderest bloom was on the skin. It held a branch of fresh green holly in its hand; and, in singular contradiction of that wintry emblem, had its dress trimmed with summer flowers. But the strangest thing about it was that from the crown of its head there sprang a bright, clear jet of light by which all this was visible; and which was doubtless the occasion of its using, in its duller moments, a great extinguisher for a cap, which it now held under its arm.

"Are you the spirit, sir, whose coming was foretold to me?"

"I am!"

"Who and what are you?"

"I am the Ghost of Christmas Past."

"Long past?"

"No. Your past. The things that you will see with me are shadows of the things that have been; they will have no consciousness of us."

Scrooge then made bold to inquire what business brought him there.

"Your welfare. Rise and walk with me!"

It would have been in vain for Scrooge to plead that the weather and the hour were not adapted to pedestrian purposes; that bed was warm, and the thermometer a long way below freezing; that he was clad but lightly in his slippers, dressing gown, and nightcap; and that he had a cold upon him at that time. The grasp, though gentle as a woman's hand, was not to be resisted. He rose; but finding that the spirit made toward the window, clasped its robe in supplication.

"I am a mortal, and liable to fall."

"Bear but a touch of my hand *there*," said the spirit, laying it upon his heart, "and you shall be upheld in more than this!"

As the words were spoken, they passed through the wall and stood in the busy thoroughfares of a city. It was made plain enough by the dressing of the shops that here, too, it was Christmastime. The ghost stopped at a certain warehouse door and asked Scrooge if he knew it.

"Know it! I was apprenticed here!"

They went in. At sight of an old gentleman in a Welsh wig, sitting behind such a high desk that, if he had been two inches taller, he must have knocked his head against the ceiling, Scrooge cried in great excitement: "Why, it's old Fezziwig! Bless his heart, it's Fezziwig, alive again!"

Old Fezziwig laid down his pen and looked up at the clock, which pointed to the hour of seven. He rubbed his hands; adjusted his capacious waistcoat; laughed all over himself, from his shoes to his organ of benevolence;[17] and called out in a comfortable, oily, rich, fat, jovial voice: "Yo ho, there! Ebenezer! Dick!"

A living and moving picture of Scrooge's former self, a young man, came briskly in, accompanied by his fellow apprentice.

"Dick Wilkins, to be sure!" said Scrooge to the ghost. "My old fellow 'prentice, bless me, yes. There he is. He was very much attached to me, was Dick. Poor Dick! Dear, dear!"

"Yo ho, my boys!" said Fezziwig. "No more work tonight. Christmas Eve, Dick. Christmas, Ebenezer! Let's have the shutters up, before a man can say 'Jack Robinson'! Clear away, my lads, and let's have lots of room here!"

Clear away! There was nothing they wouldn't have cleared away, or couldn't have cleared away, with old Fezziwig looking on. It was done in a minute. Every movable was packed off, as if it were dismissed from public life forevermore; the floor was swept and watered, the lamps were trimmed, fuel was heaped upon the fire; and the warehouse was as snug and warm and dry and bright a ball-

room as you would desire to see on a winter night.

In came a fiddler with a music book, and went up to the lofty desk, and made an orchestra of it, and tuned like fifty stomachaches. In came Mrs. Fezziwig, one vast substantial smile. In came the three Miss Fezziwigs, beaming and lovable. In came the six young followers whose hearts they broke. In came all the young men and women employed in the business. In came the housemaid, with her cousin, the baker. In came the cook, with her brother's particular friend, the milkman. In they all came one after another; some shyly, some boldly, some gracefully, some awkwardly, some pushing, some pulling; in they all came, anyhow and everyhow. Away they all went, twenty couples at once; hands half round and back again the other way; down the middle and up again;

Mr. Fezziwig's Ball.

round and round in various stages of affectionate grouping; old top couple always turning up in the wrong place; new top couple starting off again, as soon as they got there; all top couples at last, and not a bottom one to help them. When this result was brought about, old Fezziwig, clapping his hands to stop the dance, cried out, "Well done"; and the fiddler plunged his hot face into a pot of porter[18] especially provided for that purpose.

There were more dances, and there were forfeits[19] and more dances, and there was cake, and there was negus,[20] and there was a great piece of cold roast, and there was a great piece of cold boiled,[21] and there were mince pies, and plenty of beer. But the great effect of the evening came after the roast and boiled, when the fiddler struck up "Sir Roger de Coverley."[22] Then old Fezziwig stood out to dance with Mrs. Fezziwig. Top couple, too; with a good stiff piece of work cut out for them; three- or four-and-twenty pairs of partners; people who were not to be trifled with; people who *would* dance, and had no notion of walking.

But if they had been twice as many—four times—old Fezziwig would have been a match for them, and so would Mrs. Fezziwig. As to *her,* she was worthy to be his partner in every sense of the term. A positive light appeared to issue from Fezziwig's calves. They shone in every part of the dance. You couldn't have predicted, at any given time, what would become of 'em next. And when old Fezziwig and Mrs. Fezziwig had gone all through the dance—advance and retire, turn your partner, bow and curtsy, corkscrew, thread the needle, and

back again to your place—Fezziwig "cut"—cut so deftly, that he appeared to wink with his legs.

When the clock struck eleven this domestic ball broke up. Mr. and Mrs. Fezziwig took their stations, one on either side of the door, and, shaking hands with every person individually as he or she went out, wished him or her a Merry Christmas. When everybody had retired but the two 'prentices, they did the same to them; and thus the cheerful voices died away, and the lads were left to their beds, which were under a counter in the back shop.

"A small matter," said the ghost, "to make these silly folks so full of gratitude. He has spent but a few pounds of your mortal money—three or four perhaps. Is that so much that he deserves this praise?"

"It isn't that," said Scrooge, heated by the remark, and speaking unconsciously like his former, not his latter, self—"it isn't that, Spirit. He has the power to render us happy or unhappy; to make our service light or burdensome; a pleasure or a toil. Say that his power lies in words and looks; in things so slight and insignificant that it is impossible to add and count 'em up: what then? The happiness he gives is quite as great as if it cost a fortune."

He felt the spirit's glance, and stopped.

"What is the matter?"

"Nothing particular."

"Something, I think?"

"No, no. I should like to be able to say a word or two to my clerk just now. That's all."

"My time grows short," observed the spirit. "Quick!"

This was not addressed to Scrooge, or to anyone whom he could see, but it produced an immediate effect. For again he saw himself. He was older now; a man in the prime of life.

He was not alone, but sat by the side of a fair

---

18. **porter:** dark brown beer.
19. **forfeits** (fôr′fĭts): a game in which the players must forfeit, or give up, something if they lose.
20. **negus** (nē′gəs): punch.
21. **boiled:** boiled beef.
22. **"Sir Roger de Coverley":** a square-dance tune.

young girl in a black dress, in whose eyes there were tears.

"It matters little," she said softly to Scrooge's former self. "To you very little. Another idol has displaced me; and if it can comfort you in time to come, as I would have tried to do, I have no just cause to grieve."

"What idol has displaced you?"

"A golden one. You fear the world too much. I have seen your nobler aspirations fall off one by one, until the master passion, gain, engrosses you. Have I not?"

"What then? Even if I have grown so much wiser, what then? I am not changed toward you. Have I ever sought release from our engagement?"

"In words, no. Never."

"In what, then?"

"In a changed nature; in an altered spirit; in another atmosphere of life; another hope as its great end. If you were free today, tomorrow, yesterday, can even I believe that you would choose a dowerless[23] girl; or, choosing her, do I not know that your repentance and regret would surely follow? I do; and I release you. With a full heart, for the love of him you once were."

"Spirit! remove me from this place."

"I told you these were shadows of the things that have been," said the ghost. "That they are what they are, do not blame me!"

"Remove me!" Scrooge exclaimed. "I cannot bear it! Leave me! Take me back! Haunt me no longer!"

As he struggled with the spirit, he was conscious of being exhausted and overcome by an irresistible drowsiness; and, further, of being in his own bedroom. He had barely time to reel to bed before he sank into a heavy sleep.

23. **dowerless** (dou′ər-lĭs): without a dowry, the money and property that a woman formerly brought to her husband at marriage.

Stave Three:
The Second of the Three Spirits

Scrooge awoke in his own bedroom. There was no doubt about that. But it and his own adjoining sitting room, into which he shuffled in his slippers, attracted by a great light there, had undergone a surprising transformation. The walls and ceiling were so hung with living green that it looked a perfect grove. The leaves of holly, mistletoe, and ivy reflected back the light, as if so many little mirrors had been scattered there; and such a mighty blaze went roaring up the chimney, as that petrifaction[24] of a hearth had never known in Scrooge's time, or Marley's, or for many and many a winter season gone. Heaped upon the floor, to form a kind of throne, were turkeys, geese, game, brawn,[25] great joints of meat, suckling pigs, long wreaths of sausages, mince pies, plum puddings, barrels of oysters, red-hot chestnuts, cherry-cheeked apples, juicy oranges, luscious pears, immense twelfth-cakes,[26] and great bowls of punch. In easy state upon this couch there sat a giant glorious to see, who bore a glowing torch, in shape not unlike Plenty's horn, and who raised it high to shed its light on Scrooge, as he came peeping round the door.

"Come in—come in! and know me better, man! I am the Ghost of Christmas Present. Look upon me! You have never seen the like of me before?"

"Never."

"Have never walked forth with the younger members of my family; meaning (for I am very young) my elder brothers born in these later years?" pursued the phantom.

24. **petrifaction** (pĕt′rə-făk′shən): something petrified, or turning to stone. The hearth, or fireplace, is cold and hard because it has never known a generous fire.
25. **brawn:** boar meat.
26. **twelfth-cakes:** fruitcakes made for Epiphany, or Twelfth Day, a holiday that occurs on January 6, twelve days after Christmas.

Scrooge's Third Visitor.

Scrooge and the ghost passed on, invisible, straight to Scrooge's clerk's; and on the threshold of the door the spirit smiled, and stopped to bless Bob Cratchit's dwelling with the sprinklings of his torch. Think of that! Bob had but fifteen "bob"[28] a week himself; he pocketed on Saturdays but fifteen copies of his Christian name; and yet the Ghost of Christmas Present blessed his four-roomed house!

Then up rose Mrs. Cratchit, Cratchit's wife, dressed out but poorly in a twice-turned[29] gown, but brave in ribbons, which are cheap and make a goodly show for sixpence; and she laid the cloth, assisted by Belinda Cratchit, second of her daughters, also brave in ribbons; while Master Peter Cratchit plunged a fork into the saucepan of potatoes, and, getting the corners of his monstrous shirt collar (Bob's private property, conferred upon his son and heir in honor of the day) into his mouth, rejoiced to find himself so gallantly attired, and yearned to show his linen in the fashionable parks. And now two smaller Cratchits, boy and girl, came tearing in, screaming that outside the baker's[30] they had smelled the goose and known it for their own; and basking in luxurious thoughts of sage and onion, these young Cratchits danced about the table, and exalted Master Peter Cratchit to the skies, while he (not proud, although his collar nearly choked him) blew the fire until the slow potatoes, bubbling up, knocked loudly at the saucepan lid to be let out and peeled.

"What has ever got your precious father then?" said Mrs. Cratchit. "And your brother Tiny Tim! And Martha warn't as late last Christmas Day by half an hour!"

"I don't think I have; I am afraid I have not. Have you had many brothers, Spirit?"

"More than eighteen hundred."[27]

"A tremendous family to provide for! Spirit, conduct me where you will. I went forth last night on compulsion, and I learned a lesson which is working now. Tonight, if you have aught to teach me, let me profit by it."

"Touch my robe!"

Scrooge did as he was told, and held it fast.

The room and its contents all vanished instantly, and they stood in the city streets upon a snowy Christmas morning.

27. **More . . . hundred:** Since this story was written in 1843, the Ghost of Christmas Present would have more than eighteen hundred brothers.

28. **"bob":** slang for "shilling" (or "shillings"), a former British coin worth one twentieth of a pound.
29. **twice-turned:** remade twice so that worn parts would not show.
30. **the baker's:** In the days when people of small means had fireplaces but no ovens, they would rent space in the local baker's oven to roast poultry or large pieces of meat.

"Here's Martha, Mother!" said a girl, appearing as she spoke.

"Here's Martha, Mother!" cried the two young Cratchits. "Hurrah! There's *such* a goose, Martha!"

"Why, bless your heart alive, my dear, how late you are!" said Mrs. Cratchit, kissing her a dozen times, and taking off her shawl and bonnet for her.

"We'd a deal of work to finish up last night," replied the girl, "and had to clear away this morning, Mother!"

"Well! Never mind so long as you are come," said Mrs. Cratchit. "Sit ye down before the fire, my dear, and have a warm, Lord bless ye!"

"No, no! There's Father coming," cried the two young Cratchits, who were everywhere at once. "Hide, Martha, hide!"

So Martha hid herself, and in came little Bob, the father, with at least three feet of comforter, exclusive of the fringe, hanging down before him; and his threadbare clothes darned up and brushed, to look seasonable; and Tiny Tim upon his shoulder. Alas for Tiny Tim, he bore a little crutch and had his limbs supported by an iron frame!

"Why, where's our Martha?" cried Bob Cratchit, looking round.

"Not coming," said Mrs. Cratchit.

"Not coming!" said Bob, with a sudden declension[31] in his high spirits; for he had been Tim's blood horse all the way from church, and had come home rampant[32]—"not coming upon Christmas Day!"

Martha didn't like to see him disappointed, if it were only in joke; so she came out prematurely from behind the closet door, and ran into his arms, while the two young Cratchits hustled Tiny Tim, and bore him off into the washhouse, that he might hear the pudding singing in the copper.

"And how did little Tim behave?" asked Mrs. Cratchit, when she had rallied Bob on his credulity,[33] and Bob had hugged his daughter to his heart's content.

"As good as gold," said Bob, "and better. Somehow he gets thoughtful, sitting by himself so much, and thinks the strangest things you ever heard. He told me, coming home, that he hoped the people saw him in the church because he was a cripple, and it might be pleasant to them to remember, upon Christmas Day, who made lame beggars walk and blind men see."

Bob's voice was tremulous when he told them this, and trembled more when he said that Tiny Tim was growing strong and hearty.

His active little crutch was heard upon the floor, and back came Tiny Tim before another word was spoken, escorted by his brother and sister to his stool beside the fire; and while Bob, turning up his cuffs—as if, poor fellow, they were capable of being made more shabby—compounded some hot mixture in a jug with gin and lemons, and stirred it round and round, and put it on the hob to simmer, Master Peter and the two ubiquitous[34] young Cratchits went to fetch the goose, with which they soon returned in high procession.

Mrs. Cratchit made the gravy (ready beforehand in a little saucepan) hissing hot; Master Peter mashed the potatoes with incredible vigor; Miss Belinda sweetened up the applesauce; Martha dusted the hot plates; Bob took Tiny Tim beside him in a tiny corner at the table; the two young Cratchits set chairs for everybody, not forgetting themselves, and,

---

31. **declension:** sinking or falling off.
32. **rampant:** rearing up like a horse; here, high-spirited.

33. **rallied Bob on his credulity** (krə-dōō′lə-tē): teased Bob for being so easily fooled by their joke.
34. **ubiquitous** (yōō-bik′wə-təs): being everywhere at the same time.

mounting guard upon their posts, crammed spoons into their mouths, lest they should shriek for goose before their turn came to be helped. At last the dishes were set on, and grace was said. It was succeeded by a breathless pause, as Mrs. Cratchit, looking slowly all along the carving knife, prepared to plunge it in the breast; but when she did, and when the long-expected gush of stuffing issued forth, one murmur of delight arose all around the board, and even Tiny Tim, excited by the two young Cratchits, beat on the table with the handle of his knife, and feebly cried; "Hurrah!"

There never was such a goose. Bob said he didn't believe there ever was such a goose cooked. Its tenderness and flavor, size and cheapness, were the themes of universal admiration. Eked out by applesauce and mashed potatoes, it was a sufficient dinner for the whole family; indeed, as Mrs. Cratchit said with great delight (surveying one small atom of a bone upon the dish), they hadn't ate[35] it all at last! Yet everyone had had enough, and the youngest Cratchits in particular were steeped in sage and onion to the eyebrows! But now, the plates being changed by Miss Belinda, Mrs. Cratchit left the room alone—too nervous to bear witnesses—to take the pudding up and bring it in.

Suppose it should not be done enough! Suppose it should break in turning out! Suppose somebody should have got over the wall of the backyard and stolen it while they were merry with the goose—a supposition at which the two young Cratchits became livid![36] All sorts of horrors were supposed.

Hallo! A great deal of steam! The pudding was out of the copper. A smell like a washing day! That was the cloth.[37] A smell like an eating house and a pastry cook's next door to each other, with a laundress' next door to that! That was the pudding! In half a minute Mrs. Cratchit entered—flushed but smiling proudly—with the pudding, like a speckled cannonball, so hard and firm, blazing in half of half a quartern[38] of ignited brandy and bedight[39] with Christmas holly stuck into the top.

Oh, a wonderful pudding! Bob Cratchit said, and calmly too, that he regarded it as the greatest success achieved by Mrs. Cratchit since their marriage. Mrs. Cratchit said that now the weight was off her mind, she would confess she had had her doubts about the quantity of flour. Everybody had something to say about it, but nobody said or thought it was at all a small pudding for a large family. Any Cratchit would have blushed to hint at such a thing.

At last the dinner was all done, the cloth was cleared, the hearth swept, and the fire made up. The compound in the jug being tasted, and considered perfect, apples and oranges were put upon the table, and a shovelful of chestnuts on the fire.

Then all the Cratchit family drew round the hearth, in what Bob Cratchit called a circle, and at Bob Cratchit's elbow stood the family display of glass—two tumblers, and a custard cup without a handle.

These held the hot stuff from the jug, however, as well as golden goblets would have done; and Bob served it out with beaming looks, while the chestnuts on the fire spluttered and crackled noisily. Then Bob proposed:

"A Merry Christmas to us all, my dears. God bless us!"

---

35. **ate** (ĕt): an alternate form of *eaten*, used in Great Britain.
36. **livid:** pale.

37. **cloth:** The pudding was wrapped in cloth and then boiled.
38. **quartern:** one fourth of a pint.
39. **bedight** (bĭ-dīt′): decorated.

Which all the family reechoed.

"God bless us every one!" said Tiny Tim, the last of all.

He sat very close to his father's side, upon his little stool. Bob held his withered little hand in his, as if he loved the child and wished to keep him by his side, and dreaded that he might be taken from him.

Scrooge raised his head speedily, on hearing his own name.

"Mr. Scrooge!" said Bob; "I'll give you Mr. Scrooge, the Founder of the Feast!"

"The Founder of the Feast indeed!" cried Mrs. Cratchit, reddening. "I wish I had him here. I'd give him a piece of my mind to feast upon, and I hope he'd have a good appetite for it."

"My dear," said Bob, "the children! Christmas Day."

"It should be Christmas Day, I am sure," said she, "on which one drinks the health of such an odious, stingy, hard, unfeeling man as Mr. Scrooge. You know he is, Robert! Nobody knows it better than you do, poor fellow!"

"My dear," was Bob's mild answer, "Christmas Day."

"I'll drink his health for your sake and the day's," said Mrs. Cratchit, "not for his. Long life to him! A Merry Christmas and a Happy New Year! He'll be very merry and very happy, I have no doubt!"

The children drank the toast after her. It was the first of their proceedings which had no heartiness in it. Tiny Tim drank it last of all, but he didn't care twopence for it. Scrooge was the ogre of the family. The mention of his name cast a dark shadow on the party, which was not dispelled for full five minutes.

After it had passed away, they were ten times merrier than before from the mere relief of Scrooge the Baleful[40] being done with. Bob

Cratchit told them how he had a situation in his eye for Master Peter, which would bring him, if obtained, full five and sixpence weekly. The two young Cratchits laughed tremendously at the idea of Peter's being a man of business; and Peter himself looked thoughtfully at the fire from between his collars, as if he were deliberating what particular investments he should favor when he came into the receipt of that bewildering income. Martha, who was a poor apprentice at a milliner's, then told them what kind of work she had to do, and how many hours she worked at a stretch, and how she meant to lie abed tomorrow morning for a good long rest—tomorrow being a holiday she passed at home. Also how she had seen a countess and a lord some days before, and how the lord "was much about as tall as Peter"; at which Peter pulled up his collars so high that you couldn't have seen his head if you had been there. All this time the chestnuts and the jug went round and round; and by and by they had a song about a lost child traveling in the snow from Tiny Tim, who had a plaintive little voice, and sang it very well indeed.

There was nothing of high mark in this. They were not a handsome family; they were not well dressed; their shoes were far from being waterproof; their clothes were scanty; and Peter might have known, and very likely did, the inside of a pawnbroker's. But they were happy, grateful, pleased with one another, and contented with the time; and when they faded, and looked happier yet in the bright sprinklings of the spirit's torch at parting, Scrooge had his eye upon them, and especially on Tiny Tim, until the last.

It was a great surprise to Scrooge, as this scene vanished, to hear a hearty laugh. It was a much greater surprise to Scrooge to recognize it as his own nephew's, and to find himself in a bright, dry, gleaming room, with the spirit

40. **Baleful:** wretched.

standing smiling by his side and looking at that same nephew.

It is a fair, even-handed, noble adjustment of things, that while there is infection in disease and sorrow, there is nothing in the world so irresistibly contagious as laughter and good humor. When Scrooge's nephew laughed, Scrooge's niece by marriage laughed as heartily as he. And their assembled friends, being not a bit behindhand, laughed out lustily.

"He said that Christmas was a humbug, as I live!" cried Scrooge's nephew. "He believed it, too!"

"More shame for him, Fred!" said Scrooge's niece, indignantly. Bless those women! they never do anything by halves. They are always in earnest.

She was very pretty; exceedingly pretty. With a dimpled, surprised-looking, capital face; a ripe little mouth that seemed made to be kissed—as no doubt it was; all kinds of good little dots about her chin that melted into one another when she laughed; and the sunniest pair of eyes you ever saw in any little creature's head. Altogether she was what you would have called provoking, but satisfactory, too. Oh, perfectly satisfactory.

"He's a comical old fellow," said Scrooge's nephew, "that's the truth, and not so pleasant as he might be. However, his offenses carry their own punishment, and I have nothing to say against him. Who suffers by his ill whims? Himself, always. Here he takes it into his head to dislike us, and he won't come and dine with us. What's the consequence? He don't lose much of a dinner."

"Indeed, I think he loses a very good dinner," interrupted Scrooge's niece. Everybody else said the same, and they must be allowed to have been competent judges, because they had just had dinner; and, with the dessert upon the table, were clustered round the fire, by lamplight.

"Well, I am very glad to hear it," said Scrooge's nephew, "because I haven't any great faith in these young housekeepers. What do *you* say, Topper?"

Topper clearly had his eye on one of Scrooge's niece's sisters, for he answered that a bachelor was a wretched outcast, who had no right to express an opinion on the subject. Whereat Scrooge's niece's sister—the plump one with the lace tucker,[41] not the one with the roses—blushed.

After tea they had some music. For they were a musical family and knew what they were about when they sang a glee or catch,[42] I can assure you—especially Topper, who could growl away in the bass like a good one, and never swell the large veins in his forehead, or get red in the face over it.

But they didn't devote the whole evening to music. After a while they played at forfeits; for it is good to be children sometimes, and never better than at Christmas, when its mighty Founder was a child himself. There was first a game at blindman's buff though. And I no more believe Topper was really blinded than I believe he had eyes in his boots. Because the way in which he went after that plump sister in the lace tucker was an outrage on the credulity of human nature. Knocking down the fire irons, tumbling over the chairs, bumping up against the piano, smothering himself among the curtains; wherever she went, there went he! He always knew where the plump sister was. He wouldn't catch anybody else. If you had fallen up against him, as some of them did, and stood there, he would have made a feint[43] of endeavoring to seize you, which would have been an affront to your under-

41. **tucker:** a covering for the neck and shoulders, something like a large collar.
42. **glee; catch:** songs for three or more voices, unaccompanied by instruments.
43. **feint** (fānt): pretense.

standing, and would instantly have sidled off in the direction of the plump sister.

"Here is a new game," said Scrooge. "One half-hour, Spirit, only one!"

It was a game called Yes and No, where Scrooge's nephew had to think of something, and the rest must find out what; he only answering to their questions Yes or No, as the case was. The fire of questioning to which he was exposed elicited from him that he was thinking of an animal, a live animal, rather a disagreeable animal, a savage animal, an animal that growled and grunted sometimes, and talked sometimes, and lived in London, and walked about the streets, and wasn't made a show of, and wasn't led by anybody, and didn't live in a menagerie, and was never killed in a market, and was not a horse, or an ass, or a cow, or a bull, or a tiger, or a dog, or a pig, or a cat, or a bear. At every new question put to him, this nephew burst into a fresh roar of laughter, and was so inexpressibly tickled, that he was obliged to get up off the sofa and stamp. At last the plump sister cried out: "I have found it out! I know what it is, Fred! I know what it is!"

"What is it?" cried Fred.

"It's your Uncle Scro-o-o-oge!"

Which it certainly was. Admiration was the universal sentiment, though some objected that the reply to "Is it a bear?" ought to have been "Yes."

Uncle Scrooge had imperceptibly become so gay and light of heart, that he would have drunk to the unconscious company in an inaudible speech. But the whole scene passed off in the breath of the last word spoken by his nephew; and he and the spirit were again upon their travels.

Much they saw, and far they went, and many homes they visited, but always with a happy end. The spirit stood beside sickbeds, and they were cheerful; on foreign lands, and they were close at home; by struggling men, and they were patient in their greater hope; by poverty, and it was rich. In almshouse, hospital, and jail, in misery's every refuge, where vain man in his little brief authority had not made fast the door and barred the spirit out, he left his blessing, and taught Scrooge his precepts.[44] Suddenly, as they stood together in an open place, the bell struck twelve.

Scrooge looked about him for the ghost, and saw it no more. As the last stroke ceased to vibrate, he remembered the prediction of old Jacob Marley, and, lifting up his eyes, beheld a solemn phantom, draped and hooded, coming like a mist along the ground toward him.

Stave Four:
The Last of the Spirits

The phantom slowly, gravely, silently approached. When it came near him, Scrooge bent down upon his knee; for in the air through which this spirit moved it seemed to scatter gloom and mystery.

It was shrouded in a deep black garment, which concealed its head, its face, its form, and left nothing of it visible save one outstretched hand. He knew no more, for the spirit neither spoke nor moved.

"I am in the presence of the Ghost of Christmas Yet to Come? Ghost of the Future! I fear you more than any specter I have seen. But as I know your purpose is to do me good, and as I hope to live to be another man from what I was, I am prepared to bear you company, and do it with a thankful heart. Will you not speak to me?"

It gave him no reply. The hand was pointed straight before them.

"Lead on! Lead on! The night is waning fast, and it is precious time to me, I know. Lead on, Spirit!"

44. **precepts** (prē′sĕpts′): rules of living.

They scarcely seemed to enter the city; for the city rather seemed to spring up about them. But there they were in the heart of it; on 'Change, among the merchants.

The spirit stopped beside one little knot of businessmen. Observing that the hand was pointed to them, Scrooge advanced to listen to their talk.

"No," said a great fat man with a monstrous chin. "I don't know much about it either way. I only know he's dead."

"When did he die?" inquired another.

"Last night, I believe."

"Why, what was the matter with him? I thought he'd never die."

"Goodness knows," said the first, with a yawn.

"What has he done with his money?" asked a red-faced gentleman.

"I haven't heard," said the man with the large chin. "Company, perhaps. He hasn't left it to me. That's all I know. Bye-bye."

Scrooge was at first inclined to be surprised that the spirit should attach importance to conversation apparently so trivial, but feeling assured that it must have some hidden purpose, he set himself to consider what it was likely to be. It could scarcely be supposed to have any bearing on the death of Jacob, his old partner, for that was past, and this ghost's province was the future.

He looked about in that very place for his own image; but another man stood in his accustomed corner, and though the clock pointed to his usual time of day for being there, he saw no likeness of himself among the multitudes that poured in through the porch. It gave him little surprise, however; for he had been revolving in his mind a change of life, and he thought and hoped he saw his newborn resolutions carried out in this.

They left this busy scene and went into an obscure part of the town to a low shop where iron, old rags, bottles, bones, and greasy offal[45] were bought. A gray-haired rascal, of great age, sat smoking his pipe. Scrooge and the phantom came into the presence of this man just as a woman with a heavy bundle slunk into the shop. But she had scarcely entered, when another woman, similarly laden, came in too; and she was closely followed by a man in faded black. After a short period of blank astonishment, in which the old man with the pipe had joined them, they all three burst into a laugh.

"Let the charwoman[46] alone to be the first!" cried she who had entered first. "Let the laundress alone to be the second; and let the undertaker's man alone to be the third. Look here, old Joe, here's a chance! If we haven't all three met here without meaning it!"

"You couldn't have met in a better place. You were made free of it long ago, you know; and the other two ain't strangers. What have you got to sell? What have you got to sell?"

"Half a minute's patience, Joe, and you shall see."

"What odds then! What odds, Mrs. Dilber?" said the woman. "Every person has a right to take care of themselves. *He* always did! Who's the worse for the loss of a few things like these? Not a dead man, I suppose."

Mrs. Dilber, whose manner was remarkable for general propitiation,[47] said, "No, indeed, ma'am."

"If he wanted to keep 'em after he was dead, a wicked old screw, why wasn't he natural in his lifetime? If he had been, he'd have had somebody to look after him when he was struck with death, instead of lying gasping out his last there, alone by himself."

45. **offal** (ôf′əl): the waste parts of an animal that has been butchered for meat.
46. **charwoman:** a woman employed to clean a house or an office.
47. **propitiation** (prō-pĭsh′ē-ā′shən): ability to keep the peace.

"It's the truest word that ever was spoke, it's a judgment on him."

"I wish it was a little heavier judgment, and it should have been, you may depend upon it, if I could have laid my hands on anything else. Open that bundle, old Joe, and let me know the value of it. Speak out plain. I'm not afraid to be the first, nor afraid for them to see it."

Joe went down on his knees for the greater convenience of opening the bundle, and dragged out a large and heavy roll of some dark stuff.

"What do you call this? Bed curtains!"

"Ah! Bed curtains! Don't drop that oil upon the blankets, now."

"*His* blankets?"

"Whose else's do you think? He isn't likely to take cold without 'em, I dare say. Ah! You may look through that shirt till your eyes ache; but you won't find a hole in it, nor a threadbare place. It's the best he had, and a fine one too. They'd have wasted it by dressing him up in it, if it hadn't been for me."

Scrooge listened to this dialogue in horror.

"Spirit! I see, I see. The case of this unhappy man might be my own. My life tends that way, now. Merciful Heaven, what is this?"

The scene had changed, and now he almost touched a bare, uncurtained bed. A pale light, rising in the outer air, fell straight upon this bed; and on it, unwatched, unwept, uncared for, was the body of this plundered unknown man.

"Spirit, let me see some tenderness connected with a death, or this dark chamber, Spirit, will be forever present to me."

The ghost conducted him to poor Bob Cratchit's house—the dwelling he had visited before—and found the mother and the children seated round the fire.

Quiet. Very quiet. The noisy little Cratchits were as still as statues in one corner and sat looking up at Peter, who had a book before him. The mother and her daughters were engaged in needlework. But surely they were very quiet!

" 'And he took a child, and set him in the midst of them.' "[48]

Where had Scrooge heard those words? He had not dreamed them. The boy must have read them out, as he and the spirit crossed the threshold. Why did he not go on?

The mother laid her work upon the table and put her hand up to her face. "The color hurts my eyes," she said.

The color? Ah, poor Tiny Tim!

"They're better now again. It makes them weak by candlelight; and I wouldn't show weak eyes to your father when he comes home, for the world. It must be near his time."

"Past it rather," Peter answered, shutting up his book. "But I think he has walked a little slower than he used, these few last evenings, Mother."

"I have known him walk with—I have known him walk with Tiny Tim upon his shoulder, very fast indeed."

"And so have I," cried Peter. "Often."

"And so have I," exclaimed another. So had all.

"But he was very light to carry, and his father loved him so, that it was no trouble—no trouble. And there is your father at the door!"

She hurried out to meet him; and little Bob in his comforter—he had need of it, poor fellow—came in. His tea was ready for him on the hob, and they all tried who should help him to it most. Then the two young Cratchits got upon his knees and laid, each child, a little cheek against his face, as if they said, "Don't mind it, Father. Don't be grieved!"

Bob was very cheerful with them, and spoke

---

48. **"And he . . . them"**: a quotation from Mark 9:36.

pleasantly to all the family. He looked at the work upon the table, and praised the industry and speed of Mrs. Cratchit and the girls. They would be done long before Sunday, he said.

"Sunday! You went today, then, Robert?"

"Yes, my dear," returned Bob. "I wish you could have gone. It would have done you good to see how green a place it is. But you'll see it often. I promised him that I would walk there on a Sunday. My little, little child! My little child!"

He broke down all at once. He couldn't help it. If he could have helped it, he and his child would have been farther apart, perhaps, than they were.

"Specter," said Scrooge, "something informs

The Last of the Spirits.

me that our parting moment is at hand. I know it, but I know not how. Tell me what man that was, with the covered face, whom we saw lying dead?"

The Ghost of Christmas Yet to Come conveyed him to a dismal, wretched, ruinous churchyard.

The spirit stood among the graves, and pointed down to one.

"Before I draw nearer to that stone to which you point, answer me one question. Are these the shadows of the things that will be, or are they shadows of the things that may be only?"

Still the ghost pointed downward to the grave by which it stood.

"Men's courses will foreshadow certain ends, to which, if persevered in, they must lead. But if the courses be departed from, the ends will change. Say it is thus with what you show me!"

The spirit was immovable as ever.

Scrooge crept toward it, trembling as he went; and following the finger, read upon the stone of the neglected grave his own name— EBENEZER SCROOGE.

"Am *I* that man who lay upon the bed? No, Spirit! Oh no, no! Spirit! hear me! I am not the man I was. I will not be the man I must have been but for this intercourse. Why show me this, if I am past all hope? Assure me that I yet may change these shadows you have shown me by an altered life."

For the first time the kind hand faltered.

"I will honor Christmas in my heart, and try to keep it all the year. I will live in the Past, the Present, and the Future. The spirits of all three shall strive within me. I will not shut out the lessons that they teach. Oh, tell me I may sponge away the writing on this stone!"

Holding up his hands in one last prayer to have his fate reversed, he saw an alteration in the phantom's hood and dress. It shrunk, collapsed, and dwindled down into a bedpost.

Stave Five:
The End of It

Yes! and the bedpost was his own. The bed was his own, the room was his own. Best and happiest of all, the time before him was his own, to make amends in!

"I will live in the Past, the Present, and the Future!" Scrooge repeated, as he scrambled out of bed. "The spirits of all three shall strive within me. Oh, Jacob Marley! Heaven and the Christmastime be praised for this! I say it on my knees, old Jacob, on my knees!"

He was so fluttered and so glowing with his good intentions that his broken voice would scarcely answer to his call. He had been sobbing violently in his conflict with the spirit, and his face was wet with tears.

"They are not torn down," cried Scrooge, folding one of his bed curtains in his arms; "they are not torn down, rings and all. They are here; I am here; the shadows of the things that would have been may be dispelled. They will be. I know they will!"

His hands were busy with his garments all this time; turning them inside out, putting them on upside down, tearing them, mislaying them, making them parties to every kind of extravagance.

"I don't know what to do!" cried Scrooge, laughing and crying in the same breath, and making a perfect Laocoon[49] of himself with his stockings. "I am as light as a feather; I am as happy as an angel; I am as merry as a schoolboy; I am as giddy as a drunken man. A Merry Christmas to everybody! A Happy New Year to all the world. Hallo here! Whoop! Hallo!"

He had frisked into the sitting room, and was now standing there perfectly winded.

"There's the saucepan that the gruel was in!" cried Scrooge, starting off again and frisking round the fireplace. "There's the door by which the ghost of Jacob Marley entered! There's the corner where the Ghost of Christmas Present sat! There's the window where I saw the wandering spirits! It's all right; it's all true; it all happened. Ha, ha, ha!"

Really, for a man who had been out of practice for so many years, it was a splendid laugh, a most illustrious laugh. The father of a long, long line of brilliant laughs!

"I don't know what day of the month it is!" said Scrooge. "I don't know how long I've been among the spirits. I don't know anything. I'm quite a baby. Never mind. I don't care. I'd rather be a baby. Hallo! Whoop! Hallo here!"

He was checked in his transports,[50] by the churches' ringing out the lustiest peals he had ever heard. Clash, clang, hammer, ding, dong, bell. Bell, dong, ding, hammer, clang, clash! Oh, glorious, glorious!

Running to the window, he opened it and put out his head. No fog, no mist; clear, bright, jovial, stirring cold; cold, piping for the blood to dance to; golden sunlight; heavenly sky; sweet fresh air; merry bells. Oh, glorious. Glorious!

"What's today?" cried Scrooge, calling downward to a boy in Sunday clothes, who perhaps had loitered in to look about him.

"Eh?" returned the boy, with all his might of wonder.

"What's today, my fine fellow?" said Scrooge.

"Today!" replied the boy. "Why, CHRISTMAS DAY."

"It's Christmas Day!" said Scrooge to himself. "I haven't missed it. The spirits have done it all in one night. They can do anything they like. Of course they can. Of course they can. Hallo, my fine fellow?"

49. **Laocoon** (lā-ŏk′ō-ŏn′): a character in a Greek myth who was strangled by sea serpents.

50. **transports:** feelings of great joy.

"Hallo!" returned the boy.

"Do you know the poulterer's,[51] in the next street but one, at the corner?" Scrooge inquired.

"I should hope I did," replied the lad.

"An intelligent boy!" said Scrooge. "A remarkable boy! Do you know whether they've sold the prize turkey that was hanging up there? Not the little prize turkey; the big one?"

"What, the one as big as me?" returned the boy.

"What a delightful boy!" said Scrooge. "It's a pleasure to talk to him. Yes, my buck!"

"It's hanging there now," replied the boy.

"Is it?" said Scrooge. "Go buy it."

"Walk-ER!"[52] exclaimed the boy.

"No, no," said Scrooge, "I am in earnest. Go and buy it, and tell 'em to bring it here, that I may give them the direction where to take it. Come back with the man, and I'll give you a shilling. Come back with him in less than five minutes, and I'll give you half a crown!"[53]

The boy was off like a shot. He must have had a steady hand at a trigger who could have got a shot off half so fast.

"I'll send it to Bob Cratchit's!" whispered Scrooge, rubbing his hands, and splitting with a laugh. "He shan't know who sends it. It's twice the size of Tiny Tim. No one ever made such a joke as sending it to Bob's will be!"

The hand in which he wrote the address was not a steady one, but write it he did, somehow, and went downstairs to open the street door, ready for the coming of the poulterer's man. As he stood there, waiting his arrival, the knocker caught his eye.

"I shall love it as long as I live!" cried Scrooge, patting it with his hand. "I scarcely ever looked at it before. What an honest expression it has in its face! It's a wonderful knocker! Here's the turkey. Hallo! Whoop! How are you? Merry Christmas!"

It *was* a turkey! He could never have stood upon his legs, that bird. He would have snapped 'em off short in a minute, like sticks of sealing wax.

"Why, it's impossible to carry that to Camden Town," said Scrooge. "You must have a cab."

The chuckle with which he said this, and the chuckle with which he paid for the turkey, and the chuckle with which he paid for the cab, and the chuckle with which he recompensed the boy were only to be exceeded by the chuckle with which he sat down, breathless, in his chair again, and chuckled till he cried.

Shaving was not an easy task, for his hand continued to shake very much; and shaving requires attention, even when you don't dance while you are at it. But if he had cut the end of his nose off, he would have put a piece of sticking plaster over it, and been quite satisfied.

He dressed himself "all in his best," and at last got out into the streets. The people were by this time pouring forth, as he had seen them with the Ghost of Christmas Present; and walking with his hands behind him, Scrooge regarded everyone with a delighted smile. He looked so irresistibly pleasant, in a word, that three or four good-humored fellows said, "Good morning, sir! A Merry Christmas to you!" And Scrooge said often, afterward, that of all the blithe[54] sounds he had ever heard, those were the blithest in his ears.

He had not gone far, when coming on toward him he beheld the portly gentleman who had walked into his countinghouse the day before and said, "Scrooge and Marley's, I

---

51. **poulterer's:** shop where poultry is sold.

52. **Walk-ER!:** a slang word used to express disbelief, equivalent to "You're kidding!"

53. **half a crown:** a coin equal to one eighth of a pound.

54. **blithe** (blīth): cheerful.

believe?" It sent a pang across his heart to think how this old gentleman would look upon him when they met; but he knew what path lay straight before him, and he took it.

"My dear sir," said Scrooge, quickening his pace, and taking the old gentleman by both his hands. "How do you do? I hope you succeeded yesterday. It was very kind of you. A Merry Christmas to you, sir!"

"Mr. Scrooge?"

"Yes," said Scrooge. "That is my name, and I fear it may not be pleasant to you. Allow me to ask your pardon. And will you have the goodness——" Here Scrooge whispered in his ear.

"Lord bless me!" cried the gentleman, as if his breath were gone. "My dear Mr. Scrooge, are you serious?"

"If you please," said Mr. Scrooge. "Not a farthing[55] less. A great many back payments are included in it, I assure you. Will you do me that favor?"

"My dear sir," said the other, shaking hands with him, "I don't know what to say to such munifi——"[56]

"Don't say anything, please," retorted Scrooge. "Come and see me. Will you come and see me?"

"I will!" cried the old gentleman. And it was clear he meant to do it.

"Thankee," said Scrooge. "I am much obliged to you. I thank you fifty times. Bless you!"

He went to church, and walked about the streets, and watched the people hurrying to and fro, and patted children on the head, and questioned beggars, and looked down into the kitchens of houses, and up to the windows; and found that everything could yield him pleasure. He had never dreamed that any walk—that anything—could give him so much happiness. In the afternoon, he turned his steps toward his nephew's house.

He passed the door a dozen times before he had the courage to go up and knock. But he made a dash, and did it.

"Is your master at home, my dear?" said Scrooge to the girl. Nice girl! Very.

"Yes, sir."

"Where is he, my love?" said Scrooge.

"He's in the dining room, sir, along with mistress. I'll show you upstairs, if you please."

"Thankee. He knows me," said Scrooge, with his hand already on the dining-room lock. "I'll go in here, my dear."

He turned it gently, and sidled his face in round the door. They were looking at the table (which was spread out in great array); for these young housekeepers are always nervous on such points, and like to see that everything is right.

"Fred!" said Scrooge.

Dear heart alive, how his niece by marriage started! Scrooge had forgotten, for the moment, about her sitting in the corner with the footstool, or he wouldn't have done it, on any account.

"Why, bless my soul!" cried Fred. "Who's that?"

"It is I. Your Uncle Scrooge. I have come to dinner. Will you let me in, Fred?"

Let him in! It is a mercy he didn't shake his arm off. He was at home in five minutes. Nothing could be heartier. His niece looked just the same. So did Topper when *he* came. So did the plump sister when *she* came. So did everyone when *they* came. Wonderful party, wonderful games, wonderful unanimity,[57] wonderful happiness!

---

55. **farthing** (fär′thĭng): a former British coin worth one quarter of a penny.
56. **munificence** (myo͞o-nĭf′ə-səns): great generosity. Scrooge prevents the gentleman from finishing the word.

57. **unanimity** (yo͞o′-nə-nĭ′mĭ-tē): agreement.

But he was early at the office next morning. Oh, he was early there. If he could only be there first, and catch Bob Cratchit coming late! That was the thing he had set his heart upon.

And he did it; yes, he did! The clock struck nine. No Bob. A quarter past. No Bob. He was full eighteen minutes and a half behind his time. Scrooge sat with his door wide open, that he might see him come into the tank.

His hat was off before he opened the door; his comforter too. He was on his stool in a jiffy, driving away with his pen as if he were trying to overtake nine o'clock.

"Hallo!" growled Scrooge, in his accustomed voice as near as he could feign it. "What do you mean by coming here at this time of day?"

"I am very sorry, sir," said Bob. "I *am* behind my time."

"You are?" repeated Scrooge. "Yes, I think you are. Step this way, sir, if you please."

"It's only once a year, sir," pleaded Bob, appearing from the tank. "It shall not be repeated. I was making rather merry yesterday, sir."

"Now, I'll tell you what, my friend," said Scrooge, "I am not going to stand this sort of thing any longer. And therefore," he continued, leaping from his stool, and giving Bob such a dig in the waistcoat that he staggered back into the tank again, "and therefore I am about to raise your salary!"

Bob trembled, and got a little nearer to the ruler. He had a momentary idea of knocking Scrooge down with it, holding him, and calling to the people in the court for help and a strait waistcoat.[58]

"A Merry Christmas, Bob!" said Scrooge, with an earnestness that could not be mistaken, as he clapped him on the back. "A merrier Christmas, Bob, my good fellow, than I have

Scrooge and Bob Cratchit.

given you for many a year! I'll raise your salary, and endeavor to assist your struggling family, and we will discuss your affairs this very afternoon, over a Christmas bowl of smoking bishop,[59] Bob! Make up the fires, and buy another coal scuttle before you dot another *i*, Bob Cratchit!"

Scrooge was better than his word. He did it all, and infinitely more; and to Tiny Tim, who did *not* die, he was a second father. He became as good a friend, as good a master, and as good a man, as the good old city knew, or any other good old city, town, or borough, in the good old world. Some people laughed to see the alteration in him, but he let them laugh, and little heeded them; for he was wise enough to know that nothing ever happened on this globe, for good, at which some people did not have their fill of laughter in the outset; and

58. **strait waistcoat:** a straitjacket.

59. **bishop:** a hot drink made of spiced port wine.

knowing that such as these would be blind anyway, he thought it quite as well that they should wrinkle up their eyes in grins, as have the malady in less attractive forms. His own heart laughed, and that was quite enough for him.

He had no further intercourse with spirits, but lived upon the total-abstinence principle,[60] ever afterward; and it was always said of him that he knew how to keep Christmas well, if any man alive possessed the knowledge. May that be truly said of us, and all of us! And so, as Tiny Tim observed, God Bless Us, Every One!

60. **total-abstinence** (ăb′stə-nəns) **principle:** the giving up of "spirits" completely, usually alcoholic "spirits," but here ghostly "spirits."

Reading Check

1. Who was Jacob Marley?
2. Why do the two gentlemen visit Scrooge in his countinghouse on Christmas Eve?
3. What is the first supernatural event?
4. Why does Marley's spirit visit Scrooge?
5. What two scenes from his past does Scrooge relive?
6. What toast does Bob Cratchit make on Christmas Day?
7. What vow does Scrooge make to the last spirit?
8. What is Scrooge's first charitable act?
9. Why does Scrooge hesitate before visiting his nephew?
10. How does Scrooge help Bob Cratchit?

Analyzing and Interpreting the Story

Character

1. "A Christmas Carol" contains many sequences with supernatural characters and events. Yet it is Ebenezer Scrooge, the human being, who is the center of attention. It is his transformation, or change, that forms the central action of the story. How is Scrooge different at the end of the story?

2. At the beginning of the story, the author must convince you that Scrooge is a hardhearted miser. He does this through direct and indirect characterization. He *tells* you that Scrooge is a "tightfisted hand at the grindstone"—in other words, a stingy person. Locate other passages that *tell* you how miserly Scrooge is. You learn that in his countinghouse, Scrooge keeps the coalbox in his own room, and that his clerk tries to warm himself at his candle. This scene *shows* you how stingy Scrooge is. Point out other passages that *show* Scrooge's miserliness. (For a review of direct and indirect characterization, see page 240.)

3. During the visit of each Christmas spirit, Scrooge learns something about himself that helps him to change. At the end of Stave Two, for example, Scrooge realizes that he lost his fiancée through his own greed and stupidity. **a.** What does Scrooge learn about himself by the end of Stave Three? **b.** By the end of Stave Four?

4. At the beginning of the story, Scrooge is described as a "squeezing, wrenching, grasping, scraping, clutching, covetous old sinner!" What words would you use to describe him at the end of the story?

Plot

5. The plot of a story turns upon a conflict, or struggle, of some kind. What is the conflict in

this story? (For a review of conflict, see page 218.)

6. The first thing the author tells you is that Marley is dead. **a.** What later events are being foreshadowed? **b.** You are also told that Scrooge is a man of no "fancy," or imagination (page 279). Why is it important to emphasize this fact about Scrooge?

7. Which scene in the story forms the climax, the point at which Scrooge makes a decision to change?

Setting

8. An important part of the action of the story is set in Scrooge's rooms. **a.** In what way are the rooms a reflection of Scrooge's character? **b.** How is this setting transformed, or changed, by the appearance of the Ghost of Christmas Present? **c.** How is the spirit of Christmas reflected in Fezziwig's warehouse? **d.** In the homes of Bob Cratchit and of Scrooge's nephew?

Point of View

9. Dickens has chosen an omniscient point of view for the story. Find passages that reveal Scrooge's innermost thoughts and feelings before and after his transformation.

10. Although the narrator doesn't appear in the story, he makes his opinions of the characters and events known to us. For example, on page 290, when he describes the game of blindman's buff at Fred's home, he says, "And I no more believe Topper was really blinded than I believe he had eyes in his boots."Where else does the narrator comment on the characters and actions in his own person?

Theme

11. Marley's ghost tells Scrooge, "Mankind was my business . . . charity, mercy, forbearance, benevolence, were all my business" (page 281). **a.** What does the word *business* mean in

Marley's statement? **b.** How do you know by the end of the story that Scrooge has made mankind *his* business? **c.** What does the story suggest is everyone's business?

12. Scrooge asks the Ghost of Christmas Yet to Come if the visions he has seen are shadows of what will be or what may be (page 294). What does the conclusion of "A Christmas Carol" imply about the ability of people to determine their own futures?

Literary Elements

Recognizing Onomatopoeia

Many words in English imitate sounds. For example, when you say the word *buzz*, you hear the sound of buzzing at the end of the word. When you say *plop*, you hear the sound that is made by an object when it strikes water. The technical name for this use of words is **onomatopoeia** (ŏn′ə-măt′ə-pē′ə).

In "A Christmas Carol" there is a "clanking" of chains before Marley's ghost enters; Mrs. Cratchit makes the gravy "hissing" hot; and you are told that the chestnuts "crackled" in the fire. The words *clank, hiss,* and *crackle* imitate the sounds made by dragging chains, steaming gravy, and roasting chestnuts, respectively. When Dickens uses these words, he helps you experience vividly what he is describing.

Writers may also use the sounds of words to suggest something about character. Read aloud these lines describing Scrooge:

> Oh! But he was a tightfisted hand at the grindstone, was Scrooge! A squeezing, wrenching, grasping, scraping, clutching, covetous old sinner!

Many sounds in the passage are harsh sounds. The sound **s** suggests hissing. How often is the sound **s** repeated? Can you find repeated **r** sounds that give you the impression of someone growling or grumbling angrily? Where do you hear the harsh sound **k**? The repetition of these harsh sounds reinforces what the reader already knows about Scrooge—that he is a hard-hearted and unfeeling man.

Language and Vocabulary

Recognizing Analogies

You are familiar with vocabulary questions that ask you to identify synonyms or antonyms. These questions usually involve a pair of words. Some other vocabulary questions, called **analogies,** involve two pairs of words. You must first decide what relationship exists between the words in the first pair. The same relationship applies to the second pair.

An analogy question has a special format and uses special symbols. This is one type of analogy question:

little : small :: strong : _____
a. tiny   **b.** great   **c.** powerful   **d.** large

The two dots (:) stand for "is to"; the four dots (::) stand for "as." The example, therefore, reads "Little *is to* small *as* strong *is to* _____." Since the first two words, *little* and *small*, are synonyms, the correct answer is *c*. The word that is a synonym for *strong* is *powerful.*

Here are some questions involving synonym and antonym relationships. Before you complete the analogies, check the meanings of words in your glossary or in a dictionary.

1. covetous : greedy :: destitute : _____
   a. hateful
   b. sad
   c. determined
   d. poor
2. melancholy : cheerful :: trivial : _____
   a. significant
   b. motionless
   c. unimportant
   d. cautious
3. apparition : phantom :: aspiration : _____
   a. scorn
   b. ambition
   c. self-control
   d. good will
4. inexplicable : clear :: inaudible : _____
   a. deceitful
   b. low
   c. deafening
   d. noticeable

Writing About Literature

Discussing the Theme of the Story

Although "A Christmas Carol" has elements of fantasy, the theme of the story is realistic. Dickens' anger at human folly and greed and his sympathy for the poor and unfortunate come through. In what ways does this story reveal the true meaning of Christmas? Develop your answer in a short essay.

Extending Your Study

Evaluating Illustrations

The illustrations reproduced here were made by John Leech for the edition of *A Christmas Carol* published in 1846. How do the details in these illustrations capture the spirit of Dickens' story?

Find other illustrated editions of this great classic and compare the illustrations with those of Leech. Which do you prefer and why? In your discussion, tell what criteria you used in arriving at your conclusions.

Charles Dickens   (1812–1870)

Charles Dickens spent the happiest years of his childhood in Chatham, a dockyard town near London. He was a keen observer of the city life around him. He roamed the area, observing the great black prisons that jutted out over the Medway River and the gray, square ruins of Rochester Castle. He saw the inhumane conditions existing in the local hospitals, prisons, and poorhouses.

Dickens was an avid reader. He spent many free hours reading the works of Shakespeare and *The Arabian Nights,* and rummaging through old novels piled up in the attic of his home. Dickens' schooling was cut short when his father fell deeply into debt. At the age of twelve, he was forced to take a job in a warehouse, where he worked twelve hours a day, pasting labels on bottles. This experience was shattering, and it aroused in Dickens a fierce determination to fight poverty and social injustice—an ideal he expressed passionately in many of his books.

Dickens' literary career began in 1836, when he published *Sketches by Boz,* a collection of short, fictional pieces based on his observations of London life. Shortly afterward, he was asked to write a comic narrative to accompany a set of engravings by a well-known artist. The result was *The Pickwick Papers,* which brought him instant fame. In such classics as *Oliver Twist* (1837–1838), *David Copperfield* (1850), and *Great Expectations* (1861), he created some of the most vivid characters and memorable situations in English literature.

Dickens also acted in amateur plays and gave readings from his works in England and in America. The version of "A Christmas Carol" that appears in this book was prepared by Dickens for his public readings.

DEVELOPING SKILLS
IN CRITICAL THINKING

Establishing Criteria for Evaluation

This unit has introduced you to certain basic elements that can help you read short stories with greater pleasure and understanding. Before completing your study, you may wish to consider the criteria to be used in reading and *evaluating,* or judging, the merits of other short stories.

Plot

1. *Is the main conflict of the story well developed?* Does the author make clear what the conflict or conflicts are? Do the episodes of the story grow logically out of the conflict? Is the resolution of the conflict acceptable or is it improbable?

2. *Are the elements of suspense and foreshadowing handled skillfully?* Is your interest sustained?

How does the story "Rikki-tikki-tavi" show skillful use of all these plot elements?

Character

3. *Are the characters believable and consistent in their actions?* Are their actions well motivated? Are you adequately prepared for any change in a character's actions or thoughts?

4. *Are the characters presented effectively?* Does the author reveal characters directly or indirectly? Are the characters clearly individualized or are they types?

How do these criteria apply to all the characters in "A Christmas Carol"?

Setting

5. *What role does the setting play?* Does it have an important connection to the plot or is it irrelevant? Does the setting help to create atmosphere or to reveal characters' moods?

What is the importance of setting in stories as different as "The Landlady" and "Zlateh the Goat"?

Point of View

6. *What point of view is used and what is its purpose?* How does the author use point of view to control your reactions to the characters and events?

How, for example, does Irving's narrator control your reactions to Rip Van Winkle and Dame Van Winkle?

Irony

7. *How is irony used and how does it affect the story?*

How is the situation in "The Landlady" ironic? Why is this irony essential to the story?

Theme

8. *Does the story offer some insight into human experience?*

What is the theme of "The Erne from the Coast"? Test your statement of theme by seeing if it includes all important aspects of the story.

PRACTICE IN
READING AND WRITING

Writing Stories

A short story makes use of many of the techniques used in good descriptive and narrative writing. In addition, a short story has a particular structure, which places characters in a specific situation and setting. Here are some suggestions to guide you in writing your own short stories.

Prewriting

One of the best sources for ideas is your own experience. Consider some of the conflicts you observe every day: external conflicts between motorists and cyclists, children on a playground, salespeople and customers; internal conflicts between self-control and indulgence, feelings of anger and love.

Good ideas often can be found in newspaper articles. A skillful writer can invent characters and episodes to flesh out the lead paragraph in a news story.

Once you have decided on your situation and main character or characters, gather details for your story by asking the 5W-How questions: *Who? What? Where? When? Why?* and *How?* Then plan the sequence of events that grow out of the conflict. What will be the climax and how will the conflict be resolved?

Choose a point of view. Will you tell the story in first-person or third-person point of view?

Where will the action take place? Will there be one setting or several settings?

Writing

The opening of the story can set a mood for the story or establish the conflict. In either case it needs to arouse the reader's interest.

Introduce your major character or characters early. Use both direct and indirect methods of characterization. Carefully select only those details that are essential to the story. Prepare the reader for any change in a character's actions, thoughts, or feelings.

If you use dialogue, make sure that the language suits the characters.

Keep the point of view consistent. If you have started with an omniscient narrator, do not shift to a first-person point of view.

Evaluating, Revising, and Proofreading

In evaluating your story, ask yourself if the opening paragraph catches the reader's interest. If it is dull, revise by opening with dialogue, an anecdote, or a more vivid description of setting.

Ask yourself if the events in the plot are clearly organized. If not, think about reorganizing the incidents in the plot. Would a flashback help to make the conflict clear? Would it help to illuminate character?

As you evaluate, also ask yourself if the main character seems "real." If the main character is not sufficiently developed, add actions, dialogue, or thoughts to make the character more convincing.

Proofread your story to see that you have eliminated errors in grammar, usage, and mechanics. If your story includes dialogue, be sure to check punctuation carefully.

Prepare a final copy and share your story with another student or a small group.

For Further Reading

Bennett, George, editor, *Great Tales of Action and Adventure* (paperback, Dell, 1959)

The classic tales of suspense in this collection include "The Most Dangerous Game" by Richard Connell, "The Pit and the Pendulum" by Edgar Allan Poe, and "To Build a Fire" by Jack London.

Bradbury, Ray, *The Vintage Bradbury* (paperback, Vintage, 1965)

This collection of science-fiction stories includes "The Veldt," "The Fog Horn," and "There Will Come Soft Rains."

Doyle, Sir Arthur Conan, *The Adventures of Sherlock Holmes* (many editions)

Readers who like mysteries will enjoy these stories about the most famous and most brilliant detective in literature. Some of the best-known stories are "The Red-Headed League," "The Adventure of the Speckled Band," and "The Hound of the Baskervilles."

Edmonds, Walter D., *The Night Raider and Other Stories* (Little, Brown, 1980)

All four stories are set in New York State.

Fenner, Phyllis, R., editor, *Midnight Prowlers: Stories of Cats and Their Enslaved Owners* (William Morrow, 1981)

Here are ten stories about cats.

Henry, O. (many collections of stories)

O. Henry is the writer who perfected surprise endings. Favorite stories include "The Gift of the Magi," "The Last Leaf," "The Ransom of Red Chief," and "After Twenty Years."

Irving, Washington (many collections of stories)

Among Irving's well-known stories are "The Legend of Sleepy Hollow," "The Specter Bridegroom," and "The Moor's Legacy."

Kipling, Rudyard, *The Jungle Book* and *The Second Jungle Book* (many editions)

Kipling's tales about the jungles of India include the story of Mowgli, a boy who was raised by animals.

Singer, Isaac Bashevis, *Stories for Children* (Farrar, Straus, 1984)

This collection includes more than thirty stories about growing up in Poland.

DRAMA

There is a great difference between seeing a play performed in a theater or on a screen and reading that play in class or at home. When you watch a performance, you are seeing the results of other people's imaginative efforts. For many weeks or months before a play is produced, there is careful planning. Sets must be created; costumes must be designed and fitted; actors and actresses must study and rehearse their parts. When you read a play, you must rely on your own imagination to create the performance. You must visualize the setting and costumes; you must imagine the shifting tones of voice in which the performers would deliver their lines. You must interpret the different roles as they would be interpreted for you by the players.

Theatre du Gymnase in Paris (1856) by Adolph Von Menzel. Oil on canvas.
Nationalgalerie Staatliche Museen Preussischer Kulturbesitz, West Berlin

307

CLOSE READING OF A PLAY

Developing Skills in Critical Thinking

While many of the elements studied in connection with short stories are relevant to the study of drama, there are several additional elements that need to be taken into account. Dramatists frequently make use of stage directions to create setting and to give players instructions for acting. Sound effects are often important in creating setting and mood. Sometimes, a dramatist may use a narrator to comment on the action, as Pearl Buck does in *The Big Wave* (page 357). Generally, however, dialogue is the dramatist's most important device for presenting character and for moving the action along.

Here is a one-act play by Milton Geiger, called *In the Fog*. Read the play carefully, using the sidenotes as a guide. Then turn to the analysis on page 316.

In the Fog

MILTON GEIGER

Sets: *A signpost on Pennsylvania Route 30. A rock or stump in the fog. A gas station pump.*

Night. At first we can only see fog drifting across a dark scene devoid of[1] detail. Then, out of the fog, there emerges toward us a white roadside signpost with a number of white painted signboards pointing to right and to left. The marker is a Pennsylvania State Route—marked characteristically "PENNA-30." Now, a light as from a far headlight sweeps the signs.

An automobile approaches. The car pulls up close. We hear the car door open and slam, and a man's footsteps approaching on the concrete. Now the signs are lit up again by a more localized, smaller source of light. The light grows stronger as the man, offstage, approaches. The Doctor *en-*

Thinking Model

Fog and darkness create an eerie mood.

Setting is a roadside in Pennsylvania, with signposts pointing in different directions.

Automobile indicates that the action takes place in recent times.

1. **devoid** (dĭ-void′) **of:** without.

ters, holding a flashlight before him. He scrutinizes[2] the road marker. He flashes his light up at the arrows. We see the legends on the markers. Pointing off right there are markers that read: York, Columbia, Lancaster; pointing left the signs read: Fayetteville, McConnellsburg, Pennsylvania Turnpike.

The Doctor's face is perplexed and annoyed as he turns his flashlight on a folded road map. He is a bit lost in the fog. Then his flashlight fails him. It goes out!

Doctor. Darn! (*He fumbles with the flashlight in the gloom. Then a voice is raised to him from offstage.*)

Eben (*offstage, strangely*). Turn around, mister. . . .

[*The* Doctor *turns sharply to stare offstage.*]

Zeke (*offstage*). You don't have to be afraid, mister. . . .

[*The* Doctor *sees two men slowly approaching out of the fog. One carries a lantern below his knees. The other holds a heavy rifle. Their features are utterly indistinct as they approach, and the rifleman holds up his gun with quiet threat.*]

Eben. You don't have to be afraid.

Doctor (*more indignant than afraid*). So you say! Who are you, man?

Eben. We don't aim to hurt you none.

Doctor. That's reassuring. I'd like to know just what you mean by this? This gun business! Who *are* you?

Zeke (*mildly*). What's your trade, mister?

Doctor. I . . . I'm a doctor. Why?

Zeke (*to* Eben). Doctor.

Eben (*nods; then to* Doctor). Yer the man we want.

---

2. **scrutinizes** (skrōōt'n-īz'əz): examines carefully.

Doctor is checking his location; presumably, he is lost.

What is the significance of these place names?

Total darkness creates a sense of danger.

Chilling effect of voices coming out of the darkness.

Strangers are menacing, despite their claim that they mean no harm.

Zeke. Ye'll do proper, we're thinkin'.

Eben. So ye'd better come along, mister.

Zeke. Aye.

Doctor. Why? Has—anyone been hurt?

Eben. It's for you to say if he's been hurt nigh to the finish.

Zeke. So we're askin' ye to come along, doctor.

[*The* Doctor *looks from one to another in indecision and puzzlement.*]

Eben. In the name o' mercy.

Zeke. Aye.

Doctor. I want you to understand—I'm not afraid of your gun! I'll go to your man all right. Naturally, I'm a doctor. But I demand to know who you are.

Zeke (*patiently*). Why not? Raise yer lantern, Eben. . . .

Eben (*tiredly*). Aye.

[Eben *lifts his lantern. Its light falls on their faces now, and we see that they are terrifying. Matted beards, clotted with blood; crude head bandages, crusty with dirt and dry blood. Their hair, stringy and disheveled. Their faces are lean and hollow-cheeked; their eyes sunken and tragic. The* Doctor *is shocked for a moment—then bursts out——*]

Doctor. Good heavens!—

Zeke. That's Eben; I'm Zeke.

Doctor. What's happened? Has there been an accident or . . . what?

Zeke. Mischief's happened, stranger.

Eben. Mischief enough.

Doctor (*looks at rifle at his chest*). There's been gunplay—hasn't there?

Zeke (*mildly ironic*). Yer tellin' us there's been gunplay!

Doctor. And I'm telling you that I'm not at all frightened! It's my duty to report this, and report it I will!

Note archaic character of strangers' speech.

Imagine the sudden, dramatic effect of seeing these faces surrounded by darkness.

Answers are evasive.

Zeke. Aye, mister. You do that.

Doctor. You're arrogant about it now! You don't think you'll be caught and dealt with. But people are losing patience with you men. . . . You . . . you moonshiners![3] Running wild . . . a law unto yourselves . . . shooting up the countryside!

Zeke. Hear that, Eben? Moonshiners.

Eben. Mischief's happened, mister, we'll warrant[4] that. . . .

Doctor. And I don't like it!

Zeke. Can't say we like it better'n you do, mister. . . .

Eben (*strangely sad and remote*). What must be, must.

Zeke. There's no changin' or goin' back, and all 'at's left is the wishin' things were different.

Eben. Aye.

Doctor. And while we talk, your wounded man lies bleeding, I suppose—worthless though he may be. Well? I'll have to get my instrument bag, you know. It's in the car.

[Eben *and* Zeke *part to let* Doctor *pass between them. The* Doctor *reenters, carrying his medical bag.*]

Doctor. I'm ready. Lead the way.

[Eben *lifts his lantern a bit and goes first.* Zeke *prods the* Doctor *ever so gently and apologetically, but firmly with the rifle muzzle. The* Doctor *leaves.* Zeke *strides off slowly after them.*

A wounded man is lying against a section of stone fence. He, too, is bearded, though very young, and his shirt is dark with blood. He breathes but never stirs otherwise. Eben *enters, followed by the* Doctor *and* Zeke.]

---

3. **moonshiners:** people who distill liquor illegally.
4. **warrant** (wôr′ənt, wŏr′): declare positively.

Doctor assumes that Eben and Zeke are making and selling whiskey unlawfully.

They neither affirm nor deny the charge.

Why are they sad?

What do they regret?

Suspense mounts. Whom is the Doctor going to attend? What will happen to him?

Zeke. Ain't stirred a mite since we left 'im.

Doctor. Let's have that lantern here! (*The* Doctor *tears the man's shirt for better access to the wound. Softly*) Dreadful! Dreadful . . .!

Zeke's voice (*off scene*). Reckon it's bad in the chest like that, hey?

Doctor (*taking pulse*). His pulse is positively racing . . . ! How long has he been this way?

Zeke. A long time, mister. A long time. . . .

Doctor (*to* Eben). You! Hand me my bag.

[Eben *puts down lantern and hands bag to* Doctor. *The* Doctor *opens bag and takes out a couple of retractors.*[5] Zeke *holds lantern close now.*]

Doctor. Lend me a hand with these retractors. (*He works on the man.*) All right . . . when I tell you to draw back on the retractors—draw back.

Eben. Aye.

Zeke. How is 'e, mister?

Doctor (*preoccupied*). More retraction. Pull them a bit more. Hold it. . . .

Eben. Bad, ain't he?

Doctor. Bad enough. The bullet didn't touch any lung tissue far as I can see right now. There's some pneumothorax[6] though. All I can do now is plug the wound. There's some cotton and gauze wadding in my bag. Find it. . . .

[Zeke *probes about silently in the bag and comes up with a small dark box of gauze.*]

Doctor. That's it. (*Works a moment in silence*) I've never seen anything quite like it.

Eben. Yer young, doctor. Lot's o' things you've never seen.

Notice how evasive answers are.

How does the Doctor's comment add to the mystery?

5. **retractors** (rĭ-trăk′tərz): surgical instruments for holding back the flesh at the edge of a wound.

6. **pneumothorax** (noo′mō-thôr′ăks, nyoo′): air or gas in the chest cavity.

Doctor. Adhesive tape!

[Zeke *finds a roll of three-inch tape and hands it to the* Doctor, *who tears off long strips and slaps them on the dressing and pats and smooths them to man's chest.* Eben *replaces equipment in Doctor's bag and closes it with a hint of the finality to come. A preview of dismissal, so to speak.*]

Doctor (*at length*). There. So much for that. Now then—(*Takes man's shoulders*) give me a hand here.

Zeke (*quiet suspicion*). What fer?

Doctor. We've got to move this man.

Zeke. What fer?

Doctor (*stands; indignantly*). We've got to get him to a hospital for treatment; a thorough cleansing of the wound; irrigation.[7] I've done all I can for him here.

Zeke. I reckon he'll be all right 'thout no hospital.

Doctor. Do you realize how badly this man's hurt!

Eben. He won't bleed to death, will he?

Doctor. I don't think so—not with that plug and pressure dressing. But bleeding isn't the only danger we've got to——

Zeke (*interrupts*). All right, then. Much obliged to you.

Doctor. This man's dangerously hurt!

Zeke. Reckon he'll pull through now, thanks to you.

Doctor. I'm glad you feel that way about it! But I'm going to report this to the Pennsylvania State Police at the first telephone I reach!

Zeke. We ain't stoppin' ye, mister.

Eben. Fog is liftin', Zeke. Better be done with this, I say.

Zeke (*nods, sadly*). Aye. Ye can go now, mister . . . and thanks. (*Continues*) We never

Why should they refuse to have the wounded man moved?

Why should the fog be significant?

---

7. **irrigation:** here, flushing out a wound with water or other fluid.

meant a mite o' harm, I can tell ye. If we
killed, it was no wish of ours.
Eben. What's done is done. Aye.
Zeke. Ye can go now, stranger. . . .

[Eben *hands* Zeke *the* Doctor's *bag. Zeke
hands it gently to the* Doctor.]

Doctor. Very well. You haven't heard the
last of this, though!
Zeke. That's the truth, mister. We've killed,
aye; and we've been hurt for it. . . .
Eben. Hurt bad.

[*The* Doctor's *face is puckered with doubt and
strange apprehension.*]

Zeke. We're not alone, mister. We ain't the
only ones. (*Sighs*) Ye can go now, doctor . . .
and our thanks to ye. . . .

[*The* Doctor *leaves the other two, still gazing at
them in strange enchantment and wonder and a
touch of indignation.*]

Eben's voice. Thanks mister. . . .
Zeke's voice. In the name o' mercy. . . . We
thank you. . . .
Eben. In the name o' mercy.
Zeke. Thanks, mister. . . .
Eben. In the name o' kindness. . . .

[*The two men stand with their wounded comrade
at their feet—like a group statue in the park. The
fog thickens across the scene. Far off the long, sad
wail of a locomotive whimpers in the dark.*

The scene now shifts to a young Attendant
*standing in front of a gasoline pump taking a
reading and recording it in a book as he prepares
to close up. He turns as he hears the car approach
on the gravel drive.*

Note how the mood
changes in this scene.

The Doctor *enters.*]

Attendant (*pleasantly*). Good evening, sir. (*Nods off at car*) Care to pull 'er up to this pump, sir? Closing up.

Doctor (*impatiently*). No. Where's your telephone, please? I've just been held up!

Attendant. Pay station inside, sir. . . .

Doctor. Thank you! (*The* Doctor *starts to go past the* Attendant.)

Attendant. Excuse me, sir. . . .

Doctor (*stops*). Eh, what is it, what is it?

Attendant. Uh . . . what sort of looking fellows were they?

Doctor. Oh—two big fellows with a rifle; faces and heads bandaged and smeared with dirt and blood. Friend of theirs with a gaping hole in his chest. I'm a doctor, so they forced me to attend him. Why?

Attendant. *Those* fellers, huh?

Doctor. Then you know about them!

Attendant. I guess so.

Doctor. They're armed and they're desperate!

Attendant. That was about two or three miles back, would you say?

Doctor (*fumbling in pocket*). Just about—I don't seem to have the change. I wonder if you'd spare me change for a quarter . . . ?

Attendant (*makes change from metal coin canister at his belt*). Certainly, sir. . . .

Doctor. What town was that back there, now?

Attendant (*dumps coins in other's hand*). There you are, sir.

Doctor (*impatient*). Yes, thank you. I say— what town was that back there, so I can tell the police?

Attendant. That was . . . Gettysburg, mister. . . .

Doctor. Gettysburg . . . ?

Attendant. Gettysburg and Gettysburg battlefield. . . . (*Looks off*) When it's light and the fog's gone, you can see the gravestones. Meade's men . . . Pickett's men, Robert E. Lee's.[8] . . .

How does this information clear up the mystery?

[*The* Doctor *is looking off with the* Attendant; *now he turns his head slowly to stare at the other man.*]

Attendant (*continues*). On nights like this—well—you're not the first those men've stopped . . . or the last. (*Nods off*) Fill 'er up, mister?

Doctor. Yes, fill 'er up. . . .

8. **Meade's men . . . Lee's:** The Battle of Gettysburg was a turning point in the Civil War. On July 1–3, 1863, the Confederacy's forces, under Robert E. Lee, met the Union forces, under George Gordon Meade. The climax of the battle came when 15,000 Confederate soldiers, led by George Pickett, charged Cemetery Ridge and were repelled. The North suffered about 23,000 casualties; the South about 20,000.

Analysis

The dramatist of *In the Fog* has taken care to make the setting specific. The legends on the signpost tell us that the action takes place at a junction on Route 30 in southern Pennsylvania.

The opening scene arouses and sustains a foreboding mood. It is night, and dense fog makes it difficult for drivers to read the road signs. It is a lonely, dismal place to be lost.

A solitary car approaches and comes to a stop. A motorist enters carrying a flashlight. When the man, a doctor, starts to examine his road map, his flashlight goes out, and the stage is plunged into complete darkness and silence.

Suddenly we are startled by voices coming out of the darkness. Then two men enter. Because one of them is carrying a lantern below his knees, we cannot make out their faces, but there is sufficient light to see that the second man is holding a rifle. When the lantern is raised, we see two bloody, terrifying figures. Not only their appearance is frightening. The men speak in a strangely archaic way and answer the Doctor's questions evasively. Within moments the dramatist has created a menacing, suspenseful situation.

This mood is sustained when the men refuse to tell him how their comrade has been wounded and when they refuse to have him moved to a hospital. The Doctor is baffled by their attitude and by the bullet wound, which is different from anything in his experience.

The identity of these figures becomes clear in the final scene when we learn that the Doctor has encountered the strangers at Gettysburg. We now understand the significance of their bloodied appearance, their archaic language, the references to gunplay, and their sad, evasive replies. The dramatist has carefully prepared us for this eerie outcome.

Guidelines for Reading a Play

1. *Note any information that establishes the setting and the situation.* The setting of *In the Fog* is a roadside on a foggy night. The signpost on the stage identifies the site as a junction on Pennsylvania State Route 30. It is apparent that the main action of the play will grow out of the Doctor's encounter with the two strangers.

2. *Note clues that tell you what the players are doing or how the lines are spoken.* Stage directions indicate that the Doctor's voice is "indignant." His expression, as he looks at the strangers, is puzzled and indecisive. Even though their appearance is menacing, the two strangers speak "patiently" and "mildly"; their voices are "strangely sad and remote."

3. *Anticipate the action that will develop out of each scene.* The strangers do not deny or affirm the charge that they are moonshiners. From their archaic speech and their evasive answers, we get the sense that this is no ordinary case the Doctor is asked to attend.

4. *Be alert to the mood of the play.* An eerie mood is created immediately by the fog and the darkness. This note of foreboding is sustained by the mysterious character of the strangers.

The Mazarin Stone

MICHAEL AND MOLLY HARDWICK

Adapted from a story by
Sir Arthur Conan Doyle

Conflict, as you have seen, is not always physical. The conflict in this play is a battle of wits between Sherlock Holmes and the criminals who have stolen the great yellow Mazarin Stone. As you read, observe how Holmes uses his intelligence to outwit his opponents.

Characters

Sherlock Holmes
Dr. Watson, Holmes's friend and associate
Billy, Holmes's attendant
Count Negretto Sylvius, a big-game hunter and adventurer
Sam Merton, a boxer
Lord Cantlemere, a nobleman of high standing and political influence
Police Sergeant
Constables[1]

The play takes place in London around the beginning of the twentieth century.

Setting: *The parlor of 221B Baker Street. For this play, whose entire action takes place here, a curtain at the back of the stage must be capable of being drawn aside to reveal an alcove, backed by a window with blinds drawn. Seated beside this window, in profile to it and to the audience, is a dummy representing Sherlock Holmes. It is wearing an old dressing*

gown, *and sits in a large, high-backed chair. If the window blind were not down, it would appear to occupants of the houses opposite that Holmes himself is seated there. When the play begins, the chair and its occupant are concealed from the audience by the alcove curtain.*

Two doorways are necessary: one for characters arriving and departing—"parlor door"—and one leading off into Holmes's bedroom—"bedroom door." As the course of the action will reveal, an offstage route is necessary between the "bedroom" and the alcove.

The lamp is lit. A parasol stands against a chair. Billy, the page boy, *is holding up Holmes's ulster,[2] brushing it vigorously.*

There is a tap at the parlor door. It opens, and Watson's head peers round.

Billy. Dr. Watson, sir! Come in, sir!

[Watson *enters, closing the door.*]

---

1. **Constables** (kŏn′stə-bəlz): in England, policemen.

2. **ulster:** a long, loose overcoat made of heavy material, usually worn with a belt.

Watson. Well, Billy, my boy! Keeping the moths at bay?

Billy. That's it, sir.

[*He folds the coat and puts it down on a chair, as* Watson *lays aside his hat and stick.* Watson *glances round the room.*]

Watson. It doesn't seem to have changed much, Billy.

Billy. Not much, sir.

Watson. You don't change, either. I hope the same can be said of *him*?

Billy. I think he's in bed and asleep.

Watson (*laughs*). At seven o'clock of a lovely summer's evening. He *hasn't* changed, then! I suppose it means a case?

Billy. Yes, sir. He's very hard at it just now. Fair frightens me.

Watson. What does?

Billy. His health, Dr. Watson. He gets paler, and thinner, and he never eats nothing. I heard Mrs. Hudson asking him when he would take his dinner. "Seven thirty," he told her— *"the day after tomorrow!"*

Watson (*sighs*). Yes, Billy, I know how it is.

Billy (*confidentially*). I can tell you one thing, sir—he's following somebody.

[Watson, *amused, copies* Billy's *manner and leans towards him conspiratorially.*]

Watson. Really?

Billy. One disguise after another. Yesterday he was a workman, looking for a job. Today he was an old woman. Fairly took me in, he did— and I ought to know his ways by now. (*He picks up the parasol briefly.*) Part of the old girl's outfit.

Watson (*laughs*). What's it all about, Billy?

Billy (*glancing round cautiously*). I don't mind telling you, sir—but it shouldn't go no farther. . . . (Watson *gives his head a meaningful shake and places a finger to his lips.*) It's this case of the Crown diamond.[3]

Watson. What—the hundred-thousand-pound burglary?

Billy. Yes, sir. They must get it back. Why, we've had the Prime Minister and Home Secretary[4] both sat in this very room!

Watson. You don't say!

Billy. Mr. Holmes was very nice to them. Promised he would do all he could. Then there's Lord Cantlemere.

Watson (*dismally*). Oh!

Billy. Ah, you know what that means, Dr. Watson! He's a stiff 'un, and no mistake. Now, I can get along with the Prime Minister—and I've nothing against the Home Secretary. . . . But I can't *stand* His Lordship! (Watson *laughs heartily.*) Mr. Holmes can't, neither, sir! You can tell, Lord Cantlemere don't believe in Mr. Holmes. He was against employing him, and he'd rather he failed.

Watson. And Mr. Holmes knows it?

Billy. Mr. Holmes *always* knows what there is to know.

Watson (*hastily*). Oh, quite, quite! Well, Billy, we'll just hope that he won't fail, and then Lord Cantlemere will be confounded. But I'd better be getting home to my wife. (*He moves towards his hat and stick, but catches sight of the curtain.*) I say, Billy! Bit early to have the curtains drawn and the lamp lit, isn't it?

Billy. Well—there's something funny behind there.

Watson. Something *funny*?

Billy. You can see it, sir. (Billy *draws the curtain, revealing the dummy.*)

Watson. Bless my soul!

Billy. Yes, sir.

---

3. **Crown diamond:** a diamond belonging to the monarchy.
4. **Home Secretary:** a British Cabinet minister in charge of keeping internal law and order, with authority over the London police.

Watson (*examining the figure*). A perfect replica of Sherlock Holmes! Dressing gown and all!

[Billy *turns the chair so that the dummy chances to finish up with its back to the parlor door.*]

Billy. We put it at different angles every now and then, like this, so's it'll look more lifelike. Mind, I wouldn't dare touch it if the blind wasn't drawn. When it's up you can see this from right across the way.

Watson. We used something of the sort once before, you know.

Billy. Before my time, sir.

Watson. Er—yes.

[*Unseen by either of them the bedroom door opens and* Holmes *appears in his dressing gown.*]

Billy. There's folk who watch us from over yonder, sir. You may catch a peep of them now. (*He is about to pull back a corner of the blind to enable* Watson *to look out.*)

Holmes (*sharply*). That will do, Billy!

[Billy *and* Watson *spin round.*]

Watson. Holmes!

Holmes (*severely*). You were in danger of your life, then, my boy. I can't do without you just yet.

Billy. (*humbly*). Yes, sir.

Holmes. That will be all for now.

Billy. Very good, sir. (*He exits by the parlor door.*)

Holmes. That boy is a problem, Watson. How far am I justified in letting him be in danger?

Watson. Danger of what, Holmes?

Holmes. Of sudden death.

Watson. Holmes!

Holmes. But it's good to see you in your old quarters once again, my dear Watson!

Watson (*concerned*). Holmes—this talk of sudden death. What are you expecting?

Holmes (*simply*). To be murdered.

Watson. Oh, come now! You're joking!

Holmes. Even my limited sense of humor could evolve a better joke than that, Watson. (*Brightening*) But we may be comfortable in the meantime, mayn't we? Let me see you once more in the customary chair.

Watson. Pleasure, Holmes! But why not eat?

Holmes. Because the faculties[5] become refined when you starve them. Surely, as a doctor, you must admit that what your digestion gains in the way of blood supply is so much lost to the brain? *I* am a brain, Watson. The rest of me is mere appendix. Therefore, it's the brain I must consider.

Watson. But—this danger . . . ?

Holmes. Ah, yes. Just in case it should come off, it would be as well for you to know the name of the murderer. You can give it to Scotland Yard, with my love and a parting blessing.

Watson. Holmes!

Holmes. His name is Sylvius—Count Negretto Sylvius, No. 136 Moorside Gardens, London N.W. Got it?

Watson. Yes. (*Hesitantly*) Er—Holmes . . . I've got nothing to do for a day or two. Count me in.

Holmes (*sadly shaking his head*). Your morals don't improve, Watson.

Watson. My *morals*?

Holmes. You've added fibbing to your other vices. You bear every sign of the busy medical man, with calls on him every hour.

Watson. Not such important ones. But—can't you have this fellow arrested?

Holmes. Yes, Watson, I could. That's what worries him so.

Watson. Then why don't you?

Holmes. Because I don't know where the diamond is.

5. **faculties** (făk′əl-tēz): natural abilities.

Scenes on pages 321, 323, 330, and 332 are from early films based on Sherlock Holmes stories. Basil Rathbone (*shown at right*) played Sherlock Holmes; Nigel Bruce played Dr. Watson.

Watson. Ah! Billy was telling me—the missing Crown jewel!

Holmes. The great yellow Mazarin Stone. I've cast my net and I have my fish. But I have *not* got the stone. Yes, I could make the world a better place by laying *them* by the heels; but it's the stone I want.

Watson. And is Count Sylvius one of your fish?

Holmes. Yes—and he's a *shark*. He bites. The other is Sam Merton, the boxer. Not a bad fellow, Sam, but the Count has used him. Sam's just a great, big, silly, bull-headed gudgeon;[6] but he's flopping about in my net, all the same.

Watson. Where is Count Sylvius now?

Holmes. I've been at his elbow all morning. (*He gets up.*) You've seen me as an old lady, Watson?

---

6. **gudgeon** (gŭj'ən): a small fish that is easily caught and used for bait; here, a person who is easily tricked or used.

Watson (*chuckling*). Oh, yes indeed!

[Holmes *assumes the posture and walk of an old lady.*]

Holmes (*in a cracked old voice*). I was never more convincing, Doctor. Never! (Watson *laughs as* Holmes *straightens up. Normal voice*) He actually picked up my parasol for me once. (Holmes *picks up the parasol and gesticulates with it.*)

Watson. He didn't!

[Holmes *makes an elaborate bow, holding out the parasol in both hands.*]

Holmes (*mimicking* Sylvius). By your leave, madam. (Holmes *resumes his normal voice and manner and lays the parasol aside.*) He's half Italian, you know. Full of the Southern[7] graces when he's in the mood. But he's a devil incarnate[8] in the other mood. Life is full of whimsical happenings, Watson.

Watson (*with a snort*). Whimsical! It might have been tragedy!

Holmes. Well, perhaps it might. Anyway, I followed him to old Straubenzee's workshop in the Minories.[9] Straubenzee made the air gun—a very pretty bit of work, as I understand. I fancy it's in the opposite window at present, ready to put a bullet through this dummy's beautiful head whenever I choose to raise that blind.

[*Knock at parlor door, which opens.* Billy *enters, carrying a salver.*[10]]

Billy. Mr. Holmes, sir . . .

Holmes. What is it, Billy?

Billy. There's a gentleman to see you, sir.

[Holmes *takes the visiting card from the salver and looks at it.*]

Holmes. Thank you. (*He replaces the card.*) The man himself, Watson!

Watson. Sylvius!

Holmes (*nods*). I'd hardly expected this. Grasp the nettle,[11] eh! A man of nerve, Watson. But possibly you've heard of his reputation as a big-game shooter? It'd be a triumphant ending to his excellent sporting record if he added me to his bag.

Watson. Send for the police, Holmes!

Holmes. I probably shall—but not just yet. Would you just glance carefully out of the window and see if anyone is hanging about in the street?

Watson. Certainly. (*He goes to the window and peeps cautiously round the corner of the blind.*) Yes—there's a rough-looking fellow near the door.

Holmes. That will be Sam Merton—the faithful but rather fatuous[12] Sam. Billy, where is Count Sylvius?

Billy. In the waiting room, sir.

Holmes. Show him up when I ring.

Billy. Yes, sir.

Holmes. If I'm not in the room, show him in all the same.

Billy. Very good, Mr. Holmes. (*He leaves by the parlor door.*)

Watson. Look here, Holmes, this is simply ridiculous. This is a desperate man who sticks at nothing, you'd have me believe. He may have *come* to murder you.

---

7. **Southern:** The reference is to southern Europe. The Count is from Italy.
8. **devil incarnate** (ĭn-kär′nĭt): a devil in human form.
9. **Minories:** a street in London, once famous for its gun makers.
10. **salver:** a small tray.

11. **Grasp the nettle:** a proverbial expression meaning "Act boldly to gain an advantage over someone." A nettle is a plant with delicate thorns. If the plant is touched gently, the thorns sting. If it is grasped firmly, they feel soft.
12. **fatuous** (făch′ōō-əs): foolish.

Holmes. I shouldn't be surprised.

Watson. Then I insist on staying with you!

Holmes. You'd be horribly in the way.

Watson. In *his* way!

Holmes. No, my dear fellow—in mine.

[Watson *sits down stubbornly.*]

Watson. Be that as it may, I can't possibly leave you.

Holmes. Yes you can, Watson. And you will—for you've never failed to play the game. I'm sure you'll play it to the end. (*He crosses to his desk and begins to scribble a note.*) This man has come for his own purpose, but he may stay for mine. I want you to take a cab to Scotland Yard and give this note to Youghal, of the C.I.D.[13] Come back with the police.

13. **C.I.D.:** Criminal Investigation Department, a division of the London Police.

Watson (*rising*). I'll do that with joy!

Holmes (*handing* Watson *the note*). Before you get back I may just have time to find out where the stone is. Now, I'll just ring for Billy to show him up, and I think we'll go out through the bedroom. (Holmes *presses a bell, while* Watson *gathers his things.* Holmes *ushers him towards the bedroom door.*) This second exit is exceedingly useful, you know. I rather want to see my shark without his seeing me.

[Watson *halts.*]

Watson. The dummy! Shouldn't the curtain be drawn over it again?

Holmes. No, no. We'll leave it as it is. (*He moves swiftly to the dummy.*) Perhaps just a touch to this noble head . . . (*He adjusts the head to bow upon the breast*) as though somewhere in the middle of forty winks. (*He ensures that the dummy has its back to the parlor door.*) There! Now, come along.

Watson. I hope you know what you're doing, that's all!

[*They exit by the bedroom door, closing it behind them. A slight pause, then the parlor door opens.* Billy *enters and* Count Sylvius *walks in past him.*]

Billy. If you'll just wait, sir.

[Sylvius *ignores him.* Billy *withdraws, closing the door behind him.* Sylvius *looks round the room for a moment, then notices the dummy. He grips his stick more firmly and creeps a cautious pace or two towards it. Satisfied that the figure is dozing, he steps forward and raises his stick to strike.* Holmes *enters silently from the bedroom.*]

Holmes. Don't break it, Count Sylvius!

[Sylvius *whirls round, his stick still upraised, a look of disbelief on his face.*]

Sylvius. What!

Holmes. It's a pretty little thing. (Sylvius *lowers the stick and walks round to look at the dummy in astonishment.*) Tavernier, the French modeler, made it. He's as good at waxworks as your friend Straubenzee is at air guns. (Holmes *turns the chair to face the window. The dummy is now completely hidden from the audience.*)

Sylvius. Air guns? What do you mean, sir?

Holmes. Put your stick on the side table, before you're tempted to do any other form of damage.

[*There is a momentary hesitation, in which we think* Sylvius *might spring at* Holmes. *But* Holmes *stands still, looking at him hard, one hand in his pocket, in which we sense him to have a revolver.* Sylvius *relaxes and obeys.*]

Sylvius. Very well.

Holmes. Thank you. Would you care to put your revolver out, also? (*At the mention of "revolver"* Sylvius' *hand flies to his hip pocket. He does not draw, but stands poised defiantly. Blandly*) Oh, very well, if you prefer to sit on it. (Holmes *moves to a chair and sits.*) Your visit is really most opportune, Count Sylvius. I wanted badly to have a few minutes' chat with you.

[Sylvius *stumps over to a chair opposite* Holmes.]

Sylvius. I, too, wished to have some words with you, Holmes! That is why I am here. Because you have gone out of your way to annoy me. Because you have put your creatures on my track!

Holmes. Oh, I assure you no!

Sylvius. I have had them followed! Two can play at that game, Holmes!

Holmes. It's a small point, Count Sylvius, but perhaps you would kindly give me my prefix[14]

14. **prefix:** here, a title, such as *Dr., Mr.,* or *Mrs.,* before a person's name.

when you address me? You can understand that, with my routine of work, I should find myself on familiar terms with half the rogues' gallery,[15] and you'll agree that exceptions are invidious.[16]

Sylvius (*sneering*). Well, *Mr.* Holmes, then.

Holmes. That's better. But I assure you that you're mistaken about my alleged agents.

Sylvius (*laughs contemptuously*). Other people can observe as well as you! Yesterday there was an old sporting man. Today it was an elderly woman. They kept me in view all day.

Holmes. Really, sir, you compliment me! Old Baron Dowson said the night before he was hanged that in my case what the law had gained the stage had lost.

Sylvius. It . . . It was you?

Holmes. You can see in the corner the parasol which you so politely handed to me in the Minories before you began to suspect.

Sylvius. If I had known that, you might never have . . .

Holmes. . . . have seen this humble abode again? I was well aware of that. But, as it happens, you did *not* know, so here we are!

Sylvius. So it was not your agents, but your play-acting, busybodying self! You admit that you dogged me. Why?

Holmes. Come now, Count: you used to shoot lions in Algeria.

Sylvius. What about it?

Holmes. Why did you?

Sylvius. The sport—the excitement—the danger.

Holmes. And, no doubt, to free the country from a pest?

Sylvius. Exactly.

Holmes. My reasons in a nutshell!

15. **rogues' gallery:** photographs of criminals kept in police files for purposes of identification.
16. **invidious** (ĭn-vĭd′ē-əs): unfair; offensive. Holmes isn't on familiar terms with criminals and says (jokingly) that it wouldn't be fair to make an exception in the Count's case.

[Sylvius *springs to his feet in fury and reaches instinctively towards his revolver pocket.*]

Sylvius. For that, I will . . . !

Holmes. Sit down, sir, sit down! (*He gives Sylvius a steely stare. Sylvius hesitates for a moment, then obeys.*) I had another, more practical reason for following your movements. I want that yellow diamond.

[Sylvius *begins to relax and chuckle. He stretches his legs and makes himself comfortable.*]

Sylvius. Upon my word—*Mr.* Holmes!

Holmes. You know that I was after you for that. The real reason why you're here tonight is to find out how much I know and how far my removal is absolutely essential. Well, I should say that from *your* point of view it *is* absolutely essential. You see, I know all about the diamond—save only one thing, which you are about to tell me.

Sylvius. Indeed? Pray, what is this missing fact?

Holmes. Where the Crown diamond now is.

Sylvius. And how should I be able to tell you that?

Holmes. You can, and you will.

Sylvius. You astonish me!

Holmes. You can't bluff me, Count Sylvius. You are absolute plate glass. I can see to the very back of your mind.

Sylvius. Oh! Then, of course, you can see where the diamond is.

Holmes (*delighted*). Then you *do* know!

Sylvius. No!

Holmes. You've admitted it.

Sylvius. I admit nothing!

[Holmes *gets up and goes to a drawer, which he opens.*]

Holmes. Now, Count, if you'll be reasonable we can do business.

Sylvius. And *you* talk about bluff!

[Holmes *takes a notebook from the drawer.*]

Holmes. Do you know what I keep in this book?

Sylvius. No, sir. I do not.

Holmes. I keep *you* in it.

Sylvius. Me?

Holmes. You are all here—every action of your vile and dangerous life.

Sylvius. There are limits to my patience, Holmes!

Holmes (*waving the book at* Sylvius). Yes, it's all here: the real facts about the death of old Mrs. Harold, who left you the Blymer estate to gamble away. (Holmes *taunts* Sylvius *with the book,* Sylvius *making a grab for it whenever it approaches, but always missing.*)

Sylvius. You're dreaming!

Holmes. And the complete life history of Miss Minnie Warrender.

Sylvius. You'll make nothing of that!

Holmes. There's plenty more, Count: the robbery in the train-de-luxe to the Riviera[17] on February 13, 1892; the forged check in the same year on the Credit Lyonnais.[18]

Sylvius. No! There you *are* mistaken!

Holmes. Then I *am* right on the others! (*He throws the book into the drawer, which he closes, resuming his seat.*) Now, Count, you're a card player. You know that when the other fellow has all the trumps it saves time to throw in your hand.

Sylvius. Just what has all this talk to do with the jewel?

Holmes. Gently, Count! Restrain that eager mind! Let me get to the points in my own humdrum fashion. (*Gesturing towards the closed drawer*) I have all that against you. But, above all, I have a clear case against you and your fighting bully in the theft of the Crown diamond.

Sylvius. Indeed?

Holmes (*enumerating the points on his fingers*). I have the cabman who took you to Whitehall,[19] and the cabman who brought you away. I have the commissionaire[20] who saw you near the case. I have Ikey Sanders, who refused to cut the stone up for you. Ikey has talked, Count, and the game is up!

Sylvius. I don't believe you!

Holmes. That's the hand I play from. I put it all on the table. Only one card is missing. It's the King of Diamonds. I don't know where the stone is. (*He presses the bell.*)

Sylvius. And you never will! Why are you ringing that bell? (*He gets to his feet suspiciously.*)

Holmes. Be reasonable, Count! Consider the situation. You are going to be locked up for twenty years. So is Sam Merton. What good are you going to get out of your diamond? None in the world. But if you hand it over—well, I'm prepared to compound a felony.[21] We don't want you or Sam. We want the stone. Give that up, Count Sylvius, and so far as I'm concerned you can go free. But if you make another slip in the future . . . ! Well, it'll be the last.

Sylvius. And if I refuse?

Holmes (*sighs*). Then I'm afraid it must be you, and not the stone.

[*Knock at parlor door.* Billy *enters.*]

Billy. Did you ring, sir?

---

17. **Riviera** (rĭv′ē-âr′ə): a resort area along the Mediterranean Sea.
18. **Credit Lyonnais** (krĕ′dē lē′ō-nā′): a French bank.
19. **Whitehall:** a London street where many government departments are located.
20. **commissionaire** (kə-mĭsh′ə-nâr′): in England, a doorman.
21. **compound a felony:** to add to a crime by not telling the police.

Holmes. Yes, Billy. You will see a large and ugly gentleman outside the front door. Ask him to come up.

Billy. Yes, sir. (*He is about to go, but hesitates.*) What if he won't, sir?

Holmes. Oh, no violence, Billy! Don't be rough with him! If you tell him that Count Sylvius wants him he will come.

Billy. Very good, sir. (*He exits with a grin, closing the door.*)

Holmes. I think it would be as well to have your friend Sam at this conference. After all, his interests should be represented.

[Sylvius *resumes his seat.*]

Sylvius. Just what do you intend to do now?

Holmes. I was remarking to my friend, Dr. Watson, a short while ago that I had a shark and a gudgeon in my net. Now I'm drawing in the net, and up they come together.

Sylvius. You won't die in your bed, Holmes!

Holmes. I've often had that same idea. But does it matter very much? After all, Count, your own exit is more likely to be perpendicular than horizontal. (Sylvius' *hand jerks towards his gun pocket.* Holmes *waves an admonishing finger.*) It's no use, my friend. Even if I gave you time to draw it, you know perfectly well you daren't use it. Nasty, noisy things, revolvers. Better stick to air guns. (*Knock at parlor door.* Billy *shows in* Sam Merton *coldly and withdraws without speaking.* Merton *glares about him, tensed for action.*) Good day, Mr. Merton. Rather dull in the street, isn't it?

Merton. What's up, Count?

Holmes. If I may put it in a nutshell, Mr. Merton, I should say the *game* was up.

Merton. 'Ere! Is this cove[22] trying to be funny? I'm not in the funny mood meself.

Holmes. I think I can promise you'll feel even less humorous as the evening advances.

[Merton *lumbers aggressively towards* Holmes, *but is halted by a gesture from* Sylvius.]

Sylvius. That will do, Sam!

Holmes. Thank you, Count. (Holmes *gets to his feet.*) Now, look here—I'm a busy man and I can't waste time. I'm going into that bedroom to try over the *Hoffmann* "Barcarolle"[23] on my violin. You can explain to your friend how the matter lies, without the restraint of my presence. (Holmes *goes to the bedroom door.*) In five minutes I shall return for your final answer. You quite grasp the alternative, don't you? Shall we take you, or shall we have the stone?

[Holmes *exits, closing the bedroom door behind him.* Sylvius *jumps up and paces about thoughtfully.*]

Merton. 'Offmann who? What's the chap on about?

Sylvius. Shut up, Sam! Let me think!

[*Sounds of violin strings being plucked and tuned in the bedroom.*]

Merton. If it's trouble, why didn't you plug 'im?

Sylvius. You're a fool, Sam! Anyone but you could have seen he was holding a revolver in his dressing-gown pocket.

Merton. Aw! (*The violin begins to play the* "Barcarolle" *from* The Tales of Hoffmann. *It is expertly played. Having established it, diminish somewhat under following dialogue. Disgustedly*) Cor!

Sylvius. Ikey Sanders has split[24] on us.

---

22. **cove:** slang for "fellow."

23. **"Barcarolle"** (bär′kə-rōl′): a famous piece of music in *The Tales of Hoffmann,* an opera by Jacques Offenbach.
24. **split:** slang for "informed on one's partners."

Merton. Split, 'as 'e? I'll do 'im a thick 'un for that, if I swing for it!

Sylvius. How do you think that will help us? We've got to make up our minds what to do.

Merton. (*lowering his voice*). 'Arf a mo',[25] Count! That's a leary cove[26] in there. D'you suppose 'e's listening?

Sylvius. How can he listen and play that thing?

Merton. Aw, that's right!

Sylvius. Now *you* listen! He can lag[27] us over this stone, but he's offered to let us slip if we only tell him where it is.

Merton. Wot! Give up a 'undred thousand quid![28]

Sylvius. It's one or the other. He knows too much.

Merton. Well . . . listen! 'E's alone in there. Let's do 'im! Then we've nothing to fear of.

Sylvius. He's armed and ready. If we shot him we could hardly get away in a place like this. Besides, it's likely enough the police know he's on to something. Listen! (*They listen. The violin plays steadily on.*) It was just a noise in the street, I think.

Merton. Look, guv'nor—you've got the brains. If slugging's no use, then it's up to you.

Sylvius. I've fooled better men than Holmes. The stone's here, in my secret pocket. I take no chances leaving it about. It can be out of England tonight and cut into four pieces in Amsterdam before Sunday. One of us must slip round to Lime Street with the stone and tell Van Seddar to get off by the next boat.

Merton. But the false bottom ain't ready yet. Van Seddar don't expect to go till next week!

Sylvius. He must go now, and chance it. As to Holmes, we can fool him. We'll promise him

the stone, then put him on the wrong track; and by the time he finds out we'll be in Holland, too.

Merton. Now you're talking, Count!

Sylvius. You go now and see the Dutchman, Sam. Here . . . (Sylvius *pulls* Sam *aside.*) Just in case, come out of line with that keyhole.

[Sylvius *reaches into his secret pocket and produces a large yellow gem. The "dummy" in the chair near the window begins to move cautiously, and we see that during the preceding dialogue* Holmes *has contrived to seat himself in its place. Unobserved by* Sylvius *or* Merton *he sidles towards them. He has a revolver in his hand.*]

Merton. I don't know 'ow you dare carry it about!

Sylvius. Where could I keep it safer? If we could take it out of Whitehall, someone else could easily take it from my lodgings.

[Holmes *sneaks quickly forward and plucks the stone from* Sylvius' *hand.*]

Holmes. Or out of your hand! (Sylvius *and* Merton *are too flabbergasted to react. They stare speechlessly at* Holmes, *and then at the chair.*) Thank you, Count. It will be safe with me.

Merton. There was a blooming waxworks in that chair!

[*He jerks the chair round; it is empty.* Holmes *moves carefully back to a position from where he can cover them both.*]

Holmes. Your surprise is very natural, Mr. Merton. You are not aware, of course, that a second door from my bedroom leads behind that curtain. I fancied you must have heard me, Count, as I slipped into the dummy's chair, but luck and a passing cab were on my side. They enabled me to listen to your racy

---

25. **'Arf a mo':** Merton's pronunciation of "Half a mo'," an expression meaning "Wait a moment."
26. **leary cove:** slang for "clever fellow."
27. **lag:** slang for "arrest."
28. **quid** (kwĭd): slang for "pound" (or "pounds"), the basic unit of British money.

conversation, which would have been painfully constrained had you been aware of my presence.

[Sylvius *lurches towards* Holmes, *who raises the revolver slightly.*]

Sylvius. Deuce take you, Holmes!
Holmes. No violence, gentlemen! Consider the furniture! (*They stand still.*) It must be very clear to you that the position is an impossible one. The police are waiting below.
Merton. Guv'nor? Shall I . . .?
Sylvius (*resignedly*). No, Sam. I give you best, Holmes. I believe you are the devil himself.
Holmes. Not *far* from him, at any rate.

[Merton *suddenly points to the bedroom door.*]

Merton. 'Ere! That blooming fiddle! It's playing itself!
Holmes. Oh, let it play. These modern gramophones[29] are a remarkable invention!
Merton. Aw!

[*Men's voices approaching the parlor door. It opens suddenly.* Watson *hastens in.*]

Watson. This way, officers!

[*A Police Sergeant and two Constables hurry after him and seize* Sylvius *and* Merton.]

Sergeant. Come on, Sam! We've been waiting to get hold of you!
Merton. Gar!
Sylvius. Take your hands off me, my man!
Constable. Not blooming likely![30]

[*They are led away, struggling. At the door,* Merton *stops, looks back into the room, then at* Holmes.]

29. **gramophones:** phonographs.
30. **Not blooming likely:** slang for "not very likely."

Merton. Waxworks! Grammerphones! Garrr! (*He is led off as* Billy *enters.*)
Billy (*with distaste*). Lord Cantlemere is here, sir.

[Holmes *goes to the bedroom door.*]

Holmes. Show His Lordship up, Billy, while I turn off the—er—"grammerphone."
Billy. Very good, sir.

[Holmes *and* Billy *exit by the bedroom and parlor doors respectively, leaving both of them open.* Watson *lays down his hat and stick. The music ceases abruptly and* Holmes *returns, shutting the bedroom door.* Billy *reenters the parlor door.*]

Billy. Lord Cantlemere, sir. (*He steps aside to let* Cantlemere *enter, then goes out, closing the door.*)
Cantlemere. What on earth's going on here, Holmes? Constables and fellahs all over the place!
Holmes. How do you do, Lord Cantlemere? May I introduce my friend and colleague, Dr. Watson?
Watson. How d'you do, my lord?
Cantlemere (*brusquely*). D'yer do?
Holmes. Watson, pray help me with His Lordship's overcoat. (Holmes *takes hold of the coat, preparing to take it off.*)
Cantlemere. No, thank you. I will not take it off.

[Holmes *pawing the coat.*]

Holmes. Oh, but my friend Dr. Watson would assure you that it is most unhealthy to retain a coat indoors, even at this time of the year.
Cantlemere (*releasing himself*). I am quite comfortable as I am, sir! I have no need to stay. I have simply looked in to know how your self-appointed task is progressing.

[Holmes *assumes a troubled air.*]

Holmes. It's difficult—very difficult.
Cantlemere (*with gleeful malice*). Ha! I feared you'd find it so! Every man finds his limitations, Holmes—but at least it cures us of the weakness of self-satisfaction.
Holmes. Yes, sir. I admit I have been much perplexed.
Cantlemere. No doubt!

Holmes. Especially upon one point. Perhaps you could help me?

[Cantlemere *takes a chair.* Holmes *sits opposite him,* Watson *standing behind his chair.*]

Cantlemere. You apply for my advice rather late in the day. I thought you had your own self-sufficient methods. Still, I am ready to help you.

Holmes. Your Lordship is most obliging. You see, we can no doubt frame a case against the actual thieves.

Cantlemere. *When* you've caught them.

Holmes. Exactly. But the question is, how shall we proceed against the receiver?

Cantlemere. Receiver? Isn't this rather premature?

Holmes. It's as well to have our plans ready. Now, what would you regard as final evidence against the receiver?

Cantlemere. The actual possession of the stone, of course.

Holmes. You'd arrest him on that?

Cantlemere. Undoubtedly.

Holmes (*slyly*). In that case, my dear sir, I shall be under the painful necessity of advising your arrest!

[Cantlemere *leaps to his feet.*]

Cantlemere. Holmes! In fifty years of official life I cannot recall such a liberty being taken! I am a busy man, engaged upon important affairs, and I have neither time nor taste for foolish jokes. (Holmes *slowly rises.*) I may tell you frankly, sir, that I have never been a believer in your powers. I have always been of the opinion that the matter was far safer in the hands of the regular police force. Your conduct confirms all my conclusions. (*He moves stiffly towards the parlor door.*) I have the honor, sir, to wish you good evening!

Holmes. One moment, sir! (Cantlemere *turns to face him inquiringly.*) Actually to go off with the Mazarin Stone would be an even more serious offense than to be found in temporary possession of it!

Cantlemere. Sir, this is intolerable!

Holmes. Put your hand in the right-hand pocket of your overcoat.

Cantlemere. What? What do you mean?

Holmes. Come, come! Do what I ask!

[Cantlemere *splutters with fury, but feels in his pocket.*]

Cantlemere. I'll make an end to this charade,[31] and you'll wish you'd never begun it! I . . . I . . . (*His fury suddenly abates, giving way to surprise, then astonishment, as he slowly withdraws from his pocket the Mazarin Stone and holds it up.*)

Watson. Great heavens!

Holmes. Too bad of me, Lord Cantlemere. My old friend here will tell you that I have an impish habit of practical joking. Also that I can never resist a dramatic situation. I took the liberty—the very great liberty, I confess—of putting the stone into your pocket at the beginning of our interview.

Cantlemere. I . . . I'm bewildered! This *is* the Mazarin Stone! (Holmes *bows slightly.*) Hol . . . *Mr.* Holmes, we are greatly your debtors. Your sense of humor may, as you admit, be somewhat perverted, and its exhibition untimely— remarkably untimely! (Watson *stifles a grin.*) But at least I withdraw any reflection I have made upon your professional powers.

Holmes. Thank you, Lord Cantlemere. I hope your pleasure in reporting this successful result in the exalted circle to which you return will be some small atonement for my joke. I will supply the full particulars in a written report.

[Cantlemere *bows and goes to the parlor door.* Watson *hastens to open it for him.*]

Cantlemere. Once more, good evening. (*He nods to* Watson.) And to you, sir, good evening.

Watson. ⎱
Holmes. ⎰ Good evening.

[Cantlemere *exits.* Watson *gives him a rigid mili-*

31. **charade** (shə-rād′): game; pretense.

tary salute behind his retreating back, then closes the door.]

Watson. *Well,* Holmes.
Holmes. He's an excellent and loyal person, but rather of the old regime.[32] (*He goes to* Watson *and claps him on the shoulder.*) And now, my dear Watson, pray touch the bell, and Mrs. Hudson shall lay dinner for two—as of old!

[*Final curtain.*]

32. **old regime** (rə-zhēm′): the old order of things, now out of date.

Reading Check

1. What prop has Holmes used in his disguise as an old woman?
2. Which nobleman opposed putting Holmes on the case?
3. Why is Holmes going without food?
4. Why hasn't Holmes had Sylvius arrested?
5. What instruction does Holmes give Watson?
6. What information is contained in Holmes's notebook?
7. What does Holmes offer Sylvius in exchange for the diamond?
8. Who is Sylvius' accomplice?
9. Where has Sylvius hidden the diamond?
10. What does Holmes do with the Crown diamond?

For Study and Discussion

Analyzing and Interpreting the Play

1. One of Holmes's well-known talents is "play-acting." How does he show that he is skillful at disguise?

2. Holmes is expert at tricking criminals into telling him what he wants to know. How does he trick the Count into admitting that he knows where the diamond is?

3. Holmes is sure that the Count has stolen the diamond. What evidence has he used in building his case?

4. Describe Holmes's plan for recovering the diamond. What part do the dummy and the gramophone play in this plan?

5. The Count claims that he has fooled better men than Holmes. **a.** How does he plan to

get away with the diamond? **b.** How does Holmes prevent his escape?

6a. Why does Holmes play a practical joke on Lord Cantlemere? **b.** How does Lord Cantlemere become convinced that Holmes is a "brain"?

Literary Elements

Imagining a Play in Performance

In reading a play, you let your imagination do the work that would be done for you in a theater by actors, costumes, scenery, lighting, and sound effects. You imagine how the characters would be dressed, how they would speak their lines, what facial expressions they would use, and what movements they would make.

A playwright often gives players instructions for acting. These are called **stage directions**. Stage directions appear in italics within parentheses or brackets. A stage direction may tell the actor how a line should be spoken.

> **Watson** (*dismally*). Oh!
> **Holmes** (*sharply*). That will do, Billy!
> **Billy** (*humbly*). Yes, sir.

A stage direction may call for a specific action or movement.

> **Holmes** (*sadly shaking his head*). Your morals don't improve, Watson.

> [Holmes *makes an elaborate bow, holding out the parasol in both hands.*]

Stage directions may tell an actor what kind of facial expression to use.

> [Sylvius *whirls round, his stick still upraised, a look of disbelief on his face.*]

Most of the time, directions for acting are built into the dialogue of the play. As you read the speeches of the characters, you must imagine what they feel and think as well as what they do with their voices, their expressions, and their gestures.

Here is some dialogue from the play. Decide how the actors would speak these lines. How would they move? What facial expressions would they use?

> **Watson.** Look here, Holmes, this is simply ridiculous. This is a desperate man who sticks at nothing, you'd have me believe. He may have *come* to murder you. (page 322)

> **Sylvius.** I, too, wished to have some words with you, Holmes! That is why I am here. Because you have gone out of your way to annoy me. Because you have put your creatures on my track! (page 324)

> **Holmes.** Oh, no violence, Billy! Don't be rough with him! If you tell him that Count Sylvius wants him he will come. (page 327)

> **Cantlemere.** I'll make an end to this charade, and you'll wish you'd never begun it! I . . . I . . . (page 331)

Understanding Plot

In a play, as in a short story, the **plot**, or sequence of events, follows a certain pattern. The action generally develops out of one or more conflicts or problems. At the opening of *The Mazarin Stone*, we learn that a diamond has been stolen and that Holmes has been called in on the case. Holmes's problem is to get the criminals to assist him in recovering the stone. The central conflict of the play is not physical—it is a battle of wits between Sherlock Holmes and the thieves. That battle is won and the conflict resolved when Holmes takes the diamond from the thieves and has them arrested.

What is Holmes's conflict with Lord Cantlemere? How is it resolved?

Language and Vocabulary

Recognizing Cockney Speech

In drama characters are distinguished not only by their actions and words but by their manner of speech. Sam Merton, Sylvius' accomplice, speaks a London dialect known as *cockney*. Originally the word referred to someone born close to the church of Saint Mary-le-Bow in the East End of London. One characteristic of the cockney dialect is loss of the letter *h* at the beginning of words: *'im* for *him*. Find examples of this characteristic in Merton's speeches.

For Dramatization

Improvising a Scene

A good way to learn about writing and performing plays is to improvise. When you improvise, you act without a script. You do not plan what you will say or do. You make up the words and actions as you go along, responding to what the other actors say and do.

Try improvising one of the following situations with one or more partners. Notice that each situation contains a conflict. Before you begin, make sure that you know who you are, where you are, and what you want. Pay no attention to the audience, but speak loudly enough for them to hear you. All will go well if you relax and use your imagination.

> You have not practiced your music. You try to distract the teacher so that your hour will be up before you have to play.
>
> You would like to go to the beach. Your friends would like to go to the mountains. You try to persuade them to go to the beach.
>
> You are trying to persuade your parents to give you some money. They think you should earn it.
>
> You are at a sale counter. Two other people wish to buy the article you have selected.
>
> Several people are trapped in an elevator with you. You do not agree with them about what is to be done.

About The Author

Sir Arthur Conan Doyle   (1859–1930)

Sir Arthur Conan Doyle began writing detective fiction while he was practicing medicine. His greatest creation was Sherlock Holmes, one of the most famous characters in all English fiction. Holmes first appeared in *A Study in Scarlet,* published in 1887. He became a great success with readers. The demand for new books about Holmes meant that Doyle had to spend more and more time creating new adventures for his popular hero. Tiring of his creation or perhaps running out of ideas, Doyle had Holmes killed off in *The Memoirs of Sherlock Holmes.* However, Sherlock Holmes's fans had become so numerous and their appetite for new stories so strong that Doyle was persuaded to bring him back. He explained that Holmes had merely disappeared, not died.

A Sunny Morning

SERAFÍN AND JOAQUÍN QUINTERO

In stories some characters remain the same while other characters undergo some kind of change. In drama, also, characters may be static or dynamic. As you read this comedy, ask yourself how the characters change and how the dramatists make that change believable.

Characters

Doña (dō′nyä)[1] Laura
Petra
Don Gonzalo
Juanito (hwä-nē′tō)

Scene: *A sunny morning in a retired corner of a park in Madrid. Autumn. A bench at right.*

Doña Laura, *a handsome, white-haired old lady of about seventy, refined in appearance, her bright eyes and entire manner giving evidence that despite her age her mental faculties are unimpaired, enters leaning upon the arm of her maid,* Petra. *In her free hand she carries a parasol, which serves also as a cane.*

Doña Laura. I am so glad to be here. I feared my seat would be occupied. What a beautiful morning!

Petra. The sun is hot.

Doña Laura. Yes, you are only twenty. (*She sits down on the bench.*) Oh, I feel more tired today than usual. (*Noticing* Petra, *who seems impatient*) Go, if you wish to chat with your guard.

Petra. He is not mine, señora;[2] he belongs to the park.

Doña Laura. He belongs more to you than he does to the park. Go find him, but remain within calling distance.

Petra. I see him over there waiting for me.

Doña Laura. Do not remain more than ten minutes.

Petra. Very well, señora. (*Walks toward the right*)

Doña Laura. Wait a moment.

Petra. What does the señora wish?

Doña Laura. Give me the bread crumbs.

Petra. I don't know what is the matter with me.

Doña Laura (*smiling*). I do. Your head is where your heart is—with the guard.

Petra. Here, señora. (*She hands* Doña Laura *a small bag. Exit* Petra *by the right.*)

Doña Laura. Adiós.[3] (*Glances toward trees at the right*) Here they come! They know just when to expect me. (*She rises, walks toward the right, and throws three handfuls of bread crumbs.*) These are for the spryest, these for the gluttons, and these for the little ones which are the most per-

---

1. **Doña:** a Spanish title of courtesy used with a woman's given name. The title *Don* is used with a man's given name.

2. **señora** (sān-yōr′ä): a title for a married woman, like *Mrs.* or *madam* in English.
3. **Adiós** (äd′ē-ōs′): Spanish for "goodbye."

sistent. (*Laughs. She returns to her seat and watches, with a pleased expression, the pigeons feeding.*) There, that big one is always first! I know him by his big head. Now one, now another, now two, now three—That little fellow is the least timid. I believe he would eat from my hand. That one takes his piece and flies up to that branch alone. He is a philosopher. But where do they all come from? It seems as if the news had spread. Ha, ha! Don't quarrel. There is enough for all. I'll bring more tomorrow.

[*Enter* Don Gonzalo *and* Juanito *from the left center.* Don Gonzalo *is an old gentleman of seventy, gouty and impatient. He leans upon* Juanito's *arm and drags his feet somewhat as he walks.*]

Don Gonzalo. Idling their time away! They should be saying Mass.
Juanito. You can sit here, señor.[4] There is only a lady.

[Doña Laura *turns her head and listens.*]

Don Gonzalo. I won't, Juanito. I want a bench to myself.
Juanito. But there is none.
Don Gonzalo. That one over there is mine.
Juanito. There are three priests sitting there.
Don Gonzalo. Rout them out. Have they gone?
Juanito. No, indeed. They are talking.
Don Gonzalo. Just as if they were glued to the seat. No hope of their leaving. Come this way, Juanito. (*They walk toward the birds, right.*)
Doña Laura (*indignantly*). Look out!
Don Gonzalo. Are you speaking to me, señora?
Doña Laura. Yes, to you.
Don Gonzalo. What do you wish?

Doña Laura. You have scared away the birds who were feeding on my crumbs.
Don Gonzalo. What do I care about the birds?
Doña Laura. But I do.
Don Gonzalo. This is a public park.
Doña Laura. Then why do you complain that the priests have taken your bench?
Don Gonzalo. Señora, we have not met. I cannot imagine why you take the liberty of addressing me. Come, Juanito. (*Both go out right.*)
Doña Laura. What an ill-natured old man! (*Looking toward the right*) I am glad. He lost that bench, too. Serves him right for scaring the birds. He is furious. Yes, yes; find a seat if you can. Poor man! he is wiping the perspiration from his face. Here he comes. A carriage would not raise more dust than his feet.

[*Enter* Don Gonzalo *and* Juanito *by the right and walk toward the left.*]

Don Gonzalo. Have the priests gone yet, Juanito?
Juanito. No, indeed, señor. They are still there.
Don Gonzalo. The authorities should place more benches here for these sunny mornings. Well, I suppose I must resign myself and sit on the bench with the old lady. (*Muttering to himself, he sits at the extreme end of* Doña Laura's *bench and looks at her indignantly. Touches his hat as he greets her.*) Good morning.
Doña Laura. What, you here again?
Don Gonzalo. I repeat that we have not met.
Doña Laura. I was responding to your salute.[5]
Don Gonzalo. "Good morning" should be answered by "good morning," and that is all you should have said.

---

4. **señor** (sān´yōr´): a Spanish title of courtesy, like *Mr.* or *sir* in English.

5. **salute:** here, a greeting.

Doña Laura. You should have asked permission to sit on this bench, which is mine.

Don Gonzalo. The benches here are public property.

Doña Laura. Why, you said the one the priests have was yours.

Don Gonzalo. Very well, very well. I have nothing more to say. (*Between his teeth*) She ought to be at home knitting and counting her beads.[6]

Doña Laura. Don't grumble anymore. I'm not going to leave just to please you.

Don Gonzalo (*brushing the dust from his shoes with his handkerchief*). If the ground were sprinkled a little it would be an improvement.

Doña Laura. Do you use your handkerchief as a shoebrush?

Don Gonzalo. Why not?

Doña Laura. Do you use a shoebrush as a handkerchief?

Don Gonzalo. What right have you to criticize my actions?

Doña Laura. A neighbor's right.

Don Gonzalo. Juanito, my book. I do not care to listen to nonsense.

Doña Laura. You are very polite.

Don Gonzalo. Pardon me, señora, but never interfere with what does not concern you.

Doña Laura. I generally say what I think.

Don Gonzalo. And more to the same effect. Give me the book, Juanito.

Juanito. Here, señor.

[Juanito *takes a book from his pocket, hands it to* Don Gonzalo, *then exits by right.* Don Gonzalo, *casting indignant glances at* Doña Laura, *puts on an enormous pair of glasses, takes from his pocket a reading glass, adjusts both to suit him, and opens his book.*]

Doña Laura. I thought you were taking out a telescope.

6. **counting her beads:** praying with a rosary.

Don Gonzalo. Was that you?

Doña Laura. Your sight must be keen.

Don Gonzalo. Keener than yours is.

Doña Laura. Yes, evidently.

Don Gonzalo. Ask the hares and partridges.

Doña Laura. Ah! Do you hunt?

Don Gonzalo. I did, and even now—

Doña Laura. Oh, yes, of course!

Don Gonzalo. Yes, señora. Every Sunday I take my gun and dog, you understand, and go to one of my estates near Aravaca and kill time.

Doña Laura. Yes, kill time. That is all you kill.

Don Gonzalo. Do you think so? I could show you a wild boar's head in my study—

Doña Laura. Yes, and I could show you a tiger's skin in my boudoir. What does that prove?

Don Gonzalo. Very well, señora, please allow me to read. Enough conversation.

Doña Laura. Well, you subside, then.

Don Gonzalo. But first I shall take a pinch of snuff.[7] (*Takes out snuffbox*) Will you have some? (*Offers box to* Doña Laura)

Doña Laura. If it is good.

Don Gonzalo. It is of the finest. You will like it.

Doña Laura (*taking pinch of snuff*). It clears my head.

Don Gonzalo. And mine.

Doña Laura. Do you sneeze?

Don Gonzalo. Yes, señora, three times.

Doña Laura. And so do I. What a coincidence!

[*After taking the snuff, they await the sneezes, both anxiously, and sneeze alternately three times each.*]

Don Gonzalo. There, I feel better.

Doña Laura. So do I. (*Aside*) The snuff has made peace between us.

7. **snuff** (snŭf): finely ground tobacco, inhaled through the nostrils.

Don Gonzalo. You will excuse me if I read aloud?

Doña Laura. Read as loud as you please; you will not disturb me.

Don Gonzalo (*reading*). "All love is sad, but sad as it is, it is the best thing that we know." That is from Campoamor.[8]

Doña Laura. Ah!

Don Gonzalo (*reading*). "The daughters of the mothers I once loved kiss me now as they would a graven image."[9] Those lines, I take it, are in a humorous vein.

Doña Laura (*laughing*). I take them so, too.

Don Gonzalo. There are some beautiful poems in this book. Here. "Twenty years pass. He returns."

Doña Laura. You cannot imagine how it affects me to see you reading with all those glasses.

Don Gonzalo. Can you read without any?

Doña Laura. Certainly.

Don Gonzalo. At your age? You're jesting.

Doña Laura. Pass me the book, then. (*Takes book; reads aloud*)

> "Twenty years pass. He returns.
> And each, beholding the other, exclaims—
> Can it be that this is he?
> Heavens, is it she?"

[Doña Laura *returns the book to* Don Gonzalo.]

Don Gonzalo. Indeed, I envy you your wonderful eyesight.

Doña Laura (*aside*). I know every word by heart.

Don Gonzalo. I am very fond of good verses, very fond. I even composed some in my youth.

Doña Laura. Good ones?

Don Gonzalo. Of all kinds. I was a great friend of Espronceda, Zorrilla, Bécquer,[10] and others. I first met Zorrilla in America.

Doña Laura. Why, have you been in America?

Don Gonzalo. Several times. The first time I went I was only six years old.

Doña Laura. You must have gone with Columbus in one of his caravels!

Don Gonzalo (*laughing*). Not quite as bad as that. I am old, I admit, but I did not know Ferdinand and Isabella. (*They both laugh.*) I was also a great friend of Campoamor. I met him in Valencia. I am a native of that city.

Doña Laura. You are?

Don Gonzalo. I was brought up there and there I spent my early youth. Have you ever visited that city?

Doña Laura. Yes, señor. Not far from Valencia there was a villa that, if still there, should retain memories of me. I spent several seasons there. It was many, many years ago. It was near the sea, hidden away among lemon and orange trees. They called it—let me see, what did they call it—Maricela.

Don Gonzalo (*startled*). Maricela?

Doña Laura. Maricela. Is the name familiar to you?

Don Gonzalo. Yes, very familiar. If my memory serves me right, for we forget as we grow old, there lived in that villa the most beautiful woman I have ever seen, and I assure you I have seen many. Let me see—what was her name? Laura—Laura—Laura Llorente.

Doña Laura (*startled*). Laura Llorente?

Don Gonzalo. Yes.

---

8. **Campoamor:** Ramon de Campoamor (rä-mōn′ dā käm′ pō-ä-mōr′), once a popular Spanish poet, known for his humorous short poems (1817–1901).

9. **graven image:** an idol carved in stone or wood. In other words, he is treated with respect rather than affection.

10. **Espronceda . . . Bécquer:** José de Espronceda (hō-sā′ dā äs′prōn-thā′*th*ä), a Spanish romantic poet (1808–1842), known as the Spanish Byron; José Zorrilla y Moral (hō-sā′ thô-rē′lyä ē mō-räl′), a Spanish poet and dramatist (1817–1893); Gustavo Adolfo Bécquer (gōō-stä′vō ä-dôl′fō bā′kĕr), a Spanish poet and writer known for his romantic tales (1836–1870).

Detail from *The Balcony*
(1869) by Édouard Manet
(1832–1883).
Oil on canvas.
The Louvre, Paris

[*They look at each other intently.*]

Doña Laura (*recovering herself*). Nothing. You reminded me of my best friend.

Don Gonzalo. How strange!

Doña Laura. It is strange. She was called "The Silver Maiden."

Don Gonzalo. Precisely, "The Silver Maiden." By that name she was known in that locality. I seem to see her as if she were before me now, at that window with the red roses. Do you remember that window?

Doña Laura. Yes, I remember. It was the window of her room.

Don Gonzalo. She spent many hours there. I mean in my day.

Doña Laura (*sighing*). And in mine, too.

Don Gonzalo. She was ideal. Fair as a lily, jet-black hair and black eyes, with an uncommonly sweet expression. She seemed to cast a radiance wherever she was. Her figure was beautiful, perfect. "What forms of sovereign[11] beauty God models in human clay!" She was a dream.

Doña Laura (*aside*). If you but knew that dream was now by your side, you would realize what dreams come to. (*Aloud*) She was very unfortunate and had a sad love affair.

Don Gonzalo. Very sad.

[*They look at each other.*]

Doña Laura. Did you hear of it?

Don Gonzalo. Yes.

11. **sovereign** (sŏv′ər-ən): supreme.

Doña Laura. The ways of Providence are strange. (*Aside*) Gonzalo!

Don Gonzalo. The gallant lover, in the same affair—

Doña Laura. Ah, the duel?

Don Gonzalo. Precisely, the duel. The gallant lover was—my cousin, of whom I was very fond.

Doña Laura. Oh, yes, a cousin? My friend told me in one of her letters the story of that affair, which was truly romantic. He, your cousin, passed by on horseback every morning down the rose path under her window, and tossed up to her balcony a bouquet of flowers which she caught.

Don Gonzalo. And later in the afternoon the gallant horseman would return by the same path, and catch the bouquet of flowers she would toss him. Am I right?

Doña Laura. Yes. They wanted to marry her to a merchant whom she would not have.

Don Gonzalo. And one night, when my cousin waited under her window to hear her sing, this other person presented himself unexpectedly.

Doña Laura. And insulted your cousin.

Don Gonzalo. There was a quarrel.

Doña Laura. And later a duel.

Don Gonzalo. Yes, at sunrise, on the beach, and the merchant was badly wounded. My cousin had to conceal himself for a few days and later to fly.

Doña Laura. You seem to know the story well.

Don Gonzalo. And so do you.

Doña Laura. I have explained that a friend repeated it to me.

Don Gonzalo. As my cousin did to me. (*Aside*) This is Laura!

Doña Laura (*aside*). Why tell him? He does not suspect.

Don Gonzalo (*aside*). She is entirely innocent.

Doña Laura. And was it you, by any chance, who advised your cousin to forget Laura?

Don Gonzalo. Why, my cousin never forgot her!

Doña Laura. How do you account, then, for his conduct?

Don Gonzalo. I will tell you. The young man took refuge in my house, fearful of the consequences of a duel with a person highly regarded in that locality. From my home he went to Seville, then came to Madrid. He wrote Laura many letters, some of them in verse. But undoubtedly they were intercepted by her parents, for she never answered at all. Gonzalo then, in despair, believing his love lost to him forever, joined the army, went to Africa, and there, in a trench, met a glorious death, grasping the flag of Spain and whispering the name of his beloved Laura—

Doña Laura (*aside*). What an atrocious lie!

Don Gonzalo (*aside*). I could not have killed myself more gloriously.

Doña Laura. You must have been prostrated[12] by the calamity.

Don Gonzalo. Yes, indeed, señora. As if he were my brother. I presume, though, on the contrary, that Laura in a short time was chasing butterflies in her garden, indifferent to regret.

Doña Laura. No, señor, no!

Don Gonzalo. It is woman's way.

Doña Laura. Even if it were woman's way, "The Silver Maiden" was not of that disposition. My friend awaited news for days, months, a year, and no letter came. One afternoon, just at sunset, as the first stars were appearing, she was seen to leave the house, and with quickening steps wend her way toward the beach, the beach where her beloved had risked his life. She wrote his name on the sand, then sat down upon a rock, her gaze fixed upon the horizon. The waves murmured their eternal threnody[13] and slowly crept up to the rock where the

---

12. **prostrated** (prŏs′trā′təd): overcome.
13. **threnody** (thrĕn′ə-dē): lament.

maiden sat. The tide rose with a boom and swept her out to sea.

Don Gonzalo. Good heavens!

Doña Laura. The fishermen of that shore, who often tell the story, affirm that it was a long time before the waves washed away that name written on the sand. (*Aside*) You will not get ahead of me in decorating my own funeral.

Don Gonzalo (*aside*). She lies worse than I do.

Doña Laura. Poor Laura!

Don Gonzalo. Poor Gonzalo!

Doña Laura (*aside*). I will not tell him that I married two years later.

Don Gonzalo (*aside*). In three months I ran off to Paris with a ballet dancer.

Doña Laura. Fate is curious. Here are you and I, complete strangers, met by chance, discussing the romance of old friends of long ago! We have been conversing as if we were old friends.

Don Gonzalo. Yes, it is curious, considering the ill-natured prelude to our conversation.

Doña Laura. You scared away the birds.

Don Gonzalo. I was unreasonable, perhaps.

Doña Laura. Yes, that was evident. (*Sweetly*) Are you coming again tomorrow?

Don Gonzalo. Most certainly, if it is a sunny morning. And not only will I not scare away the birds, but I will bring a few crumbs.

Doña Laura. Thank you very much. Birds are grateful and repay attention. I wonder where my maid is? Petra! (*Signals for her maid*)

Don Gonzalo (*aside, looking at* Laura, *whose back is turned*). No, no, I will not reveal myself. I am grotesque[14] now. Better that she recall the gallant horseman who passed daily beneath her window tossing flowers.

Doña Laura. Here she comes.

Don Gonzalo. That Juanito! He plays havoc with the nursemaids. (*Looks to the right and signals with his hand*)

14. **grotesque** (grō-tĕsk'): ugly in appearance.

Doña Laura (*aside, looking at* Gonzalo, *whose back is turned*). No, I am too sadly changed. It is better he should remember me as the black-eyed girl tossing flowers as he passed among the roses in the garden.

[Juanito *enters by the right,* Petra *by the left. She has a bunch of violets in her hand.*]

Doña Laura. Well, Petra! At last!

Don Gonzalo. Juanito, you are late.

Petra (*to* Doña Laura). The guard gave me these violets for you, señora.

Doña Laura. How very nice! Thank him for me. They are fragrant. (*As she takes the violets from her maid a few loose ones fall to the ground.*)

Don Gonzalo. My dear lady, this has been a great honor and a great pleasure.

Doña Laura. It has also been a pleasure to me.

Don Gonzalo. Goodbye until tomorrow.

Doña Laura. Until tomorrow.

Don Gonzalo. If it is sunny.

Doña Laura. A sunny morning. Will you go to your bench?

Don Gonzalo. No, I will come to this—if you do not object?

Doña Laura. This bench is at your disposal.

Don Gonzalo. And I will surely bring the crumbs.

Doña Laura. Tomorrow, then?

Don Gonzalo. Tomorrow!

[Laura *walks away toward the right, supported by her maid.* Gonzalo, *before leaving with* Juanito, *trembling and with a great effort, stoops to pick up the violets* Laura *dropped. Just then* Laura *turns her head and surprises him picking up the flowers.*]

Juanito. What are you doing, señor?

Don Gonzalo. Juanito, wait—

Doña Laura (*aside*). Yes, it is he!

Don Gonzalo (*aside*). It is she, and no mistake.

[Doña Laura *and* Don Gonzalo *wave farewell.*]

Doña Laura. "Can it be that this is he?"
Don Gonzalo. "Heavens, is it she?"

[*They smile once more, as if she were again at the window and he below in the rose garden, and then disappear upon the arms of their servants.*]

[*Curtain.*]

Reading Check

1. Why is Don Gonzalo forced to share a bench with Doña Laura?
2. How does Don Gonzalo make peace with Doña Laura?
3. Why is Doña Laura able to read Don Gonzalo's book without glasses?
4. What was the name of Don Gonzalo's great love?
5. What was the outcome of the duel Don Gonzalo fought?

For Study and Discussion

Analyzing and Interpreting the Play

1. The plot of this play depends on a coincidence. Two elderly people, who once were lovers but who no longer recognize each other, chance to meet in a park one sunny morning. In the course of casual conversation, they reveal who they are and what their relationship was in the past. Why do you think Doña Laura and Don Gonzalo wish to keep their identities a secret from each other?

2. Don Gonzalo is reading a book of love poems, which Doña Laura claims to know by heart. How is this interest in romance reflected in the portraits they paint of each other as youthful lovers?

3. Both Doña Laura and Don Gonzalo got over their love affair rather painlessly. Why, then, do they want each other to believe that they suffered and died for their love?

4. When they first meet in the park, Doña Laura and Don Gonzalo take an immediate dislike to each other. Given their past relationship as lovers, why is this conflict amusing?

5. The reunion of lovers is often handled as a touching, emotional scene. In this play, however, the reunion is light and comical. How do the characters of Don Gonzalo and Doña Laura contribute to the lighthearted mood of the play?

6a. What change does Don Gonzalo undergo after he meets Doña Laura? **b.** What does the ending of the play imply about their future relationship?

Writing About Literature

Analyzing Character

Write a short essay telling how one of the characters changes in the course of the play. State your *thesis* at the opening of your essay in this fashion: *When we first meet him, Don Gonzalo is a cranky, peevish old man who seems to live only for his memories, but after he recognizes Doña Laura, he becomes interested again in life and in romance.*

About the Authors

Serafín Alvárez Quintero (1871–1938)
Joaquín Alvárez Quintero (1873–1944)

The Quintero brothers had their first play produced when they were still teen-agers. They collaborated on more than fifty plays, most of which are set in Andalusia, Spain. Some of their best-known plays are *Lady from Alfaqueque, One Hundred Years Ago,* and *Fortunato.*

The Governess

NEIL SIMON

Based on a Short Story by
Anton Chekhov°

A theme is the basic meaning of a literary work. It is an idea about life or an interpretation of experience. What is the theme of this play?

Mistress. Julia! (*Calls again*) Julia!

[*A young governess,* Julia, *comes rushing in. She stops before the desk and curtsies.*]

Julia (*head down*). Yes, madame?
Mistress. Look at me, child. Pick your head up. I like to see your eyes when I speak to you.
Julia (*lifts her head up*). Yes, madame. (*But her head has a habit of slowly drifting down again.*)
Mistress. And how are the children coming along with their French lessons?
Julia. They're very bright children, madame.
Mistress. Eyes up . . . They're bright, you say. Well, why not? And mathematics? They're doing well in mathematics, I assume?
Julia. Yes, madame. Especially Vanya.
Mistress. Certainly. I knew it. I excelled in mathematics. He gets that from his mother, wouldn't you say?
Julia. Yes, madame.
Mistress. Head up . . . (*She lifts head up.*) That's it. Don't be afraid to look people in the eyes,

my dear. If you think of yourself as inferior, that's exactly how people will treat you.
Julia. Yes, ma'am.
Mistress. A quiet girl, aren't you? . . . Now then, let's settle our accounts. I imagine you must need money although you never ask me for it yourself. Let's see now, we agreed on thirty rubles[1] a month, did we not?
Julia (*surprised*). Forty, ma'am.
Mistress. No, no, thirty. I made a note of it. (*Points to the book*) I always pay my governesses thirty . . . Who told you forty?
Julia. You did, ma'am. I spoke to no one else concerning money . . .
Mistress. Impossible. Maybe you *thought* you heard forty when I said thirty. If you kept your head up, that would never happen. Look at me again and I'll say it clearly. *Thirty rubles a month.*
Julia. If you say so, ma'am.
Mistress. Settled. Thirty a month it is . . . Now then, you've been here two months exactly.
Julia. Two months and five days.
Mistress. No, no. Exactly two months. I made

°**Chekhov** (chĕk'ôf'): a major Russian dramatist and short-story writer (1860–1904).

1. **rubles** (rōō'bəlz): The ruble is the Russian unit of money, like the dollar in the United States.

a note of it. You should keep books the way I do so there wouldn't be these discrepancies.[2] So—we have two months at thirty rubles a month . . . comes to sixty rubles. Correct?

Julia (*curtsies*). Yes, ma'am. Thank you, ma'am.

Mistress. Subtract nine Sundays . . . We did agree to subtract Sundays, didn't we?

Julia. No, ma'am.

Mistress. Eyes! Eyes! . . . Certainly we did. I've always subtracted Sundays. I didn't bother making a note of it because I always do it. Don't you recall when I said we will subtract Sundays?

Julia. No, ma'am.

Mistress. Think.

Julia (*thinks*). No, ma'am.

Mistress. You weren't thinking. Your eyes were wandering. Look straight at my face and look hard . . . Do you remember now?

Julia (*softly*). Yes, ma'am.

Mistress. I didn't hear you, Julia.

Julia (*louder*). Yes, ma'am.

Mistress. Good. I was sure you'd remember. . . . Plus three holidays. Correct?

Julia. Two, ma'am. Christmas and New Year's.

Mistress. And your birthday. That's three.

Julia. I worked on my birthday, ma'am.

Mistress. You did? There was no need to. My governesses never worked on their birthdays . . .

Julia. But I did work, ma'am.

Mistress. But that's not the question, Julia. We're discussing financial matters now. I will, however, only count two holidays if you insist . . . Do you insist?

Julia. I did work, ma'am.

Mistress. Then you *do* insist.

Julia. No, ma'am.

Mistress. Very well. That's three holidays;

therefore we take off twelve rubles. Now then, four days little Kolya was sick, and there were no lessons.

Julia. But I gave lessons to Vanya.

Mistress. True. But I engaged you to teach two children, not one. Shall I pay you in full for doing only half the work?

Julia. No, ma'am.

Mistress. So we'll deduct it . . . Now, three days you had a toothache and my husband gave you permission not to work after lunch. Correct?

Julia. After four. I worked until four.

Mistress (*looks in the book*). I have here: "Did not work after lunch." We have lunch at one and are finished at two, not at four, correct?

Julia. Yes, ma'am. But I——

Mistress. That's another seven rubles . . . Seven and twelve is nineteen . . . Subtract . . . that leaves . . . forty-one rubles . . . Correct?

Julia. Yes, ma'am. Thank you, ma'am.

Mistress. Now then, on January fourth you broke a teacup and saucer, is that true?

Julia. Just the saucer, ma'am.

Mistress. What good is a teacup without a saucer, eh? . . . That's two rubles. The saucer was an heirloom. It cost much more, but let it go. I'm used to taking losses.

Julia. Thank you, ma'am.

Mistress. Now then, January ninth, Kolya climbed a tree and tore his jacket.

Julia. I forbad him to do so, ma'am.

Mistress. But he didn't listen, did he? . . . Ten rubles . . . January fourteenth, Vanya's shoes were stolen . . .

Julia. By the maid, ma'am. You discharged her yourself.

Mistress. But you get paid good money to watch everything. I explained that in our first meeting. Perhaps you weren't listening. Were you listening that day, Julia, or was your head in the clouds?

Julia. Yes, ma'am.

Mistress. Yes, your head was in the clouds?

2. **discrepancies** (dĭs-krĕp′ən-sēz): disagreements.

Julia. No, ma'am. I was listening.

Mistress. Good girl. So that means another five rubles off. (*Looks in the book*) . . . Ah yes . . . the sixteenth of January I gave you ten rubles.

Julia. You didn't.

Mistress. But I made a note of it. Why would I make a note of it if I didn't give it to you?

Julia. I don't know, ma'am.

Mistress. That's not a satisfactory answer, Julia . . . Why would I make a note of giving you ten rubles if I did not in fact give it to you, eh? . . . No answer? . . . Then I must have given it to you, mustn't I?

Julia. Yes, ma'am. If you say so, ma'am.

Mistress. Well, certainly I say so. That's the point of this little talk. To clear these matters up . . . Take twenty-seven from forty-one, that leaves . . . fourteen, correct?

Julia. Yes, ma'am. (*She turns away, softly crying.*)

Mistress. What's this? Tears? Are you crying? Has something made you unhappy, Julia? Please tell me. It pains me to see you like this. I'm so sensitive to tears. What is it?

Julia. Only once since I've been here have I ever been given any money and that was by your husband. On my birthday he gave me three rubles.

Mistress. Really? There's no note of it in my book. I'll put it down now. (*She writes in the book.*) Three rubles. Thank you for telling me. Sometimes I'm a little lax with my accounts . . . Always shortchanging myself. So then, we take three more from fourteen . . . leaves eleven . . . Do you wish to check my figures?

Julia. There's no need to, ma'am.

Mistress. Then we're all settled. Here's your salary for two months, dear. Eleven rubles. (*She puts the pile of coins on the desk.*) Count it.

Julia. It's not necessary, ma'am.

Mistress. Come, come. Let's keep the records straight. Count it.

Julia (*reluctantly counts it*). One, two, three, four, five, six, seven, eight, nine, ten . . .? There's only ten, ma'am.

Mistress. Are you sure? Possibly you dropped one . . . Look on the floor; see if there's a coin there.

Julia. I didn't drop any, ma'am. I'm quite sure.

Mistress. Well, it's not here on my desk and I *know* I gave you eleven rubles. Look on the floor.

Julia. It's all right, ma'am. Ten rubles will be fine.

Mistress. Well, keep the ten for now. And if we don't find it on the floor later, we'll discuss it again next month.

Julia. Yes, ma'am. Thank you, ma'am. You're very kind, ma'am. (*She curtsies and then starts to leave.*)

Mistress. Julia! (Julia *stops, turns.*) Come back here. (*She crosses back to the desk and curtsies again.*) Why did you thank me?

Julia. For the money, ma'am.

Mistress. For the money? . . . But don't you realize what I've done? I've cheated you . . . *Robbed* you! I have no such notes in my book. I made up whatever came into my mind. Instead of the eighty rubles which I owe you, I gave you only ten. I have actually stolen from you and still you thank me . . . Why?

Julia. In the other places that I've worked, they didn't give me anything at all.

Mistress. Then they cheated you even worse than I did . . . I was playing a little joke on you. A cruel lesson just to teach you. You're much too trusting, and in this world that's very dangerous . . . I'm going to give you the entire eighty rubles. (*Hands her an envelope*) It's all ready for you. The rest is in this envelope. Here, take it.

Julia. As you wish, ma'am. (*She curtsies and starts to go again.*)

Mistress. Julia! (Julia *stops.*) Is it possible to be so spineless? Why don't you protest? Why don't you speak up? Why don't you cry out against this cruel and unjust treatment? Is it really possible to be so guileless,[3] so innocent, such a—pardon me for being so blunt—such a simpleton?

Julia (*the faintest trace of a smile on her lips*). Yes, ma'am . . . it's possible.

[*She curtsies again and runs off. The* Mistress *looks after her a moment, a look of complete bafflement on her face. The lights fade.*]

3. **guileless** (gīl′lĭs): simple; without deceit.

Reading Check

1. Why has the Mistress summoned Julia?
2. How many children does Julia take care of?
3. What subjects does the Mistress inquire about during the interview?
4. How much money does the Mistress actually give Julia?

For Study and Discussion

Analyzing and Interpreting the Play

1. The **turning point** of a play occurs when there is a decisive change or turn in the action. What is the turning point in *The Governess*?

2a. What is the "lesson" Julia's mistress wishes to teach her?   **b.** Do you think she is successful?

3. This play is based on a short story called "A Nincompoop." A *nincompoop* is a person who is easily deceived. Do you believe Julia gives in so easily because she is stupid, or do you think there is another explanation for her meekness?

4. What do you think is the author's attitude toward Julia? Is he critical? sympathetic?

5. What insight into human nature does this play give?

Extending Your Study

Comparing the Play with the Story

Locate a copy of "A Nincompoop" in a collection of Chekhov's stories. Compare *The Governess* with its source. What similarities are there in details and characterization? What changes did Simon make? Why do you think he made these changes?

About the Author

Neil Simon   (1927–   )

Neil Simon was born in New York City and studied engineering at New York University and the University of Denver. Before his first play, *Come Blow Your Horn,* opened on Broadway, in 1961, Simon wrote scripts for television shows. He is best known for his comedies, including *Barefoot in the Park, The Prisoner of Second Avenue, The Sunshine Boys,* and *Brighton Beach Memoirs.* He has adapted many of his plays for film, and he has also written original screenplays. His comedy *The Odd Couple* was made into a movie and also inspired a television series. *The Governess* is one of nine scenes in *The Good Doctor.*

FROM
The Boy David

JAMES BARRIE

David and Goliath

This episode from Barrie's play is based on the Biblical account of David and Goliath in I Samuel 17. The Bible tells how the champion of the Philistines, Goliath of Gath, issued a challenge to King Saul and the Israelites. Goliath was a giant ten feet tall ("six cubits and a span"). His armor alone weighed one hundred fifty pounds. When he walked, he resembled a fortress of gleaming brass. Only David, a young shepherd boy with no formal training in weapons or warfare, possessed the courage and the faith to answer Goliath's challenge.

The events of the play take place nearly three thousand years ago. As you read, note how Barrie creates a sense of time and place through language.

Characters

Abner
David
Jonathan } Israelites
Ophir
Slingers

Armor-bearer
Goliath of Gath } Philistines
Soldiers   (fĭ-lĭs′tĭnz, -tēnz)

Armor-bearer. Wake up, you Slingers of this outpost of Saul, and listen to me, the Armor-bearer of Goliath. Find you not that forty days sufficeth you[1] for one sleeping? Come out

from the rocks where you are hiding, and hearken again to the challenge of my master, Goliath of Gath.

All. Come out! cowards.

Armor-bearer. Nay, then, lurk in your hiding holes, you dogs, till he sends servants with whips to lash you out.

First Philistine. We are the whips!

Second Philistine. The whips of Goliath!

Armor-bearer. Thus says Goliath: "Am I not a Philistine and ye the cravens of Saul! Go out into your camp and search among all your captains, and let one come there to the Vale of Elah where Goliath awaits him."

All. Your champion.

Armor-bearer. "Then shall the tent of Goliath become his and the spear of Goliath become his. But if I prevail against him and kill him,

---

1. **sufficeth** (sə-fīs′əth) **you:** is enough.

David and Goliath   **347**

Detail from *David and Goliath*. Twelfth-century illuminated manuscript, Winchester, England.

then shall ye be our servants and serve us, ye and your gods."

All. You shall be our servants.

Third Philistine. The servants of the men of Goliath!

[Ophir *jumps up fiercely but* Jonathan *pulls him out of sight.*]

Armor-bearer. There is no man among you, no, not one! Dogs of Israel, the challenge is still open. Get you a champion. Haul him hither by a rope. His bugle has but to sound, and Goliath is ready. (*He again blows his challenge.*) Behold!

Fourth Philistine. Get you a champion.

All. Haul him!

Armor-bearer. His bugle of defiance has but to sound, and lo, the spear of Goliath will be ready in the vale.

[*He returns up the rocks right, blows his bugle, and they all exit exultantly.*

There is now no one left on the Philistine rocks. The Captain of the Slingers, Abner, signals to the Israelites *to arise, and they do so, raging at the indignity they have had to endure. Some of them leap into the arena, slings in evidence, to pursue the* Philistines, *but he drives them back.*]

A Slinger. You dogs.
Abner. We may not fight. The King forbids.
A Slinger. Skulkers! It is what we are!
Another. Ay, it is what we are.
Another. If we may not let loose our slings, why should we carry them?
Another. If we may not fight, why carry our slings?
Another. To show no longer are we fighting men?
A Third. Down with our slings, I say—no longer are we fighting men.
All. Down with our slings!

[*Several throw down their weapons.* Abner *draws his sword on them.*]

Abner. Up with your swords or you shall die by your captain's hands.
A Slinger. We have no captain who could stand up against him.
All. We have no captain.
Another. Must we wait another forty days till *our* horn answers?
Others. The horns of Israel are broken.
All. Broken, broken, the horns of Israel are broken.

[*An unseen horn, different in tone, is heard from* back at right as from some distance, low yet clear, and all are stirred.]

A Slinger. Did you hear?
Another. Some one accepts the challenge!
Another. Who could he be?
Abner. If only I could be he!
Another. A champion for Israel.
All. A champion for Israel.
Others. At last!
Another. He comes down the hill.
A Slinger. Where is he?
Another. Now he is behind a rock.
A Slinger. Where?
Another. Over there.
Another. Now I see him.
Another. He comes this way.

[*Similar cries from* Others.]

All. He comes! He comes!
A Slinger. He comes.
Another. A boy. Lo, it is a boy riding on an ass!

[Others *crowd round upstage and their excitement changes into mirth.*]

Behold the champion of Israel!

[David *comes riding forward at back on the ass and with a horn in his hand. He is in his exalted condition, and it should have the effect of keeping the scene serious, which is essential. He is now a boy of high resolve, with no playfulness about him.*]

David (*with dignity*). Greetings to this outpost of the Slingers of Israel. (*All murmur* "Greetings.")
Abner (*roughly*). Whence come you?
David. I am David, the son of Jesse, and lo——
Abner. I care not whose son you be. What seek you here?

[Ophir *and* Jonathan *enter.*]

David. I seek here a lion who is called Goliath of Gath.
Abner. And when you have found him?
David (*calm and resolved and simple, and without any boasting*). Then shall I slay him.
Abner. With your sling or with your harp?
David (*with dignity*). It is to be with my sling.
A Slinger. Behold the champion of Israel!
David. Deride me not because I am a boy. This day shall I slay Goliath.
A Slinger. What say you?
Another. Hast ever heard the like?
Another. This poor Goliath!

[*His quiet assurance impresses the* Slingers, *and they are perplexed and ponder.*]

A Slinger. What cast of boy is this? (*All start murmuring.*)
Abner (*also puzzled*). What I would know is, how came it to pass that they let you ride unchecked through the camp of Saul?
David. All were kind and sped me on my way, and they did give me this horn on which to blow my challenge, and behold I will blow it again. (*He is about to do so.*)
Abner. Hold him!
Several. Hold him!

[Slingers *restrain* David.]

A Slinger. They sped him on his way!
Another. It is unbelievable——
Another. Yet the poor soul believes it.
Another (*with awe*). Is he bereft?[2]
David. I am not bereft. I am exalted.
A Slinger. There are things happening in these days that pass the wit of man.

2. **bereft:** deprived of (his senses).

[Ophir *and* Jonathan *have remained down left in this scene, hardly noticed; but they have listened intently, and* Ophir *now comes forward.*]

Ophir. Abner!
Abner (*relieved to see a superior officer*). Now are you pleasant in my eyes, Ophir, for you are a captain of five hundred and I but of fifty, and there is that to decide which I shall gladly leave to you. This boy——
Ophir. I have heard all. (*He signs to the* Slingers *to stand back.*)
Abner. What to do with him? There is something untoward[3] about this boy.
Ophir. Ay, more so than you know of. I have known it since he came here riding on an ass.
Abner. He says that all he met in the camp encouraged him on his way.
Ophir. Ay, but that I *cannot* believe. (*He goes to* David.) Say you, boy, that no guards opposed your coming hither through the camp of this uttermost outpost of the slingers? How could it be so?
David. At first they did stay me ribaldly, dragging me from the ass and otherwise misusing me, but when I showed it to them they all did speed me on my way.
Abner. They were mocking you.
Ophir. What showed you to them that did make so great a man of you?
David. This which he gave me. (*He puts the token into the hands of* Ophir, *whom it startles.*)

[*He shows it to* Abner.]

Abner (*equally taken aback*). The token of Saul!
Ophir. Ay! (*He calls to* David.) How came you by this?
David. A shepherd did give it to me in a clearing in the wood.

3. **untoward** (ŭn'tôrd', -tōrd'): unfavorable.

Abner. Shepherd?

Ophir. He was once that. (*To* David.) How did he look?

David. He did look noble, and he sat on an open space in the wood in a purple cloak, and a javelin was near by.

[Ophir *and* Abner *exchange glances.*]

Ophir. He spoke with you?

David. He did so. He is my greatest friend, and I am *his* greatest friend.

Ophir (*to* Abner). Be wary, Abner, the boy knows not who it was. A shepherd he believes; and so Saul wants him to believe. What do you conceive is now in the secret mind of Saul?

Abner. The token of the King. No thinking is needed. All know its meaning: "Do as the Bearer asks, or incur the wrath of Saul."

Ophir. Ay, so it means—and what asks this Bearer?—To fight Goliath!

Abner. That turns it all to folly.

Ophir (*grimly*). Does it? Let me think. (*He moves about, brooding.*)

Jonathan. Let the boy go unharmed, Ophir. You can see what hand has touched him—he is afflicted.

Ophir. My prince, do you forget the words of but an hour ago—"One who shall come riding on an ass"?

Jonathan. Samuel did not say a boy.

Ophir. He said: "To that one who comes riding on an ass must be given the first blow, or a boy shall rule in the place of Saul."

Jonathan. He meant me.

Ophir. So we thought, but it has now come to me that this is the boy he meant—and so I believe has it come to the King. (*This is a shock to* Jonathan.) What asks the boy? To fight Goliath. What orders this token? To grant him that boon!

Jonathan. Of death!

Ophir. Ay, but in that one stroke he is removed forever from the path of Saul.

Jonathan. Poor shepherd boy!

Ophir (*whose loyalty to the King is still a redeeming feature*). See you not also that, with the fate of the boy, Samuel falls in the eyes of Israel?

Jonathan. The people know not that this champion is the choice of Samuel.

Ophir. Mine the part to let them know.

Jonathan. If thus my father wanted he would have made his meaning clear.

Ophir. Kings speak not their wishes clear but leave it to their servants to interpret them.

Jonathan. Consider your peril, Ophir—what if you interpret him awry?

Ophir. I have considered it. Yet even if I err the King would still be unharmed. He would but seem to have followed in the way he was told. This prophet is a deep one, but he shall find that I am deeper.

Jonathan. It is not, I think, the deepness of you that commends you to the King. If you read him wrongly now——

Ophir (*finely*). It would be the end of Ophir, but what matter if I was seeking to serve Saul?

Jonathan (*touched by his devotion*). Truly you love him!

Ophir (*passionately*). Ay, do I!

[*Shouts and declamation of the soldiers as they return.* Abner *pushes forward in front of them.*]

A Slinger. Away with the child. Thus say we all.

All. All. All. All.

Ophir. How now?

Abner (*who has* David's *horn in his hand*). His horn. They took it from him, crying that to let such a one face the man of Gath would be to make sport of us before the Philistines.

[*Cries of corroboration of this rend the air*—"We will not have him—Shall Israel be shamed?

What means Saul by giving us such a champion?"]

Ophir. First hear me.

[*The turmoil subsides.*]

Israelites, the boy comes not from Saul, he is the choice of Samuel. Saul scorns this champion, but Samuel proclaims that this boy and no other shall strike the first blow. For forty days has Saul hungered to fall upon the Philistines, but he cannot because he has been under the weight of a vow to the Prophet.
First Slinger. A vow to the Prophet?
Second Slinger. Saul is under a vow to Samuel.
Third Slinger. I have heard of this.
Fourth Slinger. What is this vow?
Fifth Slinger. We know this vow.
Sixth Slinger. It is not to fight.
Seventh Slinger. Samuel orders it.
Eighth Slinger. Yes, he orders it.
Ninth Slinger. Does Samuel rule in Israel?
Tenth Slinger. Ophir, speak. Tell us why Saul obeys him—this Samuel.
Ophir. I bring word to you from Saul. Thus says Saul to his people, "Let Samuel have his wish." At such a moment what is the life of a boy or the triumph of a braggart? Samuel's be the shame.
All. Yes, Samuel's be the shame.
Ophir. For listen, soldiers. With that first blow Saul is absolved of his vow! Then will he straightway give battle.
All. The battle! The battle!
First Slinger. Saul will be absolved of his vow!
Second Slinger. The forty days are over!
All. The forty days are over!
Ophir. See him again this day, Israel, as you have been wont[4] to see him in your front, Saul our king, as he bends backward, astride your enemies, his javelin in his hand. He calls to you once more to smite[5] the Philistines.

[*He casts the horn onto the glade where* David *is alone.*]

Abner. Know, boy, there is none in Israel who will face this monster.
A Slinger. None.
All. None of us.
Abner. For he is as one left over from the giants who were drowned in a deluge and now mourn and groan in hell beneath the waters. Such is this Goliath, crying mockingly that Israel is without a god.
David. Who is the God of Israel?
Abner. Our Maker, the Lord of Hosts, Whom this Goliath defies.
David. Can it be? (*He looks up, shuts his eyes, then crosses to where the horn lies.*)
Jonathan (*coming to* David). Touch not the horn, David.
A Slinger. Touch not the horn.
Jonathan. Surely now, you are afraid.

[David *shivers, and for a moment his courage is gone.*]

Ophir (*jeering*). Ah, see how Samuel's champion trembles! In vain do we await the blast that was to be great in the history of Israel.
A Slinger. He fears!
David (*though still in a quiver and rather childlike*). Perhaps I am afraid—but thus does David.

[*He lifts the horn and blows a clear challenging blast. The answer comes from the Philistine camp. All cringe and work around to the left of stage.*]

Armor-bearer (*offstage*). Goliath awaits the

4. **wont** (wônt, wōnt, wŭnt): accustomed to.

5. **smite** (smīt): destroy.

champion of Israel. Here in the Vale of Elah.
All. He is doomed.

[*The scene becomes darker.*]

A Slinger. A darkness comes upon the land.
All. A darkness comes upon the land.
A Slinger. Who sends it?
Another. The Lord deserts us.
Abner. Or has the boy a friend we know not of?
Ophir. He has no friend.

[*The stage is now quite dark.*]

All. Smite the Philistines!
Ophir. Then shall their cattle be thine, and their wines and their horses and their camels shall be thine, and their chariots shall be thine, and at last there will be workers of iron in this land to forge us swords and spears. Are you ready to be magnified, O Israel? Is it to be the battle?

[*His outburst is gradually received with clamorous cries of* "The battle, the battle—the forty days are over. Let the boy perish—Hail the King," *ending with* "But where is the boy?"

David, *who has been neglected and lost to sight, is now discovered in a parting of the crowd, quite regardless of them, testing pebbles in the water. They regard him wonderingly.*]

Abner. What are you doing, boy?
David (*looking up*). I am gathering pebbles for my sling.
A Slinger. Truly this one is not as others are.
David (*to* Jonathan). Who are you, boy?
Jonathan. My name is Jonathan.
David. My name is David. (*More secretively*) Hearken, Jonathan. They say that he who kills Goliath acquires his tent and his spear.
Jonathan. It is so, but woe unto you.

David (*very worried*). I fear not to sleep in his tent if there is a lamp. But his spear! Jonathan, if his spear is like unto a weaver's beam, as they say, how shall I able to carry it on my shoulder?
Jonathan (*astounded*). Is that all that in this dire moment afflicts your mind?
David. It is chiefly that.
Jonathan. Thou pitiful!
A Slinger. Ophir, are we men that we can give him to the spear of the Philistines?
Ophir. It is not we who give him. It is Samuel.
A Slinger. Ay, true, it is not Saul who sends this one to the man of Gath. Samuel's the blame.
All. Ay, Samuel's the blame.
Ophir. The boy's own be the decision.
A Slinger. Death awaits him.
Another. Let the boy do as he will.

[Ophir *takes horn from* Abner.]

Ophir (*who sees that he must act quickly before a fickle crowd*). This is his horn. Let him sound it if he dares.
Armor-bearer (*off*). Goliath awaits.

[*Challenging trumpets are heard from the Philistine camp. All the Israelites creep away, leaving only David and* Jonathan. David *hesitates, then slowly walks up center and goes toward the Philistine camp. He backs, appalled by what he has seen.* Jonathan *creeps up to him.*]

Jonathan (*in whisper*). David! David, did you see him?
David. I saw him.
Jonathan. What think you?
David. He is of a size even more huge than they said. Jonathan, I am not *quite* sure now that I shall win.

Jonathan. Fly with me quickly, David. I can save you still.

David. No.

Goliath (*off*). Now shall Israel be shamed for mocking me with such a champion. Look, insect, upon Goliath of Gath.

David. Lo, I have looked and you are smaller than they said.

The Triumph of David by Francisco Solimena (1657–1747). Black chalk drawing.
The Metropolitan Museum of Art, Harry G. Sperling Fund

Goliath. How many pebbles, little one, are in your wallet?

David. There are five, but I think I shall not need them all.

Goliath. I curse thee by my gods. Come to me and I will give thy flesh to the fowls of the air and to the beasts of the field, thou Israelite who art without a god.

David. Thou comest to me with a sword and with a spear and with a shield, but I come to thee in the Name of Him Whom thou hast defied. This day will He deliver thee into mine

hands and I will smite thee, that all the earth will know there is a God in Israel.

[*Poised on the rock,* David *discharges his sling at the unseen* Goliath. *The stone whistles through the air. There is a moment of intense silence, followed by the echoing sound of Goliath's fall.* David *runs offstage in the direction from which the sound comes. The darkness gradually lifts, and one by one, very slowly and anxiously, Israelites come on, bewildered and unable to understand what has happened. They do not speak, but stare in the direction of the Philistines.*

Abner *is amongst them. This situation lasts a full minute. Suddenly an Israelite comes on from the side of the Philistines, crying breathlessly and hoarsely:* "David has slain Goliath! David has slain Goliath! David has slain Goliath!" *Repeating the same words again and again like a madman, he crosses the stage until he disappears from sight. Behind the scene you still hear him repeating this incredible news— spreading the miracle through the tents, his voice growing louder. The few men on the stage are awestruck, whisperingly asking one another,* "David has slain Goliath," *as though unable to believe their own words.*

Then there comes a long-drawn cry from the Philistines, "David has slain Goliath!!!" *With barbaric dancing and wild shouts Israelites pour onto the scene until the stage is quite full. Throughout all the clamor the words* "David has slain Goliath!" *are continuously heard, taken up by more and more of the thronging Israelites until at last the sentence rises to a jubilant roar.*

Finally David *comes on with* Goliath's *great spear. Being unable to raise it, he is dragging it along the ground with both hands. The Israelites dance wildly around him until one cries out:* "The battle! The battle!" *This idea is taken up by more and more, until with one accord they all rush off in the direction of the Philistines, their voices mingling in one unanimous cry:* "The battle! The battle!"]

Reading Check

1. For how long does Goliath taunt the Israelites?
2. How does David get past the camp guards?
3. What vow has King Saul taken?
4. Who offers to save David?
5. What does David do with Goliath's weapon?

For Study and Discussion

Analyzing and Interpreting the Play

1. Why are the Israelite soldiers demoralized at the opening of this episode?

2. How do the Israelite soldiers react when David appears in their camp?

3a. How does Barrie emphasize David's youth and inexperience? **b.** How does he emphasize the boy's faith?

4. Why does Ophir encourage David to answer Goliath's challenge?

5. The story of the small or young hero who vanquishes a bigger or tougher opponent has always been popular. **a.** Why do such stories have permanent appeal? **b.** What other situations can you think of, in literature or in life, that are parallels to the story of David and Goliath?

Writing About Literature

Analyzing a Character's Motivation

Write an essay in which you analyze the reasons for Ophir's actions. In your paper, answer these questions: What are Ophir's attitudes toward Saul and toward Samuel? What is Ophir's plan and how does he intend to use David in order to succeed?

About the Author

Sir James Matthew Barrie (1860–1937)

Barrie was born in Scotland. He studied at Edinburgh University and worked as a journalist before beginning his career as a free-lance writer. Barrie was successful as a short-story writer, novelist, and playwright. He is best known for his play *Peter Pan,* which was first performed on the stage in 1904. This popular work has also appeared in film and television versions. Some critics have suggested that Barrie himself is the boy who lived in Never-Never-Land, refusing to grow up. In 1913 he received the title of baronet, and in 1922 he was awarded the Order of Merit for service to his country during World War I. *The Boy David,* his last play, appeared in 1936.

The Big Wave

PEARL BUCK

Dramatized for Television

In the preface to her book The Big Wave, *Pearl Buck tells how she came to write the story of Jiya and Kino. One day in Japan she saw an ancient village swept away by a tidal wave. This had happened many times before. "Yet every time the fishermen and their families, those who survive the big wave, come back to build once more the little village lying low between two mountains and surrounded on two sides by the sea."*

As you read, ask yourself why these people come back and continue to live "in the presence of death."

Characters

Narrator
Kino Uchiyama (kē′nō o͞o′chē-yä′mä), a farmer's son
Mother
Father, the farmer
Setsu (set′so͞o), Kino's sister
Jiya (jē′yä), a fisherman's son
Jiya's Father, the fisherman
Old Gentleman, a wealthy landowner
Two Menservants
Gardener
First Man
Second Man
Woman
Child

Act One

Open on: *A scene in Japan, sea and mountainside, and in the distance Fuji.[1]*

Dissolve to:[2] *A small farmhouse, built on top of terraces.*

This, as the Narrator *speaks, dissolves to: The inside of the house, a room with the simplest of Japanese furniture.*

Narrator. Kino lives on a farm. The farm lies on the side of a mountain in Japan. The fields are terraced by walls of stone, each one of them like a broad step up the mountain. Centuries ago, Kino's ancestors built the stone walls that hold up the fields. Above the fields stands this farmhouse, which is Kino's home. Sometimes he feels the climb is hard, especially

1. **Fuji** (fo͞o′jē): the highest peak in Japan, a volcano extinct since 1707.
2. **Dissolve to:** Fade from one picture into another.

The Coast of Tago from *Thirty-six Views of Fuji* (c. 1823) by Katsushika Hokusai (1760–1849). Woodblock print.
The Metropolitan Museum of Art, Rogers Fund

when he has been working in the lowest field and he is hungry.

[Dissolve to: Kino *comes into the room. He is a sturdy boy of about thirteen, dressed in shorts and a Japanese jacket, open on his bare chest.*]

Kino. Mother!

[Mother *hurries in. She is a small, serious-looking woman dressed in an everyday cotton kimono,[3] sleeves tucked up. She is carrying a jar of water.*]

Mother. Dinner is ready. Where's your father?
Kino. Coming. I ran up the terraces. I'm starving.

3. **kimono** (kə-mō′nə): a loose robe with wide sleeves and a sash, worn as an outer garment by Japanese men and women.

Mother. Call Setsu. She is playing outside.

Kino (*turning his head*). Setsu!

Father. Here she is. (*He comes in, holding by the hand a small roguish girl.*) Getting so big! I can't lift her any more. (*But he does lift her so high that she touches the low rafters.*)

Setsu. Don't put me down. I want to eat my supper up here.

Father. And fall into the soup?

Kino. How that would taste!

Setsu (*willfully*). It would taste nice.

Mother. Come, come . . .

[*They sit on the floor around the little table. The* Mother *serves swiftly from a small bucket of rice, a bowl of soup, a bowl of fish. She serves the* Father *first, then* Kino, *then* Setsu, *and herself.*]

Father. Kino, don't eat so fast.

Kino. I have promised Jiya to swim in the sea with him.

Mother. Obey your father.

Father (*smiling*). Let him eat fast. (*He puts a bit of fish in* Setsu's *bowl.*) There—that's a good bit.

Kino. Father, why is it that Jiya's father's house has no window to the sea?

Father. No fisherman wants windows to the sea.

Mother. The sea is their enemy.

Kino. Mother, how can you say so? Jiya's father catches fish from the sea and that is how their family lives.

Father. Do not argue with your mother. Ask Jiya your question. See what he says.

Kino. Then may I go?

Father. Go.

[*Dissolve to: A sandy strip of seashore at the foot of the mountain. A few cottages stand there.*

Dissolve to: A tall slender boy, Jiya. *He stands at the edge of the sea, looking up the mountain.*]

Jiya (*calling through his hands*). Kino!

Kino. Coming!

[*He is running and catches* Jiya's *outstretched hand, so that they nearly fall down. They laugh and throw off their jackets.*]

Kino. Wait—I am out of breath. I ate too much.

Jiya (*looking up the mountain*). There's Old Gentleman standing at the gate of his castle.

Kino. He is watching to see whether we are going into the sea.

Jiya. He's always looking at the sea—at dawn, at sunset.

[*Dissolve to: Old Gentleman, standing on a rock, in front of his castle, halfway up the mountain. The wind is blowing his beard. He wears the garments of an aristocrat. Withdraw the cameras to the beach again.*]

Jiya. He is afraid of the sea—always watching!

Kino. Have you ever been in his castle?

Jiya. Only once. Such beautiful gardens—like a dream in a fairy tale. The old pines are bent with the wind, and under them the moss is deep and green and so smooth. Every day men sweep the moss with brooms.

Kino. Why does he keep looking at the sea?

Jiya. He is afraid of it, I tell you.

Kino. Why?

Jiya. The sea is our enemy. We all know it.

Kino. Oh, how can you say it? When we have so much fun——

Jiya. It is our enemy. . . .

Kino. Not mine—let's swim to the island!

Jiya. No. I must find clams for my mother.

Kino. Then let's swim to the sand bar. There are millions of clams there!

Jiya. But the tide is ready to turn. . . .

Kino. It's slow—we'll have time.

[*They plunge into the sea and swim to the sand bar.* Jiya *has a small, short-handled hoe hanging from his* girdle. *He digs into the sand.* Kino *kneels to help him. But* Jiya *digs only for a moment; then he pauses to look out over the sea.*]

Kino. What are you looking for?

Jiya. To see if the sea is angry with us.

Kino (*laughing*). Silly—the sea can't be angry with people!

Jiya. Down there, a mile down, the old sea god lives alone. When he is angry he heaves and rolls, and the waves rush back and forth. Then he gets up and he stamps his feet, and earth shakes at the bottom of the sea. . . . I wish I were a farmer's son, like you. . . .

Kino. And I wish I were a fisherman's son. It is stupid to plow and plant and cut sheaves, when I could just sit in a boat and reap fish from the sea!

Jiya. The earth is safe.

Kino. When the volcano is angry the earth shakes, too.

Jiya. The angry earth helps the angry sea.

Kino. They work together.

Jiya. But fire comes out of the volcano.

[*Meanwhile, the tide is coming in and swirls about their feet.*]

Jiya (*noticing*). Oh—we have not half-enough clams. . . .

[*They fall to digging frantically.*

    Dissolve to: *The empty seashore and the tide rushing in. A man paces the sand at the water's edge. He wears shorts and a fisherman's jacket, open over his bare breast. It is* Jiya's Father. *He calls, his hands cupped at his mouth.*]

Jiya's Father. Ji—ya!

[*There is only the sound of the surf. He wades into the water, still calling. Suddenly he sees the boys, their heads out of water, swimming, and he beckons*

fiercely. *They come in, and he gives a hand to each and pulls them out of the surf.*]

Jiya's Father. Jiya! You have never been so late before!

Jiya. Father, we were on the sand bar, digging clams. We had to leave them.

Jiya's Father (*shaking his shoulder*). Never be so late!

Kino (*wondering*). You are afraid of the sea, too.

Jiya's Father. Go home, farmer's son! Your mother is calling you.

[*In the distance a woman's voice is calling* Kino's *name. He hears and runs toward the mountain.*]

Jiya. Father, I have made you angry.

Jiya's Father. I am not angry.

Jiya. Then why do you seem angry?

Jiya's Father. Old Gentleman sent down word that a storm is rising behind the horizon. He sees the cloud through his great telescope.

Jiya. Father, why do you let Old Gentleman make you afraid? Just because he is rich and lives in a castle, everybody listens to him.

Jiya's Father. Not because he is rich—not because he lives in the castle, but because he is old and wise and he knows the sea. He doesn't want anybody to die. (*He looks over the sea, and his arm tightens about his son, and he mutters as though to himself.*) Though all must die . . .

Jiya. Why must all die, Father?

Jiya's Father. Who knows? Simply, it is so.

[*They stand, looking over the sea.*]

Act Two

Open on: *The Japanese scene of sea and mountainside, with Fuji in the distance, as in Act One.*

Narrator. Yet there was much in life to enjoy. Kino had a good time every day. In the winter he went to school in the fishing village, and he and Jiya shared a bench and a writing table. They studied reading and arithmetic and learned what all children must learn in school. But in summer Kino had to work hard on the farm. Even Setsu and the mother had to help when the rice seedlings were planted in the watery terraced fields. On those days Kino could not run down the mountainside to find Jiya. When the day was ended he was so tired he fell asleep over his supper.

There were days when Jiya, too, could not play. Schools of fish came into the channel between the shore and the island, and early in the morning Jiya and his father sailed their boats out to sea to cast their nets at dawn. If they were lucky, their nets came up so heavy with fish that it took all their strength to haul them in, and soon the bottom of the boat was flashing and sparkling with wriggling fish.

Sometimes, if it were not seedtime or harvest, Kino went with Jiya and his father. It was exciting to get up in the night and put on his warm padded jacket; for even in summer the wind was cool over the sea at dawn. However early he got up, his mother was up even earlier to give him a bowl of hot rice soup and some bean curd[1] and tea before he went. She packed for him a lunch in a clean little wooden box— cold rice and fish and a radish pickle. Down the stone steps of the mountain path, Kino ran straight to the narrow dock where the fishing boats bobbed up and down with the tide. Jiya and his father were already there, and in a few minutes their boat was nosing its way past the sand bar toward the open sea. Sails set and filling with wind, they sped straight into the dawnlit horizon. Kino crouched down in the bow, and his heart rose with joy and excitement. It was like flying into the sky. The winds were so mild, the sea lay so calm and blue, that

1. **bean curd:** a soft cheese made from soybeans.

it was hard to believe it could be cruel and angry. Actually it was the earth that brought the big wave.

One day, as Kino helped his father plant turnips, a cloud came over the sun.

[Dissolve to: *A field, and* Kino *and his* Father. *The volcano is in the background.*]

Kino. Look, Father, the volcano is burning again!
Father (*straightens and gazes anxiously at the sky*). It looks very angry. I shall not sleep tonight. We must hurry home.
Kino. Why should the volcano be angry, Father?
Father. Who knows? Simply, the inner fire burns. Come—make haste.

[*They gather their tools.*
Dissolve to: *Night. The threshing floor outside the farmhouse.* Kino's Father *sits on a bench outside the door. He gets up and walks to and fro and gazes at the red sky above the volcano. The* Mother *comes to the door.*]

Mother. Can you put out the volcano fire by not sleeping?
Father. Look at the fishing village! Every house is lit. And the lamps are lit in the castle. Shall I sleep like a fool?
Mother (*silent, troubled, watching him*). I have taken the dishes from the shelves and put away our good clothes in boxes.
Father (*gazing down at the village*). If only I knew whether it would be earth or sea! Both work evil together. The fires rage under the sea, the rocks boil. The volcano is the vent unless the sea bottom breaks.
Kino (*coming to the door*). Shall we have an earthquake, Father?
Father. I cannot tell.

Mother. How still it is! There's no wind. The sea is purple.

Kino. Why is the sea such a color?

Father. Sea mirrors sky. Sea and earth and sky—if they work against man, who can live?

Kino (*coming to his* Father's *side*). Where are the gods? Do they forget us?

Father. There are times when the gods leave men alone. They test us to see how able we are to save ourselves.

Kino. What if we are not able?

Father. We must be able. Fear makes us weak. If you are afraid, your hands tremble, your feet falter. Brain cannot tell hands what to do.

Setsu (*her voice calling from inside the house*). Mother, I'm afraid!

Mother. I am coming! (*She goes away.*)

Father. The sky is growing black. Go into the house, Kino.

Kino. Let me stay with you.

Father. The red flag is flying over the castle. Twice I've seen that red flag go up, both times before you were born. Old Gentleman wants everybody to be ready.

Kino (*frightened*). Ready for what?

Father. For whatever must be.

[*A deep-toned bell tolls over the mountainside.*]

Kino. What is that bell? I've never heard it before.

Father. It rang twice before you were born. It is the bell inside Old Gentleman's temple. He is calling to the people to come up out of the village and shelter within his walls.

Kino. Will they come?

Father. Not all of them. Parents will try to make their children go, but the children will not want to leave their parents. Mothers will not want to leave fathers, and the fathers will stay by the boats. But some will want to be sure of life.

[*The bell continues to ring urgently. Soon from the village comes a straggling line of people, nearly all of them children.*]

Kino (*gazing at them*). I wish Jiya would come. (*He takes off his white cloth girdle and waves it.*)

[Dissolve to: Jiya *and his* Father *by their house. Sea in the background, roaring.*]

Jiya's Father. Jiya, you must go to the castle.

Jiya. I won't leave you . . . and Mother.

Jiya's Father. We must divide ourselves. If we die, you must live after us.

Jiya. I don't want to live alone.

Jiya's Father. It's your duty to obey me, as a good Japanese son.

Jiya. Let me go to Kino's house.

Jiya's Father. Only go . . . go quickly.

[Jiya *and his* Father *embrace fiercely, and* Jiya *runs away, crying, to leap up the mountainside.*

Dissolve to: *Terrace and farmhouse, and center on* Kino *and his* Father, *who put out their hands to help* Jiya *up the last terrace. Suddenly* Kino *screams.*]

Kino. Look . . . look at the sea!

Father. May the gods save us.

[*The bell begins to toll, deep, pleading, incessant.*]

Jiya (*shrieking*). I must go back. . . . I must tell my father. . . .

Father (*holding him*). It is too late. . . .

[Dissolve to: *The sea rushes up in a terrible wave and swallows the shore. The water roars about the foot of the mountain.* Jiya, *held by* Kino *and his* Father, *stares transfixed, and then sinks unconscious to the ground. The bell tolls on.*]

The Hollow of the Deep-Sea Wave by Katsushika Hokusai.

Act Three

Narrator. So the big wave came, swelling out of the sea. It lifted the horizon while the people watched. The air was filled with its roar and shout. It rushed over the flat, still waters of the sea; it reached the village and covered it fathoms deep in swirling, wild water—green, laced with fierce white foam. The wave ran up the mountainside until the knoll upon which the castle stood was an island. All who were still climbing the path were swept away, mere tossing scraps in the wicked waters. Then with a great sucking sigh, the wave ebbed into the sea, dragging everything with it—trees, rocks, houses, people. Once again it swept over the village, and once again returned to the sea, subsiding, sinking into great stillness.

Upon the beach, where the village had stood, not a house remained, no wreckage of

The Big Wave   **363**

wood or fallen stone wall, no street of little shops, no docks, not a single boat. The beach was as clean of houses as if no human beings had ever lived there. All that had been was now no more.

[Dissolve to: *Inside the farmhouse. The farm family is gathered about the mattress on which* Jiya *lies.*]

Mother. This is not sleep. . . . Is it death?
Father. Jiya is not dead. His soul has withdrawn for a time. He is unconscious. Let him remain so until his own will wakes him.
Mother (*rubbing* Jiya's *hands and feet*). Kino, do not cry.

[Kino *cannot stop crying, though silently.*]

Father. Let him cry. Tears comfort the heart. (*He feels* Kino's *hands and cheeks.*) He is cold. Heat a little rice soup for him and put some ginger in it. I will stay with Jiya.

[Mother *goes out.* Setsu *comes in, rubbing her eyes and yawning.*]

Father. Sleepy eyes! You have slept all through the storm. Wise one!
Setsu (*coming to stare at* Jiya). Is Jiya dead?
Father. No, Jiya is living.
Setsu. Why doesn't he open his eyes?
Father. Soon he will open his eyes.
Setsu. If Jiya is not dead, why does Kino stand there crying?
Father. As usual, you are asking too many questions. Go back to the kitchen and help your mother.

[Setsu *goes out, staring and sucking her finger.* Father *puts his arm around* Kino.]

Father. The first sorrow is always the hardest to bear.

Kino. What will we say to Jiya when he wakes? How can we tell him?
Father. We will not talk. We will give him warm food and let him rest. We will help him to feel he still has a home.
Kino. Here?
Father. Here. I have always wanted another son, and Jiya will be that son. As soon as he knows this is his home, we must help him to understand what has happened. Ah, here is Mother, with your hot rice soup. Eat it, my son—food for the body is food, too, for the heart, sometimes.

[Kino *takes the bowl from his* Mother *with both hands and drinks. The parents look at each other and at him, sorrowfully and tenderly.* Setsu *comes in and leans her head against her* Mother.

Dissolve to: *Evening. The same room, the same scene except that* Mother *and* Setsu *are not there.* Father *sits beside* Jiya's *bed.* Kino *is at the open door.*]

Kino. The sky is golden, Father, and the sea is smooth. How cruel——
Father. No, it is wonderful that after the storm the sea grows calm again, and the sky is clear. It was not the sea or the sky that made the evil storm.
Kino (*not turning his head*). Who made it?
Father. Ah, no one knows who makes evil storms. (*He takes* Jiya's *hand and rubs it gently.*) We only know that they come. When they come we must live through them as bravely as we can, and after they are gone we must feel again how wonderful is life. Every day of life is more valuable now than it was before the storm.
Kino. But Jiya's father and mother . . . and the other fisherfolk . . . so good and kind . . . all of them . . . lost. (*He cannot go on.*)
Father. We must think of Jiya—who lives. (*He stops.* Jiya *has begun to sob softly in his unconsciousness.*) Quick, Kino—call your mother and

Setsu. He will open his eyes at any moment, and we must all be here—you to be his brother, I his father, and the mother, the sister. . . .

[Kino *runs out.* Father *kneels beside* Jiya, *who stirs, still sobbing.* Kino *comes back with* Mother *and* Setsu. *They kneel on the floor beside the bed.* Jiya's *eyelids flutter. He opens his eyes and looks from one face to the other. He stares at the beams of the roof, the walls of the room, the bed, his own hands. All are quiet except* Setsu, *who cannot keep from laughing. She claps her hands.*]

Setsu. Oh, Jiya has come back. Jiya, did you have a good dream?
Jiya (*faintly*). My father, my mother . . .
Mother (*taking his hand in both hers*). I will be your mother now, dear Jiya.
Father. I will be your father.
Kino. I am your brother now, Jiya. (*He falters.*)
Setsu (*joyfully*). Oh, Jiya, you will live with us.

[Jiya *gets up slowly. He walks to the door, goes out, and looks down the hillside.*

Dissolve to: *The peaceful empty beach. Then back to the farmhouse and* Jiya, *standing outside and looking at the sea.* Setsu *comes to him.*]

Setsu. I will give you my pet duck. He'll follow you—he'll make you laugh.
Mother (*leaving the room*). We ought all to eat something, I have a fine chicken for dinner.
Kino (*coming to* Jiya). Mother makes such good chicken soup.
Setsu. I'm hungry, I tell you.
Father. Come, Jiya, my son.

[Jiya *still stands dazed.*]

Kino. Eat with us, Jiya.
Jiya. I am tired . . . very tired.
Kino. You have been sleeping so long.

Jiya (*slowly*). I shall never see them again. (*He puts his hands over his eyes.*) I shall keep thinking about them . . . floating in the sea.
Mother (*coming in*). Drink this bowl of soup at least, Jiya, my son.

[Jiya *drinks and lets the bowl fall. It is wooden and does not break.*]

Jiya. I want to sleep.
Father. Sleep, my son. Sleep is good for you. (*He leads* Jiya *to the bed and covers him with the quilt. To them all*) Jiya is not yet ready to live. We must wait.
Kino. Will he die?
Father. Life is stronger than death. He will live.

Act Four

Narrator. The body heals first, and the body heals the mind and the soul. Jiya ate food, he got out of bed sometimes, but he was still tired. He did not want to think or remember. He only wanted to sleep. He woke to eat, and then he went to sleep again. In the quiet, clean room Jiya slept, and the mother spread the quilt over him and closed the door and went away.

All through these days Kino did not play about as once he had. He was no longer a child. He worked hard beside his father in the fields. They did not talk much, and neither of them wanted to look at the sea. It was enough to look at the earth, dark and rich beneath their feet.

One evening Kino climbed the mountain behind the house and looked up at the volcano. The heavy cloud of smoke had gone away, and the sky was clear. He was glad that the volcano was no longer angry, and he went down again to the house. On the threshold his father was smoking his usual evening pipe. In the house his mother was giving Setsu her evening bath.

Kino (*dropping down on the bench beside his* Father). Is Jiya asleep again?

Father. Yes, and it is a good thing for him. When he sleeps enough, he will wake and remember.

Kino. But should he remember?

Father. Only when he dares to remember his parents will he be happy again.

[*A silence.*]

Kino. Father, are we not very unfortunate people to live in Japan?

Father. Why do you think so?

Kino. The volcano is behind our house, and the sea is in front. When they work together to make earthquake and big wave, we are helpless. Always, many of us are lost.

Father. To live in the presence of death makes us brave and strong. That is why our people never fear death. We see it too often, and we do not fear it. To die a little sooner or a little later does not matter. But to live bravely, to love life, to see how beautiful the trees are and the mountains—yes, and even the sea—to enjoy work because it produces food—in these we are fortunate people. We love life because we live in danger. We do not fear death, for we understand that death and life are necessary to each other.

Kino. What is death?

Father. Death is the great gateway.

Kino. The gateway . . . where?

Father. Can you remember when you were born?

Kino. I was too small.

Father (*smiling*). I remember very well. Oh, how hard you thought it was to be born. You cried and you screamed.

Kino (*much interested*). Didn't I want to be born?

Father. You did not. You wanted to stay just where you were, in the warm dark house of the unborn. But the time came to be born, and the gate of life opened.

Kino. Did I know it was the gate of life?

Father. You did not know anything about it, and so you were afraid. But see how foolish you were! Here we were waiting for you, your parents, already loving you and eager to welcome you. And you have been very happy, haven't you?

Kino. Until the big wave came. Now I am afraid again because of the death the big wave brought.

Father. You are only afraid because you don't know anything about death. But someday you will wonder why you were afraid, even as today you wonder why you once feared to be born.

Kino. I think I understand. . . . I begin to understand. . . .

Father. Do not hurry yourself. You have plenty of time. (*He rises to his feet.*) Now what do I see? A lantern coming up the hill.

Kino (*running to the edge of the threshold*). Who can be coming now? It is almost night.

Father. A visitor . . . ah, why, it's Old Gentleman!

[Old Gentleman *indeed is climbing the hill. He is somewhat breathless in spite of his long staff. His* Manservant *carries the lantern and, when they arrive, steps to one side.*]

Old Gentleman (*to* Manservant). Is this the house of Uchiyama, the farmer?

Manservant. It is—and this is the farmer himself and his son.

Father (*bowing deeply*). Please, Honored Sir, what can I do for you?

Old Gentleman. Do you have a lad here by the name of Jiya?

Father. He lies sleeping in my house.

Old Gentleman. I wish to see him.

Father. Sir, he suffered the loss of his parents

when the big wave came. Now sleep heals him.

Old Gentleman. I will not wake him. I only wish to look at him.

Father. Please come in.

[Dissolve to: Jiya *asleep. The* Manservant *holds the lantern so that the light does not fall on* Jiya's *face directly.* Old Gentleman *looks at him carefully.*]

Old Gentleman. Tall and strong for his age—intelligent—handsome. Hmm . . . yes. (*He motions to the* Manservant *to lead him away, and the scene returns to the dooryard. To* Father) It is my habit, when the big wave comes, to care for those who are orphaned by it. Thrice in my lifetime I have searched out the orphans, and I have fed them and sheltered them. But I have heard of this boy Jiya and wish to do more for him. If he is as good as he is handsome, I will take him for my own son.

Kino. But Jiya is ours!

Father (*sternly*). Hush. We are only poor people. If Old Gentleman wants Jiya, we cannot say we will not give him up.

Old Gentleman. Exactly. I will give him fine clothes and send him to a school, and he may become a great man and an honor to our whole province and even to the nation.

Kino. But if he lives in the castle we can't be brothers!

Father. We must think of Jiya's good. (*He turns to* Old Gentleman.) Sir, it is very kind of you to propose this for Jiya. I had planned to take him for my own son, now that he has lost his birth parents; but I am only a poor farmer, and I cannot pretend that my house is as good as yours or that I can afford to send Jiya to a fine school. Tomorrow when he wakes I will tell him of your kind offer. He will decide.

Old Gentleman. Very well. But let him come and tell me himself.

Father (*proudly*). Certainly. Jiya must speak for himself.

[Old Gentleman *bows slightly and prepares to depart.* Father *bows deeply and taps* Kino *on the head to make him bow.* Old Gentleman *and his* Manservant *return down the mountain.*]

Kino. If Jiya goes away, I shall never have a brother.

Father. Kino, don't be selfish. You must allow Jiya to make his own choice. It would be wrong to persuade him. I forbid you to speak to him of this matter. When he wakes, I will tell him myself.

Kino (*pleading*). Don't tell him today, Father.

Father. I must tell him as soon as he wakes. It would not be fair to Jiya to let him grow used to thinking of this house as his home. He must make the choice today, before he has time to put down his new roots. Go now, Kino, and weed the lower terrace.

[Dissolve to: Kino *working in the terrace, weeding. It is evident that he has worked for some time. He looks hot and dusty, and he has quite a pile of weeds. He stops to look up at the farmhouse, but he sees no one and resigns himself again to his task. Suddenly his name is called.*]

Father. Kino!

Kino. Shall I come?

Father. No, I am coming—with Jiya.

[Kino *stands, waiting.* Father *and* Jiya *come down the terraces.* Jiya *is very sad. When he sees* Kino, *he tries not to cry.*]

Father (*putting his arm about* Jiya's *shoulder*). Jiya, you must not mind that you cry easily. Until now you couldn't cry because you weren't fully alive. You had been hurt too much. But today you are beginning to live, and so your tears flow. It is good for you. Let your tears come—don't stop them. (*He turns to* Kino.) I have told Jiya that he must not decide where he will live until he has seen the inside of the castle. He must see all that Old Gentleman can give him. Jiya, you know how our house is— four small rooms, and the kitchen, this farm, upon which we have to work hard for our food. We have only what our hands earn for us. (*He holds out his two workworn hands.*) If you live in the castle, you need never have hands like these.

Jiya. I don't want to live in the castle.

Father. You don't know whether you do or not; you have never seen the castle inside. (*He turns to* Kino.) Kino, you are to go with Jiya, and when you reach the castle you must persuade him to stay there for his own sake.

Kino. I will go and wash myself—and put on my good clothes.

Father. No—go as you are. You are a farmer's son.

[Kino *and* Jiya *go, reluctantly, and* Father *stands looking after them.*

   Dissolve to: *The mountainside and the two boys nearing the gate of the castle. The gate is open, and inside an old* Gardener *is sweeping moss under pine trees. He sees them.*]

Gardener. What do you want, boys?

Kino. My father sent us to see the honored Old Gentleman.

Gardener. Are you the Uchiyama boy?

Kino. Yes, please, and this is Jiya, whom Old Gentleman wishes to come and live here.

Gardener (*bowing to* Jiya). Follow me, young sir.

[*They follow over a pebbled path under the leaning pine trees. In the distance the sun falls upon a flowering garden and a pool with a waterfall.*]

Kino (*sadly*). How beautiful it is—of course you will want to live here. Who could blame you?

[Jiya *does not answer. He walks with his head held high. They come to a great door, where a* Manservant *bids them take off their shoes. The* Gardener *leaves them.*]

Manservant. Follow me.

[*They follow through passageways into a great room decorated in the finest Japanese fashion. In the distance at the end of the room, they see* Old Gentleman *sitting beside a small table. Behind him the open panels reveal the garden.* Old Gentleman *is writing. He holds his brush upright in his hand, and he is carefully painting letters on a scroll, his silver-rimmed glasses sliding down his nose. When the two boys approach, the* Manservant *announces them.*]

Manservant. Master, the two boys are here.

Old Gentleman (*to boys*). Would you two like to know what I have been writing?

[Jiya *looks at* Kino, *who is too awed to speak.*]

Jiya. Yes, Honored Sir, if you please.

Old Gentleman (*taking up the scroll*). It is not my own poem. It is the saying of a wise man of India, but I like it so much that I have painted it on this scroll to hang there in the alcove where I can see it every day. (*He reads clearly and slowly.*)

> "The children of God are very dear,
> But very queer—
> Very nice, but very narrow."

(*He looks up over his spectacles.*) What do you think of it?

Jiya (*looking at* Kino, *who is too shy to speak*). We do not understand it, sir.

Old Gentleman (*shaking his head and laughing softly*). Ah, we are all children of God! (*He takes off his spectacles and looks hard at* Jiya.) Well? Will you be my son?

Kuwana: The Mouth of the Seven-League Ferry (c. 1834)
by Ando Hiroshige (1797–1858).

[Jiya, *too embarrassed to speak, bites his lip, looks away, etc.*]

Old Gentleman. Say yes or no. Either word is not hard to speak.

Jiya. I will say . . . no. (*He feels this is too harsh, and he smiles apologetically.*) I thank you, sir, but I have a home . . . on a farm.

Kino (*trying to repress his joy and speaking very solemnly as a consequence*). Jiya, remember how poor we are.

Old Gentleman (*smiling, half sad*). They are certainly very poor and here, you know, you would have everything. You can even invite this farm boy to come and play, sometimes, if you like. And I am quite willing for you to give the family some money. It would be suitable as my son for you to help the poor.

Jiya (*suddenly, as though he had not heard*). Where are the others who were saved from the big wave?

Old Gentleman. Some wanted to go away, and

The Big Wave **369**

the ones who wanted to stay are out in the backyard with my servants.

Jiya. Why do you not invite them to come into this castle and be your sons and daughters?

Old Gentleman (*somewhat outraged by this*). Because I don't want them for my sons and daughters. You are a bright, handsome boy. They told me you were the best boy in the village.

Jiya. I am not better than the others. My father was a fisherman.

Old Gentleman (*taking up his spectacles and his brush*). Very well—I will do without a son.

[*The* Manservant *motions to the boys to come away, and they follow.*]

Manservant (*to* Jiya). How foolish you are! Our Old Gentleman is very kind. You would have everything here.

Jiya. Not everything . . .

Kino. Let's hurry home—let's hurry—hurry . . .

[*They run down the mountain and up the hill to the farmhouse.* Setsu *sees them and comes flying to meet them, the sleeves of her bright kimono like wings, and her feet clattering in their wooden sandals.*]

Setsu. Jiya has come home—Jiya, Jiya . . .

[Jiya *sees her happy face and opens his arms and gives her a great hug.*]

Act Five

Narrator. Now happiness began to live in Jiya, though secretly and hidden inside him, in ways he did not understand. The good food warmed him, and his body welcomed it. Around him the love of the four people who received him for their own glowed like a warm and welcoming fire upon his heart.

Time passed. Eight years. Jiya grew up in the farmhouse to be a tall young man, and Kino grew at his side, solid and strong, but never as tall as Jiya. Setsu grew, too, from a mischievous laughing child into a gay, willful, pretty girl. But time, however long, was split in two parts, the time before and the time after the big wave. The big wave had changed everybody's life.

In all these years no one returned to live on the empty beach. The tides rose and fell, sweeping the sands clear every day. Storms came and went, but there was never such a wave as the big one. At last people began to think that never again would there be such a big wave. The few fishermen who had listened to the tolling bell from the castle, and were saved with their wives and children, went to other shores to fish, and they made new fishing boats. Then, as time passed, they told themselves that no beach was quite as good as the old one. There, they said, the water was deep and great fish came close to the shore. They did not need to go far out to sea to find the booty.

Jiya and Kino had not often gone to the beach, either. At first they had walked along the empty sands where once the street had been, and Jiya searched for some keepsake from his home that the sea might have washed back to the shore. But nothing was ever found. So the two boys, as they grew to be young men, did not visit the deserted beach. When they went to swim in the sea, they walked across the farm and over another fold of the mountains to the shore.

Yet Jiya had never forgotten his father and mother. He thought of them every day, their faces, their voices, the way his father talked, his mother's smile. The big wave had changed him forever. He did not laugh easily or speak carelessly. In school he had earnestly learned all he could, and now he worked hard on the farm. Now, as a man, he valued deeply everything that was good. Since the big wave had been so cruel, he was never cruel, and he grew kind and gentle. Jiya never spoke of his loneliness. He did not want others to be sad because of his sadness. When he laughed at some mischief of Setsu's, when she teased him, his laughter was wonderful to hear because it was whole and real. And sometimes, in the morning, he went to the door of the farmhouse and looked at the empty beach below, searching with his eyes as though something might one day come back. One day he did see something. . . .

Jiya. Kino, come here! (Kino *comes out, his shoes in his hand.*) Look—is someone building a house on the beach?
Kino. Two men—pounding posts into the sand——
Jiya. And a woman . . . yes, and even a child.
Kino. They can't be building a house.
Jiya. Let's go and see.

[Dissolve to: *The beach. The two* Men, Jiya *and* Kino, Woman *and* Child.]

Jiya (*out of breath*). Are you building a house?
First Man (*wiping sweat from his face*). Our father used to live here, and we with him. We are two brothers. During these years we have lived in the houses of the castle, and we have fished from other shores. Now we are tired of having no homes of our own. Besides, this is still the best beach for fishing.
Kino. What if the big wave comes again?
Second Man (*shrugging his shoulders*). There was a big wave, too, in our great-grandfather's time. All the houses were swept away. But our grandfather came back. In our father's time there was again the big wave. Now we return.
Kino (*soberly*). What of your children?
First Man. The big wave may never come back.

[*The* Men *begin to dig again. The* Woman *takes the* Child *into her arms and gazes out to sea. Suddenly there is a sound of a voice calling. All look up the mountain.*]

First Man. Here comes our Old Gentleman.
Second Man. He's very angry or he wouldn't have left the castle.

[*Both throw down their shovels and stand waiting. The* Woman *sinks to a kneeling position on the sand, still holding the* Child. Old Gentleman *shouts as he comes near, his voice high and thin. He is very old now, and is supported by two* Menservants. *His beard flies in the wind.*]

Old Gentleman. You foolish children! You leave the safety of my walls and come back to this dangerous shore, as your father did before you! The big wave will return and sweep you into the sea.
First Man. It may not, Ancient Sir.
Old Gentleman. It will come. I have spent my whole life trying to save foolish people from the big wave. But you will not be saved.
Jiya (*stepping forward*). Sir, here is our home. Dangerous as it is, threatened by the volcano and by the sea, it is here we were born.
Old Gentleman (*looking at him*). Don't I know you?
Jiya. Sir, I was once in your castle.
Old Gentleman (*nodding*). I remember you. I wanted you for my son. Ah, you made a great mistake, young man. You could have lived safely in my castle all your life, and your children would have been safe there. The big wave never reaches me.
Kino. Sir, your castle is not safe, either. If the earth shakes hard enough, even your castle will crumble. There is no refuge for us who live on these islands. We are brave because we must be.
Second Man. Ha—you are right.

[*The two* Men *return to their building.*]

Old Gentleman (*rolling his eyes and wagging his beard*). Don't ask me to save you the next time the big wave comes!

Jiya (*gently*). But you will save us, because you are so good.

Old Gentleman (*looking at him and then smiling sadly*). What a pity you would not be my son! (*He turns and, leaning on his* Menservants, *climbs the mountain.*)

[Dissolve to: *His arrival at the castle gate. He enters, and the gates clang shut.*

Dissolve to: *The field, where* Father *and* Jiya *and* Kino *are working.*]

Father (*to* Jiya). Did you soak the seeds for the rice?

Jiya (*aghast*). I forgot.

Kino. I did it.

Jiya (*throwing down his hoe*). I forget everything these days.

Father. I know you are too good a son to be forgetful on purpose. Tell me what is on your mind.

Jiya. I want a boat. I want to go back to fishing.

[Father *does not pause in his hoeing; but* Kino *flings down his hoe.*]

Kino. You, too, are foolish!

Jiya (*stubbornly*). When I have a boat, I shall build my house on the beach.

Kino. Oh, fool, fool!

Father. Be quiet! Jiya is a man. You are both men. I shall pay you wages from this day.

Jiya. Wages! (*He falls to hoeing vigorously.*)

[Dissolve to: *The beach, where* Kino *and* Jiya *are inspecting a boat.*]

Jiya. I knew all the time that I had to come back to the sea.

Kino. With this boat, you'll soon earn enough to build a house. But I'm glad I live on the mountain.

[*They continue inspecting the boat, fitting the oars, etc., as they talk.*]

Jiya (*abruptly*). Do you think Setsu would be afraid to live on the beach?

Kino (*surprised*). Why would Setsu live on the beach?

Jiya (*embarrassed but determined*). Because when I have my house built, I want Setsu to be my wife.

Kino (*astonished*). Setsu? You would be foolish to marry her.

Jiya (*smiling*). I don't agree with you.

Kino (*seriously*). But why . . . why do you want her?

Jiya. Because she makes me laugh. It is she who made me forget the big wave. For me, she is life.

Kino. But she is not a good cook. Think how she burns the rice when she runs outside to look at something.

Jiya. I don't mind burned rice, and I will run out with her to see what she sees.

Kino (*with all the gestures of astonishment and disbelief*). I can't understand. . . .

[Dissolve to: *The farmhouse, and* Father, *who is looking over his seeds.*]

Kino (*coming in stealthily*). Do you know that Jiya wants to marry Setsu?

Father. I have seen some looks pass between them.

Kino. But Jiya is too good for Setsu.

Father. Setsu is very pretty.

Kino. With that silly nose?

Father (*calmly*). I believe that Jiya admires her nose.

Kino. Besides, she is such a tease.

Father. What makes you miserable will make him happy.

Kino. I don't understand that, either.

Father (*laughing*). Someday you will understand.

[Dissolve to: Narrator.]

Narrator. One day, one early summer, Jiya and Setsu were married. Kino still did not understand, for up to the last, Setsu was naughty and mischievous. Indeed on the very day of her wedding she hid Kino's hairbrush under his bed. "You are too silly to be married," Kino said, when he had found it. "I feel sorry for Jiya," he said. Setsu's big brown eyes laughed at him, and she stuck out her red tongue. "I shall always be nice to Jiya," she said.

But when the wedding was over and the family had taken the newly married pair down the hill to the new house on the beach, Kino felt sad. The farmhouse was very quiet without Setsu. Already he missed her. Every day he could go to see Jiya, and many times he would go fishing with him. But Setsu would not be in the farmhouse kitchen, in the rooms, in the garden. He would miss even her teasing. And then he grew very grave indeed. What if the big wave came again?

[Dissolve to: *The new house.* Kino, Jiya, Father, Mother, *and* Setsu *are standing outside.* Kino *turns to* Jiya.]

Kino. Jiya, it is all very pretty—very nice. But, Setsu—what if the big wave comes again?

Jiya. I have prepared for that. Come—all of you. (*He calls the family in.*) This is where we will sleep at night, and where we will live by day. But look——

[*The family stands watching, and* Jiya *pushes back a long panel in the wall. Before their eyes is the sea,* swelling and stirring under the evening wind. The sun is sinking into the water.]

Jiya. I have opened my house to the sea. If ever the big wave comes back, I shall be ready. I face it, night and day. I am not afraid.

Kino. Tomorrow I'll go fishing with you, Jiya—shall I?

Jiya (*laughing*). Not tomorrow, brother!

Father. Come—come! (Setsu *comes to his side and leans against him, and he puts his arm about her.*) Yes, life is stronger than death. (*He turns to his family.*) Come, let us go home.

[Father *and* Mother *and* Kino *bow and leave.* Jiya *and* Setsu *stand looking out to sea.*]

Jiya. Life is stronger than death—do you hear that, Setsu?

Setsu. Yes, I hear.

Reading Check

1. Why does Old Gentleman keep looking at the sea?
2. What does the red flag signify?
3. Why does Old Gentleman have the bell in the temple rung?
4. Where does Jiya live after his home is destroyed?
5. Why do people return to the shore and begin building houses there?

The Big Wave **373**

For Study and Discussion

Analyzing and Interpreting the Play

1. The characters in this play depend upon the land and the sea for their livelihood. How are they threatened by these natural elements?

2. Before the tidal wave strikes, what warnings are there of the coming disaster?

3. Old Gentleman wants to adopt Jiya as his son. Why does Jiya choose to live with Kino and his family?

4. The statement "Life is stronger than death" occurs several times in the play. How does Jiya's decision to return to the beach prove his faith in this statement?

5. In Act One, Jiya says, "The sea is our enemy." Why, then, does Jiya open his house to the sea at the end of the play?

6. In a play, as in a short story, there is conflict. **a.** How would you describe Jiya's conflict? **b.** How does he resolve this conflict?

7. How is the Narrator in this play like the narrator in a short story or novel?

Language and Vocabulary

Recognizing Formal Speech

Good dialogue can be natural; that is, it can sound like everyday speech. Good dialogue can also be formal. Pearl Buck uses formal speech for the characters in *The Big Wave*. The dialogue contains almost no contractions, no slang, and few broken thoughts.

> **Kino.** Father, are we not very unfortunate people to live in Japan?
> **Father.** Why do you think so?
> **Kino.** The volcano is behind our house, and the sea is in front. When they work together to make earthquake and big wave, we are helpless. Always, many of us are lost.
> **Father.** To live in the presence of death makes us brave and strong. That is why our people never fear death. We see it too often, and we do not fear it. To die a little sooner or a little later does not matter. But to live bravely, to love life, to see how beautiful the trees are and the mountains—yes, and even the sea—to enjoy work because it produces food—in these we are fortunate people. We love life because we live in danger. We do not fear death, for we understand that death and life are necessary to each other.
> **Kino.** What is death?
> **Father.** Death is the great gateway.

This language has the effect of making the action of the play seem distant, timeless, and foreign. Father and Old Gentleman make thoughtful statements about the meaning of life. Formal speech is more appropriate for these statements than everyday speech would be. The language helps us understand and appreciate the deeper meanings of the characters' experiences.

Find another passage that illustrates the characteristics of formal speech.

For Dramatization

Assembling a Director's Notebook

Suppose you were asked to direct *The Big Wave*. You would have to make many decisions about how to film the play for a television audience. Read through the play again, scene by scene, and jot down what you might need under the following headings:

Sets. How many separate sets would you need? Could you use a travel poster for the opening view of Japan, with Mount Fuji in the background? How realistic would you want your sets to be? If you were working on a low budget, could any of the sets be combined? What furniture would you need?

Costumes. Some costumes are specified in the stage directions: kimonos, fishermen's jackets, shorts. Other costumes are not specified and might need to be researched. What would the aristocratic garments of Old Gentleman look like?

Props. Some props are mentioned: Jiya's clamming hoe, a lantern, Old Gentleman's scroll and brush, soup bowls, and water jars. List others. How would you provide weeds and rice plants if you were filming in a studio?

Lighting. Would lights of different colors help set the mood from moment to moment? How would you light the approach of the storm?

Sound. Would you use a real bell or sounds that have been recorded? How would you create the sounds of the sea?

Staging. Should the Narrator appear on screen? What would you show on camera during the long narrations?

About the Author

Pearl Buck (1892–1973)

Pearl Buck was born in Hillsboro, West Virginia, but spent most of her first sixteen years in Chinkiang, a city on the Yangtse River in China. Her parents, who were missionaries, took her there when she was only three months old. Since she grew up among the Chinese, she learned to speak Chinese before she learned English. Encouraged by her mother, who taught her "the beauty that lies in words and in what words will say," she began writing at an early age.

Her novel *The Good Earth* (1931) brought her international fame. One of the most popular novels of this century, it was adapted for stage and screen and was translated into more than thirty languages. In 1938 she received the Nobel Prize for literature. Before her death at the age of eighty, she filled more than eighty-five novels and collections of short stories with a unique richness. *The Big Wave* is based on a book of the same title, which she wrote after a trip to Japan.

DEVELOPING SKILLS IN CRITICAL THINKING

Understanding Cause-and-Effect Relationships

In literature, a single act can often lead to a chain of events. In *A Sunny Morning* (page 335), two people are brought together by a chance meeting at a park bench. This meeting leads to a series of disclosures about their relationship in the past, the rekindling of emotions, and the start of a new friendship.

In order to develop a short story or a play, a writer depends upon cause-and-effect relationships. Recognizing cause-and-effect relationships helps you to follow the action and to understand characters' *motivations*—the reasons for their actions.

As you read the following passages, note the causes and effects of actions. Answer the questions that follow the passages.

Billy. His health, Dr. Watson. He gets paler, and thinner, and he never eats nothing. I heard Mrs. Hudson asking him when he would take his dinner. "Seven thirty," he told her—*"the day after tomorrow!"*
Watson (*sighs*). Yes, Billy, I know how it is.
Billy (*confidentially*). I can tell you one thing, sir—he's following somebody.
　　　　　　　　　　—*The Mazarin Stone*

Don Gonzalo. And one night, when my cousin waited under her window to hear her sing, this other person presented himself unexpectedly.
Doña Laura. And insulted your cousin.
Don Gonzalo. There was a quarrel.
Doña Laura. And later a duel.
Don Gonzalo. Yes, at sunrise, on the beach, and the merchant was badly wounded. My cousin had to conceal himself for a few days and later to fly.
　　　　　　　　　　—*A Sunny Morning*

---

1. In the first passage, we are told the effect before we are told the cause. What is the effect? What is the cause?
2. In the second passage, we learn that two men meet unexpectedly under the window of a woman in whom they are both interested. What is the effect of that meeting?

PRACTICE IN
READING AND WRITING

Writing a Play

The following dialogue appears in Pearl Buck's play *The Big Wave*. As you read it, put your imagination to work. How should the lines be spoken to show the moods of the characters?

> **Father** (*to* Jiya). Did you soak the seeds for the rice?
> **Jiya** (*aghast*). I forgot.
> **Kino.** I did it.
> **Jiya** (*throwing down his hoe*). I forget everything these days.
> **Father.** I know you are too good a son to be forgetful on purpose. Tell me what is on your mind.
> **Jiya.** I want a boat. I want to go back to fishing.
>
> [Father *does not pause in his hoeing; but* Kino *flings down his hoe.*]
>
> **Kino.** You, too, are foolish!

1. Note the stage directions that tell how speeches are to be spoken and what the players are doing.

What do the stage directions in this brief scene tell you about the characters' feelings and actions?

2. Note clues in the speeches themselves that tell what the players are doing or how their speeches are to be delivered.

Stage directions cannot tell everything, of course. What other actions do you picture the characters carrying out in this scene?

3. Imagine the actions that are not indicated in stage directions or in the speeches.

What expressions do you imagine on the characters' faces?

Suggestions for Writing

Choose one of the stories you have read and adapt it or a portion of it as a play for the stage, for radio, or for television. Turn passages of description and narration into scenes of action with dialogue. You may need to create additional dialogue to make clear what the characters are thinking or feeling.

Choose an episode from history in which the character or characters must deal with a conflict.

Columbus faces the threat of mutiny from his crew.
A colonial family resists the Quartering Act.
Elizabeth Blackwell defies the prejudice of the community against women physicians.
A pioneer family crossing the prairie in a covered wagon becomes separated from their wagon train.

Write a sequel to one of the plays you have read in this unit, inventing additional characters and new situations.

Write a play celebrating a holiday.

Prewriting

- Choose a conflict or problem your characters must face. Every play centers on some kind of dramatic situation.
- Decide on a setting for the play. Where and when will the action take place?
- Choose the characters for the play and decide what they will reveal about themselves, about each other, and about the conflict in their dialogue.
- Decide what stage directions you must include to describe the characters' actions and feelings and the sounds or events occurring around them.

Writing

As you write your play, be sure that the dialogue sounds natural for the characters and that the conflict or problem is clear. Also include a cast of characters and a title for your play.

Evaluating and Revising

Evaluate the draft of your play by answering the following questions. Then revise your draft by adding, cutting, reordering, or replacing words.

- Have you provided a description of the setting that will guide the readers or the actors?
- Have you included stage directions that provide information readers or actors will need to imagine the characters' feelings and actions?
- Does the dialogue sound natural for the characters? Does it tell something about the characters or about the actions in the play?
- Have you included a conflict or problem the characters must face? Is the problem solved in the play?

Proofreading

Reread your revised draft and correct any mistakes in grammar, usage, spelling, and mechanics. Then prepare a final copy. You might enjoy sharing your play with your classmates, perhaps by having a small group act out the parts.

For Further Reading

Aiken, Joan, *The Mooncusser's Daughter* (Viking, 1974)

A mooncusser is a person who deliberately wrecks ships. In this humorous play, a lighthouse keeper, his blind wife, and a ghost try to prevent a gang of thieves from gaining a treasure. *Winterthing* (Holt, Rinehart & Winston, 1972), another play by the same author, is a fantasy (with music and lyrics) about four children and their aunt, who live on Winter Island off the coast of Scotland.

Barrie, James M., *The Boy David* (Samuel French, 1936)

This play, in three acts, is based on the Biblical account of David.

Henshaw, James Ene, *The Jewels of the Shrine,* in *Voices from the Black Experience: African and Afro-American Literature*, edited by Darwin T. Turner, Jean M. Bright, and Richard Wright (Ginn, 1972)

In this folk play from Nigeria, Okorie, a shrewd old man, manages to outwit his selfish grandsons.

Hughes, Ted, *The Tiger's Bones and Other Plays for Children* (Viking, 1974)

Hughes, who is one of the greatest living English poets, has written several plays based on folklore and myth. Included in this collection are *Beauty and the Beast* and *Orpheus.*

Kamerman, Sylvia, E., editor, *Dramatized Folk Tales of the World* (Plays, Inc., 1971)

This is a useful collection for student actors because it contains very short plays based on folk tales from all over the world.

Lamb, Wendy, *Meeting the Winter Bike Rider and Other Prize-Winning Plays* (Dell, 1986)

Here are eight plays by writers aged ten to eighteen from the 1983 and 1984 Young Playwrights Festival.

L'Engle, Madeline, *The Journey with Jonah* (Farrar, Straus & Giroux, 1967)

This is a dramatization of the story of Jonah from the Bible.

Lerner, Alan Jay, *My Fair Lady* (Coward McCann, 1956; paperback, New American Library)

An English professor transforms a flower girl into a genteel lady in this musical comedy based on George Bernard Shaw's *Pygmalion.*

Lipton, Betty Jean, editor, *Contemporary Children's Theater* (Avon, 1974)

The eight plays in this collection represent a variety of forms and approaches: plays based on legend and folk tales, science-fiction plays, and plays in which the audience participates.

Simon, Neil, *A Defenseless Creature,* in *The Good Doctor* (Random House, 1974)

In this comedy, adapted from a story by Anton Chekhov, a woman proves that she is not a "defenseless creature."

Stein, Joseph, *Fiddler on the Roof* (Crown, 1965; paperback, Pocket Books)

Sholom Aleichem's stories of Jewish life in a Russian village in 1905 are the basis of this lively musical drama about Tevye, the milkman, and his family.

Swortzell, Lowell, editor, *All the World's a Stage: Modern Plays for Young People* (Delacorte, 1972)

This collection of twenty-one plays includes *The Genie of Sutton Place,* a TV comedy by Kenneth Heuer and George Selden; *The Man with the Heart in the Highlands* by William Saroyan; *The Post Office* by the Hindu poet Rabindranath Tagore; and *Poem-Plays,* experimental dramas by Ruth Krauss.

Valency, Maurice, *Feathertop,* in *Fifteen American One-Act Plays,* edited by Paul Kozelka (paperback, Washington Square Press, 1961)

In this fantasy, adapted from a story by Nathaniel Hawthorne, a scarecrow is brought to life and then falls in love.

Wilder, Thornton, *The Long Christmas Dinner,* in *The Long Christmas Dinner and Other Plays in One Act* (Harper & Row, 1963; paperback, Avon, 1980)

This play traces the lives of several generations of an American family. *The Happy Journey to Trenton and Camden,* another play about family life, is also in this collection.

NONFICTION

Nonfiction deals with facts, but, like other forms of literature, it appeals to the imagination. In nonfiction, real people are the characters, and real life is the setting.

There are many kinds of nonfiction. Newspaper and magazine articles, biographies and autobiographies, serious and humorous essays, interviews, memoirs, diaries, speeches, letters, and scientific articles all fall into this broad category of literature.

In this unit you will find a naturalist's observations of the schooling of animals, a humorous inventory of dogs with peculiar habits, the story of a rattlesnake hunt in the Everglades, a blind man's account of using facial vision, and recollections of childhood on a Texas ranch.

Metropolitan Tower (1912) by Guy C. Wiggins. Oil on canvas.
The Metropolitan Museum of Art, George A. Hearn Fund

CLOSE READING
OF AN ESSAY

The essay is a literary form that can be adapted to many different purposes. An essay can be informative or instructive; it can be entertaining; it can be persuasive. It is customary to divide essays into two types: *informal* and *formal*. The informal essay is light, personal, and often humorous. The formal essay is serious and impersonal.

When you read an essay, determine the writer's main *purpose*. Is it to give information, to provide entertainment, to offer an explanation, or to influence thinking? Pay close attention to *style*—the way the writer uses language.

The following selection is from *River Notes,* a collection of brief meditations about a mountain river, in which naturalist Barry Holstun Lopez discovers and conveys the beauty of the wilderness. In this entry he captures the awesome destructive power of a storm. As you read, note how he combines specific details with imaginative comparisons. Use the questions in the margin to guide your reading. Then turn to the analysis on page 384.

FROM

River Notes

BARRY HOLSTUN LOPEZ

Thinking Model

A storm came this year, against which all other storms were to be measured, on a Saturday in October, a balmy afternoon. Men in the woods cutting firewood for winter, and children outside with melancholy thoughts lodged somewhere in the memory of summer. It built as it came up the valley as did every fall storm, but the steel-gray

How does the opening sentence prepare you for the power of the storm?

thunderheads,[1] the first sign of it anyone saw, were higher, much higher, too high. In the stillness before it hit, men looked at each other as though a fast and wiry man had pulled a knife in a bar. They felt the trees falling before they heard the wind, and they dropped tools and scrambled to get out. The wind came up suddenly and like a scythe, like piranha[2] after them, like seawater through a breach in a dike. The first blow bent trees half to the ground, the second caught them and snapped them like kindling, sending limbs raining down and twenty-foot splinters hurtling through the air like mortar shells to stick quivering in the ground. Bawling cattle running the fences, a loose lawnmower bumping across a lawn, a stray dog lunging for a child racing by. The big trees went down screaming, ripping open holes in the wind that were filled with the broken-china explosion of a house and the yawing screech of a pickup rubbed across asphalt, the rivet popping and twang of phone and electric wires.

It was over in three or four minutes. The eerie, sucking silence it left behind seemed palpably[3] evil, something that would get into the standing timber, like insects, a memory.

No one was killed. Roads were cut off, a bridge buckled. No power. A few had to walk in from places far off in the steep wooded country, arriving home later than they'd ever been up. Some said it pulled the community together, others how they hated living in the trees with no light. No warning. The next day it rained and the woods smelled like ashes. It was four or five days

How does the author convey the shock effect of the storm?

What three comparisons suggest the terrifying destructiveness of the storm?
What is the effect of the storm on the trees?

How does the writer interpret the silence that follows the storm?

1. **thunderheads:** dense clouds that appear before a thunderstorm.
2. **piranha** (pĭ-rän′yə, -răn′yə): carnivorous fish with very sharp teeth.
3. **palpably** (păl′pə-blē): distinctly, as of something that can be touched or felt.

before they got the roads opened and the phones working, electricity back. Three sent down to the hospital in Holterville. Among the dead, Cawley Besson's dog. And two deer, butchered and passed quietly in parts among neighbors.

Of the trees that fell into the river, a number came up like beached whales among willows at the tip of an island.

What makes the final image effective?

Analysis

Lopez conveys the character of a storm unusual in its approach and destructive fury. Through precise details and through imaginative comparisons, he helps us experience one of nature's most awesome and brutal forces.

The storm is unannounced. It catches people off guard as they are preparing for the change of seasons. The thunderclouds, which should be a warning sign, are much too high. In the first of several arresting comparisons, Lopez tells us that the shock effect is like that of seeing someone suddenly draw a knife out of concealment. The men cutting firewood are forced to drop their tools and flee as the wind begins knocking over trees.

Lopez suggests the sharp, cutting power of the wind by comparing it to a scythe, a tool with a long blade used in cutting grass, and to piranha, fish with razor-sharp teeth, known for attacking animals, including human beings. He suggests the uncontrollable force of the wind by comparing it to the flood of seawater through an opening in a dike. The noises are terrible: the bawling of cattle, the explosion of broken china, the screech of a pickup truck rubbing across asphalt, the popping of bolts and twang of wires.

Our greatest sympathy is evoked for the trees that fall helplessly before the murderous wind. Lopez uses the imagery of war to describe the assault on the trees. Their limbs are torn off and sent flying through the air "like mortar shells" that become embedded in the ground. As the trees topple, they rip open holes in the wind. When the storm has ended, its presence is still felt, not only in the damage to property and in the inconvenience of being without power. Lopez says that the storm leaves behind an evil memory that is retained by the trees. Even the rain on the following day does not wash it away: the woods smell like ashes, as if the trees had been burned. The most poignant image in the essay appears at its close. The trees uprooted by the wind and cast into the river are washed ashore like beached whales.

Guidelines for Reading an Essay

1. *Determine the tone of the essay.* A formal essay is serious in tone and generally objective. An informal essay, like that by Lopez, is told from a personal point of view.

2. *Determine the purpose of the essay.* The purpose may be to inform, to entertain, to explain, to persuade, or some combination of these objectives. Lopez is chiefly interested in explaining what he himself experienced and communicating his impressions to the reader.

3. *Pay close attention to style.* Writers make use of different kinds of writing: *description,* to give a picture and to communicate sensory impressions; *narration,* to relate a series of events; *exposition,* to present information; and *persuasion,* to influence the reader's ideas. As Lopez demonstrates, nonfiction writers make imaginative use of language.

4. *State the main idea of the essay.* The main idea is not always expressed directly, but may be implied. Look for the single idea that gives focus to the essay. Lopez begins his essay by saying the storm became the basis against which all other storms would be measured. He then goes on to demonstrate that this assertion is true, that the storm was exceptionally powerful and destructive.

Animals Go to School

EDWIN WAY TEALE

Teale's essay is primarily instructive. His purpose is to share information, but you will find his observations entertaining as well. What is the main idea that emerges from this essay?

Loons are calling in the late-summer dusk on this lonely Adirondack lake.[1] At night I hear the cry of the great horned owl. Swallows—cliff and tree—have moved down from the north at the start of their long migration. Each evening, in my cabin backed by dark forests that go up and up to the very top of a mountain, I light a kerosene lamp and in its yellow glow set down the events of the day. Sitting here, this evening, while the last light has flowed westward out of the sky, I have been remembering an occurrence of the afternoon, a little adventure in Nature's summer school.

1. **Adirondack** (ăd′ə-rŏn′dăk′) **lake:** lake in the Adirondack Mountains, a branch of the Appalachian Mountains in northeast New York State.

I was coming slowly down a trail so thick with moss that it deadened my footfalls like a plush rug. The only sound that I could hear was the thin shrilling of a distant cicada.[2] All the creatures of the woods seemed slumbering in the hushed heat of the afternoon. The trail crossed the dry bed of a brook and climbed a hillside. At the top, it turned sharply and entered a little open space floored with ferns and uneven with the moldering mounds of old logs. The hillside, to the right of the path, fell away in a steep descent.

Just as I reached the edge of this clearing, a grayish form scuttled across the path and a shrill, high crying, like the squealing of a pig, broke the silence of the woods. The gray form dodged this way and that. It ran among the fern clumps to the left of the trail. It appeared and disappeared while the squealing continued. Then, to the right, there was a sudden windy roaring of wings. A whole brood of partly grown ruffed grouse[3] skimmed away down the slope and disappeared among the trees. The squealing ceased; the mother bird disappeared. She had attracted my attention while the young birds silently ran to the right and launched themselves into the air. The brood had received one of those lessons in caution and escape which, through the wisdom of instinct, mother birds teach their young during the summer months of their earliest growth.

It is during the summertime that most young wild creatures go to school. They are growing up during those long, warm days of plenty. They are learning lessons continually that will aid them in many ways in later life. In Nature's summer school, they acquire knowledge by example, by observation, and by experience.

2. **cicada** (sĭ-kā′də): an insect that makes a high-pitched sound.
3. **ruffed grouse:** birds with a ring of neck feathers resembling a stiff collar.

Because the red fox is legendary for its cunning and resourcefulness, it is not surprising to find that the schooling that red-fox kits receive is almost human in its program of progressive training. The parents use an elaborate and careful system for educating their offspring in the art of making a living.

As soon as the kits are weaned, the mother fox begins bringing captured mice, birds, and rabbits into the den. As the young foxes grow older, the food is dropped at the entrance instead of being brought inside. A little later, it is deposited a few feet outside the entrance. Then it is placed several yards away and, finally, the kits have to search over an area of several hundred square yards to find their dinners. During the last part of the training, the parent foxes begin hiding the captured birds or rabbits beneath leaves and rubbish, thus forcing the kits to use their sense of smell as well as their eyes in making their discoveries. In this practical, progressive manner, the school for foxes educates the young animals for the vital work of hunting.

The primary lesson taught to most wild creatures is who and what to fear. Over and over again, the need for eternal vigilance and caution is impressed upon them.

A friend of mine was walking down a village street lined with maple trees, one summer morning, when a baby gray squirrel scrambled fearlessly down a nearby trunk. It came directly toward him in a series of little loping hops, its tiny tail flipping at every jump. When it was six feet away, it came to a sudden stop. An ear-piercing chatter had reached it from the branches overhead. Rattling over the bark, the mother squirrel came racing down the tree. She scurried to the baby, scolding at the top of her lungs. She gave him a nip that made him jump. Then she grabbed him by the back of the neck and lugged him, kittenwise, to the foot of the tree trunk. The youngster had

learned a lesson in caution, a lesson that might save its life on a later day.

A knowledge of the dangers of the world is far from instinctive in many creatures. When kittens and mice grow up together, the mice show no instinctive fear of the cats. That fear is learned. Young crows are far more fearless than their parents. Among the Indiana dunes, I once passed close to a dead tree in which two young crows perched, eyeing me without any sign of concern while their parents circled at a distance, cawing their alarm.

On this Adirondack lake, the other morning, I rounded a rocky headland in my canoe and came upon a family of merganser ducks.[4] At the mother's warning quack, the ducklings dis-

appeared behind a jutting rock. Then, quacking continually, rushing about, skittering over the surface of the lake, the mother merganser sought to hold my attention. Her performance was so good it defeated its purpose. The baby ducks peered out from behind their rock, then paddled out in a string, bobbing up and down in the choppy water, to watch the show. Like backward pupils, they still had to learn the primary lesson of their wild classroom, how to act in the presence of possible danger.

In contrast with these too-trusting mergansers, some creatures go to the other extreme. They have to be taught self-confidence. A farmboy, coming down a lonely backwoods road, witnessed such a lesson being taught to young mink. Near an old bridge which spanned a brook, he saw a procession of a mother mink and five quarter-grown babies

4. **merganser** (mər-găn′sər) **ducks:** fish-eating, diving ducks.

appear from the bushes at the side of the road. The mother trotted on across. Then she looked back. The youngsters were huddled together, fearfully, in the bushes. They were afraid to enter the open roadway. She ran back and tried to encourage them. Time after time, the procession would start on across the road. And each time, the little mink would lose their courage and scurry back into the protection of the bushes. This went on until the mother lost patience. One by one, she grabbed them by the back of the neck and carried them to the other side. There the procession formed once more and, single file, the animals disappeared in the bushes.

What not to fear as well as what to fear is one of the basic studies in the school of the out-of-doors. A few blocks from my home, a bluejay, that had tumbled out of the nest before it was able to fly, was raised in the protection of a greenhouse. As it gained the use of its wings, it would dart back and forth within its transparent world, investigating, with bright eyes and sharp bill, every hole and cranny. One August day, a tiger swallowtail butterfly was released in the greenhouse. As it bobbed about in the sunshine, the young bluejay screamed in terror and fled to the farthest corner of the building. It had never seen a butterfly before and, lacking the outdoor training its wild kindred had received, it viewed it as an unknown and mortal foe.

A sagacious scientist once remarked that our consciences are the sum total of our mothers' scoldings. Similarly, much of the wisdom of the wild that is not instinctive is the product of the reprimands of the parents. Obedience is essential to safety. From the dappled fawn, remaining immobile in the presence of danger, to the young opossums, clinging pickaback with their tails curled about the arching tail of their mother, baby animals have to learn the lesson of obedience in order to sidestep danger.

Their very lives may depend upon it. Punishment for failure in Nature's school is often swift and fatal.

On all sides, in woods and fields, during the summer days and nights, young animals and birds are learning specialized skills as well as fundamental knowledge. Baby raccoons, ambling along like miniature bears, follow their parents through the darkness to brooks and ponds there to learn the art of catching frogs and crayfish. Young barn swallows dart out from perches to scoop insects from the air that have been dropped close to them by their hovering parents and thus learn to secure their food on the wing. Young otters, riding on their mothers' backs, are carried out into the water and gradually taught to swim.

On the south shore of Long Island, a bayman once observed a marsh hawk schooling its offspring in catching prey. With its parent, the young bird was circling over a wide stretch of sea moor, tilting this way and that in the light breeze. Below the two hawks, a flicker[5] darted from the edge of a woods. Rising and falling, with quick, strong thrusts of its wings, it passed below. The parent bird swept downward and snatched the woodpecker from the air. Then it did a surprising thing. It flapped upward to a height of several hundred feet, closely followed by the young hawk. At the height of its climb, it suddenly released the woodpecker. The young hawk swooped after it, overtook it, and grasped it in its talons before it could reach the protection of the trees. It had learned a valuable lesson in overtaking prey aloft, learned it by observation and personal experience.

Learning by doing, of course, plays an important part in the education of most creatures of the wild. In an open field, just north of my Insect Garden, I once almost stepped on a

5. **flicker:** a woodpecker.

baby cottontail rabbit crouching in the grass. It bolted away. Instinct told it to run. Instinct told it to dodge this way and that. But only experience could teach it that it couldn't make right-angled turns when going at top speed. Four times, as it shot in one direction and then in another in its panic, it turned so abruptly it lost its balance. With its feet running in the air so fast they became almost a blur, it lay kicking on its side. Then it would right itself only to bolt off and repeat the procedure. It was discovering what it couldn't do. It was learning, and experience was its teacher.

An old beaver trapper, who for half a century had followed a trapline through the Dead River region of northern Maine, once told me that far back in the woods young beavers sometimes make practice dams of mud and twigs across rivulets. The youngsters of the beaver colony were gaining, in a kind of play, experience that someday would prove of real importance.

Similarly, as summer nears its end, young woodchucks begin digging practice burrows which they never use. On one sandy hillside in northern Indiana, I recall a place where six such holes were excavated among the mullein[6] stalks and the sandburs[7] within the space of a hundred yards. Young woodchucks from a burrow under a pine stump nearby were trying out their skill in making practice tunnels. Before winter came, each of the animals had made a satisfactory burrow—thanks, at least in part, to the experience of warm, late-summer days and nights.

All animals, even the most humble, appear to have some ability to learn from experience. An earthworm can learn to turn to the right or the left when it is placed in a maze in which it receives an unpleasant electric shock when it makes a wrong turn. Its nervous system records the lesson thus learned and the earthworm will even continue to make the correct turn after its head has been cut off. Crayfish can be taught to come to a certain spot for feeding. Frogs can remember the correct path through a laboratory maze after a lapse of a month. In one experiment, a single tentacle of a sea anemone[8] learned, independently of all

8. **sea anemone** (ə-něm′ə-nē): a flowerlike animal with colorful tentacles, or armlike parts, which attaches itself to underwater rocks.

6. **mullein** (mŭl′ən): a tall plant with woolly leaves.
7. **sandburs:** shrubby weeds.

the other tentacles, to reject wads of paper when they were offered as food. Even one-celled protozoa[9] have individuals that are able to learn simple lessons such as avoiding over-acid water or dye particles among their food.

Always, the things a creature learns are in line with its inherited capacities. A meadow-lark, sailing out over a hayfield, will drop down near its nest amid a sea of waving grass. How does it recognize the place? How does it find landmarks where everything looks the same? Tiny differences are caught by its keen eyes, differences which its inherited ability and its training fit it to see.

In truth, that accomplishment—over which I never cease to marvel—is far less surprising than the performance of two work horses I once saw standing in the shade of a tree at the edge of a pasture. They remained side by side, facing in opposite directions. In this position, the swishing of their tails kept them both, front and back, free from flies. This scheme, hit upon by chance or by experience, was advantageous to them both. All larks possess the ability to find their nests amid acres of moving grass; but only a few horses ever make use of the rational stratagem that aided those two animals under the pasture tree.

9. **protozoa** (prō′tə-zō′ə): the simplest forms of animal life, visible only under a microscope.

Reading Check

1. According to Teale, what are the three ways animals gain knowledge?
2. How does the mother squirrel teach its youngster to be cautious?
3. How does the mother mink teach confidence to its youngsters?
4. What role does play have for young beavers and woodchucks?

For Study and Discussion

Analyzing and Interpreting the Essay

1. Teale says that the primary lesson baby animals must learn is "who and what to fear." Give three examples from the selection that show how animals are taught caution.

2. Teale says that the schooling of red-fox kits is "almost human in its program of progressive training." The word *progressive* here means "step-by-step." a. What steps are used in training baby foxes to become hunters? b. In what way is the training almost human?

3. In addition to behavior that is instinctive, animals learn new behavior through firsthand experience. How are both kinds of behavior shown in the actions of the cottontail rabbit?

4. Teale marvels over the ability of the meadowlark to find its nest in a sea of waving grass. a. Why does he find the stratagem of the two work horses even more remarkable? b. What have the horses learned through chance or experience?

5. How would you describe Teale's feelings for the natural world?

6. What is the main idea of this essay?

Literary Elements

Finding the Main Idea of a Paragraph

The word *paragraph* comes from two Greek words: *para*, meaning "beside," and *graphein*, meaning "to write." Centuries ago, when books were copied by hand, scribes did not divide a manuscript into paragraphs as we do today. Instead they wrote a certain mark beside the place where a new idea began. This mark was called a paragraph.

Today, of course, we use the word *paragraph* to refer to a series of sentences that develop a single idea or topic. We indicate the beginning of a paragraph by indenting the first sentence in the series.

Sometimes a writer will state the main idea or topic of a paragraph in a sentence called the **topic sentence.** The topic sentence is usually placed at the beginning of the paragraph.

Look at this paragraph from "Animals Go to School." Which sentence states the main idea of the paragraph?

> A knowledge of the dangers of the world is far from instinctive in many creatures. When kittens and mice grow up together, the mice show no instinctive fear of the cats. That fear is learned. Young crows are far more fearless than their parents. Among the Indiana dunes, I once passed close to a dead tree in which two young crows perched, eyeing me without any sign of concern while their parents circled at a distance, cawing their alarm.

What examples does Teale give in the paragraph? How do they support the main idea?

Language and Vocabulary

Analyzing Words from a Latin Root

How are *education* and *duke* related? The answer is that they both come from the Latin verb *ducere,* meaning "to lead." Because it is the source of several English words, *ducere* is called a **root word.** It usually appears in the form *-duce* (as in pro*duce*) or in the form *-duct* (as in pro*duct*).

Many English words are related because they come from the same root word. Such related words are considered members of a **word family.** Here are some other members of the *ducere* family:

reduce	conduct	induct

Reduce comes from a Latin word meaning "to lead back." What happens when you *reduce* fractions to their lowest terms? Someone who *conducts* an orchestra leads or guides the indi-

vidual musicians. What is the meaning of *induct*?

Look up the meanings of the following words in a dictionary. What does each word have to do with the Latin root word meaning "to lead"?

adduce	deduct	ductile
conducive	educe	traduce

Expository Writing

Supporting a Statement with Evidence

Teale says that all animals have some ability to learn from experience. Think of some observation of your own that supports this statement. Have you watched professional trainers work with theatrical or circus animals? Have you ever trained a dog to follow commands, to fetch a newspaper, or to do tricks? In a paragraph explain one example in detail. To review the elements of expository writing, see page 196.

About the Author

Edwin Way Teale   (1899–1980)

Edwin Way Teale was born in Joliet, Illinois, and educated at Earlham College and Columbia University. He was one of America's foremost authors of nature books. His major work is *The Circle of Seasons* (1953), a series of books on the seasons in America. Teale's book *Wandering Through Winter* won a Pulitzer Prize in 1966. The selection in this book is a chapter from *Lost in the Woods.*

Dogs That Have Known Me

JEAN KERR

The title of an essay often indicates its tone—*the attitude the writer wants you to take toward his or her subject. This humorous essay consists of several anecdotes about pet dogs. What is the idea that unifies the essay?*

I never meant to say anything about this, but the fact is that I have never met a dog that didn't have it in for me. You take Kelly, for instance. He's a wire-haired fox terrier and he's had us for three years now. I wouldn't say that he was terribly handsome but he does have a very nice smile. What he *doesn't* have is any sense of fitness.[1] All the other dogs in the neighborhood spend their afternoons yapping at each other's heels or chasing cats. Kelly spends his whole day, every day, chasing swans on the millpond. I don't actually worry because he will never catch one. For one thing, he can't swim. Instead of settling for a simple dogpaddle like everybody else, he has to show off and try some complicated overhand stroke, with the result that he always sinks and has to be fished out. Naturally, people talk, and I never take him for a walk that somebody doesn't point him out and say, "There's that crazy dog that chases swans."

Another thing about that dog is that he absolutely refuses to put himself in the other fel-

1. **fitness:** here, the proper way to behave.

low's position. We have a pencil sharpener in the kitchen and Kelly used to enjoy having an occasional munch on the plastic cover. As long as it was just a nip now and then, I didn't mind. But one day he simply lost his head and ate the whole thing. Then I had to buy a new one and of course I put it up high out of Kelly's reach. Well, the scenes we were treated to—and the sulking! In fact, ever since he has been eating things I know he doesn't like just to get even. I don't mean things like socks and mittens and paper napkins, which of course are delicious. Lately he's been eating plastic airplanes, suede brushes, and light bulbs. Well, if he wants to sit under the piano and make low and loving growls over a suede brush just to show me, okay. But frankly I think he's lowering himself.

Time and again I have pointed out to Kelly that with discriminating dogs, dogs who are looking for a finer, lighter chew—it's bedroom slippers two to one. I have even dropped old, dilapidated bedroom slippers here and there behind the furniture, hoping to tempt him. But the fact is, that dog wouldn't touch a bedroom slipper if he was starving.

Although we knew that, as a gourmet,[2] he was a washout, we did keep saying one thing about Kelly. We kept saying, "He's a good little old watchdog." Heaven knows why we thought so, except that he barks at the drop of a soufflé.[3] In fact, when he's in the basement a stiff toothbrush on the third floor is enough to set him off into a concerto of deep, murderous growls followed by loud hysterical yappings. I used to take real pleasure in imagining the chagrin of some poor intruder who'd bring that cacophony[4] upon himself. Last month we had an intruder. He got in the porch window and

took twenty-two dollars and my wristwatch while Kelly, that good little old watchdog, was as silent as a cathedral. But that's the way it's been.

The first dog I remember well was a large black and white mutt that was part German shepherd, part English sheepdog, and part collie—the wrong part in each case. With what strikes me now as unforgivable whimsy, we called him Ladadog from the title by Albert Payson Terhune.[5] He was a splendid dog in many respects but, in the last analysis, I'm afraid he was a bit of a social climber. He used to pretend that he was just crazy about us. I mean, if you just left the room to comb your hair he would greet you on your return with passionate lickings, pawings, and convulsive tail-waggings. And a longer separation—let's

2. **gourmet** (go͞or-mā'): someone who enjoys and is a good judge of fine foods.
3. **soufflé** (so͞o-flā'): baked dish with a light, puffy crust.
4. **cacophony** (kă-kŏf'ə-nē): harsh, jarring sounds.

5. **Albert Payson Terhune:** an author of popular stories about dogs, including *Lad: A Dog.*

say you had to go out on the front porch to pick up the mail—would send Ladadog off into such a demonstration of rapture and thanksgiving that we used to worry for his heart.

However, all this mawkish, slobbering sentiment disappeared the moment he stepped over the threshold. I remember we kids used to spot him on our way home from school, chasing around the Parkers' lawn with a cocker friend of his, and we'd rush over to him with happy squeals of "Laddy, oleboy, oleboy, oleboy," and Ladadog would just stand there looking slightly pained and distinctly cool. It wasn't that he cut us dead. He nodded, but it was with the remote air of a celebrity at a cocktail party saying, "Of *course* I remember you, and how's Ed?"

We kept making excuses for him and even worked out an elaborate explanation for his behavior. We decided that Ladadog didn't see very well, that he could only recognize us by smell and that he couldn't smell very well in the open air. However, the day came when my mother met Ladadog in front of the A & P. She was wearing her new brown coat with the beaver collar, and, lo and behold, Ladadog greeted her with joy and rapture. After that we just had to face the truth—that dog was a snob.

He also had other peculiarities. For instance, he saved lettuce. He used to beg for lettuce and then he would store it away in the cellar behind the coalbin. I don't know whether he was saving up to make a salad or what, but every so often we'd have to clean away a small, soggy lump of decayed vegetation.

And every time the phone rang he would run from wherever he was and sit there beside the phone chair, his tail thumping and his ears bristling, until you'd make some sort of an announcement like "It's just the Hoover man" or "Eileen, it's for you." Then he would immediately disappear. Clearly, this dog had put a call

in to someone, but we never did figure out who.

Come to think of it, the dog that gave us the most trouble was a beagle named Murphy. As far as I'm concerned, the first thing he did wrong was to turn into a beagle. I had seen him bouncing around in the excelsior[6] of a pet-shop window, and I went in and asked the man, "How much is that adorable fox terrier in the window?" Did he say, "That adorable fox terrier is a beagle"? No, he said, "Ten dollars, lady." Now, I don't mean to say one word against beagles. They have rights just like other people. But it is a bit of a shock when you bring home a small ball of fluff in a shoebox, and three weeks later it's as long as the sofa.

Murphy had a habit that used to leave us open to a certain amount of criticism from our

6. **excelsior** (ĕk-sĕl′sē-ər): wood shavings.

friends, who were not dogophiles.[7] He never climbed up on beds or chairs or sofas. But he always sat on top of the piano. In the beginning we used to try to pull him off of there. But after a few noisy scuffles in which he knocked a picture off the wall, scratched the piano, and smashed a lamp, we just gave in— only to discover that, left to his own devices, he hopped up and down as delicately as a ballet dancer. We became quite accustomed to it, but at parties at our house it was not unusual to hear a guest remark, "I don't know what I'm drinking but I think I see a big dog on the piano."

It's not just our own dogs that bother me. The dogs I meet at parties are even worse. I don't know what I've got that attracts them; it just doesn't bear thought. My husband swears I rub chopped meat on my ankles. But at every party it's the same thing. I am sitting in happy conviviality with a group in front of the fire when all of a sudden the large mutt of mine host appears in the archway. Then, without a single bark of warning, he hurls himself upon me. It always makes me think of that line from *A Streetcar Named Desire*[8]—"Baby, we've had this date right from the beginning." My martini flies into space and my stockings are torn before he finally settles down peacefully in the lap of my new black faille.[9] I blow out such quantities of hair as I haven't swallowed and glance at my host, expecting to be rescued. He murmurs, "Isn't that wonderful? You know, Brucie is usually so distant with strangers."

At a dinner party in Long Island last week, after I had been mugged by a large sheepdog, I announced quite piteously, "Oh dear, he seems to have swallowed one of my earrings." The hostess looked really distressed for a mo-

ment, until she examined the remaining earring. Then she said, "Oh, I think it will be all right. It's small and it's round."

Nowadays if I go anywhere I just ask if they have a dog. If they do, I say, "Maybe I'd better keep away from him—I have this bad allergy." This does not tend to endear me to my hostess. But it is safer. It really is.

Reading Check

1. Why is there no danger of Kelly catching any swans?
2. What does Kelly like to eat?
3. What was Ladadog in the habit of saving?
4. According to the author, which dog was the most troublesome?
5. Where did the pet beagle like to sit?

For Study and Discussion

Analyzing and Interpreting the Essay

1. Kelly is described as a dog with no "sense of fitness." How is his behavior different from that of other dogs?

2a. What led the family to believe that Kelly would make a good watchdog? **b.** How did he surprise them?

3. Snobbishness is ordinarily associated with human beings, not with animals. Yet the author refers to Ladadog as "a snob" (page 395). **a.** Why? **b.** What other peculiarities does the author recall about Ladadog?

4. In describing Murphy, the author says she has nothing against beagles: "They have rights just like other people" (page 395). Find other examples in the essay where she refers to dogs as if they were people.

5. What is the unifying idea of this essay?

---

7. **dogophiles:** a made-up word meaning "dog lovers."
8. *A Streetcar Named Desire:* a play by Tennessee Williams.
9. **faille** (fāl): a dress made of a soft, slighty ribbed fabric.

Literary Elements

Finding Humor in the Unexpected

Laughter is often a reaction to something unexpected or surprising. For example, we expect lions to roar and birds to chirp. But imagine a chirping lion or a roaring bird.

In Jean Kerr's essay, dogs behave in odd and unexpected ways. Their actions surprise us. Consider this description of Murphy:

> He never climbed up on beds or chairs or sofas. But he always sat on top of the piano. In the beginning we used to try to pull him off of there. But after a few noisy scuffles in which he knocked a picture off the wall, scratched the piano, and smashed a lamp, we just gave in—only to discover that, left to his own devices, he hopped up and down as delicately as a ballet dancer.

Most pet dogs enjoy resting quietly on soft furniture, such as beds, chairs, and sofas. What is unusual about Murphy's behavior?

Find another example of odd or unexpected behavior in the essay and tell why it is humorous.

Language and Vocabulary

Recognizing Informal Language

Jean Kerr uses several expressions that are considered informal or conversational. She says that Ladadog "used to pretend that he was just *crazy* about us." The word *crazy* in this context is used in the **colloquial** (kə-lō′kwē-əl), or conversational, sense of "enthusiastic" or "eager." She says that Kelly "was a *washout*" as a gourmet. The word *washout* is **slang** for "a complete failure." Slang is highly informal language that tends to be colorful or humorous. Slang often has a short career; either it disappears or it enters standard usage.

What does each of these italicized expressions mean? Check your answers in a dictionary.

. . . I have never met a dog that didn't *have it in for* me.

I remember we kids used to *spot* him on our way home from school . . .

It wasn't that he *cut* us *dead.*

Narrative Writing

Writing About a Pet

In her essay Jean Kerr conveys the distinct personality and habits of her pet dogs. Have you ever owned or known of a pet that possessed very individual characteristics? Write a short narrative telling about a single incident involving that animal. Use words that reveal the pet's special personality.

About the Author

Jean Kerr (1923–   )

When she was eight years old, Jean Kerr decided that all she wanted when she grew up was to be able to sleep until noon every day. She concluded that the fastest way to arrive at this goal was to become a professional writer.

She is the author of several successful plays, including *Song of Bernadette,* which she adapted with her husband, critic Walter Kerr. She has also contributed many autobiographical essays to magazines. Her first collection of these essays resulted in her most famous book, *Please Don't Eat the Daisies,* from which the selection "Dogs That Have Known Me" is taken. Jean Kerr has been called one of the funniest writers of her generation.

Rattlesnake Hunt

MARJORIE KINNAN RAWLINGS

This selection is from Cross Creek, *a collection of remembrances. Like a short story, this narrative has a conflict that builds to a climax and then is resolved. As you read, note how Rawlings makes you aware of the changes in her attitude.*

Ross Allen, a young Florida herpetologist,[1] invited me to join him on a hunt in the upper Everglades[2]—for rattlesnakes.

The hunting ground was Big Prairie, south of Arcadia and west of the northern tip of Lake Okeechobee. Big Prairie is a desolate cattle country, half marsh, half pasture, with islands of palm trees and cypresses and oaks. At that time of year the cattlemen and Indians were burning the country, on the theory that the young fresh wire grass that springs up from the roots after a fire is the best cattle forage. Ross planned to hunt his rattlers in the forefront of the fires. They lived in winter, he said, in gopher holes, coming out in the midday warmth to forage, and would move ahead of the flames and be easily taken. We joined forces with a big fellow named Will, his snake-hunting companion of the territory, and set out in early morning, after a long rough drive over deep-rutted roads into the open wilds.

I hope never in my life to be so frightened as I was in those first few hours. I kept on Ross's footsteps, I moved when he moved, sometimes jolting into him when I thought he might leave me behind. He does not use the forked stick of conventional snake hunting, but a steel prong, shaped like an L, at the end of a long stout stick. He hunted casually, calling my attention to the varying vegetation, to hawks overhead, to a pair of the rare whooping cranes that flapped over us. In midmorning he stopped short, dropped his stick, and brought up a five-foot rattlesnake draped limply over the steel L. It seemed to me that I should drop in my tracks.

"They're not active at this season," he said quietly. "A snake takes on the temperature of its surroundings. They can't stand too much heat for that reason, and when the weather is cool, as now, they're sluggish."

The sun was bright overhead, the sky a translucent blue, and it seemed to me that it was warm enough for any snake to do as it willed. The sweat poured down my back. Ross dropped the rattler in a crocus sack[3] and Will carried it. By noon, he had caught four. I felt faint and ill. We stopped by a pond and went

---

1. **herpetologist** (hûr′pə-tŏl′ə-jĭst): a person who studies reptiles and amphibians.
2. **Everglades:** a large area of swampland in southern Florida.
3. **crocus sack:** a sack made of coarse material, such as burlap.

swimming. The region was flat, the horizon limitless, and as I came out of the cool blue water I expected to find myself surrounded by a ring of rattlers. There were only Ross and Will, opening the lunch basket. I could not eat. Ross never touches liquor and it seemed to me that I would give my hope of salvation for a dram of whiskey. Will went back and drove his truck closer, for Ross expected the hunting to be better in the afternoon. The hunting was much better. When we went back to the truck to deposit two more rattlers in the wire cage, there was a rattlesnake lying under the truck.

Ross said, "Whenever I leave my car or truck with snakes already in it, other rattlers always appear. I don't know whether this is because they scent or sense the presence of other snakes, or whether in this arid area they come to the car for shade in the heat of the day."

The problem was scientific, but I had no interest.

That night Ross and Will and I camped out in the vast spaces of the Everglades prairies. We got water from an abandoned well and cooked supper under buttonwood bushes by a flowing stream. The campfire blazed cheerfully under the stars and a new moon lifted in the sky. Will told tall tales of the cattlemen and the Indians and we were at peace.

Ross said, "We couldn't have a better night for catching water snakes."

After the rattlers, water snakes seemed innocuous[4] enough. We worked along the edge of the stream and here Ross did not use his L-shaped steel. He reached under rocks and along the edge of the water and brought out harmless reptiles with his hands. I had said nothing to him of my fears, but he understood them. He brought a small dark snake from under a willow root.

"Wouldn't you like to hold it?" he asked. "People think snakes are cold and clammy, but they aren't. Take it in your hands. You'll see that it is warm."

Again, because I was ashamed, I took the snake in my hands. It was not cold, it was not clammy, and it lay trustingly in my hands, a thing that lived and breathed and had mortality[5] like the rest of us. I felt an upsurgence of spirit.

The next day was magnificent. The air was crystal, the sky was aquamarine, and the far horizon of palms and oaks lay against the sky. I felt a new boldness and followed Ross bravely. He was making the rounds of the gopher holes. The rattlers came out in the mid-morning warmth and were never far away. He could tell by their trails whether one had come out or was still in the hole. Sometimes the two men dug the snake out. At times it was down so long and winding a tunnel that the digging was hopeless. Then they blocked the entrance and went on to other holes. In an hour or so they made the original rounds, unblocking the holes. The rattler in every case came out hurriedly, as though anything was preferable to being shut in. All the time Ross talked to me, telling me the scientific facts he had discovered about the habits of the rattlers.

"They pay no attention to a man standing perfectly still," he said, and proved it by letting Will unblock a hole while he stood at the entrance as the snake came out. It was exciting to watch the snake crawl slowly beside and past the man's legs. When it was at a safe distance he walked within its range of vision, which he had proved to be no higher than a man's knee, and the snake whirled and drew back in an attitude[6] of fighting defense. The rattler strikes only for paralyzing and killing its food, and for defense.

"It is a slow and heavy snake," Ross said. "It lies in wait on a small game trail and strikes the rat or rabbit passing by. It waits a few minutes, then follows along the trail, coming to the small animal, now dead or dying. It noses it from all sides, making sure that it is its own kill, and that it is dead and ready for swallowing."

A rattler will lie quietly without revealing itself if a man passes by and it thinks it is not seen. It slips away without fighting if given the chance. Only Ross's sharp eyes sometimes picked out the gray and yellow diamond pattern, camouflaged among the grasses. In the cool of the morning, chilled by the January air, the snakes showed no fight. They could be looped up limply over the steel L and dropped

---

4. **innocuous** (ĭ-nŏk′yō͞o-əs): harmless.
5. **had mortality** (môr-tăl′ĭ-tē): like all living things, would someday die.

6. **attitude:** here, a position of the body.

in a sack or up into the wire cage on the back of Will's truck. As the sun mounted in the sky and warmed the moist Everglades earth, the snakes were warmed too, and Ross warned that it was time to go more cautiously. Yet having learned that it was we who were the aggressors;[7] that immobility meant complete safety; that the snakes, for all their lightning flash in striking, were inaccurate in their aim, with limited vision; having watched again and again the liquid grace of movement, the beauty of pattern, suddenly I understood that I was drinking in freely the magnificent sweep of the horizon, with no fear of what might be at the moment under my feet. I went off hunting by myself, and though I found no snakes, I should have known what to do.

The sun was dropping low in the west.

7. **aggressors** (ə-grĕs′ərz): those who attack first.

Masses of white cloud hung above the flat marshy plain and seemed to be tangled in the tops of distant palms and cypresses. The sky turned orange, then saffron. I walked leisurely back toward the truck. In the distance I could see Ross and Will making their way in too. The season was more advanced than at the Creek, two hundred miles to the north, and I noticed that spring flowers were blooming among the lumpy hummocks. I leaned over to pick a white violet. There was a rattlesnake under the violet.

If this had happened the week before, if it had happened the day before, I think I should have lain down and died on top of the rattlesnake, with no need of being struck and poisoned. The snake did not coil, but lifted its head and whirred its rattles lightly. I stepped back slowly and put the violet in a buttonhole. I reached forward and laid the steel L across

the snake's neck, just back of the blunt head. I called to Ross: "I've got one."

He strolled toward me.

"Well, pick it up," he said.

I released it and slipped the L under the middle of the thick body.

"Go put it in the box."

He went ahead of me and lifted the top of the wire cage. I made the truck with the rattler, but when I reached up the six feet to drop it in the cage, it slipped off the stick and dropped on Ross's feet. It made no effort to strike.

"Pick it up again," he said. "If you'll pin it down lightly and reach just back of its head with your hand, as you've seen me do, you can drop it in more easily."

I pinned it and leaned over.

"I'm awfully sorry," I said, "but you're pushing me a little too fast."

He grinned. I lifted it on the stick and again as I had it at head height, it slipped off, down Ross's boots and on top of his feet. He stood as still as a stump. I dropped the snake on his feet for the third time. It seemed to me that the most patient of rattlers might in time resent being hauled up and down, and for all the man's quiet certainty that in standing motionless there was no danger, would strike at whatever was nearest, and that would be Ross.

I said, "I'm just not man enough to keep this up any longer," and he laughed and reached down with his smooth quickness and lifted the snake back of the head and dropped it in the cage. It slid in among its mates and settled in a corner. The hunt was over and we drove back over the uneven trail to Will's village and left him and went on to Arcadia and home. Our catch for the two days was thirty-two rattlers.

I said to Ross, "I believe that tomorrow I could have picked up that snake."

Back at the Creek, I felt a new lightness. I had done battle with a great fear, and the victory was mine.

Reading Check

1. Why were cattlemen and Indians burning the land in Big Prairie?
2. Where do the rattlesnakes live during the winter?
3. Why are the rattlesnakes sluggish?
4. What kinds of snakes does Ross catch at night?
5. Why are rattlesnakes often inaccurate in aim?

For Study and Discussion

Analyzing and Interpreting the Selection

1. During the first day of the rattlesnake hunt, how does the author show her terror?

2. Ross Allen is a herpetologist—an expert on reptiles and amphibians. At the start of the hunt, he calmly picks up a five-foot rattlesnake with a steel prong. Why is he able to hunt so "casually"?

3. At first, the author thinks snakes are cold and clammy. **a.** What does she discover when she holds a small, dark snake in her own hands? **b.** How does this new knowledge affect her?

4. Why is she less frightened on the second day of the hunt?

5. The author's new-found courage is put to a test when she encounters a rattlesnake on her own. **a.** What small gesture indicates that she is no longer afraid (see page 401)? **b.** How successful is she in catching the snake?

6. At the end of the selection, the author indicates that she has gained control over her fear. How does she now feel?

Language and Vocabulary

Forming Words with -logy

In "Rattlesnake Hunt," Ross Allen is described as a *herpetologist,* someone who specializes in *herpetology.* The word *herpetology* has two parts. The first part, *herpeto-,* comes from a Greek word meaning "reptile." The second part, *-logy,* also comes from Greek and means "the science or study of something." *Herpetology* is the science or study of reptiles.

Geo- is a root meaning "of the earth." What is *geology? Biology? Zoology?* Check your answers in a dictionary.

Look up the following roots in a dictionary. What does each one mean?

anthropo-   ethno-   theo-

What word is formed by adding *-logy* to each root? Tell what each word means.

Narrative Writing

Writing About a Personal Experience

The narrator's attitude toward snakes begins to change after she holds a water snake in her hands.

> Again, because I was ashamed, I took the snake in my hands. It was not cold, it was not clammy, and it lay trustingly in my hands, a thing that lived and breathed and had mortality like the rest of us. I felt an upsurgence of spirit.

Up to this moment, the narrator has been terrified of snakes. After she touches the water snake, her fears begin to diminish. She feels "an upsurgence of spirit."

Think about the first time you tried to do something that took courage—performing in a school play, singing in a chorus, diving from a board, getting on a roller coaster, going to a dance. Describe the experience in a short paragraph, telling as specifically as you can what your reactions were. Use words that convey your feelings.

About the Author

Marjorie Kinnan Rawlings   (1896–1953)

Marjorie Kinnan Rawlings grew up on a farm in Maryland. She attended the University of Wisconsin, where she was active in theater productions and literary magazines. In 1919 she married Charles Rawlings, a newspaperman. The next ten years involved a great deal of moving and traveling, and during that time, she worked as a newspaper reporter. She disliked this kind of work, however, and began to devote time to writing fiction.

In 1938 she published her most famous novel, *The Yearling,* a story about a boy's love for his pet fawn. This book, which won the Pulitzer Prize, is now considered an American classic. In 1942 she published a collection of remembrances, *Cross Creek,* from which the selection "Rattlesnake Hunt" is taken.

FROM

Sound-Shadows of the New World

VED MEHTA

Ved Mehta has been blind since the age of four. When he was fifteen, he left his native India to enroll in the Arkansas School for the Blind, in Little Rock, Arkansas. In these excerpts from his autobiographical narrative, Sound-Shadows of the New World, *he describes a mobility program that trained blind boys and girls to sense objects by using "facial vision."*

At the start of one social-adjustment period, Miss Harper took us into the gymnasium and lined us up at the edge of the floor, saying, "Mr. Woolly has just come back from San Francisco, where he attended a conference of the American Association of Workers for the Blind. At the conference, he heard rehabilitation workers complain that youngsters are coming out of residential schools for the blind without mobility—without the skills to get around by themselves out on the streets. If they can't get to regular jobs, then there's no hope of their ever leading a life outside the sheltered workshops for the blind. We've therefore decided to go all out for our mobility program and help you youngsters develop your facial vision. As y'all know, facial vision is a term for the ability many of you totally blind boys and girls have to sense objects through echoes and changes in air pressure around the ear." She added, "I'm sure the gym sounds very different to you boys and girls from the way it usually does."

But the gymnasium always sounds different, I thought. It sounds different with mats on the floor when we are doing calisthenics,[1] without mats when we are getting it ready for a party, and with people dancing on the wooden floor during a party. At any of those times, though, it sounds full near the floor and hollow near the ceiling. Now, however, I, along with others, suddenly realized it was the other way around. The sound-shadows were floating like airy, ghostlike shapes around and above our heads.

"What is it?"

"What are they?"

"What's happening?"

1. **calisthenics** (kăl′əs-thĕn′ĭks): exercises for physical fitness.

"Mr. Tyson strung up some cotton-pickin' mannequins[2] to show us what'll happen if we don't do well in mobility?" Oather asked Miss Harper.

Miss Harper laughed, and then explained that suspended on tracks from the ceiling were lightweight fiberboard panels of various sizes. The panels, which she could raise or lower by means of ropes and pulleys, formed a movable obstacle course. "The purpose of the obstacle course is to help y'all develop your facial vision," she said. "As y'all walk through it, we'll see how easily you're able to spot panels, big or

2. **mannequins** (măn′ĭ-kĭns): life-size dummies such as those used by window dressers.

small, and avoid running into them. Some of y'all may not do well at first, but the more you do it the better you should get at it."

Everyone talked at once.

"How am I going to keep from bumping into those things and getting all bruised up?" Lois Woodward asked. She was known for fretting about such matters, as if the smallest bruise could disfigure her.

"We've got plenty of obstacles around the school—why do they have to go and invent some more?" Oather asked. He went on to answer his own question. "I guess these panels are better than glass doors." When Oather was about nine, he had run into the door of the boys' solarium. His arm had gone right through its glass pane, and had never completely recovered from the injury. But this hadn't stopped him from tearing around the school like a racing car.

"I thought that people good in facial vision went blind when they were really little, and grew up having it," Treadway said. "I didn't think you could teach it later on."

"I'm not going to mention any names, but there are people standing right here who went blind when they were little who crash around like a bird in a cage," Oather said. He himself was a perfect example of what Treadway was talking about, but, as usual, he was playing the devil's advocate.[3]

"Well, maybe their mothers didn't let them run around when they were little, so they weren't able to develop facial vision and coordination," Miss Harper said. She added that she didn't know for certain whether people were born with facial vision or could acquire it with training, but that the obstacle course was a good experiment and we should all cooperate.

"Miss Harper, why do we need classes in fa-

cial vision when we can get ourselves Seeing Eye dogs?" a boy I'll call Branch Hill asked, as if he had just woken up. The boys referred to Branch as another Dumb Joe Wright, but, unlike Joe, Branch was totally blind.

Many of us jumped on Branch, because we thought that Seeing Eye dogs were really for blind people who didn't want to help themselves and wanted people to feel sorry for them.

"Even if you somehow get a Seeing Eye dog, you won't regret having good facial vision," Miss Harper said.

There was some more discussion in this vein, and then Miss Harper said, "Y'all are getting het up[4] about some little old panels that will just swing away if you bump into them. Yet when you get to traveling around town you're going to meet up with all kinds of real, dangerous obstacles, like lampposts and mailboxes, ladders and scaffolding. Everywhere, you'll come across parking meters and fire hydrants, and manholes left uncovered. You'll have to learn to navigate around them, so you might as well get started here, right now, and try to train your facial vision."

I imagined the gymnasium with its obstacle course as a forest that one had to find one's way through with the perceptiveness[5] of a dog, the cunning of a fox, the fearlessness of a tiger. I felt excited, and hoped that Miss Harper would call on me to walk through it first. But she called on Bruton.

Bruton, who was known for his prowess on the wrestling mat, sounded uncharacteristically timorous going through the obstacle course.

"No hands out in front of you, please," Miss Harper said to him. "Keep your arms at your sides. . . . You're doing fine. . . . Don't stop."

3. **devil's advocate:** someone who deliberately takes the opposite side or wrong side of an argument.

4. **het up:** slang for "excited" or "angry."

5. **perceptiveness** (pər-sĕp′tĭv-nəs): awareness; sensitivity.

Treadway and Vernelle, perhaps becoming restive at having nothing to do, started working out the harmony for "Button Up Your Overcoat."

"Please tell them to be quiet," Bruton said to Miss Harper, from the middle of the floor. "Their singing is interfering with my facial vision."

Miss Harper shushed Treadway and Vernelle but then said to Bruton that in the gymnasium he had only a little singing to contend with, while on the street there might be wind or jackhammers. He had to learn to put up with all kinds of noises.

Bruton bumped his head against a panel, cursed, and returned to the edge of the floor. However much Miss Harper coaxed him, he wouldn't go back out. "I'm resting now," he said.

Miss Harper called on Branch next. He went around the floor bumping into panel after panel, as if the purpose of the exercise were to score hits. People called out to him that he was doing really fine—that that was the only way to go at those blooming panels. He seemed to take their goading good-naturedly, and kept on going.

Finally, I myself was in the midst of the obstacle course. I got so caught up in the spirit of the moment, felt so happy and self-confident, that I imagined that my whole childhood of running around in Indian *gullis*[6] and compounds,[7] of flying kites and riding my bicycle, of living in different places and having to adjust constantly to new surroundings had been a preparation only for this obstacle course. Here was a big panel, which I was sure I could have detected even with a pneumatic drill hammering in my ear. Here was a small panel just above my eyebrow, which I was able to deftly

6. *gullis* (gŭl′ēz): back lanes.
7. **compound:** an enclosed area, usually encircled by a high wall.

avoid, although I didn't notice it until I was almost upon it. There, just ahead, was a panel at chin level. I easily went around it, tilting my head a little bit. As I weaved my way through the obstacle course, going now one way, now another, Miss Harper noiselessly pulled up panels so high that the gymnasium felt open, like a field, and dropped them down so close together that it felt like a thicket. Some of the panels that suddenly appeared in front of my face were even harder to detect than the slim lampposts at home, which would materialize out of nowhere when I was walking with an inattentive sighted companion, and bruise me, as if they had a will of their own. Then I would imagine that the gods were punishing me for my misdeeds, such as pinching Usha, my little sister. I now decided that if I got through the obstacle course without brushing against a single panel I would best the gods.

I skirted panels, ducked under them, sprinted past them. I put my hands in my pockets and whistled under my breath. Just ahead was a panel that hung down to my chest. I easily walked around it, but then I slipped on the short incline that framed the floor and fell. In the game of mobility, one concentrates on the signals from the region of the face only to be tripped up by things around the feet, I thought. Perhaps there is no way of besting the gods after all.

"You fell because you got overconfident," Miss Harper said primly after she had rushed over to me and I had assured her that I wasn't hurt.

In subsequent social-adjustment periods, we were made to go through the obstacle course again and again. Although the avowed purpose of the exercise was to improve our facial vision, no one ever seemed to do better or worse than before. Years later, Mr. Woolly told me, "In your time, it was the vogue to try to teach and develop facial vision. That's why we spent endless hours making every blind young-ster walk through that obstacle course over and over. It was a long time before we learned that either people have facial vision or they don't—or, at least, that there is no scientific evidence that the skill can be taught. In fact, we're not sure anymore what facial vision is, or even if there *is* such a thing. The only thing we are sure of is that some blind people have an extra sensitivity—some kind of combination of all the senses they've got—that somehow enables them to detect the presence of obstacles."

On Saturday morning, Mr. Hartman walked out with me onto the school's front drive to send me off downtown. "As you must know from your trips with partially sighted boys, the trolley goes along West Markham Street all the way to downtown and turns onto Main Street," he said. "Main Street runs north and south, while the numbered streets, which intersect it, run east and west. Now, if you're walking south on Main Street from West Markham, the num-bers of the cross streets will be going up. You can count the blocks, and you'll always know what cross street you're at." As Mr. Hartman talked, I imagined Little Rock as a checker-board set up for the game of mobility. In that game, I would use feet in place of fingers to make my moves, playing against people, cars, and obstacles.

"It seems that American towns are orderly and simple—that's a blind person's dream," I said, recalling how streets at home twisted and turned and snaked in such a way that it was hard for me ever to know exactly where I was.

"Don't go getting any such notion in your head," Mr. Hartman said. "Wait till you start moving around just here in Little Rock by yourself, boy. There are all kinds of excep-tions. What should be called First Street is just the stretch of West Markham Street that runs through downtown. If a blind individual didn't know that, he could spend hours going in cir-cles looking for First Street."

I still thought that American towns sounded relatively orderly and simple compared with those at home, but I didn't press the point. In-stead, I asked, "How high up do the numbered streets go?"

"They go up to at least Ninth Street—you'll never need to go beyond that."

"And what are the names of the streets on ei-ther side of Main Street?"

"To the west is Louisiana Street. To the west of that, there are two other streets—I've for-gotten their names, but you won't need to fool with either of them. We visually handicapped people only need to worry about where we can buy what we need, and where we live and work."

I said I wondered what the names and num-bers of the streets were between the school and downtown.

"I don't know," Mr. Hartman said. "I've al-ways gone downtown on the trolley." He added vaguely, "There must be houses and things there."

I decided that I would have to think of the area between the school and downtown as a mysterious trolley run until such time as I could somehow come up with the information for myself.

"You'll know when a trolley's coming be-cause the power lines it runs on bang and rattle like Jezebel's teeth," Mr. Hartman was saying. "The trolley will stay on West Markham until the second right-hand turn, which is onto Main Street, and you, boy, get off at the stop right after that turn."

Mr. Hartman gave me three tokens—one for going downtown, one for coming back, and an extra one for any emergency. He also gave me a couple of dollars and told me to go into the Rexall drugstore on the southeast corner of Main and Fifth and buy for him and his wife a black Ace pocket comb, two sixty-watt light bulbs, a pair of brown shoelaces, and a packet of bobby pins. "You spend the morning going around the town and getting acquainted with it," he said. "I'll meet you at one o'clock at the restaurant in Pfeifer's department store. I'll buy you a milkshake." He added jokingly, "That is, if you're still alive."

"Will you be following me—watching me?"

"Boy, this is no piddling trip to Stifft's Station,[8] with me ready to rush to your side if you land yourself in trouble. The only way you're ever going to learn to do things by yourself is to do them. Sink or swim—"

"I know—that's your philosophy."

Finally, I was on my way, thinking that it was typical of Mr. Hartman to test me by loading me up with so much last-minute information and instruction. I stepped along the front drive smartly, swinging and tapping my cane in front of my feet and feeling like a soldier going out on a dangerous mission. But as I approached the gate the *tap-tap* of the cane made me feel shy and self-conscious. "Tap-tap, here comes a blind boy from the blind school—look out!" the cane seemed to shout.

I stopped at the school gate to reflect on why I disliked the cane so much. I had always disapproved of the boys who wore dark glasses inside the school building, as if to hide their blind eyes from visitors, because it seemed to me that they were denying their blindness. But there was all the difference in the world between covering up the fact of blindness with dark glasses and not wanting to advertise it with a cane. I conceded that a cane might be useful to blind people less adept than I was, but I felt that in my case it could be only an impediment to my acceptance as just another normal person on the street or on the trolley.

After all, the point of mobility was to win that acceptance.

I stood there holding my cane. It seemed to extend from my hand like an embarrassing appendage that, do what I might, could not be quieted, hidden, laid to rest—a symbol of all that was awkward and adolescent in my blindness. I whacked the cane on the ground, thinking that it was weighing down my hopes of being as independent as the sighted.

I held the cane poised just above the ground, in the grip of an idea. After listening to make sure that no one was around, I caught up the cane by both ends, put my foot in the middle, and tried to break it. But it would yield only to spring back. I flung it in the gutter by the side of the drive, making a mental note of the spot, so I could pick it up later if anyone asked for it, and hurried across West Markham. I got across it so easily that I couldn't imagine why I had ever needed sighted attendants, why I had waited until that day to strike out on my own for downtown. (Somehow, the crossing to Stifft's Station earlier that week didn't seem to count now, because Mr. Hartman had been tailing me.)

The sun was out in its full April glory. The air around my face was fresh, the sidewalk underfoot was smooth. I felt like bursting out in song.

I was at the trolley stop, but it was so pleasant that I decided to continue walking and explore the route. To my right, there was no steady sound-shadow of a wall or a fence to guide me along the sidewalk; there was just empty, undifferentiated[9] space. To my left, there was a steady stream of cars going both ways at about forty miles an hour, with an occasional large vehicle whose passing sounded like the roar of an airplane and temporarily

8. **Stifft's Station:** the place where Ved had gone on an earlier trip.

9. **undifferentiated** (ŭn-dĭf′ə-rĕn′shē-āt′əd): without any differences or distinctions.

paralyzed my facial vision. But my facial vision—or whatever it is that enables the blind to perceive obstacles—soon got more or less adjusted to the noise of the traffic echoing in that undifferentiated space. Happily, I imagined that I was by the sea listening to the waves breaking at high tide.

The sidewalk suddenly ended in an abrupt drop. It's a manhole, I thought. My cane, my cane! But the drop turned out to be a high curb that had not been preceded by the usual signal of a footworn depression. I regained my balance, and although I had no idea whether I was in an alleyway or had come to the end of the sidewalk, I stepped along, if a little shakily. Soon the sidewalk resumed.

There was the clanging vibration of the trolley wires overhead and, almost a block behind, a smooth rumble with a slight whistle in it, reminiscent of the sound effects in the outer-space radio program "Dimension X." It was the trolley. A sighted teacher may be in the trolley, I thought guiltily. They may be checking up on me. It's childish to think that I can leave the school authorities behind like my cane.

The trolley was getting closer. I felt that eyes were staring out at me, burning a hole in the back of my neck. I ran for the trolley stop, which I supposed must be just ahead, and narrowly avoided signs and posts that appeared as suddenly as the panels in the gymnasium.

The trolley passed me. I was at an intersection. I could hear the "Dimension X" rumble and whistle of the trolley on the other side of the intersection, and the light was against me.

I remembered that trolleys came at intervals of twenty minutes or more, and I put my arms out in front of me, held my breath, and stepped off the curb. I recalled in a flash what Mamaji used to say when I was riding my bicycle in the compound with my hands off the handlebars: "You'll kill yourself." I used to reply smugly, "Death only comes once." But now, with cars honking all around me, I had a vision of something much worse than death—losing a limb and being confined to a wheelchair for life. I said a quick prayer.

Somehow, I was across—and in one piece. I kept on running, and gaining on the trolley, its "Dimension X" rumble and whistle ever louder in my ear. A few feet ahead, I finally sensed the trolley stop. I heard the whoosh and clatter of the trolley door opening and the clicking of the coin box inside. I made a dash for the door but crashed into the bench at the stop, which I sensed too late to avoid. I missed the trolley. . . .

I was finally downtown: in a metropolis, as I thought of it, with Main Street, with M. M. Cohn's and Pfeifer's department stores, with McLellan's and Woolworth's dime stores, with the Rexall drugstore and the Lido restaurant—all the landmarks we heard advertised on the radio. I got off at the first downtown stop, at West Markham and Main. I had more than half an hour at my disposal before I was supposed to meet Mr. Hartman, so I started slowly walking up to the Rexall drugstore, trying at once to get a sense of downtown and to practice my mobility. I had walked Main Street with friends repeatedly, but I felt I was noticing some things for the first time, like the fact that there were so many shops in a block. Also, I had previously imagined that I would have difficulty telling the intersections, but I found that they almost announced themselves, being preceded by an interruption in the sound-shadows of the buildings, by a sense of openness, by an increase in the noise of the cross-street traffic, and by the footworn depression at the curb. How different walking downtown is from walking in quiet Stifft's Station, I thought. Here, there is so much traffic, and so many people are rushing in and out of doorways or barreling along the street, hardly looking where they're going. No obstacle course could have prepared me for this. But what an excellent place to test my senses to the limit. I must make a mental note of the shops I'm passing, so that I can come back and explore further. What's this? It's a whiff of a clean paper smell—I must be passing a stationer's. Now I'm walking through a dull roasted aroma—this must be a nut shop. Here is a strong odor of leather and polish, but it's hard to tell if it's being given off by a shoeshop or a leather-goods store. Now, here is a store that's unmistakable—this peanutty exhaust could only be pumped out of a dime store.

I was at Fifth and Main, just across from the Rexall drugstore. The light was in my favor, but I didn't know how long it had been that way. Deciding to play it safe for a change, I waited.

"You have the light," a man said, nudging me.

"I know."

"Why don't you walk, then? Do you need a hand?"

"I would rather wait."

The man crossed the street, exclaiming in annoyance, "I won't help *your* kind again!"

I didn't like leaving him with a bad impression of the blind. Yet I wondered what choice I had had. There had been no quick way to explain to him the logic behind my waiting—one explanation would have necessarily involved another. Anyway, I had to concentrate on getting around, not on educating strangers, say what Miss Harper might about each of us being an emissary to the country of the sighted. The only way to avoid frustrating encounters with the sighted was to act as if I had some sight, I concluded—not for the first time.

The traffic stopped on Main Street and started on Fifth. I quickly crossed over.

I listened for the sweep and brush of the revolving door to locate the Rexall drugstore, and, when there was a pause in its turning, made a dash for it.

Inside, in the front, a clerk was busy with a woman customer at the cash register. I stood a little to one side, breathing in the smell of rubbing alcohol, soap, and cough medicine, my heart beating to the screech and click of his machine. The register drawer sprang open. The woman got her change, gathered up some packages, and left.

I stepped up to the register and asked the clerk where the light bulbs were kept.

"Just look around."

I stayed put, and he looked up. "Oh. Straight to the back—the second counter to the right." He thinks I have some sight, I thought. I'm doing well.

By quietly asking sales assistants, by surreptitiously[10] touching things on the shelves, by listening to other customers, I was able to find everything Mr. Hartman had told me to buy, and to leave the shop in good order.

I was hot, and looked forward to my reward of a cold milkshake. Pfeifer's, which was barely a block up, was easy to locate—it had by far the busiest entrance on the block. I followed people in through a double set of swinging doors. Toward the back, through the ringing of festive bells, I heard an elevator door open, and walked to it briskly.

"The restaurant floor, please," I said, stepping in and surrendering myself to a waking dream: A champion wrestler had me now in a jackknife maneuver, now in a half-nelson lock; he tried to pin me, but I managed to keep one shoulder off the mat. No, it wasn't a wrestler at all but Mary Ann Lambert, and we were on our first date, walking hand in hand. The cane stuck out from my other hand like a symbol of

10. **surreptitiously** (sûr′əp-tĭsh′əs-lē): secretly or stealthily.

painful effort—like a miserable deformity. I had to get rid of it for good—be like everyone else.

"You're doing fine," a voice said.

I jumped. It took me a second to realize that it was Mr. Hartman at my elbow, and that he must have been in the elevator the whole time.

The elevator door opened, and we got out. I fell in step with Mr. Hartman, the back of my hand barely touching the sleeve of his shirt. All of a sudden, every muscle in my body relaxed, and I feared that I was going to slump to the floor.

We sat down at a table in the restaurant.

"You get everything? You have any trouble?"

"I found everything, all right."

Reading Check

1. Why are Ved and his classmates taken to the gymnasium?
2. What causes Ved to fall while he is going through the obstacle course?
3. What does Ved do with his cane before starting off for downtown Little Rock?
4. What causes Ved to miss the trolley?
5. How does Ved know when he has reached Pfeifer's?

For Study and Discussion

Analyzing and Interpreting the Selection

1a. How does Miss Harper define "facial vision"? **b.** What does the obstacle course consist of? **c.** How does Ved demonstrate that he has an extra sensitivity that enables him to detect obstacles?

2. Throughout the selection Ved uses the phrase "sound-shadows." He is able to tell the intersections because they are "preceded by an interruption in the sound-shadows of the buildings." What does he mean?

3. Ved says that his goal is "acceptance as just another normal person on the street or on the trolley." **a.** Why does he feel that carrying a cane will be an impediment to him? **b.** How does he show his need for independence when he is downtown?

4. How does Ved use his senses of smell, touch, and hearing to familiarize himself with his surroundings?

Language and Vocabulary

Using Context Clues

You have seen that you can often work out the meaning of an unfamiliar word by looking at the context in which it appears. What context clues help you determine the meaning of *timorous* in this sentence?

> Bruton, who was known for his prowess on the wrestling mat, sounded uncharacteristically *timorous* going through the obstacle course.

Did you get the meaning "afraid" or "full of fear"? What clues were supplied by the words *prowess, wrestling,* and *uncharacteristically*?

Use context clues to figure out the meanings of the italicized words in these sentences from the selection. Check your answers in the glossary or in a dictionary.

Treadway and Vernelle, perhaps becoming *restive* at having nothing to do, started working out the harmony for "Button Up Your Overcoat."

Some of the panels that suddenly appeared in front of my face were even harder to detect than the slim lampposts at home, which would *materialize* out of nowhere when I was walking with an inattentive sighted companion, and bruise me, as if they had a will of their own.

Anyway, I had to concentrate on getting around, not on educating strangers, say what Miss Harper might about each of us being an *emissary* to the country of the sighted.

Writing About Literature

Describing the Narrator

What is your impression of Ved Mehta from the account he gives of himself in this selection? What adjectives would you use to describe him: independent? rebellious? determined? daring? imaginative? In a paragraph give a brief description of his character, citing evidence from the selection.

About the Author

Ved Mehta (1934–   )

Ved Mehta was born in India. An illness at the age of four left him totally blind. For three years he attended the Arkansas School for the Blind, where he learned to use "sound-shadows" to get around by himself. He later went on to Pomona College, to Oxford, and then to Harvard.

Mehta has written a series of autobiographical books about his earlier years in India: *Daddyji* (1972), which is a portrait of his father; *Mamaji* (1979), a portrait of his mother; *Vedi* (1982) and *The Ledge Between the Streams* (1984), which tell about his childhood.

When I Was a Boy on the Ranch

BY J. FRANK DOBIE

In this autobiographical essay, J. Frank Dobie tells about his boyhood on a Texas ranch. Note that Dobie uses a leisurely plan for his essay, letting his memory carry him from one pleasant pastime to another. How does he provide transitions between these individual memories?

There were six of us children and our ranch was down in the brush country of Texas between the Nueces River[1] and the Rio Grande. The automobiles have outrun the horses since then; radios have drowned out many a cricket's voice and many a coyote's wailing cry; in many a ranch yard the lights of Delco plants[2] have dimmed the glowing points of the fireflies— "lightning bugs," we called them. But the ranch of our childhood is still a ranch. And south of it clear to the Mexican border, and northwest of it into the Rocky Mountains and on up beyond the line where Montana joins Canada, there are millions and millions of acres of other ranches on which boys and girls live.

Despite automobiles these boys and girls still ride horses. Despite radios they still listen in the evening to crickets and frogs, and some-times in the night to the wailing cries of coyotes. As for electric lights on the ranches, they light such small spaces that the fireflies in the grass and the stars in the sky never notice them. The country is still country. For all the changes brought by invention, ranches are still ranches.

So if I tell how we children lived on our ranch, I'll also be telling how children still live on other ranches scattered all over the western half of the United States.

We liked ranching so much that our best game used to be "playing ranch." There were fine live oak trees between the yard fence and the pens about the stables and barns, and it was in the shade of these trees, especially during the summer, that we built our "ranches."

To build a pasture we drove little stakes close together in the ground until a plot about as big as a kitchenette was enclosed; sometimes the pasture was made by setting up "posts" of stakes in the ground and then stretching cords, in imitation of barbed wire, from one corner of

1. **Nueces** (no͞o-ā′səs, nyo͞o-) **River:** in southwestern Texas.
2. **Delco plants:** private electrical systems used on farms and ranches.

the "pasture" to the other. Each ranch had several pastures, and of course each ranch had headquarters, where houses and corrals were built. The houses were generally of boards; the corrals were of pickets laid between pairs of upright posts.

Fencing in the pastures was never so much fun as getting them stocked. It took work to fence in land and improve it with dirt tanks, which never would hold water very long. It took patience to construct corral gates that would open and shut and to make a house that would not fall down when a turkey stepped on it or a pup ran against it. But stocking this land with cattle and horses and goats was nothing but fun.

We had two kinds of cattle—high-grade cattle and common "stuff." The horn tips of real cattle—which were clipped off at branding time—became our purebred animals. Sometimes we had hundreds of them. Our "common Mexican cattle" were represented by oak balls.

But we prized our horses far more than our cattle. Horses consisted of sewing-thread spools; most of our clothes were made on the ranch, and those clothes took an astonishing amount of thread. Moreover, when we went visiting we had our eyes open for discarded spools, but visits of any kind were rare and those that brought spools were rarer. A spool has a long "side" that can be branded and it has a long "back" that can be saddled. I can't think of any better kind of play-horse than a spool.

The ranches in our part of the country had herds of white Mexican goats. White-shelled snails were abundant in our neighborhood, and these shells became our goats. A live snail would not stay in a pasture, for he can climb straight up and carry his shell with him, so our goats were always empty shells. There were no sheep in the country; we had never heard anything particularly good connected with sheepmen; and so we had no sheep—just cattle, horses, and goats.

Each of us had a brand. Mine was ⊏NE⊐, which an uncle of mine named Neville used. Fannie's was ⊠, Elrich's was an *E;* Lee's brand was *L.* The two younger children were too small to build ranches and brand herds by themselves; consequently if Henry and Martha got into the game, they got in as "hired help." Our branding irons were short pieces of bailing wire, with a crook at one end. This kind of branding iron is called a "running iron." When we had occasion to brand, we built a fire close to ranch headquarters, heated the "running irons," and burned our brands on the spool-horses, the common oak-ball cattle, and the fine horn cattle.

Like real ranchmen, we bought and sold stock. When a trade was made, the cattle or horses—we seldom traded goats—had to be gathered up, driven to the shipping pens, loaded on the railroad cars, transported, and delivered. Then after they were delivered they had to be branded with the brand of the new owner. (A great many of the "common cattle" were decayed on the inside and when they were branded collapsed into nothing!) We had to sell cheap for the very simple reason that dollars were scarce and cattle were plentiful.

The dollars we had, however, were extraordinarily good dollars of sound coinage and pure metal. The ranch kitchen used a considerable amount of canned goods, particularly canned tomatoes, salmon, and sardines, along with some peaches and corn. We held the empty can in a fire with tongs until the solder started to run, and then caught the solder in an old spoon, pouring it into a round wooden box that had once held bluing. The diameter of this round bluing box was—and still is—about that of a silver dollar. The dollars we coined were sometimes thicker than a silver dollar and they were always heavier, but in buying cattle they were worth just as much.

We had another source of metal for our dollars. In the fall of the year hunters would be on the ranch, either camped out or staying with us at the house. They usually shot up a good many boxes of shells practicing on trees. After the shooting was over, we children gouged out the lead bullets lodged in the trees and melted them into dollars.

I spoke of shipping cattle. The train was a string of empty sardine cans coupled to each other with wire hooks. Motive power was the chief problem. We tried hitching horned frogs and green lizards to it, but neither pulled with any strength. A horned frog would sometimes pull an empty wagon made of a cardboard matchbox. Old Joe, the best dog we ever had, would pull the train pretty well if he went in a straight line, but when he didn't, he caused several bad wrecks that overturned cars and spilled cattle out. If a delivery of cattle had to be made promptly, the simplest and surest way to make the engine pull the train was to tie a string to it and pull it yourself.

Of course there were *real* horses and *real* cattle to interest us. Children brought up on a ranch usually learn to ride only a little later than they learn to walk. Old Stray, Dandy, and Baldy were the horses on our ranch that could be trusted with the youngest children. Old Stray was a common Mexican pony that some Mexican had ridden down and turned loose on our ranch. When we first saw him he was as thin as a stick-horse. Nobody claimed him, so after a while we used him. He seemed to appreciate having plenty of grass to eat but he had no intention of ever exerting himself again. In short, he was not only gentle but "pokey." If a child fell off him, he would stop and graze until the child got up again. Baldy was an enormous horse, and by the time a boy was big enough to scramble upon his back without help from a man or a friendly fence, that boy was nearly ready for "long pants."

Dandy was a black horse of thoroughbred trotting stock. He alone of all the horses was entitled to corn the year around. The other

horses lived mostly on grass. We rode Dandy sometimes as well as drove him, but he had too much life in him for mere beginners. He was as kind and intelligent as he was lively. One time when my brother Elrich was very small he toddled into Dandy's stall while Dandy was eating. The flies were bothering Dandy and he was switching his tail and stamping his feet. He knew that the little boy was in danger. He put a hind foot against the child and shoved him out of the stall. He did not kick him—just shoved him.

By the time I was eight years old I had several horses to ride. There was Maudie, a little Spanish mare, that would kick up when I punched her in the shoulder with my finger or pointed my hand down toward her flank or tail. Later there was Buck, a horse raised on the ranch. He was a bay with a white face and stocking feet. I kept him as long as he lived and he died on the ranch where he was born. He could be turned loose in camp and would not stray off. Once when I was running to head some wild steers and Buck gave a quick dodge, the saddle, which was loosely girted, turned, throwing me to the ground and nearly breaking my hip. Buck could "turn on a dime" and stop as quickly as one can snap a finger. On this occasion he stopped so suddenly that he did not drag me a foot, though I was still in the saddle when my hip struck the ground. He was the best cowhorse I ever rode. Often when we were alone I talked to him. By the time I was twelve years old and a regular ranch hand, I was sometimes on him from daylight until long after dark. More than once I went to sleep riding him. I loved him and he loved me. I think of Buck oftener now than I think of many people who have been my friends.

As range cows do not give as much milk as dairy cows, we usually had a pen full of them to milk, especially in the summertime. Each cow had her calf, and the calves were allowed

part of the milk. A Mexican man usually did the milking, but it was the privilege of us boys to bring in the calves from the calf pasture each evening and then to ride them.

Now, riding calves is about as much fun as a ranch boy can possibly have. The calf is roped around the neck, and a half hitch, called a "bosal," is put around its nose. Then, using the rope as a bridle, the boy mounts. Until the calf is gentled, it will "pitch like a bay steer." One

calf that I remember particularly was a black heifer with a white face. She became very gentle and we named her Pet. I trained Pet so well that I could mount her and guide her all over the calf pasture. Usually, no matter how well "broke" to riding, a calf won't go where you want it to go. It won't go anywhere. Saddles don't fit calves or grown cattle and, although it was sometimes fun to saddle yearlings, what actual riding we did was bareback. As we grew older we caught range cattle coming into the big pen to water and rode the calves and yearlings.

Each of us children had a few head of cattle to call our own. They were for the most part dogies or of dogie origin. A "dogie" is a motherless calf. When one was found on the range, it would be brought in and some cow with a calf of like age would be tied at night and morning and forced to let the motherless calf share her milk. We had one old muley cow that was so kind to dogies that the dogie always fared better than her own offspring. She would moo to it and lick its hair and otherwise mother it.

Pet was originally a dogie. When she grew up and had calves of her own, we milked her. If she was a good "saddle horse," a red-roan calf that she had was a better one. Pet had so many calves and those calves grew up and had so many calves of their own that the little stock of cattle coming from her helped materially to put me through college one year.

We went to a country school, which was on our own ranch, where the children of five or six other ranch families attended. Most of them rode to school horseback. One of our games was "cats and dogs." This we boys—for girls did not join in it—played at noon recess. The "cats" would set out in the brush afoot. About three minutes later the "dogs," mounted on horses and yelling like Apache Indians, would take after them. The brush had thorns and the idea of the "cat" was to get into brush so thick that the "dog" could not follow him, or to crawl into a thicket where he could not be seen. Sometimes the chase would last until long after the bell had sounded. I remember one great chase that kept us out until three o'clock. An hour later eight or nine boys were alone with the teacher and a pile of *huajilla*[3] switches.

Another game on horseback that the older boys played was "tournament." Three posts are erected in a line a hundred yards apart. Each post has an arm of wood about a yard long. Hanging from this arm is a metal ring about two inches in diameter. It is held by a spring clasp so that it can be easily disengaged. The runner takes a sharpened pole—the "tournament pole"—in his right hand and,

holding it level, with the point out in front of him, runs lickety-split down the line of rings trying to spear them. The game requires skill. Buck was a wonderfully smooth-running horse, and he and I together hooked plenty of rings.

My sisters and girl cousins joined us in playing Indian and in making houses. Our ranch was built on a dry arroyo, or creek, named Long Hollow. Just below the house this creek had bluffs about forty feet high. For years we children worked periodically at digging caves back into the bluffs. Here we played Indian. If the soil had not been so gravelly and consequently inclined to cave in, we might have made dwelling places as ample as some of the ancient cliff dwellings. As it was, we got the caves big enough for us to hide in. When Long Hollow ran water after a rain, we made water wheels of sticks and cornstalks and watched them turn.

The house of our own construction that we enjoyed most was in a tree. It was a live oak called "the Coon Tree," from the fact that a coon hungry for chickens had once been found in it. Climbing up into this tree was an enormous mustang grapevine. This grapevine afforded us a kind of ladder to the limbs of the Coon Tree. We took planks up to these limbs and nailed them so that we had a solid floor.

In our country we did not have many fruits, but around the ranch house were prolific pomegranate bushes. No matter how dry the season, these pomegranates always bore fruit. In the summertime we would pick pomegranates,[4] borrow some sugar, spoons, and glasses from the kitchen, and, with a jug of water, gather on the platform in the Coon Tree for a picnic. We had a rope with which to pull up the jug and a bucket containing the other articles.

---

3. *huajilla* (wä-hēl′yä): a shrub.

4. **pomegranate** (pŏm′grăn′ĭt, pŭm′-): fruit with a juicy red pulp containing many seeds.

The point of the picnic was to make "pomegranateade" out of sugar, the fruit seeds, and water.

Sometimes we took books and read in the Coon Tree. *Beautiful Joe* and *Black Beauty* were favorites. Our real house had matting on the floor, and when this matting was discarded and we covered the platform in the Coon Tree with it, we felt that we had reached the height of luxury. I don't understand why none of us ever fell out of the Coon Tree.

I have spoken of our life with horses and calves. There were other animals to interest us, as there always are in the country. The trees about the ranch were inhabited each spring and summer by hundreds of jackdaws, a kind of blackbird. They built their nests in the trees so flimsily that disaster to the newly hatched birds was inevitable. Before they could fly or even walk, young birds would fall out of the trees and sprawl helpless on the ground, a ready prey for cats, turkeys, and other enemies. The distressed cries of the parent jackdaws were at times almost deafening, but these parents could do nothing toward getting their young back into the nests. We used to pick up the young birds and put them in straw-filled wooden nail-kegs, which we placed on the roofs of a shed and smokehouse under the Coon Tree. I have seen three or four parent jackdaws feeding their young at the same time in one of these kegs. Sometimes each keg held as many as eight young birds.

Scissortails built their hanging nests in the very tops of the higher trees, but their young never fell out. We never tired of watching the scissortails fly, especially if they were chasing a hawk, darting at his head and driving him away. The wrens nested in tool boxes in the stable, in coils of rope, even in the leather toe-fenders—called *tapaderos*[5]—covering the stir-

5. *tapaderos* (tăp′ə-där′ōz).

rups of saddles. When we found these nests, we made it our duty to warn our father and the Mexican laborers not to disturb them. One time a saddle had to go unused for weeks until a wren that had built in the *tapadero* of one stir-rup had brought off her brood.

Under Mother's direction we raised chickens, turkeys, and guineas. The guineas were good "watchdogs," alarming, with their wild

cries, everything and everybody within hearing distance when a hawk was approaching. Hawks, chicken snakes, and coyotes were constant enemies of the barnyard. We boys sometimes set traps for the coyotes. I remember seeing my mother, before I was old enough to handle a gun, shoot one with a rifle very near the house.

The evening call of the bob-white brought—as it yet brings—a wonderful peace. In the early mornings of certain times of the year we could hear wild turkeys "yelping" out in the brush back of the field. Once a large flock of them grazed up to the schoolhouse, but the teacher would not let us out to chase them. Although deer were plentiful, and some other children in the country had a pet fawn, we never had one. Once while riding in the pasture I halted a long time to watch a doe kill a rattlesnake.

I can honestly say that we did not enjoy "tormenting" animals and that we did not rob birds' nests. But when we snared lizards with a horsehair looped on the end of a pole; when we poured buckets of water down the holes of ground squirrels to make them come out; and when we hitched horned toads to matchboxes, we no doubt did torment those animals, though we seldom injured them. I have since killed noble buck deer, mountain lions, wild boars, and other game, but no memory of hunting is so pleasant as that of rescuing little jackdaws, of restoring a tiny dove fallen from its nest, and of watching, without molesting them, baby jack-rabbits in their cotton-lined nest against the cowpen fence—memories all of a ranch boy.

Ranch girls and boys always find so many ways to play and so many creatures of nature to interest them that the days are never long enough. And no life can be long enough for a ranch-bred boy or girl to forget the full times of childhood.

Reading Check

1. When the children were "playing ranch," what did they use for horses?
2. What did the children use for money when they bought and sold their stock?
3. What is a "dogie"?
4. What games were played on horseback?
5. What did the children use the tree house for?

For Study and Discussion

Analyzing and Interpreting the Essay

1a. What is Dobie's purpose?   **b.** Where does he state it?

2a. What kinds of activities were included in "playing ranch"?   **b.** How does Dobie make a transition from the game of playing ranch to the pleasures of actual ranch life?   **c.** What responsibilities did children have in helping to run the ranch?

3a. What was involved in riding calves?   **b.** What skills were needed for the games of "cats and dogs" and "tournament"?

4. Dobie has particularly fond memories of animals on the ranch. How did the children learn to care for birds and other wild creatures?

5. Dobie describes the different activities and interests of children growing up on a ranch. In what way might their play be considered schooling or preparation for their future lives as ranchers?

Language and Vocabulary

Recognizing Ranch Terms

Dobie uses a number of words that have special meaning to someone living and working on a ranch. When he talks about riding calves, he says that before it "is gentled," a calf will "pitch like a bay steer." The word *gentle* is used here as a verb with the special meaning of "to tame or train an animal"—usually a horse. What do you suppose the expression "pitch like a bay steer" means?

Make a list of other ranch terms and expressions used in the selection and tell what they mean.

Expository Writing

Explaining a Process

Dobie gives a step-by-step description of how children made play money by melting down tin cans and lead bullets and then coining dollars out of the metal. Following Dobie's method, explain how to make or do something, or tell how something works. You might choose something that you have built or put together: a doghouse, a go-cart, holiday decorations, and the like.

About the Author

J. Frank Dobie   (1888–1964)

James Frank Dobie was born on a ranch in Live Oak County, Texas, in the brush country close to the Mexican border. He began writing in college and after receiving a Master's degree from Columbia University, he taught at the University of Texas. He left teaching to manage a ranch for his uncle. While he was working on the ranch, he grew interested in the folklore and traditions of the Southwest. When he returned to teaching, he began writing books and editing publications of the Texas Folklore Society. His works include *A Vaquero of the Brush Country; Coronado's Children,* tales of buried treasure and lost mines in the Southwest; and *The Longhorns,* a collection of tales about longhorn steers.

DEVELOPING SKILLS
IN CRITICAL THINKING

Distinguishing Between Facts and Opinions

A *fact* is something that has happened or is true. An *opinion* is a statement that represents a belief or judgment and that cannot be proved. The statement *Columbus reached the New World in 1492* is a fact. The statement *Columbus was the greatest mariner who ever lived* is opinion. Even though many people will agree that the second statement is based on sound facts, it is an assertion that cannot be proved. There is nothing inherently wrong with opinions as long as they are not presented as or mistaken for facts.

As a reader and as a listener, you need to know whether the information you receive is fact or opinion. In the following passage, which statements would you consider fact and which would you consider opinion?

The next day was magnificent. The air was crystal, the sky was aquamarine, and the far horizon of palms and oaks lay against the sky. I felt a new boldness and followed Ross bravely. He was making the rounds of the gopher holes. The rattlers came out in the midmorning warmth and were never far away. He could tell by their trails whether one had come out or was still in the hole. Sometimes the two men dug the snake out. At times it was down so long and winding a tunnel that the digging was hopeless. Then they blocked the entrance and went on to other holes. In an hour or so they made the original rounds, unblocking the holes. The rattler in every case came out hurriedly, as though anything was preferable to being shut in.

PRACTICE IN
READING AND WRITING

Nonfiction

Writers of nonfiction, like writers of fiction, often combine exposition, description, and narration. In a single passage a writer might use exposition to explain, instruct, or express an opinion; description to communicate an impression of people or places; and narration to relate events.

The following passage is from "Rattlesnake Hunt." See if you can find examples of all three kinds of writing.

A rattler will lie quietly without revealing itself if a man passes by and it thinks it is not seen. It slips away without fighting if given the chance. Only Ross's sharp eyes sometimes picked out the gray and yellow diamond pattern, camouflaged among the grasses. In the cool of the morning, chilled by the January air, the snakes showed no fight. They could be looped up limply over the steel L and dropped in a sack or up into the wire cage on the back of Will's truck. As the sun mounted in the sky and warmed the moist Everglades earth, the snakes were warmed too, and Ross warned that it was time to go more cautiously. Yet having learned that it was we who were the aggressors; that immobility meant complete safety; that the snakes, for all their lightning flash in striking, were inaccurate in their aim, with limited vision; having watched again and again the liquid grace of movement, the beauty of pattern, suddenly I understood that I was drinking in freely the magnificent sweep of the horizon, with no fear of what might be at the moment under my feet. I went off hunting by myself, and though I found no snakes, I should have known what to do.

The sun was dropping low in the west. Masses of white cloud hung above the flat marshy plain and seemed to be tangled in the tops of distant palms and cypresses. The sky turned orange, then saffron. I walked leisurely back toward the truck. In the distance I could see Ross and Will making their way in too. The season was more advanced than at the Creek, two hundred miles to the north, and I noticed that spring flowers were blooming among the lumpy hummocks. I leaned over to pick a white violet. There was a rattlesnake under the violet.

1. The events in a narrative are related to one central action. What is the main action in the passage? Over what period of time does the action occur?
2. Exposition is used to inform, to explain, or to persuade. Find the sentences that explain the habits of rattlesnakes.
3. Description creates an impression of people, places, or things, by using details that appeal to the senses. The many descriptive details in the model passage add clarity and interest to the narrative. Which details help you picture the rattlesnakes? Which sentences help you see the surrounding countryside?

Suggestions for Writing

Write a composition about an experience you have had. You may write about a "first" experience, such as the time you learned to swim or to ride a bicycle. You may write about a vacation or a visit away from home. You may combine descriptive, narrative, and expository techniques.

Prewriting

- Focus on one episode. Make a list of the important events in connection with this episode. Choose specific details and words that will help your reader imagine the place and the people involved. Provide any facts or references your reader may need to know.
- Arrange the details in some logical sequence: chronological, spatial, cause and effect, order of climax, or some other order.
- Compose a topic sentence that states the main idea of your paper or conveys your feeling about the experience.

Evaluating and Revising

- Does your opening sentence inform the reader about the subject of the paper?
- Have you included the most significant details? Have you deleted repetitive or irrelevant ideas?
- Is the sequence of events clear?
- Are there appropriate transitional words (*now, then, furthermore*) to connect your ideas?
- Have you used precise verbs and specific details?

Proofreading

- Reread your revised version and correct mistakes in grammar, usage, spelling, capitalization, and punctuation. Ask a classmate to check your revision for accuracy, and then prepare a final copy.

For Further Reading

Bradley, Bill, *Life on the Run* (paperback, Bantam, 1986)

Basketball star Bill Bradley describes the exciting but often lonely life of a professional basketball player.

Frank, Anne, *The Diary of a Young Girl,* translated by B. M. Mooyart, rev. ed. (Doubleday, 1967)

Anne Frank kept this diary while she and seven other people lived in hiding in Amsterdam during the Nazi occupation.

Hautzig, Esther, *The Endless Steppe: Growing Up in Siberia* (Thomas Y. Crowell, 1968)

The author and her family were forced to spend five years in Siberia when the Soviet Union invaded Poland in 1951. The loving spirit and humor of the family help to make "a young girl's heart . . . indestructible."

Heyerdahl, Thor, *Kon-Tiki: Across the Pacific by Raft,* rev. ed. (Rand McNally, 1984)

This is an exciting account of how the author, four other men, and a parrot spent almost one hundred days traveling across the Pacific on a raft in order to test a theory.

Keller, Helen, *The Story of My Life* (many editions)

Although she was deprived of her sight and hearing by a childhood illness, Helen Keller triumphed over her handicaps and became a legend in her own time.

Kroeber, Theodora, *Ishi, Last of His Tribe* (Parnassus, 1964; paperback, Bantam)

This is the story of the last survivor of the Yahi tribe, an Indian people of California.

Latham, Jean Lee, *Carry On, Mr. Bowditch* (Houghton Mifflin, 1955; paperback, Houghton, 1973)

Here is a lively, fast-moving biography of Nathaniel Bowditch, skilled navigator and author of the classic guide *The American Practical Navigator.* The story begins in 1779, when Nathaniel is twelve, and follows him through many adventures.

Lord, Walter, *A Night to Remember* (Holt, Rinehart and Winston, 1955; paperback, Bantam)

The author gives a minute-by-minute account of the night of April 14, 1912, when the "unsinkable" ocean liner *Titanic* struck an iceberg and sank.

Petry, Ann, *Harriet Tubman: Conductor on the Underground Railroad* (Thomas Y. Crowell, 1955; paperback, Archway)

This is the biography of a daring and devoted woman who risked her life countless times to help more than three hundred slaves escape to freedom.

Scott, Robert Falcon, *Scott's Last Expedition* (Dodd, Mead, 1941)

This is the journal of Scott's tragic expedition to the Antarctic in 1910.

Singer, Isaac Bashevis, *A Day of Pleasure: Stories of a Boy Growing Up in Warsaw* (Farrar, Straus & Giroux, 1969)

The author describes his boyhood in a Jewish ghetto from 1908 to 1918.

Stuart, Jesse, *The Thread That Runs So True* (Scribner, 1968; paperback, Scribner)

The novelist and poet tells of his experiences as a young teacher in a one-room Kentucky schoolhouse.

POETRY

You may be surprised to learn that poetry is older than any other kind of literature. Poetry developed long before prose; as a matter of fact, there was poetry long before there was a written language of any kind. In early times, poems were memorized and passed down from generation to generation by word of mouth. We know that poems were often sung. Ancient Greek poets sang to the accompaniment of a lyre, a stringed instrument something like a small harp. Our word *lyric* shows this connection between poetry and music.

In this unit you will find poems of many kinds. Some of the poems tell stories, some describe scenes, some capture a mood, and some are humorous. All of them are meant to be read aloud.

Still Life: Flowers and Fruit (c. 1850) by Severin Roesen. Oil on canvas.
The Metropolitan Museum of Art

CLOSE READING
OF A POEM

*Developing
Skills in
Critical
Thinking*

Poetry has a special language and structure. Poets rely on the suggestive power of language and choose words for their emotional effect as well as for their literal meaning. Through images and figures of speech poets appeal to the mind and to the senses. Poets also make use of patterns of sound, such as rhyme and rhythm; special forms, such as haiku; and unusual arrangements of words on a page.

In order to express themselves in effective and imaginative ways, poets take liberties with language. They do not always use complete sentences or complete thoughts. They may reverse the normal order of words. They may choose not to use conventional punctuation.

It is a good idea to read a poem several times, and aloud at least once. Often it is helpful to write a prose paraphrase of a poem, restating all its ideas in plain language (see page 442). A paraphrase is no substitute for the "meaning" of a poem, but it helps you clarify and simplify the author's ideas and language.

Read the following poem several times. Then read the explication that follows. An *explication* is a line-by-line examination of the content and technique of a work.

May Day
SARA TEASDALE

A delicate fabric of bird song
   Floats in the air,
The smell of wet wild earth
   Is everywhere.

Red small leaves of the maple   5
   Are clenched like a hand,
Like girls at their first communion°
   The pear trees stand.

7. **first communion** (kə-myōōn'yən): Girls traditionally wear white for this religious ceremony.

Oh I must pass nothing by
    Without loving it much,   10
The raindrop try with my lips,
    The grass at my touch;

For how can I be sure
    I shall see again
The world on the first of May   15
    Shining after the rain?

Explication

The title of Sara Teasdale's poem refers to the first day of May, a holiday traditionally marked by the celebration of spring. Teasdale expresses her pleasure in the natural beauty of the season, a pleasure intensified by the knowledge that she must enjoy beauty fully while she can.

The poet responds to the glory of nature with all her senses. In the first stanza she tells us what she hears and what she smells. The birds seem to be awakening to the season. They do not produce a full-throated stream of sound but a "delicate fabric of bird song" that "floats in the air," a metaphor that suggests beautifully fine, light singing. The earth, still in its "wild," or natural, uncultivated state, smells of the rain.

In the second stanza, the poet notes what she sees. New leaves, red and small, are appearing on maple trees. The lobed leaves give the impression of a tightly closed fist. Looking at the pear trees abloom with white blossoms in umbrella-like clusters, the poet thinks of girls standing in white frocks at their first communion.

At the opening of the third stanza, the poet says she wishes to make the most of her opportunities—to experience everything with love. She involves two additional senses in her appreciation of nature. She must "try," or taste, the raindrop on her lips; she must touch the grass to feel its texture.

The poem ends on a sobering note, explaining the poet's sense of urgency about the passing of time. She feels compelled to take in everything, for there is no surety that she will ever again experience such a day. What she has for certain is the memory of the immediate moment—the beauty of the world on a spring day, "shining" after the rain.

Guidelines for Reading a Poem

1. *Read the poem aloud at least once. Look for complete thoughts instead of reading line by line.* Commas, semicolons, periods, and other marks of punctuation tell you where to pause. Sara Teasdale does not expect the reader to pause at the end of each line. In the last stanza, she signals no pause until the end of the poem, signifying that she wishes no break in thought.

2. *Note the effects of specific words.* In poetry, a word often has special connotations, or associations. The word *floats,* in line 2, for example, has the denotative meaning of "drifts or moves slowly on the surface of a fluid." In the context of the poem, however, it suggests a sound that is so light and exquisite that it seems to be supported by air in the way that a buoyant object is supported by water.

3. *Note the comparisons chosen by the poet.* In lines 7–8 Teasdale compares the blossoming pear trees to girls in white dresses, an image that suggests beauty and innocence.

4. *Listen for the sound effects.* Note the emphasis achieved by Teasdale's pattern of rhyme in each stanza of the poem.

5. *Write a paraphrase of any lines that need clarification or simplification.* A paraphrase helps a reader understand imagery and figurative language. A paraphrase of the first two lines might look like this: "The notes of the song are fitted together into a pattern the way threads are woven into cloth. The sound is so soft and gentle that it seems suspended in air, as if it were lifted up and carried along." A paraphrase also supplies connections in thought where words have been omitted. A paraphrase of line 11 might read: "The poet says she must taste or sample the raindrops with her lips."

6. *Arrive at the central idea or meaning of the poem.* Try to state this theme in one or two sentences: *In "May Day," Teasdale seems to be saying that since life is short, one ought to fill time with the enjoyment of natural beauty.*

Language and Meaning

THE SPEAKER

Who is the speaker in a poem? Is the speaker always the poet? Emily Dickinson assured someone once that he must not think that; she spoke of a "supposed person" as her speaker. Of course, the poet does write the poems, but he or she may be wearing a disguise. The voice may be that of some other person or thing. As you read "The Caterpillar" and "One of the Seven Has Somewhat to Say," ask yourself whose voice is speaking. Then read each poem aloud just the way that speaker would want to be heard.

The Caterpillar

ROBERT GRAVES

Under this loop of honeysuckle,
A creeping, colored caterpillar,
I gnaw the fresh green hawthorn spray,
I nibble it leaf by leaf away.

Down beneath grow dandelions,   5
Daisies, old-man's-looking-glasses;
Rooks° flap croaking across the lane.
I eat and swallow and eat again.

7. **rooks:** birds resembling crows.

Here come raindrops helter-skelter;
I munch and nibble unregarding: 10
Hawthorn leaves are juicy and firm.
I'll mind my business: I'm a good worm.

When I'm old, tired, melancholy,
I'll build a leaf-green mausoleum°
Close by, here on this lovely spray,   15
And die and dream the ages away.

14. **mausoleum** (mô′sə-lē′əm, mô′zə-): tomb.

Some say worms win resurrection,°
With white wings beating flitter-flutter,
But wings or a sound sleep, why should
    I care?
Either way I'll miss my share.   20

Under this loop of honeysuckle,
A hungry, hairy caterpillar,
I crawl on my high and swinging seat,
And eat, eat, eat—as one ought to eat.

17. **resurrection**   (rĕz′ə-rĕk′
shən): rebirth.

For Study and Discussion

Analyzing and Interpreting the Poem

1a. Who is speaking in the poem? **b.** What is the "business" (line 12) that needs minding? **c.** Which words in the poem refer to eating?

2. What different things does the speaker ignore?

3. A caterpillar turns into a butterfly or moth. Where does the speaker refer to this change?

4a. What does the poem tell you about the habits of caterpillars? **b.** Judging from your own experiences, are these habits described accurately?

5. Is the tone of this poem serious or humorous? Explain.

One of the Seven Has Somewhat to Say

SARA HENDERSON HAY

As you read, determine the identity of the speaker, and then figure out to whom he is speaking.

Remember how it was before she came—?
The picks and shovels dropped beside the door,
The sink piled high, the meals any old time,
Our jackets where we'd flung them on the floor?
The mud tracked in, the clutter on the shelves,   5
None of us shaved, or more than halfway clean . . .
Just seven old bachelors, living by ourselves?
Those were the days, if you know what I mean.

She scrubs, she sweeps, she even dusts the ceilings;
She's made us build a tool shed for our stuff.   10
Dinner's at eight, the table setting's formal.
And if I weren't afraid I'd hurt her feelings
I'd move, until we get her married off,
And things can gradually slip back to normal.

For Study and Discussion

Analyzing and Interpreting the Poem

1a. At what point did you guess the identity of the speaker? **b.** What clues led you to your conclusion?

2a. According to the speaker, how have things changed since "she" arrived? **b.** How does he feel about the old life and the new?

3. What is the speaker's attitude toward the young woman?

Creative Writing

Assuming Another Identity

Use your imagination to pretend that you are someone else—a teacher, a television personality, a figure in the news, even an animal. Decide what the "new you" might feel angry or indignant about. Write a poem in which your "speaker" makes clear his or her views.

About the Authors

Robert Graves (1895–1985)

Robert Graves was born in Wimbledon, England. He was wounded in France during World War I. After the war, he studied at Oxford University. A well-known contemporary writer, he wrote critical essays, mythological studies, and historical novels in addition to poetry. He also translated books from other languages into English.

Sara Henderson Hay (1906–   )

Sara Henderson Hay was born in Pittsburgh, Pennsylvania. She attended Brenau and Columbia universities. She has published many poems in periodicals like *Saturday Review*, *Atlantic*, and *McCall's*. Some of her most popular collections of poetry are *Field of Honor*, *This, My Letter*, *The Delicate Balance*, and *The Stone and the Shell*.

DICTION

Diction refers to a writer's choice of words or manner of expression. Poets choose words carefully for precise effects, to arouse particular moods or sensations. They depend on the rich associations, or *connotations*, of words as well as on their literal, or *denotative*, meanings.

The diction of a poem may be formal or informal. In "One of the Seven Has Somewhat to Say" (page 435), the speaker refers to "our stuff" in line 10. The word *stuff* is an informal word for "belongings."

Sometimes poets take freedom with language, making up new words, running words together, or using unusual word order. In the hands of a poet like E. E. Cummings (page 439), this *poetic license* results in striking effects.

Poets will also change the normal order of words in a sentence. This technique, called *inversion,* is used most often when the poet wishes to give emphasis to a word or an idea.

Fog

CARL SANDBURG

In this poem, fog is compared to a cat. Note how effectively Sandburg uses simple, familiar words.

The fog comes
on little cat feet.

It sits looking
over harbor and city
on silent haunches
and then moves on.

The 1st

LUCILLE CLIFTON

The words in this poem are extremely simple, yet charged with emotional feeling. What is the effect of the repetition in the last two lines?

What I remember about that day
is boxes stacked across the walk
and couch springs curling through the air
and drawers and tables balanced on the curb
and us, hollering,
leaping up and around
happy to have a playground;

nothing about the emptied rooms
nothing about the emptied family

For Study and Discussion

Analyzing and Interpreting the Poem

1. The first of the month is generally the day when rent is due. What details in the poem tell you what is happening to the family?

2a. What words does the speaker use to describe herself and the other children in lines 5–7? **b.** How do the words in the last two lines change the emotional feeling of the poem?

3a. What do you think the phrase "emptied family" means? **b.** How is the connotation of "emptied rooms" different from "emptied family"?

4. Why do you suppose the speaker repeats the words *nothing* and *emptied* in the last two lines?

Literary Elements

Understanding the Role of Diction

Precise, clear diction helps the reader understand exactly what is happening in a poem. In Clifton's poem the couch springs are *curling* upward. We can see the coils that have come through the worn padding. The children are *hollering*—shouting in play, unaware of what is happening to the family. The furniture is *balanced* on the curb.

Effective diction is one of the elements through which a poet reveals emotional meaning. What phrase conveys the family's feeling of loss as they leave their home?

in Just-

E. E. CUMMINGS

Cummings wants his readers to approach his poems as original and fresh works. What kinds of poetic license does he use here?

in Just-
spring   when the world is mud-
luscious the little
lame balloonman

whistles   far   and wee   5

and eddieandbill come
running from marbles and
piracies and it's
spring

when the world is puddle-wonderful   10

the queer
old balloonman whistles
far   and   wee
and bettyandisbel come dancing

from hop-scotch and jump-rope and   15

it's
spring
and
     the

          goat-footed°   20

balloonMan   whistles
far
and
wee

20. **goat-footed:** Pan, a god of woods and fields in Greek mythology, was represented with the legs of a goat.

For Study and Discussion

Analyzing and Interpreting the Poem

1a. When is "Just-spring"? **b.** From the point of view of a young child, why might the world be "mud-luscious" and "puddle-wonderful" at this time? **c.** What games do the children in the poem play?

2. The word *wee,* meaning "very small or little," is often used in children's stories. It also sounds like *whee,* a word used by children when they are excited or happy. What other word might be intended?

3. The sound of the balloonman's whistle is first heard in line 5. Notice the space between the words *whistles, far,* and *and wee.* **a.** What happens to the space between these words in lines 12–13? **b.** In lines 21–24? **c.** What do you think is happening to the sound of the whistle?

4. The balloonman is described as "goat-footed." As explained in the note to line 20, Pan was believed to have the legs of a goat. He was fond of music and dancing, and was thought to be the inventor of the shepherd's pipes. Why do you think the balloonman is associated with Pan?

5. How is the movement of the lines across the page like the movement of the children in the poem?

Literary Elements

Understanding the Purpose of Poetic License

In his poem Cummings wishes the reader to experience spring as it is experienced by children who are filled with wonder and happiness. Note the hyphenated words *mud-luscious* and *puddle-wonderful.* Why are these words more effective than the words *muddy* and *wet*? To a child, what makes mud *luscious*? What makes a puddle *wonderful*?

Cummings also runs together the names *eddieandbill* and *bettyandisbel,* and he does not capitalize the names, perhaps to suggest that the individual names are not important—the names of other children could easily be substituted. In the phrase *Just-spring,* Cummings capitalizes the word *Just.* What does he wish to emphasize about the season?

When you look at the poem, the lines have an irregular pattern, and the eye is forced to skip across spaces. How does this arrangement capture the spirit of the children and their movement?

What other examples of poetic license have you found in Cummings' poem? Can you explain the purpose for these elements?

The Chipmunk's Day

RANDALL JARRELL°

Sometimes the most familiar things take on new significance as the result of a poet's fresh observations. How does the poet's language capture the movements of the chipmunk?

In and out the bushes, up the ivy,
Into the hole
By the old oak stump, the chipmunk flashes.
Up the pole

To the feeder full of seeds he dashes,   5
Stuffs his cheeks,
The chickadee and titmouse scold him.
Down he streaks.

Red as the leaves the wind blows off the maple,
Red as a fox,   10
Striped like a skunk, the chipmunk whistles
Past the love seat, past the mailbox,

Down the path,
Home to his warm hole stuffed with sweet
Things to eat.   15
Neat and slight and shining, his front feet

Curled at his breast, he sits there while the sun
Stripes the red west
With its last light: the chipmunk
Dives to his rest.   20

° **Jarrell** (jə-rĕl′).

Analyzing and Interpreting the Poem

1. List the verbs that describe the chipmunk's movements. What kind of movement is emphasized?

2. The first sentence of the poem is interrupted three times by commas. Read these lines aloud. How do the lines suggest the chipmunk's movements?

Literary Elements

Understanding the Purpose of Inversion

Most sentences in the English language follow a pattern in which the subject comes before the predicate. Consider the effect of varying this pattern in a line from a familiar nursery rhyme.

Jack and Jill went up the hill
Up the hill went Jack and Jill

What change in emphasis occurs when the order of words is shifted?

A reversal of the normal arrangement of words in a sentence is called **inversion**. Inverting word order calls attention to the word or phrase that has been shifted. A poet can give a word or phrase special importance by placing it at the beginning or at the end of a line.

What would be the normal order of the words in the following lines?

In and out the bushes, up the ivy,
Into the hole
By the old oak stump, the chipmunk flashes.

What does the poet emphasize by inversion in these lines?

Locate another example of inversion in the poem and tell what its purpose is.

Writing About Literature

Paraphrasing a Poem

A **paraphrase** is a summary of a literary work. When you paraphrase a poem, you restate its language and ideas in your own words. A paraphrase is helpful in clarifying what a poem means.

The first three lines of Jarrell's poem might be paraphrased in this way:

The chipmunk moves swiftly in and out of the bushes, up the ivy vine, and into the hole near the stump of the old oak tree.

Paraphrase the rest of the poem. Check to see that your paraphrase includes all the details in the poem.

When the Frost Is on the Punkin

JAMES WHITCOMB RILEY

Dialect *is a form of speech belonging to a particular region or to a particular group of people. A dialect may be distinguished by characteristics of vocabulary, grammar, and pronunciation.*

This poem is written in a dialect that was spoken in rural Indiana many years ago. If you read the poem out loud, you will have no problem understanding words like russel *and* medder.

When the frost is on the punkin and the fodder's in the shock,°
And you hear the kyouck and gobble of the struttin' turkey
    cock,
And the clackin' of the guineys,° and the cluckin' of the hens,
And the rooster's hallylooyer as he tiptoes on the fence;
O, it's then's the time a feller is a-feelin' at his best,   5
With the risin' sun to greet him from a night of peaceful rest,
As he leaves the house, bareheaded, and goes out to feed the
    stock,
When the frost is on the punkin and the fodder's in the shock.

They's something kindo' harty-like about the atmusfere
When the heat of summer's over and the coolin' fall is here—   10
Of course we miss the flowers, and the blossums on the trees,
And the mumble of the hummin'birds and buzzin' of the bees;
But the air's so appetizin'; and the landscape through the haze
Of a crisp and sunny morning of the airly autumn days
Is a pictur' that no painter has the colorin' to mock—   15
When the frost is on the punkin and the fodder's in the shock.

The husky, rusty russel of the tossels of the corn,
And the raspin' of the tangled leaves, as golden as the morn;
The stubble in the furries—kindo' lonesome-like, but still
A-preachin' sermuns to us of the barns they growed to fill;   20
The strawstack in the medder, and the reaper in the shed;
The hosses in theyr stalls below—the clover overhead!—
O, it sets my hart a-clickin' like the tickin' of a clock,
When the frost is on the punkin and the fodder's in the shock!

1. **shock:** a pile of stalks and leaves set in a field to dry.

3. **guineys** (gĭn′ēz): guinea fowls.

Then your apples all is gethered, and the ones a feller keeps   25
Is poured around the celler floor in red and yeller heaps;
And your cider makin's over, and your wimmern folks is
    through
With theyr mince and apple butter, and theyr souse and
    sausage, too!
I don't know how to tell it—but ef sich a thing could be
As the Angels wantin' boardin', and they'd call around on *me*—   30
I'd want to 'commodate 'em—all the whole indurin' flock—
When the frost is on the punkin and the fodder's in the shock!

For Study and Discussion

Analyzing and Interpreting the Poem

1. Who is the speaker in this poem?

2. This poem tells what life was like on an Indiana farm during early autumn many years ago. In the first stanza the speaker notes the sounds he hears early in the morning. Which words imitate the sounds of farm animals?

3. In the second stanza the speaker describes the "atmusfere" of early fall. What characteristics of the morning does he enjoy?

4. Autumn is the time when crops are harvested. **a.** What details in the third stanza tell you that the harvesting is over? **b.** What are the "tossels" in line 17? **c.** The "furries" in line 19?

5. What tasks of the autumn season are described in the last stanza?

6. Why do you think autumn fills the speaker with such a sense of well-being?

Literary Elements

Understanding the Role of Dialect

The use of dialect in literature is a way of giving authenticity to a region and its people. If you have read "The Erne from the Coast" (page 208), you may remember that the characters use a dialect spoken in the sheep country of Great Britain. They say *aboot* for "about" and *aw reet* for "all right." In *The Mazarin Stone* (page 318), Sam Merton speaks a variety of English called *cockney*, which is associated with the East End of London. One characteristic of this dialect is the dropping of the letter *h*: '*ere* for "here."

James Whitcomb Riley makes use of dialect to give us the flavor of a particular place and time. What would be lost if you substituted standard speech for the dialect?

Carl Sandburg (1878–1967)

Carl Sandburg was born in Galesburg, Illinois. He left school at thirteen and helped support his family by working at odd jobs. After serving in the Spanish-American War, he decided to enroll in college. In 1914 his poem "Chicago," a vibrant picture of this Midwestern city, was published in *Poetry* magazine and won the Levinson Prize. His volume *Chicago Poems,* which came out in 1916, received wide acclaim. Five more volumes of poetry followed. Sandburg spent fifteen years writing a six-volume biography of Abraham Lincoln, his boyhood hero. He also wrote tales and lyrics for children and edited a collection of folk songs called *The American Songbag.* Sandburg was awarded the Pulitzer Prize for both poetry and history.

Lucille Clifton (1936–   )

Lucille Clifton was born in Depew, New York, and attended Howard University. Among her collections of poetry are *Good Times, An Ordinary Woman,* and *Two-Headed Woman.* She has also written novels, short stories, children's fiction, and a memoir of her family called *Generations.* Her work has been published in a number of periodicals, including *The Massachusetts Review, Black World,* and *Negro Digest.* She lives in Baltimore.

E. E. Cummings (1894–1962)

For a biography of Cummings, see page 70.

Randall Jarrell (1914–1965)

Randall Jarrell was born in Nashville, Tennessee. He enjoyed a distinguished career as a poet, teacher, and literary critic. He served as Consultant in Poetry at the Library of Congress. In 1961 he won the National Book Award for poetry. In addition to poetry, he wrote a novel and two volumes of essays. "The Chipmunk's Day" is from *The Bat Poet,* a story about a bat that writes poems.

James Whitcomb Riley (1849–1916)

James Whitcomb Riley, known as "the Hoosier poet," worked for some years as a sign painter, an actor, and a small-town journalist. Then he went to work for the *Indianapolis Daily Journal,* which regularly published his poems. Riley had a keen eye for the local scene and characters, and sometimes made use of the Hoosier (Indiana country) dialect. One of his best-known poems is "Little Orphant Annie."

IMAGERY

Imagery is language that appeals to the senses. Imagery in poetry is most often visual, but it can appeal to any of the other senses—hearing, smell, taste, and touch. Riley's poem "When the Frost Is on the Punkin" (page 443) appeals to all the senses. Riley uses visual imagery when he describes the apples "poured around the celler floor in red and yeller heaps." The "gobble" of the turkey cock and the "buzzin" of the bees appeal to the sense of hearing. The reference to "mince and apple butter, and theyr souse and sausage" appeals to the sense of taste. "The stubble in the furries" appeals to the sense of touch.

Imagery is one of the elements through which a poet reveals meaning. As you read "Trade Winds" and "A Parrot," note how the poets select images that appeal to your imagination and that also convey meaning.

Trade Winds

JOHN MASEFIELD

In the colonial period, Spanish merchant ships traveled in the Caribbean Sea, which became known as the Spanish Main. The Trade Winds, which blow toward the equator from the east, are still very important to navigators.

In the harbor, in the island, in the Spanish Seas,
Are the tiny white houses and the orange trees,
And daylong, nightlong, the cool and pleasant breeze
    Of the steady Trade Winds blowing.

There is the red wine, the nutty Spanish ale,   5
The shuffle of the dancers, the old salt's° tale,
The squeaking fiddle, and the soughing° in the sail
    Of the steady Trade Winds blowing.

And o' nights there's fireflies and the yellow moon,
And in the ghostly palm trees the sleepy tune   10
Of the quiet voice calling me, the long low croon°
    Of the steady Trade Winds blowing.

6. **old salt:** an experienced sailor.

7. **soughing** (sŭf′əng, sou′əng): soft rustling.

11. **croon:** soft singing.

For Study and Discussion

Analyzing and Interpreting the Poem

1a. What is the setting of the poem? **b.** What impression do you receive of the setting from the imagery in the poem?
2a. Who is the speaker in the poem? **b.** What clues are there to his identity?

3a. What are the pleasures that the speaker enjoys on land? **b.** What is the "voice" that calls to him in line 11?

4. Repetition of a word or a line in a poem is usually done for emphasis. What is the effect of repeating the same line at the end of each stanza?

A Parrot

MAY SARTON

My parrot is emerald green,
His tail feathers, marine.°
He bears an orange half-moon
Over his ivory beak.
He must be believed to be seen,   5
This bird from a Rousseau° wood.
When the urge is on him to speak,
He becomes too true to be good.

He uses his beak like a hook
To lift himself up with or break   10
Open a sunflower seed,
And his eye, in a bold white ring,
Has a lapidary° look.
What a most astonishing bird,
Whose voice when he chooses to sing   15
Must be believed to be heard.

That stuttered staccato scream
Must be believed not to seem
The shriek of a witch in the room.
But he murmurs some muffled words   20
(Like someone who talks through a
    dream)
When he sits in the window and sees
The to-and-fro wings of wild birds
In the leafless improbable trees.

2. **marine:** here, a blue-green color. 6. **Rousseau** (rōō-sō′): Henri Rousseau (1844–1910), a French painter known for the vivid colors of his canvases. 13. **lapidary** (lăp′ə-dĕr′ē): precious stone.

Analyzing and Interpreting the Poem

1. The poet uses chiefly color imagery in the first two stanzas to describe the parrot. Why does the bird seem to be something out of a painting?

2. Why does the speaker call the parrot "a most astonishing bird"?

3a. What kinds of sounds does the bird make? **b.** How does he react to the sight of wild birds? **c.** Why would the trees outdoors seem *improbable* to him?

4. We usually say that something must be seen to be believed, or that something is too good to be true. **a.** How has the poet changed these expressions? **b.** Can you suggest a reason for these changes?

Creative Writing

Composing a Poem

In a poem describe some unusual plant or animal you have seen at the botanical garden, a pet shop, or the zoo. Use language that appeals to the senses. If you wish, accompany your poem with an illustration.

About the Authors

John Masefield (1878–1967)

John Masefield was born in Ledbury, England. When he was fourteen, he ran away to sea. After two years, he landed in New York City with only five dollars to his name. He worked at various jobs, all the while reading as many books as he could buy at secondhand bookshops. His first volume of poems, *Salt-Water Ballads,* told of the ships and seamen he had known. One of his most famous novels is *Jim Davis.* In 1930 Masefield became poet laureate of England.

May Sarton (1912–)

May Sarton was born in Belgium. Her family emigrated to the United States two years later. Although she is best known as a poet, she has also written short stories, essays, novels, and screenplays. Among her volumes of poetry are *Encounter in April, The Leaves of the Tree,* and *Halfway to Silence.* She won the Human Dignity Award in 1984 and the American Book Award in 1985. She lives in Maine.

FIGURATIVE LANGUAGE

Figurative language is language that is not intended to be understood in a strict literal sense. Many everyday expressions are figurative. When you ask someone "to lend a hand," you are speaking figuratively. You are asking for that person's help. When used imaginatively, figurative language adds a dimension of meaning to speech or writing.

The term *figure of speech* is often used for a specific kind of figurative language. Two common figures of speech are *simile* and *metaphor*. A simile uses a word such as *like* or *as* to express some kind of likeness between two different things. In "May Day" (page 430), Teasdale says that the small leaves of the maple are "clenched *like* a hand." A metaphor draws a comparison between two unlike things by identifying them. Had Teasdale written "The leaves of the maple are clenched hands," she would have used a metaphor.

As you read the following poems, identify the figures of speech and note how they appeal to your imagination.

Living Tenderly

MAY SWENSON

This is a riddle poem. In order to guess the identity of the speaker, you must correctly interpret the figurative language.

My body a rounded stone
with a pattern of smooth seams.
My head a short snake,
retractive,° projective.°
My legs come out of their sleeves   5
or shrink within,
and so does my chin.
My eyelids are quick clamps.

My back is my roof.
I am always at home.   10
I travel where my house walks.
It is a smooth stone.
It floats within the lake,
or rests in the dust.
My flesh lives tenderly   15
inside its bone.

4. **retractive** (rĭ-trăk′tĭv): capable of drawing back. **projective** (prə-jĕk′tĭv): capable of moving forward.

Analyzing and Interpreting the Poem

1a. What does the poem describe? **b.** What details in the poem give you the answer?

2a. What does the "pattern of smooth seams" refer to? **b.** What are the "sleeves" referred to in line 5?

3a. Describe the way a clamp works. **b.** Why do you think the eyelids are called "quick clamps"?

4. State in your own words what the last two lines of the poem mean.

Understanding Figurative Language

Look again at the opening lines of the poem:

My body a rounded stone
with a pattern of smooth seams.

In these lines a body is identified with a stone. In reality, that is not possible: a body cannot be a stone. But the poet is not speaking **literally**—that is, in terms of reality. She is speaking **figuratively**—that is, in terms of poetic imagination. The poet means to suggest that there is some similarity between two different things.

To speak of a body as if it were a stone suggests something about the shape and feel of that body. What do the lines suggest to you?

In the opening lines the poet is using a kind of figurative language called **metaphor**. A metaphor draws a comparison between two things that are basically different. Explain the metaphors in line 3 and in line 8.

In addition to metaphor, poets use a figurative device called **simile**. Like metaphor, a simile draws a comparison between two unlike things. However, a simile uses a word such as *like, as,* or *than* to express the comparison. Explain the simile in these lines:

And green and blue his sharp eyes twinkled,
Like a candle flame where salt is sprinkled . . .

What two things are compared in this simile?

My heart is like an apple tree
  Whose boughs are bent with thickset fruit.

Identify the metaphors and similes in the following lines. Explain each comparison.

Deep in the sun-scorched growths the dragonfly
Hangs like a blue thread, loosened from the sky.

The lightning is a yellow fork
From tables in the sky. . .

The day is done, and the darkness
  Falls from the wings of night,
As a feather is wafted downward
  From an eagle in his flight.

The Spider

ROBERT P. TRISTRAM COFFIN

*What is the speaker's attitude toward the spider? How is that attitude revealed
in the metaphors of the poem?*

With six small diamonds for his eyes
He walks upon the Summer skies,
Drawing from his silken blouse
The lacework of his dwelling house.

He lays his staircase as he goes   5
Under his eight thoughtful toes
And grows with the concentric° flower
Of his shadowless, thin bower.°

His back legs are a pair of hands,
They can spindle out the strands   10
Of a thread that is so small
It stops the sunlight not at all.

He spins himself to threads of dew
Which will harden soon into
Lines that cut like slender knives   15
Across the insects' airy lives.

He makes no motion but is right,
He spreads out his appetite
Into a network, twist on twist,
This little ancient scientist.   20

He does not know he is unkind,
He has a jewel for a mind
And logic deadly as dry bone,
This small son of Euclid's° own.

7. concentric (kən-sĕn′trĭk): having circles, one within another, with a common center.
8. bower: here, dwelling place.

24. Euclid (yōō′klĭd): Greek mathematician of third century B.C., who wrote a basic work in geometry.

Analyzing and Interpreting the Poem

1. Although the word *web* is not used, it is clear that the poem is figuratively describing the spider spinning a web. **a.** What are the "silken blouse," the "lacework," and the "dwelling house" referred to in the first stanza? **b.** What is the "staircase" in line 5? **c.** Are these appropriate metaphors?

2. We are told that the web is so delicate that the thread "stops the sunlight not at all." How are we also reminded of the deadly nature of the web?

3. In the final lines, the spider is compared to a scientist and to a mathematician. What is the basis for these comparisons?

4a. What is the speaker's attitude toward the spider? **b.** What is the spider's logic and why is it deadly?

May Swenson (1919–   )

May Swenson was born in Logan, Utah, and attended Utah State University. She worked as a reporter on the Salt Lake City *Deseret News* before moving to New York. A winner of many fellowships and awards, she has taught poetry seminars at a number of major universities. Her poems are notable for their close observation of nature. She lives in Sea Cliff, New York.

Robert P. Tristram Coffin (1892–1955)

Robert Peter Tristram Coffin was a Maine author who graduated from Bowdoin College. He was a Rhodes scholar at Oxford University and became a professor of English at Wells College in New York. Besides his many volumes of poetry, he wrote essays, biographies, and novels. His poetry often focuses on the hearty outdoors life and on closely observed wonders of nature.

THE IDEAS IN A POEM

All the elements you have studied thus far are ways for the poet to communicate meaning. Some poems yield their meaning at a single reading. More complex poems can be read on several levels and interpreted in more than one way.

Like other forms of literature, a poem often has an underlying idea, or *theme*, that offers a point of view about life or gives some insight into human experience. As you read, learn to explore poetry for these deeper meanings.

Stopping by Woods
on a Snowy Evening

ROBERT FROST

This poem tells the story of a man who stops to watch snow falling in the woods. Most readers of the poem think that Frost is using a simple, everyday experience to reveal some deep truth or understanding about life.

Whose woods these are I think I know.
His house is in the village, though;
He will not see me stopping here
To watch his woods fill up with snow.

My little horse must think it queer   5
To stop without a farmhouse near
Between the woods and frozen lake
The darkest evening of the year.

He gives his harness bells a shake
To ask if there is some mistake.   10
The only other sound's the sweep
Of easy wind and downy flake.

The woods are lovely, dark, and deep,
But I have promises to keep,
And miles to go before I sleep,   15
And miles to go before I sleep.

For Study and Discussion

Analyzing and Interpreting the Poem

1a. Why has the speaker stopped? **b.** How do you know that it is unusual for the speaker to stop in these woods?

2a. Describe the scene that you see in the poem. **b.** What does the phrase "the darkest evening of the year" tell you?

3a. Why can't the speaker linger to look at the woods? **b.** What do you think his "promises" are?

4. This poem has been interpreted in a number of ways. Some readers believe that the woods in Frost's poem represent an escape from the world and its pressures. Others believe that the poem is about the obligations that keep people from enjoying the beauty of the world. Still others suggest that the word *sleep* in the last two lines of the poem is a reference to death. Do you agree with any of these interpretations? Give reasons for your answer.

The Listeners

WALTER DE LA MARE

This poem contains many mysterious elements. What explanation can you offer
for its strange events?

"Is there anybody there?" said the Traveler,
    Knocking on the moonlit door;
And his horse in the silence champed the grasses
    Of the forest's ferny floor;
And a bird flew up out of the turret,   5
    Above the Traveler's head:
And he smote upon the door again a second time;
    "Is there anybody there?" he said.
But no one descended to the Traveler;
    No head from the leaf-fringed sill   10

Leaned over and looked into his gray eyes,
    Where he stood perplexed and still.
But only a host of phantom listeners
    That dwelt in the lone house then
Stood listening in the quiet of the moonlight   15
    To that voice from the world of men:
Stood thronging the faint moonbeams on the dark stair
    That goes down to the empty hall,
Hearkening in an air stirred and shaken
    By the lonely Traveler's call.   20
And he felt in his heart their strangeness,
    Their stillness answering his cry,
While his horse moved, cropping the dark turf,
    'Neath the starred and leafy sky;
For he suddenly smote on the door, even   25
    Louder, and lifted his head—
"Tell them I came, and no one answered,
    That I kept my word," he said.
Never the least stir made the listeners,
    Though every word he spake   30
Fell echoing through the shadowiness of the still house
    From the one man left awake:
Aye, they heard his foot upon the stirrup,
    And the sound of iron on stone,
And how the silence surged softly backward,   35
    When the plunging hoofs were gone.

Analyzing and Interpreting the Poem

1. "The Listeners" tells of a man who knocks three times at the door of a house in a forest and, receiving no answer, mounts his horse and gallops away. **a.** Who do you think the Traveler is? **b.** Who do you think the listeners are?

2. Words like *phantom* in line 13 and *shadowiness* in line 31 add mystery to the poem. What other words can you find that contribute to the poem's eerie effect?

3. Why do you think the Traveler has come to the house? (What meaning do you see in lines 27–28?)

4. The Traveler is the central figure in the poem. Yet the poem is called "The Listeners." Why do you think the poet chose this title?

Writing About Literature

Interpreting a Poem

In a short essay give your interpretation of "Stopping by Woods on a Snowy Evening" or "The Listeners." Support your interpretation with evidence from the poem. For assistance in planning and writing your paper, see the section called *Writing About Literature* at the back of this textbook.

About the Authors

Robert Frost (1874–1963)

For a biography of the author, see page 179.

Walter de la Mare (1873–1956)

Walter de la Mare, who created magical worlds in his poems and stories, spent nearly twenty years as a bookkeeper in the London office of an oil company. In 1908 he received a grant that enabled him to become a full-time writer. Over a period of forty years he published many collections of enchanting poems and tales. "The Listeners" is famous for its beautiful music and its eerie mystery. According to one account, de la Mare got the idea for the poem from a class reunion. On the day that he and his former classmates were to meet at a school, no one but de la Mare appeared. The empty rooms and corridors of the building inspired him to write the poem.

Sound and Meaning

REPETITION AND RHYME

You have seen that poets carefully select and arrange words to appeal to your senses, your imagination, and your emotions. To convey meaning, poets also use devices of sound. One of the most important devices at the poet's disposal is *repetition*. Repetition may occur in the form of *rhyme*, in which similar sounds are repeated within or at the end of lines. Repetition may also occur with a single letter or group of letters, as in this line from "A Parrot" (page 448): "That *s*tuttered *s*taccato *s*cream." This kind of repetition is called *alliteration* (ə-lĭt′ə-rā′shən). The poet may also choose to repeat a word, a phrase, or an entire line. The term for this kind of repetition is *refrain*. In John Masefield's poem "Trade Winds" (page 447), the refrain appears at the end of each stanza.

While repetition is one of the elements that give us pleasure in reading and listening to poetry, it is also a way of emphasizing and communicating meaning.

Annabel Lee

EDGAR ALLAN POE

Poe claimed that in his poetry he chose each sound to produce a desired effect. Read this poem aloud, noting particularly his use of repetition and rhyme. Then ask yourself how these sounds help reinforce the speaker's feelings.

It was many and many a year ago,
    In a kingdom by the sea,
That a maiden there lived whom you may know
    By the name of Annabel Lee;
And this maiden she lived with no other thought   5
    Than to love and be loved by me.

I was a child and *she* was a child,
　　In this kingdom by the sea,
But we loved with a love that was more than love—
　　I and my Annabel Lee—   10
With a love that the wingèd seraphs° of Heaven
　　Coveted° her and me.

11. **seraphs** (sĕr′əfs): angels.

12. **Coveted** (kŭv′ĭ-tĭd): envied.

And this was the reason that, long ago,
　　In this kingdom by the sea,
A wind blew out of a cloud, chilling   15
　　My beautiful Annabel Lee;
So that her highborn kinsmen came
　　And bore her away from me,
To shut her up in a sepulcher°
　　In this kingdom by the sea.   20

19. **sepulcher** (sĕp′əl-kər): a tomb or burial place.

The angels, not half so happy in Heaven,
　　Went envying her and me:
Yes!—that was the reason (as all men know,
　　In this kingdom by the sea)
That the wind came out of the cloud by night,   25
　　Chilling and killing my Annabel Lee.

But our love it was stronger by far than the love
　　Of those who were older than we—
　　Of many far wiser than we—
And neither the angels in Heaven above,   30
　　Nor the demons down under the sea,
Can ever dissever° my soul from the soul
　　Of the beautiful Annabel Lee:

32. **dissever** (dĭ-sĕv′ər): separate.

For the moon never beams, without bringing me dreams
　　Of the beautiful Annabel Lee;   35
And the stars never rise, but I feel the bright eyes
　　Of the beautiful Annabel Lee:
And so, all the nighttide,° I lie down by the side
Of my darling—my darling—my life and my bride,
　　In the sepulcher there by the sea—   40
　　In her tomb by the sounding sea.

38. **nighttide:** nighttime.

Annabel Lee   **461**

Annabel Lee (1911) by W. L. Taylor. Watercolor.

Analyzing and Interpreting the Poem

1. What do you learn about Annabel Lee in the first three stanzas of the poem?

2a. Whom does the speaker blame for Annabel Lee's death? **b.** What reason does he give in lines 11–12 and lines 21–22?

3a. Why does the speaker believe that his soul and the soul of Annabel Lee cannot be separated? **b.** How is he continually reminded of her?

4a. Which sounds are repeated with frequency? **b.** How do these sounds reinforce the overall mood and meaning of the poem?

Literary Elements

Understanding Repetition in Poetry

In "Annabel Lee" Poe repeats certain words, sounds, and phrases. The name Annabel Lee appears at least once in every stanza. What other words and phrases are repeated several times? What ideas and feelings are emphasized by these repetitions?

Rhyme is a form of repetition. What words are repeatedly linked together through rhyme?

Sometimes words within a single line are rhymed. This kind of rhyme is called **internal rhyme**. Look at line 26:

Chilling and *killing* my Annabel Lee.

How many times does Poe use internal rhyme in the last stanza?

For Oral Reading

Avoiding Singsong

In reading poetry aloud, people sometimes enjoy the sounds so much that they ignore the meaning of individual lines. Unfortunately, they may read in a monotonous pattern called *singsong*.

One way to avoid singsong is to read a poem naturally. Do not stress rhyme by overstressing accented syllables, by raising your voice, or by pausing mechanically at the end of each line. Follow the punctuation and meaning of the poem.

In "Annabel Lee," how would you read lines 3–4 in the first stanza? Lines 9–10 in the second stanza? Lines 23–25 in the fourth stanza? Practice reading the poem aloud, paying close attention to meaning as well as sound.

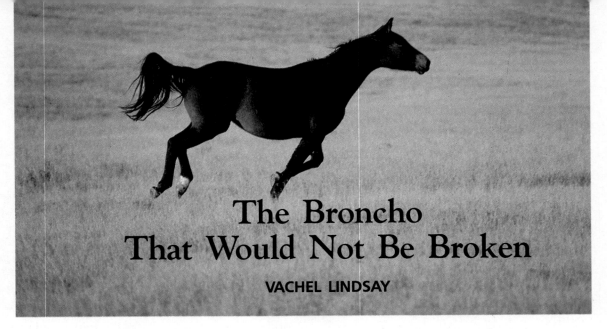

The Broncho That Would Not Be Broken

VACHEL LINDSAY

In this poem, note the refrain at the end of each stanza. What other patterns of repetition can you find? How do they reinforce the meaning of the poem?

A little colt—broncho, loaned to the farm
To be broken in time without fury or harm,
Yet black crows flew past you, shouting alarm,
Calling "Beware," with lugubrious° singing. . . .
The butterflies there in the bush were romancing,   5
The smell of the grass caught your soul in a trance,
So why be a-fearing the spurs and the traces,
O broncho that would not be broken of dancing?

You were born with the pride of the lords great and olden
Who dance, through the ages, in corridors golden.   10
In all the wide farmplace the person most human.
You spoke out so plainly with squealing and capering,
With whinnying, snorting, contorting, and prancing,
As you dodged your pursuers, looking askance,
With Greek-footed figures, and Parthenon° paces,   15
O broncho that would not be broken of dancing.

The grasshoppers cheered. "Keep whirling," they said.
The insolent sparrows called from the shed,
"If men will not laugh, make them wish they were dead."
But arch° were your thoughts, all malice displacing.   20

4. lugubrious (lōō-gōō′brē-əs): sad.

15. Parthenon (pär′thə-nän′): an ancient Greek temple decorated with sculptures of lively horses.

20. arch: sly.

Though the horse-killers came, with snakewhips advancing.
You bantered and cantered away your last chance.
And they scourged you with hell in their speech and their
    faces,
O broncho that would not be broken of dancing.

"Nobody cares for you," rattled the crows,   25
As you dragged the whole reaper, next day, down the rows.
The three mules held back, yet you danced on your toes.
You pulled like a racer, and kept the mules chasing.
You tangled the harness with bright eyes side-glancing,
While the drunk driver bled you—a pole for a lance—   30
And the giant mules bit at you—keeping their places.
O broncho that would not be broken of dancing.

In that last afternoon your boyish heart broke.
The hot wind came down like a sledge-hammer stroke.
The blood-sucking flies to a rare feast awoke.   35
And they searched out your wounds, your death warrant
    tracing.
And the merciful men, their religion enhancing,
Stopped the red reaper to give you a chance.
Then you died on the prairie, and scorned all disgraces,
O broncho that would not be broken of dancing.   40

For Study and Discussion

Analyzing and Interpreting the Poem

1. What does the word *dancing* tell you about the broncho's natural grace and spirit?

2. What words in the poem describe the broncho's playfulness?

3. How do the men try to subdue the colt and break its spirit?

4. Other animals witness what is happening to the broncho. **a.** Which of them are in sympathy with the colt? **b.** In what way are the "broken" creatures cruel to the colt?

5. By dying, the broncho "scorned all disgraces." What disgraces would he have endured had he continued to live?

6. Explain in your own words what this poem is saying about "breaking," or destroying, nature's creatures.

Literary Elements

Understanding the Refrain

A phrase or line that is repeated regularly in a poem is called a **refrain**. A refrain usually occurs at the end of a stanza. A line that is repeated often in a poem can be easily learned and remembered. In folk songs and ballads, you will often find refrains at the end of each stanza, where an audience is expected to join in the singing.

What is the refrain in Lindsay's poem? How does it foreshadow the broncho's fate?

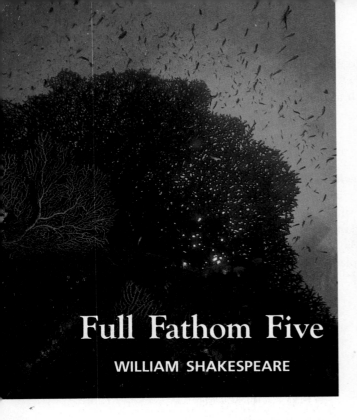

Full Fathom Five

WILLIAM SHAKESPEARE

This song is sung by Ariel, an airy spirit in The Tempest, *one of Shakespeare's plays. Prince Ferdinand believes that his father has been drowned in a shipwreck. The song tells him of a magical transformation that has taken place. Read the poem aloud. What mood is evoked by the music of its sounds?*

Full fathom° five thy father lies:
    Of his bones are coral made;
Those are pearls that were his eyes;
    Nothing of him that doth fade
But doth suffer° a sea-change
Into something rich and strange.
Sea nymphs° hourly ring his knell:°
           Ding-dong.
Hark! now I hear them—ding-dong, bell.

1. **fathom** (făth'əm): a depth of 6 feet (about 2 meters). 5. **suffer:** undergo. 7. **Sea nymphs** (nĭmfs): goddesses once thought to inhabit the sea. **knell** (nĕl): the tolling of a death bell.

For Study and Discussion

Analyzing and Interpreting the Poem

1a. According to the song, what change has the sea made in Ferdinand's father? **b.** Why is this change "rich and strange"?

2. How would you describe the mood of this poem?

Literary Elements

Understanding How Sounds Convey Feeling

You have seen that a poet makes music by repeating key words and lines and by using rhyme. A poet also makes music by repeating the sounds of certain consonants and vowels.

Look again at the opening line of Shakespeare's poem: "*Full fathom five thy father lies.*" Shakespeare uses several words that begin with the same consonant sound: **f.** He also repeats sounds in the middle of words. The sound **th** is repeated in *fathom, thy,* and *father.* This technique is known as **alliteration** (ə-lit'ə-rā'shən).

The sounds **f** and **th** are gentle sounds. They do not explode the way the sound **p** does in this line: "Peter Piper picked a peck of pickled peppers." The long vowel sound in *five, thy,* and *lies* helps slow up the movement of the line and thereby contributes to the mood of the poem.

What sounds are repeated in lines 3–5? Can you find another example of alliteration in the poem?

Edgar Allan Poe (1809–1849)

Edgar Allan Poe was born in Boston to a family of traveling actors. After his mother died, he was taken into the home of a wealthy Virginia merchant named John Allan. Although Poe took Allan as his middle name, his relations with his guardian were always strained. In 1826 he entered the University of Virginia but had to leave within a year because of his heavy gambling debts. He then enlisted in the army and served two years. John Allan helped him secure an appointment to West Point, but Poe got himself dismissed for misconduct. At this point he turned to writing and editing in order to earn a living. In 1836 he married his young cousin Virginia, but this marriage ended tragically in 1847, when Virginia died of tuberculosis. Poe died in poverty at the age of forty.

Despite his personal difficulties, Poe produced a remarkable body of short stories, poems, and essays. His short-story masterpieces include "The Tell-Tale Heart," "The Cask of Amontillado," "The Pit and the Pendulum," and "The Fall of the House of Usher"—strange tales of terror and fantasy. Among his most beautiful and melodic poems are "Eldorado," "The Raven," and "The Bells."

Vachel Lindsay (1879–1931)

Vachel Lindsay was born in Springfield, Illinois. As a young man, he took long, solitary walking tours throughout America. Called the "vagabond poet," he hoped to convert people to a doctrine of life's beauty and social reform. He became famous with the publication of his poems "General William Booth Enters into Heaven" (1913) and "The Congo" (1914). Like many of Lindsay's poems, these lend themselves to being chanted or sung, which is how the poet himself delivered them before large and enthusiastic audiences.

William Shakespeare (1564–1616)

William Shakespeare is generally considered the greatest dramatist—some believe the greatest writer—in the English language. He was born in Stratford-on-Avon in England. As a young man, he journeyed to London, where he joined an acting company. He wrote thirty-seven plays—comedies, tragedies, romances, and historical dramas. In addition to plays, he wrote some of the most magnificent sonnets in our language. Today he is probably the world's most widely read and performed playwright.

ONOMATOPOEIA AND RHYTHM

In "The Wreck of the *Hesperus*" (page 164), Longfellow describes the snow falling into the sea by saying that the "snow fell hissing in the brine." The word *hissing* to some degree imitates the actual sound made. Longfellow is making use of *onomatopoeia* (ŏn′ə-măt′ə-pē′ə), a technique that is commonly used by poets.

Rhythm is the pattern of stressed and unstressed sounds in a line of poetry. Rhythm contributes to the musical quality of a poem. It can also be used to imitate action and to give emphasis to key words and ideas.

The Highwayman

ALFRED NOYES

Historically, the highwayman was an outlaw who held up travelers on public roads. In literature, he often appears as a handsome, bold, and romantic figure. This poem is well known for its exciting story and captivating sound. As you read the poem aloud, see if you can hear the rhythm of horses' hoofs.

Part 1

The wind was a torrent of darkness among the gusty trees,
The moon was a ghostly galleon° tossed upon cloudy seas,
The road was a ribbon of moonlight over the purple moor,
And the highwayman came riding—
  Riding—riding—   5
The highwayman came riding, up to the old inn door.

He'd a French cocked hat on his forehead, a bunch of lace
  at his chin,
A coat of the claret° velvet, and breeches of brown doe skin;
They fitted with never a wrinkle: his boots were up to the
  thigh!
And he rode with a jeweled twinkle,   10
  His pistol butts a-twinkle,
His rapier hilt° a-twinkle, under the jeweled sky.

2. **galleon** (găl′ē-ən): a large sailing ship.

8. **claret** (klăr′ət): deep red, like claret wine.

12. **rapier** (rā′pē-ər) **hilt:** the handle of a light sword.

Over the cobbles he clattered and clashed in the dark
  innyard
And he tapped with his whip on the shutters, but all was
  locked and barred;
He whistled a tune to the window, and who should be
  waiting there   15
But the landlord's black-eyed daughter,
  Bess, the landlord's daughter,
Plaiting° a dark red love knot into her long black hair.

18. Plaiting: braiding.

And dark in the dark old innyard a stable wicket creaked
Where Tim the ostler° listened; his face was white and peaked;   20
His eyes were hollows of madness, his hair like moldy hay,
But he loved the landlord's daughter,
  The landlord's red-lipped daughter,
Dumb as a dog he listened, and he heard the robber say—

20. ostler (ŏs′lər): stableman; also called *hostler* (hŏs′lər).

"One kiss, my bonny sweetheart, I'm after a prize tonight,   25
But I shall be back with the yellow gold before the morning
  light;
Yet, if they press me sharply, and harry° me through the day,
Then look for me by moonlight,
  Watch for me by moonlight,
I'll come to thee by moonlight, though hell should bar the
  way."   30

27. harry: attack repeatedly.

He rose upright in the stirrups; he scarce could reach her
  hand,
But she loosened her hair i' the casement!° His face burned
  like a brand
As the black cascade of perfume came tumbling over his
  breast;
And he kissed its waves in the moonlight,
  (Oh, sweet black waves in the moonlight!)   35
Then he tugged at his rein in the moonlight, and galloped
  away to the west.

32. casement: a window that opens outward on hinges.

Part 2

He did not come in the dawning; he did not come at noon;
And out o' the tawny sunset, before the rise o' the moon,
When the road was a gypsy's ribbon, looping the purple moor,
A redcoat troop came marching—   40
  Marching—marching—
King George's men came marching, up to the old inn door.

They said no word to the landlord, they drank his ale instead,
But they gagged his daughter and bound her to the foot of
    her narrow bed;
Two of them knelt at her casement, with muskets at their side!   45
There was death at every window;
   And hell at one dark window;
For Bess could see, through her casement, the road that *he*
    would ride.

They had tied her up to attention, with many a sniggering jest;
They had bound a musket beside her, with the barrel
    beneath her breast!   50
"Now keep good watch!" and they kissed her. She heard the
    dead man say—
Look for me by moonlight;
   Watch for me by moonlight;
I'll come to thee by moonlight, though hell should bar the way!

She twisted her hands behind her; but all the knots held good!   55
She writhed her hands till her fingers were wet with sweat
    or blood!
They stretched and strained in the darkness, and the hours
    crawled by like years,
Till, now, on the stroke of midnight,
   Cold, on the stroke of midnight,
The tip of one finger touched it! The trigger at least was hers!   60

The tip of one finger touched it; she strove no more for the
    rest!
Up, she stood to attention, with the barrel beneath her breast,
She would not risk their hearing; she would not strive
    again;
For the road lay bare in the moonlight;
   Blank and bare in the moonlight;   65
And the blood in her veins in the moonlight throbbed to
    her love's refrain.

Tlot-tlot; tlot-tlot! Had they heard it? The horse hoofs ringing
    clear;
Tlot-tlot, tlot-tlot, in the distance? Were they deaf that they
    did not hear?
Down the ribbon of moonlight, over the brow of the hill,
The highwayman came riding,   70
   Riding, riding!
The redcoats looked to their priming! She stood up, straight
    and still!

Tlot-tlot, in the frosty silence! *Tlot-tlot,* in the echoing night!
Nearer he came and nearer! Her face was like a light!
Her eyes grew wide for a moment; she drew one last deep
    breath,   75
Then her finger moved in the moonlight,
  Her musket shattered the moonlight,
Shattered her breast in the moonlight and warned him—
    with her death.

He turned; he spurred to the westward; he did not know
    who stood
Bowed, with her head o'er the musket, drenched with her
    own red blood!   80
Not till the dawn he heard it, his face grew gray to hear
How Bess, the landlord's daughter,
  The landlord's black-eyed daughter,
Had watched for her love in the moonlight, and died in the
    darkness there.

Back, he spurred like a madman, shrieking a curse to the sky,   85
With the white road smoking behind him, and his rapier
    brandished high!
Blood-red were his spurs i' the golden noon; wine-red his
    velvet coat,
When they shot him down on the highway,
  Down like a dog on the highway,
And he lay in his blood on the highway, with a bunch of
    lace at his throat.   90

And still of a winter's night, they say, when the wind is in the trees,
When the moon is a ghostly galleon tossed upon cloudy seas,
When the road is a ribbon of moonlight over the purple moor,
A highwayman comes riding—
    Riding—riding—   95
A highwayman comes riding, up to the old inn door.

Over the cobbles he clatters and clangs in the dark innyard;
And he taps with his whip on the shutters, but all is locked and barred;
He whistles a tune to the window, and who should be waiting there
But the landlord's black-eyed daughter,   100
    Bess, the landlord's daughter,
Plaiting a dark red love knot into her long black hair.

For Study and Discussion

Analyzing and Interpreting the Poem

1. This poem tells a story. Where and when does the story take place? Find details in the poem that help you to establish the time and place. (What do lines 40–42 tell you?)

2a. Who are the major characters in the story? **b.** What details in the poem tell you what they look like? **c.** What role does Tim the ostler play in the story?

3. There are many references to moonlight in the poem. The meeting of lovers by moonlight is traditional in stories of romance. Why is moonlight also important to the action of the story?

4a. Which lines in the fifth stanza are echoed in the second part of the poem? **b.** Why do you think the poet wants you to recall these lines?

5. How do the last two stanzas add to the mystery and romance of the poem?

Literary Elements

Understanding How Sound Imitates Action

In poetry words are often chosen because their sounds seem to imitate the action they describe. In line 13 of Noyes's poem, we read

    Over the cobbles he clattered and clashed in the dark innyard

The words *clattered* and *clashed* suggest the actual sounds of hoofs on the cobbles. We call this effect **onomatopoeia** (ŏn′ə-măt′ə-pē′ə). What other examples of onomatopoeia can you find in the poem?

Find examples of onomatopoeia in the following poems and tell what each sound suggests:

"When the Frost Is on the Punkin" page 443, stanza 2
"Trade Winds" page 447, stanza 2
"The Broncho That Would Not Be Broken" page 464, stanza 2
"Full Fathom Five" page 466

Responding to Rhythm

Rhythm refers to the pattern of stressed and unstressed sounds in a line of poetry. Rhythm contributes to the musical quality of a poem. Rhythm can also be used to imitate the action being described in the poem.

Reread the first two lines of "The Highwayman" and listen to the way your voice rises and falls on the syllables of the words:

> The **wind** was a **tor**rent of **dark**ness a**mong** the **gust**y **trees**,
> The **moon** was a **ghost**ly **gall**eon **tossed** upon **cloud**y **seas**,

The syllables in boldface are those that are stressed when the lines are read aloud. The other syllables are unstressed.

Using your finger, tap out the rhythm of lines 3–6. What pattern do you get?

Below are lines 3–6. The stressed syllables are marked ('); the unstressed syllables (˘). Is this the pattern you tapped out?

> The road was a ribbon of moonlight over the purple moor,
> And the highwayman came riding—
> Riding—riding—
> The highwayman came riding, up to the old inn door.

Do you hear the rhythm of horses' hoofs? Reread the poem, listening carefully to its rhythm.

For Oral Reading

Presenting a Choral Reading

"The Highwayman" lends itself well to choral presentation. In the choral reading of a poem, speaking voices are used much as singing voices are used in a chorus. Some lines are assigned to individuals as solo parts; some lines are assigned to small groups of voices; some are assigned to all voices.

Choral reading takes a good deal of preparation and practice. You must decide which lines are best for solo voices and which are best for many voices. You must interpret how lines are to be read. You must determine when the voices should be raised or lowered and when the pace of reading should be stepped up or slowed down.

When you have decided how you wish to read the poem, choose a chorus leader. The chorus leader acts as a conductor who signals when different members of the chorus are to speak. If there is a tape recorder available, record your practice sessions. Listen to the tapes and suggest ways to improve the performance of the group.

About the Author

Alfred Noyes   (1880–1958)

Alfred Noyes drew material for some of his best-known poems from England's real and legendary past. He wrote "The Highwayman" at night while he was visiting Bagshot Heath, a lonely moor in England that outlaws had roamed two centuries before. Besides poetry, Noyes wrote plays, literary criticism, and an autobiography called *Two Worlds from Memory*. The first of his worlds was England, and the second was America. Noyes taught English literature at Princeton University from 1914 to 1923.

Types of Poetry

NARRATIVE POETRY

A *narrative* poem tells a story, and like a short story, it has characters, a setting, and action. You have already read some well-known stories in verse: "The Wreck of the *Hesperus*" (page 164), "The Listeners" (page 457), "Annabel Lee" (page 460), and "The Highwayman" (page 468).

One special kind of narrative poem with a long history is the *ballad*. The original ballads, called *folk ballads*, have no known authors. They were not written down; they were passed down by word of mouth from one generation to another.

One of the most popular subjects in English ballads is the legendary Robin Hood, who appears in about forty ballads. Some ballads celebrate historical events and battles. Many ballads tell tragic love stories and tales of jealousy, betrayal, and revenge.

A great many of the old ballads were brought to America by early colonists. In addition to these imported ballads, which underwent change, Americans have composed original ballads, such as "Casey Jones" and "John Henry."

One of the poems included here is an old folk ballad. The other poem, by Robert Browning, is based on an old German legend about an unusual musician.

The Golden Vanity

A great many ballads have come down to us in more than one version. This is an American version of an English sea ballad about a ship called the **Golden Vanity**. *In older texts it is known as the* **Sweet Trinity**, *which supposedly was the name of Sir Walter Raleigh's flagship.*

'Twas all on board a ship down in a southern sea,
And she goes by the name of the *Golden Vanity*;
I'm afraid that she'll be taken by this Spanish crew,
   As she sails along the Lowlands,
   As she sails along the Lowlands low.   5

Then up speaks our saucy cabin boy, without fear or joy,
Saying, "What will you give me, if I will her destroy?"
"I'll give you gold and silver, my daughter fine and gay,
   If you'll destroy her in the Lowlands,
   If you'll sink her in the Lowlands low."   10

The boy filled his chest and so boldly leaped in,
The boy filled his chest and then began to swim;
He swam alongside of the bold Spanish ship,
   And he sank her in the Lowlands,
   And he sank her in the Lowlands low.   15

Some were playing cards and some were playing dice,
And some were in their hammocks sleeping very nice;
He bored two holes into her side, he let the water in,
   And he sank her in the Lowlands,
   And he sank her in the Lowlands low.   20

The boy then swam back unto our good ship's side,
And being much exhausted, bitterly he cried;
"Captain, take me in, for I'm going with the tide,
   And I'm sinking in the Lowlands,
   And I'm sinking in the Lowlands low."   25

"I will not take you in," our captain then replied,
"I'll shoot you and I'll stab you and I'll sink you in the tide,
   And I'll sink you in the Lowlands,
   And I'll sink you in the Lowlands low."

The boy then swam around next the larboard° side,   30
And being more exhausted, bitterly he cried,
"Messmates, take me in, for I'm going with the tide,
   And I'm sinking in the Lowlands,
   And I'm sinking in the Lowlands low."

They hove the boy a rope and they hoisted him on deck,   35
They laid him on the quarter deck, the boy here soon died;
They sewed him up in a canvas sack, they hove him in the tide,
   And they buried him in the Lowlands,
   So they buried him in the Lowlands low.

30. **larboard** (lär′bərd): the port side, the left-hand side of the ship.

To think we buy gowns lined with ermine   25
For dolts that can't or won't determine
What's best to rid us of our vermin!
You hope, because you're old and obese,°

28. **obese** (ō-bēs'): extremely fat.

To find in the furry civic robe ease?
Rouse up, Sirs! Give your brains a racking   30
To find the remedy we're lacking,
Or, sure as fate, we'll send you packing!"
At this the Mayor and Corporation
Quaked with a mighty consternation.

IV

An hour they sat in council;   35
   At length the Mayor broke silence:
"For a guilder° I'd my ermine gown sell,

37. **guilder** (gĭl'dər): silver or gold coin.

   I wish I were a mile hence!
It's easy to bid one rack one's brain—
I'm sure my poor head aches again,   40
I've scratched it so, and all in vain.
Oh for a trap, a trap, a trap!"
Just as he said this, what should hap
At the chamber door but a gentle tap?
"Bless us," cried the Mayor, "what's that?"   45
(With the Corporation as he sat,
Looking little though wondrous fat;
Nor brighter was his eye, nor moister
Than a too-long-opened oyster,
Save when at noon his paunch grew mutinous   50
For a plate of turtle green and glutinous)°

51. **glutinous** (glōot'n-əs): gluey, thick.

"Only a scraping of shoes on the mat?
Anything like the sound of a rat
Makes my heart go pit-a-pat!"

V

"Come in!"—the Mayor cried, looking bigger: 55
And in did come the strangest figure!
His queer long coat from heel to head
Was half of yellow and half of red,
And he himself was tall and thin,
With sharp blue eyes, each like a pin,   60
And light loose hair, yet swarthy skin,
No tuft on cheek nor beard on chin,
But lips where smiles went out and in;

There was no guessing his kith and kin:
And nobody could enough admire
The tall man and his quaint attire.
Quoth one: "It's as my great-grandsire,
Starting up at the Trump of Doom's tone,°
Had walked this way from his painted tombstone!"

65

68. **Trump of Doom:** the trumpet of doomsday, the end of the world.

VI

He advanced to the council table:
And, "Please your honors," said he, "I'm able,
By means of a secret charm, to draw
   All creatures living beneath the sun,
   That creep or swim or fly or run,
After me so as you never saw!
And I chiefly use my charm
On creatures that do people harm,
The mole and toad and newt and viper;
And people call me the Pied Piper."
(And here they noticed round his neck
   A scarf of red and yellow stripe,
To match with his coat of the selfsame check;
   And at the scarf's end hung a pipe;
And his fingers, they noticed, were ever straying
As if impatient to be playing
Upon this pipe, as low it dangled
Over his vesture so old-fangled.)
"Yet," said he, "poor piper as I am,
In Tartary° I freed the Cham,°
   Last June, from his huge swarms of gnats;
I eased in Asia the Nizam°
   Of a monstrous brood of vampire bats:
And as for what your brain bewilders,
   If I can rid your town of rats
Will you give me a thousand guilders?"
"One? fifty thousand!"—was the exclamation
Of the astonished Mayor and Corporation.

70

75

80

85

90

95

89. **Tartary** (tär'tə-rē): a region in Asia and eastern Europe. **Cham** (kăm): khan (archaic).

91. **Nizam** (nĭ-säm', -zăm', nī-): title of the ruler of Hyderabad (hī'dər-ə-băd', bäd'), a former state in India.

VII

Into the street the Piper stepped,
   Smiling first a little smile,
As if he knew what magic slept
   In his quiet pipe the while;
Then, like a musical adept,°

100

102. **adept** (ə-dĕpt'): expert.

To blow the pipe his lips he wrinkled,
And green and blue his sharp eyes twinkled,
Like a candle flame where salt is sprinkled;   105
And ere three shrill notes the pipe uttered,
You heard as if an army muttered;
And the muttering grew to a grumbling;
And the grumbling grew to a mighty rumbling;
And out of the houses the rats came tumbling.   110
Great rats, small rats, lean rats, brawny rats,
Brown rats, black rats, gray rats, tawny rats,
Grave old plodders, gay young friskers,
   Fathers, mothers, uncles, cousins,
Cocking tails and pricking whiskers,   115
   Families by ten and dozens,
Brothers, sisters, husbands, wives—
Followed the Piper for their lives.
From street to street he piped advancing,
And step for step they followed dancing,   120
Until they came to the river Weser,
   Wherein all plunged and perished!
—Save one who, stout as Julius Caesar,
Swam across and lived to carry
   (As he, the manuscript he cherished°)   125
To Rat-land home his commentary:
Which was, "At the first shrill notes of the pipe,
I heard a sound as of scraping tripe,
And putting apples, wondrous ripe,
Into a cider press's gripe: 130
And a moving away of pickle-tub boards,
And a leaving ajar of conserve cupboards,
And a drawing the corks of train-oil° flasks,
And a breaking the hoops of butter casks:
And it seemed as if a voice   135
   (Sweeter far than by harp or by psaltery°
Is breathed) called out, 'Oh rats, rejoice!
   The world is grown to one vast drysaltery!°
So munch on, crunch on, take your nuncheon,°
Breakfast, supper, dinner, luncheon!'   140
And just as a bulky sugar-puncheon,°
All ready staved, like a great sun shone
Glorious scarce an inch before me,
Just as methought it said, 'Come, bore me!'
—I found the Weser rolling o'er me."   145

125. Once, when his ship was captured, Julius Caesar swam to shore, carrying his journals.

133. **train-oil:** fish oil.

136. **psaltery** (sôl′tə-rē): an ancient stringed instrument.

138. **drysaltery:** a store selling salted foods.
139. **nuncheon:** snack.

141. **sugar-puncheon:** sugar cask.

VIII

You should have heard the Hamelin people
Ringing the bells till they rocked the steeple.
"Go," cried the Mayor, "and get long poles,
Poke out the nests and block up the holes!
Consult with carpenters and builders,   150
And leave in our town not even a trace
Of the rats!"—when suddenly, up the face
Of the Piper perked in the marketplace,
With a "First, if you please, my thousand guilders!"

IX

A thousand guilders! The Mayor looked blue;   155
So did the Corporation too.
For council dinners made rare havoc
With Claret, Moselle, Vin-de-Grave, Hock;°
And half the money would replenish
Their cellar's biggest butt° with Rhenish.°   160
To pay this sum to a wandering fellow
With a gipsy coat of red and yellow!
"Beside," quoth the Mayor with a knowing wink,
"Our business was done at the river's brink;
We saw with our eyes the vermin sink,   165
And what's dead can't come to life, I think.
So, friend, we're not the folks to shrink
From the duty of giving you something for drink,
And a matter of money to put in your poke;
But as for the guilders, what we spoke   170
Of them, as you very well know, was in joke.
Beside, our losses have made us thrifty.
A thousand guilders! Come, take fifty!"

X

The Piper's face fell, and he cried,
"No trifling! I can't wait, beside!   175
I've promised to visit by dinnertime
Bagdad, and accept the prime
Of the Head Cook's pottage,° all he's rich in,
For having left, in the Caliph's° kitchen,
Of a nest of scorpions no survivor: 180
With him I proved no bargain-driver,
With you, don't think I'll bate° a stiver!°
And folks who put me in a passion
May find me pipe after another fashion."

158. **Claret, Moselle** (mō-zĕl′), **Vin-de-Grave** (văN-də-gràv′), **Hock:** wines.
160. **butt:** cask. **Rhenish** (rĕn′ĭsh): Rhine wine.

178. **pottage** (pŏt′ĭj): thick soup.
179. **Caliph** (kā′lĭf, kăl′ĭf): ruler in a Moslem country.

182. **bate:** subtract. **stiver** (stī′vər): one-twentieth of a guilder.

XI

"How?" cried the Mayor, "d'ye think I brook   185
Being worse treated than a Cook?
Insulted by a lazy ribald
With idle pipe and vesture piebald?
You threaten us, fellow? Do your worst,
Blow your pipe there till you burst!"   190

XII

Once more he stepped into the street,
   And to his lips again
   Laid his long pipe of smooth straight cane;
And ere he blew three notes (such sweet
Soft notes as yet musician's cunning   195
   Never gave the enraptured air)
There was a rustling that seemed like a bustling
Of merry crowds justling at pitching and hustling;
Small feet were pattering, wooden shoes clattering,
Little hands clapping and little tongues chattering,   200
And, like fowls in a farm-yard when barley is scattering,
Out came the children running.
All the little boys and girls,
With rosy cheeks and flaxen curls,
And sparkling eyes and teeth like pearls,   205
Tripping and skipping, ran merrily after
The wonderful music with shouting and laughter.

XIII

The Mayor was dumb, and the Council stood
As if they were changed into blocks of wood,
Unable to move a step, or cry   210
To the children merrily skipping by,
—Could only follow with the eye
That joyous crowd at the Piper's back.
But how the Mayor was on the rack,°
And the wretched Council's bosoms beat,   215
As the Piper turned from the High Street
To where the Weser rolled its waters
Right in the way of their sons and daughters!
However, he turned from South to West,
And to Koppelberg Hill his steps addressed,   220
And after him the children pressed;
Great was the joy in every breast.

214. **on the rack:** a metaphor for "suffering." The rack was an instrument of torture.

"He never can cross that mighty top!
He's forced to let the piping drop,
And we shall see our children stop!"   225
When, lo, as they reached the mountainside,
A wondrous portal opened wide,
As if a cavern was suddenly hollowed;
And the Piper advanced and the children followed,
And when all were in to the very last,   230
The door in the mountainside shut fast.
Did I say, all? No! One was lame,
   And could not dance the whole of the way;
And in after years, if you would blame
   His sadness, he was used to say,—   235
"It's dull in our town since my playmates left!
I can't forget that I'm bereft

Of all the pleasant sights they see,
Which the Piper also promised me.
For he led us, he said, to a joyous land,   240
Joining the town and just at hand,
Where waters gushed and fruit trees grew.
And flowers put forth a fairer hue,
And everything was strange and new;
The sparrows were brighter than peacocks here,   245
And their dogs outran our fallow deer,°

246. fallow deer: small, pale-colored deer.

And honeybees had lost their stings,
And horses were born with eagles' wings;
And just as I became assured
My lame foot would be speedily cured,   250
The music stopped and I stood still,
And found myself outside the hill,
Left alone against my will,
To go now limping as before,
And never hear of that country more!"   255

XIV

Alas, alas for Hamelin!
    There came into many a burgher's° pate°
    A text which says, that heaven's gate
    Opes to the rich at as easy rate

257. burgher (bûr′gər): town-dweller. **pate** (pāt): head.

As the needle's eye takes a camel in!°   260
The Mayor sent East, West, North and South,
To offer the Piper, by word of mouth,
    Wherever it was men's lot to find him,
Silver and gold to his heart's content,
If he'd only return the way he went,   265
    And bring the children behind him.

260. This text is from the Bible (Matthew 19:24): "It is easier for a camel to go through the eye of a needle, than for a rich man to enter into the kingdom of God."

But when they saw 'twas a lost endeavor,
And Piper and dancers were gone forever,
They made a decree that lawyers never
    Should think their records dated duly   270
If, after the day of the month and year,
These words did not as well appear,
"And so long after what happened here
    On the Twenty-second of July,
Thirteen hundred and seventy-six":   275
And the better in memory to fix
The place of the children's last retreat,
They called it, the Pied Piper's Street—

Where anyone playing on pipe or tabor°
Was sure for the future to lose his labor. 280
Nor suffered they hostelry° or tavern
   To shock with mirth a street so solemn;
But opposite the place of the cavern
   They wrote the story on a column,
And on the great church window painted 285
The same, to make the world acquainted
How their children were stolen away,
And there it stands to this very day.
And I must not omit to say
That in Transylvania there's a tribe 290
Of alien people who ascribe
The outlandish ways and dress
On which their neighbors lay such stress,
To their fathers and mothers having risen
Out of some subterraneous prison 295
Into which they were trepanned°
Long time ago in a mighty band
Out of Hamelin town in Brunswick land,
But how or why, they don't understand.

XV

So, Willy, let me and you be wipers 300
Of scores out with all men—especially pipers!
And, whether they pipe us free from rats or from mice,
If we've promised them aught, let us keep our promise!

279. **tabor** (tā′bər): small drum.

281. **hostelry** (hŏs′tǝl-rē): inn.

296. **trepanned** (trĭ-pănd′): trapped.

For Study and Discussion

Analyzing and Interpreting the Poem

1. At the opening of the poem, Hamelin is overrun by rats. What are the ways in which the townsfolk suffer?

2a. What characteristics of the Mayor and the Corporation are stressed in lines 23–54? **b.** How do these characteristics affect your reaction to the town officials?

3a. Describe the Pied Piper's appearance. **b.** What impression does he make?

4a. What claims does the Pied Piper make for his abilities? **b.** What evidence does he offer for his successes? **c.** What agreement is reached?

5. Read aloud the description in Part VII, of how the Piper charms the rats into following him. What parts of the description are particularly vivid and amusing?

6. One rat survives to bring the news to "Ratland." According to him, what is the charm in the Piper's music?

7. The Mayor and the Corporation refuse to live up to their agreement with the Piper. **a.** Is this behavior consistent with their characters? **b.** What is the Piper's revenge for their treachery?

8. One child, who is lame, never reaches the door in the mountainside. What does he reveal about the Piper's music?

9. How do the people of Hanover commemorate the tragedy?

10. What conclusion to the legend is suggested in lines 289–299?

11. The poem ends with four lines of advice to Willy, the little boy for whom Browning wrote the poem. **a.** What is the advice? **b.** How does it apply to the legend of Hamelin?

12. The events in this poem are actually found in the town records of Hamelin. The disaster is said to have occurred in 1284. **a.** What is Browning's attitude toward this disaster? **b.** Is your judgment of the events the same?

Language and Vocabulary

Recognizing Denotative and Connotative Meanings

You have seen that poets rely on the denotative and connotative meanings of words. Look at the meanings of the word *ermine* in line 25:

Word	Denotation	Connotation
ermine	soft, white fur from a kind of weasel	rich and splendid fur, often worn by royalty

Using this chart as a model, find the denotative and connotative meanings of the following words in the poem:

vermin (line 9)
quaint (line 66)
flaxen (line 204)

About the Author

Robert Browning (1812–1889)

As a young man, Robert Browning read most of the books in his father's huge library, traveled in Europe, and wrote poetry. Almost from the first, his poetry showed a keen understanding of human nature and a mastery of difficult poetic forms. In 1846, Browning eloped with Elizabeth Barrett, a well-known poet whose father had virtually imprisoned her at home. During their life together, she was the better known writer, but after her death, his reputation grew steadily. With the publication of a long poem, *The Ring and the Book,* he became recognized as one of the major poets of his day.

LYRIC POETRY

A *lyric* poem is the form used for the expression of personal thoughts and feelings. Most lyrics tend to be brief. "Full Fathom Five" (page 466) is a pure lyric, intended to be sung. A lyric poem generally leaves the reader with a single, intense impression.

Snowflakes

HENRY WADSWORTH LONGFELLOW

In this poem Longfellow is drawing an analogy, *or comparison, between certain natural events and certain human feelings. What similarity does he find?*

Out of the bosom of the Air,
  Out of the cloud-folds of her garments shaken,
Over the woodlands brown and bare,
  Over the harvest-fields forsaken,
    Silent and soft and slow   5
    Descends the snow.

Even as our cloudy fancies take
  Suddenly shape in some divine expression,
Even as the troubled heart doth make
  In the white countenance confession,   10
    The troubled sky reveals
    The grief it feels.

This is the poem of the air,
  Slowly in silent syllables recorded;
This is the secret of despair,   15
  Long in its cloudy bosom hoarded,
    Now whispered and revealed
    To wood and field.

For Study and Discussion

Analyzing and Interpreting the Poem

1. Although the title of this poem is "Snow-flakes," it is clear that the poet is speaking about some deep, personal grief that has been held in check and that suddenly has found release. Longfellow sees a relationship between the "troubled heart" and the "troubled sky." What do they have in common?

2. The "divine expression" in line 8 might refer to poetry, in which the poet's "cloudy fancies," or gloomy ideas, are revealed. What is the "poem of the air" (line 13)?

3. What eventually happens to the "secret of despair"?

4. Consider the connotative meanings of the words *bare, forsaken, troubled, grief, despair*. How do they contribute to the mood of the poem?

Literary Elements

Recognizing Personification

In poetry, an animal, an object, or an idea is often given personality, or described as if it were human. Longfellow talks about the air as if it were a woman shaking snow out of her garments, the clouds. This is a figure of speech known as **personification.** How does Longfellow personify the sky in lines 11–12?

Little Things

JAMES STEPHENS

How does the repetition of the word little *add to the effectiveness of this poem?*

Little things, that run, and quail,
And die, in silence and despair!

Little things, that fight, and fail,
And fall, on sea, and earth, and air!

All trapped and frightened little things,   5
The mouse, the coney°, hear our prayer!

As we forgive those done to us,
—The lamb, the linnet, and the hare—

Forgive us all our trespasses,
Little creatures, everywhere!   10

6. **coney** (kō′nē): rabbit.

I'm Nobody

EMILY DICKINSON

What is the speaker's attitude toward fame?

I'm nobody! Who are you?
Are you nobody, too?
Then there's a pair of us—don't tell!
They'd banish us, you know.

How dreary to be somebody!
How public, like a frog
To tell your name the livelong day
To an admiring bog!

For Study and Discussion

Analyzing and Interpreting the Poem

1. How does the poet create sympathy for the creatures in this poem?

2a. What is a trespass? **b.** What special meaning does the word have in this poem?

3. What single, intense impression does this poem make?

For Study and Discussion

Analyzing and Interpreting the Poem

1. What does the speaker mean by the words *nobody* and *somebody*?

2a. Why does the speaker enjoy anonymity? **b.** What is her attitude toward those who have achieved reputation or renown?

3a. To whom is she talking? **b.** Might she be speaking directly to the reader?

4. The tone of Emily Dickinson's poetry is often described as playful and witty. Does this poem share those characteristics?

Haiku

A haiku (hī′kōō) is a three-line poem, of Japanese origin, containing seventeen syllables. There are five syllables in the first line, seven syllables in the second line, and five syllables in the third line. Such a poem must communicate meaning through very few words. The subject matter of a haiku is usually drawn from nature.

The lightning flashes!
And slashing through the darkness,
A night-heron's screech.

Matsuo Bashō

Broken and broken
again on the sea, the moon
so easily mends.

Chosu

I must go begging
for water . . . morning glories
have captured my well.

Chiyo

Flowers and Birds by Seshu Toyo.

For Study and Discussion

Analyzing and Interpreting the Poems

1a. What images do you see and hear in the first haiku?   **b.** What words suggest pain or violence?

2. The second haiku uses the word *broken* in an unusual way. We speak of breaking an object such as a dish. In what way is the moon "broken" repeatedly on the sea?

3. What image is suggested by the word *captured* in the third haiku?

Literary Elements

Understanding Haiku

Harry Behn, who has translated Japanese haiku, believes that the best haiku are as "natural as breathing." He writes that a haiku "is made by speaking of something natural and simple suggesting spring, summer, autumn, or winter. There is no rhyme. Everything mentioned is just what it is, wonderful, here, but still beyond."

Haiku often use contrasts that catch the reader by surprise. What examples of this kind of contrast can you find in the poems on page 491?

Creative Writing

Composing a Haiku

Writing a haiku can be challenging and fun. You might start by recalling one striking or memorable image that made a special impression on you. This image, along with your feelings about it, should be compressed into no more than seventeen syllables, in three lines. The lines should have five, seven, and five syllables, respectively.

For example, if a beautiful red sun going down slowly behind the water at a beach made an impression on you, you might come up with a haiku similar to this:

A bright flaming ball,	5 syllables
Nestling down on the water	7 syllables
That swallows it whole.	5 syllables

Write at least one haiku, selecting your words carefully to appeal to your reader's senses and imagination. You may work in a little surprise in the third line. If you wish, illustrate your haiku and then read it aloud to a small group of students or to the rest of the class.

About the Authors

Henry Wadsworth Longfellow (1807–1882)

For a biography of the author, see page 169.

James Stephens (1882–1950)

James Stephens did not have a formal education, but he was deeply interested in reading, art, and folk music. A fascinating storyteller, Stephens enjoyed entertaining others with Irish stories, legends, and poetry. He is known for his novels and poems.

Emily Dickinson (1830–1886)

Emily Dickinson was born into one of the leading families of Amherst, Massachusetts. She attended Mount Holyoke Female Seminary, the first women's college. Gradually, she became a recluse, dressing all in white and rarely seeing visitors. While some people think she was disappointed in love, others believe she deliberately secluded herself to write the almost two thousand poems she kept neatly stitched together in her bureau. She allowed only eight or nine poems to be published during her lifetime. Today she is considered one of the greatest American poets.

DRAMATIC POETRY

Dramatic poems present characters who speak to other characters or to some unidentified listener. Most dramatic poems contain dialogue. Others, like the *dramatic monologue*, contain a single speech by one character.

Father William

LEWIS CARROLL

This poem is a parody, or humorous imitation, of a poem by Robert Southey called "The Old Man's Comforts." Carroll's poem is a father and son dialogue, with some delightful surprises.

"You are old, Father William," the young man said,
    "And your hair has become very white;
And yet you incessantly stand on your head—
    Do you think, at your age, it is right?"

"In my youth," Father William replied to his son,   5
    "I feared it might injure the brain;
But now that I'm perfectly sure I have none,
    Why, I do it again and again."

Illustrations by John Tenniel.

"You are old," said the youth, "as I mentioned before,
    And have grown most uncommonly fat;   10
Yet you turned a back somersault in at the door—
    Pray, what is the reason of that?"

"In my youth," said the sage, as he shook his gray locks,
    "I kept all my limbs very supple
By the use of this ointment—one shilling the box—   15
    Allow me to sell you a couple."

"You are old," said the youth, "and your jaws are too weak
    For anything tougher than suet;
Yet you finished the goose, with the bones and the beak;
    Pray, how did you manage to do it?"   20

"In my youth," said his father, "I took to the law,
    And argued each case with my wife;
And the muscular strength which it gave to my jaw,
    Has lasted the rest of my life."

"You are old," said the youth; "one would hardly suppose   25
    That your eye was as steady as ever;
Yet you balanced an eel on the end of your nose—
    What made you so awfully clever?"

"I've answered three questions, and that is enough,"
    Said his father; "don't give yourself airs!   30
Do you think I can listen all day to such stuff?
    Be off, or I'll kick you downstairs!"

For Study and Discussion

Analyzing and Interpreting the Poem

1. The son in the poem asks his father a number of questions. **a.** What are they? **b.** How does the father respond to each question?

2. How does the father's attitude toward growing older differ from the son's attitude?

3. What do you think is the most humorous aspect of this poem?

About the Author

Lewis Carroll (1832–1898)

Lewis Carroll was the pen name of Charles Lutwidge Dodgson, who was a professor of mathematics at Oxford University in England. *Alice's Adventures in Wonderland* (1865) and *Through the Looking-Glass* (1871), his two most famous books, were written to entertain the children of friends. Carroll's books are great fun, but they are also subtle and complex works that have fascinated readers for more than a hundred years.

COMIC VERSE

Some poets, like Edward Lear and Ogden Nash, have specialized in writing humorous poetry. One kind of comic verse that is extremely popular is the *limerick*.

The Bearded Man

EDWARD LEAR

A limerick is a humorous poem of five lines with a characteristic rhythm and rhyme pattern. See if you can determine this pattern as you read.

There was an old man with a beard,
Who said, "It is just as I feared!
  Two owls and a hen,
  Four larks and a wren
Have *all* built their nests in my beard!"

The Lama

OGDEN NASH

Nash's poetry is known for its comic rhymes and unusual spellings. Find examples in this poem of both devices.

The one-l lama,
He's a priest.
The two-l llama,
He's a beast.
And I will bet
A silk pyjama
There isn't any
Three-l lllama.

A Tutor

CAROLYN WELLS

A tutor who tooted the flute
Tried to tutor two tooters to toot.
Said the two to the tutor,
"Is it harder to toot, or
To tutor two tooters to toot?"

Creative Writing

Writing a Limerick

Limericks have a definite form. Which lines rhyme? Which lines are shorter than the others? The rhymes are often funny and unexpected. What comic rhymes can you find in the limericks on these pages?

Write a limerick of your own. Here are two lines you might use to begin:"

There once was a student named Wayne,
Whose homework was lost on a train. . . .

DEVELOPING SKILLS IN CRITICAL THINKING

Analyzing Poetry

A poem generally gains in meaning the more closely you study it. Read the following poem slowly and carefully. After you have read it, pause and think about it, and then read it again. The steps outlined below will guide you in analyzing the poem.

Lost
CARL SANDBURG

Desolate and lone
All night long on the lake
Where fog trails and mist creeps,
The whistle of a boat
Calls and cries unendingly,
Like some lost child
In tears and trouble
Hunting the harbor's breast
And the harbor's eyes.

1. *Look for complete thoughts instead of reading line by line.* How many sentences are there in Sandburg's poem? In reading the poem aloud, where should you pause?

2. *Note the effects of specific words and images.* What feelings are suggested by the title of the poem? What are the connotations of the word *desolate?* What feelings are suggested by the image of a foggy lake at night?

3. *Note the comparisons chosen by the poet.* Sandburg compares the whistle of a boat at night to the crying of a lost child. What feelings are suggested by this simile? How does the metaphor in the last two lines add to the overall effect of the poem?

4. *Listen for the sound effects.* Notice that the **l** sound in the title is repeated in the first two lines of the poem. What emphasis or connection does Sandburg achieve by repetition of this sound? Find other examples of alliteration in the poem.

5. *Express the meaning of the poem in your own words.* What experience do you think the poet wishes to share with the reader? What do you think he may have felt or thought?

PRACTICE IN READING AND WRITING

Writing Poetry

Choose one of the images suggested below or think of another image that appeals to you. Write a brief poem that communicates a feeling or an idea about the image. Your poem may or may not use rhyme, and it may be serious or humorous. You might try comparing the subject of your poem with something else, as Sandburg has done in "Lost."

A worn-out pair of shoes
A siren in the night
The buzzing of a fly in a quiet room
Bare feet on a hot pavement or on cool grass
City streets on a rainy night

Consider the titles of the poems you have read in this unit. If you wish, write your own poem for one of these titles.

Use the writing process to develop your poem. In the prewriting stage, gather your ideas. Start with a feeling, an image, or a word. Jot down ideas that come to you. Try to think in images and in sounds as you record your ideas. In the writing stage, use these notes to write a first draft of your poem. Then evaluate your work. Have you chosen words with the right connotations for your poem? Are your images specific? Might any of your ideas be expressed effectively in figurative language? If you have decided to use rhyme, have you established a pattern? Use your evaluation to revise your poem and then proofread your work. Before you prepare a final copy, have a fellow student read your poem. Give your poem a title.

For Further Reading

Adoff, Arnold, editor, *I Am the Darker Brother: An Anthology of Modern Poems by Negro Americans* (paperback, Macmillan, 1970)
> Twenty-eight black poets—including Gwendolyn Brooks, Paul Laurence Dunbar, and Langston Hughes—write about the past and future of black Americans, their feelings, hopes, and dreams.

Atwood, Ann, *Haiku, the Mood of Earth* (Scribner, 1971)
> The book presents twenty-five haiku, each illustrated with two full-color photographs.

Bogan, Louise, and William Jay Smith, editors, *The Golden Journey: Poems for Young People* (Regnery, 1965)
> The poems in this collection are grouped under these categories: rhymes, country poems, love poems, nonsense verses, war poems, and poems of dreams and fancies.

Brewton, Sara, and John E. Brewton, editors, *Laughable Limericks* (Thomas Y. Crowell, 1965)
> "Crawlers, Croakers, and Creepers" is one of the chapter titles in this collection of old and new limericks.

Cole, William, editor, *Good Dog Poems* (Charles Scribner's Sons, 1981)
> This is a collection of eighty-eight poems about dogs, arranged in ten sections.

Dickinson, Emily, *Poems for Youth,* edited by Alfred Leete Hampson (Little, Brown, 1934)
> Emily Dickinson wrote many of these poems for her nieces and nephews.

Dunning, Stephen, et al., editors, *Reflections on a Gift of Watermelon Pickles* (Lothrop, 1967)
> Here are one hundred fourteen poems selected by English teachers. Another collection edited by this group is *Some Haystacks Don't Even Have Any Needle* (Lothrop, 1969)

Eliot, T. S., *Old Possum's Book of Practical Cats* (Harcourt Brace Jovanovich, 1982)
> This delightful volume containing humorous character sketches of fifteen kinds of cats provided the inspiration for the hit musical *Cats.*

Janeczko, Paul B, editor, *Strings: A Gathering of Family Poems* (Bradbury, 1984)
> Included here are more than a hundred poems by a variety of modern poets, including Stephen Spender, Richard Wilbur, and Anne Sexton.

Lewis, Richard, editor, *Miracles: Poems by Children of the English-Speaking World* (Simon and Schuster, 1984)
> Here are more than two hundred poems written by children about their thoughts, feelings, and experiences. Another collection by Richard Lewis, *Out of the Earth I Sing: Poetry and Songs of Primitive Peoples of the World* (Norton, 1968), contains traditional songs and chants from many different countries.

Lindsay, Vachel, *Johnny Appleseed and Other Poems* (Buccaneer, 1981)
> This anthology includes Lindsay's nonsense rhymes, lyrics, and historical poems.

Livingston, Myra Cohn, *A Lollygag of Limericks* (Atheneum, 1978)
> This funny collection includes a gallery of misfits accompanied by droll line drawings.

Peck, Richard, editor, *Pictures That Storm Inside My Head: Poems for the Inner You* (Avon, 1976)
> Here are many short poems on a variety of emotions by such poets as May Sarton, Richard Wilbur, and Nikki Giovanni.

Plotz, Helen, editor, *Saturday's Children: Poems of Work* (Greenwillow Books, 1982)
> The poems in this collection are about different occupations and range from the Bible to contemporary literature.

Sandburg, Carl, *Wind Song* (Harcourt Brace Jovanovich, 1960; paperback, Harcourt)
> Sandburg selected these poems especially for young people and grouped them into such chapters as "Blossom Themes," "Night," and "Wind, Sea, and Sky."

THE NOVEL

Road to Adventure (1940) by Dale Nichols.
Oil on canvas.
Joslyn Art Museum

The novel is a popular form of literature with readers of all ages. There are *historical* novels, like Charles Dickens' *A Tale of Two Cities,* which is set in the period of the French Revolution. There are *adventure* novels, like Robert Louis Stevenson's *Treasure Island,* which tells about pirates and buried treasure. There are *Western* novels, like Jack Schaefer's *Shane,* dealing with the problems of homesteaders in Wyoming; *detective* novels with thrilling plots, like Wilkie Collins' *The Moonstone;* *gothic* novels, which are suspenseful horror stories, like Mary Shelley's *Frankenstein;* and *science fiction* novels, set in strange worlds of the future, like Ray Bradbury's *The Martian Chronicles.*

A novel may be defined as a long work of prose fiction that makes use of the same basic elements found in the short story: *plot, character, setting, point of view,* and *theme.* There are, however, important differences. In a short story, there is generally a single plot. In the novel, there may be one or more subsidiary plots, or *subplots,* interwoven with the main plot. In a short story, characters must be developed economically. The novelist has more room to present a character and may focus on many different aspects of major and minor figures. Setting is often given more emphasis in a novel than in a short story. The novelist has greater scope to provide background and to create atmosphere and mood. Whereas a short story tends to have a single theme, a novel may explore several ideas in depth.

In this unit, you will read *Old Yeller,* a contemporary novel by Fred Gipson. Here are suggestions to guide you in reading the novel.

Guidelines for Reading a Novel

1. *Read actively, asking questions as you read.* For example, as you read, try to predict how some incident or event will turn out. Try to determine the author's purpose as you work through the novel.

2. *Become aware of information that establishes the setting.* The language of characters, for example, can help to set the time and place.

3. *Look for clues that reveal what characters are like: key speeches, important actions, or descriptive details.* Discover how characters develop and change as the novel progresses.

4. *Determine what forms the major action of the novel.* As you read, consider how individual episodes are connected to the main plot.

5. *Note the point of view of the novel.* Seek to understand the author's reason in selecting this point of view.

6. *Consider how all the elements of the novel contribute to its theme.* Try to clarify your own understanding of the author's underlying idea.

Old Yeller

FRED GIPSON

PART I

One

We called him Old Yeller. The name had a sort of double meaning. One part meant that his short hair was a dingy yellow, a color that we called "yeller" in those days. The other meant that when he opened his head, the sound he let out came closer to being a yell than a bark.

I remember like yesterday how he strayed in out of nowhere to our log cabin on Birdsong Creek. He made me so mad at first that I wanted to kill him. Then, later, when I had to kill him, it was like having to shoot some of my own folks. That's how much I'd come to think of the big yeller dog.

He came in the late 1860s, the best I remember. Anyhow, it was the year that Papa and a bunch of other Salt Licks settlers formed a "pool herd" of their little separate bunches of steers and trailed them to the new cattle market at Abilene, Kansas.

This was to get "cash money," a thing that all Texans were short of in those years right after the Civil War. We lived then in a new country and a good one. As Papa pointed out the day the men talked over making the drive, we had plenty of grass, wood, and water. We had wild game for the killing, fertile ground for growing bread corn, and the Indians had been put onto reservations with the return of U.S. soldiers to the Texas forts.

"In fact," Papa wound up, "all we lack having a tight tail-holt on the world is a little cash money. And we can get that at Abilene."

Well, the idea sounded good, but some of the men still hesitated. Abilene was better than six hundred miles north of the Texas hill country we lived in. It would take months for the men to make the drive and ride back home. And all that time the womenfolks and children of Salt Licks would be left in a wild frontier settlement to make out the best they could.

Still, they needed money, and they realized that whatever a man does, he's bound to take some risks. So they talked it over with each other and with their women and decided it was the thing to do. They told their folks what to do in case the Indians came off the reservation or the coons got to eating the corn or the bears got to killing too many hogs. Then they gathered their cattle, burned a trail brand on their hips, and pulled out on the long trail to Kansas.

I remember how it was the day Papa left. I remember his standing in front of the cabin with his horse saddled, his gun in his scabbard, and his bedroll tied on back of the cantle.[1] I remember how tall and straight and handsome he looked, with his high-crowned hat and his

1. **cantle** (kăn′təl): the rear part of the saddle that sticks up.

Scenes on pages 504, 509, 518, 520–521, 530, 536, 547, 549, 557, and 563 are from a film version of *Old Yeller*.

black mustaches drooping in cow-horn curves past the corners of his mouth. And I remember how Mama was trying to keep from crying because he was leaving and how Little Arliss, who was only five and didn't know much, wasn't trying to keep from crying at all. In fact, he was howling his head off; not because Papa was leaving, but because he couldn't go, too.

I wasn't about to cry. I was fourteen years old, pretty near a grown man. I stood back and didn't let on for a minute that I wanted to cry.

Papa got through loving up Mama and Little Arliss and mounted his horse. I looked up at him. He motioned for me to come along. So I walked beside his horse down the trail that led under the big live oaks and past the spring.

When he'd gotten out of hearing of the house, Papa reached down and put a hand on my shoulder.

"Now, Travis," he said, "you're getting to be a big boy; and while I'm gone, you'll be the man of the family. I want you to act like one. You take care of Mama and Little Arliss. You

look after the work and don't wait around for your mama to point out what needs to be done. Think you can do that?"

"Yessir," I said.

"Now, there's the cows to milk and wood to cut and young pigs to mark and fresh meat to shoot. But mainly there's the corn patch. If you don't work it right or if you let the varmints eat up the roasting ears, we'll be without bread corn for the winter."

"Yessir," I said.

"All right, boy. I'll be seeing you this fall."

I stood there and let him ride on. There wasn't any more to say.

Suddenly I remembered and went running down the trail after him, calling for him to wait.

He pulled up his horse and twisted around in the saddle. "Yeah, boy," he said. "What is it?"

"That horse," I said.

"What horse?" he said, like he'd never heard me mention it before. "You mean you're wanting a horse?"

"Now, Papa," I complained. "You know I've been aching all over for a horse to ride. I've told you time and again."

I looked up to catch him grinning at me and felt foolish that I hadn't realized he was teasing.

"What you're needing worse than a horse is a good dog."

"Yessir," I said, "but a horse is what I'm wanting the worst."

"All right," he said. "You act a man's part while I'm gone, and I'll see that you get a man's horse to ride when I sell the cattle. I think we can shake on that deal."

He reached out his hand, and we shook. It was the first time I'd ever shaken hands like a man. It made me feel big and solemn and important in a way I'd never felt before. I knew then that I could handle whatever needed to be done while Papa was gone.

I turned and started back up the trail toward the cabin. I guessed maybe Papa was right. I guessed I could use a dog. All the other settlers had dogs. They were big fierce cur dogs that the settlers used for catching hogs and driving cattle and fighting coons out of the cornfields. They kept them as watchdogs against the depredations[2] of loafer wolves, bears, panthers, and raiding Indians. There was no question about it: for the sort of country we lived in, a good dog around the place was sometimes worth more than two or three men. I knew this as well as anybody, because the summer before I'd had a good dog.

His name was Bell. He was nearly as old as I was. We'd had him ever since I could remember. He'd protected me from rattlesnakes and bad hogs while I was little. He'd hunted with me when I was bigger. Once he'd dragged me

2. **depredations** (dĕp′rə-dā′shəns): instances of preying upon or stealing.

out of Birdsong Creek when I was about to drown and another time he'd given warning in time to keep some raiding Comanches from stealing and eating our mule, Jumper.

Then he'd had to go act a fool and get himself killed.

It was while Papa and I were cutting wild hay in a little patch of prairie back of the house. A big diamondback rattler struck at Papa and Papa chopped his head off with one quick lick of his scythe. The head dropped to the ground three or four feet away from the writhing body. It lay there, with the ugly mouth opening and shutting, still trying to bite something.

As smart as Bell was, you'd have thought he'd have better sense than to go up and nuzzle that rattler's head. But he didn't, and a second later, he was falling back, howling and slinging his own head till his ears popped. But it was too late then. That snake mouth had snapped shut on his nose, driving the fangs in so deep that it was a full minute before he could sling the bloody head loose.

He died that night, and I cried for a week. Papa tried to make me feel better by promising to get me another dog right away, but I wouldn't have it. It made me mad just to think about some other dog's trying to take Bell's place.

And I still felt the same about it. All I wanted now was a horse.

The trail I followed led along the bank of Birdsong Creek through some bee myrtle bushes. The bushes were blooming white and smelled sweet. In the top of one a mockingbird was singing. That made me recollect how Birdsong Creek had got its name. Mama had named it when she and Papa came to settle. Mama had told me about it. She said she named it the first day she and Papa got there, with Mama driving the ox cart loaded with our house plunder,[3] and with Papa driving the cows and horses. They'd meant to build closer to the other settlers, over on Salt Branch. But they'd camped there at the spring; and the bee myrtle had been blooming white that day, and seemed like in every bush there was a mockingbird, singing his fool head off. It was all so pretty and smelled so good and the singing birds made such fine music that Mama wouldn't go on.

"We'll build right here," she'd told Papa.

And that's what they'd done. Built themselves a home right here on Birdsong Creek and fought off the Indians and cleared a corn patch and raised me and Little Arliss and lost a little sister who died of a fever.

Now it was my home, too. And while Papa was gone, it was up to me to look after it.

I came to our spring that gushed clear cold water out of a split in a rock ledge. The water poured into a pothole about the size of a wagon bed. In the pothole, up to his ears in the water, stood Little Arliss. Right in our drinking water!

I said: "*Arliss!* You get out of that water."

Arliss turned and stuck out his tongue at me.

"I'll cut me a sprout!" I warned.

All he did was stick out his tongue at me again and splash water in my direction.

I got my knife out and cut a green mesquite[4] sprout. I trimmed all the leaves and thorns off, then headed for him.

Arliss saw then that I meant business. He came lunging up out of the pool, knocking water all over his clothes lying on the bank. He lit out for the house, running naked and screaming bloody murder.

Mama heard him and came rushing out of the cabin. She saw Little Arliss running naked.

She saw me following after him with a mesquite sprout in one hand and his clothes in the other. She called out to me.

"Travis," she said, "what on earth have you done to your little brother?"

I said, "Nothing yet. But if he doesn't keep out of our drinking water, I'm going to wear him to a frazzle."

That's what Papa always told Little Arliss when he caught him in the pool. I figured if I had to take Papa's place, I might as well talk like him.

Mama stared at me for a minute. I thought she was fixing to argue that I was getting too big for my britches. Lots of times she'd tell me that. But this time she didn't. She just smiled suddenly and grabbed Little Arliss by one ear and held on. He went to hollering and jumping up and down and trying to pull away, but she held on till I got there with his clothes. She put them on him and told him: "Look here, young squirrel. You better listen to your big brother Travis if you want to keep out of trouble." Then she made him go sit still awhile in the dog run.

The dog run was an open roofed-over space between the two rooms of our log cabin. It was a good place to eat watermelons in the hot summer or to sleep when the night breezes weren't strong enough to push through the cracks between the cabin logs. Sometimes we hung up fresh-killed meat there to cool out.

Little Arliss sat in the dog run and sulked while I packed water from the spring. I packed the water in a bucket that Papa had made out of the hide of a cow's leg. I poured the water into the ash hopper that stood beside the cabin. That was so the water could trickle down through the wood ashes and become lye water. Later Mama would mix this lye water with hog fat and boil it in an iron pot when she wanted to make soap.

When I went to cut wood for Mama, though,

3. **plunder** (plŭn′dər): here, household goods.
4. **mesquite** (mĕs-kēt′, mə-skēt′): a shrub or small tree that grows in the southwestern United States and Mexico. Its pods are used as fodder.

Little Arliss left the dog run to come watch me work. Like always, he stood in exactly the right place for the chips from my axe to fly up and maybe knock his eyeballs out. I said: "You better skin out for that house, you little scamp!" He skinned out, too. Just like I told him. Without even sticking out his tongue at me this time.

And he sat right there till Mama called us to dinner.

After dinner, I didn't wait for Mama to tell me that I needed to finish running out the corn middles. I got right up from the table and went out and hooked Jumper to the double shovel. I started in plowing where Papa had left off the day before. I figured that if I got an early start, I could finish the corn patch by sundown.

Jumper was a dun mule with a narrow black stripe running along his backbone between his mane and tail. Papa had named him Jumper because nobody yet had ever built a fence he couldn't jump over. Papa claimed Jumper could clear the moon if he took a notion to see the other side of it.

Jumper was a pretty good mule, though. He was gentle to ride: you could pack in fresh meat on him; and he was willing about pulling a plow. Only, sometimes when I plowed him and he decided quitting time had come, he'd stop work right then. Maybe we'd be out in the middle of the field when Jumper got the notion that it was time to quit for dinner. Right then, he'd swing around and head for the cabin, dragging down corn with the plow and paying no mind whatever to my hauling back on the reins and hollering "Whoa!"

Late that evening, Jumper tried to pull that stunt on me again; but I was laying for him. With Papa gone, I knew I had to teach Jumper a good lesson. I'd been plowing all afternoon, holding a green cedar club between the plow handles.

I still lacked three or four corn rows being finished when sundown came and Jumper decided it was quitting time. He let out a long bray and started wringing his tail. He left the middle he was traveling in. He struck out through the young corn, headed for the cabin.

I didn't even holler "Whoa!" at him. I just threw the looped reins off my shoulder and ran up beside him. I drew back my green cedar club and whacked him so hard across the jawbone that I nearly dropped him in his tracks.

You never saw a worse surprised mule. He snorted, started to run, then just stood there and stared at me. Like maybe he couldn't believe that I was man enough to club him that hard.

I drew back my club again. "Jumper," I said, "if you don't get back there and finish this plowing job, you're going to get more of the same. You understand?"

I guess he understood, all right. Anyhow, from then on till we were through, he stayed right on the job. The only thing he did different from what he'd have done with Papa was to travel with his head turned sideways, watching me every step of the way.

When finally I got to the house, I found that Mama had done the milking and she and Little Arliss were waiting supper on me. Just like we generally waited for Papa when he came in late.

I crawled into bed with Little Arliss that night, feeling pretty satisfied with myself. Our bed was a cornshuck mattress laid over a couple of squared-up cowhides that had been laced together. The cowhides stood about two feet off the dirt floor, stretched tight inside a pole frame Papa had built in one corner of the room. I lay there and listened to the corn shucks squeak when I breathed and to the owls hooting in the timber along Birdsong Creek. I guessed I'd made a good start. I'd done my work without having to be told. I'd taught Little Arliss and Jumper that I wasn't to be trifled with. And Mama could already see that I was man enough to wait supper on.

I guessed that I could handle things while Papa was gone just about as good as he could.

Two

It was the next morning when the big yeller dog came.

I found him at daylight when Mama told me to step out to the dog run and cut down a side of middling meat[1] hanging to the pole rafters.

The minute I opened the door and looked up, I saw that the meat was gone. It had been tied to the rafter with bear-grass blades braided together for string. Now nothing was left hanging to the pole but the frazzled ends of the snapped blades.

I looked down then. At the same instant, a dog rose from where he'd been curled up on the ground beside the barrel that held our cornmeal. He was a big ugly slick-haired yeller dog. One short ear had been chewed clear off and his tail had been bobbed so close to his rump that there was hardly stub enough left to wag. But the most noticeable thing to me about him was how thin and starved looking he was, all but for his belly. His belly was swelled up as tight and round as a pumpkin.

It wasn't hard to tell how come that belly was so full. All I had to do was look at the piece of curled-up rind lying in the dirt beside him, with all the meat gnawed off. That side of meat had been a big one, but now there wasn't enough meat left on the rind to interest a pack rat.

Well, to lose the only meat we had left from last winter's hog butchering was bad enough.

But what made me even madder was the way the dog acted. He didn't even have the manners to feel ashamed of what he'd done. He rose to his feet, stretched, yawned, then came romping toward me, wiggling that stub tail and yelling *Yow! Yow! Yow!* Just like he belonged there and I was his best friend.

"Why, you thieving rascal!" I shouted and kicked at him as hard as I could.

He ducked, just in time, so that I missed him by a hair. But nobody could have told I missed, after the way he fell over on the ground and lay there, with his belly up and his four feet in the air, squawling, and bellering[2] at the top of his voice. From the racket he made, you'd have thought I had a club and was breaking every bone in his body.

Mama came running to stick her head through the door and say, "What on earth, Travis?"

"Why, this old stray dog has come and eaten our middling meat clear up," I said.

I aimed another kick at him. He was quick and rolled out of reach again, just in time, then fell back to the ground and lay there, yelling louder than ever.

Then out came Little Arliss. He was naked, like he always slept in the summer. He was hollering "A dog! A dog!" He ran past me and fell on the dog and petted him till he quit howling, then turned on me, fighting mad.

"You quit kicking my dog!" he yelled fiercely. "You kick my dog, and I'll wear you to a frazzle!"

The battling stick that Mama used to beat the dirt out of clothes when she washed stood leaning against the wall. Now, Little Arliss grabbed it up in both hands and came at me, swinging.

It was such a surprise move, Little Arliss

1. **middling meat:** salt pork.

2. **squawling . . . bellering:** squalling and bellowing; crying loudly.

making fight at me that way, that I just stood there with my mouth open and let him clout me a good one before I thought to move. Then Mama stepped in and took the stick away from him.

Arliss turned on her, ready to fight with his bare fists. Then he decided against it and ran and put his arms around the big dog's neck. He began to yell: "He's my dog. You can't kick him. He's my dog!"

The big dog was back up on his feet now, wagging his stub tail again and licking the tears off Arliss' face with his pink tongue.

Mama laughed. "Well, Travis," she said, "it looks like we've got us a dog."

"But Mama," I said. "You don't mean we'd keep an old ugly dog like that. One that will come in and steal meat right out of the house."

"Well, maybe we can't keep him," Mama said. "Maybe he belongs to somebody around here who'll want him back."

"He doesn't belong to anybody in the settlement," I said. "I know every dog at Salt Licks."

"Well, then," Mama said. "If he's a stray, there's no reason why Little Arliss can't claim him. And you'll have to admit he's a smart dog. Mighty few dogs have sense enough to figure out a way to reach a side of meat hanging that high. He must have climbed up on top of that meal barrel and jumped from there."

I went over and looked at the wooden lid on top of the meal barrel. Sure enough, in the thin film of dust that had settled over it were dog tracks.

"Well, all right," I admitted. "He's a smart dog. But I still don't want him."

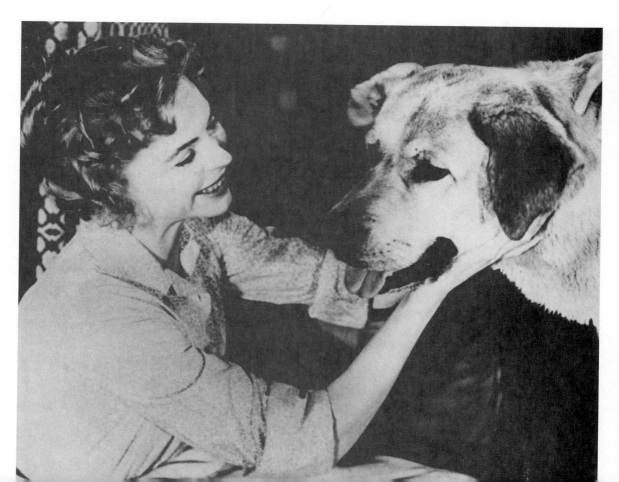

"Now, Travis," Mama said. "You're not being fair. You had you a dog when you were little, but Arliss has never had one. He's too little for you to play with, and he gets lonely."

I didn't say any more. When Mama got her mind set a certain way, there was no use in arguing with her. But I didn't want that meat-thieving dog on the place, and I didn't aim to have him. I might have to put up with him for a day or so, but sooner or later, I'd find a way to get rid of him.

Mama must have guessed what was going on in my mind, for she kept handing me sober looks all the time she was getting breakfast.

She fed us cornmeal mush cooked in a pot swung over the fireplace. She sweetened it with wild honey that Papa and I had cut out of a bee tree last fall, and added cream skimmed off last night's milk. It was good eating; but I'd had my appetite whetted for fried middling meat to go with it.

Mama waited till I was done, then said: "Now, Travis, as soon as you've milked the cows, I think you ought to get your gun and try to kill us a fat young doe for meat. And while you're gone, I want you to do some thinking on what I said about Little Arliss and this stray dog."

Three

All right, I was willing to go make a try for a fat doe. I was generally more than willing to go hunting. And while I was gone, I might do some thinking about Little Arliss and that thieving stray dog. But I didn't much think my thinking would take the turn Mama wanted.

I went and milked the cows and brought the milk in for Mama to strain. I got my rifle and went out to the lot and caught Jumper. I tied a rope around his neck, half-hitched a noose around his nose and pitched the rest of the rope across his back. This was the rope I'd rein him with. Then I got me a second rope and tied it tight around his middle, just back of his withers.[1] This second rope I'd use to tie my deer onto Jumper's back—if I got one.

Papa had shown me how to tie a deer's feet together and pack it home across my shoulder, and I'd done it. But to carry a deer very far like that was a sweat-popping job that I'd rather leave to Jumper. He was bigger and stronger.

I mounted Jumper bareback and rode him along Birdsong Creek and across a rocky hog-back ridge.[2] I thought how fine it would be if I was riding my own horse instead of an old mule. I rode down a long sweeping slope where a scattering of huge, ragged-topped live oaks stood about in grass so tall that it dragged against the underside of Jumper's belly. I rode to within a quarter of a mile of the Salt Licks, then left Jumper tied in a thicket and went on afoot.

I couldn't take Jumper close to the Licks for a couple of reasons. In the first place, he'd get to swishing his tail and stomping his feet at flies and maybe scare off my game. On top of that, he was gun shy. Fire a gun close to Jumper, and he'd fall to staves.[3] He'd snort and wheel to run and fall back against his tie rope, trying to break loose. He'd bawl and paw the air and take on like he'd been shot. When it came to gunfire Jumper didn't have any more sense than a red ant in a hot skillet.

It was a fine morning for hunting, with the air still and the rising sun shining bright on the tall green grass and the greener leaves of the timber. There wasn't enough breeze blowing for me to tell the wind direction, so I licked one finger and held it up. Sure enough, the side next to me cooled first. That meant that what little push there was to the air was away from

1. **withers** (wĭth' ərz): the high point of the back, located between the shoulder blades.
2. **hog-back ridge:** a long, narrow hill with steeply sloping sides.
3. **fall to staves:** fall apart.

me, toward the Salt Licks. Which wouldn't do at all. No deer would come to the Licks if he caught wind of me first.

I half circled the Licks till I had the breeze moving across them toward me and took cover under a wild grapevine that hung low out of the top of a gnarled oak. I sat down with my back against the trunk of the tree. I sat with my legs crossed and my rifle cradled on my knees. Then I made myself get as still as the tree.

Papa had taught me that, 'way back when I was little, the same as he'd taught me to hunt downwind from my game. He always said: "It's not your shape that catches a deer's eye. It's your moving. If a deer can't smell you and can't see you move, he won't ever know you're there."

So I sat there, holding as still as a stump, searching the clearing around the Licks.

The Licks was a scattered outcropping of dark rocks with black streaks in them. The black streaks held the salt that Papa said had got mixed up with the rocks a jillion years ago. I don't know how he knew what had happened so far back, but the salt was there, and all the hogs and cattle and wild animals in that part of the country came there to lick it.

One time, Papa said, when he and Mama had first settled there, they'd run clean out of salt and had to beat up pieces of the rock and boil them in water. Then they'd used the salty water to season their meat and cornbread.

Wild game generally came to lick the rocks in the early mornings or late evenings, and those were the best times to come for meat. The killer animals, like bear and panther and bobcats, knew this and came to the Licks at the same time. Sometimes we'd get a shot at them. I'd killed two bobcats and a wolf there while waiting for deer; and once Papa shot a big panther right after it had leaped on a mule colt and broken its neck with one slap of its heavy forepaw.

I hoped I'd get a shot at a bear or panther this morning. The only thing that showed up, however, was a little band of javelina hogs,[4] and I knew better than to shoot them. Make a bad shot and wound one so that he went to squealing, and you had the whole bunch after you, ready to eat you alive. They were small animals. Their tushes[5] weren't as long as those of the range hogs we had running wild in the woods. They couldn't cut you as deep, but once javelinas got after you, they'd keep after you for a lot longer time.

Once Jed Simpson's boy Rosal shot into a bunch of javelinas and they took after him. They treed him up a mesquite and kept him there from early morning till long after suppertime. The mesquite was a small one, and they nearly chewed the trunk of it in two trying to get to him. After that Rosal was willing to let the javelinas alone.

The javelinas moved away, and I saw some bobwhite quail feed into the opening around the Licks. Then here came three cows with young calves and a roan bull. They stood and licked at the rocks. I watched them awhile, then got to watching a couple of squirrels playing in the top of a tree close to the one I sat under.

The squirrels were running and jumping and chattering and flashing their tails in the sunlight. One would run along a tree branch, then take a flying leap to the next branch. There it would sit, fussing, and wait to see if the second one had the nerve to jump that far. When the second squirrel did, the first one would set up an excited chatter and make a run for a longer leap. Sure enough, after a while, the leader tried to jump a gap that was too wide. He missed his branch, clawed at some leaves, and came tumbling to the ground. The

4. **javelina** (hä-və-lē′nə) **hogs:** jabalina, or wild hogs.
5. **tushes:** tusks.

second squirrel went to dancing up and down on his branch then, chattering louder than ever. It was plain that he was getting a big laugh out of how that show-off squirrel had made such a fool of himself.

The sight was so funny that I laughed, myself, and that's where I made my mistake.

Where the doe had come from and how she ever got so close without my seeing her, I don't know. It was like she'd suddenly lit down out of the air like a buzzard or risen right up out of the bare ground around the rocks. Anyhow, there she stood, staring straight at me, sniffing and snorting and stomping her forefeet against the ground.

She couldn't have scented me, and I hadn't moved; but I had laughed out loud a little at those squirrels. And that sound had warned her.

Well, I couldn't lift my gun then, with her staring straight at me. She'd see the motion and take a scare. And while Papa was a good enough shot to down a running deer, I'd never tried it and didn't much think I could. I figured it smarter to wait. Maybe she'd quit staring at me after a while and give me a chance to lift my gun.

But I waited and waited, and still she kept looking at me, trying to figure me out. Finally, she started coming toward me. She'd take one dancing step and then another and bob her head and flap her long ears about, then start moving toward me again.

I didn't know what to do. It made me nervous, the way she kept coming at me. Sooner or later she was bound to make out what I was. Then she'd whirl and be gone before I could draw a bead on[6] her.

She kept doing me that way till finally my heart was flopping around inside my chest like a catfish in a wet sack. I could feel my muscles

6. **draw a bead on:** aim at.

tightening up all over. I knew then that I couldn't wait any longer. It was either shoot or bust wide open, so I whipped my gun up to my shoulder.

Like I'd figured, she snorted and wheeled, so fast that she was just a brown blur against my gunsights. I pressed the trigger, hoping my aim was good.

After I fired, the black powder charge in my gun threw up such a thick fog of blue smoke that I couldn't see through it. I reloaded, then leaped to my feet and went running through the smoke. What I saw when I came into the clear again made my heart drop down into my shoes.

There went the frightened, snorting cattle, stampeding through the trees with their tails in the air like it was heel-fly time. And right beside them went my doe, running all humped up and with her white, pointed tail clamped tight to her rump.

Which meant that I'd hit her but hadn't made a killing shot.

I didn't like that. I never minded killing for meat. Like Papa had told me, every creature has to kill to live. But to wound an animal was something else. Especially one as pretty and harmless as a deer. It made me sick to think of the doe's escaping, maybe to hurt for days before she finally died.

I swung my gun up, hoping yet to get in a killing shot. But I couldn't fire on account of the cattle. They were too close to the deer. I might kill one of them.

Then suddenly the doe did a surprising thing. 'Way down in the flat there, nearly out of sight, she ran head on into the trunk of a tree. Like she was stone blind. I saw the flash of her light-colored belly as she went down. I waited. She didn't get up. I tore out, running through the chin-tall grass as fast as I could.

When finally I reached the place, all out of breath, I found her lying dead, with a bullet hole through her middle, right where it had to have shattered the heart.

Suddenly I wasn't sick any more. I felt big and strong and sure of myself. I hadn't made a bad shot. I hadn't caused an animal a lot of suffering. All I'd done was get meat for the family, shooting it on the run, just like Papa did.

I rode toward the cabin, sitting behind the gutted doe that I'd tied across Jumper's back. I rode, feeling proud of myself as a hunter and a provider for the family. Making a killing shot like that on a moving deer made me feel bigger and more important. Too big and important, I guessed, to fuss with Little Arliss about that old yeller dog. I still didn't think much of the idea of keeping him, but I guessed that when you are nearly a man, you have to learn to put up with a lot of aggravation from little old bitty kids. Let Arliss keep the thieving rascal. I guessed I could provide enough meat for him, too.

That's how I was feeling when I crossed Birdsong Creek and rode up to the spring under the trees below the house. Then suddenly, I felt different. That's when I found Little Arliss in the pool again. And in there with him was the big yeller dog. That dirty stinking rascal, romping around in our drinking water!

"Arliss!" I yelled at Little Arliss. "You get that nasty old dog out of the water!"

They hadn't seen me ride up, and I guess it was my sudden yell that surprised them both so bad. Arliss went tearing out of the pool on one side and the dog on the other. Arliss was screaming his head off, and here came the big dog with his wet fur rising along the ridge of his backbone, baying me like I was a panther.

I didn't give him a chance to get to me. I was too quick about jumping off the mule and grabbing up some rocks.

I was lucky. The first rock I threw caught the big dog right between the eyes, and I was throwing hard. He went down, yelling and pitching and wallowing. And just as he came to his feet again, I caught him in the ribs with another one. That was too much for him. He turned tail then and took out for the house, squawling and bawling.

But I wasn't the only good rock thrower in the family. Arliss was only five years old, but I'd spent a lot of time showing him how to throw a rock. Now I wished I hadn't. Because about then, a rock nearly tore my left ear off. I whirled around just barely in time to duck another that would have caught me square in the left eye.

I yelled, "Arliss, you quit that!" but Arliss wasn't listening. He was too scared and too mad. He bent over to pick up a rock big enough to brain me with if he'd been strong enough to throw it.

Well, when you're fourteen years old, you can't afford to mix in a rock fight with your five-year-old brother. You can't do it, even when you're in the right. You just can't explain a thing like that to your folks. All they'll do is point out how much bigger you are, how unfair it is to your little brother.

All I could do was turn tail like the yeller dog and head for the house, yelling for Mama. And right after me came Little Arliss, naked and running as fast as he could, doing his dead-level best to get close enough to hit me with the big rock he was packing.

I outran him, of course; and then here came Mama, running so fast that her long skirts were flying, and calling out: "What on earth, boys!"

I hollered, "You better catch that Arliss!" as I ran past her. And she did; but Little Arliss was so mad that I thought for a second he was going to hit her with the rock before she could get it away from him.

Well, it all wound up about like I figured.

Mama switched Little Arliss for playing in our drinking water. Then she blessed me out good and proper for being so bossy with him. And the big yeller dog that had caused all the trouble got off scot free.

It didn't seem right and fair to me. How could I be the man of the family if nobody paid any attention to what I thought or said?

I went and led Jumper up to the house. I hung the doe in the live oak tree that grew beside the house and began skinning it and cutting up the meat. I thought of the fine shot I'd made and knew it was worth bragging about to Mama. But what was the use? She wouldn't pay me any mind—not until I did something she thought I shouldn't have done. Then she'd treat me like I wasn't any older than Little Arliss.

I sulked and felt sorry for myself all the time I worked with the meat. The more I thought about it, the madder I got at the big yeller dog.

I hung the fresh cuts of venison up in the dog run, right where Old Yeller had stolen the hog meat the night he came. I did it for a couple of reasons. To begin with, that was the handiest and coolest place we had for hanging fresh meat. On top of that, I was looking for a good excuse to get rid of that dog. I figured if he stole more of our meat, Mama would have to see that he was too sorry and no account to keep.

But Old Yeller was too smart for that. He gnawed around on some of the deer's leg bones that Mama threw away; but not once did he ever even act like he could smell the meat we'd hung up.

Four

A couple of days later, I had another and better reason for wanting to get rid of Old Yeller. That was when the two longhorn range bulls met at the house and pulled off their big fight.

We first heard the bulls while we were eating our dinner of cornbread, roasted venison, and green watercress gathered from below the spring. One bull came from off a high rocky ridge to the south of the cabin. We could hear his angry rumbling as he moved down through the thickets of catclaw and scrub oak.

Then he lifted his voice in a wild brassy blare that set echoes clamoring in the draws and canyons for miles around.

"That old bull's talking fight," I told Mama and Little Arliss. "He's bragging that he's the biggest and toughest and meanest. He's telling all the other bulls that if they've got a lick of sense, they'll take to cover when he's around."

Almost before I'd finished talking, we heard the second bull. He was over about the Salt Licks somewhere. His bellering was just as loud and braggy as the first one's. He was telling the first bull that his fight talk was all bluff. He was saying that *he* was the he bull of the range, that *he* was the biggest and meanest and toughest.

We sat and ate and listened to them. We could tell by their rumblings and bawlings that they were gradually working their way down through the brush toward each other and getting madder by the minute.

I always liked to see a fight between bulls or bears or wild boars or almost any wild animals. Now, I got so excited that I jumped up from the table and went to the door and stood listening. I'd made up my mind that if the bulls met and started a fight, I was going to see it. There was still plenty of careless weeds and crabgrass that needed hoeing out of the corn, but I guessed I could let them go long enough to see a bullfight.

Our cabin stood on a high knoll about a hundred yards above the spring. Years ago, Papa had cleared out all the brush and trees from around it, leaving a couple of live oaks near the house for shade. And while I stood there at the door, the first bull entered the clearing.

He was a leggy, mustard-colored bull with black freckles speckling his jaws and the underside of his belly. He had one great horn set for hooking, while the other hung down past his jaw like a tallow candle that had drooped in the heat. He was what the Mexicans called a *chongo* or "droop horn."

He trotted out a little piece into the clearing, then stopped to drop his head low. He went to snorting and shaking his horns and pawing up the dry dirt with his forefeet. He flung the dirt back over his neck and shoulders in great clouds of dust.

I couldn't see the other bull yet, but I could tell by the sound of him that he was close and coming in a trot. I hollered back to Mama and Little Arliss.

"They're fixing to fight right here, where we can all see it."

There was a split-rail fence around our cabin. I ran out and climbed up and took a seat on the top rail. Mama and Little Arliss came and climbed up to sit beside me.

Then, from the other side of the clearing came the second bull. He was the red roan I'd seen at the Salt Licks the day I shot the doe. He wasn't as tall and long-legged as the *chongo* bull, but every bit as heavy and powerful. And while his horns were shorter, they were both curved right for hooking.

Like the first bull, he came blaring out into the clearing, then stopped, to snort and sling his wicked horns and paw up clouds of dust. He made it plain that he wanted to fight just as bad as the first bull.

About that time, from somewhere behind the cabin, came Old Yeller. He charged through the rails, bristled up[1] and roaring al-

most as loud as the bulls. All their bellering and snorting and dust pawing sounded like a threat to him. He'd come out to run them away from the house.

I hollered at him. "Get back there, you rascal," I shouted. "You're fixing to spoil our show."

That stopped him, but he still wasn't satisfied. He kept baying the bulls till I jumped down and picked up a rock. I didn't have to throw it. All I had to do was draw back like I was going to. That sent him flying back into the yard and around the corner of the cabin, yelling like I'd murdered him.

That also put Little Arliss on the fight.

He started screaming at me. He tried to get down where he could pick up a rock.

But Mama held him. "Hush, now, baby," she said. "Travis isn't going to hurt your dog. He just doesn't want him to scare off the bulls."

Well, it took some talking, but she finally got Little Arliss' mind off hitting me with a rock. I climbed back up on the fence. I told Mama that I was betting on Chongo. She said she was betting her money on Roany because he had two fighting horns. We sat there and watched the bulls get ready to fight and talked and laughed and had ourselves a real good time. We never once thought about being in any danger.

When we learned different, it was nearly too late.

Suddenly, Chongo quit pawing the dirt and flung his tail into the air.

"Look out!" I shouted. "Here it comes."

Sure enough, Chongo charged, pounding the hardpan with his feet and roaring his mightiest. And here came Roany to meet him, charging with his head low and his tail high in the air.

I let out an excited yell. They met head on, with a loud crash of horns and a jar so solid that it seemed like I could feel it clear up there

1. **bristled** (brĭs'əld) **up:** made his hair stand on end, in excitement.

on the fence. Roany went down. I yelled louder, thinking Chongo was winning.

A second later, though, Roany was back on his feet and charging through the cloud of dust their hoofs had churned up. He caught Chongo broadside. He slammed his sharp horns up to the hilt in the shoulder of the mustard-colored bull. He drove against him so fast and hard that Chongo couldn't wheel away. All he could do was barely keep on his feet by giving ground.

And here they came, straight for our rail fence.

"Land sakes!" Mama cried suddenly and leaped from the fence, dragging Little Arliss down after her.

But I was too excited about the fight. I didn't see the danger in time. I was still astride the top rail when the struggling bulls crashed through the fence, splintering the posts and rails, and toppling me to the ground almost under them.

I lunged to my feet, wild with scare, and got knocked flat on my face in the dirt.

I sure thought I was a goner. The roaring of the bulls was right in my ears. The hot, reeking scent of their blood was in my nose. The bone-crushing weight of their hoofs was stomping all around and over me, churning up such a fog of dust that I couldn't see a thing.

Then suddenly Mama had me by the hand and was dragging me out from under, yelling in a scared voice: "Run, Travis, run!"

Well, she didn't have to keep hollering at me. I was running as fast as I ever hoped to run. And with her running faster and dragging me along by the hand, we scooted through the open cabin door just about a quick breath before Roany slammed Chongo against it.

They hit so hard that the whole cabin shook. I saw great big chunks of dried-mud chinking fall from between the logs. There for a second, I thought Chongo was coming through that

door, right on top of us. But turned broadside like he was, he was too big to be shoved through such a small opening. Then a second later, he got off Roany's horns somehow and wheeled on him. Here they went, then, down alongside the cabin wall, roaring and stomping and slamming their heels against the logs.

I looked at Mama and Little Arliss. Mama's face was white as a bed sheet. For once, Little Arliss was so scared that he couldn't scream. Suddenly, I wasn't scared any more. I was just plain mad.

I reached for a braided rawhide whip that hung in a coil on a wooden peg driven between the logs.

That scared Mama still worse. "Oh, no, Travis," she cried. "Don't go out there!"

"They're fixing to tear down the house, Mama," I said.

"But they might run over you," Mama argued.

The bulls crashed into the cabin again. They grunted and strained and roared. Their horns and hoofs clattered against the logs.

I turned and headed for the door. Looked to me like they'd kill us all if they ever broke through those log walls.

Mama came running to grab me by the arm. "Call the dog!" she said. "Put the dog after them!"

Well, that was a real good idea. I was half aggravated with myself because I hadn't thought of it. Here was a chance for that old yeller dog to pay back for all the trouble he'd made around the place.

I stuck my head out the door. The bulls had fought away from the house. Now they were busy tearing down more of the yard fence.

I ducked out and around the corner. I ran through the dog run toward the back of the house, calling, "Here, Yeller! Here Yeller! Get 'em, boy! Sic 'em!"

Old Yeller was back there, all right. But he

didn't come and he didn't sic 'em. He took one look at me running toward him with that bullwhip in my hand and knew I'd come to kill him. He tucked his tail and lit out in a yelling run for the woods.

If there had been any way I could have done it, right then is when I would have killed him.

But there wasn't time to mess with a fool dog. I had to do something about those bulls. They were wrecking the place, and I had to stop it. Papa had left me to look after things while he was gone, and I wasn't about to let two mad bulls tear up everything we had.

I ran up to the bulls and went to work on them with the whip. It was a heavy sixteen-footer and I'd practiced with it a lot. I could crack that rawhide popper louder than a gunshot. I could cut a branch as thick as my little finger off a green mesquite with it.

But I couldn't stop those bulls from fighting. They were too mad. They were hurting too much already; I might as well have been spitting on them. I yelled and whipped them till I gave clear out. Still they went right on with their roaring bloody battle.

I guess they would have kept on fighting till they leveled the house to the ground if it hadn't been for a freak accident.

We had a heavy two-wheeled Mexican cart that Papa used for hauling wood and hay. It happened to be standing out in front of the house, right where the ground broke away in a sharp slant toward the spring and creek.

It had just come to me that I could get my gun and shoot the bulls when Chongo crowded Roany up against the cart. He ran that long single horn clear under Roany's belly. Now he gave such a big heave that he lifted Roany's feet clear off the ground and rolled him in the air. A second later, Roany landed flat on his back inside the bed of that dump cart, with all four feet sticking up.

I thought his weight would break the cart to pieces, but I was wrong. The cart was stronger than I'd thought. All the bull's weight did was tilt it so that the wheels started rolling. And away the cart went down the hill, carrying Roany with it.

When that happened, Chongo was suddenly the silliest-looking bull you ever saw. He stood with his tail up and his head high, staring after the runaway cart. He couldn't for the life of him figure out what he'd done with the roan bull.

The rolling cart rattled and banged and careened its way down the slope till it was right beside the spring. There, one wheel struck a big boulder, bouncing that side of the cart so high that it turned over and skidded to a stop. The roan bull spilled right into the spring. Water flew in all directions.

Roany got his feet under him. He scrambled up out of the hole. But I guess that cart ride and sudden wetting had taken all the fight out of him. Anyhow, he headed for the timber, running with his tail tucked. Water streamed down out of his hair, leaving a dark wet trail in the dry dust to show which way he'd gone.

Chongo saw Roany then. He snorted and went after him. But when he got to the cart, he slid to a sudden stop. The cart, lying on its side now, still had that top wheel spinning around and around. Chongo had never seen anything like that. He stood and stared at the spinning wheel. He couldn't understand it. He lifted his nose up close to smell it. Finally he reached out a long tongue to lick and taste it.

That was a bad mistake. I guess the iron tire of the spinning wheel was roughed up pretty badly and maybe had chips of broken rock and gravel stuck to it. Anyhow, from the way Chongo acted, it must have scraped all the hide off his tongue.

Chongo bawled and went running backward. He whirled away so fast that he lost his footing and fell down. He came to his feet and took out in the opposite direction from the roan bull. He ran, slinging his head and flopping his long tongue around, bawling like he'd stuck it into a bear trap. He ran with his tail clamped just as tight as the roan bull's.

It was enough to make you laugh your head off, the way both those bad bulls had gotten the wits scared clear out of them, each one thinking he'd lost the fight.

But they sure had made a wreck of the yard fence.

Five

That Little Arliss! If he wasn't a mess! From the time he'd grown up big enough to get out of the cabin, he'd made a practice of trying to catch and keep every living thing that ran, flew, jumped, or crawled.

Every night before Mama let him go to bed, she'd make Arliss empty his pockets of whatever he'd captured during the day. Generally, it would be a tangled-up mess of grasshoppers and worms and praying bugs and little rusty tree lizards. One time he brought in a horned toad that got so mad he swelled out round and flat as a Mexican *tortilla* and bled at the eyes. Sometimes it was stuff like a young bird that had fallen out of its nest before it could fly, or a green-speckled spring frog or a striped water snake. And once he turned out of his pocket a wadded-up baby copperhead that nearly threw Mama into spasms. We never did figure out why the snake hadn't bitten him, but Mama took no more chances on snakes. She switched Arliss hard for catching that snake. Then she made me spend better than a week, taking him out and teaching him to throw rocks and kill snakes.

That was all right with Little Arliss. If Mama wanted him to kill his snakes first, he'd kill them. But that still didn't keep him from sticking them in his pockets along with everything else he'd captured that day. The snakes might

be stinking by the time Mama called on him to empty his pockets, but they'd be dead.

Then, after the yeller dog came, Little Arliss started catching even bigger game. Like cottontail rabbits and chaparral birds[1] and a baby possum that sulled[2] and lay like dead for the first several hours until he finally decided that Arliss wasn't going to hurt him.

Of course, it was Old Yeller that was doing the catching. He'd run the game down and turn it over to Little Arliss. Then Little Arliss could come in and tell Mama a big fib about how he caught it himself.

I watched them one day when they caught a

---

1. **chaparral** (shăp′ə-răl′) **birds:** another name for road runners. Chaparral is a thicket of thorny bushes and small trees that grows in the Southwest.
2. **sulled:** played dead.

blue catfish out of Birdsong Creek. The fish had fed out into water so shallow that his top fin was sticking out. About the time I saw it, Old Yeller and Little Arliss did, too. They made a run at it. The fish went scooting away toward deeper water, only Yeller was too fast for him. He pounced on the fish and shut his big mouth down over it and went romping to the bank, where he dropped it down on the grass and let it flop. And here came Little Arliss to fall on it like I guess he'd been doing everything else. The minute he got his hands on it, the fish finned him and he went to crying.

But he wouldn't turn the fish loose. He just grabbed it up and went running and squawling toward the house, where he gave the fish to Mama. His hands were all bloody by then, where the fish had finned him. They swelled up and got mighty sore; not even a mesquite thorn hurts as bad as a sharp fish fin when it's run deep into your hand.

But as soon as Mama had wrapped his hands in a poultice of mashed-up prickly-pear root to draw out the poison, Little Arliss forgot all about his hurt. And that night when we ate the fish for supper, he told the biggest windy I ever heard about how he'd dived 'way down into a deep hole under the rocks and dragged that fish out and nearly got drowned before he could swim to the bank with it.

But when I tried to tell Mama what really happened, she wouldn't let me. "Now, this is Arliss' story," she said. "You let him tell it the way he wants to."

I told Mama then, I said: "Mama, that old yeller dog is going to make the biggest liar in Texas out of Little Arliss."

But Mama just laughed at me, like she always laughed at Little Arliss' big windies after she'd gotten off where he couldn't hear her. She said for me to let Little Arliss alone. She said that if he ever told a bigger whopper than the ones I

used to tell, she had yet to hear it.

Well, I hushed then. If Mama wanted Little Arliss to grow up to be the biggest liar in Texas, I guessed it wasn't any of my business.

All of which, I figure, is what led up to Little Arliss' catching the bear. I think Mama had let him tell so many big yarns about his catching live game that he'd begun to believe them himself.

When it happened, I was down the creek a ways, splitting rails to fix up the yard fence where the bulls had torn it down. I'd been down there since dinner, working in a stand of tall slim post oaks. I'd chop down a tree, trim off the branches as far up as I wanted, then cut away the rest of the top. After that I'd start splitting the log.

I'd split the log by driving steel wedges into the wood. I'd start at the big end and hammer in a wedge with the back side of my axe. This would start a little split running lengthways of the log. Then I'd take a second wedge and drive it into this split. This would split the log further along and, at the same time, loosen the first wedge. I'd then knock the first wedge loose and move it up in front of the second one.

Driving one wedge ahead of the other like that, I could finally split a log in two halves. Then I'd go to work on the halves, splitting them apart. That way, from each log, I'd come out with four rails.

Swinging that chopping axe was sure hard work. The sweat poured off me. My back muscles ached. The axe got so heavy I could hardly swing it. My breath got harder and harder to breathe.

An hour before sundown, I was worn down to a nub. It seemed like I couldn't hit another lick. Papa could have lasted till past sundown, but I didn't see how I could. I shouldered my axe and started toward the cabin, trying to think up some excuse to tell Mama to keep her from knowing I was played clear out.

That's when I heard Little Arliss scream.

Well, Little Arliss was a screamer by nature. He'd scream when he was happy and scream when he was mad and a lot of times he'd scream just to hear himself make a noise. Generally, we paid no more mind to his screaming than we did to the gobble of a wild turkey.

But this time was different. The second I heard his screaming, I felt my heart flop clear over. This time I knew Little Arliss was in real trouble.

I tore out up the trail leading toward the cabin. A minute before, I'd been so tired out with my rail splitting that I couldn't have struck a trot. But now I raced through the tall trees in that creek bottom, covering ground like a scared wolf.

Little Arliss' second scream, when it came, was louder and shriller and more frantic-sounding than the first. Mixed with it was a whimpering crying sound that I knew didn't come from him. It was a sound I'd heard before and seemed like I ought to know what it was, but right then I couldn't place it.

Then, from way off to one side came a sound that I would have recognized anywhere. It was the coughing roar of a charging bear. I'd just heard it once in my life. That was the time Mama had shot and wounded a hog-killing bear and Papa had had to finish it off with a knife to keep it from getting her.

My heart went to pushing up into my throat, nearly choking off my wind. I strained for every lick of speed I could get out of my running legs. I didn't know what sort of fix Little Arliss had got himself into, but I knew that it had to do with a mad bear, which was enough.

The way the late sun slanted through the trees had the trail all cross-banded with streaks of bright light and dark shade. I ran through

these bright and dark patches so fast that the changing light nearly blinded me. Then suddenly, I raced out into the open where I could see ahead. And what I saw sent a chill clear through to the marrow of my bones.

There was Little Arliss, down in that spring hole again. He was lying half in and half out of the water, holding onto the hind leg of a little black bear cub no bigger than a small coon. The bear cub was out on the bank, whimpering and crying and clawing the rocks with all three of his other feet, trying to pull away. But Little Arliss was holding on for all he was worth, scared now and screaming his head off. Too scared to let go.

How come the bear cub ever to prowl close enough for Little Arliss to grab him, I don't know. And why he didn't turn on him and bite

loose, I couldn't figure out, either. Unless he was like Little Arliss, too scared to think.

But all of that didn't matter now. What mattered was the bear cub's mama. She'd heard the cries of her baby and was coming to save him. She was coming so fast that she had the brush popping and breaking as she crashed through and over it. I could see her black heavy figure piling off down the slant on the far side of Birdsong Creek. She was roaring mad and ready to kill.

And worst of all, I could see that I'd never get there in time!

Mama couldn't either. She'd heard Arliss, too, and here she came from the cabin, running down the slant toward the spring, screaming at Arliss, telling him to turn the bear cub loose. But Little Arliss wouldn't do it. All he'd

do was hang with that hind leg and let out one shrill shriek after another as fast as he could suck in a breath.

Now the she bear was charging across the shallows in the creek. She was knocking sheets of water high in the bright sun, charging with her fur up and her long teeth bared, filling the canyon with that awful coughing roar. And no matter how fast Mama ran or how fast I ran, the she bear was going to get there first!

I think I nearly went blind then, picturing what was going to happen to Little Arliss. I know that I opened my mouth to scream and not any sound came out.

Then, just as the bear went lunging up the creek bank toward Little Arliss and her cub, a flash of yellow came streaking out of the brush.

Old Yeller **521**

It was that big yeller dog. He was roaring like a mad bull. He wasn't one-third as big and heavy as the she bear, but when he piled into her from one side, he rolled her clear off her feet. They went down in a wild, roaring tangle of twisting bodies and scrambling feet and slashing fangs.

As I raced past them, I saw the bear lunge up to stand on her hind feet like a man while she clawed at the body of the yeller dog hanging to her throat. I didn't wait to see more. Without ever checking my stride, I ran in and jerked Little Arliss loose from the cub. I grabbed him by the wrist and yanked him up out of that water and slung him toward Mama like he was a half-empty sack of corn. I screamed at Mama. "Grab him, Mama! Grab him and run!" Then I swung my chopping axe high and wheeled, aiming to cave in the she bear's head with the first lick.

But I never did strike. I didn't need to. Old Yeller hadn't let the bear get close enough. He couldn't handle her; she was too big and strong for that. She'd stand there on her hind feet, hunched over, and take a roaring swing at him with one of those big front claws. She'd slap him head over heels. She'd knock him so far that it didn't look like he could possibly get back there before she charged again, but he always did. He'd hit the ground rolling, yelling his head off with the pain of the blow; but somehow he'd always roll to his feet. And here he'd come again, ready to tie into her for another round.

I stood there with my axe raised, watching them for a long moment. Then from up toward the house, I heard Mama calling: "Come away from there, Travis. Hurry, son! Run!"

That spooked me. Up till then, I'd been ready to tie into that bear myself. Now, suddenly, I was scared out of my wits again. I ran toward the cabin.

But like it was, Old Yeller nearly beat me there. I didn't see it, of course; but Mama said that the minute Old Yeller saw we were all in the clear and out of danger, he threw the fight to that she bear and lit out for the house. The bear chased him for a little piece, but at the rate Old Yeller was leaving her behind, Mama said it looked like the bear was backing up.

But if the big yeller dog was scared or hurt in any way when he came dashing into the house, he didn't show it. He sure didn't show it like we all did. Little Arliss had hushed his screaming, but he was trembling all over and clinging to Mama like he'd never let her go. And Mama was sitting in the middle of the floor, holding him up close and crying like she'd never stop. And me, I was close to crying, myself.

Old Yeller, though, all he did was come bounding in to jump on us and lick us in the face and bark so loud that there, inside the cabin, the noise nearly made us deaf.

The way he acted, you might have thought that bear fight hadn't been anything more than a rowdy romp that we'd all taken part in for the fun of it.

Reading Check

1. What is the time and place of the action?
2. Who are Travis, Arliss, and Old Yeller?
3. What is Travis' major responsibility?
4. How did Old Yeller come into the family?
5. What brave act did Old Yeller commit?

Analyzing and Interpreting the Novel

1. Travis, the narrator of the story, says that Old Yeller's name had a "double meaning." Explain what he means.

2. Travis' father tells him to act "a man's part." What is Travis expected to do in his father's absence?

3a. In what way is shooting the doe a "test" for Travis? **b.** What other "tests" does he meet in these early chapters?

4a. Discuss Travis' relationship with Little Arliss. **b.** In what way is his relationship to Old Yeller very similar?

5a. In what way does Old Yeller show that he is an unusual animal? **b.** Are his emotions and behavior believable?

6. Old Yeller runs away when he is needed to scare off the bulls. Yet he attacks the she bear and saves Little Arliss' life. How do you account for his behavior in both episodes?

You have learned that an author may use both direct and indirect methods of characterization in presenting character. Give one example of what you have learned about each character through direct and indirect characterization.

Plot

4. In this early part of the novel, Travis is involved in a number of conflicts. **a.** Which of these conflicts do you think is the major conflict Travis faces? **b.** Is it an external or internal conflict?

5. You have seen that in a short story an author uses foreshadowing to hint at what is to come later. What clues does the author give you to what lies ahead?

Point of View

6. We witness everything from the point of view of Travis. **a.** How does the author convince us that the narrator is a fourteen-year-old boy growing up on the frontier? **b.** Locate at least three details that make the narrator sound authentic.

Literary Elements

Understanding the Novel

Setting

1. The early chapters of *Old Yeller* establish the setting of the novel. List five specific details that help you picture how the family lives.

Character

2. The story focuses on Travis' development as he copes with each new challenge of frontier life. Consider the various situations he faces. Tell how he shows evidence of the following qualities: courage, perseverance, self-reliance.

3. The four major characters in the novel are introduced in these opening chapters.

Language and Vocabulary

Explaining Similes

Poets are not the only writers who use imaginative figures of speech. Travis uses a number of colorful similes. Explain each comparison in the following quotations:

"His belly was swelled up as tight and round as a pumpkin" (page 508).

"When it came to gunfire Jumper didn't have any more sense than a red ant in a hot skillet" (page 510).

"She kept doing me that way till finally my heart was flopping around inside my chest like a catfish in a wet sack" (page 512).

"I could crack that rawhide popper louder than a gunshot" (page 517).

"One time he brought in a horned toad that got so mad he swelled out round and flat as a Mexican *tortilla* and bled at the eyes" (page 518).

"But now I raced through the tall trees in that creek bottom, covering ground like a scared wolf" (page 520).

"He was roaring like a mad bull" (page 522).

"I grabbed him by the wrist and yanked him up out of that water and slung him toward Mama like he was a half-empty sack of corn" (page 522).

Creative Writing

Using Similes in Description

Each of the similes on pages 523–524 is drawn from nature. A simile can be drawn from any subject. For example, we could rewrite the first comparison, using a simile from the world of sports:

"His belly was swelled up as tight and round as a *basketball*."

Rewrite any of the similes on pages 523–524, supplying a comparison of your own.

Writing About Literature

Comparing and Contrasting Experiences

In reading *Old Yeller*, we can experience imaginatively what it was like growing up in the frontier wilderness of our country, more than a century ago. Compare the daily routines of Travis' life with the typical routines of a fourteen-year-old in today's society. What important similarities and differences can you find? Write a short essay developing the points of comparison and contrast.

Examining Aspects of Travis' Character

In the early days after his father leaves him in charge, Travis has moments of great confidence and moments of self-doubt. Write a short essay illustrating both aspects of Travis' character. Cite specific evidence from the novel to support your statements.

Giving an Impression of Old Yeller

Old Yeller is an important and interesting character. Write a short essay giving your impression of the animal.

PART II

Six

Till Little Arliss got us mixed up in that bear fight, I guess I'd been looking on him about like most boys look on their little brothers. I liked him, all right, but I didn't have a lot of use for him. What with his always playing in our drinking water and getting in the way of my chopping axe and howling his head off and chunking me with rocks when he got mad, it didn't seem to me like he was hardly worth the bother of putting up with.

But that day when I saw him in the spring, so helpless against the angry she bear, I learned different. I knew then that I loved him as much as I did Mama and Papa, maybe in some ways even a little bit more.

So it was only natural for me to come to love the dog that saved him.

After that, I couldn't do enough for Old Yeller. What if he was a big ugly meat-stealing rascal? What if he did fall over and yell bloody murder every time I looked crossways at him? What if he had run off when he ought to have helped with the fighting bulls? None of that made a lick of difference now. He'd pitched in and saved Little Arliss when I couldn't possibly have done it, and that was enough for me.

I petted him and made over him till he was wiggling all over to show how happy he was. I felt mean about how I'd treated him and did everything I could to let him know. I searched his feet and pulled out a long mesquite thorn that had become embedded between his toes. I held him down and had Mama hand me a stick with a coal of fire on it, so I could burn off three big bloated ticks that I found inside one of his ears. I washed him with lye soap and water, then rubbed salty bacon grease into his

hair all over to rout the fleas. And that night after dark, when he sneaked into bed with me and Little Arliss, I let him sleep there and never said a word about it to Mama.

I took him and Little Arliss squirrel hunting the next day. It was the first time I'd ever taken Little Arliss on any kind of hunt. He was such a noisy pest that I always figured he'd scare off the game.

As it turned out, he was just as noisy and pesky as I'd figured. He'd follow along, keeping quiet like I told him, till he saw maybe a pretty butterfly floating around in the air. Then he'd set up a yell you could have heard a mile off and go chasing after the butterfly. Of course, he couldn't catch it; but he would keep yelling at me to come help him. Then he'd get mad because I wouldn't and yell still louder. Or maybe he'd stop to turn over a flat rock. Then he'd stand yelling at me to come back and look at all the yellow ants and centipedes and crickets and stinging scorpions that went scurrying away, hunting new hiding places.

Once he got hung up in some briars and yelled till I came back to get him out. Another time he fell down and struck his elbow on a rock and didn't say a word about it for several minutes—until he saw blood seeping out of a cut on his arm. Then he stood and screamed like he was being burnt with a hot iron.

With that much racket going on, I knew we'd scare all the game clear out of the country. Which, I guess we did. All but the squirrels. They took to the trees where they could hide from us. But I was lucky enough to see which tree one squirrel went up; so I put some of Little Arliss' racket to use.

I sent him in a circle around the tree, beating on the grass and bushes with a stick, while I stood waiting. Sure enough, the squirrel got to watching Little Arliss and forgot me. He kept turning around the tree limb to keep it between him and Little Arliss, till he was on my side in plain sight. I shot him out of the tree the first shot.

After that, Old Yeller caught onto what game we were after. He went to work then, trailing and treeing the squirrels that Little Arliss was scaring up off the ground. From then on, with Yeller to tree the squirrels and Little Arliss to turn them on the tree limbs, we had pickings. Wasn't but a little bit till I'd shot five, more than enough to make us a good squirrel fry for supper.

A week later, Old Yeller helped me catch a wild gobbler that I'd have lost without him. We had gone up to the corn patch to pick a bait[1] of blackeyed peas. I was packing my gun. Just as we got up to the slabrock fence that Papa had built around the corn patch, I looked over and spotted this gobbler doing our pea-picking for us. The pea pods were still green yet, most of them no further along than snapping size. This made them hard for the gobbler to shell, but he was working away at it, pecking and scratching so hard that he was raising a big dust out in the field.

"Why, that old rascal," Mama said. "He's just clawing those pea vines all to pieces."

"Hush, Mama," I said. "Don't scare him." I lifted my gun and laid the barrel across the top of the rock fence. "I'll have him ready for the pot in just a minute."

It wasn't a long shot, and I had him sighted in, dead to rights. I aimed to stick a bullet right where his wings hinged to his back. I was holding my breath and already squeezing off when Little Arliss, who'd gotten behind, came running up.

"Whatcha shootin' at, Travis?" he yelled at the top of his voice. "Whatcha shootin' at?"

Well, that made me and the gobbler both jump. The gun fired, and I saw the gobbler go down. But a second later, he was up again, streaking through the tall corn, dragging a broken wing.

For a second, I was so mad at Little Arliss I could have wrung his neck like a frying chicken's. I said, "*Arliss!* Why can't you keep your mouth shut? You've made me lose that gobbler!"

Well, Little Arliss didn't have sense enough to know what I was mad about. Right away, he puckered up and went to crying and leaking tears all over the place. Some of them splattered clear down on his bare feet, making dark splotches in the dust that covered them. I always did say that when Little Arliss cried he could shed more tears faster than any crier I ever saw.

"Wait a minute!" Mama put in. "I don't think you've lost your gobbler yet. Look yonder!"

She pointed, and I looked, and there was Old Yeller jumping the rock fence and racing toward the pea patch. He ran up to where I'd knocked the gobbler down. He circled the place one time, smelling the ground and wiggling his stub tail. Then he took off through the corn the same way the gobbler went, yelling like I was beating him with a stick.

When he barked "treed" a couple of minutes later, it was in the woods the other side of the corn patch. We went to him. We found him jumping at the gobbler that had run up a stooping live oak and was perched there, panting, just waiting for me.

So in spite of the fact that Little Arliss had caused me to make a bad shot, we had us a real sumptuous supper that night. Roast turkey with cornbread dressing and watercress and wild onions that Little Arliss and I found growing down in the creek next to the water.

But when we tried to feed Old Yeller some of the turkey, on account of his saving us from losing it, he wouldn't eat. He'd lick the meat and wiggle his stub tail to show how grateful he

---

1. **bait:** here, an adequate amount of something.

was, but he didn't swallow down more than a bite or two.

That puzzled Mama and me because, when we remembered back, we realized that he hadn't been eating anything we'd fed him for the last several days. Yet he was fat and with hair as slick and shiny as a dog eating three square meals a day.

Mama shook her head. "If I didn't know better," she said, "I'd say that dog was sucking eggs. But I've got three hens setting and one with biddy chickens, and I'm getting more eggs from the rest of them than I've gotten since last fall. So he can't be robbing the nests."

Well, we wondered some about what Old Yeller was living on, but didn't worry about it. That is, not until the day Bud Searcy dropped by the cabin to see how we were making out.

Bud Searcy was a red-faced man with a bulging middle who liked to visit around the settlement and sit and talk hard times and spit tobacco juice all over the place and wait for somebody to ask him to dinner.

I never did have a lot of use for him and my folks didn't, either. Mama said he was shiftless. She said that was the reason the rest of the men left him at home to sort of look after the womenfolks and kids while they were gone on the cow drive. She said the men knew that if they took Bud Searcy along, they'd never get to Kansas before the steers were dead with old age. It would take Searcy that long to get through visiting and eating with everybody between Salt Licks and Abilene.

But he did have a little white-haired granddaughter that I sort of liked. She was eleven and different from most girls. She would hang around and watch what boys did, like showing how high they could climb in a tree or how far they could throw a rock or how fast they could swim or how good they could shoot. But she never wanted to mix in or try to take over and boss things. She just went along and watched and didn't say much, and the only thing I had against her was her eyes. They were big solemn brown eyes and right pretty to look at; only when she fixed them on me, it always seemed like they looked clear through me and saw everything I was thinking. That always made me sort of jumpy, so that when I could, I never would look right straight at her.

Her name was Lisbeth and she came with her grandpa the day he visited us. They came riding up on an old shad-bellied[2] pony that didn't look like he'd had a fill of corn in a coon's age. She rode behind her grandpa's saddle, holding to his belt in the back, and her white hair was all curly and rippling in the sun. Trotting behind them was a blue-ticked[3] she dog that I always figured was one of Bell's pups.

Old Yeller went out to bay them as they rode up. I noticed right off that he didn't go about it like he really meant business. His yelling bay sounded a lot more like he was just barking because he figured that's what we expected him to do. And the first time I hollered at him, telling him to dry up all that racket, he hushed. Which surprised me, as hardheaded as he generally was.

By the time Mama had come to the door and told Searcy and Lisbeth to get down and come right in, Old Yeller had started a romp with the blue-ticked dog.

Lisbeth slipped to the ground and stood staring at me with those big solemn eyes while her grandpa dismounted. Searcy told Mama that he believed he wouldn't come in the house. He said that as hot as the day was, he figured he'd like it better sitting in the dog run. So Mama had me bring out our four cowhide

2. **shad-bellied:** having a flat belly.
3. **blue-ticked:** having a white coat flecked with bluish gray.

bottom chairs. Searcy picked the one I always liked to sit in best. He got out a twist of tobacco and bit off a chew big enough to bulge his cheek and went to chewing and talking and spitting juice right where we'd all be bound to step in it and pack it around on the bottoms of our feet.

First he asked Mama if we were making out all right, and Mama said we were. Then he told her that he'd been left to look after all the families while the men were gone, a mighty heavy responsibility that was nearly working him to death, but that he was glad to do it. He said for Mama to remember that if the least little thing went wrong, she was to get in touch with him right away. And Mama said she would.

Then he leaned his chair back against the cabin wall and went to telling what all was going on around in the settlement. He told about how dry the weather was and how he looked for all the corn crops to fail and the settlement folks to be scraping the bottoms of their meal barrels long before next spring. He told how the cows were going dry and the gardens were failing. He told how Jed Simpson's boy Rosal was sitting at a turkey roost, waiting for a shot, when a fox came right up and tried to jump on him, and Rosal had to club it to death with his gun butt. This sure looked like a case of hydrophobia[4] to Searcy, as anybody knew that no fox in his right mind was going to jump on a hunter.

Which reminded him of an uncle of his that got mad-dog bit down in the piney woods of East Texas. This was 'way back when Searcy was a little boy. As soon as the dog bit him, the man knew he was bound to die; so he went and got a big log chain and tied one end around the bottom of a tree and the other end to one of his legs. And right there he stayed till the sick-

ness got him and he lost his mind. He slobbered at the mouth and moaned and screamed and ran at his wife and children, trying to catch them and bite them. Only, of course, the chain around his leg held him back, which was the reason he'd chained himself to the tree in the first place. And right there, chained to that tree, he finally died and they buried him under the same tree.

Bud Searcy sure hoped that we wouldn't have an outbreak of hydrophobia in Salt Licks and all die before the men got back from Kansas.

Then he talked awhile about a panther that had caught and killed one of Joe Anson's colts and how the Anson boys had put their dogs on the trail. They ran the panther into the cave and Jeff Anson followed in where the dogs had more sense than to go and got pretty badly panther-mauled for his trouble; but he did get the panther.

Searcy talked till dinnertime, said not a word all through dinner, and then went back to talking as quick as he'd swallowed down the last bite.

He told how some strange varmint that wasn't a coyote, possum, skunk, or coon had recently started robbing the settlement blind. Or maybe it was even some*body*. Nobody could tell for sure. All they knew was that they were losing meat out of their smokehouses, eggs out of their hens' nests, and sometimes even whole pans of cornbread that the womenfolks had set out to cool. Ike Fuller had been barbecuing some meat over an open pit and left it for a minute to go get a drink of water and came back to find that a three- or four-pound chunk of beef ribs had disappeared like it had gone up in smoke.

Salt Licks folks were getting pretty riled about it, Searcy said, and guessed it would go hard with whatever or whoever was doing the raiding if they ever learned what it was.

4. **hydrophobia** (hī′drǝ-fō′bē-ǝ): rabies, a disease that attacks the nervous system and that can be spread by the bite of an infected animal.

Listening to this, I got an uneasy feeling. The feeling got worse a minute later when Lisbeth motioned me to follow her off down to the spring.

We walked clear down there, with Old Yeller and the blue-tick dog following with us, before she finally looked up at me and said, "It's him."

"What do you mean?" I said.

"I mean it's your big yeller dog," she said. "I saw him."

"Do what?" I asked.

"Steal that bait of ribs," she said. "I saw him get a bunch of eggs, too. From one of our nests."

I stopped then and looked straight at her and she looked straight back at me and I couldn't stand it and had to look down.

"But I'm not going to tell," she said.

I didn't believe her. "I bet you do," I said.

"No, I won't," she said, shaking her head. "I wouldn't, even before I knew he was your dog."

"Why?"

"Because Miss Prissy is going to have pups."

"Miss Prissy?"

"That's the name of my dog, and she's going to have pups and your dog will be their papa, and I wouldn't want their papa to get shot."

I stared at her again, and again I had to look down. I wanted to thank her, but I didn't know the right words. So I fished around in my pocket and brought out an Indian arrowhead that I'd found the day before and gave that to her.

She took it and stared at it for a little bit, with her eyes shining, then shoved it deep into a long pocket she had sewn to her dress.

"I won't never, never tell," she said, then whirled and tore out for the house, running as fast as she could.

I went down and sat by the spring awhile. It seemed like I liked Bud Searcy a lot better than I ever had before, even if he did talk too much and spit tobacco juice all over the place. But I was still bothered. If Lisbeth had caught Old Yeller stealing stuff at the settlement, then somebody else might, too. And if they did, they were sure liable to shoot him. A family might put up with one of its own dogs stealing from them if he was a good dog. But for a dog that left home to steal from everybody else— well, I didn't see much chance for him if he ever got caught.

After Bud Searcy had eaten a hearty supper and talked awhile longer, he finally rode off home, with Lisbeth riding behind him. I went then and gathered the eggs and held three back. I called Old Yeller off from the house and broke the eggs on a flat rock, right under his nose and tried to get him to eat them. But he wouldn't. He acted like he'd never heard tell that eggs were fit to eat. All he'd do was stand there and wiggle his tail and try to lick me in the face.

It made me mad. "You thievin' rascal," I said. "I ought to get a club and break your back—in fourteen different places."

But I didn't really mean it, and I didn't say it loud and ugly. I knew that if I did, he'd fall over and start yelling like he was dying. And there I'd be—in a fight with Little Arliss again.

"When they shoot you, I'm going to laugh," I told him.

But I knew that I wouldn't.

Seven

I did considerable thinking on what Lisbeth Searcy had told me about Old Yeller and finally went and told Mama.

"Why, that old rogue!" she said. "We'll have to try to figure some way to keep him from prowling. Everybody in the settlement will be mad at us if we don't."

"Somebody'll shoot him," I said.

"Try tying him," she said.

So I tried tying him. But we didn't have any bailing wire in those days, and he could chew through anything else before you could turn your back. I tried him with rope and then with big thick rawhide string that I cut from a cowhide hanging across the top rail of the yard fence. It was the same thing in both cases. By the time we could get off to bed, he'd done chewed them in two and was gone.

"Let's try the corncrib," Mama said on the third night.

Which was a good idea that might have worked if it hadn't been for Little Arliss.

I took Old Yeller out and put him in the corncrib and the second that he heard the door shut on him, he set up a yelling and a howling that brought Little Arliss on the run. Mama and I both tried to explain to him why we needed to shut the dog up, but Little Arliss was too mad to listen. You can't explain things very well to somebody who is screaming his head off and chunking you with rocks as fast as he can pick them up. So that didn't work, either.

"Well, it looks like we're stumped," Mama said.

I thought for a minute and said, "No, Mama. I believe we've got one other chance. That's to shut him up in the same room with me and Little Arliss every night."

"But he'll sleep in the bed with you boys," Mama said, "and the first thing you know, you'll both be scratching fleas and having mange and breaking out with ringworms."[1]

"No, I'll put him a cowhide on the floor and make him sleep there," I said.

So Mama agreed and I spread a cowhide on the floor beside our bed and we shut Old Yeller in and didn't have a bit more trouble.

1. **mange** (mānj) . . . **ringworms:** contagious skin diseases.

Of course, Old Yeller didn't sleep on the cowhide. And once, a good while later, I did break out with a little ringworm under my left arm. But I rubbed it with turpentine, just like Mama always did, and it soon went away. And after that, when we fed Old Yeller cornmeal mush or fresh meat, he ate it and did well on it and never one time bothered our chicken nests.

About that time, too, the varmints got to pestering us so much that a lot of times Old Yeller

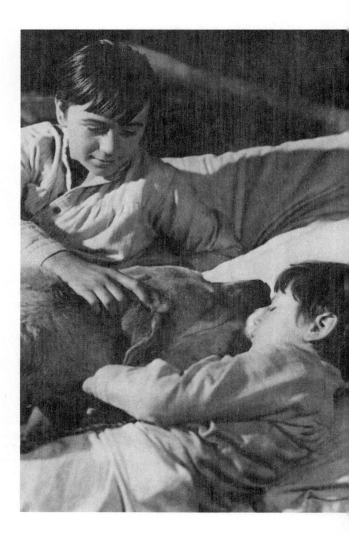

and I were kept busy nearly all night long.

It was the coons, mainly. The corn was ripening into roasting ears now, and the coons would come at night and strip the shucks back with their little hands, and gnaw the milky kernels off the cob. Also, the watermelons were beginning to turn red inside and the skunks would come and open up little round holes in the rinds and reach in with their forefeet and drag out the juicy insides to eat. Sometimes the coyotes would come and eat watermelons, too; and now and then a deer would jump into the field and eat corn, melons, and peas.

So Old Yeller and I took to sleeping in the corn patch every night. We slept on the cowhide that Yeller never would sleep on at the house. That is, we did when we got to sleep. Most of the night, we'd be up fighting coons. We slept out in the middle of the patch, where Yeller could scent a coon clear to the fence on every side. We'd lie there on the cowhide and look up at the stars and listen to the warm night breeze rustling the corn blades. Sometimes I'd wonder what the stars were and what kept them hanging up there so high and bright and if Papa, 'way off up yonder in Kansas, could see the same stars I could see.

I was getting mighty lonesome to see Papa. With the help of Old Yeller, I was taking care of things all right; but I was sure beginning to wish that he'd come back home.

Then I'd think awhile about the time when I'd get big enough to go off on a cow drive myself, riding my own horse, and see all the big new country of plains and creeks and rivers and mountains and timber and new towns and Indian camps. Then, finally, just about the time I started drifting off to sleep, I'd hear Old Yeller rise to his feet and go padding off through the corn. A minute later, his yelling bay would lift from some part of the corn patch, and I'd hear the fighting squawl of some coon caught stealing corn. Then I'd jump to my feet and go running through the corn, shouting encouragement to Old Yeller.

"Git him, Yeller," I'd holler. "Tear him up!"

And that's what Old Yeller would be trying to do; but a boar coon isn't an easy thing to tear up. For one thing, he'll fight you from sundown till sunup. He's not big for size, but the longer you fight him, the bigger he seems to get. He fights you with all four feet and every tooth in his head and enough courage for an animal five times his size.

On top of that, he's fighting inside a thick hide that fills a dog's mouth like a wad of loose sacking. The dog has a hard time ever really biting him. He just squirms and twists around inside that hide and won't quit fighting even after the dog's got enough and is ready to throw the fight to him. Plenty of times, Papa and I had seen a boar coon whip Bell, run him off, then turn on us and chase us clear out of a cornfield.

It was easy for me to go running through the dark cornfields, yelling for Old Yeller to tear up a thieving coon, but it wasn't easy for Old Yeller to do it. He'd be yelling and the coon would be squawling and they'd go wallowing and clawing and threshing through the corn, popping the stalks as they broke them off, making such an uproar in the night that it sounded like murder. But, generally, when the fight was all over, the coon went one way and Old Yeller the other, both of them pretty well satisfied to call it quits.

We didn't get much sleep of a night while all this was going on, but we had us a good time and saved the corn from the coons.

The only real bad part of it was the skunks. What with all the racket we made coon fighting, the skunks didn't come often. But when one did come, we were in a mess.

Old Yeller could handle a skunk easy enough. All he had to do was rush in, grab it by the head and give it a good shaking. That would break the skunk's neck, but it wouldn't end the trouble. Because not even a hoot owl can kill a skunk without getting sprayed with his scent. And skunk scent is a smell that won't quit. After every skunk killing, Old Yeller would get so sick that he could hardly stand it. He'd snort and drool and slobber and vomit. He'd roll and wallow in the dirt and go dragging his body through tall weeds, trying to get the scent off; but he couldn't. Then finally, he'd give up and come lie down on the cowhide with me. And of course he'd smell so bad that I couldn't stand him and have to go off and try to sleep somewhere else. Then he'd follow me and get his feelings hurt because I wouldn't let him sleep with me.

Papa always said that breathing skunk scent was the best way in the world to cure a head cold. But this was summertime, when Old Yeller and I didn't have head colds. We would just as soon that the skunks stayed out of the watermelons and let us alone.

Working there, night after night, guarding our precious bread corn from the varmints, I came to see what I would have been up against if I'd had it to do without the help of Old Yeller. By myself, I'd have been run to death and still probably wouldn't have saved the corn. Also, look at all the fun I would have missed if I'd been alone, and how lonesome I would have been. I had to admit Papa had been right when he'd told me how bad I needed a dog.

I saw that even more clearly when the spotted heifer had her first calf.

Our milk cows were all old-time longhorn cattle and didn't give a lot of milk. It was real hard to find one that would give much more than her calf could take. What we generally had to do was milk five or six cows to get enough milk for just the family.

But we had one crumpled-horn cow named Rose that gave a lot of milk, only she was getting old, and Mama kept hoping that each of her heifer calves would turn out to be as good a milker as Rose. Mama had tried two or three, but none of them proved to be any good. And then along came this spotted one that was just rawboned and ugly enough to make a good milk cow. She had the bag for it, too, and Mama was certain this time that she'd get a milk cow to replace Rose.

The only trouble was, this heifer Spot, as we called her, had been snaky wild from the day she was born. Try to drive her with the other cattle, and she'd run off and hide. Hem her up in a corner and try to get your hands on her, and she'd turn on you and make fight. Mama had been trying all along to get Spot gentled before she had her first calf, but it was no use. Spot didn't want to be friends with anybody. We knew she was going to give us a pile of trouble when we set out to milk her.

I failed to find Spot with the rest of our milk cows one evening, and when I went to drive them up the next day, she was still gone.

"It's time for her to calve," Mama said, "and I'll bet she's got one."

So the next morning I went further back in the hills and searched all over. I finally came across her, holed up in a dense thicket of bee myrtle close to a little seep spring. I got one brief glimpse of a wobbly, long-legged calf before Spot snorted and took after me. She ran me clear to the top of the next high ridge before she turned back.

I made another try. I got to the edge of the thicket and picked me up some rocks. I went to hollering and chunking into the brush, trying to scare her and the calf out. I got her out, all right, but she wasn't scared. She came straight for me with her horns lowered, bawling her threats as she came. I had to turn tail a second time, and again she chased me clear to the top of that ridge.

I tried it one more time, then went back to the house and got Old Yeller. I didn't know if he knew anything about driving cattle or not, but I was willing to bet that he could keep her from chasing me.

And he did. I went up to the edge of the thicket and started hollering and chunking rocks into it. Here came the heifer, madder than ever, it looked like. I yelled at Old Yeller. "Get her, Yeller," I hollered. And Yeller got her. He pulled the neatest trick I ever saw a dog pull on a cow brute.

Only I didn't see it the first time. I was getting away from there too fast. I'd stumbled and fallen to my knees when I turned to run from Spot's charge, and she was too close behind for me to be looking back and watching what Old Yeller was doing. I just heard the scared bawl she let out and the crashing of the brush as Old Yeller rolled her into it.

I ran a piece further, then looked back. The heifer was scrambling to her feet in a cloud of dust and looking like she didn't know any more about what had happened than I did. Then she caught sight of Old Yeller. She snorted, stuck her tail in the air and made for him. Yeller ran like he was scared to death, then cut back around a thicket. A second later, he was coming in behind Spot.

Without making a sound, he ran up beside her, made his leap and set his teeth in her nose.

I guess it was the weight of him that did it. I saw him do it lots of times later, but never did quite understand how. Anyway, he just set his teeth in her nose, doubled himself up in a tight ball, and swung on. That turned the charging heifer a flip. Her heels went straight up in the air over her head. She landed flat on her back with all four feet sticking up. She hit the ground so hard that it sounded like she ought to bust wide open.

I guess she felt that way about it, too. Anyhow, after taking that second fall, she didn't have much fight left in her. She just scrambled to her feet and went trotting back into the thicket, lowing to her calf.

I followed her, with Old Yeller beside me, and we drove her out and across the hills to the cow lot. Not one time did she turn on us again. She did try to run off a couple of times, but all I had to do was send Old Yeller in to head her. And the second she caught sight of him, she couldn't turn fast enough to get headed back in the right direction.

It was the same when we got her into the cow pen. Her bag was all in a strut[2] with milk that the calf couldn't hold. Mama said we needed to get that milk out. She came with a bucket and I took it, knowing I had me a big kicking fight on my hands if I ever hoped to get any milk.

The kicking fight started. The first time I touched Spot's bag, she reached out with a flying hind foot, aiming to kick my head off and coming close to doing it. Then she wheeled on me and put me on top of the rail fence as quick as a squirrel could have made it.

Mama shook her head. "I was hoping she wouldn't be that way," she said. "I always hate to have to tie up a heifer to break her for milking. But I guess there's no other way with this one."

I thought of all the trouble it would be, having to tie up that Spot heifer, head and feet, twice a day, every day, for maybe a month or more. I looked at Old Yeller, standing just outside the pen.

"Yeller," I said, "you come in here."

Yeller came bounding through the rails.

Mama said: "Why, son, you can't teach a heifer to stand with a dog in the pen. Especially one with a young calf. She'll be fighting at him all the time, thinking he's a wolf or something trying to get her calf."

I laughed. "Maybe it won't work," I said,

2. **in a strut:** bulging.

"but I bet you one thing. She won't be fighting Old Yeller."

She didn't, either. She lowered her horns and rolled her eyes as I brought Old Yeller up to her.

"Now, Yeller," I said, "you stand here and watch her."

Old Yeller seemed to know just what I wanted. He walked right up to where he could almost touch his nose to hers and stood there, wagging his stub tail. And she didn't charge him or run from him. All she did was stand there and sort of tremble. I went back and milked out her strutted bag and she didn't offer to kick me one time, just flinched and drew up a little when I first touched her.

"Well, that does beat all," Mama marveled. "Why, at that rate, we'll have her broke to milk in a week's time."

Mama was right. Within three days after we started, I could drive Spot into the pen, go right up and milk her, and all she'd do was stand there and stare at Old Yeller. By the end of the second week, she was standing and belching and chewing her cud—the gentlest cow I ever milked.

After all that, I guess you can see why I nearly died when a man rode up one day and claimed Old Yeller.

Eight

The man's name was Burn Sanderson. He was a young man who rode a good horse and was mighty nice and polite about taking his hat off to Mama when he dismounted in front of our cabin. He told Mama who he was. He said he was a newcomer to Salt Licks. He said that he'd come from down San Antonio way with a little bunch of cattle that he was grazing over in the Devil's River country. He said he couldn't afford to hire riders, so he'd brought along a couple of dogs to help him herd his cattle. One

of these dogs, the best one, had disappeared. He'd inquired around about it at Salt Licks, and Bud Searcy had told him that we had the dog.

"A big yeller dog?" Mama asked, looking sober and worried.

"Yessum," the man said, then added with a grin, "and the worse egg sucker and camp robber you ever laid eyes on. Steal you blind, that old devil will; but there was never a better cow dog born."

Mama turned to me. "Son, call Old Yeller," she said.

I stood frozen in my tracks. I was so full of panic that I couldn't move or think.

"Go on, Son," Mama urged. "I think he and Little Arliss must be playing down about the creek somewhere."

"But Mama!" I gasped. "We can't do without Old Yeller. He's—"

"Travis!"

Mama's voice was too sharp. I knew I was whipped. I turned and went toward the creek, so mad at Bud Searcy that I couldn't see straight. Why couldn't he keep his blabber mouth shut?

"Come on up to the house," I told Little Arliss.

I guess the way I said it let him know that something real bad was happening. He didn't argue or stick out his tongue or anything. He just got out of the water and followed me back to the house and embarrassed Mama and the young man nearly to death because he came packing his clothes in one hand instead of wearing them.

I guess Burn Sanderson had gotten an idea of how much we thought of Old Yeller, or maybe Mama had told some things about the dog while I was gone to the creek. Anyhow, he acted uncomfortable about taking the dog off. "Now, Mrs. Coates," he said to Mama, "your man is gone, and you and the boys don't have much protection here. Bad as I need that old dog, I can make out without him until your man comes."

But Mama shook her head.

"No, Mr. Sanderson," she said. "He's your dog; and the longer we keep him, the harder it'll be for us to give him up. Take him along. I can make the boys understand."

The man tied his rope around Old Yeller's neck and mounted his horse. That's when Little Arliss caught onto what was happening. He threw a walleyed[1] fit. He screamed and he hollered. He grabbed up a bunch of rocks and went to throwing them at Burn Sanderson. One hit Sanderson's horse in the flank. The horse bogged his head and went to pitching and bawling and grunting. This excited Old Yeller. He chased after the horse, baying him at the top of his voice. And what with Mama running after Little Arliss, hollering for him to shut up and quit throwing those rocks, it was altogether the biggest and loudest commotion that had taken place around our cabin for a good long while.

When Burn Sanderson finished riding the pitch out of his scared horse, he hollered at Old Yeller. He told him he'd better hush up that racket before he got his brains beat out. Then he rode back toward us, wearing a wide grin.

His grin got wider as he saw how Mama and I were holding Little Arliss. We each had him by one wrist and were holding him clear off the ground. He couldn't get at any more rocks to throw that way, but it sure didn't keep him from dancing up and down in the air and screaming.

"Turn him loose," Sanderson said with a big laugh. "He's not going to throw any more rocks at me."

He swung down from his saddle. He came and got Little Arliss and loved him up till he hushed screaming. Then he said: "Look, boy, do you really want that thieving old dog?"

He held Little Arliss off and stared him straight in the eyes, waiting for Arliss to answer. Little Arliss stared straight back at him and didn't say a word.

"Well, do you?" he insisted.

Finally, Little Arliss nodded, then tucked his chin and looked away.

"All right," Burn Sanderson said. "We'll make a trade. Just between you and me. I'll let you keep the old rascal, but you've got to do something for me."

He waited till Little Arliss finally got up the nerve to ask what, then went on: "Well, it's like this. I've hung around over there in that cow camp, eating my own cooking till I'm so starved out, I don't hardly throw a shadow. Now, if you could talk your mama into feeding me a real jam-up[2] meal of woman-cooked grub, I think it would be worth at least a one-eared yeller dog. Don't you?"

I didn't wait to hear any more. I ran off. I was so full of relief that I was about to pop. I knew that if I didn't get out of sight in a hurry, this Burn Sanderson was going to catch me crying.

Mama cooked the best dinner that day I ever ate. We had roast venison and fried catfish and stewed squirrel and blackeyed peas and cornbread and flour gravy and butter and wild honey and hog-plum jelly and fresh buttermilk. I ate till it seemed like my eyeballs would pop out of my head, and still didn't make anything like the showing that Burn Sanderson made. He was a slim man, not nearly as big as Papa, and I never could figure out where he was putting all that grub. But long before he fi-

1. **walleyed:** with wild, glaring eyes; with the whites of the eyes prominent.

2. **jam-up:** very good.

nally sighed and shook his head at the last of the squirrel stew, I was certain of one thing: he sure wouldn't have any trouble throwing a shadow on the ground for the rest of that day. A good, black shadow.

After dinner, he sat around for a while, talking to me and Mama and making Little Arliss some toy horses out of dried cornstalks. Then he said his thank-yous to Mama and told me to come with him. I followed with him while he led his horse down to the spring for water. I remembered how Papa had led me away from the house like this the day he left and knew by that that Burn Sanderson had something he wanted to talk to me about.

At the spring, he slipped the bits out of his horse's mouth to let him drink, then turned to me.

"Now, boy," he said, "I didn't want to tell your mama this. I didn't want to worry her. But there's a plague of hydrophobia making the rounds, and I want you to be on the lookout for it."

I felt a scare run through me. I didn't know much about hydrophobia, but after what Bud Searcy had told about his uncle that died, chained to a tree, I knew it was something bad. I stared at Burn Sanderson and didn't say anything.

"And there's no mistake about it," he said. "I've done shot two wolves, a fox, and one skunk that had it. And over at Salt Licks, a woman had to kill a bunch of house cats that her younguns had been playing with. She wasn't sure, but she couldn't afford to take any chances. And you can't, either."

"But how will I know what to shoot and what not to?" I wanted to know.

"Well, you can't hardly tell at first," he said. "Not until they have already gone to foaming at the mouth and are reeling with the blind staggers. Any time you see a critter acting that way, you know for sure. But you watch for others that aren't that far along. You take a pet cat. If he takes to spitting and fighting at you for no reason, you shoot him. Same with a dog. He'll get mad at nothing and want to bite you. Take a fox or a wildcat. You know they'll run from you; when they don't run, and try to make fight at you, shoot 'em. Shoot anything that acts unnatural, and don't fool around about it. It's too late after they've already bitten or scratched you."

Talk like that made my heart jump up in my throat till I could hardly get my breath. I looked down at the ground and went to kicking around some rocks.

"You're not scared, are you, boy? I'm only telling you because I know your papa left you in charge of things. I know you can handle whatever comes up. I'm just telling you to watch close and not let anything—*anything*—get to you or your folks with hydrophobia. Think you can do it?"

I swallowed. "I can do it," I told him. "I'm not scared."

The sternness left Burn Sanderson's face. He put a hand on my shoulder, just as Papa had the day he left.

"Good boy," he said. "That's the way a man talks."

Then he gripped my shoulder real tight, mounted his horse and rode off through the brush. And I was so scared and mixed up about the danger of hydrophobia that it was clear into the next day before I even thought about thanking him for giving us Old Yeller.

Nine

A boy, before he really grows up, is pretty much like a wild animal. He can get the wits scared clear out of him today and by tomorrow have forgotten all about it.

At least, that's the way it was with me. I was plenty scared of the hydrophobia plague that Burn Sanderson told me about. I could hardly sleep that night. I kept picturing in my mind mad dogs and mad wolves reeling about with the blind staggers, drooling slobbers and snapping and biting at everything in sight. Maybe biting Mama and Little Arliss, so that they got the sickness and went mad, too. I lay in bed and shuddered and shivered and dreamed all sorts of nightmare happenings.

Then, the next day, I went to rounding up and marking hogs and forgot all about the plague.

Our hogs ran loose on the range in those days, the same as our cattle. We fenced them out of the fields, but never into a pasture; we had no pastures. We never fed them, unless maybe it was a little corn that we threw to them during a bad spell in the winter. The rest of the time, they rustled for themselves.

They slept out and ate out. In the summertime, they slept in the cool places around the water holes, sometimes in the water. In the winter, they could always tell at least a day ahead of time when a blizzard was on the way; then they'd gang up and pack tons of leaves and dry grass and sticks into some dense thicket or cave. They'd pile all this into a huge bed and sleep on until the cold spell blew over.

They ranged all over the hills and down into the canyons. In season, they fed on acorns, berries, wild plums, prickly-pear apples, grass, weeds, and bulb plants which they rooted out of the ground. They especially liked the wild black persimmons that the Mexicans called *chapotes*.[1]

Sometimes, too, they'd eat a newborn calf if the mama cow couldn't keep them horned away. Or a baby fawn that the doe had left hidden in the tall grass. Once, in a real dry time, Papa and I saw an old sow standing belly deep in a drying up pothole of water, catching and

1. *chapotes* (chə-pōd'ēs).

eating perch that were trapped in there and couldn't get away.

Most of these meat eaters were old hogs, however. Starvation, during some bad drought or extra cold winter had forced them to eat anything they could get hold of. Papa said they generally started out by feeding on the carcass of some deer or cow that had died, then going from there to catching and killing live meat. He told a tale about how one old range hog had caught him when he was a baby and his folks got there just barely in time to save him.

It was that sort of thing, I guess, that always made Mama so afraid of wild hogs. The least little old biting shoat could make her take cover. She didn't like it a bit when I started out to catch and mark all the pigs that our sows had raised that year. She knew we had it to do, else we couldn't tell our hogs from those of the neighbors. But she didn't like the idea of my doing it alone.

"But I'm not working hogs alone, Mama," I pointed out. "I've got Old Yeller, and Burn Sanderson says he's a real good hog dog."

"That doesn't mean a thing," Mama said. "All hog dogs are good ones. A good one is the only kind that can work hogs and live. But the best dog in the world won't keep you from getting cut all to pieces if you ever make a slip."

Well, Mama was right. I'd worked with Papa enough to know that any time you messed with a wild hog, you were asking for trouble. Let him alone, and he'll generally snort and run from you on sight, the same as a deer. But once you corner him, he's the most dangerous animal that ever lived in Texas. Catch a squealing pig out of the bunch, and you've got a battle on your hands. All of them will turn on you at one time and here they'll come, roaring and popping their teeth, cutting high and fast with gleaming white tushes that they keep whetted to the sharpness of knife points. And there's no bluff to them, either. They mean business.

They'll kill you if they can get to you; and if you're not fast footed and don't keep a close watch, they'll get to you.

They had to be that way to live in a country where the wolves, bobcats, panther, and bear were always after them, trying for a bait of fresh hog meat. And it was because of this that nearly all hog owners usually left four or five old barrows, or "bar' hogs," as we called them, to run with each bunch of sows. The bar' hogs weren't any more vicious than the boars, but they'd hang with the sows and help them protect the pigs and shoats, when generally the boars pulled off to range alone.

I knew all this about range hogs, and plenty more; yet I still wasn't bothered about the job facing me. In fact, I sort of looked forward to it. Working wild hogs was always exciting and generally proved to be a lot of fun.

I guess the main reason I felt this way was because Papa and I had figured out a quick and nearly foolproof way of doing it. We could catch most of the pigs we needed to mark without ever getting in reach of the old hogs. It took a good hog dog to pull off the trick; but the way Burn Sanderson talked about Old Yeller, I was willing to bet that he was that good.

He was, too. He caught on right away.

We located our first bunch of hogs at a seep spring at the head of a shallow dry wash that led back toward Birdsong Creek. There were seven sows, two long-tushed old bar' hogs, and fourteen small shoats.

They'd come there to drink and to wallow around in the potholes of soft cool mud.

They caught wind of us about the same time I saw them. The old hogs threw up their snouts and said "Woo-oof!" Then they all tore out for the hills, running through the rocks and brush almost as swiftly and silently as deer.

"Head 'em, Yeller," I hollered. "Go get 'em, boy!"

But it was a waste of words. Old Yeller was done gone.

He streaked down the slant, crossed the draw, and had the tail-end pig caught by the hind leg before the others knew he was after them.

The pig set up a loud squeal. Instantly, all the old hogs wheeled. They came at Old Yeller with their bristles up, roaring and popping their teeth. Yeller held onto his pig until I thought for a second they had him. Then he let go and whirled away, running toward me, but running slow. Slow enough that the old hogs kept chasing him, thinking every second that they were going to catch him the next.

When they finally saw that they couldn't, the old hogs stopped and formed a tight circle. They faced outward around the ring, their rumps to the center, where all the squealing pigs were gathered. That way, they were ready to battle anything that wanted to jump on them. That's the way they were used to fighting bear and panther off from their young, and that's the way they aimed to fight us off.

But we were too smart, Old Yeller and I. We knew better than to try to break into that tight ring of threatening tushes. Anyhow, we didn't need to. All we needed was just to move the hogs along to where we wanted them, and Old Yeller already knew how to do this.

Back he went, right up into their faces, where he pestered them with yelling bays and false rushes till they couldn't stand it. With an angry roar, one of the barrows broke the ring to charge him. Instantly, all the others charged, too.

They were right on Old Yeller again. They were just about to get him. Just let them get a few inches closer, and one of them would slam a four-inch tush into his soft belly.

The thing was, Old Yeller never would let them gain that last few inches on him. They cut and slashed at him from behind and both sides, yet he never was quite there. Always he was just a little bit beyond their reach, yet still so close that they couldn't help thinking that the next try was sure to get him.

It was a blood-chilling game Old Yeller played with the hogs, but one that you could see he enjoyed by the way he went at it. Give him time, and he'd take that bunch of angry hogs clear down out of the hills and into the pens at home if that's where I wanted them— never driving them, just leading them along.

But that's where Papa and I had other hog hunters out-figured. We almost never took our hogs to the pens to work them any more. That took too much time. Also, after we got them penned, there was still the dangerous job of catching the pigs away from the old ones.

I hollered at Old Yeller. "Bring 'em on, Yeller," I said. Then I turned and headed for a big gnarled live oak tree that stood in a clear patch of ground down the draw apiece.

I'd picked out that tree because it had a huge branch that stuck out to one side. I went and looked the branch over and saw that it was just right. It was low, yet still far enough above the ground to be out of reach of the highest-cutting hog.

I climbed up the tree and squatted on the branch. I unwound my rope from where I'd packed it coiled around my waist and shook out a loop. Then I hollered for Old Yeller to bring the hogs to me.

He did what I told him. He brought the fighting hogs to the tree and rallied them in a ring around it. Then he stood back, holding them there while he cocked his head sideways at me, wanting to know what came next.

I soon showed him. I waited till one of the pigs came trotting under my limb. I dropped my loop around him, gave it a quick yank, and lifted him, squealing and kicking, up out of the shuffling and roaring mass of hogs below. I clamped him between my knees, pulled out my knife, and went to work on him. First I folded his right ear and sliced out a three-cornered gap in the top side, a mark that we called an overbit. Then, from the under side of his left ear, I slashed off a long strip that ran clear to the point. That is what we called an underslope. That had him marked for me. Our mark was overbit the right and underslope the left.

Other settlers had other marks, like crop the right and underbit the left, or two underbits in the right ear, or an overslope in the left and an overbit in the right. Everybody knew the hog mark of everybody else and we all respected them. We never butchered or sold a hog that didn't belong to us or marked a pig following a sow that didn't wear our mark.

The squealing of the pig and the scent of his blood made the hogs beneath me go nearly wild with anger. You never heard such roaring and teeth-popping, as they kept circling the tree and rearing up on its trunk, trying to get to me. The noise they made and the hate and anger that showed in their eyes was enough to chill your blood. Only, I was used to the feeling and didn't let it bother me. That is, not much. Sometimes I'd let my mind slip for a minute and get to thinking how they'd slash me to pieces if I happened to fall out of the tree, and I'd feel a sort of cold shudder run all through me. But Papa had told me right from the start that fear was a right and natural feeling for anybody, and nothing to be ashamed of.

"It's a thing of your mind," he said, "and you can train your mind to handle it just like you can train your arm to throw a rock."

Put that way, it made sense to be afraid; so I hadn't bothered about that. I'd put in all my time trying to train my mind not to let fear stampede me. Sometimes it did yet, of course, but not when I was working hogs. I'd had enough experience at working hogs that now I could generally look down and laugh at them.

I finished with the first pig and dropped it to the ground. Then, one after another, I roped the others, dragged them up into the tree, and worked them over.

A couple of times, the old hogs on the ground got so mad that they broke ranks and charged Old Yeller. But right from the start, Old Yeller had caught onto what I wanted. Every time they chased him from the tree, he'd just run off a little way and circle back, then stand off far enough away that they'd rally around my tree again.

In less than an hour, I was done with the job, and the only trouble we had was getting the hogs to leave the tree after I was finished. After going to so much trouble to hold the hogs under the tree, Old Yeller had a hard time understanding that I finally wanted them out of the way. And even after I got him to leave, the hogs were so mad and so suspicious that I had to squat there in the tree for nearly an hour longer before they finally drifted away into the brush, making it safe for me to come down.

Ten

With hogs ranging in the woods like that, it was hard to know for certain when you'd found them all. But I kept a piece of ear from every pig I marked. I carried the pieces home in my pockets and stuck them on a sharp-pointed stick which I kept hanging in the corn crib. When the count reached forty-six and I couldn't seem to locate any new bunches of hogs, Mama and I decided that was all the pigs the sows had raised that year. So I had left off hog hunting and started getting ready to gather corn when Bud Searcy paid us another visit. He told me about one bunch of hogs I'd missed.

"They're clear back in that bat cave country,

the yonder side of Salt Branch," he said. "Rosal Simpson ran into them a couple of days ago, feeding on pear apples in them prickly-pear flats. Said there was five pigs following three sows wearing your mark. Couple of old bar' hogs ranging with them."

I'd never been that far the other side of Salt Branch before, but Papa told me about the bat cave. I figured I could find the place. So early the next morning, I set out with Old Yeller, glad for the chance to hunt hogs a while longer before starting in on the corn gathering. Also, if I was lucky and found the hogs early, maybe I'd have time left to visit the cave and watch the bats come out.

Papa had told me that was a real sight, the way the bats come out in the late afternoon. I was sure anxious to go see it. I always like to go see the far places and strange sights.

Like one place on Salt Branch that I'd found. There was a high, undercut cliff there and some birds building their nests against the face of it. They were little gray, sharp-winged swallows. They gathered sticky mud out of a hog wallow and carried it up and stuck it to the bare rocks of the cliff, shaping the mud into little bulging nests with a single hole in the center of each one. The young birds hatched out there and stuck their heads out through the holes to get at the worms and bugs the grown birds brought to them. The mud nests were so thick on the face of the cliff that, from a distance, the wall looked like it was covered with honeycomb.

There was another place I liked, too. It was a wild, lonesome place, down in a deep canyon that was bent in the shape of a horseshoe. Tall trees grew down in the canyon and leaned out over a deep hole of clear water. In the trees nested hundreds of long-shanked herons, blue ones and white ones with black wing tips. The herons built huge ragged nests of sticks and trash and sat around in the trees all day long, fussing and staining the tree branches with their white droppings. And beneath them, down in the clear water, yard-long catfish lay on the sandy bottom, waiting to gobble up any young birds that happened to fall out of the nests.

The bat cave sounded like another of those wild places I liked to see. I sure hoped I could locate the hogs in time to pay it a visit while I was close by.

We located the hogs in plenty of time; but before we were done with them, I didn't want to go see a bat cave or anything else.

Old Yeller struck the hogs' trail at a water hole. He ran the scent out into a regular forest of prickly pear. Bright red apples fringed the edges of the pear pads. In places where the hogs had fed, bits of peel and black seeds and red juice stain lay on the ground.

The sight made me wonder again how a hog could be tough enough to eat prickly-pear apples with their millions of little hairlike spines. I ate them, myself, sometimes; for pear apples are good eating. But even after I'd polished them clean by rubbing them in the sand, I generally wound up with several stickers in my mouth. But the hogs didn't seem to mind the stickers. Neither did the wild turkeys or the pack rats or the little big-eared ringtail cats. All of those creatures came to the pear flats when the apples started turning red.

Old Yeller's yelling bay told me that he'd caught up with the hogs. I heard their rumbling roars and ran through the pear clumps toward the sound. They were the hogs that Rosal Simpson had sent word about. There were five pigs, three sows, and a couple of bar' hogs, all but the pigs wearing our mark. Their faces bristled with long pear spines that they'd got stuck with, reaching for apples. Red juice stain was smeared all over their snouts. They stood, backed up against a big prickly-pear clump. Their anger had their bristles standing in high fierce ridges along their backbones. They roared and popped their teeth and dared me or Old Yeller to try to catch one of the squealing pigs.

I looked around for the closest tree. It stood better than a quarter of a mile off. It was going to be rough on Old Yeller, trying to lead them to it. Having to duck and dodge around in those prickly pear, he was bound to come out bristling with more pear spines than the hogs had in their faces. But I couldn't see any other place to take them. I struck off toward the tree, hollering at Old Yeller to bring them along.

A deep cut-bank draw[1] ran through the pear flats between me and the huge mesquite tree I was heading for, and it was down in the bottom of this draw that the hogs balked. They'd found a place where the flood waters had undercut one of the dirt banks to form a shallow cave.

They'd backed up under the bank, with the pigs behind them. No amount of barking and pestering by Old Yeller could get them out. Now and then, one of the old bar' hogs would break ranks to make a quick cutting lunge at the dog. But when Yeller leaped away, the hog wouldn't follow up. He'd go right back to fill the gap he'd left in the half circle his mates had formed at the front of the cave. The hogs knew they'd found a natural spot for making a fighting stand, and they didn't aim to leave it.

I went back and stood on the bank above them, looking down, wondering what to do. Then it came to me that all I needed to do was go to work. This dirt bank would serve as well as a tree. There were the hogs right under me. They couldn't get to me from down there, not without first having to go maybe fifty yards down the draw to find a place to get out. And Old Yeller wouldn't let them do that. It wouldn't be easy to reach beneath that under-cut bank and rope a pig, but I believed it could be done.

I took my rope from around my waist and shook out a loop. I moved to the lip of the cut bank. The pigs were too far back under me for a good throw. Maybe if I lay down on my stomach, I could reach them.

I did. I reached back under and picked up the first pig, slick as a whistle. I drew him up and worked him over. I dropped him back and watched the old hogs sniff his bloody wounds. Scent of his blood made them madder, and they roared louder.

I lay there and waited. A second pig moved out from the back part of the cave that I couldn't quite see. He still wasn't quite far enough out. I inched forward and leaned further down, to where I could see better. I could reach him with my loop now.

I made my cast, and that's when it happened. The dirt bank broke beneath my weight. A wagon load of sand caved off and spilled down over the angry hogs. I went with the sand.

I guess I screamed. I don't know. It happened too fast. All I can really remember is the wild heart-stopping scare I knew as I tumbled, head over heels, down among those killer hogs.

The crumbling sand all but buried the hogs. I guess that's what saved me, right at the start. I remember bumping into the back of one old bar' hog, then leaping to my feet in a smothering fog of dry dust. I jumped blindly to one side as far as I could. I broke to run, but I was too late. A slashing tush caught me in the calf of my right leg.

A searing pain shot up into my body. I screamed. I stumbled and went down. I screamed louder then, knowing I could never get to my feet in time to escape the rush of angry hogs roaring down upon me.

It was Old Yeller who saved me. Just like

1. **draw:** here, a gully.

he'd saved Little Arliss from the she bear. He came in, roaring with rage. He flung himself between me and the killer hogs. Fangs bared, he met them head on, slashing and snarling. He yelled with pain as the savage tushes ripped into him. He took the awful punishment meant for me, but held his ground. He gave me that one-in-a-hundred chance to get free.

I took it. I leaped to my feet. In wild terror, I ran along the bed of that dry wash,[2] cut right up a sloping bank. Then I took out through the forest of prickly pear. I ran till a forked stick tripped me and I fell.

It seemed like that fall, or maybe it was the long prickly-pear spines that stabbed me in the hip, brought me out of my scare. I sat up, still panting for breath and with the blood hammering in my ears. But I was all right in my mind again. I yanked the spines out of my hip, then pulled up my slashed pants to look at my leg. Sight of so much blood nearly threw me into another panic. It was streaming out of the cut and clear down into my shoe.

I sat and stared at it for a moment and shivered. Then I got hold of myself again. I wiped away the blood. The gash was a bad one, clear to the bone, I could tell, and plenty long. But it didn't hurt much; not yet, that is. The main hurting would start later, I guessed, after the bleeding stopped and my leg started to get stiff. I guessed I'd better hurry and tie up the place and get home as quick as I could. Once that leg started getting stiff, I might not make it.

I took my knife and cut a strip off the tail of my shirt. I bound my leg as tight as I could. I got up to see if I could walk with the leg wrapped as tight as I had it, and I could.

But when I set out, it wasn't in the direction of home. It was back along the trail through the prickly pear.

2. **wash:** here, the dry bed of a stream.

I don't quite know what made me do it. I didn't think to myself: "Old Yeller saved my life and I can't go off and leave him. He's bound to be dead, but it would look mighty shabby to go home without finding out for sure. I have to go back, even if my hurt leg gives out on me before I can get home."

I didn't think anything like that. I just started walking in that direction and kept walking till I found him.

He lay in the dry wash, about where I'd left it to go running through the prickly pear. He'd tried to follow me, but was too hurt to keep going. He was holed up under a broad slab of red sandstone rock that had slipped off a high bank and now lay propped up against a round boulder in such a way as to form a sort of cave. He'd taken refuge there from the hogs. The hogs were gone now, but I could see their tracks in the sand around the rocks, where they'd tried to get at him from behind. I'd have missed him, hidden there under that rock slab, if he hadn't whined as I walked past.

I knelt beside him and coaxed him out from under the rocks. He grunted and groaned as he dragged himself toward me. He sank back to the ground, his blood-smeared body trembling while he wiggled his stub tail and tried to lick my hog-cut leg.

A big lump came up into my throat. Tears stung my eyes, blinding me. Here he was, trying to lick my wound, when he was bleeding from a dozen worse ones. And worst of all was his belly. It was ripped wide open and some of his insides were bulging out through the slit.

It was a horrible sight. It was so horrible that for a second I couldn't look at it. I wanted to run off. I didn't want to stay and look at something that filled me with such a numbing terror.

But I didn't run off. I shut my eyes and made myself run a hand over Old Yeller's head. The stickiness of the blood on it made my flesh crawl, but I made myself do it. Maybe I couldn't do him any good, but I wasn't going to run off and leave him to die, all by himself.

Then it came to me that he wasn't dead yet and maybe he didn't have to die. Maybe there was something that I could do to save him. Maybe if I hurried home, I could get Mama to come back and help me. Mama'd know what to do. Mama always knew what to do when somebody got hurt.

I wiped the tears from my eyes with my shirt sleeves and made myself think what to do. I took off my shirt and tore it into strips. I used a sleeve to wipe the sand from the belly wound. Carefully, I eased his entrails[3] back into place. Then I pulled the lips of the wound together and wound strips of my shirt around Yeller's body. I wound them tight and tied the strips together so they couldn't work loose.

All the time I worked with him, Old Yeller didn't let out a whimper. But when I shoved him back under the rock where he'd be out of the hot sun, he started whining. I guess he knew that I was fixing to leave him, and he wanted to go, too. He started crawling back out of his hole.

I stood and studied for a while. I needed something to stop up that opening so Yeller couldn't get out. It would have to be something too big and heavy for him to shove aside. I thought of a rock and went looking for one. What I found was even better. It was an uprooted and dead mesquite tree, lying on the bank of the wash.

The stump end of the dead mesquite was big and heavy. It was almost too much for me to drag in the loose sand. I heaved and sweated and started my leg to bleeding again. But I managed to get that tree stump where I wanted it.

I slid Old Yeller back under the rock slab. I scolded him and made him stay there till I could haul the tree stump into place.

Like I'd figured, the stump just about filled the opening. Maybe a strong dog could have squeezed through the narrow opening that was left, but I didn't figure Old Yeller could. I figured he'd be safe in there till I could get back.

Yeller lay back under the rock slab now, staring at me with a look in his eyes that made that choking lump come into my throat again. It was a begging look, and Old Yeller wasn't the kind to beg.

I reached in and let him lick my hand. "Yeller," I said, "I'll be back. I'm promising that I'll be back."

Then I lit out for home in a limping run. His howl followed me. It was the most mournful howl I ever heard.

Reading Check

1. Identify the three new characters who make their appearance in this part of the novel.
2. How does Travis keep Old Yeller from prowling at night?
3. Why does the family want to replace Rose?
4. What causes Travis to fall into the gully among the hogs?
5. Where does Travis leave Old Yeller?

---

3. **entrails** (ĕn′trālz′, -trəlz): internal organs of the body; the intestines.

Analyzing and Interpreting the Novel

1. In this part of the novel we see a marked change in Travis' attitude toward Old Yeller. How does he show his affection for the dog?

2. In the opening chapter of the book we learned that Travis once had a "good dog" named Bell. How does Old Yeller also prove to be a "good dog"?

3. Travis says that Bud Searcy liked to "talk hard times." **a.** What does he reveal about the hardships faced by other settlers? **b.** Why is Travis upset by Searcy's news?

4. How does Burn Sanderson confirm Searcy's suspicion that there is hydrophobia in Salt Licks?

5. What new "tests" of skill and courage does Travis face in this part of the novel?

6. Old Yeller heroically throws himself between Travis and the angry hogs. What earlier episodes have prepared us for his bravery and loyalty?

Literary Elements

Understanding the Novel

Setting

1. On the frontier a dog was clearly more than a household pet. Judging from the accounts of Travis and Burn Sanderson, in what ways were the settlers dependent upon their dogs?

2. The settlers of communities like Salt Licks had no newspapers, telephones, or other modern means of communication. How was news spread?

Character

3. You have seen that for characters to be believable they must behave consistently. In Part II of the novel, we discover that Old Yeller has

been stealing food from the settlers. How is this thieving consistent with his behavior in Part I?

4. When characters change or develop in a narrative, the changes in attitude or action have to be explained in some reasonable way. **a.** How does Travis explain the change in his feelings toward Old Yeller? **b.** Do you believe this change is natural?

5. The animal characters in *Old Yeller* are carefully individualized. Earlier in the novel, we met Jumper the mule. In this part we are introduced to a heifer named Spot. What characteristics make her so difficult to handle?

Plot

6. In this part of the novel, as well as in Part I, there are hints of what is to come. Find an example of foreshadowing and tell what you think will happen.

7. Rounding up and marking the hogs is Travis' most dangerous task. How does the author build suspense during this episode?

Point of View

8. How do you know that Travis appreciates the natural world? Find passages in which he reveals his love for nature.

Writing About Literature

Discussing Frontier Education

Although Travis does not go to school, he gets an education in the qualities and skills necessary to live on the frontier. Consider some of the specialized information Travis needs to cope with the responsibilities of getting food, running a farm, managing animals, and other hardships. Write an essay in which you discuss the "subjects" of Travis' daily education.

PART III

Eleven

It looked like I'd never get back to where I'd left Old Yeller. To begin with, by the time I got home, I'd traveled too far and too fast. I was so hot and weak and played out that I was trembling all over. And that hog-cut leg was sure acting up. My leg hadn't gotten stiff like I'd figured. I'd used it too much. But I'd strained the cut muscle. It was jerking and twitching long before I got home; and after I got there, it wouldn't stop.

That threw a big scare into Mama. I argued and fussed, trying to tell her what a bad shape Old Yeller was in and how we needed to hurry back to him. But she wouldn't pay me any mind.

She told me: "We're not going anywhere until we've cleaned up and doctored that leg. I've seen hog cuts before. Neglect them, and they can be as dangerous as snakebite. Now, you just hold still till I get through."

I saw that it wasn't any use, so I held still while she got hot water and washed out the cut. But when she poured turpentine into the place, I couldn't hold still. I jumped and hollered and screamed. It was like she'd burnt me with a red-hot iron. It hurt worse than when the hog slashed me. I hollered with hurt till Little Arliss tuned up and went to crying, too. But when the pain finally left my leg, the muscle had quit jerking.

Mama got some clean white rags and bound up the place. Then she said, "Now, you lie down on that bed and rest. I don't want to see you take another step on that leg for a week."

I was so stunned that I couldn't say a word. All I could do was stare at her. Old Yeller, lying 'way off out there in the hills, about to die if he didn't get help, and Mama telling me I couldn't walk.

I got up off the stool I'd been sitting on. I said to her, "Mama, I'm going back after Old Yeller. I promised him I'd come back, and that's what I aim to do." Then I walked through the door and out to the lot.

By the time I got Jumper caught, Mama had her bonnet on. She was ready to go, too. She looked a little flustered, like she didn't know what to do with me, but all she said was, "How'll we bring him back?"

"On Jumper," I said. "I'll ride Jumper and hold Old Yeller in my arms."

"You know better than that," she said. "He's too big and heavy. I might lift him up to you, but you can't stand to hold him in your arms that long. You'll give out."

"I'll hold him," I said. "If I give out, I'll rest. Then we'll go on again."

Mama stood tapping her foot for a minute while she gazed off across the hills. She said, like she was talking to herself, "We can't use the cart. There aren't any roads, and the country is too rough."

Suddenly she turned to me and smiled. "I know what. Get that cowhide off the fence. I'll go get some pillows."

"Cowhide?"

"Tie it across Jumper's back," she said. "I'll show you later."

I didn't know what she had in mind, but it didn't much matter. She was going with me.

I got the cowhide and slung it across Jumper's back. It rattled and spooked him so that he snorted and jumped from under it.

"You Jumper!" I shouted at him. "You hold still."

He held still the next time. Mama brought the pillows and a long coil of rope. She had me tie the cowhide to Jumper's back and bind the pillows down on top of it. Then she lifted Little

Arliss up and set him down on top of the pillows.

"You ride behind him," she said to me. "I'll walk."

We could see the buzzards gathering long before we got there. We could see them wheeling black against the blue sky and dropping lower and lower with each circling. One we saw didn't waste time to circle. He came hurtling down at a long-slanted dive, his ugly head outstretched, his wings all but shut against his body. He shot past, right over our heads, and the *whooshing* sound his body made in splitting the air sent cold chills running all through me.

I guessed it was all over for Old Yeller.

Mama was walking ahead of Jumper. She looked back at me. The look in her eyes told me that she figured the same thing. I got so sick that it seemed like I couldn't stand it.

But when we moved down into the prickly-pear flats, my misery eased some. For suddenly, up out of a wash ahead rose a flurry of flapping wings. Something had disturbed those buzzards and I thought I knew what it was.

A second later, I was sure it was Old Yeller. His yelling bark sounded thin and weak, yet just to hear it made me want to holler and run

and laugh. He was still alive. He was still able to fight back!

The frightened buzzards had settled back to the ground by the time we got there. When they caught sight of us, though, they got excited and went to trying to get off the ground again. For birds that can sail around in the air all day with hardly more than a movement of their wing tips, they sure were clumsy and awkward about getting started. Some had to keep hopping along the wash for fifty yards, beating the air with their huge wings, before they could finally take off. And then they were slow to rise. I could have shot a dozen of them before they got away if I'd thought to bring my gun along.

There was a sort of crazy light shining in Old Yeller's eyes when I looked in at him. When I reached to drag the stump away, he snarled and lunged at me with bared fangs.

I jerked my hands away just in time and shouted "Yeller!" at him. Then he knew I wasn't a buzzard. The crazy light went out of his eyes. He sank back into the hole with a loud groan like he'd just had a big load taken off his mind.

Mama helped me drag the stump away. Then we reached in and rolled his hurt body over on its back and slid him out into the light.

Without bothering to examine the blood-caked cuts that she could see all over his head and shoulders, Mama started unwinding the strips of cloth from around his body.

Then Little Arliss came crowding past me, asking in a scared voice what was the matter with Yeller.

Mama stopped. "Arliss," she said, "do you think you could go back down this sandy wash here and catch Mama a pretty green-striped lizard? I thought I saw one down there around that first bend."

Little Arliss was as pleased as I was surprised. Always before, Mama had just sort of put up with his lizard-catching. Now she was wanting him to catch one just for her. A delighted grin spread over his face. He turned and ran down the wash as hard as he could go.

Mama smiled up at me, and suddenly I understood. She was just getting Little Arliss out of the way so he wouldn't have to look at the terrible sight of Yeller's slitted belly.

She said to me: "Go jerk a long hair out of Jumper's tail, Son. But stand to one side, so he won't kick you."

I went and stood to one side of Jumper and jerked a long hair out of his tail. Sure enough, he snorted and kicked at me, but he missed. I took the hair back to Mama, wondering as much about it as I had about the green-striped lizard. But when Mama pulled a long sewing needle from her dress front and poked the small end of the tail hair through the eye, I knew then.

"Horse hair is always better than thread for sewing up a wound," she said. She didn't say why, and I never did think to ask her.

Mama asked me if any of Yeller's entrails had been cut and I told her that I didn't think so.

"Well, I won't bother them then," she said. "Anyway, if they are, I don't think I could fix them."

It was a long, slow job, sewing up Old Yeller's belly. And the way his flesh would flinch and quiver when Mama poked the needle through, it must have hurt. But if it did, Old Yeller didn't say anything about it. He just lay there and licked my hands while I held him.

We were wrapping him up in some clean rags that Mama had brought along when here came Little Arliss. He was running as hard as he'd been when he left. He was grinning and hollering at Mama. And in his right hand he carried a green-striped lizard, too.

How on earth he'd managed to catch anything as fast running as one of those green-striped lizards, I don't know; but he sure had one.

You never saw such a proud look as he wore on his face when he handed the lizard to Mama. And I don't guess I ever saw a more helpless look on Mama's face as she took it. Mama had always been squeamish about lizards and snakes and bugs and things, and you could tell that it just made her flesh crawl to have to touch this one. But she took it and admired it and thanked Arliss. Then she asked him if he'd keep it for her till we got home. Which Little Arliss was glad to do.

"Now, Arliss," she told him, "we're going to play a game. We're playing like Old Yeller is sick and you are taking care of him. We're going to let you both ride on a cowhide, like the sick Indians do sometimes."

It always pleased Little Arliss to play any sort of game, and this was a new one that he'd never heard about before. He was so anxious to get started that we could hardly keep him out from underfoot till Mama could get things ready.

As soon as she took the cowhide off Jumper's back and spread it hair-side down upon the ground, I began to get the idea. She placed the soft pillows on top of the hide, then helped me to ease Old Yeller's hurt body onto the pillows.

"Now, Arliss," Mama said, "you sit there on the pillows with Old Yeller and help hold him on. But remember now, don't play with him or get on top of him. We're playing like he's sick, and when your dog is sick, you have to be real careful with him."

It was a fine game, and Little Arliss fell right in with it. He sat where Mama told him to. He held Old Yeller's head in his lap, waiting for the ride to start.

It didn't take long. I'd already tied a rope around Jumper's neck, leaving the loop big enough that it would pull back against his

shoulders. Then, on each side of Jumper, we tied another rope into the one knotted about his shoulders, and carried the ends of them back to the cowhide. I took my knife and cut two slits into the edge of the cowhide, then tied a rope into each one. We measured to get each rope the same length and made sure they were far enough back that the cowhide wouldn't touch Jumper's heels. Like most mules, Jumper was mighty fussy about anything touching his heels.

"Now, Travis, you ride him," Mama said, "and I'll lead him."

"You better let me walk," I argued. "Jumper's liable to throw a fit with that hide rattling along behind him, and you might not can hold him by yourself."

"You ride him," Mama said. "I don't want you walking on that leg any more. If Jumper acts up one time, I'll take a club to him!"

We started off, with Little Arliss crowing at what a fine ride he was getting on the dragging hide. Sure enough, at the first sound of that rattling hide, old Jumper acted up. He snorted and tried to lunge to one side. But Mama yanked down on his bridle and said, "Jumper, you wretch!" I whacked him between the ears with a dead stick. With the two of us coming at him like that, it was more than Jumper wanted. He settled down and went to traveling as quiet as he generally pulled a plow, with just now and then bending his neck around to take a look at what he was dragging. You could tell he didn't like it, but I guess he figured he'd best put up with it.

Little Arliss never had a finer time than he did on that ride home. He enjoyed every long hour of it. And a part of the time, I don't guess it was too rough on Old Yeller. The cowhide dragged smooth and even as long as we stayed in the sandy wash. When we left the wash and took out across the flats, it still didn't look bad. Mama led Jumper in a long roundabout way, keeping as much as she could to the openings where the tall grass grew. The grass would bend down before the hide, making a soft cushion over which the hide slipped easily. But this was a rough country, and try as hard as she could, Mama couldn't always dodge the rocky places. The hide slid over the rocks, the same as over the grass and sand, but it couldn't do it without jolting the riders pretty much.

Little Arliss would laugh when the hide raked along over the rocks and jolted him till his teeth rattled. He got as much fun out of that as the rest of the ride. But the jolting hurt Old Yeller till sometimes he couldn't hold back his whinings.

When Yeller's whimperings told us he was hurting too bad, we'd have to stop and wait for him to rest up. At other times, we stopped to give him water. Once we got water out of a little spring that trickled down through the rocks. The next time was at Birdsong Creek.

Mama'd pack[1] water to him in my hat. He was too weak to get up and drink; so Mama would hold the water right under his nose and I'd lift him up off the pillows and hold him close enough that he could reach down and lap the water up with his tongue.

Having to travel so far and so slow and with so many halts, it looked like we'd never get him home. But we finally made it just about the time it got dark enough for the stars to show.

By then, my hurt leg was plenty stiff, stiff and numb. It was all swelled up and felt as dead as a chunk of wood. When I slid down off Jumper's back, it wouldn't hold me. I fell clear to the ground and lay in the dirt, too tired and hurt to get up.

Mama made a big to-do about how weak and hurt I was, but I didn't mind. We'd gone and brought Old Yeller home, and he was still alive. There by the starlight, I could see him licking Little Arliss' face.

Little Arliss was sound asleep.

Twelve

For the next couple of weeks, Old Yeller and I had a rough time of it. I lay on the bed inside the cabin and Yeller lay on the cowhide in the dog run, and we both hurt so bad that we were wallowing and groaning and whimpering all the time. Sometimes I hurt so bad that I didn't quite know what was happening. I'd hear grunts and groans and couldn't tell if they were mine or Yeller's. My leg had swelled up till it was about the size of a butter churn. I had such a wild hot fever that Mama nearly ran herself to death, packing fresh cold water from the spring, which she used to bathe me all over, trying to run my fever down.

When she wasn't packing water, she was out

1. **pack:** carry.

digging prickly-pear roots and hammering them to mush in a sack, then binding the mush to my leg for a poultice.

We had lots of prickly pear growing close to the house, but they were the big tall ones and their roots were no good. The kind that make a good poultice are the smaller size. They don't have much top, but lots of knotty roots, shaped sort of like sweet potatoes. That kind didn't grow close to the house. Along at the last, Mama had to go clear over to the Salt Licks to locate that kind.

When Mama wasn't waiting on me, she was taking care of Old Yeller. She waited on him just like she did me. She was getting up all hours of the night to doctor our wounds, bathe us in cold water, and feed us when she could get us to eat. On top of that, there were the cows to milk, Little Arliss to look after, clothes to wash, wood to cut, and old Jumper to worry with.

The bad drouth[1] that Bud Searcy predicted had come. The green grass all dried up till Jumper was no longer satisfied to eat it. He took to jumping the field fence and eating the corn that I'd never yet gotten around to gathering.

Mama couldn't let that go on; that was our bread corn. Without it, we'd have no bread for the winter. But it looked like for a while that there wasn't any way to save it. Mama would go to the field and run Jumper out; then before she got her back turned good, he'd jump back in and go to eating corn again.

Finally, Mama figured out a way to keep Jumper from jumping. She tied a drag to him. She got a rope and tied one end of it to his right forefoot. To the other end, she tied a big heavy chunk of wood. By pulling hard, Jumper could move his drag along enough to graze and get to water; but any time he tried to

1. **drouth:** a long period without rain. Also spelled *drought.*

rear up for a jump, the drag held him down.

The drag on Jumper's foot saved the corn but it didn't save Mama from a lot of work. Jumper was always getting his chunk of wood hung up behind a bush or rock, so that he couldn't get away. Then he'd have himself a big scare and rear up, fighting the rope and falling down and pitching and bawling. If Mama didn't hear him right away, he'd start braying, and he'd keep it up till she went and loosened the drag.

Altogether, Mama sure had her hands full, and Little Arliss wasn't any help. He was too little to do any work. And with neither of us to play with, he got lonesome. He'd follow Mama around every step she made, getting in the way and feeling hurt because she didn't have time to pay him any mind. When he wasn't pestering her, he was pestering me. A dozen times a day, he'd come in to stare at me and say: "Whatcha doin' in bed, Travis? Why doncha get up? Why doncha get up and come play with me?"

He nearly drove me crazy till the day Bud Searcy and Lisbeth came, bringing the pup.

I didn't know about the pup at first. I didn't even know that Lisbeth had come. I heard Bud Searcy's talk to Mama when they rode up, but I was hurting too bad even to roll over and look out the door. I remember just lying there, being mad at Searcy for coming. I knew what a bother he'd be to Mama. For all his talk of looking after the women and children of Salt Licks while the men were gone, I knew he'd never turn a hand to any real work. You wouldn't catch him offering to chop wood or gather in a corn crop. All he'd do was sit out under the dog run all day, talking and chewing tobacco and spitting juice all over the place. On top of that, he'd expect Mama to cook him up a good dinner and maybe a supper if he took a notion to stay that long. And Mama had ten times too much to do, like it was.

In a little bit, though, I heard a quiet step at the door. I looked up. It was Lisbeth. She stood with her hands behind her back, staring at me with her big solemn eyes.

"You hurting pretty bad?" she asked.

I was hurting a-plenty, but I wasn't admitting it to a girl. "I'm doing all right," I said.

"We didn't know you'd got hog cut, or we'd have come sooner," she said.

I didn't know what to say to that, so I didn't say anything.

"Well, anyhow," she said, "I brung you a surprise."

I was too sick and worn out to care about a surprise right then; but there was such an eager look in her eyes that I knew I had to say "What?" or hurt her feelings, so I said "What?"

"One of Miss Prissy's pups!" she said.

She brought her hands around from behind her back. In the right one, she held a dog pup about as big as a year-old possum. It was a dirty white in color and speckled all over with blue spots about the size of cow ticks. She held it by the slack hide at the back of its neck. It hung there, half asleep, sagging in its own loose hide like it was dead.

"Born in a badger hole," she said. "Seven of them. I brung you the best one!"

I thought: If that puny-looking thing is the best one, Miss Prissy must have had a sorry litter of pups. But I didn't say so. I said: "He sure looks like a dandy."

"He is," Lisbeth said. "See how I've been holding him, all this time, and he hasn't said a word."

I'd heard that one all my life—that if a pup didn't holler when you held him up by the slack hide of his neck, he was sure to turn out to be a gritty one. I didn't think much of that sign. Papa always put more stock in what color was inside a pup's mouth. If the pup's mouth was black inside, Papa said that was the one to choose. And that's the way I felt about it.

But right now I didn't care if the pup's mouth was pea green on the inside. All I wanted was just to quit hurting.

I said, "I guess Little Arliss will like it," then knew I'd said the wrong thing. I could tell by the look in her eyes that I'd hurt her feelings, after all.

She didn't say anything. She just got real still and quiet and kept staring at me till I couldn't stand it and had to look away. Then she turned and went out of the cabin and gave the pup to Little Arliss.

It made me mad, her looking at me like that. What did she expect, anyhow? Here I was laid up with a bad hog cut, hurting so bad I could hardly get my breath, and her expecting me to make a big to-do over a little old puny speckled pup.

I had me a dog. Old Yeller was all cut up, worse than I was, but he was getting well. Mama had told me that. So what use did I have for a pup? Be all right for Little Arliss to play with. Keep him occupied and out from underfoot. But when Old Yeller and I got well and took to the woods again, we wouldn't have time to wait around on a fool pup, too little to follow.

I lay there in bed, mad and fretful all day, thinking how silly it was for Lisbeth to expect me to want a pup when I already had me a full-grown dog. I lay there, just waiting for a chance to tell her so, too; only she never did come back to give me a chance. She stayed outside and played with Little Arliss and the pup till her grandpa finally wound up his talking and tobacco spitting and got ready to leave. Then I saw her and Little Arliss come past the door, heading for where I could hear her grandpa saddling his horse. She looked in at me, then looked away, and suddenly I wasn't mad at her anymore. I felt sort of mean. I wished now I could think of the right thing to say about the pup, so I could call her back and tell her. I didn't want her to go off home with her feelings still hurt.

But before I could think of anything, I heard her grandpa say to Mama: "Now Mrs. Coates, you all are in a sort of bind here, with your man gone and that boy crippled up. I been setting out here all evening, worrying about it. That's my responsibility, you know, seeing that everybody's taken care of while the men are gone, and I think now I've got a way figured. I'll just leave our girl Lisbeth here to help you all out."

Mama said in a surprised voice: "Why, Mr. Searcy, there's no need for that. It's mighty kind of you and all, but we'll make out all right."

"No, now, Mrs. Coates; you got too big a load to carry, all by yourself. My Lisbeth, she'll be proud to help out."

"But," Mama argued, "she's such a little girl, Mr. Searcy. She's probably never stayed away from home of a night."

"She's little," Bud Searcy said, "but she's stout[2] and willing. She's like me; when folks are in trouble, she'll pitch right in and do her part. You just keep her here now. You'll see what a big help she'll be."

Mama tried to argue some more, but Bud Searcy wouldn't listen. He just told Lisbeth to be a good girl and help Mama out, like she was used to helping out at home. Then he mounted and rode on off.

Thirteen

I was like Mama. I didn't think Lisbeth Searcy would be any help around the place. She was too little and too skinny. I figured she'd just be an extra bother for Mama.

But we were wrong. Just like Bud Searcy said, she was a big help. She could tote water

2. **stout**: here, brave; determined.

from the spring. She could feed the chickens, pack in wood, cook corn bread, wash dishes, wash Little Arliss, and sometimes even change the prickly-pear poultice on my leg.

She didn't have to be told, either. She was right there on hand all the time, just looking for something to do. She was a lot better about that than I ever was. She wasn't as big and she couldn't do as much as I could, but she was more willing.

She didn't even back off when Mama hooked Jumper to the cart and headed for the field to gather in the corn. That was a job I always hated. It was hot work, and the corn shucks made my skin itch and sting till sometimes I'd wake up at night scratching like I'd stumbled into a patch of bull nettles.

But it didn't seem to bother Lisbeth. In fact, it looked like she and Mama and Little Arliss had a real good time gathering corn. I'd see them drive past the cabin, all three of them sitting on top of a cartload of corn. They would be laughing and talking and having such a romping big time, playing with the speckled pup, that before long I half wished I was able to gather corn too.

In a way, it sort of hurt my pride for a little old girl like Lisbeth to come in and take over my jobs. Papa had left me to look after things. But now I was laid up, and here was a girl handling my work about as good as I could. Still, she couldn't get out and mark hogs or kill meat or swing a chopping axe. . . .

Before they were finished gathering corn, however, we were faced with a trouble a whole lot too big for any of us to handle.

The first hint of it came when the Spot heifer failed to show up one evening at milking time. Mama had come in too late from the corn gathering to go look for her before dark, and the next morning she didn't need to. Spot came up, by herself; or rather, she came past the house.

I heard her first. The swelling in my leg was about gone down. I was weak as a rain-chilled chicken, but most of the hurting had stopped. I was able to sit up in bed a lot and take notice of things.

I heard a cow coming toward the house. She was bawling like cows do when they've lost a calf or when their bags are stretched too tight with milk. I recognized Spot's voice.

Spot's calf recognized it, too. It had stood hungry in the pen all night and now it was nearly crazy for a bait of milk. I could hear it blatting[1] and racing around in the cowpen, so starved it could hardly wait.

I called to Mama. "Mama," I said, "you better go let old Spot in to her calf. I hear her coming."

"That pesky Spot," I heard her say impatiently. "I don't know what's got into her, staying out all night like that and letting her calf go hungry."

I heard Mama calling to Spot as she went out to the cow pen. A little later, I heard Spot beller like a fighting bull, then Mama's voice rising high and sharp. Then here came Mama, running into the cabin, calling for Lisbeth to hurry and bring in Little Arliss. There was scare in Mama's voice. I sat up in bed as Lisbeth came running in, dragging Little Arliss after her.

Mama slammed the door shut, then turned to me. "Spot made fight at me," she said. "I can't understand it. It was like I was some varmint that she'd never seen before."

Mama turned and opened the door a crack. She looked out, then threw the door wide open and stood staring toward the cow pen.

"Why, look at her now," she said. "She's not paying one bit of attention to her calf. She's just going on past the cow pen like her calf wasn't there. She's acting as crazy as if she'd got hold of a bait of pea vine."

1. **blatting:** bleating.

There was a little pea vine that grew wild all over the hills during wet winters and bloomed pale lavender in the spring. Cattle and horses could eat it, mixed with grass, and get fat on it. But sometimes when they got too big a bait of it alone, it poisoned them. Generally, they'd stumble around with the blind staggers for a while, then gradually get well. Sometimes, though, the pea vine killed them.

I sat there for a moment, listening to Spot. She was bawling again, like when I first heard her. But now she was heading off into the brush again, leaving her calf to starve. I wondered where she'd gotten enough pea vine to hurt her.

"But Mama," I said, "she couldn't have eaten pea vine. The pea vine is all dead and gone this time of year."

Mama turned and looked at me, then looked away. "I know," she said. "That's what's got me so worried."

I thought of what Burn Sanderson had told me about animals that didn't act right. I said, "Cows don't ever get hydrophobia, do they?"

I saw Lisbeth start at the word. She stared at me with big solemn eyes.

"I don't know," Mama said. "I've seen dogs with it, but I've never heard of a cow brute having it. I just don't know."

In the next few days, while Old Yeller and I healed fast, we all worried and watched.

All day and all night, Spot kept right on doing what she did from the start: she walked and she bawled. She walked mostly in a wide circle that brought her pretty close to the house about twice a day and then carried her so far out into the hills that we could just barely hear her. She walked with her head down. She walked slower and her bawling got weaker as she got weaker; but she never stopped walking and bawling.

When the bull came, he was worse, and a lot more dangerous. He came two or three days later. I was sitting out under the dog run at the time. I'd hobbled out to sit in a chair beside Old Yeller, where I could scratch him under his chewed-off ear. That's where he liked to be scratched best. Mama was in the kitchen, cooking dinner. Lisbeth and Little Arliss had gone off to the creek below the spring to play with the pup and to fish for catfish. I could see them running and laughing along the bank, chasing after grasshoppers for bait.

Then I heard this moaning sound and turned to watch a bull come out of the brush. He was the roan bull, the one that the droopy-horned *chongo* had dumped into the Mexican cart the day of the fight. But he didn't walk like any bull I'd ever seen before. He walked with his head hung low and wobbling. He reeled and staggered like he couldn't see where he was going. He walked head on into a mesquite tree like it wasn't there, and fell to his knees when he hit it. He scrambled to his feet and came on, grunting and staggering and moaning, heading toward the spring.

Right then, for the first time since we'd brought him home, Old Yeller came up off his cowhide bed. He'd been lying there beside me, paying no attention to sight or sound of the bull. Then, I guess the wind must have shifted and brought him the bull's scent; and evidently that scent told him for certain what I was only beginning to suspect.

He rose, with a savage growl. He moved out toward the bull, so trembly weak that he could hardly stand. His loose lips were lifted in an ugly snarl, baring his white fangs. His hackles[2] stood up in a ragged ridge along the back of his neck and shoulders.

Watching him, I felt a prickling at the back of my own neck. I'd seen him act like that before, but only when there was the greatest danger. Never while just facing a bull.

2. **hackles** (hăk′əlz): the hair on the back of the neck.

Suddenly, I knew that Mama and I had been fooling ourselves. Up till now, we'd been putting off facing up to facts. We'd kept hoping that the heifer Spot would get over whatever was wrong with her. Mama and Lisbeth had kept Spot's calf from starving by letting it suck another cow. They'd had to tie the cow's hind legs together to keep her from kicking the calf off; but they'd kept it alive, hoping Spot would get well and come back to it.

Now, I knew that Spot wouldn't get well, and this bull wouldn't, either. I knew they were both deathly sick with hydrophobia. Old Yeller had scented that sickness in this bull and somehow sensed how fearfully dangerous it was.

I thought of Lisbeth and Little Arliss down past the spring. I came up out of my chair, calling for Mama. "Mama!" I said. "Bring me my gun, Mama!"

Mama came hurrying to the door. "What is it, Travis?" she wanted to know.

"That bull!" I said, pointing. "He's mad with hydrophobia and he's heading straight for Lisbeth and Little Arliss."

Mama took one look, said "Oh, my Lord!" in almost a whisper. She didn't wait to get me my gun or anything else. She just tore out for the creek, hollering for Lisbeth and Little Arliss to run, to climb a tree, to do anything to get away from the bull.

I called after her, telling her to wait, to give me a chance to shoot the bull. I don't guess she ever heard me. But the bull heard her. He tried to turn on her, stumbled and went to his knees. Then he was back on his feet again as Mama went flying past. He charged straight for her. He'd have gotten her, too, only the sickness had his legs too wobbly. This time, when he fell, he rooted his nose into the ground and just lay there, moaning, too weak even to try to get up again.

By this time, Old Yeller was there, baying the bull, keeping out of his reach, but ready to eat him alive if he ever came to his feet again.

I didn't wait to see more. I went and got my gun. I hobbled down to where I couldn't miss and shot the roan bull between the eyes.

Fourteen

We couldn't leave the dead bull to lie there that close to the cabin. In a few days, the scent of rotting flesh would drive us out. Also, the carcass lay too close to the spring. Mama was afraid it would foul up our drinking water.

"We'll have to try to drag it further from the cabin and burn it," she said.

"Burn it?" I said in surprise. "Why can't we just leave it for the buzzards and varmints to clean up?"

"Because that might spread the sickness," Mama said. "If the varmints eat it, they might get the sickness too."

Mama went to put the harness on Jumper. I sent Lisbeth to bring me a rope. I doubled the rope and tied it in a loop around the bull's horns. Mama brought Jumper, who snorted and shied away at the sight of the dead animal. Jumper had smelled deer blood plenty of times, so I guess it was the size of the bull that scared him. Or maybe like Yeller, Jumper could scent the dead bull's sickness. I had to talk mean and threaten him with a club before we could get him close enough for Mama to hook the singletree[1] over the loop of rope I'd tied around the bull's horns.

Then the weight of the bull was too much for him. Jumper couldn't drag it. He leaned into his collar and dug in with his hoofs. He grunted and strained. He pulled till I saw the big muscles of his haunches flatten and start quivering. But the best he could do was slide the bull carcass along the ground for about a foot before he gave up.

1. **singletree:** the crossbar to which the harness traces are fastened, also called *whiffletree.*

I knew he wasn't throwing off. Jumper was full of a lot of pesky, aggravating mule tricks; but when you called on him to move a load, he'd move it or bust something.

I called on him again. I drove him at a different angle from the load, hoping he'd have better luck. He didn't. He threw everything he had into the collar, and all he did was pop a link out of his right trace chain. The flying link whistled past my ear with the speed of a bullet. It would have killed me just as dead if it had hit me.

Well, that was it. There was no moving the dead bull now. We could patch up that broken trace chain for pulling an ordinary load. But it would never be strong enough to pull this one. Even if Jumper was.

I looked at Mama. She shook her head. "I guess there's nothing we can do but burn it here," she said. "But it's going to take a sight of wood gathering."

It did, too. We'd lived there long enough to use up all the dead wood close to the cabin. Now, Mama and Lisbeth had to go 'way out into the brush for it. I got a piece of rawhide string and patched up the trace chain, and Mama and Lisbeth used Jumper to drag up big dead logs. I helped them pile the logs on top of the bull. We piled them up till we had the carcass completely covered, then set fire to them.

In a little bit, the fire was roaring. Sheets of hot flame shot high into the air. The heat and the stench of burnt hair and scorching hide drove us back.

It was the biggest fire I'd ever seen. I thought there was fire enough there to burn three bulls. But when it began to die down a couple of hours later, the bull carcass wasn't half burnt up. Mama and Lisbeth went back to dragging up more wood.

It took two days and nights to burn up that bull. We worked all day long each day, with

Mama and Lisbeth dragging up the wood and me feeding the stinking fire. Then at night, we could hardly sleep. This was because of the howling and snarling and fighting of the wolves lured to the place by the scent of the roasting meat. The wolves didn't get any of it; they were too afraid of the hot fire. But that didn't keep them from gathering for miles around and making the nights hideous with their howlings and snarlings.

And all night long, both nights, Old Yeller crippled back and forth between the fire and the cabin, baying savagely, warning the wolves to keep away.

Both nights, I lay there, watching the eyes of the shifting wolves glow like live mesquite coals in the firelight, and listening to the weak moaning bawl of old Spot still traveling in a circle. I lay there, feeling shivery with a fearful dread that brought up pictures in my mind of Bud Searcy's uncle.

I sure did wish Papa would come home.

As soon as the job of burning the bull was over, Mama told us we had to do the same for the Spot heifer. That was all Mama said about it, but I could tell by the look in her eyes how much she hated to give up. She'd had great hopes for Spot's making us a real milk cow, especially after Old Yeller had gentled her so fast; but that was all gone now.

Mama looked tired, and more worried than I think I'd ever seen her. I guess she couldn't help thinking what I was thinking—that if hydrophobia had sickened one of our cows, it just might get them all.

Old Yeller **557**

"I'll do the shooting," I told her. "But I'm going to follow her out a ways from the house to do it. Closer to some wood."

"How about your leg?" Mama asked.

"That leg's getting all right," I told her. "Think it'll do it some good to be walked on."

"Well, try to kill her on bare ground," Mama cautioned. "As dry as it is now, we'll be running a risk of setting the woods afire if there's much old grass around the place."

I waited till Spot circled past the cabin again, then took my gun and followed her, keeping a safe distance behind.

By now, Spot was so sick and starved I could hardly stand to look at her. She didn't look like a cow; she looked more like the skeleton of one. She was just skin and bones. She was so weak that she stumbled as she walked. Half a dozen times she went to her knees and each time I'd think she'd taken her last step. But she'd always get up and go on again—and keep bawling.

I kept waiting for her to cross a bare patch of ground where it would be safe to build a fire. She didn't; and I couldn't drive her, of course. She was too crazy mad to be driven anywhere. I was afraid to mess with her. She might be like the bull. If I ever let her know I was anywhere about, she might go on the fight.

I guess she was a mile from the cabin before I saw that she was about to cross a dry sandy wash, something like the one where Yeller and I had got mixed up with the hogs. That would be a good place, I knew. It was pretty far for us to have to come to burn her, but there was plenty of dry wood around. And if I could drop her out there in that wide sandy wash, there'd be no danger of a fire getting away from us.

I hurried around and got ahead of her. I hid behind a turkey-pear bush on the far side of the wash. But as sick and blind as she was, I think I could have stood out in the broad open without her ever seeing me. I waited till she came stumbling across the sandy bed of the wash, then fired, dropping her in the middle of it.

I'd used up more of my strength than I knew, following Spot so far from the cabin. By the time I got back, I was dead beat. The sweat was pouring off me and I was trembling all over.

Mama took one look at me and told me to get to bed. "We'll go start the burning," she said. "You stay on that leg any longer, and it'll start swelling again."

I didn't argue. I knew I was too weak and tired to take another walk that far without rest. So I told Mama where to find Spot and told her to leave Little Arliss with me, and watched her and Lisbeth head out, both mounted on Jumper. Mama was carrying a panful of live coals to start the fire with.

At the last minute, Yeller got up off his cowhide. He stood watching them a minute, like he was trying to make up his mind about something; then he went trotting after them. He was still thin and rough looking and crippling pretty badly in one leg. But I figured he knew better than I did whether or not he was able to travel. I didn't call him back.

As it turned out, it's a good thing I didn't. Only, afterward, I wished a thousand times that I could have had some way of looking ahead to what was going to happen. Then I would have done everything I could to keep all of them from going.

With Little Arliss to look after, I sure didn't mean to drop off to sleep. But I did and slept till sundown, when suddenly I jerked awake, feeling guilty about leaving him alone so long.

I needn't have worried. Little Arliss was right out there in the yard, playing with the speckled pup. They had themselves a game going. Arliss was racing around the cabin, dragging a short piece of frayed rope. The pup was chasing the rope. Now and then he'd get close enough to pounce on it. Then he'd let out a growl and set teeth into it and try to shake it and hang on at the same time. Generally, he got jerked off his feet and turned a couple of somersets,[2] but that didn't seem to bother him. The next time Arliss came racing past, the pup would tie into the rope again.

I wondered if he wouldn't get some of his baby teeth jerked out at such rough play, but guessed it wouldn't matter. He'd soon be shedding them, anyhow.

I wondered, too, what was keeping Mama and Lisbeth so long. Then I thought how far it was to where the dead cow lay and how long it would take for just the two of them to drag up enough wood and get a fire started, and figured they'd be lucky if they got back before dark.

I went off to the spring after a bucket of fresh water and wondered when Papa would come back. Mama had said a couple of days ago that it was about that time, and I hoped so. For one thing, I could hardly wait to see what sort of horse Papa was going to bring me. But mainly, this hydrophobia plague had me scared. I'd handled things pretty well until that came along. Of course, I'd gotten a pretty bad hog cut, but that could have happened to anybody, even a grown man. And I was about to get well of that. But if the sickness got more of our cattle, I wouldn't know what to do.

Fifteen

It wasn't until dark came that I really began to get uneasy about Mama and Lisbeth. Then I could hardly stand it because they hadn't come home. I knew in my own mind why they hadn't: it had been late when they'd started

out; they'd had a good long piece to go; and even with wood handy, it took considerable time to drag up enough for the size fire they needed.

And I couldn't think of any real danger to them. They weren't far enough away from the cabin to be lost. And if they were, Jumper knew the way home. Also, Jumper was gentle; there wasn't much chance that he'd scare and throw them off. On top of all that, they had Old Yeller along. Old Yeller might be pretty weak and crippled yet, but he'd protect them from just about anything that might come their way.

Still, I was uneasy. I couldn't help having the feeling that something was wrong. I'd have gone to see about them if it hadn't been for Little Arliss. It was past his suppertime; he was getting hungry and sleepy and fussy.

I took him and the speckled pup inside the kitchen and lit a candle. I settled them on the floor and gave them each a bowl of sweet milk into which I'd crumbled cold corn bread. In a little bit, both were eating out of the same bowl. Little Arliss knew better than that and I ought to have paddled him for doing it. But I didn't. I didn't say a word; I was too worried.

I'd just about made up my mind to put Little Arliss and the pup to bed and go look for Mama and Lisbeth when I heard a sound that took me to the door in a hurry. It was the sound of dogs fighting. The sound came from 'way out there in the dark; but the minute I stepped outside, I could tell that the fight was moving toward the cabin. Also, I recognized the voice of Old Yeller.

It was the sort of raging yell he let out when he was in a fight to the finish. It was the same savage roaring and snarling and squawling that he'd done the day he fought the killer hogs off me.

The sound of it chilled my blood. I stood, rooted to the ground, trying to think what

2. **somersets:** somersaults.

it could be, what I ought to do.

Then I heard Jumper snorting keenly and Mama calling in a frightened voice. "Travis! Travis! Make a light, Son, and get your gun. And hurry!"

I came alive then. I hollered back at her, to let her know that I'd heard. I ran back into the cabin and got my gun. I couldn't think at first what would make the sort of light I needed, then recollected a clump of bear grass that Mama'd recently grubbed out,[1] where she wanted to start a new fall garden. Bear grass has an oily sap that makes it burn bright and fierce for a long time. A pile of it burning would make a big light.

I ran and snatched up four bunches of the half-dried bear grass. The sharp ends of the stiff blades stabbed and stung my arms and chest as I grabbed them up. But I had no time to bother about that. I ran and dumped the bunches in a pile on the bare ground outside the yard fence, then hurried to bring a live coal from the fireplace to start them burning.

I fanned fast with my hat. The bear-grass blades started to smoking, giving off their foul smell. A little flame started, flickered and wavered for a moment, then bloomed suddenly and leaped high with a roar.

I jumped back, gun held ready, and caught my first glimpse of the screaming, howling battle that came wheeling into the circle of light. It was Old Yeller, all right, tangled with some animal as big and savage as he was.

Mama called from outside the light's rim. "Careful, Son. And take close aim; it's a big loafer wolf, gone mad."

My heart nearly quit on me. There weren't many of the gray loafer wolves in our part of the country, but I knew about them. They were big and savage enough to hamstring a horse or drag down a full-grown cow. And

here was Old Yeller, weak and crippled, trying to fight a mad one!

I brought up my gun, then held fire while I hollered at Mama. "Y'all get in the cabin," I yelled. "I'm scared to shoot till I know you're out of the line of fire!"

I heard Mama whacking Jumper with a stick to make him go. I heard Jumper snort and the clatter of his hoofs as he went galloping in a wide circle to come up behind the cabin. But even after Mama called from the door behind me, I still couldn't fire. Not without taking a chance on killing Old Yeller.

I waited, my nerves on edge, while Old Yeller and the big wolf fought there in the fire-light, whirling and leaping and snarling and slashing, their bared fangs gleaming white, their eyes burning green in the half light.

Then they went down in a tumbling roll that stopped with the big wolf on top, his huge jaws shut tight on Yeller's throat. That was my chance, and one that I'd better make good. As weak as Old Yeller was, he'd never break that throat hold.

There in the wavering light, I couldn't get a true bead on the wolf. I couldn't see my sights well enough. All I could do was guess-aim and hope for a hit.

I squeezed the trigger. The gunstock slammed back against my shoulder, and such a long streak of fire spouted from the gun barrel that it blinded me for a second; I couldn't see a thing.

Then I realized that all the growling and snarling had hushed. A second later, I was running toward the two still gray forms lying side by side.

For a second, I just knew that I'd killed Old Yeller, too. Then, about the time I bent over him, he heaved a big sort of sigh and struggled up to start licking my hands and wagging that stub tail.

I was so relieved that it seemed like all the

1. **grubbed out:** dug out by the roots.

strength went out of me. I slumped to the ground and was sitting there, shivering, when Mama came and sat down beside me.

She put one arm across my shoulders and held it there while she told me what had happened.

Like I'd figured, it had taken her and Lisbeth till dark to get the wood dragged up and the fire to going around the dead cow. Then they'd mounted old Jumper and headed for home. They'd been without water all this time and were thirsty. When they came to the crossing on Birdsong Creek, they'd dismounted to get a drink. And while they were lying down, drinking, the wolf came.

He was right on them before they knew it. Mama happened to look up and see the dark hulk of him come bounding toward them across a little clearing. He was snarling as he came, and Mama just barely had time to come to her feet and grab up a dead chinaberry pole before he sprang. She whacked him hard across the head, knocking him to the ground. Then Old Yeller was there, tying into him.

Mama and Lisbeth got back on Jumper and tore out for the house. Right after them came the wolf, like he had his mind fixed on catching them, and nothing else. But Old Yeller fought him too hard and too fast. Yeller wasn't big and strong enough to stop him, but he kept him slowed down and fought away from Jumper and Mama and Lisbeth.

"He had to've been mad, Son," Mama wound up. "You know that no wolf in his right senses would have acted that way. Not even a big loafer wolf."

"Yessum," I said, "and it's sure a good thing that Old Yeller was along to keep him fought off." I shuddered at the thought of what could have happened without Old Yeller.

Mama waited a little bit, then said in a quiet voice: "It was a good thing for us, Son; but it wasn't good for Old Yeller."

The way she said that gave me a cold feeling in the pit of my stomach. I sat up straighter. "What do you mean?" I said. "Old Yeller's all right. He's maybe chewed up some, but he can't be bad hurt. See, he's done trotting off toward the house."

Then it hit me what Mama was getting at. All my insides froze. I couldn't get my breath.

I jumped to my feet, wild with hurt and scare. "But Mama!" I cried out. "Old Yeller's just saved your life! He's saved my life. He's saved Little Arliss' life! We can't—"

Mama got up and put her arm across my shoulders again. "I know, Son," she said. "But he's been bitten by a mad wolf."

I started off into the blackness of the night while my mind wheeled and darted this way and that, like a scared rat trying to find its way out of a trap.

"But Mama," I said. "We don't know for certain. We could wait and see. We could tie him or shut him up in the corncrib or some place till we know for sure!"

Mama broke down and went to crying then. She put her head on my shoulder and held me so tight that she nearly choked off my breath.

"We can't take a chance, Son," she sobbed. "It would be you or me or Little Arliss or Lisbeth next. I'll shoot him if you can't, but either way, we've got it to do. We just can't take the chance!"

It came clear to me then that Mama was right. We couldn't take the risk. And from everything I had heard, I knew that there was very little chance of Old Yeller's escaping the sickness. It was going to kill something inside me to do it, but I knew then that I had to shoot my big yeller dog.

Once I knew for sure I had it to do, I don't think I really felt anything. I was just numb all over, like a dead man walking.

Quickly, I left Mama and went to stand in the light of the burning bear grass. I reloaded my gun and called Old Yeller back from the house. I stuck the muzzle of the gun against his head and pulled the trigger.

Sixteen

Days went by, and I couldn't seem to get over it. I couldn't eat. I couldn't sleep. I couldn't cry. I was all empty inside, but hurting. Hurting worse than I'd ever hurt in my life. Hurting with a sickness there didn't seem to be any cure for. Thinking every minute of my big yeller dog, how we'd worked together and romped together, how he'd fought the she bear off Little Arliss, how he'd saved me from the killer hogs, how he'd fought the mad wolf off Mama and Lisbeth. Thinking that after all this, I'd had to shoot him the same as I'd done the roan bull and the Spot heifer.

Mama tried to talk to me about it, and I let her. But while everything she said made sense, it didn't do a thing to that dead feeling I had.

Lisbeth talked to me. She didn't say much; she was too shy. But she pointed out that I had another dog, the speckled pup.

"He's part Old Yeller," she said. "And he was the best one of the bunch."

But that didn't help any either. The speckled pup might be part Old Yeller, but he wasn't Old Yeller. He hadn't saved all our lives and then been shot down like he was nothing.

Then one night it clouded up and rained till daylight. That seemed to wash away the hydrophobia plague. At least, pretty soon afterward, it died out completely.

But we didn't know that then. What seemed important to us about the rain was that the next morning after it fell, Papa came riding home through the mud.

The long ride to Kansas and back had Papa drawn down till he was as thin and knotty as a fence rail. But he had money in his pockets, a big shouting laugh for everybody, and a saddle horse for me.

The horse was a cat-stepping blue roan with a black mane and tail. Papa put me on him the first thing and made me gallop him in the clearing around the house. The roan had all the pride and fire any grown man would want in his best horse, yet was as gentle as a pet.

"Now, isn't he a dandy?" Papa asked.

I said "Yessir!" and knew that Papa was right and that I ought to be proud and thankful. But I wasn't. I didn't feel one way or another about the horse.

Papa saw something was wrong. I saw him look a question at Mama and saw Mama shake her head. Then late that evening, just before supper, he called me off down to the spring, where we sat and he talked.

"Your mama told me about the dog," he said.

I said "Yessir," but didn't add anything.

"That was rough," he said. "That was as rough a thing as I ever heard tell of happening to a boy. And I'm mighty proud to learn how my boy stood up to it. You couldn't ask any more of a grown man."

He stopped for a minute. He picked up some little pebbles and thumped them into the water, scattering a bunch of hairy-legged water bugs. The bugs darted across the water in all directions.

"Now the thing to do," he went on, "is to try to forget it and go on being a man."

"How?" I asked. "How can you forget a thing like that?"

He studied me for a moment, then shook his head. "I guess I don't quite mean that," he said. "It's not a thing you can forget. I don't guess it's a thing that you ought to forget. What I mean is, things like that happen. They may seem mighty cruel and unfair, but that's how life is a part of the time.

"But that isn't the only way life is. A part of the time, it's mighty good. And a man can't afford to waste all the good part, worrying about the bad parts. That makes it all bad. . . . You understand?"

"Yessir," I said. And I did understand. Only, it still didn't do me any good. I still felt just as dead and empty.

That went on for a week or better, I guess, before a thing happened that brought me alive again.

It was right at dinnertime. Papa had sent me out to the lot to feed Jumper and the horses. I'd just started back when I heard a commotion in the house. I heard Mama's voice lifted high and sharp. "Why, you thieving little whelp!" she cried out. Then I heard a shrieking yelp, and out the kitchen door came the speckled pup with a big chunk of corn bread clutched in his mouth. He raced around the house, running with his tail clamped. He was yelling and squawling like somebody was beating him to death. But that still didn't keep him from hanging onto that piece of corn bread that he'd stolen from Mama.

Inside the house, I heard Little Arliss. He was fighting and screaming his head off at Mama for hitting his dog. And above it all, I could hear Papa's roaring laughter.

Right then, I began to feel better. Sight of that little old pup, tearing out for the brush with that piece of corn bread seemed to loosen something inside me.

I felt better all day. I went back and rode my horse and enjoyed it. I rode 'way off out in the brush, not going anywhere especially, just riding and looking and beginning to feel proud of owning a real horse of my own.

Then along about sundown, I rode down into Birdsong Creek, headed for the house. Up at the spring, I heard a splashing and hollering. I looked ahead. Sure enough, it was Little Arliss. He was stripped naked and romping in our drinking water again. And right in there, romping with him, was that bread-stealing speckled pup.

I started to holler at them. I started to say: *"Arliss!* You get that nasty old pup out of our drinking water."

Then I didn't. Instead, I went to laughing. I sat there and laughed till I cried. When all the time I knew that I ought to go beat them to a frazzle for messing up our drinking water.

When finally I couldn't laugh and cry another bit, I rode on up to the lot and turned my horse in. Tomorrow, I thought, I'll take Arliss and that pup out for a squirrel hunt. The pup was still mighty little. But the way I figured it, if he was big enough to act like Old Yeller, he was big enough to start learning to earn his keep.

1. Why does Old Yeller try to attack Travis when he clears the stump away?
2. How does Mama save Yeller's life?
3. How does Bud Searcy help the Coates family?
4. What is the first indication that hydrophobia has spread to the Coates farm?
5. How does Yeller contract the sickness?

For Study and Discussion

Analyzing and Interpreting the Novel

1. Tell how Old Yeller is rescued by Travis and his mother.

2. Pioneer women had to work as hard as men. **a.** How does Mrs. Coates show she is resourceful in running the farm? **b.** How does Lisbeth Searcy assist her?

3. Why does it become necessary for Travis to kill Old Yeller?

4a. How does Travis' father help him deal with his loss? **b.** How does the speckled pup help Travis get over the pain of losing Old Yeller?

Literary Elements

Understanding the Novel

Setting

1. On the frontier settlers had to depend on home remedies and nursing skills in times of sickness. Recall Mrs. Coates' "doctoring" of Little Arliss, Travis, and Old Yeller. How does she "treat" each of her patients?

2. Settlers had to combat serious illnesses without the help of doctors or present-day miracle drugs. What measures are taken to prevent the spread of hydrophobia?

Character

3. Old Yeller's last act is a heroic struggle that costs him his life. **a.** How have we been prepared for his sacrifice? **b.** At what other points has he shown courage in the face of great personal danger?

4. Although Travis is in great pain after being attacked by the hogs, he insists on returning to save Old Yeller's life. **a.** Do you find his behavior believable? **b.** Is his action consistent with other actions earlier in the book?

5. When Lisbeth first brings the speckled pup, Travis rejects it. **a.** How do you account for his attitude? **b.** Why does he later change his mind about the pup?

6. In what way is Travis' shooting of Old Yeller the greatest test he has had to face?

Plot

7. The most exciting or intense part of a narrative is called its **climax**. What point in this novel do you consider the climax?

8. The **resolution** of a story tells how the conflict or conflicts are worked out. What is the resolution that forms the conclusion of the novel?

Point of View

9. Imagine this story told by one of the other characters or by an omniscient author. What do you think is gained by having Travis tell about his experiences in his own words?

Theme

10. **Theme** is the basic meaning of a literary work, the main idea it expresses about human nature. The central theme in this novel is about the experiences that shape one boy's character as he learns to cope with the problems and responsibilities of the adult world. As

Travis grows up, we see his relationships to his family and to Old Yeller change and deepen. Find a sentence or a passage in the book that comes close to stating the basic truth Travis learns about life.

Writing About Literature

Writing a Character Sketch

In literature an animal character may be developed fully and may have as individual a personality as any human character. Consider what you have learned about Old Yeller directly and indirectly. Select three dominant aspects of his character and discuss them in an essay. Cite evidence from the novel to support your statements.

Explaining the Function of Minor Characters

The minor characters in *Old Yeller* play an important role in the story. What purpose is served by Bud Searcy and Burn Sanderson? By Lisbeth Searcy? Explain in a brief essay.

Extending Your Study

Reporting on the Role of Dogs in the Old West

On the frontier, dogs were important not only as pets and companions, but also as work animals. Find out what functions dogs performed for settlers in the Old West. Present your findings in a written or oral report. Be sure to cite the sources for your information.

To locate relevant information, you may have to look under several different headings in an index or table of contents. For example:

Uses of the Dog
History of the Dog
Domesticated Canines
Work Animals

About the Author

Fred Gipson   (1908–1973)

Fred(erick Benjamin) Gipson was born in Mason, Texas. He attended the University of Texas at Austin. He worked as a farm and ranch hand. He became a reporter and columnist for several newspapers. In 1960 he assumed the position of President of the Texas Institute of Letters. In addition to *Old Yeller*, his books include *The Trail-Driving Rooster* and *Savage Sam,* a sequel to *Old Yeller*. He wrote screenplays for three films based on his novels. Gipson was a strong regionalist and hoped to teach something about American history through his books.

DEVELOPING SKILLS
IN CRITICAL THINKING

Making Use of Analysis and Synthesis

You have seen that different activities go on when you think: you make inferences, you compare and contrast, you draw conclusions, you evaluate, and the like. Two very important methods of reasoning are *analysis* and *synthesis*, which often go together. Analysis is a method of taking something apart to see how the individual parts function. Synthesis is a recombination of ideas to form something new. In the study of literature, the term *analysis* frequently stands for both thinking processes.

Suppose you were asked to analyze the plot structure of *Old Yeller*. One way to handle analysis is to ask questions and then answer them, in this fashion:

1. *What is the major conflict in the novel?* Travis must prove himself. He must play a man's part in his father's absence.

2. *What are the major incidents that serve as "tests" for Travis?* He has to discipline Jumper, the mule, when he is plowing the corn patch; he has to watch out for his brother; he has to provide meat for the family; he has to keep the fighting bulls from tearing down the house; he has to keep Old Yeller from raiding the settlement; he has to protect the corn patch from varmints; he has to mark the pigs; he has to bring Old Yeller home from the wash; he has to shoot the rabid bull, the Spot heifer, and the wolf; and he has to kill Old Yeller.

3. *Which incident is the climax of the novel?* The most difficult test Travis has to pass is to kill the dog he loves in order to protect his family.

4. *How is the conflict resolved?* Travis learns to accept the death of Old Yeller and recognizes that part of growing up is accepting the bad as well as the good things in life.

Once you have completed your analysis of plot structure, you can proceed with the synthesis of your ideas. Your central idea is best expressed in the form of a *thesis statement* such as this one:

Old Yeller is a story about a boy who has to assume the responsibilities and burdens of a man and who learns to face up to pain and loss.

Write a paragraph developing this thesis statement, or write another thesis statement for your paragraph.

PRACTICE IN READING AND WRITING

Writing a Book Report on a Novel

A book report generally has two purposes: to summarize the overall content of the book and to give your opinion of the book. A good book report does not have to be long, but it should have a clear focus and organization.

In writing a book report about a novel, you are expected to tell about the main action in the story. What is the conflict about? What begins the struggle? You should describe elements of the setting (time and place) that are important to the story. You should identify the major characters and indicate which character traits contribute to the conflict. Be prepared to tell one incident in detail to give the flavor of the book. You should tell what you think of the book.

Remember what you have learned about the writing process. In the prewriting stage, gather your ideas and plan how you will organize them. Write a first draft of your report and then evaluate your work. Use your evaluation to revise the report. Add or delete ideas, rearrange sentences, and rephrase as necessary. Proofread your work and prepare a final copy for your audience.

Here are some guidelines to follow when you write a book report about a novel:

1. *Include the title of the book and the name of the author. Underline the title.*

2. *Identify the kind of novel it is.* Is the book a mystery, a romance, an adventure story, or an historical novel?

3. *Summarize the content of the book briefly.* Do not tell everything that happens. Identify the setting, the central action of the story, and the main characters. Note the most interesting or important incidents.

4. *State your opinion of the book, and support your opinion with specific reasons.* Does the author describe action and events vividly? Is the story interesting? Is it enjoyable? Would you want to read other books by the same author?

Here is a sample book report on *The Call of the Wild* for analysis.

The Call of the Wild, an animal story by Jack London, takes place in Alaska during the time of the Gold Rush, when the only form of transportation across the frozen North was by sled. The central character is a dog named Buck, who is part Saint Bernard and part Scottish shepherd. Buck is stolen from his California home and shipped to Alaska to be trained as a sled dog. He is treated cruelly by several masters, and under this harsh treatment he comes to understand "the law of club and fang." Finally, he finds a kind master in John Thornton, whom he comes to worship. The most exciting incident in the book occurs when Buck wins a bet for Thornton by pulling a thousand-pound load. Although Buck loves Thornton, he is torn between devotion to his master and the "call of the wild." At the end of the story, Buck becomes the leader of a pack of wolves.

This is one of the best dog stories I have ever read. Buck seems more human than animal. Because London tells the story from Buck's point of view, the reader is able to see into Buck's mind, to feel as Buck feels about his enemies and his friends, and to understand why his primitive instincts are aroused by the savage experiences he undergoes. I also learned a great deal about what life was like in the Alaskan wilderness at the close of the nineteenth century.

Choose a novel from one of the recommended lists in this book or from a list suggested by your teacher. Write a book report of two paragraphs. In the first paragraph, summarize what the book is about. In the second paragraph, give your opinion of the book, supported by reasons.

For Further Reading

Armstrong, Sperry, *Call It Courage* (Macmillan, 1968)
A boy who lives in the South Seas learns to conquer his fear of the sea.

Carroll, Lewis, *Alice's Adventures in Wonderland* (many editions)
In this fantasy, Alice talks to a Cheshire cat, visits a Mad Tea Party, and plays croquet with the Queen.

————, *Through the Looking-glass* (many editions)
In this continuation of her adventures, Alice meets Humpty Dumpty, Tweedledum and Tweedledee, and other comic characters.

Kipling, Rudyard, *Captains Courageous* (many editions)
A rich boy who falls overboard from an ocean liner finds himself on a simple fishing boat.

Kjelgaard, Jim, *Big Red* (paperback, Bantam, 1976)
This is a story about a boy and his dog, an Irish setter.

Knight, Eric, *Lassie Come-Home* (many editions)
In this famous story, a collie makes a 400-mile journey home.

Sandoz, Mari, *Winter Thunder* (paperback, University of Nebraska Press, 1986)
A group of children are trapped in a blizzard when their bus breaks down.

Steinbeck, John, *The Red Pony* (reissue, Viking, 1986)
Here is a collection of stories about Jody Tiflin, a young boy growing up on a California ranch.

Street, James, *Goodbye, My Lady* (Lippincott, 1954)
This is a touching story about a boy and a dog that he finds in a swamp.

Twain, Mark, *The Prince and the Pauper* (many editions)
Edward Tudor, heir to the throne of England, and Tom Canty, a boy of the London slums, have their identities switched.

Verne, Jules, *Twenty Thousand Leagues Under the Sea* (many editions)
This is an early science-fiction novel about Captain Nemo and his submarine, the *Nautilus*.

LITERARY HERITAGE

CLASSICAL MYTHOLOGY

The Parthenon by Frederic Edwin Church (1826–1920). Oil on canvas.

Myths are stories that have come down to us from the distant past. They have survived for many centuries because they are appealing stories for old and young alike. The main characters in myths are generally gods and goddesses, but if you read carefully, you will find that myths have much to say about human nature.

Every people has its own body of myths, or *mythology*. Classical myths, the name given to the myths of the ancient Greeks and Romans, are the best-known myths in Western culture. These stories were first told by the ancient Greeks more than twenty-five hundred years ago. Later the stories were retold by the Romans, who substituted the names of their own gods and goddesses for those of the Greeks. The Roman god Jupiter was identified with the Greek god Zeus, the Roman goddess Juno with the Greek goddess Hera, and so on. For this reason, many gods and goddesses in classical mythology are known by both Greek and Roman names.

Here are some guidelines to follow in reading the myths in this unit.

Guidelines for Reading the Myths

1. *Read for enjoyment and for understanding.* The myths are highly entertaining as literature. They also provide insight into universal human characteristics such as courage and honor. Moreover, they yield a good deal of information about words in our language and many aspects of our own culture.

2. *Become familiar with the major figures in classical mythology.* Many of the characters appear in various myths, and often in different roles. Apollo, for example, who is god of the sun, is also the god of youth, music, prophecy, archery, and healing. In the myth of Midas, he appears in his attribute or function as the god of music. In the myth of Niobe, he is an avenging archer. As you read the myths in this unit, you may want to refer to the chart on pages 576–577. For help with the pronunciation of names, see the *Index of Names* on pages 629–632.

3. *Determine the function of individual myths.* Some myths are attempts to explain natural phenomena like the seasons. Other myths are concerned with the proper relationship of mortals to the gods and goddesses, and offer lessons in acceptable and unacceptable behavior.

4. *Note the individual characteristics valued by ancient Greeks and Romans.* Determine which of these characteristics have value in our own society. For example, are there parallels for the Greek ideal of moderation in the contemporary world?

The Gods and Goddesses of Mount Olympus°

OLIVIA COOLIDGE

This selection will introduce you to the most important figures in classical mythology—Zeus and his family. What reasons does the author give for the continued popularity of this literature?

Greek legends have been favorite stories for many centuries. They are mentioned so often by famous writers that it has become impossible to read widely in English, or in many other literatures, without knowing what the best of these tales are about. Even though we no longer believe in the Greek gods, we enjoy hearing of them because they appeal to our imagination.

The Greeks thought all the forces of nature were spirits, so that the whole earth was filled with gods. Each river, each woodland, even each great tree had its own god or nymph.[1] In the woods lived the satyrs,[2] who had pointed ears and the shaggy legs of goats. In the sea danced more than three thousand green-haired, white-limbed maidens. In the air rode wind gods, cloud nymphs, and the golden chariot of the sun. All these spirits, like the

Head of Zeus. Roman copy of lost Greek original. Marble, fourth century B.C.
Pio Clementino Museum, Vatican Art Collection

° **Olympus** (ō-lĭm′pəs).
1. **nymph** (nĭmf): a goddess who inhabited a part of nature, such as a river, a mountain, or a tree.
2. **satyrs** (sā′tərz): woodland creatures who were part man and part goat.

CLASSICAL GODS AND GODDESSES

GREEK	ROMAN	DESCRIPTION
Zeus	Jupiter, Jove	king of the gods; god of the sky and the weather
Hera	Juno	queen of the gods; goddess of marriage and childbirth
Poseidon	Neptune	god of the sea
Hades, Pluto	Pluto	god of the underworld
Demeter	Ceres	goddess of grain, plants, and fruit
Athena, Athene, or Pallas Athena	Minerva	goddess of wisdom, arts, crafts, and war; protector of Athens
Hephaestus	Vulcan	god of fire and metalworking
Aphrodite	Venus	goddess of love and beauty
Ares	Mars	god of war
Apollo, Phoebus Apollo	Apollo, Phoebus Apollo	god of youth, music, prophecy, archery, healing, and the sun

Procession of twelve gods and goddesses. From left:
Persephone, Hermes, Aphrodite, Ares, Demeter, Hephaestus,
Hera, Poseidon, Athena, Zeus, Artemis, Apollo. Marble relief.
Walters Art Gallery, Baltimore

GREEK	ROMAN	DESCRIPTION
Artemis	Diana	goddess of hunting, childbirth, wild animals, and the moon
Hermes	Mercury	messenger of the gods; god of travelers, merchants, and thieves
Persephone	Proserpina	goddess of spring and the underworld; Demeter's daughter
Dionysus, Bacchus	Bacchus	god of wine, fertility, and drama
Eros	Cupid	god of love; Aphrodite's son
Iris	Iris	goddess of the rainbow; messenger of the gods
Muses	Muses	nine goddesses who inspired artists
Fates	Fates	three goddesses who determined human destiny

forces of nature, were beautiful and strong, but sometimes unreliable and unfair. Above all, however, the Greeks felt that they were tremendously interested in mankind.

From very early times the Greeks began to invent stories to account for the things that went on—the change of seasons, the sudden storms, the good and bad fortune of the farmer's year. These tales were spread by travelers from one valley to another. They were put together and altered by poets and musicians, until at last a great body of legends arose from the whole of Greece. These did not agree with one another in details, but, on the whole, gave a clear picture of who the chief gods were, how men should behave to please them, and what their relationships had been with heroes of the past.

The ruler of all the gods was Zeus, the sky god, titled by courtesy "Father of gods and men." He lived in the clouds with most of the great gods in a palace on the top of Mount Olympus, the tallest mountain in Greece. Lightning was the weapon of Zeus, thunder was the rolling of his chariot, and when he nodded his head, the whole earth shook.

Zeus, though the ruler of the world, was not the eldest of the gods. First had come a race of monsters with fifty heads and a hundred arms each. Next followed elder gods called Titans, the leader of whom, Cronus, had reigned before Zeus. Then arose mighty Giants, and finally Zeus and the Olympians. Zeus in a series of wars succeeded in banishing the Titans and imprisoning the Giants in various ways. One huge monster, Typhon, lay imprisoned under the volcano of Aetna, which spouted fire when he struggled. Atlas, one of the Titans, was forced to stand holding the heavens on his shoulders so that they should not fall upon the earth.

Almost as powerful as Zeus were his two brothers, who did not live on Olympus: Posei-

Bust of Poseidon. Bronze.

don,[3] ruler of the sea, and Hades,[4] gloomy king of the underworld, where the spirits of the dead belong. Queen of the gods was blue-eyed, majestic Hera. Aphrodite,[5] the laughing, sea-born goddess, was queen of love and most beautiful of all.

Apollo and Artemis were twins, god of the sun and goddess of the moon. Apollo was the more important. Every day he rode the heavens in a golden chariot from dawn to sunset. The sun's rays could be gentle and healing, or they could be terrible. Apollo, therefore, was a great healer and the father of the god of medicine. At the same time he was a famous archer, and the arrows from his golden bow were arrows of infection and death. Apollo was also god of poetry and song; his instrument was a

3. **Poseidon** (pō-sī′dən).
4. **Hades** (hā′dēz).
5. **Aphrodite** (ăf′rə-dī′tē).

golden lyre, and the nine Muses, goddesses of music and the arts, were his attendants. He was the ideal of young manhood and the patron of athletes.

Apollo was also god of prophecy. There were temples of Apollo, known as oracles, at which a man could ask questions about the future. The priestesses of Apollo, inspired by the god, gave him an answer, often in the form of a riddle which was hard to understand. Nevertheless, the Greeks believed that if a man could interpret the words of the oracle, he would find the answer to his problem.

Artemis, the silver moon goddess, was goddess of unmarried girls and a huntress of wild beasts in the mountains. She also could send deadly arrows from her silver bow.

Gray-eyed Athene,[6] the goddess of wisdom,

6. **Athene** (ə-thē′-nē): also called *Athena* (ə-thē′nə).

was patron of Athens. She was queen of the domestic arts, particularly spinning and weaving. Athene was warlike too; she wore helmet and breastplate, and carried a spear. Ares, however, was the real god of war, and the maker of weapons was Hephaestus,[7] the lame smith and metalworker.

One more god who lived on Olympus was Hermes, the messenger. He wore golden, winged sandals which carried him dry-shod over sea and land. He darted down from the peaks of Olympus like a kingfisher dropping to

7. **Hephaestus** (hĭ-fĕs′təs).

Athena. Roman copy of Greek original. Stone, fourth century B.C.

Hermes Running. Attributed to the Tithonos Painter. Red-figured vase, 475 B.C.

catch a fish, or came running down the sloping sunbeams bearing messages from Zeus to men. Mortal eyes were too weak to behold the dazzling beauty of the immortals; consequently the messages of Zeus usually came in dreams. Hermes was therefore also a god of sleep, and of thieves because they prowl by night. Healing was another of his powers. His rod, a staff entwined by two snakes, is commonly used as a symbol of medicine.

The Greeks have left us so many stories about their gods that it hardly would be possible for everyone to know them all. We can still enjoy them because they are good stories. In spite of their great age we can still understand them because they are about nature and about people. We still need them to enrich our knowledge of our own language and of the great masterpieces of literature.

Reading Check

1. According to mythology, where did most of the Greek gods and goddesses live?
2. Who were the Titans?
3. Who kept the heavens from falling on the earth?
4. Where did Poseidon and Hades live?
5. Who were the Muses?
6. What did human beings learn from the oracles?
7. Why were the words of the oracles difficult to interpret?
8. Who was the messenger of the gods?
9. Which of the Olympians were twins?
10. Name two Olympians associated with war.

For Study and Discussion

Analyzing and Interpreting the Selection

1. The ancient Greeks believed that all of nature was ruled by divine beings. **a.** How did they explain lightning and thunder? **b.** What did they believe happened when Zeus nodded his head?

2. The ancient Greeks believed that each of the gods and goddesses had control over a special area of life. For example, Hephaestus was the god of fire and metalworking. Blacksmiths would have prayed to him to help them in their craft. To which god or goddess would the following persons have prayed for special help?

athletes	robbers	soldiers
hunters	sailors	weavers

3. Why do people still read stories about the ancient Greek gods and goddesses? Give two reasons stated by the author.

Literary Elements

Recognizing Gods and Goddesses by Their Titles

The gods and goddesses in classical mythology are often identified by their titles rather than by their names. Zeus is known by several titles: "the sky god," "father of gods and men," "king of the gods." Writers frequently refer to Apollo by one of his titles: "god of the sun," "god of poetry and song," "god of prophecy."

The gods and goddesses are also identified by certain of their physical characteristics. For example, Hera is often described as "the ox-eyed goddess." She is also described as "the goddess of the white arms." Athena is described as "gray-eyed" or "bright-eyed." Aphrodite is called "the pale-gold goddess." "Broad-browed" and "dark-misted" are often used to describe Zeus.

Sometimes the gods and goddesses are identified by their special powers. Zeus, for example, is referred to as "the summoner of clouds." Artemis is known as "goddess of wild things."

Which of the gods do you think is known as "the thunderer"?

Why would Poseidon be called the "blue-maned" god?

Why would Hephaestus be described as "strong-handed"?

Extending Your Study

Learning About the Olympic Games

In classical times the Olympic Games were a festival held every four years at Olympia, a plain in the southern part of Greece, to honor Zeus. The festival was first celebrated in 776 B.C. and was discontinued in A.D. 394. It consisted of contests not only in sports but also in poetry and music. The events included foot races, chariot racing, the discus throw, the javelin throw, the broad jump, boxing, wrestling, and the pentathlon (a contest of five events). Greek women did not participate in the Olympic Games, but held games of their own called *Heraea,* in honor of the goddess Hera. The modern international revival of the Olympic Games began at Athens in 1896.

Choose one of these topics for research, and present your findings in a short essay.

The Foundation of the Olympic Games
The Origin of the Olympic Marathon Footrace
The Events of the Heraea

About the Author

Olivia Coolidge (1908–   )

Olivia Coolidge started teaching in 1931 in Potsdam, Germany, and for the next fifteen years she was an instructor of Latin, Greek, and English in England and America. She has written on a variety of subjects, including mythology and history. Among her books are *Greek Myths, Legends of the North, The Trojan War,* and *Churchill and the History of Two World Wars.* She also has several biographies to her credit, including volumes on Edith Wharton, Eugene O'Neill, and Gandhi, and two on Abraham Lincoln.

Prometheus°
the Fire-Bringer

Retold by
JEREMY INGALLS

For people of early times, mythology was part of religion. The myths of gods, goddesses, and heroes were sacred stories. But mythology also served another function. Through myths these early people provided explanations for natural events that puzzled them.

The ancient Greeks believed that the secret of making fire once belonged only to the gods. As you read the following myth, ask yourself why the Greeks came to regard one of the Titans as their friend.

Fire itself, and the civilized life which fire makes possible—these were the gifts of Prometheus to the men of ancient times. Prometheus himself was not of the oldest race of men. He was not alive in the first age of mankind.

Ancient writers tell us there were three ages of men on earth before the fourth age, in which we are now living. Each of the previous ages ended in terrible disasters which destroyed a large part of the human race. A raging fire ended the first age of the world. At the end of the second age, vast floods engulfed plains and mountains. According to the oldest poets, these misfortunes were punishments the gods visited upon men for their wickedness and wrongdoing.

The story of Prometheus, remembered by the Greeks and set down in their books, tells of the days when Zeus was king of the world and Prometheus was his chief councilor. From their ancestors they and their companions upon Mount Olympus had inherited the secrets of fire, of rain, of farming and metalworking. This knowledge gave them a power so great that they appeared as gods to the men who served them.

After the flood which destroyed many of the men of the second age, Zeus, with the help of Prometheus, had bred a new race of men in Arcadia.[1] But Zeus did not find life on earth so simple for men and gods as it had been in earlier times.

When Cronus, the father of Zeus, had ruled the earth, summer had been the only season. Great land masses toward the north had barred all the icy winds. The age of Cronus

° **Prometheus** (prə-mē′thē-əs).

1. **Arcadia** (är-kā′dē-ə): a pleasant, mountainous district in Greece.

Zeus and His Eagle. Base of a Laconian cup, c. 550 B.C.
Louvre Museum

was an age of contentment. No man had needed to work for food or clothes or a house to shelter him.

After the first flood, the land masses were broken. Winter winds blew upon countries which before had known only summer.

The race of gods did not suffer. They warmed their houses, having the secret of fire. And the women of the race were weavers of cloth, so that the gods were clothed and defended from the north wind.

But winter was a harsh season for the men and women who did not live on the gods' mountain. Without defense from the cold, they huddled with the animals. They complained against the gods, whom they must serve for what little comfort they might find of food and warmth. They scarcely believed the stories which their ancestors had handed down to them of a time when men had lived in endless summer weather, when men were friends and favorites of the gods.

Men became rebels and grumblers. For this reason Zeus, seeing winter coming on again, determined to destroy the people of Arcadia. Then Prometheus, his chief councilor, sought to save this third race of man from destruction.

"They quarrel among themselves," said Zeus angrily. "They start trouble in the fields. We must train up a new race of men who will learn more quickly what it means to serve the gods."

Zeus was walking across the bronze floor of his mountain palace. A tremendous, tall figure of a man he was, the king god Zeus. But he who stood beside him, Prometheus of the family of Titans, was even taller.

"Worthless," Zeus was saying as if to himself. "Worthless," he repeated again, "the whole race. They complain of the winters. They are too weak a race for the climate of these times. Why should we continue to struggle with them? Better to be rid of them, every man and woman of the troublesome tribe."

"And then?" inquired Prometheus. "What if you create a new race to provide manpower for the farms and the bigger buildings? That race, too, will rebel while they can see and envy our knowledge and our power."

"Even so, I will destroy these Arcadians," insisted Zeus stubbornly. "Men are our creatures. Let them learn to serve us, to do our will."

"Up here on your mountain," observed Prometheus thoughtfully, "you make men and destroy them. But what about the men themselves? How can they learn wisdom when, time after time, you visit them with destruction?"

"You have too much sympathy for them," answered Zeus in a sharp voice. "I believe you love these huddling, sheepish men."

"They have minds and hearts," replied Prometheus warmly, "and a courage that is worth admiring. They wish to live even as the gods wish to live. Don't we feed ourselves on nectar and ambrosia[2] every day to preserve our lives?"

Prometheus was speaking rapidly. His voice was deep. "This is your way," he went on. "You won't look ahead. You won't be patient. You won't give men a chance to learn how to live. Over and over again, with floods or with cracking red thunderbolts, you destroy them."

"I have let you live, Prometheus," said Zeus in an ominous tone, "to advise me when you can. You are my cousin. But I am not your child to be scolded." Zeus was smiling, but there was thunder behind the smile.

Silently Prometheus turned away. Leaving the marble-columned hall, he went out among the gardens of Olympus, the gods' mountain. The last roses were fading before the time of winter winds and rain.

This was not the first time Prometheus had heard thunder in the voice of Zeus. Prometheus knew that someday Zeus would turn against him, betray him, and punish him. Prometheus the Titan had the gift of reading the future. He could foresee the fate hidden and waiting for him and for others and even for Zeus himself.

Climbing among the upper gardens, Prometheus stopped at last beside an ancient, twisted ash tree. Leaning against its trunk, he looked toward the south. Beyond the last canal, the last steep sea wall, he could see the ocean. He

2. **nectar and ambrosia** (ăm-brō′zhə): the drink and food of the Olympian gods.

looked far out toward that last shining circle of water. Then, with his head bent, he sat down on the tree roots bulging in thick knots above the ground.

It would be hard to tell you all the thoughts in the mind of the Titan—thoughts that coiled and twined like a nest of dragons. In his mighty brain were long memories of the past and far-reaching prophecies of what was to come.

He thought most often of the future, but the talk with Zeus just now had brought the past before him once again. He remembered once more the terrible war in which Zeus had seized the kingship of the gods. He thought of the exile and imprisonment of Cronus, the father of Zeus. He remembered the Titans, his people, now chained in the black pit of Tartarus.[3]

The great god Cronus himself, who had given peace to gods and men, where was he now? And the mighty-headed Titans, the magnificent engineers, builders of bridges and temples, where were they? All of them fallen, helpless, as good as dead.

Zeus had triumphed. Of the Titans, only two now walked the upper earth—he, Prometheus, and Epimetheus, his brother.

And now, even now, Zeus was not content. It was not enough for his glory, it seemed, to have dethroned his own father, not enough to have driven the race of Titans from the houses of the gods. Now Zeus was plotting to kill the race of men.

Prometheus had endured the war against the Titans, his own people. He had even given help to Zeus. Having seen what was to come, he had thought, "Since Zeus must win, I'll guide him. I'll control his fierce anger and his greed for power."

3. **Tartarus** (tär′tər-əs): a dark place below the underworld.

But Prometheus could not submit to this latest plot of Zeus. He would use all his wits to save the men of Arcadia from destruction.

Why were they to be destroyed? Because they were cold and full of fears, huddled together in caves like animals. It was well enough in the warm months. They worked willingly in the fields of the gods and reared the horses and bulls and guarded the sheep. But when the cold days came, they grumbled against Olympus. They grumbled because they must eat and hunt like the animals and had no hoof nor claw nor heavy fur for protection.

What did they need? What protection would be better than hoof or claw? Prometheus knew. It was fire they needed—fire to cook with, to warm them, to harden metal for weapons. With fire they could frighten the wolf and the bear and the mountain lion.

Why did they lack the gift of fire? Prometheus knew that too. He knew how jealously the gods sat guard about their flame.

More than once he had told Zeus the need men had of fire. He knew why Zeus would not consent to teach men this secret of the gods. The gift of fire to men would be a gift of power. Hardened in the fire, the spears which men might make to chase the mountain lion might also, in time, be hurled against the gods. With fire would come comfort and time to think while the flames leaped up the walls of hidden caves. Men who had time to think would have time to question the laws of the gods. Among men who asked questions disorder might breed, and rebellion stronger than any mere squabble in the fields.

"But men are worth the gift of fire," thought Prometheus, sitting against the roots of his favorite ash tree. He could see ahead dimly into that time to come when gods would lose their power. And he, Prometheus, through his love for men, must help to bring on that time.

Prometheus did not hesitate. By the fall of

night his plans were accomplished. As the sun went down, his tall figure appeared upon a sea beach. Above the sands a hundred caves, long ago deserted by the waters of the ocean, sheltered families of Arcadians. To them the Titan was bringing this very night the secret of the gods.

He came along the pebble line of high water. In his hand he carried a yellow reed.

This curious yellow stalk was made of metal, the most precious of the metals of the gods. From it the metalworkers molded rare and delicate shapes. From it they made the reedlike and hollow stalks which carried, in wisps of fennel[4] straw, coals from the gods' ever-burning fire. The gods who knew the sources of flame never built new fires in the sight of men. Going abroad on journeys, they took from their central hearth a smoldering coal.

Prometheus had left Olympus as one upon a journey. He alone knew he was not going to visit the home of Poseidon, Zeus's brother, lord of the sea—nor going into India, nor into the cold north. He was going only as far as the nearest sea beach.

He knew that, though he was going only to the sea beach, he was in truth starting upon a journey. He knew the hatred of Zeus would follow him. He knew that now he, Prometheus, could never return to the house of the gods. From this night he must live his life among the men he wished to save.

While the stars came out, bright as they are on nights when winter will soon come on, Prometheus gathered together a heap of driftwood. Opening the metal stalk, he set the flame of the gods in the waiting fuel.

Eating into the wood, the fire leaped up, fanned in the night breeze. Prometheus sat down beside the fire he had made. He was not long alone.

4. **fennel:** an herb.

Shadowy figures appeared at the mouths of caves. One by one, men, women, and children crept toward the blaze. The night was cold. North winds had blown that day. The winds had blown on the lands of men, even as they had blown on the head of Zeus in his palace above them. Now in the night they came, the people of men, to the warmth of the beckoning fire.

Hundreds there were of them now. Those nearest the tall fire-bringer, the Titan, were talking with him. They knew him well. It was not the first time Prometheus had come to talk with them. But never before had he come late, alone, and lighted a fire against the dark.

It was not the first time men had seen a fire or felt its warmth. More than once a god, walking the earth, had set a fire, lit from the coals he carried secretly. Men reverenced the slender magic wands with which, it seemed, the gods could call up flame. But never before had they stood so near a fire nor seen the firewand.

Now men might hold in their own hands the mysterious yellow rod. They said, "Look" and "See" and, fingering the metal, "How wonderfully the gods can mold what is hard in the hands."

For a while Prometheus let them talk. He watched with pleasure the gleam of firelight in their shining eyes. Then quietly he took the metal stalk from the man who held it. With a swift gesture he threw it into the heap of burning wood.

The people groaned. The fire-wrought metal crumpled against the heat. The metal which carried well a single coal melted in the blazing fire.

The people murmured among themselves, "Hasn't he taken away the secret now? Hasn't he destroyed before our eyes the source of fire?"

Patiently, silently they waited. A few asked

questions but got no answers. The cold wind cut them as the last of the burning driftwood grayed and blackened in the sand.

While the embers crumbled away, Prometheus rose, calling with him a few of the men who had asked him questions. Watching, they saw him scrape a hollow pit. Wondering, they followed his every movement, his hands holding a bronze knife, shaving chips of wood, taking from the fold of his cloak handfuls of bark and straw.

Next he set in his pit a chunk of ashwood, flat and firm, notched cleanly on one side. Beneath and around this notch he laid in bark and straw. Into the notch he set a pointed branch, slender, hard-tipped, and firm. Then slowly he swung the branch in his palms, twirled it in a steady rhythm, boring, drilling more and more rapidly with his skilled and powerful hands.

The wood grew warm. The dust ground from the ash block heated to smoldering. The straw caught. Light sputtered from the pit. Small sparks glowed, flew up, went out. Tugged by the night wind, smoke curled from the dry straw, from the bark, from the wood shavings fed gently from the heap Prometheus had made ready to his hand. At last, more suddenly than the eye could follow, out of the pit in the sand rose the living flame.

Deftly Prometheus removed the ash block, added heavier kindling. Last of all, the driftwood yielded to the strengthening fire. He knelt beside it awhile, breathing upon it, guarding, urging the blaze. At last he rose, stood back, folded his arms. As if considering a thought, half sorrow, half pleasure, he looked up at the glare of fire invading the night sky.

Whispers and murmuring first, then cries, then shouting. Men ran to scoop new hollows in the sand. They begged Prometheus' knife. The children, running from the beach to the caves and fields, hurried back with fists crammed full of straw and withered leaves.

The people of the caves were breathless with excitement. Here was no secret. The fire-wand did not breed the fire as they had thought. No nameless power of the gods bred the flame.

The hard, pale ashwood passed from hand to hand as men struggled to light their own fires. They despaired at first. New sparks flew up and died. Or the hands were weak, too weak to drill the flame. But at last came triumph. A dozen fires sprang up. Women and children ran with laden arms to feed each growing blaze.

The gods, from their distant houses, saw the glow. There to the south it shone, fighting against the starlight, the glare in the sky. Was it the end of the world? Would the terrible fire consume the earth again?

Hermes, the messenger, came at last with an answer to all their questions.

"Great Zeus," said Hermes gravely in the assembly of the gods, "Prometheus, your cousin, stands in the midst of those rising fires. He took coals from the central hearth as for a journey."

"So?" asked Zeus, nodding his head. Then, as if he were holding an argument with himself, he continued, saying, "But then? What then? The fire will die. It is not a crime for a god or for a Titan to light a fire for himself on a cold evening."

"But that fire will not die," interrupted Hermes. "That fire is not the fire of gods and Titans. Prometheus has taught men the source of fire. Those fires are their own, the fires of men. They've drilled flame out of hardwood with their own hands."

Then the gods knew the end of the world was not yet come upon them. But they knew, and Zeus most of all, that it might be their own great power that was burning away in the fires of men.

Atlas and Prometheus. Attributed to the Arkesilias Painter. Base of a Laconian cup.
Vatican Art Collection

Reading Check

1. How was Cronus related to Zeus?
2. How did the gods and goddesses preserve their lives?
3. What had happened to the Titans?
4. Why had Prometheus helped Zeus in the war against the Titans?
5. Why did Prometheus choose fire as his gift to human beings?

For Study and Discussion

Analyzing and Interpreting the Myth

1. The reign of Cronus was known in Greek mythology as the Golden Age. **a.** How was life in that age different from life in later times? **b.** Why did this "age of contentment" end?

2a. Why did Zeus want to destroy the third race of humans? **b.** What objections did Prometheus raise? Summarize Prometheus' arguments in your own words.

3a. Why was Zeus unwilling to give mortals the gift of fire? **b.** Why did Prometheus deliberately disobey Zeus's wishes? **c.** Would you call Prometheus a hero? Why or why not?

4. What human characteristics are shown by Zeus and Prometheus in this myth?

Language and Vocabulary

Distinguishing Homophones

Prometheus, we are told, is Zeus's chief councilor. The word *councilor* means "a member of a council." This word is sometimes confused with its homophone *counselor,* which means "adviser." You have probably heard the word *counselor* used in reference to a lawyer, who gives counsel, or advice. It may help you to avoid confusing these two words if you remember that a *council* is an assembly of people created for a specific purpose, as a town council elected to manage the affairs of a town. The word *counsel* means "advice" or "opinion."

Which word—*councilor* or *counselor*—would be used for the person who acts as your program adviser in school? Which word would be used for the delegate to a legislative body?

Extending Your Study

Locating Information

The myth of Pandora is part of the Prometheus story. Find the answers to these questions: How did Pandora get her name? What does the myth of Pandora explain?

An encyclopedia is a useful place to start looking for information. If there is no entry under "Pandora," what should you look under?

Whenever you need more information than an encyclopedia provides, find out if there is a special reference book on the subject you are investigating. There are dictionaries and encyclopedias of classical mythology. Your library may have a copy of the *Larousse Encyclopedia of Mythology* or *The Meridian Handbook of Classical Mythology.* Check the entry "Mythology" or "Greek Mythology" or "Classical Mythology" in the card catalog.

You can also find retellings of the myths in special collections of mythology, such as *Mythology* by Edith Hamilton and *Gods, Heroes and Men of Ancient Greece* by W. H. D. Rouse. Use the indexes at the back of these books to locate the Pandora story.

Comparing Myths

Many mythologies offer an explanation for the way human beings gained possession of fire. In American Indian mythology, where many of the heroes are animals, such as Coyote or Raven, fire is obtained through the cunning of a trickster-hero. In the mythology of the African tribes of the upper Nile, Dog is the hero who steals fire from the Rainbow and brings it to the human race.

In a collection of mythologies, locate one of these myths or another myth telling how human beings obtained fire, and compare it with the Prometheus myth. What do the myths have in common, and how do they differ?

About the Author

Jeremy Ingalls (1911–   )

Jeremy Ingalls was born in Gloucester, Massachusetts. She received her A.M. and Litt. D. from Tufts University. She writes poetry as well as prose, and won the Yale Series of Younger Poets Prize in 1941 for *The Metaphysical Sword*. Her studies also encompass comparative religion and Chinese and Japanese culture, on which she has written several books and articles. She taught American literature in Japan in 1957 and 1958, when she received grants from both the Fulbright and Rockefeller foundations, and has taught at several colleges. She now devotes her time to free-lance writing.

The Origin of the Seasons

Retold by
OLIVIA COOLIDGE

Like "Prometheus the Fire-Bringer," this is a myth explaining a natural phenomenon. How does the myth account for the cycle of the seasons?

Demeter,[1] the great earth mother, was goddess of the harvest. Tall and majestic was her appearance, and her hair was the color of ripe wheat. It was she who filled the ears with grain. In her honor white-robed women brought golden garlands of wheat as first fruits to the altar. Reaping, threshing, winnowing, and the long tables set in the shade for the harvesters' refreshment—all these were hers. Songs and feasting did her honor as the hard-working farmer gathered his abundant fruit. All the laws which the farmer knew came from her: the time for plowing, what land would best bear crops, which was fit for grapes, and which to leave for pasture. She was a goddess whom men called "the great mother" because of her generosity in giving. Her own special daughter in the family of the gods was named Persephone.[2]

Persephone was the spring maiden, young and full of joy. Sicily was her home, for it is a land where the spring is long and lovely, and where spring flowers are abundant. Here Persephone played with her maidens from day to day till the rocks and valleys rang with the sound of laughter, and gloomy Hades heard it as he sat on his throne in the dark land of the dead. Even his heart of stone was touched by her gay young beauty, so that he arose in his awful majesty and came up to Olympus to ask Zeus if he might have Persephone to wife. Zeus bowed his head in agreement, and mighty Olympus thundered as he promised.

Thus it came about that as Persephone was gathering flowers with her maidens in the vale of Enna, a marvelous thing happened. Enna was a beautiful valley in whose meadows all the most lovely flowers of the year grew at the same season. There were wild roses, purple crocuses, sweet-scented violets, tall irises, rich narcissus, and white lilies. All these the girl was gathering, yet fair as they were, Persephone herself was fairer far.

As the maidens went picking and calling to one another across the blossoming meadow, it happened that Persephone strayed apart from the rest. Then, as she looked a little ahead in the meadow, she suddenly beheld the marvelous thing. It was a flower so beautiful that none like it had ever been known. It seemed a kind of narcissus, purple and white, but from a single root there sprang a hundred blossoms, and at the sweet scent of it the very heavens and earth appeared to smile for joy. Without calling to the others, Persephone sprang forward to be the first to pick the precious bloom. As

1. **Demeter** (dĭ-mē′tər).
2. **Persephone** (pər-sĕf′ə-nē).

Persephone and Pluto. Relief, c. 500 B.C.

she stretched out her hand, the earth opened in front of her, and she found herself caught in a stranger's arms. Persephone shrieked aloud and struggled, while the armful of flowers cascaded down to earth. However, the dark-eyed Hades was far stronger than she. He swept her into his golden chariot, took the reins of his coal-black horses, and was gone amid the rumbling sound of the closing earth before the other girls in the valley could even come in sight of the spot. When they did get there, nobody was visible. Only the roses and lilies of Persephone lay scattered in wild confusion over the grassy turf.

Bitter was the grief of Demeter when she heard the news of her daughter's mysterious fate. Veiling herself with a dark cloud she sped, swift as a wild bird, over land and ocean for nine days, searching everywhere and asking all she met if they had seen her daughter. Neither gods nor men had seen her. Even the birds could give no tidings, and Demeter in despair turned to Phoebus Apollo,[3] who sees all things from his chariot in the heavens.

"Yes, I have seen your daughter," said the god at last. "Hades has taken her with the consent of Zeus, that she may dwell in the land of mist and gloom as his queen. The girl struggled and was unwilling, but Hades is far stronger than she."

3. **Phoebus** (fē′bəs) **Apollo:** Apollo, god of the sun, was sometimes called *Phoebus,* which means "shining."

The Origin of the Seasons   **593**

When she heard this, Demeter fell into deep despair, for she knew she could never rescue Persephone if Zeus and Hades had agreed. She did not care any more to enter the palace of Olympus, where the gods live in joy and feasting and where Apollo plays the lyre while the Muses sing. She took on her the form of an old woman, worn but stately, and wandered about the earth, where there is much sorrow to be seen. At first she kept away from the homes of people, since the sight of little children and happy mothers gave her pain. One day, however, as she sat by the side of a well to rest her weary feet, four girls came down to draw water. They were kindhearted and charming as they talked with her and concerned themselves about the fate of the homeless stranger-woman who was sitting at their gates. To account for herself, Demeter told them that she was a woman of good family from Crete across the sea, who had been captured by pirates and was to have been sold for a slave. She had escaped as they landed once to cook a meal on shore, and now she was wandering to find work.

The four girls listened to this story, much impressed by the stately manner of the strange woman. At last they said that their mother, Metaneira,[4] was looking for a nurse for their newborn brother, Demophoon.[5] Perhaps the stranger would come and talk with her. Demeter agreed, feeling a great longing to hold a baby once more, even if it were not her own. She went therefore to Metaneira, who was much struck with the quiet dignity of the goddess and glad to give her charge of her little son. For a while thereafter Demeter was nurse to Demophoon, and his smiles and babble consoled her in some part for her own darling daughter. She began to make plans for

Demophoon: he should be a great hero; he should become an immortal, so that when he grew up she could keep him with her.

Presently the whole household was amazed at how beautiful Demophoon was growing, the more so as they never saw the nurse feed him anything. Secretly Demeter would anoint him with ambrosia, like the gods, and from her breath as he lay in her lap, he would draw his nourishment. When the night came, she would linger by the great fireside in the hall, rocking the child in her arms while the embers burned low and the people went off to sleep. Then when all was still, she would stoop quickly down and put the baby into the fire itself. All night long the child would sleep in the red-hot ashes, while his earthly flesh and blood changed slowly into the substance of the immortals. In the morning when people came, the ashes were cold and dead, and by the hearth sat the stranger-woman, gently rocking and singing to the child.

Presently Metaneira became suspicious of the strangeness of it all. What did she know of this nurse but the story she had heard from her daughters? Perhaps the woman was a witch of some sort who wished to steal or transform the boy. In any case it was wise to be careful. One night, therefore, when she went up to her chamber, she set the door ajar and stood there in the crack silently watching the nurse at the fireside crooning over the child. The hall was very dark, so that it was hard to see clearly, but in a little while the mother beheld the dim figure bend forward. A log broke in the fireplace, a little flame shot up, and there clear in the light lay the baby on top of the fire.

Metaneira screamed loudly and lost no time in rushing forward, but it was Demeter who snatched up the baby. "Fool that you are," she said indignantly to Metaneira, "I would have made your son immortal, but that is now impossible. He shall be a great hero, but in the

4. **Metaneira** (mĕt′ə-nī′rə).
5. **Demophoon** (dĭ-mŏ′fō-ŏn′).

end he will have to die. I, the goddess Demeter, promise it." With that, old age fell from her and she grew in stature. Golden hair spread down over her shoulders, so that the great hall was filled with light. She turned and went out of the doorway, leaving the baby on the ground and Metaneira too amazed and frightened even to take him up.

All the while that Demeter had been wandering, she had given no thought to her duties as the harvest goddess. Instead she was almost glad that others should suffer because she was suffering. In vain the oxen spent their strength in dragging the heavy plowshare through the soil. In vain did the sower with his bag of grain throw out the even handfuls of white barley in a wide arc as he strode. The greedy birds had a feast off the seed corn that season, or if it started to sprout, sun baked it and rains washed it away. Nothing would grow. As the gods looked down, they saw threatening the earth a famine such as never had been known. Even the offerings to the gods were neglected by despairing men who could no longer spare anything from their dwindling stores.

At last Zeus sent Iris, the Rainbow, to seek out Demeter and appeal to her to save mankind. Dazzling Iris swept down from Olympus swift as a ray of light and found Demeter sitting in her temple, the dark cloak still around her and her head bowed on her hand. Though Iris urged her with the messages of Zeus and offered beautiful gifts or whatever powers among the gods she chose, Demeter would not lift her head or listen. All she said was that she would neither set foot on Olympus nor let fruit grow on the earth until Persephone was restored to her from the kingdom of the dead.

At last Zeus saw that he must send Hermes of the golden sandals to bring back Persephone to the light. The messenger found dark-haired Hades sitting upon his throne with Persephone beside him, pale and sad. She had neither

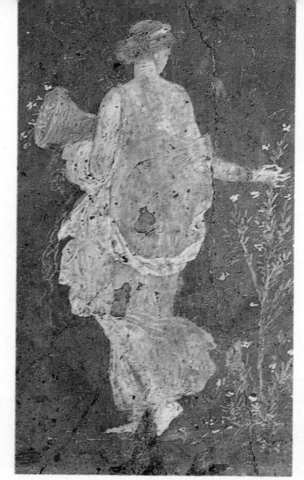

Girl picking flowers. Roman wall painting from house in Stabiae, Italy, first century A.D.

eaten nor drunk since she had been in the land of the dead. She sprang up with joy at the message of Hermes, while the dark king looked gloomier than ever, for he really loved his queen. Though he could not disobey the command of Zeus, he was crafty, and he pressed Persephone to eat or drink with him as they parted. Now, with joy in her heart, she should not refuse all food. Persephone was eager to be gone; but since the king entreated her, she took a pomegranate[6] from him to avoid argument and delay. Giving in to his pleading, she

6. **pomegranate** (pŏm′grăn′ĭt): a reddish fruit containing many seeds.

ate seven of the seeds. Then Hermes took her with him, and she came out into the upper air.

When Demeter saw Hermes with her daughter, she started up, and Persephone too rushed forward with a glad cry and flung her arms about her mother's neck. For a long time the two caressed each other, but at last Demeter began to question the girl. "Did you eat or drink anything with Hades?" she asked her daughter anxiously, and the girl replied: "Nothing until Hermes released me. Then in my joy I took a pomegranate and ate seven of its seeds."

"Alas," said the goddess in dismay, "my daughter, what have you done? The Fates have said that if you ate anything in the land of shadow, you must return to Hades and rule with him as his queen. However, you ate not the whole pomegranate, but only seven of the seeds. For seven months of the year, therefore, you must dwell in the underworld, and the remaining five you may live with me."

Thus the Fates had decreed, and even Zeus could not alter their law. For seven months of every year Persephone is lost to Demeter and rules pale and sad over the dead. At this time Demeter mourns, trees shed their leaves, cold comes, and the earth lies still and dead. But when in the eighth month Persephone returns, her mother is glad and the earth rejoices. The wheat springs up, bright, fresh, and green in the plowland. Flowers unfold, birds sing, and young animals are born. Everywhere the heavens smile for joy or weep sudden showers of gladness upon the springing earth.

Detail from a fresco, showing a garden from the house of Livia, Rome.

Arachne°

Retold by
REX WARNER

Through the power of a god or goddess, a human being could be changed into a plant, an animal, or a constellation. There are many stories of such transformations in classical mythology. The Greek word for "transformation" is meta-morphosis, a word scientists now use to describe the changes during the life cycles of such creatures as the butterfly and the frog.

In mythology, metamorphosis is sudden and magical. In this myth, the meta-morphosis explains how something in nature came to be.

Arachne was famous not for her birth or for her city, but only for her skill. Her father was a dyer of wool; her mother also was of no great family. She lived in a small village whose name is scarcely known. Yet her skill in weaving made her famous through all the great cities of Lydia. To see her wonderful work the nymphs of Tmolus would leave their vineyards, the nymphs of Pactolus would leave the golden waters of their river. It was a delight not only to see the cloth that she had woven, but to watch her at work, there was such beauty in the way she did it, whether she was winding the rough skeins into balls of wool, or smoothing it with her fingers, or drawing out the fleecy shiny wool into threads, or giving a twist to the spindle with her quick thumb, or putting in embroidery with her needle. You would think that she had learned the art from Minerva herself, the goddess of weaving.

Arachne, however, when people said this, would be offended at the idea of having had

even so great a teacher as Minerva. "Let her come," she used to say, "and weave against me. If she won, she could do what she liked with me."

Minerva heard her words and put on the form of an old woman. She put false gray hair on her head, made her steps weak and tottering, and took a staff in her hand. Then she said to Arachne: "There are some advantages in old age. Long years bring experience. Do not, then, refuse my advice. Seek all the fame you like among men for your skill, but allow the goddess to take first place, and ask her forgiveness, you foolish girl, for the words which you have spoken. She will forgive you if you ask her."

Arachne dropped the threads from her hand and looked angrily at the old woman. She hardly kept her hands off her, and her face showed the anger that she felt. Then she spoke to the goddess in disguise: "Stupid old thing, what is wrong with you is that you have lived too long. Go and give advice to your daughters, if you have any. I am quite able to look

---

° **Arachne** (ə-răk′nē).

Detail from the *Month of March: The Triumph of Minerva* by Francesco del
Cossa (1436–1478). Fresco.
Palazzo Schiffanoia, Ferrara, Italy

after myself. As for what you say, why does not the goddess come here herself? Why does she avoid a contest with me?"

"She has come," Minerva replied, and she put off the old woman's disguise, revealing herself in her true form. The nymphs bowed down to worship her, and the women also who were there. Arachne alone showed no fear. Nevertheless she started,[1] and a sudden blush came to her unwilling face and then faded away again, as the sky grows crimson at the moment of sunrise and then again grows pale. She persisted in what she had said already, and stupidly longing for the desired victory, rushed headlong to her fate.

Minerva no longer refused the contest and gave no further advice. At once they both set up their looms and stretched out on them the delicate warp. The web was fastened to the beam; reeds separated the threads and through the threads went the sharp shuttles which their quick fingers sped. Quickly they worked, with their clothes tucked up round their breasts, their skilled hands moving backward and forward like lightning, not feeling the work since they were both so good at it. In their weaving they used all the colors that are made by the merchants of Tyre—purple of the oyster and every other dye, each shading into each, so that the eye could scarcely tell the difference between the finer shades, though the extreme colors were clear enough. So, after a storm of rain, when a rainbow spans the sky, between each color there is a great difference, but still between each an insensible shading. And in their work they wove in stiff threads of gold, telling ancient stories by pictures.

Minerva, in her weaving, showed the ancient citadel of Athens and the story of the old quarrel between her and Neptune, god of the sea,

over the naming of this famous land.[2] There you could see the twelve gods as witnesses, and there Neptune striking with his huge trident[3] the barren rock from which leaped a stream of sea water. And there was Minerva herself, with shield and spear and helmet. As she struck the rock there sprang up a green olive tree, and the victory was hers. Athens was her city, named from her other name, Athene.

As for Arachne, the pictures which she wove were of the deceitful loves of the gods. There was Europa, carried away by a bull over the sea. You would have thought it a real bull and real waves of water. Then she wove Jupiter coming to Danae in a golden shower, to Aegina as a flame, to Mnemosyne,[4] mother of the Muses, in the disguise of a shepherd. There was Neptune too, disguised as a dolphin, a horse, or a ram. Every scene was different, and each scene had the surroundings that it ought to have. Round the edge of the web ran a narrow border filled with designs of flowers and sprays of ivy intertwined.

Neither Minerva nor Envy itself could find any fault with Arachne's work. Furious at the success of the mortal girl, Minerva tore to pieces the gorgeous web with its stories of the crimes of the gods. With the hard boxwood spindle that she held, she struck Arachne on the head over and over again.

Arachne could not bear such treatment. In her injured pride she put a noose round her neck and hanged herself. As she hung from the rope, Minerva, in pity, lifted her body and said: "You may keep your life, you rude and arrogant girl, but you and all your descendants will still hang."

---

1. **started:** here, made a sudden movement from fear or surprise.

2. **the naming . . . land:** a reference to a contest that was held to see which god could give the better gift to the city and thus become its protector.
3. **trident** (trīd′ənt): a spear with three prongs.
4. **Europa** (yŏŏ-rō′pə); **Danae** (dăn′ə-ē′); **Aegina** (ē-jī′nə); **Mnemosyne** (nĭ-mŏs′ə-nē): women loved by Jupiter. Danae was the mother of the hero Perseus.

Then, as she went out, she sprinkled over her some magic juices, and immediately her hair felt the poison it fell off; so did her nose and ears; her head became minute and all her body shrunk; her slender fingers were joined onto her body as legs; everything else was stomach and now, turned into a spider, she still spins threads out of her own stomach and everywhere still exercises her old craft of weaving.

Reading Check

1. How did Minerva disguise herself to visit Arachne?
2. What advice did she give Arachne?
3. What quarrel did the goddess depict in her tapestry?
4. Which scenes did Arachne choose for her tapestry?
5. Why did Arachne hang herself?

For Study and Discussion

Analyzing and Interpreting the Myth

1. The ancient Greeks connected many things in nature with the actions of gods and mortals. How does the myth of Arachne explain the characteristics of the spider?

2. The myth of Arachne reveals that human beings could choose to please or offend the gods. What sin did Arachne commit?

3. What lesson do you think the ancient Greeks drew from the myth of Arachne?

About the Author

Rex Warner   (1905–1986)

Rex Warner, an authority on classical literature, was born in England. He was educated at Oxford. Warner's books on the ancient world include *Pericles the Athenian,* *Imperial Caesar,* and *Men of Athens.* Warner also published many translations of classical works, including *Three Great Plays of Euripides,* *The Peloponnesian Wars* by Thucydides, and *Caesar's War Commentaries.* "Arachne" is from the collection of myths called *Men and Gods.*

The Reward of Baucis and Philemon°

Retold by
SALLY BENSON

In addition to being the ruler of the Olympians, Zeus was also the protector of guests. As you will see in this myth, inhospitality was considered an offense against the gods.

Once upon a time, Jupiter assumed human shape and taking his son Mercury journeyed to Phrygia.[1] Mercury had left his wings behind so that no one would know he was a god, and the two presented themselves from door to door as weary travelers, seeking rest and shelter. They found all doors closed to them as it was late, and the inhospitable inhabitants would not bother to let them in. At last, they came to a small thatched cottage where Baucis, a feeble old woman, and her husband, Philemon, lived. They were a kindly couple, not ashamed of their poverty, and when the two strangers knocked at their door, they bade them enter. The old man placed a seat, on which Baucis, bustling and attentive, spread a cloth, and begged his guests to sit down. Then Baucis raked out the coals from the ashes and kindled up a fire, fed it with leaves and dry bark, and with her scanty breath blew it into flames. She brought split sticks and dry branches out of a

corner, broke them up, and placed them under a small kettle. Philemon collected some potherbs in the garden, and she shred them from the stalks and prepared them for the pot. He reached down with a forked stick a flitch of bacon hanging in the chimney, cut a small piece, and put it in the pot to boil with the herbs. A beechen bowl was filled with warm water, that their guests might wash. Host and visitors talked amicably together.

On the bench designed for the guests, a cushion stuffed with seaweed was laid; and a cloth, only produced on great occasions, was spread over that. The old lady, with her apron on, set the table with trembling hands. When the table was fixed, she rubbed it down with sweet-smelling herbs, and upon it she set some of chaste Minerva's olives, some cornel berries preserved in vinegar, and added radishes and cheese, with eggs lightly cooked in the ashes.

° **Baucis** (bô′sĭs); **Philemon** (fĭ-lē′mən).
1. **Phrygia** (frĭj′ē-ə): an ancient country in western Asia, now part of Turkey.

Philemon and Baucis by Rembrandt van Rijn (1606–1669). Oil on canvas.
National Gallery of Art, Widener Collection

Everything was served in earthenware dishes, and an earthenware pitcher with wooden cups stood beside them. When all was ready, the stew, smoking hot, was set on the table. Some wine, mild and sweet, was served, and for dessert they offered wild apples and honey. Over and above all, there were the friendly faces and simple, hearty welcome of the old couple.

As the visitors ate and drank, Baucis and Philemon were astonished to see that the wine, as fast as it was poured out, renewed itself in the pitcher. Struck with terror, they recognized their heavenly guests and, falling to their knees, implored forgiveness for the poor entertainment. They had an old goose which they kept as the guardian of their humble cottage and they decided to sacrifice him in honor of their illustrious visitors. But the goose was too nimble and eluded the elderly couple, and at last he took shelter between the gods themselves.

Jupiter and Mercury forbade it to be slain, and spoke in these words: "We are gods. This inhospitable village shall pay the penalty of its impiety. You alone shall go free from the chastisement. Quit your house and come with us to the top of yonder hill."

Baucis and Philemon hastened to obey and labored up the steep ascent. They had reached up to an arrow's flight of the top, when they beheld all the country they had left sunk into a lake, only their own house left standing. While they gazed with wonder at the sight, their house was changed into a temple. Columns took the place of the corner posts, the thatch grew yellow and turned to gold, the floors became marble, the doors were enriched with exquisite carvings and ornaments of gold.

Then Jupiter spoke to them kindly. "Excellent old man, and woman worthy of such a husband," he said, "speak! Tell us your wishes. What favor have you to ask us?"

Philemon whispered to his wife for a few minutes, and then declared to the gods their united wish. "We ask to be priests and guardians of this your temple. And since we have passed our lives in love and concord, we wish that one and the same hour may take us both from life, that I may not live to see her grave nor be laid in my own by her."

Their prayers were granted. They were keepers of the temple as long as they lived. When they were very old, as they stood one day before the steps of the sacred temple and were telling the story of the place to some visitors, Baucis saw Philemon begin to put forth leaves, and old Philemon saw Baucis changing in a like manner. And now a leafy crown had grown over their heads. As long as they could speak they exchanged parting words. "Farewell, dear spouse," they said together, as the bark closed over their mouths.

Still on a certain hill in Phrygia, stand a linden tree and an oak enclosed by a low wall. Not far from the spot is a marsh, formerly good habitable land, but now dotted with pools, the haunt of fen birds and cormorants.[2] They are all that is left of the town and of Baucis and Philemon.

2. **fen birds and cormorants** (kôr′mər-ənts): birds that inhabit watery land.

Reading Check

1. At what point did Baucis and Philemon realize that they had been entertaining gods?
2. How did Baucis and Philemon offer to honor their visitors?
3. How was their cottage transformed?
4. What favor did Jupiter grant?

Analyzing and Interpreting the Myth

1. Why did Jupiter and Mercury punish the inhabitants of Phrygia?

2. How was the metamorphosis of Baucis and Philemon a reward?

3. What lesson do you think was drawn from the myth of Baucis and Philemon?

Creative Writing

Writing a Story About Metamorphosis

Choose some natural object, and write an original story explaining how and why someone was transformed into the object. Here are some suggestions:

a butterfly	an octopus
a diamond	a violet
a giraffe	a water lily
a lobster	a weeping willow
a mosquito	a whale

Decide which classical gods and goddesses might play a part in your story.

Extending Your Study

Using Reference Books

Here are the names of some other figures in Greek mythology who were transformed by the gods:

Adonis	Daphne	Narcissus
Alcyone	Echo	Orion
Clytie	Hyacinthus	Scylla

Choose one of these characters and find out: 1) why the person was transformed, 2) what the person was transformed into, and 3) which god or goddess was involved in the story. Then tell the story to the class in your own words.

You might begin your research by consulting a dictionary or an encyclopedia. If there is no entry in the encyclopedia under the character's name, see if the character is mentioned in the general article on "Mythology." Perhaps the encyclopedia will have a special entry on "Greek Mythology" or "Classical Mythology." Consult the special reference books listed on page 590.

About the Author

Sally Benson (1900–1972)

Sally Benson wrote short stories for *The New Yorker* beginning in 1930. A collection of her short stories, *Junior Miss,* was published in 1941, and later became the basis for a comedy. She was the joint author of the screenplay for *Anna and the King of Siam,* and also wrote *The Young and the Beautiful,* a play based on F. Scott Fitzgerald's "Josephine" stories in the *Saturday Evening Post,* and *Seventeen,* a musical comedy based on Booth Tarkington's *Seventeen.* The selection in this anthology is from *Stories of the Gods and Heroes.*

Classical Mythology in Today's World

The *zodiac* is an imaginary belt in the sky, divided into twelve parts called *signs* of the zodiac. Each of the signs is named for a different constellation. On its path through the sky, the sun passes through this imaginary circle, spending one month in each of the twelve parts.

The signs of the zodiac are shown on these pages. The first sign of the zodiac is *Aries,* "the ram." The second sign of the zodiac is *Taurus,* "the bull." The other signs, in order, are *Gemini,* "the twins"; *Cancer,* "the crab"; *Leo,* "the lion"; *Virgo,* "the maiden"; *Libra,* "the balance"; *Scorpio,* "the scorpion"; *Sagittarius,* "the archer"; *Capricorn,* "the horned goat"; *Aquarius,* "the water-bearer"; and *Pisces,* "the fish."

Each person has a sign determined by his or her date of birth. Find out what your sign is by looking up the entry for *zodiac* in a dictionary or an encyclopedia.

Find out how each of these signs is connected with classical mythology. (Consult the reference books listed on page 590.)

Aries	Leo	Capricorn
Cancer	Sagittarius	Pisces

Many of the constellations are named for figures in classical mythology. Locate, read, and summarize a myth associated with one of these constellations:

Andromeda	Perseus
Cassiopeia	Pleiades
Cepheus	Ursa Major (Big Dipper)
Cygnus	Ursa Minor (Little Dipper)

With what American holiday is the cornucopia associated? Find out why the cornucopia is associated with Zeus.

Seven of the chemical elements in this list are named for figures in classical mythology. Identify the seven elements and the figures for whom they are named.

antimony	helium	plutonium
californium	krypton	selenium
cerium	mercury	uranium
einsteinium	neptunium	yttrium

Celestial globe with clockwork, supported by Pegasus (1566–1584) by
Gerhard Emmoser. Silver, gilt, and brass.

Phaethon°

Retold by
EDITH HAMILTON

In classical mythology there are many stories of mortals who attempt too much, who try to rival the powers of the gods and goddesses. This is the story of a boy who for a few moments "felt himself the lord of the sky." How do you think Phaethon's adventure would have been viewed by the ancient Greeks—as an act of heroism or of arrogance?

The palace of the Sun was a radiant place. It shone with gold and gleamed with ivory and sparkled with jewels. Everything without and within flashed and glowed and glittered. It was always high noon there. Shadowy twilight never dimmed the brightness. Darkness and night were unknown. Few among mortals could have long endured that unchanging brilliancy of light, but few had ever found their way thither.

Nevertheless, one day a youth, mortal on his mother's side, dared to approach. Often he had to pause and clear his dazzled eyes, but the errand which had brought him was so urgent that his purpose held fast and he pressed on, up to the palace, through the burnished doors, and into the throne room where surrounded by a blinding, blazing splendor the sun god sat. There the lad was forced to halt. He could bear no more.

Nothing escapes the eyes of the Sun. He saw the boy instantly and he looked at him very kindly. "What brought you here?" he asked.

"I have come," the other answered boldly, "to find out if you are my father or not. My mother said you were, but the boys at school laugh when I tell them I am your son. They will not believe me. I told my mother and she said I had better go and ask you."

Smiling, the Sun took off his crown of burning light so that the lad could look at him without distress. "Come here, Phaethon," he said. "You are my son. Clymene[1] told you the truth. I expect you will not doubt my word too? But I will give you a proof. Ask anything you want of me and you shall have it. I call the Styx[2] to be witness to my promise, the river of the oath of the gods."

No doubt Phaethon had often watched the Sun riding through the heavens and had told himself with a feeling, half awe, half excitement, "It is my father up there." And then he would wonder what it would be like to be in that chariot, guiding the steeds along that dizzy course, giving light to the world. Now at his father's words this wild dream had become possi-

1. **Clymene** (klĭm′ə-nē).
2. **Styx** (stĭks): one of the rivers in the underworld.

° **Phaethon** (fā′ə-thən).

ble. Instantly he cried, "I choose to take your place, Father. That is the only thing I want. Just for a day, a single day, let me have your car to drive."

The Sun realized his own folly. Why had he taken that fatal oath and bound himself to give in to anything that happened to enter a boy's rash young head? "Dear lad," he said, "this is the only thing I would have refused you. I know I cannot refuse. I have sworn by the Styx. I must yield if you persist. But I do not believe you will. Listen while I tell you what this is you want. You are Clymene's son as well as mine. You are mortal and no mortal could drive my chariot. Indeed, no god except myself can do that. The ruler of the gods cannot. Consider the road. It rises up from the sea so steeply that the horses can hardly climb it, fresh though they are in the early morning. In midheaven it is so high that even I do not like to look down. Worst of all is the descent, so precipitous that the sea gods waiting to receive me wonder how I can avoid falling headlong. To guide the horses, too, is a perpetual struggle. Their fiery spirits grow hotter as they climb and they scarcely suffer[3] my control. What would they do with you?

"Are you fancying that there are all sorts of wonders up there, cities of the gods full of beautiful things? Nothing of the kind. You will have to pass beasts, fierce beasts of prey, and they are all that you will see. The Bull, the Lion, the Scorpion, the great Crab, each will try to harm you. Be persuaded. Look around you. See all the goods the rich world holds. Choose from them your heart's desire and it shall be yours. If what you want is to be proved my son, my fears for you are proof enough that I am your father."

But none of all this wise talk meant anything to the boy. A glorious prospect opened before

---

3. **suffer:** here, bear.

him. He saw himself proudly standing in that wondrous car, his hands triumphantly guiding those steeds which Jove himself could not master. He did not give a thought to the dangers his father detailed. He felt not a quiver of fear, not a doubt of his own powers. At last the Sun gave up trying to dissuade him. It was hopeless, as he saw. Besides, there was no time. The moment for starting was at hand. Already the gates of the east glowed purple, and Dawn had opened her courts full of rosy light. The stars were leaving the sky; even the lingering morning star was dim.

There was need for haste, but all was ready. The Seasons, the gatekeepers of Olympus, stood waiting to fling the doors wide. The horses had been bridled and yoked to the car. Proudly and joyously Phaethon mounted it and they were off. He had made his choice. Whatever came of it he could not change now. Not that he wanted to in that first exhilarating rush through the air, so swift that the East Wind was outstripped and left far behind. The horses' flying feet went through the low-banked clouds near the ocean as through a thin sea mist and then up and up in the clear air, climbing the height of heaven. For a few ecstatic moments Phaethon felt himself the lord of the sky. But suddenly there was a change. The chariot was swinging wildly to and fro; the pace was faster; he had lost control. Not he, but the horses were directing the course. That light weight in the car, those feeble hands clutching the reins, had told them their own driver was not there. They were the masters then. No one else could command them. They left the road and rushed where they chose, up, down, to the right, to the left. They nearly wrecked the chariot against the Scorpion; they brought up short and almost ran into the Crab. By this time the poor charioteer was half fainting with terror, and he let the reins fall.

The Fall of Phaethon by Peter Paul Rubens (1577–1640). Watercolor drawing.

That was the signal for still more mad and reckless running. The horses soared up to the very top of the sky and then, plunging headlong down, they set the world on fire. The highest mountains were the first to burn, Ida and Helicon, where the Muses dwell, Parnassus, and heaven-piercing Olympus. Down their slopes the flame ran to the low-lying valleys and the dark forest lands, until all things everywhere were ablaze. The springs turned into steam; the rivers shrank. It is said that it was then the Nile fled and hid his head, which still is hidden.

In the car Phaethon, hardly keeping his

place there, was wrapped in thick smoke and heat as if from a fiery furnace. He wanted nothing except to have this torment and terror ended. He would have welcomed death. Mother Earth, too, could bear no more. She uttered a great cry which reached up to the gods. Looking down from Olympus they saw that they must act quickly if the world was to be saved. Jove seized his thunderbolt and hurled it at the rash, repentant driver. It struck him dead, shattered the chariot, and made the maddened horses rush down into the sea.

Phaethon all on fire fell from the car through the air to the earth. The mysterious river Eridanus, which no mortal eyes have ever seen, received him and put out the flames and cooled the body. The naiads,[4] in pity for him, so bold and so young to die, buried him and carved upon the tomb:

> Here Phaethon lies who drove the sun
> god's car.
> Greatly he failed, but he had greatly
> dared.

His sisters, the Heliades, the daughters of Helios,[5] the Sun, came to his grave to mourn for him. There they were turned into poplar trees, on the bank of the Eridanus,

> Where sorrowing they weep into the
> stream forever.
> And each tear as it falls shines in the water
> A glistening drop of amber.

---

4. **naiads** (nā′ădz): nymphs who lived in rivers, springs, and lakes.
5. **Helios** (hē′lē-ŏs′): an early Greek sun god, later identified with Apollo.

Reading Check

1. Why did the Sun take off his crown when Phaethon visited him?
2. What oath did the Sun take?
3. What favor did Phaethon ask?
4. What happened to the horses when Phaethon lost control?
5. How did Jove stop the runaway chariot?

For Study and Discussion

Analyzing and Interpreting the Myth

1. According to this myth, what explanation did the ancient Greeks have for the rising and setting of the sun?

2. Why did Phaethon want to drive his father's chariot?

3a. Why was Helios forced to keep his promise to Phaethon? **b.** What arguments did he use in an attempt to change his son's mind? **c.** Why was he unsuccessful?

4. What happened to the earth when Phaethon lost control of the chariot?

5. The inscription carved on Phaethon's tomb read: "Greatly he failed, but he had greatly dared." Was Phaethon's adventure an act of great daring or great folly? Explain your answer.

Language and Vocabulary

Learning Words from the Myths

Helios, the early sun god, has given his name to a number of English words. Whenever you see a word that begins with *helio-*, you can be sure that it has something to do with the sun.

Find the meanings of these words and use each one in a sentence:

heliocentric   heliotherapy
heliograph   heliotropic

Descriptive Writing

Using Specific Words in Description

Compare the italicized verbs in these two descriptions of the Sun's palace:

It *was covered* with gold and ivory and jewels. Everything inside and outside *was* very bright and shiny.

It *shone* with gold and *gleamed* with ivory and *sparkled* with jewels. Everything without and within *flashed* and *glowed* and *glittered*.

In the second description, all six verbs specify different ways of sending out light.

Selene, Helios' sister, was an early moon goddess, later identified with Artemis. The ancient Greeks believed that Selene drove the chariot of the moon across the sky. Imagine what Selene, her palace, and her chariot looked like. Write a description, using specific verbs to describe the colors, sights, and sounds of the moon goddess' palace, or of her chariot.

About the Author

Edith Hamilton   (1867–1963)

Edith Hamilton developed an interest in ancient Greek and Roman civilizations when she was very young. However, she did not begin writing about these ancient civilizations until she was sixty-three and had already had a career as the headmistress of a girls' school. One of her best-known works, *The Greek Way,* is a study of the life and thought of ancient Greece. She followed this book with *The Roman Way,* a study of ancient Roman civilization. *Mythology,* from which "Phaethon" is taken, contains retellings of Greek, Roman, and Norse myths. For her contributions to the study of ancient Greece, she was made an honorary citizen of Athens.

Phaethon

MORRIS BISHOP

What humorous parallel does this poem draw between the myth of Phaethon and modern youth?

Apollo through the heavens rode
    In glinting gold attire;
His car was bright with chrysolite,°
    His horses snorted fire.
He held them to their frantic course   5
    Across the blazing sky.
His darling son was Phaethon,
    Who begged to have a try.

"The chargers are ambrosia-fed,
    They barely brook control;   10
On high beware the Crab, the Bear,
    The Serpent round the Pole;
Against the Archer and the Bull
    Thy form is all unsteeled!"°
But Phaethon could lay it on;   15
  Apollo had to yield.

Out of the purple doors of dawn
    Phaethon drove the horses;
They felt his hand could not command.
    They left their wonted° courses.   20
And from the chariot Phaethon
    Plunged like a falling star—
And so, my boy, no, no, my boy,
    You cannot take the car.

---

3. **chrysolite** (krĭs′ə-līt′): a greenish, transparent gem.
14. **unsteeled:** unprotected. 20. **wonted** (wôn′tĭd): habitual.

For Study and Discussion

Analyzing and Interpreting the Poem

1a. To whom is the speaker in this poem talking? **b.** Why does he tell this person the story of Phaethon?

2. The Serpent in line 12 is the constellation Draco, which is also called the Dragon. Identify the Crab, Bear, Archer, and Bull mentioned in lines 11 and 13.

3. Morris Bishop's story differs from Edith Hamilton's retelling of the myth in certain details. What differences can you find?

About the Author

Morris Bishop (1893–1973)

Morris Bishop was born in New York State and for many years was a professor of Romance languages at Cornell University. Bishop published several translations, histories, and a number of volumes of poetry. His books of verse include *Paramount Poems* (1929) and *A Bowl of Bishop* (1954).

Icarus and Daedalus°

Retold by
JOSEPHINE PRESTON PEABODY

Daedalus, we are told, was among the wisest of men, capable of reaching be-
yond even the laws of nature. What does this myth suggest about his kind of
wisdom? How does Icarus' fate suggest the need for moderation?

Among all those mortals who grew so wise that they learned the secrets of the gods, none was more cunning than Daedalus.

He once built, for King Minos of Crete,[1] a wonderful Labyrinth[2] of winding ways so cunningly tangled up and twisted around that, once inside, you could never find your way out again without a magic clue.[3] But the King's favor veered with the wind, and one day he had his master architect imprisoned in a tower. Daedalus managed to escape from his cell; but it seemed impossible to leave the island, since every ship that came or went was well guarded by order of the King.

At length, watching the sea gulls in the air— the only creatures that were sure of liberty—he thought of a plan for himself and his young son Icarus, who was captive with him.

Little by little, he gathered a store of feathers great and small. He fastened these together with thread, molded them in with wax, and so fashioned two great wings like those of a bird. When they were done, Daedalus fitted them to his own shoulders, and after one or two efforts, he found that by waving his arms he could winnow[4] the air and cleave it, as a swimmer does the sea. He held himself aloft, wavered this way and that with the wind, and at last, like a great fledgling, he learned to fly.

Without delay, he fell to work on a pair of wings for the boy Icarus and taught him carefully how to use them, bidding him beware of rash adventures among the stars. "Remember," said the father, "never to fly very low or very high, for the fogs about the earth would weigh you down, but the blaze of the sun will surely melt your feathers apart if you go too near."

For Icarus, these cautions went in at one ear and out by the other. Who could remember to be careful when he was to fly for the first time? Are birds careful? Not they! And not an idea

---

° **Daedalus** (dĕd′l-əs).
1. **King Minos** (mī′nŏs′) **of Crete:** Minos was a son of Zeus. Crete is a large island southeast of the Greek mainland.
2. **Labyrinth** (lăb′ə-rĭnth).
3. **clue:** here, a ball of thread. Theseus, an Athenian hero, was able to escape by tying one end of the thread to the entrance, unwinding the ball as he went in, and rewinding it as he came out.

4. **winnow:** beat.

The Fall of Icarus by Bernard Picart. Eighteenth-century etching.

Icarus and Daedalus   **615**

remained in the boy's head but the one joy of escape.

The day came, and the fair wind that was to set them free. The father-bird put on his wings, and, while the light urged them to be gone, he waited to see that all was well with Icarus, for the two could not fly hand in hand. Up they rose, the boy after his father. The hateful ground of Crete sank beneath them; and the country folk, who caught a glimpse of them when they were high above the treetops, took it for a vision of the gods—Apollo, perhaps, with Cupid after him.

At first there was a terror in the joy. The wide vacancy of the air dazed them—a glance downward made their brains reel. But when a great wind filled their wings, and Icarus felt himself sustained, like a halcyon bird[5] in the hollow of a wave, like a child uplifted by his mother, he forgot everything in the world but joy. He forgot Crete and the other islands that he had passed over: he saw but vaguely that winged thing in the distance before him that was his father Daedalus. He longed for one draft of flight to quench the thirst of his captivity: he stretched out his arms to the sky and made toward the highest heavens.

Alas for him! Warmer and warmer grew the air. Those arms, that had seemed to uphold him, relaxed. His wings wavered, dropped. He fluttered his young hands vainly—he was falling—and in that terror he remembered. The heat of the sun had melted the wax from his wings; the feathers were falling, one by one, like snowflakes; and there was none to help.

He fell like a leaf tossed down by the wind, down, down, with one cry that overtook Daedalus far away. When he returned and sought high and low for the poor boy, he saw nothing but the birdlike feathers afloat on the water, and he knew that Icarus was drowned.

The nearest island he named Icaria, in memory of the child; but he, in heavy grief, went to the temple of Apollo in Sicily and there hung up his wings as an offering. Never again did he attempt to fly.

Reading Check

1. Where was Daedalus imprisoned by King Minos?
2. What did Daedalus use to make the wings?
3. What instructions did he give Icarus?
4. What caused Icarus' death?
5. What did Daedalus do with his wings?

---

5. **halcyon** (hăl′sē-ən) **bird:** a legendary bird, identified with the kingfisher, which supposedly had the power of calming the winter seas.

For Study and Discussion

Analyzing and Interpreting the Myth

1. At the opening of the myth, you are told that Daedalus was so cunning that he learned the secrets of the gods. Do you think he was punished for his knowledge? Explain your answer.

2. Both Icarus and Phaethon fell from the sky to their deaths. Compare these young men. How are they alike, and how are they different?

3. Myths often show what attitudes and behavior were expected of human beings. **a.** What lesson might have been drawn from the myth of Icarus and Daedalus about obedience to the laws of nature? **b.** What lesson might have been drawn about the obedience of young people to their elders?

Language and Vocabulary

Learning Words from the Myths

Daedalus built the original Labyrinth in Crete to house the Minotaur, a monster that was half man and half bull. King Minos ordered young men and women to be fed to the Minotaur. The Labyrinth kept them from escaping.

We now use the word *labyrinth* to mean any complicated system of passageways and dead ends. The word *labyrinth* may also be used for anything that is intricate or confusing. The poet Tennyson has referred to "the *labyrinth* of the mind." What do you think the word means in this phrase?

About the Author

Josephine Preston Peabody (1874–1922)

Josephine Preston Peabody was best known as a poet and a playwright. The selection included in this anthology is from *Old Greek Folk Stories Told Anew,* a collection of stories that was written as a complement to Nathaniel Hawthorne's *Wonder Book* and *Tanglewood Tales.* Some of her works include *The Wolf of Gubbio,* a comedy; *The Wayfarers* and *Harvest Moon,* poetry; and *Fortune and Men's Eyes,* poems with a play.

To a Friend Whose Work Has Come to Triumph

ANNE SEXTON

The title of this poem alludes, or refers, to the title of a poem by William Butler Yeats, "To a Friend Whose Work Has Come to Nothing." In that poem Yeats praises the efforts of a friend whose attempts to bring a collection of French art to Dublin had been thwarted by local officials.

    Similarly, Sexton here is talking about triumph in defeat. In what way is Icarus' failure a great success?

Consider Icarus, pasting those sticky wings on,
testing that strange little tug at his shoulder blade,
and think of that first flawless moment over the lawn
of the labyrinth. Think of the difference it made!
There below are the trees, as awkward as camels;   5
and here are the shocked starlings pumping past
and think of innocent Icarus who is doing quite well:
larger than a sail, over the fog and the blast
of the plushy ocean, he goes. Admire his wings!
Feel the fire at his neck and see how casually   10
he glances up and is caught, wondrously tunneling
into that hot eye. Who cares that he fell back to the sea?
See him acclaiming the sun and come plunging down
while his sensible daddy goes straight into town.

For Study and Discussion

Analyzing and Interpreting the Poem

1. This poem is addressed to someone whose work has been unsuccessful in one sense, yet triumphant in another. **a.** Does the poet consider Icarus' death a defeat or a victory? **b.** Which lines support your answer?

2. The word *sensible* is used in line 14 to describe Daedalus. Do you think the author admires him for his caution? Explain your answer.

Extending Your Study

Tracking Down an Allusion

The authors of the poems that appear on pages 613 and 618 expect their readers to recognize the characters and events in certain classical myths. Readers who know these myths can better understand and appreciate the poems.

Writers often use references to characters and events from classical mythology. In these lines from *Childe Harold's Pilgrimage,* Byron, an English poet, compares the Rome of his day to Niobe, a character in mythology:

> The Niobe of nations! there she stands,
> Childless and crownless, in her voiceless woe.

Such a reference as this is known as an **allusion**. What does modern Rome, fallen from its past grandeur as a great empire, have in common with Niobe? In order to understand what Byron means, you need to find out Niobe's story.

You might begin tracking down this allusion by looking in a dictionary:

Ni·o·be (nī′ō bē), *n. Class. Myth.* the daughter of Tantalus and wife of Amphion of Thebes; her children were slain and Zeus turned her into stone, in which state she continued to weep over her loss.

This entry tells why Niobe was childless and why she was voiceless—she was turned to stone. But the entry does not tell why her children were slain or why Zeus turned her to stone. A different dictionary may give more information. An encyclopedia may also tell more of Niobe's story. Your best source, however, is a book of myths or an encyclopedia of mythology. Consult one of the sources suggested on page 590.

The expression "Achilles' heel" is used to refer to a person's special weakness. Locate the story of Achilles and find out how that expression came into being.

About the Author

Anne Sexton   (1928–1974)

Anne Sexton, a native of Newton, Massachusetts, was, along with Sylvia Plath and others, one of the "confessional" poets. Under the influence of Robert Lowell, this group turned to the intimate details of their own lives and feelings for their subjects. Sexton once said that poetry "should be a shock to the senses. It should almost hurt." She received a Pulitzer Prize in 1967 for her volume of poetry *Live or Die.*

Classical Mythology in Today's World

Throughout this unit you have been learning about English words that come from the myths. Many more words and phrases can be traced to classical mythology. What words can you think of that come from the names of these figures?

Hygeia, a Greek goddess of health
Hypnos, a Greek god of sleep
Oceanus, a Titan who was the father of the river gods and sea nymphs

Which planets are named for gods and goddesses of classical mythology? Use a dictionary to check your answers.

Several of our months get their names from figures in classical mythology. Which months are they and for what figures are they named?

Use a dictionary to find the origin of these words:

giant	psychology
lethargic	tantalize
music	titanic
panic	volcano

A book of maps is called an *atlas*. The word comes from the name of a figure in classical mythology. Find out who Atlas was and explain his connection with maps.

Many towns and cities in the United States have been named for characters or places in classical mythology. Here are some of them:

Atlas (Illinois, Michigan)
Hercules (California)
Juno Beach (Florida)
Jupiter (North Carolina)
Mercury (Nevada, Texas)
Mount Olympus (Utah, Washington)
Olympia (California, Kentucky, Washington)
Venus (Florida, Nebraska, Pennsylvania, Texas)

Are the names of any towns or cities in your state derived from classical mythology? Consult an almanac or an atlas.

The city of *Carthage* figures in the story of Aeneas and Dido. Aeneas was a Trojan. When Troy fell to the Greeks at the end of the Trojan War, Aeneas and many of his people escaped and began searching for a new homeland. Find out how Aeneas came to Carthage and what happened to Dido after he left.

Rome is named for Romulus. Look up the myth of Romulus and Remus. Find out how Rome, the City of the Seven Hills, was founded.

Sparta is associated in mythology with King Menelaus, who was married to Helen, the most beautiful woman in the world. Find out how Helen is connected with the Trojan War.

The island of *Ithaca* was the home of Odysseus, or Ulysses, one of the Greek heroes who fought in the Trojan War. Find out how Odysseus was responsible for the fall of Troy and why he was forced to wander for ten years before he reached his home.

What relationship is there between these place names and the characters and events in classical mythology?

Atlantic Ocean	Hellespont
Europe	Icarian Sea

The Adventures of Hercules

Retold by
EDITH HAMILTON

The greatest hero in ancient Greece was Heracles, whose Roman name was Hercules. He was the strongest man on earth. Like many other heroes in classical mythology, he was the son of a god (Zeus) and a mortal (Alcmene). Throughout his life he suffered from fits of madness that the goddess Hera sent to plague him. In one of his fits, he killed his wife and children. In order to be purified of his crime, he sought the help of a priestess of Apollo, who brought him the message of the god: For twelve long years he was to serve as a slave, carrying out all-but-impossible labors.

As you read, determine which characteristics of Hercules show that despite his superhuman strength he had certain human weaknesses.

Eurystheus[1] was by no means stupid, but of a very ingenious turn of mind, and when the strongest man on earth came to him humbly prepared to be his slave, he devised a series of penances which from the point of view of difficulty and danger could not have been improved upon. It must be said, however, that he was helped and urged on by Hera. To the end of Hercules' life she never forgave him for being Zeus's son. The tasks Eurystheus gave him to do are called "the labors of Hercules." There were twelve of them and each one was all but impossible.

The first was to kill the lion of Nemea, a beast no weapons could wound. That difficulty Hercules solved by choking the life out of him. Then he heaved the huge carcass up on his back and carried it into Mycenae.[2] After that, Eurystheus, a cautious man, would not let him inside the city. He gave him his orders from afar.

The second labor was to go to Lerna and kill a creature with nine heads called the Hydra, which lived in a swamp there. This was exceedingly hard to do, because one of the heads was immortal and the others almost as bad, inasmuch as when Hercules chopped off one, two grew up instead. However, he was helped by his nephew Iolaus,[3] who brought him a burn-

1. **Eurystheus** (yŏŏ-rĭs′thē-əs).

2. **Mycenae** (mī-sē′nē).
3. **Iolaus** (ī′ə-lā′əs).

Hercules and the Nemean Lion. Black-figured terra cotta vase, c. 560 B.C.

chased the beast from one place to another until it was exhausted; then he drove it into deep snow and trapped it.

The fifth labor was to clean the Augean stables in a single day. Augeas had thousands of cattle and their stalls had not been cleared out for years. Hercules diverted the courses of two rivers and made them flow through the stables in a great flood that washed out the filth in no time at all.

The sixth labor was to drive away the Stymphalian birds, which were a plague to the people of Stymphalus because of their enormous numbers. He was helped by Athena to drive them out of their coverts, and as they flew up he shot them.

The seventh labor was to go to Crete and fetch from there the beautiful savage bull that Poseidon had given Minos. Hercules mastered him, put him in a boat and brought him to Eurystheus.

The eighth labor was to get the man-eating mares of King Diomedes of Thrace. Hercules slew Diomedes first and then drove off the mares unopposed.

The ninth labor was to bring back the girdle[4] of Hippolyta, the Queen of the Amazons. When Hercules arrived she met him kindly and told him she would give him the girdle, but Hera stirred up trouble. She made the Amazons think that Hercules was going to carry off their queen, and they charged down on his ship. Hercules, without a thought of how kind Hippolyta had been, without any thought at all, instantly killed her, taking it for granted that she was responsible for the attack. He was able to fight off the others and get away with the girdle.

The tenth labor was to bring back the cattle of Geryon, who was a monster with three bodies living on Erythia, a western island. On his

ing brand with which he seared the neck as he cut each head off so that it could not sprout again. When all had been chopped off he disposed of the one that was immortal by burying it securely under a great rock.

The third labor was to bring back alive a stag with horns of gold, sacred to Artemis, which lived in the forests of Cerynitia. He could have killed it easily, but to take it alive was another matter and he hunted it a whole year before he succeeded.

The fourth labor was to capture a great boar which had its lair on Mount Erymanthus. He

---

4. **girdle:** here, a belt.

way there Hercules reached the land at the end of the Mediterranean and he set up as a memorial of his journey two great rocks, called the Pillars of Hercules (now Gibraltar and Ceuta). Then he got the oxen and took them to Mycenae.

The eleventh labor was the most difficult of all so far. It was to bring back the golden apples of the Hesperides,[5] and he did not know where they were to be found. Atlas, who bore the vault of heaven upon his shoulders, was the father of the Hesperides, so Hercules went to him and asked him to get the apples for him. He offered to take upon himself the burden of the sky while Atlas was away. Atlas, seeing a chance of being relieved forever from his heavy task, gladly agreed. He came back with the apples, but he did not give them to Hercules. He told Hercules he could keep on holding up the sky, for Atlas himself would take the apples to Eurystheus. On this occasion Hercules had only his wits to trust to; he had to give all his strength to supporting that mighty load. He was successful, but because of Atlas' stupidity rather than his own cleverness. He agreed to Atlas' plan, but asked him to take the sky back for just a moment so that Hercules could put a pad on his shoulders to ease the pressure. Atlas did so, and Hercules picked up the apples and went off.

The twelfth labor was the worst of all. It took him down to the lower world; and it was then that he freed Theseus from the Chair of Forgetfulness.[6] His task was to bring Cerberus, the three-headed dog, up from Hades. Pluto gave him permission provided Hercules used no weapons to overcome him. He could use his hands only. Even so, he forced the terrible monster to submit to him. He lifted him and carried him all the way up to the earth and on to Mycenae. Eurystheus very sensibly did not want to keep him and made Hercules carry him back. This was his last labor.

When all were completed and full expiation made for the death of his wife and children, he would seem to have earned ease and tranquility for the rest of his life. But it was not so. He was never tranquil and at ease. An exploit quite as difficult as most of the labors was the conquest of Antaeus,[7] a Giant and a mighty wrestler who forced strangers to wrestle with him on condition that if he was victor he should kill them. He was roofing a temple with the skulls of his victims. As long as he could touch the earth he was invincible. If thrown to the ground he sprang up with renewed strength from the contact. Hercules lifted him up and holding him in the air strangled him.

Story after story is told of his adventures. He fought the river god Achelous[8] because Achelous was in love with the girl Hercules now wanted to marry. Like everyone else by this time, Achelous had no desire to fight him and he tried to reason with him. But that never worked with Hercules. It only made him more angry. He said, "My hand is better than my tongue. Let me win fighting and you may win talking." Achelous took the form of a bull and attacked him fiercely, but Hercules was used to subduing bulls. He conquered him and broke off one of his horns. The cause of the contest, a young princess named Deianira,[9] became his wife.

He traveled to many lands and did many other great deeds. At Troy he rescued a maiden who was in the same plight as An-

5. **Hesperides** (hĕs-pĕr′ə-dēz′): sisters who guarded the golden apples belonging to Hera. These apples had been given to her as a wedding present by Gaea (jē′ə), an earth goddess.
6. **Chair of Forgetfulness:** Theseus, an Athenian hero and a cousin of Hercules, had been trapped in this chair when he accompanied a friend to Hades in order to kidnap Persephone.

7. **Antaeus** (ăn-tē′əs).
8. **Achelous** (ə-kĕl′ō-əs).
9. **Deianira** (dē′yə-nī′rə).

dromeda,[10] waiting on the shore to be devoured by a sea monster which could be appeased in no other way. She was the daughter of King Laomedon, who had cheated Apollo and Poseidon of their wages after at Zeus's command they had built for the King the walls of Troy. In return Apollo sent a pestilence, and Poseidon the sea serpent. Hercules agreed to rescue the girl if her father would give him the horses Zeus had given his grandfather. Laomedon promised, but when Hercules had slain the monster the King refused to pay. Hercules captured the city, killed the King, and gave the maiden to his friend, Telamon of Salamis, who had helped him.

On his way to Atlas to ask him about the Golden Apples, Hercules came to the Caucasus, where he freed Prometheus,[11] slaying the eagle that preyed on him.

Along with these glorious deeds there were others not glorious. He killed with a careless thrust of his arm a lad who was serving him by pouring water on his hands before a feast. It was an accident and the boy's father forgave Hercules, but Hercules could not forgive himself and he went into exile for a time. Far worse was his deliberately slaying a good friend in order to avenge an insult offered him by the young man's father, King Eurytus.[12] For this base action Zeus himself punished him: he sent

10. **Andromeda** (ăn-drăm′ə-də): a princess rescued from a sea monster by Perseus, whom she later married.

11. **Prometheus:** See "Prometheus the Fire-Bringer," page 583. Zeus had punished Prometheus for his defiance by having him chained to a mountaintop and sending an eagle each day to devour his liver, which grew back each night.
12. **Eurytus** (yŏŏr′ĭ-təs).

Detail from *Cerberus* by William Blake (1757–1827). Watercolor.
Tate Gallery

Hercules by Francisco de Zurburán (1598–1664). Oil on canvas. Hercules is
shown wearing the robe anointed with the blood of Nessus.
Prado Museum

him to Lydia to be a slave to the Queen, Omphale,[13] some say for a year, some for three
years. She amused herself with him, making
him at times dress up as a woman and do
woman's work, weave or spin. He submitted
patiently, as always, but he felt himself de-
graded by this servitude and with complete un-
reason blamed Eurytus for it and swore he

13. **Omphale** (ŏm′fə-lĕ).

would punish him to the utmost when he was
freed.

As Hercules had sworn to do while he was
Omphale's slave, no sooner was he free than
he started to punish King Eurytus because he
himself had been punished by Zeus for killing
Eurytus' son. He collected an army, captured
the King's city and put him to death. But
Eurytus, too, was avenged, for indirectly this

victory was the cause of Hercules' own death.

Before he had quite completed the destruction of the city, he sent home—where Deianira, his devoted wife, was waiting for him to come back from Omphale in Lydia—a band of captive maidens, one of them especially beautiful, Iole, the King's daughter. The man who brought them to Deianira told her that Hercules was madly in love with this Princess. This news was not so hard for Deianira as might be expected, because she believed she had a powerful love-charm which she had kept for years against just such an evil, a woman in her own house preferred before her. Directly after her marriage, when Hercules was taking her home, they had reached a river where the centaur[14] Nessus acted as ferryman, carrying travelers over the water. He took Deianira on his back and in midstream insulted her. She shrieked and Hercules shot the beast as he reached the other bank. Before he died he told Deianira to take some of his blood and use it as a charm for Hercules if ever he loved another woman more than her. When she heard about Iole, it seemed to her the time had come, and she anointed a splendid robe with the blood and sent it to Hercules by the messenger.

As the hero put it on, the effect was the same as that of the robe Medea had sent her rival whom Jason was about to marry.[15] A fearful pain seized him, as though he were in a burning fire. In his first agony he turned on Deianira's messenger, who was, of course, completely innocent, seized him and hurled him down into the sea. He could still slay others, but it seemed that he himself could not die. The anguish he felt hardly weakened him. What had instantly killed the young Princess of

14. **centaur** (sĕn'tôr'): one of a group of mountain creatures who were part man and part horse.
15. **the robe . . . marry:** Jason's intended bride, the Princess of Corinth, died in agony when she tried on the robe, which Medea had anointed with poison.

Corinth could not kill Hercules. He was in torture, but he lived and they brought him home. Long before, Deianira had heard what her gift had done to him and had killed herself. In the end he did the same. Since death would not come to him, he would go to death. He ordered those around him to build a great pyre on Mount Oeta and carry him to it. When at last he reached it he knew that now he could die and he was glad. "This is rest," he said. "This is the end." And as they lifted him to the pyre he lay down on it as one who at a banquet table lies down upon his couch.

He asked his youthful follower, Philoctetes, to hold the torch to set the wood on fire; and he gave him his bow and arrows, which were to be far-famed in the young man's hands, too, at Troy. Then the flames rushed up and Hercules was seen no more on earth. He was taken to heaven, where he was reconciled to Hera and married her daughter Hebe, and where

> After his mighty labors he has rest.
> His choicest prize eternal peace
> Within the homes of blessedness.

But it is not easy to imagine him contentedly enjoying rest and peace, or allowing the blessed gods to do so, either.

Reading Check

1. Why was it difficult for Hercules to kill the Hydra?
2. How did Hercules manage to clean the Augean stables in a day?
3. Why was the twelfth labor the worst of all?
4. In what way did Hercules defeat Antaeus?
5. Why did Hercules' wife anoint a robe with the blood of Nessus?

For Study and Discussion

Analyzing and Interpreting the Myth

1. All twelve labors required great strength, courage, and perseverance. Which labors required that Hercules also use his wits?

2a. Which labors were useful tasks that benefited humanity?   **b.** Which were simply tests of strength and patience? Explain your answer.

3. Since Hercules had superhuman strength, he could not be killed by poison. How did he die?

Language and Vocabulary

Learning Words from the Myths

The Hydra was the nine-headed monster that Hercules killed in the second of his labors. The name *Hydra* comes from a Greek word meaning "water serpent." In English the root *hydro-* (or *hydr-*) means "water." Find the meaning of these words:

    hydrant   hydroelectric
    hydraulic   hydrophobia

Creative Writing

Writing a Television Script

Imagine that you are the creator of a new television series based on the adventures of Hercules. Choose one of the episodes in his life—one of the labors or one of his other feats—and plan a script for a half-hour show. You may want to work with three or four other students in planning and writing the script.

Before you begin to write, consider these questions:

How many characters will appear in the play?
What will be the main events in the plot?
Where will the action take place?
How many different scenes will there be?
What details will have to be invented?
What dialogue will have to be written?

Extending Your Study

Using Reference Books

Hercules fought and killed the Nemean lion, the nine-headed Hydra, and other fearsome monsters. Here are some additional monsters from classical mythology:

Chimera	Gorgons	Python
Cyclopes	Harpies	Sphinx
Furies	Minotaur	Typhon

Choose four of these monsters. Consult one of the reference books listed on page 590 and identify each one in a sentence. If you like to draw, try drawing four of the monsters instead of writing about them.

INDEX OF NAMES

Where a character is known by more than one name, a separate entry has been provided for each name. For example, you will find Zeus also listed under his Roman names, Jove and Jupiter.

Aphrodite (ăf′rə-dī′tē): Greek goddess of love and beauty. She was identified with the Roman goddess **Venus.** 578

Apollo (ə-pŏl′ō): Greek and Roman god of youth, music, prophecy, archery, healing, and the sun. He was also called **Phoebus** (fē′bəs) **Apollo,** from the Greek word for "shining." 578, 593, 613

Arachne (ə-răk′nē): an arrogant young woman who boasted of her skill in weaving to Minerva and challenged the goddess to a contest. She was transformed into a spider by Minerva. 598

Ares (âr′ēz): Greek god of war. He was identified with the Roman god **Mars.** 580

Artemis (är′tə-mĭs): Greek goddess of wild animals, hunting, childbirth, and the moon. She was identified with the Roman goddess **Diana.** 579

Athena (ə-thē′nə): Greek goddess of wisdom, arts, crafts, and war, and protector of the city of Athens. She was also called **Athene** (ə-thē′nē) and **Pallas** (păl′əs) **Athena,** and was identified with the Roman goddess **Minerva.** 579

Atlas (ăt′ləs): the Titan whom Zeus punished by making him hold up the sky on his shoulders. 578, 624

Bacchus. See **Dionysus.**

Baucis (bô′sĭs): a poor Phrygian peasant. She and her husband, **Philemon** (fĭ-lē′mən), gave shelter to Jupiter and Mercury when they visited Phrygia in disguise. 602

Centaurs (sĕn′tôrz′): a race of mountain creatures, part man and part horse. 627

Ceres (sîr′ēz): Roman goddess of agriculture. She was identified with the Greek goddess **Demeter.**

Cronus (krō′nəs): the Titan who ruled the universe until he was overthrown by his son Zeus. The reign of Cronus was known as the Golden Age. He was identified with the Roman god **Saturn.** 578, 583

Cupid (kyōō′pĭd): Roman god of love. He was identified with the Greek god **Eros.** 616

The Metropolitan Museum of Art, Rogers Fund, 1943

Sleeping Eros. Bronze, third century B.C.

Daedalus (dĕd′l-əs): an Athenian inventor and architect who built the Labyrinth for King Minos of Crete. He fashioned wings for himself and his son **Icarus** (ĭk′ə-rəs), who fell to his death when he flew too close to the sun.   614, 618

Demeter (dĭ-mē′tər): Greek goddess of agriculture and fertility. She was identified with the Roman goddess **Ceres**.   592

Diana (dī-ă′nə): Roman goddess of the moon and hunting. She was identified with the Greek goddess **Artemis.**

Diana the Huntress. Roman copy of Greek statue.

Dionysus (dī′ə-nī′səs): Greek god of wine, fertility, and drama. He was also called **Bacchus** (băk′əs) by the Greeks and the Romans.

Eros (îr′ŏs′): Greek god of love, Aphrodite's son. He was identified with the Roman god **Cupid.**

Fates: three goddesses who controlled human destiny and life. **Clotho** (klō′thō) spun the thread of each person's life, **Lachesis** (lăk′ə-sĭs) determined the length of each thread, and **Atropos** (ăt′rə-pŏs′) cut each thread.   596

Hades (hā′dēz): Greek god of the underworld, and husband of **Persephone.** He was also called **Pluto** (plōō′tō) by the Greeks and the Romans.   578, 592

Helios (hē′lē-ŏs′): early Greek god of the sun. He was later identified with **Apollo.**   608

Hephaestus (hĭ-fĕs′təs): Greek god of fire and metalworking. He was identified with the Roman god **Vulcan.**   580

Hera (hîr′ə): Greek goddess of marriage and childbirth, Zeus's wife, and queen of the gods of Olympus. She was identified with the Roman goddess **Juno.**   578, 622

Heracles (hĕr′ə-klēz′): a Greek hero, the son of Zeus and **Alcmene** (ălk-mē′nē). He was known as **Hercules** to the Romans.   622

Hercules. See Heracles.

Hermes (hûr′mēz): Greek god of travelers, merchants, and thieves, and messenger of the gods. He was identified with the Roman god **Mercury.**   580, 595

Icarus. See Daedalus.

Iris (ī′rĭs): goddess of the rainbow and messenger of the gods.   595

Jove. See Jupiter.

Juno (jōō′nō): Roman goddess of marriage and childbirth, Jupiter's wife, and the queen of the gods. She was identified with the Greek goddess **Hera.**

Jupiter (jōō′pə-tər): Roman god of the sky and the weather, and king of the gods. He was also called **Jove**, and was identified with the Greek god **Zeus.** 578

Mars (märz): Roman god of war. He was identified with the Greek god **Ares.**

Coin with the head of Mars, 280–276 B.C.

Mercury (mûr′kyə-rē): Roman god of business, science, and thieves, and messenger of the gods. He was identified with the Greek god **Hermes.** 580

Minerva (mĭ-nûr-və): Roman goddess of the arts and wisdom. She was identified with the Greek goddess **Athena.** 580, 598

Muses (myōō′zəz): nine sisters, daughters of Zeus and **Mnemosyne** (nĭ-mŏs′ə-nē), who were patronesses of the arts. Each Muse was associated with a different art: **Calliope** (kə-lī′ə-pē′), epic poetry; **Clio** (klī′ō), history; **Erato** (ĕr′ə-tō′), lyric poetry; **Euterpe** (yōō-tûr′pē), music; **Melpomene** (mĕl-pŏm′ə-nē), tragedy; **Polyhymnia** (pŏl′ē-hĭm′nē-ə), religious poetry; **Terpsichore** (tûrp-sĭk′ə-rē), dance; **Thalia** (thə-lī′ə), comedy; and **Urania** (yōō-rā′nē-ə), astronomy. 579, 610

Neptune (nĕp′tōōn′): Roman god of the sea. He was identified with the Greek god **Poseidon.**

Nymphs (nĭmfs): goddesses who inhabited parts of nature, such as rivers, mountains, and trees.

Pan: Greek god of woodlands, shepherds, and goatherds. He was often represented as having the head, chest, and arms of a man, and the legs, horns, and ears of a goat.

Persephone (pər-sĕf′ə-nē): Greek goddess of spring and the underworld, Demeter's daughter. The Romans called her **Proserpina** (prō-sûr′pə-nə). 592

Phaethon (fā′ə-thən): Helios' son. He was killed when he tried to drive the chariot of the Sun. 608

Philemon. See Baucis.

Pluto. See Hades.

Poseidon (pō-sī′dən): Greek god of the sea. He was identified with the Roman god **Neptune.** 578

Prometheus (prə-mē′thē-əs): the Titan who gave fire to mortals against the wishes of Zeus. 583

Proserpina. See Persephone.

Saturn (săt′ərn): Roman god of agriculture and fertility. He was identified with the Greek god **Cronus.**

Satyrs (sā′tərz): woodland creatures who were part human and part goat. They were followers of Dionysus. 575

Selene (sə-lē′nē): early Greek goddess of the moon. She was later identified with **Artemis.** 612

Titans (tīt′nz): a family of gods who ruled the universe before the Olympians. 578

Venus (vē′nəs): Roman goddess of gardens, spring, love, and beauty. She was identified with the Greek goddess **Aphrodite.**

Vulcan (vûl′kən): Roman god of fire and metalworking. He was identified with the Greek god **Hephaestus.**

Zeus (zoos): Greek god of the sky and the weather, and king of the gods of Olympus. He was identified with the Roman god **Jupiter**, also called **Jove.** 578, 583, 593

Detail from *Venus de Milo.* Marble statue, c. 150–100 B.C.

Extending Your Study

1. In your notebook, keep a record of references to classical mythology that you find in your reading, in movies, and on television. Post some of these on a bulletin board as you find them.

2. Look in newspapers and magazines at home for advertisements that use names or symbols drawn from classical mythology. What association is the consumer expected to make? Post these advertisements on a bulletin board or paste them in your notebook.

3. Make a collection of myths that come from different cultures and share a common subject. For example, look for myths that explain the origin of the seasons. You can also look for myths in which people are transformed into animals or plants.

4. The following questions might inspire stories that are like myths:

Why does it rain?
Why are there thunder and lightning?
Why do rivers run toward the sea?

Why has the sky so many different colors at sunrise and at sunset?
Why is the moon sometimes visible during the day?
Why are there eclipses of the sun?
Why does the moon change its shape?
Why are there mountains?

Make up a story explaining one of these phenomena, to be told to the class. You will have to do some planning before you can tell your story. What characters are necessary? What happens to the characters to cause the phenomenon you are explaining?

5. Work with a group of students to retell one of the classical myths in the form of a drama. Write dialogue for the characters, and present the play to the class.

6. What do you imagine Hercules looked like? Illustrate one of the characters in a myth you have read, or show one or more scenes from a myth in the form of a collage, a poster, or a drawing.

For Further Reading

Asimov, Isaac, *Words from the Myths* (Houghton Mifflin, 1961; paperback, New American Library, 1969)

Many words and phrases in English come from classical myths. The author explains the fascinating origins of scores of words and retells the myths associated with them.

Benson, Sally, *Stories of the Gods and Heroes* (Dial Press, 1940)

This book includes simple retellings of the major classical myths.

Colum, Padraic, *The Golden Fleece* (paperback, Macmillan, 1983)

One of the greatest hero tales in Greek mythology is the story of Jason and the Argonauts and their search for the Golden Fleece.

Coolidge, Olivia, *Greek Myths* (Houghton Mifflin, 1949)

This is a collection of many well-known classical myths.

————, *The Trojan War* (Houghton Mifflin, 1952)

According to legend, the Greeks fought the Trojan War in order to recover Helen, the most beautiful woman in the world.

Graves, Robert, *Greek Gods and Heroes* (Doubleday, 1960; paperback, Dell)

The author retells some of the most famous myths in an informal, witty style. The opening chapter, "The Palace of the Gods," includes interesting information about the Olympian gods and goddesses, their temperaments, their special powers, and their emblems.

Green, Roger Lancelyn, *Heroes of Greece and Troy* (Walck, 1961)

This is a vivid narrative of the lives and deeds of the classical gods, goddesses, and heroes.

Hamilton, Edith, *Mythology* (Little, Brown, 1942; paperback, New American Library, 1971)

These retellings of the myths are based on a variety of classical sources, and there is a useful introduction. Norse myths are also included.

Hawthorne, Nathaniel, *A Wonder-Book* and *Tanglewood Tales* (many editions)

Hawthorne expands the classical myths with richness of detail, characterization, and dialogue. See especially his dramatic versions of "The Golden Fleece" and "The Golden Touch."

Picard, Barbara L., *The Odyssey of Homer* (Walck, 1952)

Here is a retelling of the exciting adventures of Odysseus: his outwitting of the Cyclops, his journey to the underworld, his narrow escape from the monsters Scylla and Charybdis, and many more.

Rouse, W. H. D., *Gods, Heroes and Men of Ancient Greece* (New American Library, 1971)

The author tells the myths "as parts of a connected whole, as the Greeks felt them to be."

Sabin, Frances Ellis, *Classical Myths That Live Today* (Silver Burdett, 1958)

This recounting of Greek and Roman myths includes examples of the way these famous stories have influenced our language, our art, and our literature.

Serraillier, Ian, *The Gorgon's Head: the Story of Perseus* (Walck, 1962)

Among the most famous heroes in mythology is Perseus, who killed Medusa, one of the Gorgons. The Gorgons were three sisters who had snakes for hair. They were so repulsive and terrifying that whoever looked at them was turned to stone.

The Lair of the Sea Serpent by Elihu Vedder (1836–1923). Oil on canvas.
The Metropolitan Museum of Art, gift of Mrs. Harold G. Henderson

NORSE MYTHOLOGY

Norse mythology consists of the myths of ancient Scandinavia and Germany. Norse mythology is very different from classical mythology. Unlike the Olympians, the gods and goddesses in Norse mythology are not all-powerful. Although they rule the worlds of humans, giants, and dwarfs, they themselves are ruled by fate and cannot change their destiny. They do not have the gift of eternal youth: in order to remain young, they must eat the apples of Idun every day. Furthermore, they are not immortal. They await a great final battle, called Ragnarok (răg'nə-räk'), which is to be fought between the gods and goddesses and their enemies, the giants. In this battle, all will perish and the earth will be destroyed. Then a new race of gods and goddesses will be reborn and a new world re-created for the human race.

There are three separate levels in the universe of Norse mythology. At the first level, there is Asgard (ăs'gärd, äz'), the world of the gods and goddesses. At the middle level, there is Midgard (mĭd'gärd'), where human beings, dwarfs, and giants dwell. At the bottom level, there is Niflheim (nĭv'əl-hām'), the world of the dead. All three levels are held together by the roots and branches of a mighty ash tree.

In this unit you will meet the major figures in Norse mythology and read some of the best stories ever told. As you read the myths in this unit, you may want to refer to this chart. Note that some names may be spelled in more than one way.

NAME	DESCRIPTION
Aesir (ă'sîr, ē'sîr)	warrior gods of Norse mythology
Asgard (ăs'gärd', äz')	home of the Aesir and slain heroes
Balder (bôl'dər)	god of daylight; wisest and most beautiful of the gods
Bifrost (bēf'räst)	rainbow bridge connecting Asgard and Midgard
Bragi (brä'gē)	god of poetry
Fenris (Fenrir) (fĕn'rĭs)	Wolf, the son of Loki
Frey (frā)	god of plenty

Dragon Ship by John Taylor Arms. Aquatint.

Names in Norse Mythology   **637**

NAME	DESCRIPTION
Freya (Freyja) (frā′ə)	goddess of love and beauty
Frig (Frigg, Frigga) (frĭg)	goddess of the heavens; Odin's wife
Heimdall (hām′däl′)	watchman of the rainbow bridge
Hel (Hela) (hĕl)	goddess of the underworld
Hermod	Odin's messenger
Hod (Hoder)	blind god of night
Honir	shining god
Idun (Iduna) (ē′do͞on)	goddess responsible for the apples of youth
Jotunheim (Iotunheim) (yô′to͞on-hām′, yō′-)	world of the giants
Loki (lō′kē)	god of fire; trickster and sky traveler
Midgard (mĭd′gärd′)	middle world inhabited by human beings
Mimir (mē′mîr)	guardian of the well of wisdom
Mjolnir (Miollnir, Mjollnir)	Thor's hammer
Niflheim (Nifelheim) (nĭv′əl-hām′)	world of the dead
Njord (Niord, Njorth) (nyôth)	wind god
Norns (nôrns)	three goddesses of destiny
Odin (ō′dĭn)	king of the gods and goddesses; god of war, wisdom, and art
Ragnarok (răg′nə-räk′)	final battle between gods and human beings, giants, and monsters
Thor (thôr)	lord of thunder
Tyr (tîr)	bravest of Aesir gods

Raging Wotan Rides to the Rock! (1910) by Arthur Rackham (1867–1939). In German mythology, Odin is sometimes called Wodan or Wotan.

NAME	DESCRIPTION
Utgard (o͞ot'gärd')	citadel of giants in Jotunheim
Valhalla (Valhall) (văl-hăl'ə)	huge hall in Asgard where slain warriors are brought and feasted
Valkyrie (Valkyr) (văl-kîr'ē, văl'kîr-ē)	warrior-maiden who carries slain warriors to Valhalla
Vanir (vä'nîr)	nature gods and goddesses who live in Asgard
Yggdrasill (ĭg'drə-sĭl, üg'-)	ash tree that supports all levels of the Norse universe

The Norse Gods and Goddesses

BARBARA LEONIE PICARD

In this selection you will meet some of the most important figures in Norse mythology. As you read, see if you can find any parallels to the Olympians in classical mythology.

Bronze statue of Odin.
Ny Carlsberg Glyptotek, Copenhagen

The gods of the Norsemen were the Aesir and the Vanir. The Vanir were the gods of nature: Niord, the god of the shore and the shallow summer sea; and his son and daughter, Frey and Freya, Frey who ruled over the elves of light and Freya the goddess of love and beauty; and Aegir,[1] the lord of the deep and

1. **Aegir** (ăg′ər).

stormy seas, with Ran his wife, who caught sailors in her net and drowned them. Aegir and Ran were not truly of the kindly Vanir, for they were cruel and more akin to the giants, but like the Vanir, they ruled over nature and were on good terms with all the other gods.

The Aesir were the gods who cared for men; Odin the Allfather, king of all the gods, wise and just and understanding; and Frigg, his queen, who presided over human marriages; Honir, Odin's brother, the shining god, who lived among the Vanir; large, noisy Thor, the god of thunder, Odin's son, who always had a special corner in his heart for the peasants and the poor and the dispossessed; Tyr, the brave god of war; Balder and Hod, the twin sons of Odin and Frigg, Balder the god of daylight, who was the most beautiful of all the gods, and Hod who was blind and ruled over the hours of darkness; Hermod, Odin's messenger; and Heimdall, the divine watchman who kept guard over Bifrost, the bridge between Asgard and the world.

And lastly there was Loki, who was neither of the Aesir nor of the Vanir, nor yet of the giant race; crafty red-haired Loki, quick to laugh and quick to change his shape, the god of the fire that burns on the hearth, good and kindly when it wishes, but a merciless destroyer when it leaves its proper place. From the earliest days Odin and Loki had sworn an oath of brotherhood; and it was this which so often saved Loki in later times, when his cunning tricks so much displeased the other gods.

In Asgard Odin had three palaces; in one the gods met in council; and in another stood his throne, Hlidskialf,[2] which served him as a watchtower from where he might see all that passed not only in Asgard, but in Midgard and Iotunheim, and even in the depths of dark Niflheim, the home of mist, as well. Here would he sit with his two ravens perched upon his shoulders. Each day he sent these birds flying forth across the world and each evening they returned to tell him of the happenings of the day. At his feet would lie his two wolves who followed him like hounds wherever he went in Asgard, and at the feasting would eat the meat that was set before him; for the

Allfather lived on mead[3] alone, and no food passed his lips so long as he was among the gods, though when he traveled through Midgard, he lived like other men.

Odin's third palace was called Valhall and was set in the midst of a grove of trees whose leaves were gleaming gold. This palace had five hundred and forty doors, and its walls were made of glittering spears and its roof of golden shields. To this hall came all those warriors who had died in battle, when death had passed away from them as a dream, to feast and tell tales of their deeds as living men, and to test their fighting skill on one another with weapons and armor made of imperishable gold. For the Norsemen were great warriors, and they believed that when a battle raged, Odin would send out his warrior-maidens, the Valkyrs, to ride across the sky and fetch the slain to Valhall, where they would be with Odin himself, and feast upon the flesh of the boar Saehrimnir,[4] which, though slaughtered and roasted each day, came back to life each night, and drink of the mead provided by the goat Heidrun.[5] Thus every Norseman longed, when the time came, to die in battle; and his greatest fear was that he should suffer a straw-death, and die in bed, lying on his straw-stuffed mattress. For the spirits of all those who did not die fighting went down to dark Niflheim.

Odin sought knowledge and wisdom, that he might use them to the good of both gods and men; and one day he went to Mimir's well, the fount of wisdom and understanding, which flowed by that root of the ash tree Yggdrasill which grew in Midgard, and asked the giant Mimir to let him drink of the magic waters.

Mimir looked long at Odin before he an-

2. **Hlidskialf** (lĭd'skē-ălf): "Hill-Opening."

3. **mead** (mēd): a drink made from fermented honey and water.
4. **Saehrimnir** (sā'rĭm-nĭr).
5. **Heidrun** (hā'drŭn).

The Ride of the Valkyries
(1910) by Arthur
Rackham.

swered, and then he said, "Even the gods must pay for knowledge."

"And what is the price of wisdom?" asked Odin.

"Give me one of your eyes as a pledge," said Mimir.

Unhesitatingly, Odin plucked out one of his eyes and gave it to Mimir, and Mimir let him drink from the well, and straightway Odin was filled with the knowledge of all things past and present, and even into the future could he look. And though his new knowledge gave him joy, it brought sorrow to him also, for he could now tell not only what was past, but also the grief that was to come. Yet he returned to Asgard to use his knowledge to help the other gods and those men who sought his aid.

And Mimir dropped Odin's eye into his well, and it lay there evermore, shining below the water, a proof of Odin's love of wisdom and his good will towards mankind.

Reading Check

1. In Norse mythology the Aesir ruled over human beings. What did the Vanir do?
2. How was Loki different from the other gods?
3. How was Asgard, the realm of the gods, connected to the earth?
4. What different functions were served by Odin's three palaces?
5. How did Odin obtain wisdom?

For Study and Discussion

Analyzing and Interpreting the Selection

1. The Norse Universe consists of three levels. Briefly describe each one.

2. Odin, the Allfather, occupies the central role in Norse mythology as Zeus does in classical mythology. Yet he is a very different figure. How is this difference shown in his attitude toward human beings?

3. In Norse mythology Loki is the Trickster god. He is sly and he enjoys making mischief. In what way are these characteristics appropriate for the god of fire?

4. How does Norse mythology reflect the importance of physical courage and military glory in the culture of the Norse people?

Language and Vocabulary

Tracing the Origins of Calendar Names

Several of our weekdays are named for Old English gods who trace their ancestry to the gods of Norse mythology. Here is an etymological entry for the word *Thursday:*

> [Middle English *thur(e)sday,* Old English *thur(e)s dâeg* (influenced by Old Norse *thōrsdagr,* "Thor's day"), from earlier *thunresdâeg,* "Thor's day" (translation of Late Latin *Jovis diēs,* "Jupiter's day"): *thunres,* genitive of *thunor,* THUNDER + *dâeg,* DAY.]

This entry tells you that our word *Thursday* appeared in Middle English (between 1100 and 1500) as *thuresday.* This word had come from Old English words (between 400 and 1100), which were influenced by the Old Norse word meaning "Thor's day." The Old Norse word, in turn, had been a translation of the Latin words meaning "Jupiter's day." Like the Roman god Jupiter, Thor was associated with thunder, as the last item of the etymological entry shows.

Use a college or unabridged dictionary to find the etymology of each of these calendar names:

Tuesday   Wednesday   Friday

Writing About Literature

Explaining Characteristics of Odin

Although Tyr is identified as the brave god of war, Odin also has characteristics of a war god. In a paragraph explain Odin's role as god of battle.

The Fenris Wolf

Retold by
OLIVIA COOLIDGE

In Norse mythology, as in classical mythology, there are many fearsome monsters, none perhaps more terrifying than the Fenris Wolf. How would the gods subdue him?

Though Loki, the fire god, was handsome and ready-witted, his nature was really evil. He was, indeed, the cause of most of the misfortunes which befell the gods. He was constantly in trouble, yet often forgiven because the gods valued his cleverness. It was he who found ways out of difficulty for them, so that for a long time they felt that they could not do without him.

In the early days Loki, though a god, had wedded a monstrous giantess, and the union of these two evil beings produced a fearful brood. The first was the great world serpent, whom Odin cast into the sea, and who became so large that he completely encircled the earth, his tail touching his mouth. The second was Hel, the grisly goddess of the underworld, who reigned in the horrible land of the dead. The third was the most dreadful of all, a huge monster called the Fenris Wolf.

When the gods first saw the Fenris Wolf, he was so young that they thought they could tame him. They took him to Asgard, therefore, and brave Tyr undertook to feed and train him. Presently, however, the black monster grew so enormous that his open jaws would stretch from heaven to earth, showing teeth as large as the trunks of oak trees and as sharply pointed as knives. The howls of the beast were so dreadful as he tore his vast meals of raw meat that the gods, save for Tyr, dared not go near him, lest he devour them.

At last all were agreed that the Fenris Wolf must be fettered if they were to save their very lives, for the monster grew more ferocious towards them every day. They forged a huge chain, but since none was strong enough to bind him, they challenged him to a trial of strength. "Let us tie you with this to see if you can snap the links," said they.

The Fenris Wolf took a look at the chain and showed all his huge white teeth in a dreadful grin. "Bind me if you wish," he growled, and he actually shut his eyes as he lay down at ease to let them put it on.

The gods stepped back, and the wolf gave a little shake. There was a loud cracking sound, and the heavy links lay scattered around him in pieces. The wolf howled in triumph until the sun and moon in heaven trembled at the noise.

Thor, the smith, called other gods to his aid, and they labored day and night at a second chain. This was half as strong again as the first, and so heavy that no one of the gods could drag it across the ground. "This is by far the largest chain that was ever made," said they.

"Even the Fenris Wolf will not be able to snap fetters such as these."

Once more they brought the chain to the wolf, and he let them put it on, though this

The Binding of Fenris by Dorothy Hardy.

time it was clear that he somewhat doubted his strength. When they had chained him, he shook himself violently, but the fetters held. His great, red eyes burned with fury, the black hair bristled on his back, and he gnashed his teeth until the foam flew. He strained heavily against the iron until the vast links flattened and lengthened, but did not break. Finally with a great bound and a howl he dashed himself against the ground, and suddenly the chain sprang apart so violently that broken pieces were hurled about the heads of the watching gods.

Now the gods realized in despair that all their strength and skill would not avail to bind the wolf. Therefore Odin sent a messenger to the dwarf people under the earth, bidding them forge him a chain. The messenger returned with a little rope, smooth and soft as a silken string, which was hammered on dwarfish anvils out of strange materials which have never been seen or heard. The sound of a cat's footfall, the breath of a fish, the flowing beard of a woman, and the roots of a mountain made the metal from which it was forged.

The gods took the little rope to the Fenris Wolf. "See what an easy task we have for you this time," they said.

"Why should I bother myself with a silken string?" asked the wolf sullenly. "I have broken your mightiest chain. What use is this foolish thing?"

"The rope is stronger than it looks," answered they. "We are not able to break it, but it will be a small matter to you."

"If this rope is strong by enchantment," said the wolf in slow suspicion, "how can I tell that you will loosen me if I cannot snap it after all? On one condition you may bind me: you must give me a hostage from among yourselves."

"How can we do this?" they asked.

The Fenris Wolf stretched himself and yawned until the sun hid behind clouds at the sight of his great, red throat. "I will let you bind me with this rope," he said, "if one of you gods will hold his hand between my teeth while I do it."

The gods looked at one another in silence. The wolf grinned from ear to ear. Without a word Tyr walked forward and laid his bare hand inside the open mouth.

The gods bound the great wolf, and he stretched himself and heaved as before. This time, however, he did not break his bonds. He gnashed his jaws together, and Tyr cried out in pain as he lost his hand. Nevertheless, the great black wolf lay howling and writhing and helplessly biting the ground. There he lay in the bonds of the silken rope as long as the reign of Odin endured. The Fates[1] declared, however, that in the last days,[2] when the demons of ice and fire should come marching against the gods to the battlefield, the great sea would give up the serpent, and the Fenris Wolf would break his bonds. The wolf would swallow Odin, and the gods would go down in defeat. Sun and moon would be devoured, and the whole earth would perish utterly.

---

1. **Fates:** the three goddesses of destiny.
2. **last days:** In Norse mythology, there is to be a final battle called Ragnarok, in which almost all life is destroyed.

Reading Check

1. Who were the three monstrous children born to Loki and the giantess?
2. Which god was responsible for feeding and training the Fenris Wolf?
3. Why was it necessary for the gods to bind the Fenris Wolf?
4. Who made the silken rope to bind the monster?
5. How did Tyr lose his hand?

For Study and Discussion

Analyzing and Interpreting the Myth

1. What makes the Fenris Wolf such a terrible threat to the gods?

2. Which characteristics does the Fenris Wolf appear to have inherited from his father, Loki?

3. In Norse mythology the dwarfs, who live under Midgard, are credited with great cunning and skill. **a.** What is the silken rope made of? **b.** What do all these things have in common?

4. In order to overcome the Fenris Wolf, the gods have to make a terrible sacrifice. What significance can you see in the bravest of the gods losing his right hand?

Writing About Literature

Analyzing the Image of the Wolf

In Norse mythology the Fenris Wolf represents the fearsome enemy of the gods, who will eventually swallow Odin. In literature the wolf is often depicted as a frightening and fierce enemy to human beings. We even use the expression "wolf down" for someone who devours food greedily. Think of the character of the wolf in fairy tales like "The Three Little Pigs" and "Little Red Ridinghood."

In other stories, however, the wolf is depicted as befriending human beings. The Roman myth of Romulus and Remus tells how twin boys are raised by a she-wolf.

Choose four different selections you have read in which a wolf appears. In a paragraph analyze the image of the wolf as enemy, as friend, or as both.

How Thor Found His Hammer

Retold by
<u>HAMILTON WRIGHT MABIE</u>

Thor, the mighty god of thunder, is a key figure in several of the best-known Norse myths. In reading this myth, can you see the reasons for his popularity?

The Frost Giants[1] were always trying to get into Asgard. For more than half the year they held the world in their grasp, locking up the streams in their rocky beds, hushing their music and the music of the birds as well, and leaving nothing but a wild waste of desolation under the cold sky. They hated the warm sunshine which stirred the wildflowers out of their sleep, and clothed the steep mountains with verdure, and set all the birds a-singing in the swaying treetops. They hated the beautiful god, Balder, with whose presence summer came back to the ice-bound earth, and, above all, they hated Thor, whose flashing hammer drove them back into Jotunheim and guarded the summer sky with its sudden gleamings of power. So long as Thor had his hammer, Asgard was safe against the giants.

One morning Thor started up out of a long, deep sleep and put out his hand for the hammer; but no hammer was there. Not a sign of it could be found anywhere, although Thor anxiously searched for it. Then a thought of the giants came suddenly in his mind, and his anger rose till his eyes flashed like great fires and his red beard trembled with wrath.

"Look, now, Loki," he shouted, "they have stolen Miolnir[2] by enchantment, and no one on earth or in heaven knows where they have hidden it."

"We will get Freyja's falcon-guise[3] and search for it," answered Loki, who was always quick to get into trouble or to get out of it again. So they went quickly to Folkvang[4] and found Freyja surrounded by her maidens and weeping tears of pure gold, as she had always done since her husband went on his long journey.

"The hammer has been stolen by enchantment," said Thor. "Will you lend me the falcon-guise that I may search for it?"

---

1. **Frost Giants:** In Norse mythology, the Frost Giants, who represent the cold Northern winter, are the enemies of the gods.

2. **Miolnir** (myəl′nər). Thor's hammer. Also spelled *Mjolnir*.
3. **falcon-guise:** a magic disguise that allowed Freyja to fly like a falcon, a small, swift hawk.
4. **Folkvang** (fōlk′vəng): "Field of Folk," Freyja's home.

Marble statue of Thor by B. E. Fogelberg.

"If it were silver, or even gold, you should have it and welcome," answered Freyja, glad to help Thor find the wonderful hammer that kept them all safe from the hands of the Frost Giants.

So the falcon-guise was brought, and Loki put it on and flew swiftly out of Asgard to the home of the giants. His great wings made broad shadows over the ripe fields as he swept along, and the reapers, looking up from their work, wondered what mighty bird was flying seaward. At last he reached Jotunheim, and no sooner had he touched ground and taken off the falcon-guise than he came upon the giant Thrym,[5] sitting on a hill twisting golden collars for his dogs and stroking the long manes of his horses.

"Welcome, Loki," said the giant. "How fares it with the gods and the elves, and what has brought you to Jotunheim?"

"It fares ill with both gods and elves since you stole Thor's hammer," replied Loki, guessing quickly that Thrym was the thief, "and I have come to find where you have hidden it."

Thrym laughed as only a giant can when he knows he has made trouble for somebody.

"You won't find it," he said at last. "I have buried it eight miles underground, and no one shall take it away unless he gets Freyja for me as my wife."

The giant looked as if he meant what he said, and Loki, seeing no other way of finding the hammer, put on his falcon-guise and flew back to Asgard. Thor was waiting to hear what news he brought, and both were soon at the great doors of Folkvang.

"Put on your bridal dress, Freyja," said Thor bluntly, after his fashion, "and we will ride swiftly to Jotunheim."

But Freyja had no idea of marrying a giant just to please Thor, and, in fact, that Thor

5. **Thrym** (thrĭm).

should ask her to do such a thing threw her into such a rage that the floor shook under her angry tread and her necklace snapped in pieces.

"Do you think I am a weak lovesick girl, to follow you to Jotunheim and marry Thrym?" she cried indignantly.

Finding they could do nothing with Freyja, Thor and Loki called all the gods together to talk over the matter and decide what should be done to get back the hammer. The gods were very much alarmed, because they knew the Frost Giants would come upon Asgard as soon as they knew the hammer was gone. They said little, for they did not waste time with idle words, but they thought long and earnestly, and still they could find no way of getting hold of Miolnir once more. At last Heimdall, who had once been a Van,[6] and could therefore look into the future, said: "We must have the hammer at once or Asgard will be in danger. If Freyja will not go, let Thor be dressed up and go in her place. Let keys jingle from his waist and a woman's dress fall about his feet. Put precious stones upon his breast, braid his hair like a woman's, hang the necklace around his neck, and bind the bridal veil around his head."

Thor frowned angrily. "If I dress like a woman," he said, "you will jeer at me."

"Don't talk of jeers," retorted Loki; "unless that hammer is brought back quickly, the giants will rule in our places."

Thor said no more, but allowed himself to be dressed like a bride, and soon drove off to Jotunheim with Loki beside him disguised as a servant-maid. There was never such a wedding journey before. They rode in Thor's chariot and the goats drew them, plunging swiftly along the way, thunder pealing through the mountains and the frightened earth blazing

and smoking as they passed. When Thrym saw the bridal party coming, he was filled with delight.

"Stand up, you giants," he shouted to his companions; "spread cushions upon the benches and bring in Freyja, my bride. My yards are full of golden-horned cows, black oxen please my gaze whichever way I look, great wealth and many treasures are mine, and Freyja is all I lack."

It was evening when the bride came driving into the giant's court in her blazing chariot. The feast was already spread against her coming, and with her veil modestly covering her face she was seated at the great table, Thrym fairly beside himself with delight. It wasn't every giant who could marry a goddess!

If the bridal journey had been so strange that anyone but a foolish giant would have hesitated to marry a wife who came in such a turmoil of fire and storm, her conduct at the table ought certainly to have put Thrym on his guard; for never had bride such an appetite before. The great tables groaned under the load of good things, but they were quickly relieved of their burden by the voracious[7] bride. She ate a whole ox before the astonished giant had fairly begun to enjoy his meal. Then she devoured eight large salmon, one after the other, without stopping to take breath; and having eaten up the part of the feast specially prepared for the hungry men, she turned upon the delicacies which had been made for the women, and especially for her own fastidious[8] appetite.

Thrym looked on with wondering eyes, and at last, when she had added to these solid foods three whole barrels of mead, his amazement was so great that, his astonishment getting the better of his politeness, he called out, "Did

6. **Van:** one of the Vanir.

7. **voracious** (vô-rā′shəs, vō-, və): greedy in eating.
8. **fastidious** (fă-stĭd′ē-əs, fə-): delicate.

anyone ever see such an appetite in a bride before, or know a maid who could drink so much mead?"

Then Loki, who was playing the part of a serving-maid, thinking that the giant might have some suspicions, whispered to him, "Freyja was so happy in the thought of coming here that she has eaten nothing for eight whole days."

Thrym was so pleased at this evidence of affection that he leaned forward and raised the veil as gently as a giant could, but he instantly dropped it and sprang back the whole length of the hall before the bride's terrible eyes.

"Why are Freyja's eyes so sharp?" he called to Loki. "They burn me like fire."

"Oh," said the cunning serving-maid, "she has not slept for a week, so anxious has she been to come here, and that is why her eyes are so fiery."

Everybody looked at the bride and nobody envied Thrym. They thought it was too much like marrying a thunderstorm.

The giant's sister came into the hall just then and, seeing the veiled form of the bride sitting there, went up to her and asked for a bridal gift. "If you would have my love and friendship, give me those rings of gold upon your fingers."

But the bride sat perfectly silent. No one had yet seen her face or heard her voice.

Thrym became very impatient. "Bring in the hammer," he shouted, "that the bride may be consecrated, and wed us in the name of Var."[9]

If the giant could have seen the bride's eyes when she heard these words, he would have

sent her home as quickly as possible and looked somewhere else for a wife.

The hammer was brought and placed in the bride's lap, and everybody looked to see the marriage ceremony; but the wedding was more strange and terrible than the bridal journey had been. No sooner did the bride's fingers close round the handle of Miolnir than the veil which covered her face was torn off and there stood Thor, the giant-queller, his terrible eyes blazing with wrath. The giants shuddered and shrank away from those flaming eyes, the sight of which they dreaded more than anything else in all the worlds; but there was no chance of escape. Thor swung the hammer round his head and the great house rocked on its foundations. There was a vivid flash of lightning, an awful crash of thunder, and the burning roof and walls buried the whole company in one common ruin.

Thrym was punished for stealing the hammer, his wedding guests got crushing blows instead of bridal gifts, and Thor and Loki went back to Asgard, where the presence of Miolnir made the gods safe once more.

---

9. **Var** (vär): goddess who hears marriage oaths.

Reading Check

1. Why do the Frost Giants hate Balder?
2. How does Thor defend Asgard from the Frost Giants?
3. Why does Loki borrow the falcon-guise?
4. Whose idea is it to send Thor in Freyja's place?
5. How does Thor keep his identity a secret?

For Study and Discussion

Analyzing and Interpreting the Myth

1. The conflict of the gods and the giants is a dominating theme in the Norse myths. What explanation is given for this antagonism at the opening of the myth?

2. In what way is Thor's hammer a symbol of the god's strength?

3. This myth shows a more attractive side of Loki, as Sky Traveler and as the Sly One. How does he outwit Thrym?

4. The Frost Giants are usually shown as evil and destructive. What characteristics are emphasized in this myth?

5. What do you think contributes most to the humor of this myth?

Writing About Literature

Comparing Myths

Write a short essay comparing the Norse explanation of the seasons with that of the classical myth "The Origin of the Seasons" (page 592).

Extending Your Study

Locating Information on Myths

Thor's hammer is a magic hammer, one of the gods' treasures forged by the dwarfs. Find out how it was made, what special properties it has, and how Thor uses it. Consult one of the sources listed on page 687.

Thor and
the Giant King

Retold by
OLIVIA COOLIDGE

*Magic and illusion are important elements in Norse mythology. As you read,
note how the gods themselves can be deceived by appearances.*

Thor and Loki in a goat-drawn chariot rumbled through the air faster than wind. As night was falling, they neared the great sea which surrounds the earth. "I see a small farmhouse," said Loki peering through the dusk. "Let us go there for shelter."

"We will descend to the earth," answered Thor, "lest we frighten the peasants here."

The great forms of the gods shrank to mortal size, and the goats trotted over the pasture with their chariot bumping behind.

Pine torches were already lit in the peasant's rude cottage. He himself was by the fireside whittling a plow handle. The son of the house was out feeding the oxen, but the peasant's wife sat sewing, while the daughter stirred a porridge of water and meal, which was all the supper they had.

"Welcome, strangers!" cried the master of the house. "You are in time to share our supper, poor though it is. Beds we have none, but Thjalfe,[1] my son, shall fetch you an armful of dry, fresh rushes. Wife, bring our guests some ale."

The old woman offered thin beer in rude,

1. **Thjalfe** (thē-ăl′fē): Also spelled *Thialfi.*

wooden cups. Thor and Loki sat down on the bench beside the fire. Presently above the smells of damp clothes and wood smoke which pervaded the air, Thor's nose detected the scent of the porridge which the daughter still stirred in the iron pot. His face went blank with disgust. "Is this all you have to set before us?" he inquired.

"We are no lords that we should eat meat every day," answered the peasant.

"Thjalfe," cried Thor, turning to the son, who had just come in, "take my two goats and kill them for supper. Only before you put them in the pot, bring me their skins."

Thjalfe hastened to do his bidding, and presently the whole family was seated around an appetizing meal. First, however, Thor spread the goatskins in a corner. "Cast all the bones in these skins," he commanded, "and be careful to break none." He did not notice that Thjalfe had broken a thigh bone before he threw it in the corner with the rest.

The next morning Thor tapped the bones of his goats with his hammer and made them arise again younger and stronger than ever, save that one was now lame. When Thor beheld this and knew that he had been diso-beyed, he was terribly angry. His great red eyebrows came down over his eyes, and he gripped his huge hammer with such force that his knuckles turned white. The unfortunate peasant and his family sank to their knees imploring his mercy.

"Spare at least my parents," pleaded Thjalfe, "for they are not at fault. As for me, I will go with you to be your servant if you will but grant me my life."

Thor's frown relaxed, and he nodded, appeased. "That is good," said he. "Thjalfe shall become my servant, and I will leave my goats here in his father's care until the broken leg is healed." Thus the two gods and their new servant set out on foot, Thjalfe carrying a bag of provisions. Across the great sea they traveled, to Giantland, a trackless country of great forests and barren heaths, where they wandered for a long time without seeing giant or dwelling.

At last as dark approached, they came to a strange hall with no doors or windows, but a great, irregular opening at one end. Inside, it was dark and empty, but since the wind blew chill, the three travelers were glad enough to sleep there on the floor.

They were awakened in the middle of the night by a terrible noise and an earthquake. Loki and Thjalfe felt their way into one of a row of small inner chambers which opened from the hall, and lay there huddled together, trying not to listen to the dreadful sounds. Thor took his hammer in his hands and sat in the great hall until daylight, when he crawled out to find the source of the fearsome roaring.

A man the size of a mountain was lying snoring across their path. The earth shook as his chest rose and fell. He was so huge that as he lay, Thor could only just reach up to shout in his ear.

"Hey! Hallo! What's that? What squeaked?" said the giant, sitting up and rubbing his eyes. "Well, little fellow, what do you want? Hey! Get out of my glove!" He picked up the strange-looking hall in which they had spent the night and fitted it on his hand.

"We are traveling in Giantland," shouted Thor. "We come in peace."

"Oho! Doubtless King Utgard-Loke[2] will be glad to hear that," laughed the giant. "You think a good deal of yourself, I see, but I warn you that at the king's court, I am not particularly large. Unless I am much mistaken, you will not be greatly regarded there."

"Where is the king's court?" asked Thor.

"To the North. I am going that way, but I am in no hurry. If you start out over the hill, I will overtake you and put you on the road."

Thjalfe shouldered his sack in haste, and the three companions set out as fast as their legs would carry them. The giant ate, slept, and waited until noon. Then in three strides he was up with the gods, who were toiling, hungry and thirsty, over a dusty plain. "I see I must carry your sack," said he good-naturedly. "Let me put it in mine. I will give it back this evening when the time comes to make a meal." He scooped up the sack of provisions from Thjalfe and was out of sight in three strides.

Thor looked grimly at his companions. "If we are to eat, we must catch up with this giant," said he. The three hastened over the hills until sunset. When it was almost dark, they made out the huge form in the distance and quickened their flagging steps.

"Here you are at last!" cried the giant. "I thought you were never coming. Take my sack

2. **Utgard-Loke** (o͞ot′gärd′ lō′kē): Utgard, the home of Utgard-Loke, is also known as Jotunheim.

Thor and the Mountain by J. C. Dollman.

and open it, for I have eaten and am ready for sleep." He tossed over his sack and lay down. Presently the whole place resounded with snores.

"I cannot open this sack," said Thjalfe.

"Let Thor try," said Loki wearily. "He is the strongest, and I am too hungry to wait any more."

Thor took the sack and tugged at the strings, but try as he would, he could neither loosen or break them. "Wake up!" he yelled to the giant, but his voice was drowned in the noise of snoring.

The three companions looked at one another in despair. "Wait a moment," said Thor between his teeth. "I have something with me that can make even giants pay attention." He took out his hammer and strode up to the monstrous head. Drawing himself up to his full height, he whirled his weapon and brought it down on the giant's forehead with the full strength of both arms.

"Ugh!" said the giant thickly. He put up a hand and turned over. "What tickled?" he asked sleepily. "Did a leaf fall out of the tree?"

Thor put up his hammer completely crestfallen. "We shall have to eat in the morning," said he to his companions with as much authority as he could muster. "You had better go to sleep."

"I am far too hungry," grumbled Loki. "Besides, he makes such an earthshaking noise!"

All three lay down, but while the snoring went on, sleep was impossible. The more Thor thought of his blow, the more certain he felt that he must have missed the giant altogether in the darkness. "Unlikely though that may seem," he said to himself, "it is less incredible than that he should not have felt Mjolnir, the mightiest weapon on earth."

Presently his fury at hunger and sleeplessness got the better of him, and he crept out to try again. He took care this time to find his way to a rock where he stood right over the giant and could feel his beard fluttering in the fierce wind of the monster's breath. He whirled the hammer three times, brought it down, and felt it sink into something yielding.

"What is the matter with this tree?" said the giant sitting up crossly. "There must be birds in it. They are throwing down twigs in my face." He lay down once more.

"I cannot believe it," said Thor grimly to himself. "I felt my hammer sink in. I must try again when it is light."

The gray light of morning dawned at last on a miserable trio, cold, sleepless, and hungry, regarding the giant with furious eyes. "Just let him wait until I can see him," said Thor at intervals all night long. "He will notice Mjolnir this time, I can promise."

By the faint light the giant's face, though indistinct, was clear enough. With a terrible blow Thor buried his hammer, head and handle, deep in the mighty forehead.

"Agh!" said the giant this time. "Those birds!" he complained. "I hope you slept out in the open. They keep throwing down moss in my face." He looked around. "Why, you are awake and ready to go. You are in a great hurry, though I fear King Utgard-Loke will not think you very important. Still, his citadel lies but a short distance ahead. My way now takes me elsewhere." With that he got up, lifted his sack, and was gone in three strides.

"There goes our breakfast," said Loki. "I hope Utgard-Loke is near!"

It was not long until they saw the giant king's citadel, but it was many hours before they came close to it. It towered so huge in front of them that, though they craned their necks, they could not see the top of the wall. The great, locked gate had bars the thickness of oak trees, but the spaces between them were so wide that the gods could easily creep through.

King Utgard-Loke sat in his hall amid a company of mountainous giants. "Who are you, little fellows?" asked he, looking down on the gods.

"I am Thor," answered the god, "and these are Loki and my servant. We have traveled hither to visit the king of Giantland."

"You are welcome, little gods," said the king. "I had not expected that you would be so small. Nevertheless, if you are indeed Thor and Loki, you should be able to show us some feats, for it is our custom to prove our guests before we sit down to the feast. Tell us, therefore, what you will do."

"I," said Loki immediately, "will eat more and faster than anyone in your company."

"That is a fine wager," said the king laughing. "Loge[3] here is considered a fast eater among us, but no doubt he is outclassed by you. We will put a trough of meat between you and let one start at each end. We shall soon see who is the better."

Loki was ravenous with hunger. Even Thor marveled at his appetite. Yet fast as he ate, Loge did equally well. When the two met finally in the middle of the trough, Loki had eaten all the meat, but Loge had eaten meat, bones, and the trough itself. He was therefore adjudged the winner. "Never mind," whispered Loki to Thor. "At least I have had my fill!"

"Loki is not very impressive," remarked the giant king. "What now will you show us?"

"I will run a race with anyone you care to put forward," cried Thjalfe, who was the swiftest of mankind.

"Come with us, Huge,"[4] said the giant king. "Let us go out to the race course."

Huge and Thjalfe were set to race, and though Thjalfe ran like the wind, Huge touched the goal and turned to face his rival

before Thjalfe could come up with him. The second time they ran, there was a long bolt shot between them. The third time, Huge turned back from the winning post to meet Thjalfe still only halfway along the course.

"I do not think Thjalfe has brought you much credit," said the king, "but now that we come to Thor himself, the tale is bound to be different. Tell us, great Thor, what will you do?"

Thor was angered at the mockery of the king's tone, and he was still somewhat cast down by his failure of the night before. Therefore he refrained from trials of strength and said sulkily, "I am called a deep drinker. Perhaps I can astonish you with that."

"Bring here my horn," cried the king. "My young men empty this at a draft. A poor drinker takes two, but I have never yet known one who could not empty it in three."

The horn seemed very long to Thor, but it was not wide. He put his lips down to the brim, lest he spill it, but as he drank more deeply, he tried to tilt it to his mouth. To his surprise, the horn would not move, and he was forced to bend over it. At last he straightened up exhausted and saw in astonishment that it was almost impossible to tell whether it were emptier than before.

"That is not much of a draft," said the king, "but perhaps you are saving your strength for your second one."

Thor bent down angrily, but the second time that he stopped for breath, he had only emptied the horn enough for it to be carried without spilling.

"I do not think your feats are as great as your reputation," remarked the king. "You have left a great deal for your last draft."

Thor bent down again and drank with all his might, but though this was the mightiest draft he had ever taken, he could not empty the horn. Its contents were visibly less, but that was

3. **Loge** (lōg′ē).
4. **Huge** (yoo′gē).

all. He pushed it away sullenly. "Let me try something else," said he.

"I have heard much of your strength," answered the king, "and I would gladly see something of it, yet I dare not set you a hard task, since I perceive you are not such a hero as I had thought. Will you try to lift my cat from the floor?"

A huge, gray cat sprang forward. Thor put his shoulders under its middle, but the cat only arched its back, and he could not lift it an inch. At last he got both hands under one paw, and by tugging and straining managed to raise it a little.

"Let be," said the king. "Every child among us could do that feat."

"I will wrestle with anyone and beat him," cried Thor, "for now my blood is up."

"I do not think I can ask my young men to wrestle with you," answered the king. "It seems hardly worth their while. Nevertheless, you may try a fall with my old nurse, Elle,[5] if you wish."

Thor advanced upon the old woman in anger, but though he put forth all his strength, he could not budge her. After a while she in her turn tightened her grasp. Thor's footing failed him, and after hard struggles he was forced down on one knee.

"That is enough," said the king. "It is not worth contesting with you. Sit down and take your supper, but in future let other people boast."

The three companions ate their meal in silence, and early next morning they took their leave. King Utgard-Loke himself went out to say farewell to them and to ask when they were likely to return.

"When I can avenge my disgrace," answered Thor sulkily.

Utgard-Loke laughed. "You are not disgraced, but rather covered with glory," he replied. "If you will promise to visit me no more, I will tell you how that is so."

"I will gladly promise," cried Thor, "if you can convince me of this."

"Know then," said Utgard-Loke, "that I was the giant you met in the forest, and that my size, which seemed so great to you, was but an illusion of magic. Do you see those hills over there?"

Thor nodded.

"That range of hills I brought between my forehead and your hammer as I lay pretending to sleep. See the three great notches you have made in them by blows such as I would have thought incredible, had I not beheld them."

"I knew you must notice Mjolnir," said Thor with a grim laugh.

"For two days I kept you without food and sleep," said the king. "I hoped that you would be discouraged and return to the earth; but if not, at least I might expect that when you came to my court, your strength would be somewhat lessened. Alas, it was not so!"

"I had not thought any of us had shown great prowess," replied Thor.

"You did not think so, but we who beheld you were frightened and amazed. First, Loki had an eating match with Loge, who is fire itself. No wonder Loge burned through bones and trough, and yet Loki ate as much meat as he, after all. As for Thjalfe, he was matched against Huge, who is my thought. It is clear that he had no chance, and yet the first time he ran, he came within an arm's length!"

"What of me, then?"

"The end of the horn that you drank from lay in the sea. When you come to the shore, you will see how greatly the water has ebbed. We all held our breath for a moment and thought that, though it was clearly impossible, you might actually drink the ocean dry. The cat in turn was none other than the serpent

---

5. **Elle** (ĕl′ē).

who lies stretched around the sea, his tail meeting his mouth. When you raised the monster's back to the sky, you appeared about to tear it from its resting place. When you actually lifted it a little, we feared lest the Day of Doom was upon us!"

"I have fought with the serpent before," said Thor. "I wish I had known the creature again, for this time it would not have escaped me."

"Last of all, you wrestled with Elle, who is Old Age. None may ever get the better of her!"

"I see you have thoroughly fooled us," said Thor, "but it is now my turn." With that he lifted his hammer, but the great form of the giant dissolved into wavering mist before his eyes. A mocking laugh sounded near him. Thor whirled in fury and beheld the outlines of the citadel and all that it contained grow dim. In another second they too had scattered into air.

"Remember your promise," said the voice. "Never again!"

"I suppose not," answered Thor glumly. "Nevertheless, should I meet you some time by chance, beware!"

"I will not leave that to chance," answered the voice. "Farewell."

Thor shouldered his weapon and set out with his companions across the long, dusty plains to the sea.

Reading Check

1. Why does one of Thor's goats become lame?
2. Who are Thor's companions on his journey to the land of the giants?
3. How does Thor try to awaken the sleeping giant?
4. What three "tests" does Thor fail?
5. What promise does Thor make to Utgard-Loke?

For Study and Discussion

Analyzing and Interpreting the Myth

1. A number of Norse myths tell of conflicts between the gods and the giants. This myth might be viewed as a comic battle between the two sides. In what way are the giants the winners and the gods the losers in this encounter?

2. Thor's hammer is an important weapon which he uses to keep law and order and to protect the gods from the giants. Why does it fail him in this myth?

3. How are Loki, Thjalfe, and Thor tricked by Utgard-Loke?

4. Consider the importance of magic and illusion in this myth. How do both Thor and Utgard-Loke make use of magic and illusion?

Writing About Literature

Discussing Elements of Magic and Disguise

In classical mythology, disguise and magic are important elements. In the myth of "Arachne" (page 598), Minerva visits Arachne in the guise of an old woman. In "The Reward of Baucis and Philemon" (page 602), Jupiter and Mercury assume human shape to travel the earth. In "The Origin of the Seasons" (page 592), the goddess Demeter uses magic to make the baby Demophoon immortal.

These elements are important in Norse mythology as well. In a brief essay, discuss the role of magic and disguise in the three myths read so far: "The Fenris Wolf" (page 644); "How Thor Found His Hammer" (page 648); and "Thor and the Giant King."

The Death of Balder

Retold by
EDITH HAMILTON

In Norse mythology, the most beautiful of all the gods is Balder, the god of sun-light. His twin brother, the god of darkness, is Hoder (or Hod), who is blind. Here is a tragic and ironic story about these brothers.

Balder was the most beloved of the gods, on earth as in heaven. His death was the first of the disasters which fell upon the gods. One night he was troubled with dreams which seemed to foretell some great danger to him. When his mother, Frigga, the wife of Odin, heard this she determined to protect him from the least chance of danger. She went through the world and exacted an oath from every-thing, all things with life and without life, never to do him harm. But Odin still feared. He rode down to Niflheim, the world of the dead, where he found the dwelling of Hela, or Hel, the goddess of the dead, all decked out in festal array. A wise woman told him for whom the house had been made ready:

The mead has been brewed for Balder.
The hope of the high gods has gone.

Odin knew then that Balder must die, but the other gods believed that Frigga had made him safe. They played a game accordingly which gave them much pleasure. They would try to hit Balder, to throw a stone at him or hurl a dart or shoot an arrow or strike him with a sword, but always the weapons fell short of him or rolled harmlessly away. Nothing would hurt Balder. He seemed raised above them by this strange exemption and all honored him for it, except one only, Loki. He was not a god, but the son of a giant, and wherever he came trou-ble followed. He continually involved the gods in difficulties and dangers, but he was allowed to come freely to Asgard because for some reason never explained Odin had sworn broth-erhood with him. He always hated the good, and he was jealous of Balder. He determined to do his best to find some way of injuring him. He went to Frigga disguised as a woman and entered into talk with her. Frigga told him of her journey to ensure Balder's safety and how everything had sworn to do him no harm. Ex-cept for one little shrub, she said, the mistletoe, so insignificant she had passed it by.

That was enough for Loki. He got the mis-tletoe and went with it to where the gods were amusing themselves. Hoder, Balder's brother, who was blind, sat apart. "Why not join in the game?" asked Loki. "Blind as I am?" said Hoder. "And with nothing to throw at Balder, either?" "Oh, do your part," Loki said. "Here is a twig. Throw it and I will direct your aim." Hoder took the mistletoe and hurled it with all his strength. Under Loki's guidance it sped to

The Death of Balder by Peter Cramer (1726–1782). Oil on canvas.
National Museum of Art, Copenhagen

Balder and pierced his heart. Balder fell to the ground dead.

His mother refused even then to give up hope. Frigga cried out to the gods for a volunteer to go down to Hela and try to ransom Balder. Hermod, one of her sons, offered himself. Odin gave him his horse Sleipnir[1] and he sped down to Niflheim.

The others prepared the funeral. They built a lofty pyre on a great ship, and there they laid Balder's body. Nanna, his wife, went to look at it for the last time; her heart broke and she fell to the deck dead. Her body was placed beside his. Then the pyre was kindled and the ship pushed from the shore. As it sailed out to sea, the flames leaped up and wrapped it in fire.

When Hermod reached Hela with the gods' petition, she answered that she would give Balder back if it were proved to her that all everywhere mourned for him. But if one thing or

1. **Sleipnir** (slāp′nîr): Odin's eight-legged horse.

one living creature refused to weep for him she would keep him. The gods dispatched messengers everywhere to ask all creation to shed tears so that Balder could be redeemed from death. They met with no refusal. Heaven and earth and everything therein wept willingly for the beloved god. The messengers rejoicing started back to carry the news to the gods. Then, almost at the end of their journey, they came upon a giantess—and all the sorrow of the world was turned to futility, for she refused to weep. "Only dry tears will you get from me," she said mockingly. "I had no good from Balder, nor will I give him good." So Hela kept her dead.

Loki was punished. The gods seized him and bound him in a deep cavern. Above his head a serpent was placed so that its venom fell upon his face, causing him unutterable pain. But his wife, Sigyn, came to help him. She took her place at his side and caught the venom in a cup. Even so, whenever she had to empty the cup and the poison fell on him, though but for a moment, his agony was so intense that his convulsions shook the earth.

Reading Check

1. How does Frigga try to protect Balder?
2. Why does Loki wish to harm Balder?
3. How is Balder killed?
4. Hela offers to return Balder on one condition. What is it?
5. How do the gods punish Loki?

For Study and Discussion

Analyzing and Interpreting the Myth

1. Irony occurs when events take a surprising or unexpected turn. In what way are the circumstances of Balder's death ironic?

2. In this myth Loki again appears as an evil, treacherous enemy of the gods. How does he cause the death of Balder?

3. The Norsemen believed that the fates of gods as well as human beings were determined by the goddesses of destiny and were impossible to escape. How is this fatalism reflected in the myth of Balder's death?

Writing About Literature

Analyzing a Character

Loki is the most complex figure in the Norse myths. In a paragraph analyze the aspects of his character revealed in the myths you have read. If you wish, use the first sentence of this paragraph as your thesis sentence.

The End of All Things

BARBARA LEONIE PICARD

The Norse gods and goddesses knew that their own end was foretold by the death of Balder. Here is the dramatic conclusion of their story.

The Norsemen believed that, as Odin had foreseen, the gods were doomed one day to perish, and this is how they told that it would come to pass.

First would there be three winters more terrible than any that had ever gone before, with snow and ice and biting winds and no power in the sun; and no summers to divide this cruel season and make it bearable, but only one long wintertime with never a respite. And at the end of that winter, Skoll,[1] the wolf who had ever pursued the sun, would leap upon it and devour it, and likewise would Hati[2] with the moon. And the stars which had been sparks from Muspellheim[3] would flicker and go out, so that there would be darkness in the world.

The mountains would shake and tremble, and the rocks would be torn from the earth; and the sea would wash over the fields and the forests as Iormungand,[4] the Midgard-Serpent, raised himself out of the water to advance on the land. And at that moment all chains would be sundered and all prisoners released; Fenris Wolf would break free from Gleipnir,[5] and Loki rise up from his prison under the ground. Out of fiery Muspellheim would come Surt the giant with his flaming sword; and out of her house would come Hel, with Garm[6] the hound at her side, to join with her father, Loki. And all the frost and storm giants would gather together to follow them.

From Bifrost, Heimdall, with his sharp eyes, would see them come, and know that the moment which the gods had feared was at hand, and he would blow his horn to summon them to defend the universe. Then the Aesir and the Vanir would put on their armor, and the spirits of the dead warriors that were feasting in Valhall take up their swords, and with Odin at their head in his golden helmet, ride forth to give battle to the enemies of good.

And in the mighty conflict which would follow, all the earth, all Asgard, even Niflheim itself, would shake with the clang and cry of war. Odin would fight against huge Fenris Wolf, and hard would be the struggle they would have. Thor, with Miolnir, would kill the

1. **Skoll** (skōl).
2. **Hati** (hä′tē).
3. **Muspellheim** (mŭs′pĕl-hām): the realm of fire. Muspell was guarded by a giant named Surt.
4. **Iormungand** (yôr′mŭn-gănd): the offspring of Loki and a giantess. See page 644.

5. **Gleipnir** (glāp′nîr): the silken rope forged by the dwarfs.
6. **Garm** (gärm).

Midgard-Serpent, as had ever been his wish to do; but he would not long survive his victory, for he would fall dead from the dying monster's poisonous breath.

Tyr and Hel's hound, Garm, would rush at each other and close to fight, and with his good left hand, brave Tyr would hew down the mighty beast; but in its last struggles it would tear the god to pieces, and so would they perish both.

Surt with his flaming sword would bear down on Frey, but Frey had given his own sword to Skirnir,[7] and as Loki had foretold, bitterly would he regret it, for he would have no more than the antler of a deer with which to defend himself. Yet would he not perish without a struggle.

As they had met and fought once before, over Freya's necklace,[8] so Loki and Heimdall would come together in battle once again, and Loki would laugh as he strove with his one-

7. **Skirnir** (skîr′nîr): Frey's messenger.
8. **necklace:** In one of the myths, Freya's necklace is stolen by Loki.

Odin and Fenris by Dorothy Hardy.

time friend. And in the same moment, each would strike the other a deadly blow, and both alike fall dead.

Though Odin would fight long and bravely with Fenris Wolf, in the end that mighty monster would be too strong for him, and the wolf with his gaping jaws would devour the father of the gods, and then perish at the hands of Vidar[9] the silent.

Then fire from Muspellheim would sweep over all, and thus would everything be destroyed; and it would indeed be the end of all things.

But the Norsemen believed that one day, out of the sea that had engulfed it, and out of the ruins, the world would grow again, fresh and green and beautiful; with fair people dwelling on it, born from Lifthrasir and Lif,[10] the only man and woman to escape the fire. And they believed that out of the ashes of old Asgard would arise another home for the gods, where would live in joy and peace the younger gods, who had not perished; the two sons of Odin, Vidar the silent god, and Vali[11] the son of Rind. And with them would be Magni,[12] the strong son of Thor, mightier even than his father; while out from the house of Hel, at last, would come Balder, and Hod, his brother. And everywhere would be happiness.

9. **Vidar** (vē′där): a son of Odin.
10. **Lifthrasir** (lĭft′rä-sîr); **Lif** (lĭf).
11. **Vali** (vä′lē): son of Odin and the goddess Rind.
12. **Magni** (măg′nē).

Reading Check

1. In Norse mythology, what supposedly will happen to the sun and moon on the day of doom?
2. What will happen to the monsters that the gods had imprisoned or chained?
3. Who will follow Odin into battle?
4. How will the earth be destroyed?
5. Which of the gods will be restored to life?

For Study and Discussion

Analyzing and Interpreting the Myth

1. What natural disasters will accompany the struggles of the gods and their enemies?

2. In what way is the ending of the gods a new beginning?

3. How will the earth be purified by the great destruction called Ragnarok?

Writing About Literature

Analyzing Heroic Characteristics

In the Norse myths the gods and goddesses are depicted as heroic figures, grander and larger than life. Analyze the heroic characteristics shown by the gods during their last battle.

FABLES

"Hares" from an illuminated manuscript, *Livre de la Chasse (Book of the Chase)*, by Gaston Phebus (M. 1044, f. 15v), Paris, c. 1410.

Fables are brief tales that combine common sense with entertainment. The stories are fun to read. At the same time, they teach useful lessons about human behavior. The characters in fables are usually animals who speak and act like human beings. The meaning of a fable is often summed up in its *moral*, a statement of the lesson to be learned, such as *Do not trust flatterers*.

No one knows when fables were first told. Some say that the credit for creating the fable form belongs to Aesop, a Greek who probably lived around the sixth century B.C. Not much is known about Aesop, but his fables have remained popular for centuries. You will find several examples of his work in this unit.

In addition to the fables by Aesop, you will find modern retellings of well-known fables. Two examples, in verse, will show you how poets have adapted the fable form to their own needs. In the fables by James Thurber, one of America's most humorous writers, you will see that the old form has been given a new twist.

Guidelines for Reading a Fable

1. *Read for pleasure and understanding.* Fables often teach their lessons through humor or through irony.

2. *Look for qualities or traits that the characters represent.* In many fables the characters stand for characteristics like industriousness or indolence.

3. *Determine the moral if it is not stated explicitly.*

4. *Try to restate the moral of the fable in your own words.* Ask yourself if the moral of the fable applies to modern-day situations.

Retold by
JOSEPH JACOBS

Belling the Cat

Long ago, the mice had a general council to consider what measures they could take to outwit their common enemy, the Cat. Some said this, and some said that; but at last a Young Mouse got up and said he had a proposal to make which he thought would meet the case. "You will all agree," said he, "that our chief danger consists in the sly and treacherous manner in which the enemy approaches us. Now, if we could receive some signal of her approach, we could easily escape from her. I venture, therefore, to propose that a small bell be procured and attached by a ribbon round the neck of the Cat. By this means we should always know when she was about and could easily retire while she was in the neighborhood."

This proposal met with general applause, until an Old Mouse got up and said, "That is all very well, but who is to bell the Cat?" The mice looked at one another and nobody spoke. Then the Old Mouse said:

"It is easy to propose impossible remedies."

"Lion, King of the Beasts" from an illuminated manuscript, *Der Renner (The Racer)*, by Hugo von Trimberg (M. 763, f. 29v), Austria, fifteenth century.
The Pierpont Morgan Library

The Town Mouse and the Country Mouse

Now you must know that a Town Mouse once upon a time went on a visit to his cousin in the country. He was rough and ready, this cousin, but he loved his town friend and made him heartily welcome. Beans and bacon, cheese and bread, were all he had to offer, but he offered them freely.

The Town Mouse rather turned up his long nose at this country fare, and said: "I cannot understand, Cousin, how you can put up with such poor food as this, but of course you cannot expect anything better in the country; come you with me and I will show you how to live. When you have been in town a week you will wonder how you could ever have stood a country life."

No sooner said than done: the two mice set off for the town and arrived at the Town Mouse's residence late at night. "You will want some refreshment after our long journey," said the polite Town Mouse, and took his friend into the grand dining room. There they found the remains of a fine feast, and soon the two mice were eating up jellies and cakes and all that was nice. Suddenly they heard growling and barking.

"What is that?" said the Country Mouse.

"It is only the dogs of the house," answered the other.

"Only!" said the Country Mouse. "I do not like that music at my dinner."

Just at that moment the door flew open, in came two huge mastiffs,[1] and the two mice had to scamper down and run off. "Goodbye, Cousin," said the Country Mouse.

"What! going so soon?" said the other.

"Yes," he replied:

"Better beans and bacon in peace than cakes and ale in fear."

1. **mastiffs:** a breed of dogs used for hunting and as watchdogs.

"The Town Rat and the Country Rat," an illustration by Gustave Doré (1832–1883) for the *Fables of La Fontaine*, c. 1860.

The Ant and the Grasshopper

In a field one summer's day a Grasshopper was hopping about, chirping and singing to its heart's content. An Ant passed by, bearing along with great toil an ear of corn he was taking to the nest.

"Why not come and chat with me," said the Grasshopper, "instead of toiling and moiling in that way?"

"I am helping to lay up food for the winter," said the Ant, "and recommend you to do the same."

"Why bother about winter?" said the Grasshopper; "we have got plenty of food at present."

But the Ant went on its way and continued its toil. When the winter came the Grasshopper had no food, and found itself dying of hunger, while it saw the ants distributing every day corn and grain from the stores they had collected in the summer. Then the Grasshopper knew:

It is best to prepare for the days of necessity.

The Ant and the Grasshopper by Christopher Sanders. Watercolor.

The Fox and the Crow

A Fox once saw a Crow fly off with a piece of cheese in its beak and settle on a branch of a tree. "That's for me, as I am a Fox," said Master Reynard, and he walked up to the foot of the tree.

"Good day, Mistress Crow," he cried. "How well you are looking today: how glossy your feathers; how bright your eye. I feel sure your voice must surpass that of other birds, just as your figure does. Let me hear but one song from you, that I may greet you as the Queen of Birds."

The Crow lifted up her head and began to caw her best, but the moment she opened her mouth, the piece of cheese fell to the ground, only to be snapped up by Master Fox.

"That will do," said he. "That was all I wanted. In exchange for your cheese I will give you a piece of advice for the future:

" *'Do not trust flatterers.'* "

For Study and Discussion

Analyzing and Interpreting the Fables

1. The animals in a fable often show contrasting traits of character. For example, in "Belling the Cat," the Young Mouse is inexperienced and foolish; the Old Mouse is experienced and wise. What contrasts in character do you find in the other fables?

2. It is possible to state the moral of a fable in different ways. The moral of "The Town Mouse and the Country Mouse" might be stated in this way: *It is better to live humbly in peace than to live luxuriously in fear.* Restate the moral of "Belling the Cat" in your own words.

3. A fable expresses a general truth or gives practical advice about life and behavior. To what modern-day situations could you apply the moral of "The Ant and the Grasshopper"?

4a. What kinds of behavior do these fables support or praise?   **b.** What kinds of behavior do they ridicule or condemn?

5. Aesop's fables were first told more than two thousand years ago, yet we continue to enjoy them today. Why do you think these fables still appeal to readers?

Recognizing Allusions

In one of Aesop's fables, there is a race between a tortoise and a hare. The hare, certain of an easy victory, becomes overconfident. Midway through the race, he decides to take a rest. As a result, he loses the race to the tortoise, who slowly but surely overtakes him. The fable makes this point: *Slow and steady wins the race*.

A number of expressions that we use in speaking and writing are **allusions**, or references, to Aesop's fables. People often use the moral *Slow and steady wins the race* when they wish to point out the rewards of perseverance and effort. In the following sentence, what kind of "race" has been run?

Everyone was surprised when Danny won the scholarship, but Danny has always believed that *slow and steady wins the race*.

Each italicized expression in the sentences below refers to a fable by Aesop. Which of these expressions have you read or heard before?

Whenever it comes to dividing a cake, Sylvia always takes the *lion's share*.

Reynaldo says that he wouldn't have attended the party even if he had been invited, but I think it's a case of *sour grapes*.

To find the meanings of the italicized expressions, look them up in a dictionary. If your library has a collection of Aesop's fables, locate "The Lion's Share" and "The Fox and the Grapes," and tell the fables to the class.

Fables in Verse

The Blind Men and the Elephant

JOHN GODFREY SAXE

This fable comes from India. Like most fables, it points up a human weakness.
Are these men blind in more than one way?

It was six men of Indostan°
　To learning much inclined,
Who went to see the Elephant
　(Though all of them were blind),
That each by observation　　　　　　5
　Might satisfy his mind.

The *First* approached the Elephant,
　And happening to fall
Against his broad and sturdy side,
　At once began to bawl:　　　　　　10
"God bless me! but the Elephant
　Is very like a wall!"

The *Second*, feeling of the tusk,
　Cried, "Ho! what have we here
So very round and smooth and sharp?　15
　To me 'tis mighty clear
This wonder of an Elephant
　Is very like a spear!"

The *Third* approached the animal,
　And happening to take　　　　　　20
The squirming trunk within his hands,
　Thus boldly up and spake:
"I see," quoth he, "the Elephant
　Is very like a snake!"

The *Fourth* reached out an eager hand,　25
　And felt about the knee.
"What most this wondrous beast is like
　Is mighty plain," quoth he;
"'Tis clear enough the Elephant
　Is very like a tree!"　　　　　　30

The *Fifth*, who chanced to touch the ear,
　Said: "E'en the blindest man
Can tell what this resembles most;
　Deny the fact who can,
This marvel of an Elephant　　　　　35
　Is very like a fan!"

1. **Indostan** (ĭn'dō-stăn'): Hindustan, an old name for India.

The *Sixth* no sooner had begun
   About the beast to grope,
Than, seizing on the swinging tail
   That fell within his scope,   40
"I see," quoth he, "the Elephant
   Is very like a rope!"

And so these men of Indostan
   Disputed loud and long,
Each in his own opinion   45
   Exceeding stiff and strong,
Though each was partly in the right,
   And all were in the wrong!

The Blind Men and the Elephant (1817) by Katsushika Hokusai (1760–1849).
Japanese woodblock print.

The Boy and the Wolf

A Fable of Aesop
adapted by

<u>LOUIS UNTERMEYER</u>

A boy employed to guard the sheep
Despised his work. He liked to sleep.
And when a lamb was lost, he'd shout,
"Wolf! Wolf! The wolves are all about!"

The neighbors searched from noon till
    nine,   5
But of the beast there was no sign,
Yet "Wolf!" he cried next morning
    when
The villagers came out again.

One evening around six o'clock
A real wolf fell upon the flock.   10
"Wolf!" yelled the boy. "A wolf
    indeed!"
But no one paid him any heed.

Although he screamed to wake the
    dead,
"He's fooled us every time," they said,
And let the hungry wolf enjoy   15
His feast of mutton, lamb—and boy.

The moral's this: The man who's wise
Does not defend himself with lies.
Liars are not believed, forsooth,°
Even when liars tell the truth.   20

19. **forsooth:** indeed.

Aesop by Diego Velázquez (1599–1660).
Oil on canvas.

For Study and Discussion

Analyzing and Interpreting the Poems

The Blind Men and the Elephant

1. Each blind man makes the same mistake in deciding what the Elephant is like. What is the mistake?

2. How would you state the moral of "The Blind Men and the Elephant"?

The Boy and the Wolf

3a. Why did the boy cry "Wolf" every time a lamb was lost?   **b.** "To cry wolf" has become a common expression in our language. What does it mean?

4. To what modern-day situations could you apply the moral of this fable?

Literary Elements

Understanding Proverbs

The moral of a fable generally gives some practical advice or warning that is intended to guide our behavior. A similar kind of common sense is contained in the sayings known as **proverbs**.

Proverbs are brief and to the point. They are often expressed in a catchy way that makes them easy to remember:

> A fool and his money are soon parted.
> Haste makes waste.
> He who laughs last laughs best.
> Better late than never.
> Where there's a will, there's a way.

Some proverbs are metaphors. "A stitch in time saves nine" tells us that we can prevent a tear or a hole from growing by catching it early with a single stitch. By extension, the proverb means that we can avoid some future difficulty or problem by acting early enough to prevent it.

Explain these proverbs in your own words.

> The early bird catches the worm.
> A rolling stone gathers no moss.

Collect some proverbs that you like. Ask the older members of your family if they remember sayings or proverbs they heard when they were children.

Writing About Literature

Analyzing the Moral of a Fable

In "The Blind Men and the Elephant," Saxe uses the men who are physically blind to point up another kind of blindness in human nature. How would you describe this kind of blindness? Why do the blind men jump to the wrong conclusions? How could they have avoided their error? In a short paper, analyze the moral of the fable.

Fables by James Thurber

In these modern fables, Thurber enjoys giving a new twist to the conventional form of the fable.

The Fairly Intelligent Fly

A large spider in an old house built a beautiful web in which to catch flies. Every time a fly landed on the web and was entangled in it the spider devoured him, so that when another fly came along he would think the web was a safe and quiet place in which to rest. One day a fairly intelligent fly buzzed around above the web so long without lighting that the spider appeared and said, "Come on down." But the fly was too clever for him and said, "I never light where I don't see other flies and I don't see any other flies in your house." So he flew away until he came to a place where there were a great many other flies. He was about to settle down among them when a bee buzzed up and said, "Hold it, stupid, that's flypaper. All those flies are trapped." "Don't be silly," said the fly, "they're dancing." So he settled down and became stuck to the flypaper with all the other flies.

Moral: There is no safety in numbers, or in anything else.

From *Fables for Our Time* by James Thurber, © 1940 by James Thurber, © 1968 Helen Thurber. Harper & Row, New York

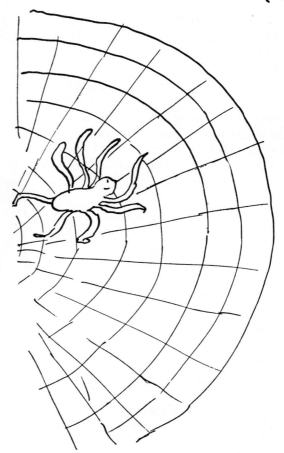

The Fairly Intelligent Fly   **679**

What Happened to Charles

A farm horse named Charles was led to town one day by his owner, to be shod. He would have been shod and brought back home without incident if it hadn't been for Eva, a duck, who was always hanging about the kitchen door of the farmhouse, eavesdropping, and never got anything quite right. Her farmmates said of her that she had two mouths but only one ear.

On the day that Charles was led away to the smithy, Eva went quacking about the farm, excitedly telling the other animals that Charles had been taken to town to be shot.

"They're executing an innocent horse!" cried Eva. "He's a hero! He's a martyr! He died to make us free!"

"He was the greatest horse in the world," sobbed a sentimental hen.

"He just seemed like old Charley to me," said a realistic cow. "Let's not get into a moony mood."

"He was wonderful!" cried a gullible goose.

"What did he ever do?" asked a goat.

Eva, who was as inventive as she was inaccurate, turned on her lively imagination. "It was butchers who led him off to be shot!" she

From *Further Fables for Our Time* by James Thurber, Simon and Schuster, New York, © 1956 by James Thurber, © 1987 by Helen Thurber.

shrieked. "They would have cut our throats while we slept if it hadn't been for Charles!"

"I didn't see any butchers, and I can see a burnt-out firefly on a moonless night," said a barn owl. "I didn't hear any butchers, and I can hear a mouse walk across moss."

"We must build a memorial to Charles the Great, who saved our lives," quacked Eva. And all the birds and beasts in the barnyard except the wise owl, the skeptical goat, and the realistic cow set about building a memorial.

Just then the farmer appeared in the lane, leading Charles, whose new shoes glinted in the sunlight.

It was lucky that Charles was not alone, for the memorial-builders might have set upon him with clubs and stones for replacing their hero with just plain old Charley. It was lucky, too, that they could not reach the barn owl, who quickly perched upon the weather vane of the barn, for none is so exasperating as he who is right. The sentimental hen and the gullible goose were the ones who finally called attention to the true culprit—Eva, the one-eared duck with two mouths. The others set upon her and tarred and unfeathered her, for none is more unpopular than the bearer of sad tidings that turn out to be false.

Moral: Get it right or let it alone. The conclusion you jump to may be your own.

The Fox and the Crow

A crow, perched in a tree with a piece of cheese in his beak, attracted the eye and nose of a fox. "If you can sing as prettily as you sit," said the fox, "then you are the prettiest singer within my scent and sight." The fox had read somewhere, and somewhere, and somewhere else, that praising the voice of a crow with a cheese in his beak would make him drop the cheese and sing. But this is not what happened to this particular crow in this particular case.

"They say you are sly and they say you are crazy," said the crow, having carefully removed the cheese from his beak with the claws of one foot, "but you must be nearsighted as well. Warblers wear gay hats and colored jackets and bright vests, and they are a dollar a hundred. I wear black and I am unique." He began nibbling the cheese, dropping not a single crumb.

"I am sure you are," said the fox, who was neither crazy nor nearsighted, but sly. "I recognize you, now that I look more closely, as the most famed and talented of all birds, and I fain would hear you tell about yourself, but I am hungry and must go."

"Tarry awhile," said the crow quickly, "and

share my lunch with me." Whereupon he tossed the cunning fox the lion's share of the cheese and began to tell about himself. "A ship that sails without a crow's-nest sails to doom," he said. "Bars may come and bars may go, but crowbars last forever. I am the pioneer of flight, I am the map maker. Last, but never least, my flight is known to scientists and engineers, geometrists and scholars, as the shortest distance between two points.[1] Any two points," he concluded arrogantly.

1. **my flight . . . two points:** A crow is said to fly in a straight line, which is the shortest distance between two points.

"Oh, every two points, I am sure," said the fox. "And thank you for the lion's share of what I know you could not spare." And with this he trotted away into the woods, his appetite appeased, leaving the hungry crow perched forlornly in the tree.

Moral: 'Twas true in Aesop's time, and La Fontaine's,[2] and now, no one else can praise thee quite so well as thou.

2. **La Fontaine** (lə fŏn-tān′): Jean la Fontaine, a seventeenth-century French poet who wrote verse fables that criticized the French court.

For Study and Discussion

Analyzing and Interpreting the Fables

The Fairly Intelligent Fly

1. The familiar moral Thurber alludes to in this fable is *There is safety in numbers.* **a.** What happens to the fly when he puts his faith in this old moral? **b.** Explain Thurber's new moral in your own words.

2a. Why do you think the fly is described as "fairly intelligent"? **b.** How might the fly have behaved if he had been "very intelligent"?

What Happened to Charles

3. What mistake does Eva, the duck, make after hearing the word *shod*?

4. In Aesop's fables the animals often reveal contrasting traits of character. **a.** Which characters in Thurber's fable are shown to be foolish or hasty? **b.** Which are shown to be wise or cautious?

5. The moral is not the only message in this fable. **a.** Find two statements that are direct comments on human behavior. **b.** What kinds of behavior is Thurber criticizing in this fable?

The Fox and the Crow

6. You have read two versions of "The Fox and the Crow," Aesop's version on page 673 and Thurber's version on page 682. Both fables have a clever fox and a vain crow. How is Thurber's crow different in character from Aesop's?

7. In Aesop's fable the fox uses flattery and succeeds in outwitting the crow. Thurber's fox also uses flattery to trick the crow. What difference is there in his approach?

8. Thurber's crow attaches a great deal of importance to words that carry his name. **a.** How do you think *crow's-nest* got its name? **b.** What does a crow have to do with a *crowbar*?

9. Compare the morals in the fables by Aesop and Thurber. What new advice does Thurber offer on the subject of flattery?

Creative Writing

Writing a Fable

A fable, as you have seen, has certain characteristics. It is brief, it has a few characters, and it teaches some lesson about human behavior. It generally ends with a moral.

Here are some common situations in fables:

A person or animal is the cause of his or her own misfortune.

A clever person or animal outwits a foolish one.

A strong person or animal preys upon a weaker one.

Write a fable of your own in prose or verse based on one of these situations. Use a moral that appears in this unit, some common saying, or an original moral of your own.

Extending Your Study

1. What moral can you think of for this Eskimo fable?

The Owl and the Two Rabbits

An Owl spotted two Rabbits playing close together and seized them, one clutched in each foot. But they were too strong for him and ran away, sliding the Owl along the ice. The Owl's wife shouted to him, "Let one of them go and kill the other!"

But he replied, "The moon will soon disappear, and then we shall be hungry. We need both of them."

The Rabbits ran on; and when they came to a boulder, one ran to the right side of it, the other to the left. The Owl did not let go quick enough, and was torn in two.

2. Collect cartoons or comic strips in which animals behave like people. What characteristics do these drawings share with fables?

DEVELOPING SKILLS
IN CRITICAL THINKING

Using Methods of Comparison and Contrast

In this unit, you have seen that a fable from India, "The Blind Men and the Elephant," has several elements in common with the fables of Aesop, who lived in Greece. Seeing relationships in literary works enhances your enjoyment and understanding of what you read.

Here is an American Indian myth about the origin of corn. As you read this myth, keep in mind the classical myths and Norse myths you read in earlier units.

The Origin of Corn

A long time ago, when Indians were first made, there lived one alone, far, far from any others. He knew not of fire, and subsisted on roots, barks, and nuts. This Indian became very lonesome for company. He grew tired of digging roots, lost his appetite, and for several days lay dreaming in the sunshine; when he awoke he saw something standing near, at which, at first, he was very much frightened. But when it spoke, his heart was glad, for it was a beautiful woman with long *light* hair, very unlike any Indian. He asked her to come to him, but she would not, and if he tried to approach her she seemed to go farther away; he sang to her of his loneliness and besought her not to leave him; at last she told him, if he would do just as she should say, he would always have her with him. He promised that he would.

She led him to where there was some very dry grass, told him to get two very dry sticks, rub them together quickly, holding them in the grass. Soon a spark flew out; the grass caught it, and quick as an arrow the ground was burned over. Then she said, "When the sun sets, take me by the hair and drag me over the burned ground." He did not like to do this, but she told him that wherever he dragged her something like grass would spring up, and he would see her hair coming from between the leaves; then the seeds would be ready for his use. He did as she said, and to this day, when they see the silk (hair) on the cornstalk, the Indians know she has not forgotten them.

1. What natural phenomenon does this myth attempt to explain? Does this recall Greek myths you have read? Are the attitudes toward nature the same or are they different?
2. What part is played by magic or the supernatural in this myth? What similar magical events can you recall in other myths?
3. Are there important differences between this myth and the other myths you have read?

PRACTICE IN
READING AND WRITING

Expressing Opinions

Persuasive writing aims to convince the reader to agree with an opinion or to take some specific action. In order to be effective, persuasive writing has to present reasons and supply evidence. Evidence can be of different kinds: it can consist of facts, statistics, or examples.

Here is a paragraph in which Edith Hamilton expresses an opinion about Norse mythology. What reasons does she give for her opinion?

> The world of Norse mythology is a strange world. Asgard, the home of the gods, is unlike any other heaven men have dreamed of. No radiancy of joy is in it, no assurance of bliss. It is a grave and solemn place, over which hangs the threat of an inevitable doom. The gods know that a day will come when they will be destroyed. Sometime they will meet their enemies and go down beneath them to defeat and death. Asgard will fall in ruins. The cause the forces of good are fighting to defend against the forces of evil is hopeless. Nevertheless, the gods will fight for it to the end.

Suggestions for Writing

Prewriting
- Choose a topic for discussion.
- Write a topic sentence that states your opinion.
- Note at least three reasons that explain your opinion.
- Arrange the reasons and evidence in order.

Writing
- Use your notes to write a draft of your essay.
- Use transitional expressions to link your ideas.

Evaluating, Revising, and Proofreading
- Does the topic sentence state your opinion clearly and concisely?
- Is there adequate development of the topic sentence?
- Are the reasons arranged in logical order?
- Are there transitions between ideas?
- Have you checked for errors in grammar, spelling, punctuation, and capitalization before preparing your final copy?

For Further Reading

Norse Mythology

Colum, Padraic, *The Children of Odin: The Book of Northern Myths* (Macmillan, 1984)
> A well-known collection of myths retold by an Irish poet.

Coolidge, Olivia E., *Legends of the North* (Houghton Mifflin, 1951)
> This book is divided into four parts: "Tales of the Northern Gods," "The Last of the Volsungs," "Tales of the Northern Heroes," and "Tales from the Sagas." Included are the stories of Sigurd, the Dragon Slayer; the Valkyrie; and Beowulf.

Crossley-Holland, Kevin, *The Norse Myths* (Pantheon Books, 1980)
> In addition to a retelling of thirty-two Norse myths, this book contains a valuable introduction exploring the sources of the myths and their structure.

Green, Roger Lancelyn, *Myths of the Norsemen* (Puffin Books, 1960; paperback, Penguin, 1970)
> The author presents the myths as a single, connected narrative.

Picard, Barbara Leonie, *Tales of the Norse Gods and Heroes* (Oxford University Press, 1953)
> Divided into two parts, this collection deals with stories of the Norse gods and tales of the great Norse heroes.

Goodrich, Norma Lorre, *Medieval Myths* (New American Library, 1961)
> Here are seven stories about different national heroes and heroines. Represented are myths from Scandinavia, Wales, France, Austria, Russia, and Spain.

Fables

Aesop, *The Fables of Aesop,* retold by Joseph Jacobs (Smith Publishers, 1979)
> Here are more than eighty of Aesop's best fables.

Gaer, Joseph, *Fables of India* (Little, Brown, 1955)
> Aesop may have based many of his fables on the fables of India. Here is a rich and varied sample of these ancient stories.

Thurber, James, *Fables for Our Time* (Paperback, Harper & Row, 1983)
> Included in this collection are "The Little Girl and the Wolf" and "The Scotty Who Knew Too Much." A second collection of fables, *Further Fables for Our Time* (Simon and Schuster, 1956), includes "The Tiger Who Would Be King" and "The Kingfisher and the Phoebe."

WRITING ABOUT LITERATURE

Developing Skills in Critical Thinking

Many of the compositions you will be asked to write in English class will be about the literature you read. The writing may be in response to an examination question, a homework assignment, or a research project. At times you may be given a topic to work on; at other times you may have to choose your own subject for a paper.

In writing about literature, you generally focus on some aspect of a work. For example, you may give your impression of a character in a short story; you may discuss the suspense that is developed in a play; you may explain the main idea of a poem. Such writing assignments are an important part of literary study, which aims at greater understanding and appreciation of the works you read.

Writing about a literary work is a way of getting to know it better. Before you write a composition about a story, a poem, or a play, you must study the selection carefully. You must sort out your thoughts and reach conclusions. In putting your thoughts down on paper, you become more fully involved with the work.

Throughout your studies you will become familiar with a great many elements that are useful in analyzing literary works. When you refer to the sequence of events in a short story or play, for instance, you may use such terms as *plot, climax,* and *resolution* in describing the action. You may concern yourself with the *conflict,* or struggle, that a *character* faces. In discussing the meaning of a poem, you may refer to its *imagery* or *figurative language.* These words are part of a common vocabulary used in writing about literature. You can assume that your readers will understand what you mean when you write about such elements. (See the *Guide to Literary Terms and Techniques,* page 706.)

The material on the following pages offers help in planning and writing papers about literature. Here you will find suggestions for answering examination questions, choosing topics, gathering evidence, organizing essays, and writing, evaluating, and revising papers. Also included are several model essays.

The Writing Process

We often refer to writing an essay as a *process,* which consists of six key stages: **prewriting, writing, evaluating, revising, proofreading,** and **making a final copy.** In this process, much of the important work—the thinking and planning—comes before writing the first draft.

In the **prewriting** stage, the writer must decide what to say and how to say it. Prewriting includes choosing a topic, gathering ideas and organizing them into a plan, and developing a *thesis*—the main idea for the paper. In the **writing** stage, the writer uses the plan to write a first draft of the essay. In the **evaluating** stage, the writer judges the first draft to identify strengths and weaknesses in content, organization, and style. **Revising,** the fourth stage, involves making changes to correct the weaknesses in the draft. The writer can revise by adding, cutting, reordering, or replacing words. In the **proofreading** stage, the writer reads the draft to locate and correct any mistakes in grammar, usage, and mechanics. The last stage, **making a final copy,** involves preparing a clean copy and then proofreading it to catch any mistakes made in copying.

The stages of the writing process are related. For this reason, there is usually a "back and forth" movement among the stages. Few writers finish one stage completely before they move on to the next one. At the same time, few writers move in a straight line from one stage to the next. For example, the writer might think up new ideas as he or she is writing a first draft. This would probably require going "back" to prewriting to restate the thesis or to locate new supporting evidence. This movement among the stages of the writing process is a natural part of writing—for all writers.

The amount of time devoted to each stage will vary with individual assignments. During a classroom examination, you will have limited time to plan your essay and to proofread your paper. For a term paper, you may have weeks or months to prepare your essay.

On the following pages the steps in this process are illustrated through the development of several model essays.

Answering Examination Questions

Often you may be asked to show your understanding of a literary work or topic by writing a short essay in class. Usually, your teacher will give you a specific question to answer. How well you do will depend not only on how carefully you have read and mastered the material, but on how carefully you read and interpret the essay question.

Before you begin to write, be sure you understand what the question calls for. If a question requires that you give three reasons for a character's actions, and you supply only two, your answer will be incomplete. If the question asks you to *contrast* two settings, be sure that you point out their differences, not their similarities. Don't use essays or short stories if the question calls for poetry. Always take some time to read the essay question carefully in order to determine how it should be answered.

Remember that you are expected to demonstrate specific knowledge of the literature. Any general statement should be supported by evidence. If you wish to show that a character changes, for example, you should refer to specific actions, dialogue, thoughts and feelings, or direct comments by the author, in order to illustrate your point. If you are allowed to use your textbook during the examination, you may occasionally quote short passages or refer to a specific page in order to provide supporting evidence.

At the start, it may be helpful to jot down some notes to guide you in writing your essay. If you have four main points to make, you may then decide what the most effective order of presentation will be. You might build up to your strongest point, or you might present your points to develop a striking contrast. Aim for a logical organization.

Also remember that length alone is not satisfactory. Your answer must be clearly related to the question, and it must be presented in acceptable, correct English. Always take some time to proofread your paper.

The key word in examination questions is the *verb*. Let us look briefly at some common instructions used in examinations.

ANALYSIS A question may ask you to *analyze* some aspect of a literary work. When you analyze something, you take it apart to see how each part works. In literary analysis you generally focus on some limited aspect of a work in order to better understand and appreciate the work as a whole. For example, you might analyze the technique of suspense in

"The Tiger's Heart" (page 170); you might analyze the role of moonlight in "The Highwayman" (page 468); you might analyze Thurber's use of exaggeration in "The Night the Bed Fell" (page 133).

COMPARISON CONTRAST

A question may ask that you *compare* (or *contrast*) two characters, two settings, two ideas. When you *compare*, you point out likenesses; when you *contrast*, you point out differences. Sometimes you will be asked to *compare and contrast*. In that event, you will be expected to deal with similarities and differences. You might, for instance, compare and contrast the characters of Emily Vanderpool and Lottie Jump in "Bad Characters" (page 52). You might compare and contrast two versions of a fable, "The Fox and the Crow," by Aesop (page 673), and by Thurber (page 682). Sometimes, the word *compare* is used to include both comparison and contrast. Always check with your teacher to make sure that you understand how the term *compare* is being used.

DEFINITION

A question may ask you to *define* a literary term—to answer the question "What is it?" To define a term, first place it in a large group. Then discuss the features or characteristics that make it different from other members of the same group. You should also include a specific example to illustrate the term. For example, if asked to define the term *irony*, you would first say it is an element of literature (large group) in which there is a contrast between what is expected to happen and what actually happens (feature). For example, in the story "You Can't Take It with You" (page 264), Uncle Basil's relatives expect him to leave his money behind. Instead he actually takes it with him by using it to line his coffin.

DESCRIPTION

If a question asks you to *describe* a setting or a character, you are expected to give a picture in words. In describing a setting, include not only details that establish the historical period and locale, but also details that evoke a mood. In describing a character, you should deal with methods of direct and indirect characterization (see pages 707–708). You might describe the scene in "Stopping by Woods on a Snowy Evening" (page 455); you might describe each of the Christmas spirits in "A Christmas Carol" (page 276).

DISCUSSION

The word *discuss* in a question is much more general than the other words we've looked at. When you are asked to discuss something, you are expected to examine it in detail. If you are asked to discuss the images in a poem, for example, you must deal with all major images; if asked to discuss the use of dialect in a story or poem, you must be sure to cover all significant examples. Suppose your assignment asked you to discuss Charles Dickens' characterization of Ebenezer Scrooge in "A Christmas Carol" (page 276). In your answer you would have to examine and provide examples of Dickens' methods of indirect and direct characterization.

EVALUATION   If a question asks you to *evaluate* a literary work, you are expected to show whether an author has achieved his or her purpose. To evaluate, you must apply standards of judgment that relate to both literary content and form. For example, you might be asked to evaluate how well Kipling has succeeded in giving distinctive personalities to his characters in "Rikki-tikki-tavi" (page 229) or how effectively Frost uses rhyme scheme to reinforce meaning in "Stopping by Woods on a Snowy Evening" (page 455).

EXPLANATION   A question may ask you to *explain* something. When you explain, you give reasons for something being the way it is. You make clear a character's actions, or you show how something has come about. For example, you might explain what happens to the *Hesperus* and its crew (page 164); you might explain Holmes's plan for recovering the Mazarin Stone (page 318).

ILLUSTRATION   The word *illustrate, demonstrate,* or *show* asks that you provide examples to support a point. You might be asked to give examples of musical devices in "Annabel Lee" (page 460). You might be asked to illustrate peculiarities of Jean Kerr's pets in "Dogs That Have Known Me" (page 393). You might be asked to select and demonstrate instances of natural dialogue in *The Governess* (page 343).

INTERPRETATION   The word *interpret* in a question asks that you give the meaning or significance of something. You might, for example, be asked to interpret "The Listeners" (page 457), a poem that is famous for its mysterious meaning.

At times it will be useful to combine approaches. In discussing a subject, you may draw upon illustration, explanation, or analysis. In comparing or contrasting two works, you may rely on description or interpretation. However, an examination question generally will have a central purpose, and you should focus on this purpose in preparing your answer.

Using the Writing Process to Answer an Essay Question

The following suggestions show how you can use the writing process to answer an essay examination question efficiently. As you write, plan your time—decide how long you can work on each stage and stick to your schedule.

PREWRITING In an essay examination, the question itself gives a narrow topic. Its key verb also suggests a way to answer the question. Several prewriting steps remain:

1. *Write a thesis statement.* A thesis statement gives the main idea of your essay. It should appear at the beginning of your essay.

2. *Develop points to support, or explain, the thesis.* The main idea should be supported by at least two main points. In a short essay all the points may be discussed in a single paragraph. In a longer essay each point may be discussed in a separate paragraph. Each point must clearly support the main idea of the essay.

3. *Locate supporting evidence from the literary work(s).* Evidence can include specific details, direct quotations, incidents, or images. This evidence should support or explain each main point you are discussing.

4. *Organize the main points and evidence.* You should arrange your ideas and details into a logical order—one that your reader can follow easily. By arranging your ideas, you will develop a plan that you can use to write your essay. This plan should include an introduction, a body, and a conclusion for your essay.

WRITING Write your essay, following the plan you made in prewriting. In the introduction, state the title of the literary work and your thesis. In the body, present the main points and the supporting evidence. In the conclusion, state your thesis again or summarize your main points. Be sure to use language that is serious enough for your purpose (to convey ideas) and for your audience (your teacher, in most cases). Also use transitional expressions (words or phrases that connect ideas, such as *first, then,* and *finally*) to make it clear how ideas are related.

EVALUATING Quickly evaluate, or judge, your essay by answering the following questions:

Purpose	1. Have I answered the specific question given?
Introduction	2. Have I included a thesis statement that expresses the main idea of my essay?
Body	3. Have I included at least two main points that support the thesis statement?
	4. Have I included evidence from the literary work to support each main point?
	5. Is the order of ideas clear and logical?
Conclusion	6. Have I included a conclusion that states the main idea again or that summarizes the main points?

REVISING   Using your evaluation, improve your essay by *adding, cutting, reordering,* or *replacing* words.

PROOFREADING   Read your essay to locate and correct any mistakes in grammar, usage, and mechanics. You can make a clean copy of your essay if your teacher says you have time to do so. If so, proofread again to catch any mistakes made in copying.

Sample Examination Questions and Answers

On the following pages you will find some sample examination questions and answers for study and discussion. Note that the assignments (shown in italics) may be phrased as direct questions or as essay topics.

I

QUESTION   *The boy in Ernest Hemingway's story "A Day's Wait" (page 242) mistakenly believes that he is going to die. Why is he confused? Explain in a single paragraph.*

DEVELOPING AN ANSWER   This question calls for reasons. Before writing, jot down some notes to guide you:

> The boy is familiar with the Celsius scale.
> The doctor uses a Fahrenheit thermometer.
> Boy has a temperature of 102°.
> On the Celsius thermometer, a temperature of 44° would be fatal.

In the opening sentence of your answer, state your *thesis,* your main point, wording it in such a way that you restate the key words of the question. Here is a model paragraph based on the writer's notes.

The boy in Hemingway's "A Day's Wait" is confused about two systems of temperature measurement. Because he has gone to school in France, he is familiar with the Celsius scale of temperature. The normal temperature on the Celsius scale is 37°. A temperature as high as 44° would be fatal. The doctor who examines the boy uses a Fahrenheit thermometer on which the normal reading is 98.6°. The boy thinks that the doctor has used a Celsius thermometer. When he learns that his temperature is 102°, he assumes he is going to die.

Length: 93 words

II

QUESTION

What is the role of the narrator in Pearl Buck's The Big Wave *(page 357)? In your analysis, refer to specific passages in the play.*

**DEVELOPING
AN ANSWER**

Begin by reviewing each act in the play. Jot down notes that indicate what the narrator does in each act. You can refer to these notes when you write your answer to the question.

**WRITING AN
ANSWER**

Here is a model answer that includes a summary of the narrator's role and a discussion of his importance in each act of the play.

Main Idea

The narrator in Pearl Buck's *The Big Wave* helps us to understand and appreciate the meaning of the characters' experiences. Like the omniscient ("all-knowing") narrator of a short story or novel, he fills us in on the background of events, provides a bridge between different episodes of the play, and comments on the action. Although he does not play an active role in the drama, he knows what every character does and thinks.

Present evidence in
a logical sequence.

In Act One, the narrator introduces us to Kino and his family. He tells us how Kino and his ancestors have lived in the Japanese fishing village. At the opening of Act Two, he describes life in the village. He tells us how the villagers spend their days at work and at play. He even describes the foods that they eat. In Acts Three and Four, the narrator comments on the events of the play, noting how the big wave brought change to the village and its inhabitants. In the final act, the narrator condenses the events of eight years so that we see a new generation of villagers confronting life.

Length: 185 words

III

QUESTION

What makes T. J. a natural leader of the boys in "Antaeus" (page 187)? Discuss his qualities of leadership, using specific references to the story.

DEVELOPING AN ANSWER

Begin by skimming the story to locate examples of T. J.'s leadership abilities. Take notes as you read, jotting down the page number of each piece of evidence you locate. Here is a list of prewriting notes that one writer developed.

Notes

T. J. had a slow, gentle voice, but he was no sissy (page 187).
He was not insecure with strangers; he reserved his opinions (page 187).
He was not ashamed of being different (page 188).
He was self-assured, not easily bullied (page 188).
He had pride in his accomplishments (page 189).
Boys were attracted to his "stolid sense of rightness and belonging" (page 189).
His imagination excited other boys (page 189).
T. J. persisted in his project, keeping others interested (page 190).
He was intelligent (page 191).
He made others share his goal (page 191).
He knew when to compromise (page 191).

There is a great deal of information to organize here. You might try grouping the prewriting notes so that you can present the evidence under three categories: perhaps self-confidence, imagination, and persistence.

WRITING AN ANSWER

Here is a model essay that builds on the writer's notes. Notice how each of T. J.'s qualities is discussed in a separate paragraph.

Main Idea

First Quality

Supporting Statements

T. J., a character in "Antaeus," is a natural leader because of his self-confidence, imagination, and persistence. **Although he is a stranger, he is not ashamed of being different.** He feels secure about himself. He does not get upset or angry when the boys in the gang begin to tease him. When Blackie laughs at him because he comes from Alabama, T. J. remains calm and assured. When Charley kids him about his name, T. J. replies without hesitation or shame. He doesn't allow himself to be bullied, and he doesn't lose his temper because he has a "stolid sense of rightness and belonging."

Second Quality

Supporting Statements

T. J. has imagination, and his ideas appeal to the other boys. He starts them thinking about a roof garden, and whenever their enthusiasm begins to wane, he renews their interest in the project. He talks to them about raising watermelons, flowers, grass, and trees. Because he is intelligent, he knows when to give in. Although he wants to grow corn and vegetables, he compromises on his dream and agrees to grow a grass lawn.

Third Quality **T. J. perseveres throughout the winter.** He gives the boys direction and organization. Even though the others become distracted, T. J. persists in carrying earth up to the roof. He works harder than any of the other boys to fulfill their mutual goal, and he inspires the others by his example.

Supporting Statements

Length: 230 words

Writing on a Topic of Your Own

Choosing a Topic

At times you may be asked to choose a topic of your own. Often it will be necessary to read a work more than once before a suitable topic presents itself.

A topic may focus on one element or technique in a work. If you are writing about fiction, you might concentrate on some aspect of plot, such as conflict. Or you might concentrate on character, setting, or theme. If you are writing about poetry, you might choose to analyze imagery or figurative language. A topic may deal with more than one aspect of a work. You might, for example, discuss several elements of a short story in order to show how an idea or theme is developed.

Above all, be sure to limit a broad subject to a manageable topic—one that is sufficiently narrow. A narrow topic is one you can discuss in the time and space you have for the essay. Once you have a topic in mind, your object is to form it into a *thesis,* a controlling idea that represents the conclusion of your findings. You would then need to present the evidence supporting your position. It may be necessary to read a work several times before you can formulate a thesis. Here are some examples:

"Guinea Pig" (page 39) and "The Night the Bed Fell" (page 133)

Topic Comparing the humor in these essays
Thesis In both essays, humor results from situations in which people's intentions misfire.

"Last Cover" (page 153)

Topic Contrasting attitudes toward nature of Colin and his father
Thesis Although Colin and his father both love nature, Colin shows a greater instinct for understanding the woods and wild things.

"You Can't Take It with You" (page 264)

Topic   Explaining the significance of a title
Thesis   The old saying about money is disproved with an ironic twist.

"Rip Van Winkle" (page 247)

Topic   Comparing the characters of Rip and Dame Van Winkle
Thesis   Both Rip and Dame Van Winkle are treated as comic stereotypes.

"A Christmas Carol" (page 276)

Topic   Analyzing the change in Scrooge's character
Thesis   During the visit of each Christmas spirit, Scrooge gets valuable insights into his own character, which help to change him from a hardhearted miser into a kind and charitable man.

The Big Wave (page 357)

Topic   Interpreting the theme of *The Big Wave*
Thesis   The statement "Life is stronger than death," which occurs at several important points in the play, may be taken as the theme, or underlying meaning, of the work.

Gathering Evidence/Developing Major Points

It is a good idea to take notes as you read, even if you do not yet have a topic in mind. Later on, when you have settled on a topic, you can discard any notes that are not relevant. Some people prefer a worksheet, others index cards. In the beginning, you should record all your reactions. A topic may emerge during this early stage. As you continue to read, you will shape your topic into a rough thesis.

When you take notes, make an effort to state ideas in your own words. If a specific phrase or line is so important that it deserves to be quoted directly, be sure to enclose the words in quotation marks. When you transfer your notes to your final paper, be sure to copy quotations exactly.

In working with a short poem, you may cite phrases and lines without identifying the quotations by line numbers. If you cite lines in a long poem, you should enclose the line numbers in parentheses following the quotation. The following note, which is for Longfellow's poem "The Wreck of the *Hesperus*" (page 164), shows you how to do this:

> When the *Hesperus* struck the breakers, the rocks "gored her side/ Like the horns of an angry bull" (lines 71–72).

The slash (/) shows the reader where line 71 ends and line 72 begins.

If you cite three or more lines of a poem, you should separate the quotation from your own text in this way.

Longfellow compares the *Hesperus* to a frightened horse that trembles, then springs from the ground when the storm strikes:

> Down came the storm, and smote amain
>   The vessel in its strength;
> She shuddered and paused, like a frighted steed,
>   Then leaped her cable's length.

(lines 25–28)

Let us suppose you have chosen to compare the following poems:

The Wind   JAMES STEPHENS

The wind stood up, and gave a shout;
He whistled on his fingers, and

Kicked the withered leaves about,
And thumped the branches with his hand,

And said he'd kill, and kill, and kill;
And so he will! And so he will!

The Wind Tapped like a Tired Man

EMILY DICKINSON

The wind tapped like a tired man,
And like a host, "Come in,"
I boldly answered; entered then
My residence within

A rapid, footless guest,   5
To offer whom a chair
Were as impossible as hand
A sofa to the air.

No bone had he to bind him,
His speech was like the push   10
Of numerous hummingbirds at once
From a superior° bush.   12. **superior:** here, high up.

His countenance° a billow,
His fingers, as he passed,
Let go a music, as of tunes   15
Blown tremulous° in glass.

He visited, still flitting;
Then, like a timid man,
Again he tapped—'twas flurriedly°—
And I became alone.   20

13. **countenance** (koun′tə-nəns): face, expression.

16. **tremulous** (trĕm′yə-ləs): vibrating, quivering.

19. **flurriedly** (flûr′ē-əd′lē): excitedly.

As your reading shows, there is common ground for comparison of these poems. You might work out a chart of this kind for taking notes, letting the letter A stand for "The Wind," and B for "The Wind Tapped like a Tired Man":

Similarities	*Differences*
The subject of both poems is the wind.	In A, the wind is a strong gale. The "withered leaves" suggest autumn. In B, the wind is a gentle breeze.
The poets compare the wind to a person.	In A, the poet describes the wind as a furious man. In B, the poet describes the wind as a shy visitor.
Both poems describe the wind in terms of human feelings and characteristics.	In A, the wind is angry and violent. It shouts and whistles. It kicks the leaves and thumps the branches. It is determined to kill.
	In B, the wind is timid. Its movements are light and rapid. It flits and taps timidly, "like a tired man." It has no visible form—no feet ("footless") and no bones, yet has speech, a face, and fingers. Its speech is like the sound of hummingbirds. Its face ("countenance") is a billow. Its fingers produce music like the sound that comes from a reed instrument. It is shy, "like a timid man," and taps "flurriedly."
Both poems suggest that nature has something in common with human beings.	

You might find at this point that a thesis statement has begun to emerge. *Although the poems are quite different in their treatment of the wind, both convey the special character of the wind by representing it as having human qualities.* You would continue to study the poems, gathering additional evidence, developing major points, and refining your thesis statement. The next step is organizing your ideas.

Organizing Ideas

Before you begin writing, organize your main ideas to provide for an introduction, a body, and a conclusion. The introduction should identify the author(s), the work(s), or the problem that is under study. It should contain a statement of your thesis as well. The body of your paper should present the evidence supporting your thesis. The conclusion should bring together your main ideas.

This is one kind of plan you might use for a short paper. It indicates the main idea of each paragraph.

INTRODUCTION

Paragraph 1   *Thesis* Although the poets describe different aspects of the wind, both choose to convey the special character of the wind by representing it as having human qualities.

BODY

Paragraph 2   Stephens' poem represents the wind as an angry, violent man, whose object is destruction.

Paragraph 3   Dickinson's poem represents the wind as a visitor with a gentle, shy temperament.

CONCLUSION

Paragraph 4   In treating the wind in terms of human feelings and characteristics, the poets make us aware of certain resemblances between nature and human beings.

Writing the Essay

As you write your essay, you should use language that is serious enough for your purpose and audience. Remember that your purpose is to convey ideas clearly, and that you are writing for your teachers or, occasionally, for your classmates. Use transitional expressions (words like *then, second,* and *therefore*) to make the order of ideas clear.

Here is a model essay developing the thesis statement. Notice how the essay follows the writer's notes.

TITLE

A COMPARISON OF JAMES STEPHENS' "THE WIND" AND
EMILY DICKINSON'S "THE WIND TAPPED LIKE A TIRED MAN"

INTRODUCTION
Identify works and authors.

Thesis

"The Wind" by James Stephens and "The Wind Tapped like a Tired Man" by Emily Dickinson deal with very different types of wind. Stephens' wind is a strong blast, perhaps a gale; Dickinson's wind is a light, gentle breeze. *Although the poets describe different aspects of the wind, both choose to convey the special character of the wind by representing it as having human qualities.*

BODY/Main Idea

Stephens' wind is a violent, raging figure. From the reference to "the withered leaves" in line 3, we can infer that it is late autumn, when powerful gusts are common. Stephens treats the characteristics of the wind—its sounds and its movements—as if they were produced by a human voice, human limbs, and human feelings. The "shout" is the sudden roar of the wind as it sweeps over the land. As it moves, it makes a high, shrill sound, its "whistle." The wind appears to be acting in fury as it lifts and scatters the leaves and pounds the branches of the trees. The wind's rage mounts as it builds to gale proportions. The repetition of the words *kill* and *will* in the concluding lines of the poem emphasizes the destructive intent of the storm.

Main Idea/Transition

While Stephens presents his wind as a threatening figure that shouts, whistles, kicks, and thumps, Dickinson gives us a gentle ghost of a wind. This wind is timid: it taps softly, "like a tired man." It has no visible form. Since it is "footless" and has no "bone," or skeleton, it cannot be seated. Its speech is a low, continuous humming, like that produced by the vibration of hummingbirds' wings. Its face ("countenance") is a great swelling or surging of air. The sound the breeze makes is attributed to the fingers of the wind, making music like that produced by glass reeds that vibrate when air is blown over them. The wind's movements are light and rapid; it flits, and shyly, "like a timid man," taps "flurriedly" and leaves.

Give evidence of close reading.

CONCLUSION By choosing to describe the wind in terms of human feelings and characteristics, the poets seem to be saying that nature has a great deal in common with human beings. The poets make us conscious of similarities we might never have discovered for ourselves.

Length: 374 words

Evaluating and Revising Papers

When you write an essay in class, you have a limited amount of time to plan and develop your essay. Nevertheless, you should save a few minutes to read over your work and make necessary corrections.

When an essay is assigned as homework, you have more time to prepare it carefully. Get into the habit of revising your work. A first draft of an essay should be treated as a rough copy of your manuscript. Chances are that reworking your first draft will result in a clearer and stronger paper.

To evaluate an essay, you judge its content, organization, and style. Your aim is to decide what the strong points and weak points are in your essay. You can then make the changes that will improve your essay. To evaluate your essay, answer the following questions:

Guidelines for Evaluating a Paper

Introduction
1. Have I included an introduction that identifies the title and author of the literary work(s)?
2. Have I included a thesis statement that gives the main idea of the essay?

Body
3. Have I included at least two main points that support the thesis statement?
4. Have I included evidence from the literary work to support each main point?

Conclusion
5. Have I included a conclusion that brings together the main points?

Coherence
6. Does the order of ideas make sense?

Style
7. Do the sentences differ in length and in the way they begin?

Word Choice
8. Is the language serious enough for the purpose and audience?
9. Have I defined unfamiliar words for the audience?
10. Have I used vivid and specific words?

Using your evaluation, you can revise your essay. Writers revise by using four basic techniques: *adding, cutting, reordering,* or *replacing.* For example, if the order of ideas is not clear, you can *add* words like *first, second,* and *finally.* If your language is not serious enough, you can *replace* slang and contractions with formal language. You can *cut* evidence that does not explain a main point, and you can *reorder* ideas that are difficult to follow.

On the following pages you will find a revised draft of the essay that appears on page 702. The notes in the margin show which revision technique the writer used. Study the two versions of the essay. As you do so, notice how the writer has revised for greater clarity, accuracy, and conciseness.

replace; add	~~In their poems,~~ *"The Wind" by* James Stephens and *"The Wind Tapped Like a Tired Man" by* Emily Dickinson deal with very different
replace; cut; cut; add	~~forces of nature.~~ *types of wind.* In Stephens' poem~~, the~~ wind is a strong blast~~.~~ *perhaps a gale;* Dickinson's wind
replace; replace; add	is a light, gentle breeze. Although the ~~poems deal with~~ *poets describe* different ~~kinds of~~ *aspects the* winds,
cut	both ~~poets~~ choose to convey the special character of the wind by representing it
	as having human qualities.
reorder	Stephens' wind is a violent, raging figure. Stephens treats the characteristics
	of the wind--its sounds and its movements--as if they were produced by a human
replace	voice, human limbs, and human feelings. *From the reference to "the withered leaves" in line 3, we can infer that it* ~~The season~~ is late autumn, when pow-
add; cut	erful gusts are common. As it sweeps over the land, ~~the wind roars. This is its~~ *The "shout" is the sudden roar of the wind*
replace; replace	~~shout. Its "whistle" is the~~ *As it moves, it makes a* high, shrill sound i~~t makes as it moves.~~ *its "whistle."* The wind ap-
reorder; cut	pears to be acting in fury as it lifts the leaves and scatters them, and pounds the

704 WRITING ABOUT LITERATURE

reorder   branches of the trees. The repetition of the words <u>kill</u> and <u>will</u> in the concluding

                               destructive intent   *rage*

replace; replace   lines of the poem emphasizes the ~~fury~~ of the storm. The wind's ~~fury~~ mounts as it

builds to gale proportions.

         While Stephens presents his wind as a threatening figure that
         shouts, whistles, kicks and thumps,

add   Dickinson gives us a gentle ghost of a wind. This wind is timid: it taps softly,

                           Since it is "footless" and has no "bone" or skeleton,

add   "like a tired man." It has no visible form. /It cannot be seated. Its speech is a

                           the vibration of

add   low, continuous humming, like that produced by hummingbirds' wings. Its face

                             the breeze makes

add   ("countenance") is a great swelling or surging of air. The sound is attributed to

                           that vibrate

add   the fingers of the wind, making music like that produced by glass reeds when air

cut   is blown over them. The wind's movements are light and rapid; it flits and ~~leaves~~

         "like a timid man," taps "flurriedly" and leaves.

add   shyly.

         By choosing to describe the wind in terms of human feelings and characteris-

tics, the poets seem to be saying that nature has a great deal in common with

                    The poets make us

replace   human beings. ~~We become~~ conscious of similarities we might never have discov-

ered for ourselves.

Proofreading and Making a Final Copy

After you revise, you should proofread your essay to correct any mistakes in grammar, usage, and mechanics. Pay special attention to the correct capitalization and punctuation of any direct quotations you use as supporting evidence. Then make a final copy of your essay by using correct manuscript form or your teacher's instructions. After writing this clean copy, proofread again to catch any mistakes made in copying.

GUIDE TO LITERARY TERMS AND TECHNIQUES

ALLITERATION   *The repetition of a sound in a group of words usually related in meaning.* Alliteration occurs in many common phrases and expressions: "*w*ild and *w*ooly *W*est," "*b*rown as a *b*erry," and so on. Alliteration is usually confined to consonants, but vowels are sometimes alliterated too. Most alliteration occurs at the beginning of words, but sometimes writers like to alliterate in the middle and at the end of words as well.

One of the uses of alliteration seems to be to gain emphasis and to make a group of words meaningful to us. This is why many advertising jingles depend on alliteration. Manufacturers use alliteration in naming their products as an aid to memory.

Politicians often use alliteration. When we are asked to put up with hardship, we are asked to "*Tigh*ten our bel*ts*," or to "*B*ite the *b*ullet." Abraham Lincoln once said, "Among free men there can be no successful appeal from the *bal*lot to the *bullet.*"

Poets use alliteration to the most obvious and memorable effect. Some examples of alliteration in poetry are:

> Blue were her eyes as the *f*airy *f*lax,
> Her cheeks like the *d*awn of *d*ay, . . .
> > Henry Wadsworth Longfellow
> > "The Wreck of the *Hesperus*"

> The angels, not *h*alf so *h*appy in *H*eaven,
> Went envying *h*er and me:
> > Edgar Allan Poe
> > "Annabel Lee"

> I *r*emembe*r*, I *r*emembe*r*
> The *r*oses, *r*ed and white
> The vio*l*ets and the *l*i*l*y cup—
> Those *f*lowers made of *l*ight!
> > Thomas Hood
> > "I Remember, I Remember"

These are serious examples, but sometimes alliteration is used simply for fun. One poet, Algernon Charles Swinburne, actually wrote a poem that made fun of his own style. He had been criticized for using too much alliteration. So he composed "Nephelidia" (little clouds), which is complicated and funny nonsense. It starts this way:

> From the *d*epth of the *d*reamy *d*ecline of the *d*awn through a *n*otable *n*imbus of *n*ebulous *n*oonshine,
> *P*allid and *p*ink as the *p*alm of the *f*lag-*f*lower that *f*lickers with *f*ear of the *f*lies as they *f*loat, . . .

Swinburne makes the point that heavily alliterated poetry can seem to mean more than it does.

Prose writers use alliteration, too, but they have to be careful not to sound too artificial. Some of the most memorable expressions from the King James translation of the Bible are alliterated: "*L*et there be *l*ight: and there was *l*ight" (Genesis). Even the famous quotation from Ecclesiastes uses alliteration: "There is *n*o *n*ew thi*n*g u*n*der the su*n*."

See **Repetition.**
See also page 466.

ALLUSION   *A reference in one work of literature to another work of literature or to a well-known event, person, or place.* Allusion can be used equally well in prose or poetry. It is used to best effect when the reference calls up appropriate associations.

Literature contains many allusions to the Bible. Characters will sometimes be described as having the patience of Job, who was noted for his patience. When Henry James called one of his stories "The Tree of Knowledge," he expected his readers to recognize the allusion to the tree that grew in the Garden of Eden. He also expected his readers to associate the word *knowledge* with a specific context—the knowledge of good and evil.

Allusions to the literature of ancient Greece and Rome are also common in literature. The great writers of years past were carefully trained to read both Latin and Greek. We do not study these languages or their literature as intensely nowadays, so we miss many of the allusions that writers like William Shakespeare, John Milton, William Wordsworth, and Alfred, Lord Tennyson took for granted.

Often literature makes allusions to famous events. When someone points out that a character has "met his Waterloo," the allusion is to the battle at which Napoleon was finally defeated by the English. Allusions to battlefields are common because much of history was decided by the outcome of battles. Therefore, references to Gettysburg, for the American Civil War; Flanders, for World War I; and the beaches of Normandy, for World War II, occur frequently. "Black Monday" is a reference to the day the stock market on Wall Street collapsed—referred to universally as "The Crash"—and all the world was plunged into the Great Depression of the 1930s.

Allusions to the media are growing more and more common, though these are not as lasting as allusions to the Bible and classical literature. In the story "Bad Characters," Emily alludes to a character in the comic strip "Katzenjammer Kids" when she compares Lottie's hat to the Inspector's hat.

See pages 619, 674.

ANECDOTE *A very short story with a simple, usually amusing point.* Many jokes are anecdotes. Often short stories are expanded anecdotes. In the essay "Dogs That Have Known Me," Jean Kerr includes several anecdotes that illustrate the amusing peculiarities of her pets. One dog

she tells about insisted on swimming with a fancy overhand stroke instead of using the dog paddle; another made a habit of collecting and hiding lettuce; still another enjoyed hopping on and off the piano.

See page 99.

BALLAD *A story told in verse and usually meant to be sung.* Ballads use regular patterns of rhythm and strong rhymes. A common element is the **refrain.** Most ballads are full of adventure, action, and romance. The earliest ballads, known as **folk ballads,** were composed anonymously and transmitted orally for generations before they were written down. A popular ballad like "Bonny Barbara Allan" has many different versions, since the story changed as it was passed down through the years. **Literary ballads** are composed by known writers who imitate the folk ballad.

See **Refrain.**
See also page 477.

BIOGRAPHY *The story of a person's life.* When a person writes his or her own biography, it is called an **autobiography.** Biography and autobiography are two of the most popular forms of **nonfiction,** and most libraries have a section set aside for these books. Almost every famous person has been the subject of a biography. One of the greatest biographies ever written is *The Life of Samuel Johnson* by James Boswell. Another is Carl Sandburg's six-volume biography of Abraham Lincoln. Well-known autobiographies include *The Story of My Life* by Helen Keller, *The Autobiography of Lincoln Steffens,* and *The Autobiography of Mark Twain.*

See pages 404, 414.

CHARACTERIZATION *The methods used to present the personality of a character in a narrative.* A writer can create a character by: (1) giving a physical description of the character; (2) showing the character's actions and letting the character speak; (3) revealing the character's thoughts and feelings; (4) revealing what others think of the character; and (5) commenting directly on the character. The first four methods are **indirect** methods of characterization. The writer shows or dramatizes the character and allows you to draw your own conclusions. The last method is **direct** characterization. The writer tells you directly what a character is like.

In "Rip Van Winkle," Washington Irving develops Rip's character through direct and indirect means. In this passage, for example, the author first comments on Rip's character and then lets Rip reveal himself through his actions.

> Rip Van Winkle, however, was one of those happy mortals, of foolish, well-oiled dispositions, who take the world easy, eat white bread or brown, whichever can be got with least thought or trouble, and would rather starve on a penny than work for a pound. If left to himself, he would have whistled life away in perfect contentment; but his wife kept continually dinning in his ears about his idleness, his carelessness, and the ruin he was bringing on his family. Morning, noon, and night, her tongue was incessantly going, and everything he said or did was sure to produce a torrent of household eloquence. Rip had but one way of replying to all lectures of the kind, and that, by frequent use, had grown into a habit. He shrugged his shoulders, shook his head, cast up his eyes, but said nothing. This, however, always provoked a fresh volley from his wife; so that he would take to the outside of the house—the only side which, in truth, belongs to a henpecked husband.

Animals can be characterized through the same techniques. Here is a description of Wolf, Rip's dog:

> True it is, in all points of spirit befitting an honorable dog, he was as courageous an animal as ever scoured the woods—but what courage can withstand the terrors of a woman's tongue? The moment Wolf entered the house his crest fell, his tail drooped to the ground, or curled between his legs, he sneaked about with a gallows air, casting many a sidelong glance at Dame Van Winkle, and at the least flourish of a broomstick or ladle, he would fly to the door, yelping.

Characterization can be sketchy, particularly if the character does not play an important role in the piece. Or, it can be extraordinarily full, as when the character is the main focus of a piece.

We often describe characters as being "flat" or "round." A "flat" character is merely sketched out for us. There is no full development. Dame Van Winkle in "Rip Van Winkle" is a flat character because she is represented as a shrew. She is never really given a chance to speak for herself or to be further characterized.

"Flat" characters are often **stereotypes**. Harry Thorburn, in "The Erne from the Coast," is an example of a "round" character, since we see him under many different circumstances and we watch him grow and change.

See **Description, Narration, Point of View.** See also pages 240, 261.

CONFLICT *The struggle that takes place between two opposing forces.* A conflict can be between a character and a natural force, like a bear or a hurricane; between two characters; or between opposing views held by separate characters or groups of characters. Such conflicts are **external conflicts**. Conflict can also be **internal**—it can exist within a character and be a psychological conflict.

Usually a conflict arises from a blocking of desires. In "The Highwayman," King George's men intend to kill the highwayman when he comes to visit his sweetheart. They literally block him from achieving his goal.

There may be more than one conflict in a work. In *The Big Wave* by Pearl Buck, the characters are involved in a struggle against the hostile forces of nature that threaten their lives and their homes. There is also an internal conflict within Jiya, the main character, who must decide what kind of life he wishes to lead. In Jean Stafford's story "Bad Characters," Emily has conflicts with her friends and with members of her family. She also has internal struggles. She is torn between her desire to be Lottie's friend and guilt over her own actions.

See **Plot.**
See also page 218.

CONNOTATION *All the emotions and associations that a word or phrase arouses.* Connotation is different from **denotation**, which is the strict literal (or "dictionary") definition of a word. For example, the word *springtime* literally means "the season of the year between the vernal equinox and the summer solstice." But *springtime* usually makes most people think of love, rebirth, youth, and romance.

Poets are especially sensitive to the connotations of words. For example, Walter de la Mare uses the words *moonlight* and *moonbeams* in "The Listeners." The two words literally mean light reflected from the moon. But *moonlight* and *moonbeams* have certain connotations associated with things mysterious and ghostly that help create the poem's eerie mood. You can imagine how different the poem would be if you substituted the word "sunshine" for *moonlight* or *moonbeam*.

See page 487.

DESCRIPTION *Any careful detailing of a person, place, thing, or event.* We associate the term with prose, both fiction and nonfiction, but poems also use description, if a bit more economically.

Description appeals to the senses. In this passage from Charles Dickens' "A Christmas Carol," note how the description of the Christmas pudding appeals to both smell and sight:

Hallo! A great deal of steam! The pudding was out of the copper. A smell like a washing day! That was the cloth. A smell like an eating house and a pastry cook's next door to each other, with a laundress' next door to that! That was the pudding! In half a minute Mrs. Cratchit entered—flushed but smiling proudly—with the pudding, like a speckled cannonball, so hard and firm, blazing in half of half a quartern of ignited brandy and bedight with Christmas holly stuck into the top.

Some description is simple, direct, and factual. But more often, description is used to establish a mood or stir an emotion. When Dickens describes the Ghost of Christmas Yet to Come, he emphasizes the shadowy and frightening appearance of the phantom:

The phantom slowly, gravely, silently approached. When it came near him, Scrooge bent down upon his knee; for in the air through which this spirit moved it seemed to scatter gloom and mystery.
It was shrouded in a deep black garment, which concealed its head, its face, its form, and left nothing of it visible save one outstretched hand.

See **Mood.**
See also page 89.

DIALECT *A representation of the speech patterns of a particular region or social group.* Dialect often is used to establish local color. Some of the regional dialects in America are the Down-East dialect of Maine, the Cajun dialect of Louisiana, the Southern and Western dialects, and, in some of the writings of the early twentieth century, a city-slang.

Mark Twain often has his characters speak in dialect. This line of dialogue appears in *Adventures of Huckleberry Finn*, which is set in a region of the Mississippi River more than a hundred years ago:

> "I've seed a raft act so before, along here . . . 'pears to me the current has most quit above the head of this bend durin' the last two years."

Twain increases local color by having his character speak ungrammatically (by traditional grammar standards) and clip the "g's" off some of his words.

See **Dialogue.**
See also pages 218, 444.

DIALOGUE *Talk or conversation between two or more characters.* Dialogue usually attempts to present the speech of characters in a realistic fashion. It is used in almost all literary forms: biography, essays, fiction, poetry, and drama. Dialogue is especially important in drama, where it forwards all the action of the play. Dialogue must move the plot, set up the action, reveal the characters, and even help establish some of the mood.

When dialogue appears in a play, there are no quotation marks to set it apart, since—besides stage directions—there is nothing but dialogue. When dialogue appears in a prose work or in a poem, it is customary to set it apart with quotation marks.

Biographies often include dialogue. In most cases the dialogue is imagined and presented as it would have sounded if it really had been delivered. Biographers take many such liberties because the use of dialogue helps to liven up their presentations.

The use of dialogue in fiction is one of the ways a writer makes a story come alive. A short story that uses dialogue extensively will seem more realistic. The following passage was written by Sarah Orne Jewett, an American writer well known in the late 1800s. It is part of a story called "A White Heron":

> "So Sylvy knows all about birds, does she?" he exclaimed, as he looked round at the little girl who sat, very demure but increasingly sleepy, in the moonlight. "I am making a collection of birds myself. I have been at it ever since I was a boy." (Mrs. Tilley smiled.) "There are two or three very rare ones I have been hunting for these five years. I mean to get them on my own ground if they can be found."
>
> "Do you cage 'em up?" asked Mrs. Tilley doubtfully, in response to this enthusiastic announcement.
>
> "Oh no, they're stuffed and preserved, dozens and dozens of them," said the ornithologist, "and I have shot or snared every one myself. I caught a glimpse of a white heron a few miles from here on Saturday, and I have followed it in this direction. They have never been found in this district at all."

The author is able, in this brief piece of dialogue, to clarify character, set the stage for the next action, and to build suspense.

See **Dialect.**
See also page 374.

DRAMA *A story acted out, usually on a stage, by actors and actresses who take the parts of specific characters.* The word *drama* comes from a Greek word meaning "act." In reading a drama it is best to try to imagine real actors as they would play their parts onstage. We usually think of two main kinds of drama: **tragedies,** serious plays generally ending in suffering and death, like William Shakespeare's *Macbeth;* and **comedies,** lighter plays that are often funny, like Shakespeare's *Twelfth Night.*

Drama involves the use of **plot,** the sequence of related events that make up the story. The plot pits characters against one another or against forces that are powerful and sometimes greater than they are. The characters carry forward the plot by means of **dialogue.**

Most playwrights include **stage directions,**

which tell the actors and actresses what to do or how to feel when certain lines are spoken. The stage directions are useful to the director, who must help the actors and actresses interpret their lines correctly. The director decides such things as the timing of a line, the speed of delivery, the way the players stand or move when speaking their lines, and what they do when they are not speaking their lines. In many productions the director is as important as the author of the play.

Most plays are presented on stages with **sets.** A set is a realistic representation of the room, landscape, or locale in which the play takes place. **Props** (short for *properties*) are representations of important items in the drama, such as telephones, radios, flashlights, working automobiles, or other objects that figure in the action. **Lighting** helps to establish the desired moods. Or, instead of establishing mood, lighting can help establish the time of day or the season.

A drama usually begins with **exposition,** which explains the action that has already occurred. It then introduces the **conflict** or difficulties that the characters must overcome. All this happens at the same time the audience is getting to know the characters. Each act may be composed of several scenes. The end of each act often includes a **climax,** which is designed to keep the audience in suspense so it will come back after the intermission. The final act of the drama usually builds to a climax or crisis greater than any that has gone before. The end of the drama involves the **resolution** of the climax, usually by death in a tragedy or by marriage in a comedy.

See **Dialogue, Plot.**
See also pages 333, 334, 377.

ESSAY *A piece of prose writing that discusses a subject in a limited way and that usually expresses a particular point of view.* The word *essay* means "an evaluation or consideration of something." Therefore, most essays tend to be thoughtful observations about a subject of interest to the author. Most essays are *expository* in nature, which means simply that they explain a situation, circumstance, or process. They often go on to consider the results or consequences of what they have explained. Edwin Way Teale's "Animals Go to School" is a good example of an expository essay.

See **Exposition.**
See also page 382.

EXPOSITION *A kind of writing that explains something or gives information about something.* Exposition can be used in fiction as well as in non-fiction. The most familiar form it takes is in **essays.** A typical piece of exposition is this passage from Henry David Thoreau's *Walden:* "It is not all books that are as dull as their readers. There are probably words addressed to our condition exactly, which, if we could really hear and understand, would be more salutary than the morning or the spring to our lives, and possibly put a new aspect on the face of things for us. How many a man has dated a new era in his life from the reading of a book." Exposition is also that part of a play in which important background information is revealed to the audience. At the opening of *The Mazarin Stone,* Holmes provides the audience with essential information when he tells Watson his plan for recovering the diamond.

See **Essay.**
See also page 196.

FABLE *A brief story with a moral, written in prose or poetry.* The characters in fables are often animals who speak and act like human beings. The most famous fables are those of Aesop, who was supposed to have lived around the sixth century B.C. Almost as famous are the fables of the seventeenth-century French writer Jean de La Fontaine (là fôn-těn').

A typical fable is Aesop's "The Wind and the Sun," in which the Wind and the Sun quarrel about which is the stronger. When they see a traveler coming down the road, they propose to settle the dispute in this way: Whichever causes the traveler to take off his coat will be considered the stronger. The Wind blows as hard as he can, but this causes the traveler to wrap himself up in his cloak. The Sun then shines down upon the traveler and causes him to remove his cloak. The moral of the story is "Kindness can achieve more than harshness."

See page 668.

FANTASY *A form of fiction, poetry, or drama that takes place in an imaginary world and makes use of unrealistic elements.* It involves combinations of an impossible sort—animals that think and talk like people, plants that move or think, or circumstances that are highly fanciful, like worlds and societies beneath the sea. Fantasy has been popular in almost all ages and among people of most cultures.

Time travel is one of the favorite themes in fantasy. In Mark Twain's novel *A Connecticut Yankee in King Arthur's Court,* a man from the nineteenth century suddenly finds himself back in the Middle Ages. In H. G. Wells's *The Time Machine,* a man builds a machine that can take him into the past and into the future.

FICTION *A prose account that is invented and not a record of things as they actually happened.* Much fiction is based on personal experience, but involves invented characters, settings, or other details that exist for the sake of the story itself. Fiction generally refers to short stories and novels.

FIGURATIVE LANGUAGE *Any language that is not intended to be interpreted in a strict literal sense.* When we call a car a "lemon," we do not mean it is a citrus fruit, but that its performance is "sour," or defective. When we hear someone refer to another person as a clown, a brick, a prince, or an angel, we can be sure that the person is none of those things. Instead, we understand that the person shares some qual-

ity with those other things. Figurative language always makes use of comparisons between different things.

The main form of figurative language used in literature is **metaphor.** Metaphor draws a comparison between two unlike things. Metaphor never uses any special language to establish a comparison. The opening stanza of "The Highwayman" contains a number of metaphors. The road is called "a ribbon of moonlight"; the moon "a ghostly galleon"; the sky is referred to as "cloudy seas." Longfellow compares himself to a castle in "The Children's Hour" and expresses his affection for his daughters through the metaphor of imprisonment:

I have you fast in my fortress,
    And will not let you depart,
But put you down into the dungeon
    In the round tower of my heart.

Similes are easier to recognize than metaphors because they do have a special language to set them off. That language is *like, as, as if, than, such as,* and other words that make an explicit comparison. When Robert Burns says, "My love is like a red, red rose," he is using a simile. Like metaphor, the simile does not use all the points of comparison for its force. It uses only some. For instance, the comparison of "my love" to a rose does not necessarily mean that the loved one is thorny, nor that she lives in a garden, nor that she has a green neck. Rather, it means that "my love" is delicate, fragrant, and beautiful as the flower is.

Similes in everyday language are common: "He was mad as a hornet"; "He roared like a bull when I told him"; "Louie laughed like a hyena"; "Float like a butterfly, sting like a bee"; "Be as firm as Gibraltar and as cool as a cucumber"; "She's like Wonder Woman"; "She sang like a bird."

See **Metaphor, Simile, Personification.**
See also pages 450, 451, 489.

FLASHBACK *An interruption of the sequence of a narrative to relate an action that happened at an earlier point in time.* The flashback is an effective technique because it is usually unexpected. A plot generally moves in chronological order: it starts at a given moment, progresses through time, and ends. A flashback interrupts that flow by suddenly shifting to past time and narrating important incidents that make the present action more intelligible.

See page 28.

FOLK TALE *A story that was not originally written down, but was passed on orally from one storyteller to another.* Folk tales often exist in several forms because they are carried by storytellers to different parts of the world. Many fairy tales, such as the story of Cinderella, are folk tales that originated in Europe, and versions of them later appeared in the Appalachian Mountains of the New World. Folk tales often involve unreal creatures, like dragons, giants, and talking animals. In the United States, folk tales have grown up about such figures as the lumberjack Paul Bunyan, the riverboatman Mike Fink, and the frontiersman Davy Crockett.

Here is a folk tale from Nigeria. In folk tales of certain cultures, the characters are animals. This particular tale shows that inhospitality is a shameful act.

How Ijapa°, Who Was Short, Became Long
Retold by Harold Courlander

Ijapa the tortoise was on a journey. He was tired and hungry, for he had been walking a long time. He came to the village where Ojola[1] the boa lived, and he stopped there,

---

° **Ijapa** (ē-jä′pä).
1. **Ojola** (ō-jō′lä).

From *Olode the Hunter and Other Tales from Nigeria* by Harold Courlander. Copyright © 1968 by Harold Courlander. Reprinted by permission of Harold Courlander.

thinking, "Ojola will surely feed me, for I am famished."

Ijapa went to Ojola's house. Ojola greeted him, saying, "Enter my house and cool yourself in the shade, for I can see you have been on the trail."

Ijapa entered. They sat and talked. Ijapa smelled food cooking over the fire. He groaned with hunger, for when Ijapa was hungry he was more hungry than anyone else. Ojola said politely: "Surely the smell of my food does not cause you pain?"

Ijapa said: "Surely not, my friend. It only made me think that if I were at home now, my wife would be cooking likewise."

Ojola said: "Let us prepare ourselves. Then we shall eat together."

Ijapa went outside. He washed himself in a bowl of water. When he came in again he saw the food in the middle of the room and smelled its odors. But Ojola the boa was coiled around the food. There was no way to get to it. Ijapa walked around and around, trying to find an opening through which he could approach the waiting meal. But Ojola's body was long, and his coils lay one atop the other, and there was no entrance through them. Ijapa's hunger was intense.

Ojola said: "Come, do not be restless. Sit down. Let us eat."

Ijapa said: "I would be glad to sit with you. But you, why do you surround the dinner?"

Ojola said: "This is our custom. When my people eat, they always sit this way. Do not hesitate any longer." The boa went on eating while Ijapa again went around and around trying to find a way to the food. At last he gave up. Ojola finished eating. He said: "What a pleasure it is to eat dinner with a friend."

Ijapa left Ojola's house hungrier than he had come. He returned to his own village. There he ate. He brooded on his experience with Ojola. He decided that he would return the courtesy by inviting Ojola to his house to eat with him. He told his wife to prepare a meal for a certain festival day. And he began to weave a long tail out of grass. He spent many days weaving the tail. When it was finished, he fastened it to himself with tree gum.

On the festival day, Ojola arrived. They greeted each other at the door, Ijapa saying, "You have been on a long journey. You are hungry. You are tired. Refresh yourself at the spring. Then we shall eat."

Ojola was glad. He went to the spring to wash. When he returned, he found Ijapa already eating. Ijapa's grass tail was coiled several times around the food. Ojola could not get close to the dinner. Ijapa ate with enthusiasm. He stopped sometimes to say: "Do not hesitate, friend Ojola. Do not be shy. Good food does not last forever."

Ojola went around and around. It was useless. At last he said: "Ijapa, how did it happen that once you were quite short but now you are very long?"

Ijapa said: "One person learns from another about such things." Ojola then remembered the time Ijapa had been his guest. He was ashamed. He went away. It was from Ijapa that came the proverb:

"The lesson that a man should be short came from his fellow man.
The lesson that a man should be tall also came from his fellow man."

FORESHADOWING   *The use of hints or clues in a narrative to suggest what action is to come.* Foreshadowing helps to build **suspense** because it alerts the reader to what is about to happen. It also helps the reader savor all the details of the buildup. Of drama, it is often said that if a loaded gun is presented in Act One, it should go off before Act Five. In other words, presenting a loaded gun or a potentially dangerous or interesting opportunity early in a literary work is an effective kind of foreshadowing.

See **Plot.**
See also pages 67, 227.

GENRE   *A literary type.* Included in this textbook are the following genres: short story, nonfiction, drama, poetry, novel, mythology, and folklore.

HAIKU   *A three-line poem with five syllables in the first line, seven syllables in the second line, and five syllables in the third line.*

See pages 491, 492.

HERO/HEROINE   *The chief character in a story.* In older heroic stories, the hero or heroine often embodies the best or most desirable qualities of the society for which the story was written. The hero or heroine in such stories is usually physically strong, courageous, and intelligent. Often the conflict involves the hero or heroine with a monster or with a force that threatens the entire social group. Nowadays, we use the term **hero** or **heroine** simply to mean the main character in any narrative.

IMAGERY   *A description that appeals to any one or any combination of the five senses.* Most images tend to be visual in nature, but they may also suggest the way things sound, smell, taste, or feel to the touch. In "A Christmas Carol," Charles Dickens associates the Ghost of Christmas Present with images that appeal not only to the visual sense but also to the sense of taste: "Heaped upon the floor, to form a kind of throne, were turkeys, geese, game, brawn, great joints of meat, suckling pigs, long wreaths of sausages, mince pies, plum puddings, barrels of oysters, red-hot chestnuts, cherry-cheeked apples, juicy oranges, luscious pears, immense twelfth-cakes, and great bowls of punch." Dickens heralds the entrance of Marley's ghost with images of noise. First Scrooge hears every bell in the house ringing. Then he hears "a clanking noise, deep down below, as if some person were dragging a heavy chain over the casks in the wine merchant's cellar."

Good images involve our sensory awareness

and help us be more responsive readers.

See pages 113, 446.

INFERENCE *A reasonable conclusion about something based on certain clues or facts.* Often the author of a literary work does not tell us everything there is to tell, but gives us the pleasure of drawing an inference about the characters, the situation, or the meaning of the work. The process of drawing an inference is pleasurable because we are actually making a discovery on our own.

In "Rip Van Winkle," Washington Irving expects his readers to grasp the truth about his hero's long sleep before it becomes evident to Rip. When Rip awakens, he is puzzled by what he finds, but the reader can infer what has happened from different clues:

> He looked round for his gun, but in place of the clean, well-oiled fowling piece, he found an old firelock lying by him, the barrel incrusted with rust, the lock falling off, and the stock worm-eaten.

> As he rose to walk, he found himself stiff in the joints.

> As he approached the village, he met a number of people, but none whom he knew, which somewhat surprised him, for he had thought himself acquainted with everyone in the country round. Their dress, too, was of a different fashion from that to which he was accustomed. They all stared at him with equal marks of surprise, and whenever they cast their eyes upon him, invariably stroked their chins. The recurrence of this gesture induced Rip to do the same, when, to his astonishment, he found his beard had grown a foot long!

See pages 86, 88, 121, 129.

INVERSION *A reversal of the usual order of words to achieve some kind of emphasis.* For exam-
ple, in this line from "The Pied Piper of Hamelin," Robert Browning inverts the subject and object: "To blow the pipe his lips he wrinkled." The device usually appears in poetry, but it occurs in prose and in speech as well. Its effect is to give special importance to a phrase or thought.

Sometimes it is not just the order of words but the actual sequence of events which is inverted. One of the most common uses of this kind of inversion in everyday language occurs in the expression, "Wait until I put on my shoes and socks." We all know that socks go on first—then come the shoes! But it is not only more effective to invert the order, but for many people more natural. We do not think of the sequence as an inversion.

A more usual kind of inversion is that which appears in Alfred, Lord Tennyson's poem "Sir Galahad":

> When down the stormy crescent goes,
> A light before me swims,
> Between dark stems the forest glows,
> I hear a noise of hymns.

It would be more normal to write: "When the stormy crescent goes down, a light swims before me; the forest glows between dark stems, and I hear a noise of hymns." But Tennyson liked the stateliness, the slightly unexpected quality he achieved by inverting these lines. The inversion is also designed to produce effective rhyme.

See page 442.

IRONY *A contrast between what is stated and what is really meant, or between what is expected to happen and what actually does happen.* Irony is used in literature for different effects, from humor to serious comments on the unpredictable nature of life. A good example of irony is found in the short story "The Landlady." Impressed by appearances, Billy Weaver thinks he has found a cheap, attractive place to live in, whereas he is actually in grave danger.

See page 268.

LEGEND *A story handed down from the past. Legends seem to have some basis in history.* A legend usually centers on some historical incident, such as a battle or a journey in search of a treasure or the founding of a city or nation. A legend usually features a great hero or heroine who struggles against some powerful force to achieve the desired goal. Most legends were passed on orally long before they were written down, so that the characters became larger than life, and their actions became fantastic and unbelievable. Browning's poem "The Pied Piper of Hamelin" is based on a well-known legend about events that occurred in the town of Hamelin in 1284.

See page 487.

LIMERICK *A comic poem written in three long and two short lines, rhymed in the pattern aabba.* No one knows if the limerick was actually invented in Limerick, Ireland, but the form of the poem is very popular throughout that country. Writing limericks is also a popular pastime in our country. Much of the fun comes in using the name of a place or person. Limericks often begin in this fashion: "There was a young girl (boy) from St. Paul." What comes later is up to the writer.

Sometimes writers twist the spellings of rhyme words to build more humor into limericks. The following Irish limerick plays on the spelling of a town south of Dublin: *Dun Laoghaire,* pronounced "dun leery."

> An ancient old man of Dun Laoghaire
> Said, "Of pleasure and joy I've grown
>   waoghaire.
>   The life that is pure,
>   Will suit me I'm sure,
> It's healthy and noble though draoghaire."

Perhaps a more typical limerick is this one, also Irish:

> There was an old man of Tralee,
> Who was bothered and bit by a flea,
>   So he put out the light,
>   Saying, "Now he can't bite,
> For he'll never be able to see."

The pattern of rhythm for lines 1, 2, and 5 is the same:

$$\smile\,'\,\smile\smile\,'\,\smile\smile\,'$$

The pattern for lines 3 and 4 is also the same:

$$\smile\smile\,'\,\smile\smile\,'$$

See page 496.

METAMORPHOSIS *A change, mainly of shape or form.* In literature, it usually involves the miraculous change of a human or god into an animal or tree or flower. The most famous examples of metamorphosis are found in classical myths. In the myth of Arachne, the goddess Minerva transforms Arachne into a spider. In the myth of Daphne and Apollo, Daphne is transformed into a laurel tree, which thereafter becomes sacred to Apollo. Classical myths often employ metamorphosis to suggest a close relationship among gods, humans, and the world of nature. The goddess Aphrodite, for instance, sprang from the foam of the sea. The goddess Athene appeared to the Greek hero Odysseus in the form of a mist. She also assumed the form of an owl when it suited her. In the myths metamorphosis reflects a sense of wonder about the nature of the world: the shapes of things are not necessarily reliable indications of what the things are. If an owl could be a goddess, then it was only wise for a Greek to be cautious of the owl and to respect it. Such respect typifies other mythologies as well: American Indian myths express the same kind of respect for the natural world.

Metamorphosis is found in many popular European folk tales. In "The Princess and the Frog," the frog metamorphoses into a handsome prince, and in "Beauty and the Beast," a prince is metamorphosed into an animal.

See pages 598, 605.

METAPHOR *A comparison between two unlike things with the intent of giving added meaning to one of them.* A metaphor is one of the most important forms of **figurative language.** It is used in virtually all forms of language, from everyday speech to formal prose and all forms of fiction and poetry.

When one says, "He was a gem to help me like that," the metaphor lies in calling a person a gem. Gems are stones; they glisten; they are usually quite small. But these are not the qualities that the metaphor above wants us to consider. The metaphor relies on our understanding that it is the person's gemlike or jewel-like value that is referred to. Thus, we see that metaphors use selected points of comparison that are supplied by the context.

Should we say, "The miser had a heart of flint," we do not mean that his heart is small, black, bloodless, and nonfunctioning. Rather, we mean he has no capacity to feel emotionally for someone else.

Unlike a **simile,** a metaphor does not use a specific word to state a comparison. The difference is illustrated in this pair of sentences. The first expresses a simile, the second a metaphor.

> Life is like a dream.
> Life is a dream.

> See **Figurative Language, Simile.**
> See also page 451.

MOOD *The emotional situation that a piece of literature tries to establish.* Mood is very closely related to atmosphere because certain kinds of atmosphere will create moods of different sorts. The mood of a piece of literature might be described in a single word: somber, gay, strange, comfortable, easy, happy, hopeful, or reflective. But more often the mood of a piece will not be easily described in a single word. More complex moods, such as those of apprehension, fear, and excitement—in combina-

tions that resist such simple definition—will be harder to describe.

Mood is apparent in all forms of literature: fiction, nonfiction, poetry, and drama. It is achieved often by description. But it can be achieved by skillful **dialogue** as well. The uses of **foreshadowing** and of **suspense** can help establish a variety of moods.

Edgar Allan Poe, a master of mood in poetry, establishes an unforgettable mood in his poem "To Helen." He uses vowel sounds such as the open **o** sound and the long **e** sound to set the mood. He then uses an unusual amount of **alliteration.** His intention is to connect Helen with the beauties of classical Greece by using language that is musical in sound. He also describes classical beauty by referring to classical ships (Nicaean barks):

> Helen, thy beauty is to me
>   Like those Nicaean barks of yore,
> That gently, o'er a perfumed sea,
>   The weary wayworn wanderer bore
>   To his own native shore.
>
> On desperate seas long wont to roam,
>   Thy hyacinth hair, thy classic face,
> Thy naiad airs have brought me home
>   To the glory that was Greece,
>   And the grandeur that was Rome.

> See **Foreshadowing, Suspense.**

MYTH *An ancient story often serving to explain a natural phenomenon and generally involving supernatural beings.* Sometimes myth, like legend, seems to have a general rooting in some historical event, but, unlike legend, myth concentrates far less on history than it does on stories that include supernatural elements. Myths explaining the origin of specific events, such as the ways in which the seas or the mountains came into being, exist in almost every culture. Likewise, almost every culture has myths that explain the beginnings of the world.

Classical mythology is the name given to the

myths developed by the ancient Greeks and the Romans. Most classical myths are about the gods and goddesses of Olympus. Norse mythology consists of myths of ancient Scandinavia and Germany.

See pages 574, 636.

NARRATION *The kind of writing or speaking that tells a story (a narrative).* Any narrative must be delivered by a narrator, whether it is the author or a character created by the author. The narrator's **point of view** can sometimes color the narration. In one famous mystery story by Agatha Christie, the reader does not realize until the last page that the narrator is the murderer. And the narrator's point of view is such that he thinks of himself as innocent.

See **Point of View.**
See also page 139.

NONFICTION *Any prose narrative that tells about things as they actually happened or that presents factual information about something.* One of the chief kinds of nonfiction is a history of someone's life. When a person writes his or her own life story, we call it **autobiography.** When someone else writes a person's life story, we call it **biography.** In each case, the purpose of the writing is to give an accounting of a person's life. Presumably, it is a true and accurate accounting. When someone writes about personal observations on some subject—as Jean Kerr does in "Dogs That Have Known Me"—the result is an **essay.** Essays are among the most common forms of nonfiction and appear in most of the magazines we see on the newsstands. Another kind of nonfiction is also to be found on newsstands: the newspaper itself. News stories, editorials, the letters to the editor, and feature stories of all kinds are forms of nonfiction. Travel stories, personal journals, and diaries are also forms of nonfiction.

See **Biography, Essay.**
See also pages 381, 425.

NOVEL *A fictional narrative in prose, generally longer than a short story.* The novel allows for greater complexity of character and plot development than the short story. The forms the novel may take cover a wide range. For example, there are the **historical novel,** in which historical characters, settings, and periods are drawn in detail; the **picaresque novel,** presenting the adventures of a rogue; and the **psychological novel,** which focuses on characters' emotions and thoughts. Other forms of the novel include the detective story, the spy thriller, and the science-fiction novel.

See page 502.

ONOMATOPOEIA *The use of a word whose sound in some degree imitates or suggests its meaning.* The names of some birds are onomatopoetic, imitating the cries of the birds named: *cuckoo, whippoorwill, owl, crow, towhee, bobwhite.* Some onomatopoetic words are *hiss, clang, rustle,* and *snap.* In these lines from Edgar Allan Poe's poem "The Bells," the word *tintinnabulation* is onomatopoetic:

> Keeping time, time, time
> In a sort of Runic rhyme,
> To the *tintinnabulation* that so musically wells
> From the bells, bells, bells, bells
> Bells, bells, bells—

See pages 300, 472.

PARAPHRASE *A summary or recapitulation of a piece of literature.* A paraphrase does not add anything to our enjoyment of a literary work. It merely tells in the simplest form what happened. A paraphrase of "The Highwayman" might go this way.

> The highwayman tells his sweetheart Bess that he will return to her with the gold he plans to steal that very night. Tim, a stableman who is in love with Bess, overhears this conversation and tells the British soldiers of the lovers' plan. A troop of soldiers comes to the inn and waits for the highwayman to return. Bess is gagged and bound to her bed,

but she is able to reach the trigger of a musket. When she hears the sound of horse hoofs in the distance, she pulls the trigger and warns the highwayman with her death. After he learns how Bess has died, the highwayman rides back for revenge, and is shot down on the highway. There is a legend that the lovers can still be seen and heard at the old inn on winter nights.

This summary gives us some essential information and is useful for checking to see just what did happen. But it is also clear that such a paraphrase is no substitute for the charm and beauty of the original poem.

See pages 432, 442.

PERSONIFICATION *A figure of speech in which something nonhuman is given human qualities.* In these lines from "Blow, Blow, Thou Winter Wind," William Shakespeare personifies the wind. He addresses it as if it were a person who could consciously act with kindness or unkindness. He also gives it teeth and breath.

Blow, blow, thou winter wind,
Thou art not so unkind
    As man's ingratitude.
Thy tooth is not so keen,
Because thou art not seen,
    Although thy breath be rude.

See page 489.

PLOT *The sequence of events or happenings in a literary work.* We generally associate plot with short stories, novels, and drama. Plot differs from narrative in that it is not merely a record of events as they happen, but an ordering of events in such a fashion as to bring them to a strongly satisfying conclusion. The use of **foreshadowing,** surprise, **suspense,** and carefully worked out **conflict** produces a tight pattern of action. Plot implies a step-by-step working out of events, in which each step takes us perceptibly closer to the unraveling of the action.

The major element in plot is **conflict,** or struggle of some kind. Sometimes the conflict is **external:** it takes place between characters and their environment—whether that be nature, the gods, or other characters. Often, the conflict is **internal,** or within the character's own mind. A plot will slowly reveal the nature of the conflict, the source of the conflict, illustrate its effects on the characters, and then show us how the conflict is resolved. If the conflict is not resolved, the plot will point toward changes in the lives of the characters that will be necessary to accommodate the conflict.

In most plots there is a point at which the intensity of the action rises to such a height we must consider it a point of **climax.** In Charles Dickens' "A Christmas Carol," the point of climax comes when Scrooge sees a vision of a tombstone bearing his name, and resolves to become a better man.

The **resolution** is the moment in the plot when the conflict ends. Not all plots have a resolution as such. In older stories, there generally is a resolution. In "A Christmas Carol," the conflict is resolved when Scrooge changes from a hardhearted miser to a warm and generous man. But many modern stories end without a resolution. They provide us with enough information so that we may draw our own inferences as to how the conflict will be resolved.

See pages 218, 333.

POETRY *Traditional poetry is language arranged in lines, with a regular rhythm and often a definite rhyme scheme. Nontraditional poetry does away with regular rhythm and rhyme, although it usually is set up in lines.* There is no satisfactory way of defining poetry, although most people have little trouble knowing when they read it. Some definitions offered by those concerned with it may help us. The English poet William Wordsworth called it "the spontaneous overflow of powerful feelings." He also called it "wisdom married to immortal verse." Matthew Arnold, an English writer and poet of the nineteenth century, defined it in this fashion:

"Poetry is simply the most beautiful, impressive, and widely effective mode of saying things."

Poetry often employs lines set up in **stanza** form. It uses **rhyme** in order to build the musicality of the language or to emphasize certain moods or effects. It uses **imagery** and **figurative language** widely. Techniques like **alliteration, repetition,** and **inversion** are often considered specifically poetic. Poetry depends heavily on strong **rhythms,** even when they are not regular.

A **narrative poem** tells a story, and like a story, it has characters, a setting, and action. A **lyric** expresses personal thoughts and feelings; it is usually brief. **Dramatic poetry** presents characters who speak to other characters or to some unidentified listener.

See the terms noted above.
See also pages 429, 430, 474, 488, 493, 498.

POINT OF VIEW *The vantage point from which a work is told.* Writers may choose a totally unlimited point of view or a narrow, limited one. In some cases the point of view will be of great importance, since we will be expected to draw inferences about the nature of the narrator. In other cases, the point of view will be of less importance, since it will have been chosen only to give us all the details of the story in the most direct way possible.

In the **third-person point of view,** the story is told by an outside observer. In the following passage, we are told that a character, Hester Martin, has made a decision. She is referred to in the third person ("she"), which is how this point of view gets its name:

Hester Martin could let the insult get her down. She could reply rudely or call for the man's manager and make a formal complaint. But she decided against both courses. Instead, she took the man aside and explained to him what it felt like to have someone who was a total stranger say some-

thing cruel, even if the man did not intend to be insulting. Whether he intended to be insulting or not, once Hester told him how she felt, he changed his manner entirely. She had done the right thing. She had educated him.

This is an example of the **omniscient,** or **all-knowing, point of view.** The author tells us things that Hester Martin does not directly think or observe. The author speculates on whether the man was consciously rude, just as the author ultimately tells us that Hester made the right decision. She does not know whether it was right or not. The author tells us so.

A **limited third-person** narrative tells only what one character sees, feels, and thinks. The same scene written from a limited third-person point of view might go this way:

Hester Martin felt her face flush. Did he notice it, too? Should she go to his manager? Should she insult him back? She took a moment to bring her emotions back under control, but when she collected herself she drew the man aside and lectured him carefully and patiently on the subject of insulting a patron. His apologies and his extraordinary politeness and caution gave her a small measure of satisfaction.

The **first-person point of view** tells everything from the "I" vantage point. Like the third-person limited point of view, this point of view tells only what the narrator knows and feels. We cannot be told what any other character thinks, except when the narrator may speculate about the character's feelings or thoughts. It is a very limited point of view, but its popularity is secure since we all identify with "I" in a story. The scene above, in the first-person narrative, might go this way:

I felt my face burn with the insult. I wondered if he noticed it. Should I go to his manager? No, I thought. And I won't stoop to his level and return the comment. When I thought I could control myself, I took the man aside and I told him in no uncertain terms that I did not like being insulted by a stranger. The only satisfaction I got was watching him try to squirm out of it, telling me he didn't mean it as an insult. But at least I got him to admit he was wrong. Maybe he learned a lesson.

See **Narration.**

See also pages 245, 275.

PROVERB   *A wise saying, usually quite old and usually of folk origin.* Proverbs are related to **morals,** the concluding lessons that are often attached to fables. A proverb like "A stitch in time saves nine," "A rolling stone gathers no moss," or "A new broom sweeps clean" could easily be the moral tag on a fable. Benjamin Franklin was one of the most prolific of modern proverb writers. His publication *Poor Richard's Almanac* always included at least one proverb per issue. One of Franklin's most famous sayings is, "A penny saved is a penny earned."

See page 678.

QUATRAIN   *A four-line stanza, usually rhymed.* Sometimes an entire poem will be in the form of a quatrain, while at other times the poem will be broken up into stanzas of quatrain length. One of the most famous quatrains in poetry is that of Edward Fitzgerald in his translation of Omar Khayám's *The Rubáiyát:*

A book of verses underneath the bough,
A jug of wine, a loaf of bread—and thou
   Beside me singing in the wilderness—
   O, Wilderness were paradise enow!

REFRAIN   *A word, phrase, line, or group of lines that is repeated regularly in a poem or song, usually at the end of each stanza.* One of the delights in refrains is in anticipating their return. Many ballads use refrains. Sometimes the refrain is repeated exactly the same way and sometimes it is varied slightly for effect.

See pages 163, 465.

REPETITION   *The return of a word, phrase, stanza form, or effect in any form of literature.* Repetition in all its forms is probably the most dependably used literary device. **Alliteration,** repeating sounds at the beginning, middle, or end of words, is one of the most common kinds of repetition in poetry. **Rhyme** is also a form of repetition. The **refrain** in ballads and songs is a form of repetition. Once we realize that these are forms of repetition, we can begin to appreciate how important the device is. We do not wholly understand how it affects us, since the device is very complex. We do know that a stanza such as the opening quatrain in Lewis Carroll's "Jabberwocky" reads at first as if it were a foreign language:

'Twas brillig, and the slithy toves
   Did gyre and gimble in the wabe;
All mimsy were the borogoves,
   And the mome raths outgrabe.

After the entire story of the boy's adventurous slaying of the Jabberwock is told, the stanza is repeated. Then it seems much clearer and much easier to read. It also takes on the odd quality of being comforting to us.

One of the great masters of repetition is Edgar Allan Poe. He actually worked out theories of how poetry affects a reader. His conclusion was that simple repetition was one of the most important and functional devices a poet could use. His poem "Annabel Lee" is filled with repetitive references to her name, since it was for him an immensely musical name. He also repeats in its entirety the phrase "kingdom by the sea." Such repetitions are not only pleasurable—they also build emotional tension in his poems. In one of his poems, "Annie," Poe tries to build a sense of feverish intensity. The subject of the poem is Annie's death. In one stanza, Poe repeats himself almost nervously:

A holier odor
   About it, of pansies—

A rosemary odor,
   Commingled with pansies—

With rue and the beautiful
    Puritan pansies.

Sometimes a poet will repeat a formula line with slight differences each time. Christina Georgina Rossetti, an English poet of the nineteenth century, wrote this stanza in her poem "A Birthday":

My heart is like a singing bird
    Whose nest is in a watered shoot;
My heart is like an apple tree
    Whose boughs are bent with thick-set
        fruit;
My heart is like a rainbow shell
    That paddles in a halcyon sea;
My heart is gladder than all these,
    Because my love is come to me.

See **Alliteration, Refrain, Rhyme.**
See also pages 460, 463.

RHYME *The repetition of sounds in words, usually, but not exclusively, at the ends of lines of poetry.* One of the primary uses of rhyme is as an aid to memory. Rhyme is used for this purpose in certain rules, such as: "Thirty days hath September, April, June, and November," and *"I before e except after c."*

The most familiar form of rhyme is the **end rhyme.** This simply means the rhymes come at the end of the lines. The following passage is from a long poem on the muse of music by the English poet Alexander Pope. He is trying to re-create the sounds of the underworld when Orpheus sang there in order to rescue his beloved wife, Eurydice:

What sounds were heard,
What scenes appeared,
    O'er all the dreary coasts!
      Dreadful gleams,
      Dismal screams,

      Fires that glow,
      Shrieks of woe,
      Sullen moans,
      Hollow groans,
And cries of tortured ghosts!

Each of these rhymes was an **exact rhyme** for Pope, although we now pronounce *heard* differently from *appeared.* (We call this a **partial rhyme**—the final consonant sounds are the same, but the vowel sounds are different.) The rhyme of *coasts* and *ghosts,* separated by six lines, is a marvelous example of **distant rhyme.**

Exact rhyme insists that the two words rhymed sound exactly the same. The most common form of exact rhyme is **strong rhyme.** Strong rhyme refers to words of one syllable that rhyme: *place/space.* It also refers to words of more than one syllable where the rhyme occurs on the stressed syllable: *approve/remove.* In **weak rhyme,** there are two or more syllables that rhyme, but the accent does not fall on the last syllable: *sínging/clínging: wéarily/dréarily.* The terms *strong* and *weak* do not have anything to do with the qualities of the sounds themselves. The first two rhymes in John Gay's poem "Song" are weak. The next two are strong:

O ruddier than the cherry!
O sweeter than the berry!
    O nymph more bright
    Than the moonshine night.

Rhyme that occurs within a line is called **internal rhyme.** Usually, the rhyme word appears in the middle of a line and rhymes with an end rhyme from the line above or from its own line. One of the masters of this technique is Edgar Allan Poe, who begins the first line of "The Raven" with the internal weak rhyme *eerie:* "Once upon a midnight dreary, while I pondered, weak and weary." Clearly, the reasons for rhyming in these poems go far beyond a simple memory device.

Rhymes in the work of Pope, Poe, or any other careful poet serve many purposes. One is to increase the musicality of the poem. Rhyme appeals to the ear. Another purpose is to give delight by rewarding our anticipation of a returning sound, such as the *coasts/ghosts* rhyme in Pope's poem. There is also the purpose of humor. Limericks, for instance, would not be half so funny if they did not rhyme—particularly when the rhymes are strained for comic effect.

See **Poetry, Repetition.**
See also pages 460, 463.

RHYTHM   *The pattern of stressed and unstressed sounds in a line of poetry.* All language has rhythm of some sort or another, but rhythm is most important in poetry, where it is carefully controlled for effect.

The effects of rhythm are several. Rhythm contributes to the musical quality of a poem, which gives the reader or listener pleasure. Rhythm can also be used to imitate the action being described in the poem. In Robert Browning's poem "How They Brought the Good News from Ghent to Aix," the lines actually imitate the galloping rhythm of horses' hoofs:

> And there was my Roland to bear the
>   whole weight,
> Of the news which alone could save Aix
>   from her fate,
> With his nostrils like pits full of blood to the
>   brim,
> And with circles of red for his eye sockets'
>   rim.

Scanning the lines—examining them for the stressed and unstressed syllables—is not easy. It requires practice. One thing to remember is that good poets usually put stress on the most important words in the line. If you say the line to yourself in a natural voice, you will hear that the most important words demand the stress.

Browning uses techniques other than just stressed and unstressed syllables to intensify his rhythm. The lines above are all one sentence and must be read in a single breath, thus building a feeling of constant motion. Even the internal rhyme of *there* and *bear* in the first line

builds rhythmic intensity, since the stresses fall on those words. In the last two lines, stressed words are accented by having them also alliterate: *b*lood/*b*rim; *r*ed/*r*im. Such devices help build even more rhythmic pressure in a poem that depends heavily on rhythm for its effect.

Rhyme also contributes to rhythm in poetry, since it causes us to feel that a passage has come to an end. When rhymes fall close together, we have the feeling that we must pause in our reading of the lines. An extreme example is from "Endymion," a long poem by John Keats:

> O sorrow!
> Why dost borrow
> The natural hue of health, from vermeil
>   lips?—
> To give maiden blushes
> To the white rose bushes?
> Or is it the dewy hand the daisy tips?

In addition to the rhymes, Keats uses another technique that many poets like to employ: that of asking questions in the poem. Any question has a natural rhythm of its own, so poets can capitalize on this fact and use it to their own purposes. Here, Keats is trying to have us read rhythmically in order to build in us a questioning sense of the meaning of things. He is asking in these lines why sorrow takes the healthy redness from some people's lips. Perhaps, he asks, it is to give the redness to the roses and the daisies.

One of the most powerful means of building rhythm in poetry is through repetition. Consider this passage, the last lines from Edgar Allan Poe's "The Bells":

> Keeping time, time, time,
> In a sort of Runic rhyme,
>   To the throbbing of the bells—
> Of the bells, bells, bells—
>   To the sobbing of the bells;
> Keeping time, time, time,
>   As he knells, knells, knells.
> In a happy Runic rhyme,

To the rolling of the bells—
  Of the bells, bells, bells:—
    To the tolling of the bells—
  Of the bells, bells, bells, bells,
    Bells, bells, bells—
To the moaning and the groaning of the bells.

The repetition of the words *bells, knells,* and *time* builds up a rhythm that suggests the repeated ringing of bells.

    See **Alliteration, Repetition, Rhyme.**
    See also pages 468, 473.

SETTING *The time and place of action.* In short stories and novels, the setting is generally established by description. Setting can be important in poetry and nonfiction as well, and the means of establishing setting is through description, as in fiction. In dramas, the setting is usually established by stage directions and then reinforced in dialogue. Since a drama normally has sets that appear before an audience, elaborate descriptions of setting are unnecessary.

In the first sentence of "The Legend of Sleepy Hollow" Washington Irving establishes the setting of the story:

> In the bosom of one of those spacious coves which indent the eastern shore of the Hudson, at that broad expansion of the river named by the ancient Dutch navigators the Tappan Zee, there lies a small market town or rural port, which by some is called Greensburgh, but which is more generally and properly known by the name of Tarrytown.

The setting establishes not only the physical locale (Tarrytown) but also something of historical moment as well. This tells us right away that history may have something to do with the story.

Setting can be of great importance in establishing mood or building emotional intensity. Here is the famous opening passage from "The Fall of the House of Usher" by Edgar Allan Poe. Note how the italicized words help to build an atmosphere of gloom:

> During the whole of a *dull, dark,* and *soundless* day in the autumn of the year, when the clouds hung *oppressively low* in the heavens, I had been passing alone, on horseback, through a *singularly dreary* tract of country, and at length found myself, as the shades of the evening drew on, within view of the *melancholy* House of Usher.

In "The Wreck of the *Hesperus,*" Henry Wadsworth Longfellow describes the setting in highly emotional terms. Longfellow uses figurative language to intensify his description of a storm at sea:

> Colder and louder blew the wind,
>   A gale from the Northeast,
> The snow fell hissing in the brine,
>   And the billows frothed like yeast.
>
>   . . .
>
> And fast through the midnight dark and
>   drear,
>   Through the whistling sleet and snow,
> Like a sheeted ghost, the vessel swept
>   Toward the reef of Norman's Woe.

    See pages 176, 260.

SIMILE *A comparison between two unlike things, using* like, as, *and similar words of comparison.* Similes are **figures of speech** and are common in everyday language and in most forms of literature. We use simile when we say: "He fought like a tiger"; "He was as mild as a dove"; and "She was cooler than a cucumber." A more poetic use of simile is this, from Lord Byron's "Stanzas for Music":

> There will be none of Beauty's daughters
>   With a magic like thee;
> And like music on the waters
>   Is thy sweet voice to me.

    See **Figurative Language.**
    See also pages 451, 523.

STANZA *A group of lines forming a unit in a poem.* Some poems have a single stanza. Other poems are divided into several stanzas, each of which has the same number of lines and the same rhyme scheme. Some poems do not repeat the same structure in each stanza, yet each group of lines is still referred to as a stanza. "The Broncho That Would Not Be Broken" by Vachel Lindsay has a regular pattern of five stanzas, each containing eight lines. "Annabel Lee" by Edgar Allan Poe has six stanzas. Three of the stanzas have six lines, one has seven lines, and two have eight lines.

See **Poetry**.

SUSPENSE *That quality in a literary work that makes the reader or audience uncertain or tense about what is to come next.* Suspense is a kind of "suspending" of our emotions. We know something is about to happen, and the longer the writer can keep us anticipating what will happen, the greater the suspense. The device is popular in all kinds of literature that involve plot, whether nonfiction, short stories, drama, or poetry. Suspense is possible even when the reader knows the outcome. At the opening of "Guinea Pig," Ruth McKenney tells us that she was almost drowned by a Red Cross Lifesaving Examiner and that she received a black eye in the cause of serving others. Although we know what to expect, we are still eager to find out what has led to these circumstances. Holding the reader off for as long as possible is part of the strategy of building suspense. Some writers feel it works even better when we know what is coming, so they let us know through **foreshadowing.**

See **Plot**.
See also page 227.

THEME *The main idea or the basic meaning of a literary work.* Not all literary works can be said to have a theme. Some stories are told chiefly for entertainment and have little to say about life or about human nature. But in those stories that try to make a comment on the human condition, theme is of great importance.

Because theme in fiction is rarely expressed directly, it is not always obvious to every reader. Theme is one of those qualities of a piece of literature that must be dug out and thought about. The reason for this is that writers develop their themes for thoughtful people. They expect that one of the rewards of reading for such people is the pleasure of inferring the theme on their own.

Usually, however, careful writers set up their stories so that one can pick out passages here and there that focus on the theme. Such "key passages" point in the right direction so that we are not totally unaided in coming to understand the theme. Key passages are recognizable because they seem to speak directly to us as readers. They also make direct statements of a philosophical nature, discussing the meaning of the action and the lessons the characters may have learned. In "A Christmas Carol," one key passage that points toward the theme of the story is this speech by Marley's ghost, warning Scrooge to change his ways before it is too late:

> "Mankind was my business. The common welfare was my business; charity, mercy, forbearance, benevolence, were all my business. The dealings of my trade were but a drop of water in the comprehensive ocean of my business!"

Some simple themes can be stated in a single sentence. Sometimes a literary work is rich and complex, and a paragraph or essay is needed to state the theme. When deciding upon what we think the theme of a story is, we must be careful to doublecheck our ideas against the action of the story. We must test our sense of theme to be sure the actions of the main characters are consistent with our conclusions. If their actions contradict the theme we have arrived at, we must go back, reread the story, and see if we have made a mistake, or if the author has used the contradiction to some literary purpose.

See page 274.

GLOSSARY

The words listed in the glossary in the following pages are found in the selections in this textbook. You can use this glossary as you would a dictionary—to look up words that are unfamiliar to you. Strictly speaking, the word *glossary* means a collection of technical, obscure, or foreign words found in a certain field of work. Of course, the words in this glossary are not "technical, obscure, or foreign," but are those that might present difficulty as you read the selections in this textbook.

Many words in the English language have several meanings. In this glossary, the meanings given are the ones that apply to the words as they are used in the selections in the textbook. Words closely related in form and meaning are generally listed together in one entry (**immobile** and **immobility**), and the definition is given for the first form. Regular adverbs (ending in *-ly*) are defined in their adjective form, with the adverb form shown at the end of the definition.

The following abbreviations are used:

    adj., adjective   *n.*, noun
    adv., adverb   *v.*, verb

For more information about the words in this glossary, consult a dictionary.

A

abash (ə-băsh′) *v.* To embarrass.—**abashed** *adj.*
abate (ə-bāt′) *v.* To lessen.
abet (ə-bĕt′) *v.* To encourage.
abnormal (ăb-nôr′məl) *adj.* Not normal; strange—**abnormally** *adv.*
abode (ə-bōd′) *n.* A home.
abrupt (ə-brŭpt′) *adj.* Sudden.—**abruptly** *adv.*
abundant (ə-bŭn′dənt) *adj.* Plentiful.
acclaim (ə-klām′) *v.* To greet; salute.
accommodate (ə-kŏm′ə-dāt′) *v.* To serve; oblige.
accomplice (ə-kŏm′plĭs) *n.* A partner in an activity, especially in a crime.

accost (ə-kôst′, ə-kŏst′) *v.* To meet and speak to first, often in an aggressive way.
acknowledgment (ăk-nŏl′ĭj-mənt) *n.* **1.** An admission. **2.** A sign of recognition.
adept (ə-dĕpt′) *adj.* Expert.
adhesive (ăd-hē′sĭv, zĭv) *adv.* Sticky.
adjoining (ə-joi′nĭng) *adj.* Next to; neighboring.
adjudge (ə-jŭj′) *v.* To determine or declare.
admonish (ăd-mŏn′ĭsh) *v.* To correct someone in a kindly manner.
adobe (ə-dō′bē) *adj.* Made of sun-dried bricks of clay and straw.
aesthetic (ĕs-thĕt′ĭk) *adj.* Relating to principles of beauty.—**aesthetically** *adv.*
affect (ə-fĕkt′) *v.* To put on; pretend.
afflict (ə-flĭkt′) *v.* To cause to suffer.—**afflicted** *adj.*
afford (ə-fôrd′, ə-fōrd′) *v.* To provide.
aggravate (ăg′-rə-vāt′) *v.* To irritate; annoy.
aghast (ə-găst′, ə-gäst′) *adj.* Shocked; horrified.
agitation (ăj′ə-tā′shən) *n.* Emotional upset.
airs (ârs) *n.* Affectation.
ajar (ə-jär′) *adj.* Slightly open.
alcove (ăl′kōv′) *n.* A recessed area in a room, as for a bed.
alienate (āl′yən-āt′, ā′lē-ən-) *v.* **1.** To make unfriendly. **2.** To turn away.
alist (ə-lĭst′) *adj.* Tilted.
allay (ə-lā′) *v.* To soothe; calm.
allege (ə-lĕj′) *v.* To declare or affirm.
alleged (ə-lĕjd′) *adj.* Supposed.
alloy (ə-loi′, ăl′oi′) *v.* To lessen or mar.
allurement (ə-lōor′mənt) *n.* A temptation.
aloof (ə-lōof′) *adj.* Unfriendly; cold.
amble (ăm′bəl) *v.* To walk in a leisurely way.
amiable (ā′mē-ə-bəl) *adj.* Friendly; agreeable.
ample (ăm′pəl) *adj.* Large; spacious.
analogous (ə-năl′ə-gəs) *adj.* Similar.
anesthetic (ăn′ĭs-thĕt′ĭk) *n.* Something that deadens physical sensations.
anguish (ăng′gwĭsh) *n.* Great suffering.
animated (ăn′ə-mā′tĭd) *adj.* Lively.—**animatedly** *adv.*

anoint (ə-noint′) *v.* To rub the body with oil.

anonymous (ə-nŏn′ə-məs) *adj.* Without a name; not identified.

antiquity (ăn-tĭk′wə-tē) *n.* The quality of being old or ancient.

anxiety (ăng-zī′ə-tē) *n.* Worry.

apparition (ăp′ə-rĭsh′ən) *n.* A ghost or phantom.

appease (ə-pēz′) *v.* To satisfy.—**appeased** *adj.*

appendage (ə-pĕn′dĭj) *n.* An attachment.

appendix (ə-pĕn′dĭks) *n.* Something added on.

appraise (ə-prāz′) *v.* To judge the value of.— **appraising** *adj.*

apprehension (ăp′rĭ-hĕn′shən) *n.* Fear.

apprehensive (ăp′rĭ-hĕn′sĭv) *adj.* Uneasy; fearful.

approbation (ap′rə-bā′shən) *n.* Approval.

aquamarine (ăk′wə-mə-rēn′, äk′wə-) *adj.* Pale blue-green.

aquiline (ăk′wə-līn′, -lĭn) *adj.* Curved like an eagle's beak.

ardent (är′dənt) *adj.* Enthusiastic; intense.

areaway (âr′ē-ə-wā′) *n.* A passageway between buildings.

arid (ăr′ĭd) *adj.* Very dry.

aristocracy (ăr′ĭs-tŏk′rə-sē) *n.* The upper class.

aristocrat (ə-rĭs′tə-krăt′, ăr′ĭs-tə-)*n.* A member of the nobility; an upper-class person.

array (ə-rā′) *n.* A large display.

arresting (ə-rĕs′tĭng) *adj.* Attracting attention.

arrogant (ăr′ə-gənt) *adj.* Excessively proud; self-important.

articulate (är-tĭk′yə-lĭt) *adj.* Able to speak clearly.

asbestos (ăs-bĕs′təs, ăz-) *adj.* Made of asbestos, which is fire-resistant.

ascent (ə-sĕnt′) *n.* An upward slope.

askance (ə-skăns′) *adv.* With a side glance.

aspen (ăs′pən) *n.* A kind of poplar tree.

aspiration (ăs′pə-rā′shən) *n.* High ambition or desire.

assail (ə-sāl′) *v.* To attack.

assault (ə-sôlt′) *n.* An attack.

assess (ə-sĕs′) *v.* To determine the value of.

asset (ăs′ĕt′) *n.* An advantage.

astride (ə-strīd′) *adj.* With one leg on each side of.

atmosphere (ăt′mə-sfîr′) *n.* The air surrounding the earth.

atonement (ə-tōn′mənt) *n.* Satisfaction or amends for wrongdoing.

atrocious (ə-trō′shəs) *adj.* Monstrous, extremely bad.

attitude (ăt′ə-tood′, -tyood′) *n.* A position of the body expressing some action or emotion.

attribute (ăt′rə-byoot′) *n.* A quality or characteristic.

atypical (ā-tĭp′ĭ-kəl) *adj.* Unusual.

aura (ôr′ə) *n.* An air or quality that seems to surround a person.

avail (ə-vāl′) *v.* To be of help or use.

avaricious (ăv′ə-rĭsh′əs) *adj.* Greedy.—**avariciously** *adv.*

avenge (ə-vĕnj′) *v.* To take revenge.

avert (ə-vûrt′) *v.* To prevent.

avowed (ə-voud′) *adj.* Confessed; admitted.

awe (ô) *n.* A feeling of great reverence for someone or something.—**awed** *adj.*

azure (ăzh′ər) *adj.* Sky-blue.

B

bafflement (băf′əl-mənt) *n.* Bewilderment; state of being confused.

balk (bôk) *v.* To stop and refuse to go on.

banish (băn′ĭsh) *v.* To force to leave.

bankrupt (băngk′rŭpt′, -rəpt) *v.* To ruin financially.

banter (băn′tər) *v.* To tease in a good-humored way.

barrette (bə-rĕt′, bä-) *n.* A clip for holding the hair in place.

bay (bā) *v.* To bark or howl.

bayonet (bā′ə-nĭt, -nĕt′, bā′ə-nĕt′) *n.* A daggerlike blade attached to a rifle.

beaker (bē′kər) *n.* A large container for liquids.

beckon (bĕk′ən) *v.* To motion to come forward.— **beckoning** *adj.*

begrudge (bĭ-grŭj′) *v.* To resent.

behest (bĭ-hĕst′) *n.* Request.

benevolence (bə-nĕv′ə-ləns) *n.* Good will.

bewilderment (bĭ-wĭl′dər-mənt) *n.* Puzzlement; confusion.

billow (bĭl′ō) *n.* A large wave.

blare (blâr) *n.* A loud, brassy sound.

bleak (blēk) *adj.* Cheerless.

ă pat/ā pay/âr care/ä father/b bib/ch church/d deed/ĕ pet/ē be/f fife/g gag/h hat/hw which/ĭ pit/ī pie/îr pier/j judge/k kick/ l lid, needle/m mum/n no, sudden/ng thing/ŏ pot/ō toe/ô paw, for/oi noise/ou out/ŏŏ took/ōŏ boot/p pop/r roar/s sauce/ sh ship, dish/t tight/th thin, path/*th* this, bathe/ŭ cut/ûr urge/v valve/w with/y yes/z zebra, size/zh vision/ə about, item, edi- ble, gallop, circus/á *Fr.* ami/œ *Fr.* feu, *Ger.* schön/ü *Fr.* tu, *Ger.* über/ĸʜ *Ger.* ich, *Scot.* loch/ɴ *Fr.* bon.

blemish (blĕm'ĭsh) *n.* A slight defect.

bloat (blōt) *v.* To swell up.

bloated (blōt'əd) *adj.* Swollen.

bloom (blōōm) *v.* To grow; flourish.

bloomers (blōō'mərs) *n.* Baggy trousers once worn by women for athletics.

blunt (blŭnt) *adj.* Frank and abrupt.

bootleg (bōōt'lĕg') *v.* To produce or sell something, such as liquor, illegally.—**bootlegger** *n.*

boudoir (bōō'dwär', -dwôr') *n.* A woman's bedroom.

bough (bou) *n.* A branch of a tree.

bound (bound) *v.* To leap up or forward.

bow (bou) *n.* The front of a ship.

brand (brănd) *n.* A piece of burning wood or a hot iron.

brandish (brăn'dĭsh) *v.* To wave in a threatening way.

bravado (brə-vä'dō) *n.* False courage.

breaker (brā'kər) *n.* A wave as it breaks, especially against the shore.

bridle (brīd'l) *v.* To put a harness on a horse.—**bridled** *adj.*

brine (brīn) *n.* The sea.

brisk (brĭsk) *adj.* Lively.—**briskly** *adv.*

bristle (brĭs'əl) *v.* To react angrily.

brood (brōōd) *n.* The young of a family.

brook (brŏŏk) *v.* To put up with; permit.

brusque (brŭsk) *adj.* Rude.—**brusquely** *adv.*

buffet (bŭf'ĭt) *v.* Hit.—**buffeted** *adj.*

burden (bûrd'n) *n.* A heavy weight.

burly (bûr'lē) *adj.* Husky.

burnish (bûr'nĭsh) *v.* To polish.—**burnished** *adj.*

butte (byōōt) *n.* A hill with steep sides.

C

cable (kā'bəl) *n.* A heavy rope or chain.

calamity (kə-lăm'ə-tē) *n.* A disaster.

calculate (kăl'kyə-lāt') *v.* To figure out; guess.

caliber (kăl'ə-bər) *n.* Quality or worth of a person or thing.

calico (kăl'ĭ-kō) *n.* A spotted cat.

camaraderie (kä'mə-rä'də-rē, kăm'ə-) *n.* A friendly feeling among people in a group.

camisole (kăm'ə-sōl') *n.* A woman's waist-length sleeveless undergarment.

camouflage (kăm'ə-fläzh', -fläj') *v.* To conceal; disguise.—**camouflaged** *adj.*

canopy (kăn'ə-pē) *n.* A covering.

canter (kăn'tər) *v.* To move at an easy pace.

capacious (kə-pā'shəs) *adj.* Able to hold a large quantity; roomy.

caper (kā'pər) *v.* To leap playfully.—**capering** *n.*

capital (kăp'ə-təl) *adj.* Excellent.

capsize (kăp'sīz', kăp-sīz') *v.* To turn over.

capsule (kăp'səl, -syōōl) *n.* A small container of medicine.

caravel (kăr'ə-vĕl') *n.* A sailing ship used in the fifteenth and sixteenth centuries.

carcass (kär'kəs) *n.* The dead body of an animal.

careen (kə-rēn') *v.* To move rapidly, out of control.

caress (kə-rĕs') *v.* To touch someone lovingly.

carrion (kăr'ē-ən) *n.* Dead, decaying flesh.

cascade (kăs-kād)' *v.* To fall in great amounts.

catapult (kăt'ə-pŭlt) *v.* To leap.

cathedral (kə-thē'drəl) *n.* A large, impressive church.

caustic (kôs'tĭk) *adj.* Sharp in speech.

celebrity (sə-lĕb'rə-tē) *n.* A famous person.

celluloid (sĕl'yə-loid') *n.* A substance used for toys, film, and toilet articles.

chaff (chăf) *n.* The waste part of grain.

chagrin (shə-grĭn') *n.* A feeling of annoyance and embarrassment.

chamois (shăm'ē) *adj.* Referring to a soft leather made from the hide of the chamois, a small antelope, or from the skin of sheep, deer, or goats.

champ (chămp) *v.* To chew on.

chaos (kā'ŏs') *n.* Extreme confusion.

charger (chär'jər) *n.* A horse trained for battle or parade.

chasm (kăz'əm) *n.* A deep opening in the earth's surface.

chaste (chāst) *adj.* Pure.

chastisement (chăs-tīz'mənt, chăs'tĭz-mənt) *n.* Punishment.

chivalrous (shĭv'əl-rəs) *adj.* Showing the gallantry and courtesy of a knight.

chops (chŏps) *n.* The mouth, the jaws.

churl (chûrl) *n.* A miser.

churn (chûrn) *v.* To move or shake vigorously.

citadel (sĭt'ə-dəl, -dĕl') *n.* A fort that protects a city.

civic (sĭv'ĭk) *adj.* Referring to a city or to a citizen.

clamber (klăm'ər, klăm'bər) *v.* To climb clumsily or with difficulty, usually on hands and knees.

clamor (klăm'ər) *n.* A loud noise. *v.* To make a loud, continuous noise.—**clamorous** *adj.*

cleave (klēv) *v.* To cut.

clientele (klī'ən-tĕl') *n.* Customers.

clutch (klŭch) *v.* To hold tightly.

cobble (kŏb′əl) *n.* A stone used to pave streets.

colleague (kŏl′ēg′) *n.* A co-worker; associate.

colossal (kə-lŏs′əl) *adj.* Gigantic.

commission (kə-mĭsh′ən) *n.* A fee or percentage paid to another for doing something.

commit (kə-mĭt′) *v.* To bind by promise; pledge.—**committed** *adj.*

commotion (kə-mō′shən) *n.* A minor upset or disturbance; confusion.

commute (kə-myo͞ot′) *v.* To travel back and forth regularly, as from one city to another.

compel (kŏm-pĕl′) *v.* To force.

competent (kŏm′pə-tənt) *adj.* Skillful.

compound (kŏm-pound′, kəm-) *v.* To mix.—(kŏm′pound) *n.* A mixture.—**compounded** *adj.*

compressor (kəm-prĕs′ər) *n.* A machine for increasing the pressure of gases.

compulsion (kəm-pŭl′shən) *n.* A force; an irresistable urge.

concede (kən-sēd′) *v.* To admit.

concerto (kən-chĕr′tō) *n.* A kind of musical composition.

concord (kŏn′kôrd, kŏng′-) *n.* Peace.

confound (kən-found′, kŏn-) *v.* To surprise and confuse.—**confounded** *adj.*

confront (kən-frŭnt′) *v.* To meet someone face to face, often in an unfriendly way.

congeal (kən-jēl′) *v.* To become solid; jell.

congenial (kən-jēn′yəl) *adj.* Pleasant; agreeable.

conjure (kŏn′jər, kŏn-jo͝or′) *v.* To call upon; bring to mind.

conquest (kŏn′kwĕst, kŏng′-) *n.* A victory.

conservatory (kən-sûr′və-tôr′ē, -tōr′ē) *n.* A school of music.

consolation (kŏn′sə-lā′shən) *n.* A comfort.

console (kən-sōl′) *v.* To comfort.—**consoled** *adj.*

conspicuous (kən-spĭk′yo͞o-əs) *adj.* Easily seen; obvious.

constrain (kən-strān′) *v.* To check; control.—**constrained** *adj.*

consume (kən-so͞om′, -syo͞om′) *v.* To destroy.

consumption (kən-sŭmp′shən) *n.* Using up.

contemplate (kŏn′təm-plāt′) *v.* To look at thoughtfully.

contemplation (kŏn′təm-plā′shən) *n.* Meditation; deep thought.

contemporary (kən-tĕm′pə-rĕr′ē) *n.* A person of about the same age as another.

contempt (kən-tĕmpt′) *n.* Scorn.

contemptuous (kən-tĕmp′cho͞o-əs) *adj.* Scornful.—**contemptuously** *adv.*

contort (kən-tôrt′) *v.* To twist into unusual shapes.

contrive (kən-trīv′) *v.* **1.** To manage to do something. **2.** To scheme or plan.—**contrivance** *n.*

contuse (kən-to͞oz′, -tyo͞oz′) *v.* To bruise.—**contusion** *n.*

conventional (kən-vĕn′shən-əl) *adj.* Usual; ordinary.

converge (kən-vûrj′) *v.* To move toward one point; to come together.

convert (kən-vûrt′) *v.* To change.

convivial (kən-vĭv′ē-əl) *adj.* Good-humored; sociable.—**conviviality** *n.*

convulsive (kən-vŭl′sĭv) *adj.* Jerky.

coral (kôr′əl, kŏr′əl) *n.* A stonelike substance used in jewelry and other ornaments.

corroborate (kə-rŏb′ə-rāt′) *v.* To confirm.

countenance (koun′tə-nəns) *n.* The face.

countinghouse (koun′tĭng-hous′) *n.* A place where accounting and other business operations take place.

covert (kŭv′ərt, kō′vərt) *n.* A hiding place.

covetous (kŭv′ə-təs) *adj.* Greedy.

covey (kŭv′ē) *n.* A small flock.

crack (krăk) *adj.* First-rate.

crafty (krăf′tē, kräf′-) *adj.* Shrewd; deceitful.

crane (krān) *v.* To stretch.

cranny (krăn′ē) *n.* A crack in a wall.

cremation (krĭ-mā′shən) *n.* The incineration of a body.

crestfallen (krĕst′fô′lən) *adj.* Low in spirits; depressed.

crevasse (krə-văs′) *n.* A deep crack in the earth.

crimson (krĭm′zən) *adj.* Deep red.

croon (kro͞on) *v.* To sing softly.

croupier (kro͞o′pē-ər, -pē-ā′) *n.* A person who takes in and pays out money at a gambling table.

crucial (kro͞o′shəl) *adj.* Decisive.

crux (krŭks, kro͝oks) *n.* The most important part.

culprit (kŭl′prĭt) *n.* A guilty person.

cumbersome (kŭm′bər-səm) *adj.* Heavy and awkward.

ă pat/ā pay/âr care/ä father/b bib/ch church/d deed/ĕ pet/ē be/f fife/g gag/h hat/hw which/ĭ pit/ī pie/îr pier/j judge/k kick/ l lid, needle/m mum/n no, sudden/ng thing/ŏ pot/ō toe/ô paw, for/oi noise/ou out/o͞o took/o͞o boot/p pop/r roar/s sauce/ sh ship, dish/t tight/th thin, path/*th* this, bathe/ŭ cut/ûr urge/v valve/w with/y yes/z zebra, size/zh vision/ə about, item, edi- ble, gallop, circus/á *Fr.* ami/œ *Fr.* feu, *Ger.* schön/ü *Fr.* tu, *Ger.* über/кн *Ger.* ich, *Scot.* loch/N *Fr.* bon.

curator (kyŏŏ-rā′tər, kyŏŏr′ə-tər) *n.* A person in charge of a museum, library, or exhibit.

cynical (sĭn′ĭ-kəl) *adj.* Sneering; sarcastic.

D

dappled (dăp′əld) *adj.* Spotted.

decamp (dĭ-kămp′) *v.* To leave.

deceitful (dĭ-sēt′fəl) *adj.* Not honest.

decipher (dĭ-sī′fər) *v.* To figure out.

declamation (dĕk′lə-mā′shən) *n.* A long, pompous speech.

decline (dĭ-klīn′) *v.* To turn down; refuse.

deform (dĭ-fôrm′) *v.* To cause to be misshapen; disfigure.

deformed (dĭ-fôrmd′) *adj.* Misshapen.

deft (dĕft) *adj.* Skillful.—**deftly** *adv.*

deliberate (dĭ-lĭb′ə-rāt′) *v.* To think about carefully. —(dĭ-lĭb′ər-ĭt) *adj.* Intentional.—**deliberately** *adv.*

deluge (dĕl′yōōj) *v.* To flood. *n.* A flood.

delve (dĕlv) *v.* To study something deeply.

deportment (dĭ-pôrt′mənt, dĭ-pōrt′-) *n.* Behavior.

depressed (dĭ-prĕst′) *adj.* Sad.

desolate (dĕs′ə-lĭt) *adj.* Deserted.—**desolateness** *n.*

desolation (dĕs′ə-lā′shən) *n.* Ruin; emptiness.

despondency (dĭ-spŏn′dən-sē) *n.* Hopelessness.

despotism (dĕs′pə-tĭz′əm) *n.* Tyranny; dictatorship.

destitute (dĕs′tə-tōōt′, -tyōōt′) *adj.* Extremely poor.

desultory (dĕs′əl-tôr′ē, -tōr′ē) *adj.* Aimless.

detect (dĭ-tĕkt′) *v.* To discover.

detonate (dĕt′n-āt′) *v.* To make explode.— **detonation** *n.*

devise (dĭ-vīz′) *v.* To plan.

dexterity (dĕk-stĕr′-ə-tē) *n.* Skill in using the hands.

diameter (dī-ăm′ĭ-tər) *n.* **1.** Width. **2.** A straight line through the center of a circle.

dilapidated (dĭ-lăp′ə-dā′tĭd) *adj.* In very bad condition.

dilate (dī-lāt′, dī′lāt′, dĭ-lāt′) *v.* To become larger.— **dilated** *adj.*

dimension (dĭ-mĕn′shən) *n.* Size; scope.

diminish (dĭ-mĭn′ĭsh) *v.* To reduce.

dingy (dĭn′jē) *adj.* Dirty; dull.

dire (dīr) *adj.* Frightening.

disability (dĭs′ə-bĭl′ə-tē) *n.* **1.** A condition that prevents someone from working. **2.** A disadvantage.

discard (dĭs-kärd′) *v.* To throw away.

discharge (dĭs-chärj′) *v.* To dismiss.

disclose (dĭs-klōz′) *v.* To reveal; to make known.

discriminate (dĭs-krĭm′ə-nāt′) *v.* **1.** To show prejudice. **2.** To draw fine distinctions.

discriminating (dĭs-krĭm′ə-nā′tĭng) *adj.* **1.** Making fine distinctions. **2.** Selective.

disengage (dĭs′ĭn-gāj′) *v.* To release or get free.

dishearten (dĭs-härt′n) *v.* To discourage; depress.— **disheartened** *adj.*

dismay (dĭs-mā′) *v.* To fill with alarm.—**dismayed** *adj.*

dismount (dĭs-mount′) *v.* To get down from a horse.

dispatch (dĭs-păch′) *v.* To send off.

dispense (dĭs-pĕns′) *v.* To give out; distribute.

disposition (dĭs′pə-zĭsh′ən) *n.* **1.** Personality; temperament. **2.** The manner in which something is arranged or settled.

dispute (dĭs-pyōōt′) *v.* To argue.

disreputable (dĭs-rĕp′yə-tə-bəl) *adj.* Not respectable; disgraceful.

dissuade (dĭ-swād′) *v.* To persuade someone not to do something.

distract (dĭs-trăkt′) *v.* To turn one's attention elsewhere.—**distracted** *adj.*

distraction (dĭs-trăk′shən) *n.* Anything that draws attention from an original focus of interest.

distress (dĭs-trĕs′) *n.* Discomfort.

divert (dĭ-vûrt′, dī-) *v.* To turn aside.—**diverted** *adj.*

divine (dĭ-vīn′) *v.* To guess; to know by intuition.

domain (dō-mān′) *n.* Territory.

domestic (də-mĕs′tĭk) *adj.* Having to do with the home.

dour (dŏŏr, dour) *adj.* Gloomy.

draggle (drăg′əl) *v.* To make dirty.—**draggled** *adj.*

dram (drăm) *n.* A small amount of something.

drench (drĕnch) *v.* To wet thoroughly.

drivel (drĭv′əl) *n.* Stupid talk.

duly (dōō′le, dyōō′-) *adv.* Properly.

dun (dŭn) *adj.* Grayish brown.

duplicate (dōō′plĭ-kĭt, dyōō′-) *n.* An exact copy.

E

ebb (ĕb) *v.* To diminish; weaken.

eccentric (ĕk-sĕn′trĭk, ĭk-) *adj.* Peculiar; odd.

eccentricity (ĕk′sĕn-trĭs′ə-tē) *n.* Peculiarity.

ecstatic (ĕk-stăt′ĭk) *adj.* Very joyful.

eddy (ĕd′ē) *n.* A current moving against another current, usually in a swirling motion.

eerie (îr′ē) *adj.* Weird.

efficiency (ĭ-fĭsh′ən-sē) *n.* Ability to get things done with little effort.

elaborate (ĭ-lăb′ər-ĭt) *adj.* Complicated.

elicit (ĭ-lĭs′ĭt) *v.* To draw out.

elocution (ĕl′ə-kyōō′shən) *n.* The art of speaking well.

eloquence (ĕl′ə-kwəns) *n.* Forceful or persuasive speech.

eloquent (el′ə-kwənt) *adj.* Expressive.

elude (ĭ-lōōd′) *v.* To escape from.

emanate (ĕm′ə-nāt′) *v.* To flow out; issue.

embed (ĕm-bĕd′, ĭm-) *v.* To fix firmly in something.

ember (ĕm′bər) *n.* A glowing piece of coal or wood from a dying fire.

emblem (ĕm′bləm) *n.* A badge.

embolden (ĕm-bōl′dən) *v.* To make bold or courageous.—**emboldened** *adj.*

emerge (ĭ-mûrj′) *v.* To appear.

emery (ĕm′ə-rē, ĕm′rē) *n.* A substance used for grinding and polishing.

emissary (ĕm′ə-sĕr′ē) *n.* Messenger or representative.

emphatic (ĕm-făt′ĭk) *adj.* Definite.—**emphatically** *adv.*

endear (ĕn-dîr′, ĭn-) *v.* To make dear or beloved.

endeavor (ĕn-dĕv′ər, ĭn-) *n.* An attempt.

engage (ĕn-gāj′, ĭn-) *v.* To employ.

engulf (ĕn-gŭlf′, ĭn-) *v.* To submerge; overwhelm.

enhance (ĕn-hăns′, -häns′, ĭn-) *v.* To make better.

enterprise (ĕn′tər-prīz′) *n.* An undertaking.

enthrall (ĕn-thrôl′, ĭn-) *v.* To hold as in a spell.—**enthralled** *adj.*

entreat (ĕn-trēt′, ĭn-) *v.* To beg.

entreaty (ĕn-trē′tē, ĭn-) *n.* A plea.

entwine (ĕn-twīn′, ĭn-) *v.* To twist around.

enumerate (ĭ-nōō′mə-rāt′, ĭ-nyōō′-) *v.* To list.

enumeration (ĭ-nōō′mə-rā′shən, ĭ-nyōō′-) *n.* A list of items.

envelop (ĕn-vĕl′əp, ĭn-) *v.* To cover completely.

enviable (ĕn′vē-ə-bəl) *adj.* Desirable.

envision (ĕn-vĭzh′ən) *v.* To imagine something that has not yet happened.

epidemic (ĕp′ə-dĕm′ĭk) *n.* A rapid spread of a disease.

equity (ĕk′wə-tē) *n.* Justice; fairness.

erratic (ĭ-răt′ĭk) *adj.* Irregular.—**erratically** *adv.*

essence (ĕs′əns) *n.* The essential nature of a person or a thing.

evolve (ĭ-vŏlv′) *v.* To develop gradually.

exact (ĕg-zăkt′, ĭg-) *v.* To demand; force.

exalt (ĕg-zôlt′, ĭg-) *v.* To raise to a high positon.—**exalted** *adj.*

exasperate (ĕg-zăs′pə-rāt, ĭg-) *v.* To make angry.—**exasperating** *adj.*

exceedingly (ĕk-sē′dĭng-lē, ĭk-) *adv.* Extremely.

excel (ĕk-sĕl′, ĭk-) *v.* To do better than others.

exemption (ĕg-zĕmp′shən) *n.* Release from obligation.

exhale (ĕks-hāl′, ĕk-sāl′, ĭk-sāl′) *v.* To breathe out.

exhilarate (ĕg-zĭl′ə-rāt′, ĭg-) *v.* To excite.—**exhilarating** *adj.*

exile (ĕg′zīl′, ĕk′sīl′) *n.* Separation from one's country.

exotic (ĕg-zŏt′ĭk, ĭg-) *adj.* Unusual and fascinating.

expectant (ĕk-spĕk′tənt, ĭk-) *adj.* Waiting for something to happen.

expiation (ĕk′spē-ā′shən) *n.* The act of making amends.

exploit (ĕks′ploit′) *n.* A daring act.

exposure (ĕk-spō′zhər, ĭk-) *n.* Being without protection from natural forces.

exquisite (ĕks′kwĭ-zĭt) *adj.* Extemely beautiful.—**exquisitely** *adv.*

extemporize (ĕk-stĕm′pə-rīz′, ĭk-) *v.* To improvise; to prepare something for temporary use.

extension (ĕk-stĕn′shən, ĭk-) *n.* An extra period of time allowed for payment of a debt.

extract (ĕk-străkt′, ĭk-) *v.* To pull out.

extricate (ĕk′strĭ-kāt′) *v.* To set free.

exude (ĕg-zōōd′, ĭg-, ĕk-sōōd′, ĭk-) *v.* To give off.

exultant (ĕg-zŭl′tənt, ĭg-) *adj.* Joyful.—**exultantly** *adv.*

exultation (ĕg′zŭl-tā′shən) *n.* Great joyfulness; triumph.

F

façade (fə-säd′) *n.* The front of a building.

fain (fān) *adv.* Willingly.

falter (fôl′tər) *v.* To show uncertainty.

famine (făm′ĭn) *n.* A severe and widespread shortage of food.

fancy (făn′sē) *v.* To imagine. *n.* Imagination; invention.

ă pat/ā pay/âr care/ä father/b bib/ch church/d deed/ĕ pet/ē be/f fife/g gag/h hat/hw which/ĭ pit/ī pie/îr pier/j judge/k kick/ l lid, needle/m mum/n no, sudden/ng thing/ŏ pot/ō toe/ô paw, for/oi noise/ou out/ŏŏ took/ōō boot/p pop/r roar/s sauce/ sh ship, dish/t tight/th thin, path/*th* this, bathe/ŭ cut/ûr urge/v valve/w with/y yes/z zebra, size/zh vision/ə about, item, edible, gallop, circus/ä *Fr.* ami/œ *Fr.* feu, *Ger.* schön/ü *Fr.* tu, *Ger.* über/кн *Ger.* ich, *Scot.* loch/ɴ *Fr.* bon.

fathom (făth′əm) v. **1.** To measure the depth of. **2.** To understand thoroughly. n. A unit of measurement equal to six feet.

feat (fēt) n. An act of great skill or courage.

feign (fān) v. To pretend.

ferocity (fə-rŏs′ə-tē) n. Fierceness.

fervent (fûr′vənt) adj. Very enthusiastic; intense.

festal (fĕs′təl) adj. Joyous; merry.

festive (fĕs′tĭv) adj. Merry.

fetter (fĕt′ər) v. To put in chains. n. A chain.

feud (fyood) n. A bitter, prolonged quarrel between two individuals or families.

flabbergast (flăb′ər-găst′) v. To shock and surprise. —**flabbergasted** adj.

flagging (flăg′ĭng) adj. Weakening.

flail (flāl) v. To move one's arms about vigorously.

flank (flăngk) v. To be on either side of. n. The side of something. —**flanked** adj.

flaw (flô) n. A defect. —**flawless** adj.

flax (flăks) n. A plant with delicate blue flowers.

fleck (flĕk) n. A spot. —**flecked** adj.

fledgling (flĕj′lĭng) n. A young bird.

flexible (flĕk′sə-bəl) adj. Capable of being bent.

flicker (flĭk′ər) v. To burn unsteadily.

flinch (flĭnch) v. To draw away; wince.

flounder (floun′dər) v. To struggle clumsily.

flush (flŭsh) v. To frighten out of a hiding place.

flustered (flŭs′tərd) adj. Upset; confused.

foible (foi′bəl) n. Weakness in character.

folly (fŏl′ē) n. Foolishness.

foolhardy (fool′här′dē) adj. Rash; foolishly daring.

forage (fôr′ĭj, fŏr′-) n. Food for domestic animals such as cattle, sheep, and horses.

foray (fôr′ā′) n. A surprise attack or raid.

forbearance (fôr-bâr′əns) n. Patience; self-control.

forlorn (fôr-lôrn′, fər-) adj. Deserted. —**forlornly** adv.

forsaken (fôr-sāk′ən) adj. Deserted.

fortitude (fôr′tə-tood′, -tyood′) n. Courage.

foul (foul) adj. Disgusting.

fount (fount) n. A source.

frantic (frăn′tĭk) adj. Wild. —**frantically** adv.

fraudulent (frô′jə-lənt) adj. Deceitful.

fray (frā) n. A fight.

frenzy (frĕn′zē) n. Violent activity.

fretful (frĕt′fəl) adj. Complaining; discontented.

fringe (frĭnj) v. To grow along the edge of.

frothing (frôth′ĭng, frŏth-) n. Enthusiasm.

functional (fŭngk′shən-əl) adj. Practical; usable.

furtive (fûr′tĭv) adj. Sneaky; sly. —**furtively** adv.

futility (fyoo-tĭl′ə-tē) n. Uselessness.

G

gait (gāt) n. A manner of walking.

gall (gôl) v. To irritate.

garble (gär′bəl) v. To mix up; confuse. —**garbled** adj.

garland (gär′lənd) n. A wreath.

gaudy (gô′dē) adj. Flashy; lacking taste.

gazebo (gə-zē′bō, -zā′bō) n. A roofed structure serving as a shelter.

gesticulate (jĕ-stĭk′yə-lāt′) v. To use gestures in place of speech.

gingerly (jĭn′jər-lē) adv. Carefully.

girth (gûrth) n. A strap that goes under the belly of an animal to secure a saddle or a pack.

glade (glād) n. An open area in a forest.

glaze (glāz) v. To apply a shiny coating. —**glazing** adj.

glower (glou′ər) v. To stare in an angry or ill-humored way.

glum (glŭm) adj. Gloomy; in low spirits. —**glumly** adv.

glutton (glŭt′n) n. One who overeats.

gouge (gouj) v. To cut or force.

greatcoat (grāt′kōt′) n. A heavy overcoat.

greenhouse (grēn′hous′) n. A glass-enclosed structure where plants are grown.

grim (grĭm) adj. Stern; unfriendly. —**grimly** adv.

grimace (grĭ-mās′, grĭm′ĭs) v. To twist or distort the face.

grisly (grĭz′lē) adj. Horrifying.

grizzle (grĭz′əl) v. To become gray. —**grizzled** adj.

grope (grōp) v. To feel one's way.

gross (grōs) adj. Referring to total income before deductions are made.

gruel (groo′əl) n. Thin watery porridge, usually made of oatmeal.

grueling (groo′ə-ling) adj. Harsh; extremely difficult.

guffaw (gə-fô′) n. A loud burst of laughter.

gullible (gŭl′ə-bəl) adj. Easily deceived or cheated.

gust (gŭst) n. A rush of wind. —**gusty** adj.

gut (gŭt) v. **1.** To destroy the insides of. **2.** To take out the inner organs. —**gutted** adj.

H

habitable (hăb′ə-tə-bəl) adj. Able to be lived in.

hamstring (hăm′strĭng′) v. To cripple by cutting the tendons in the hind legs.

hapless (hăp′lĭs) adj. Unlucky.

hark (härk) v. To listen.

harry (hăr′ē) v. To annoy constantly. —**harried** adj.

haughty (hô′tē) *adj.* Proud; arrogant.

havoc (hăv′ək) *n.* Extreme disorder.

headland (hĕd′lənd, -lănd′) *n.* A point of land that juts out into the water.

hearken (här′kən) *v.* To listen carefully.

heath (hēth) *n.* An open, uncultivated area; a moor.

heifer (hĕf′ər) *n.* A young cow.

heirloom (âr′lo͞om′) *n.* A prized family possession that is handed down from generation to generation.

helm (hĕlm) *n.* The steering wheel of a ship.

hemorrhage (hĕm′ə-rĭj) *n.* A heavy flow of blood.

hideous (hĭd′e-əs) *adj.* Ugly.

hoard (hôrd, hōrd) *v.* To store up or hide.

hobnail (hŏb′nāl) *n.* A nail put on the soles of shoes to keep them from wearing or slipping.

hoist (hoist) *v.* To lift.

homage (hŏm′ĭj, ŏm′-) *n.* Honor; respect.

hospitable (hŏs′pə-tə-bəl) *adj.* Friendly toward visitors.

hostile (hŏs′təl) *adj.* Unfriendly.

hover (hŭv′ər, hŏv′-) *v.* To remain suspended in one place in the air.

hummock (hŭm′ək) *n.* A small hill.

hunker (hŭng′kər) *v.* To crouch; squat.

hurl (hûrl) *v.* To throw vigorously.

hurtle (hûrt′l) *v.* To move with great speed.

hysteria (hĭ-stĕr′ē-ə) *n.* Uncontrolled emotion.

hysterical (hĭ-stĕr′ĭ-kəl) *adj.* Wildly emotional.

I

ignite (ĭg-nīt′) *v.* To set on fire.—**ignited** *adj.*

illuminate (ĭ-lo͞o′mə-nāt′) *v.* To light up.

immobile (ĭ-mō′bəl, -bēl′) *adj.* Not moving.—**immobility** *n.*

immortal (ĭ-môrt′l) *n.* One who will never die.—*adj.* Living forever.

impediment (ĭm-pĕd′ə-mənt) *n.* A hindrance.

imperceptible (ĭm′pər-sĕp′tə-bəl) *adj.* Barely noticeable.—**imperceptibly** *adv.*

imperial (ĭm-pîr′ē-əl) *adj.* **1.** Of superior size or quality. **2.** Majestic.

imperishable (ĭm-pĕr′ĭ-shə-bəl) *adj.* Not likely to be destroyed.

impiety (ĭm-pī′ə-tē) *n.* Lack of reverence for God; disrespect.

impish (ĭm′pĭsh) *adj.* Playful.

implore (ĭm-plôr′, -plōr′) *v.* To beg.

imposing (ĭm-pō′zĭng) *adj.* Impressive.

impressive (ĭm-prĕs′ĭv) *adj.* Creating a strong effect or impression.

improbable (ĭm-prŏb′ə-bəl) *adj.* Not likely.

inaudible (ĭn-ô′də-bəl) *adj.* Not able to be heard.

inaugurate (ĭn-ô′gyə-rāt′) *v.* To start officially.

incantation (ĭn-kăn-tā′shən) *n.* The chanting of words to cast a magic spell.

incarnate (ĭn-kär′nĭt) *adj.* In the flesh; embodied.

incessant (ĭn-sĕs′ənt) *adj.* Continuing without interruption.—**incessantly** *adv.*

incompetent (ĭn-kŏm′pə-tənt) *adj.* Lacking needed abilities; not capable.

incomprehensible (ĭn′kŏm-prĭ-hĕn′sə-bəl, ĭn-kŏm′-) *adj.* Unable to be understood; baffling.

inconspicuous (ĭn′kən-spĭk′yo͞o-əs) *adj.* Attracting little notice.

incredulous (ĭn-krĕj′ə-ləs) *adj.* Unwilling or unable to believe.

indifference (ĭn-dĭf′ər-əns) *n.* A lack of concern.—**indifferent** *adj.*—**indifferently** *adv.*

indignant (ĭn-dĭg′nənt) *adj.* Angry, especially at an injustice.—**indignantly** *adv.*

indignation (ĭn′dĭg-nā′shən) *n.* Anger, especially at an injustice.

indispensable (ĭn′dĭs-pĕn′sə-bəl) *adj.* Necessary.

induce (ĭn-do͞os′, -dyo͞os′) *v.* To persuade.

inert (ĭn-ûrt′) *adj.* Inactive.

inevitable (ĭn-ĕv′ə-tə-bəl) *adj.* Unavoidable.

inexplicable (ĭn-ĕk′splĭ-kə-bəl, ĭn′ĭk-splĭk′ə-bəl) *adj.* Not able to be explained.

infamous (ĭn′fə-məs) *adj.* Outrageous.

infatuated (ĭn-făch′o͞o-ā′tĭd) *adj.* Characterized by a foolish attraction to someone or something.

inflated (ĭn-flā′tĭd) *adj.* Expanded; puffed up.

infringe (ĭn-frĭnj′) *v.* To trespass; violate. **Infringe on** (or **upon**).

ingenious (ĭn-jēn′yəs) *adj.* Very clever.

inhospitable (ĭn-hŏs′pĭ-tə-bəl, ĭn′hŏ-spĭt′ə-bəl) *adj.* Unfriendly toward visitors.

insensible (ĭn-sĕn′sə-bəl) *adj.* So small as to be hardly noticeable.

ă pat/ā pay/âr care/ä father/b bib/ch church/d deed/ĕ pet/ē be/f fife/g gag/h hat/hw which/ĭ pit/ī pie/îr pier/j judge/k kick/ l lid, needle/m mum/n no, sudden/ng thing/ŏ pot/ō toe/ô paw, for/oi noise/ou out/o͝o took/o͞o boot/p pop/r roar/s sauce/ sh ship, dish/t tight/th thin, path/*th* this, bathe/ŭ cut/ûr urge/v valve/w with/y yes/z zebra, size/zh vision/ə about, item, edi- ble, gallop, circus/á *Fr.* ami/œ *Fr.* feu, *Ger.* schön/ü *Fr.* tu, *Ger.* über/ᴋʜ *Ger.* ich, *Scot.* loch/ɴ *Fr.* bon.

insolent (ĭn′sə-lənt) *adj.* Insulting.

insulation (ĭn′sə-lā′shən, ĭns′yə-) *n.* Something that prevents or reduces the passage of heat, electricity, sound, etc., in or out.

insuperable (ĭn-soo′pər-ə-bəl) *adj.* Unable to be overcome.

intercept (ĭn′tər-sĕpt′) *v.* To seize or stop on the way; cut off.

interlude (ĭn′tər-lood′) *n.* An intervening period of time.

interminable (ĭn-tûr′mə-nə-bəl) *adj.* Endless or seeming to be endless.—**interminably** *adv.*

intermittent (ĭn′tər-mĭt′ənt) *adj.* Stopping from time to time; not continuous.—**intermittently** *adv.*

intimate (ĭn′tə-māt′) *v.* To hint.—**intimation** *n.*

intolerable (ĭn-tŏl′ər-ə-bəl) *adj.* Unbearable.

intrude (ĭn-trood′) *n.* To enter without being welcome; to force one's way in.—**intruder** *n.*

invariable (ĭn-vâr′ē-ə-bəl) *adj.* Unchanging.—**invariably** *adv.*

invective (ĭn-vĕk′tĭv) *n.* Insulting or abusive language.

invincible (ĭn-vĭn′sə-bəl) *adj.* Not able to be conquered.

involuntary (ĭn-vŏl′ən-tĕr′ē) *adj.* Done without choice or intention.—**involuntarily** *adv.*

ironic (ī-rŏn′ĭk) *adj.* Opposite to what might be expected.—**ironically** *adv.*

irresolute (ī-rĕz′ə-loot′) *adj.* Undecided.

irrevocable (ī-rĕv′ə-kə-bəl) *adj.* Not able to be undone or recalled.

islet (ī′lĭt) *n.* A small island.

isolation (ī′sə-lā′shən) *n.* Aloneness.

J

jar (jär) *v.* To bump.

jaunty (jôn′tē, jän′-) *adj.* Gay.—**jauntily** *adv.*

jeer (jîr) *v.* To make fun of.

jetty (jĕt′ē) *n.* A pier, a landing place for ships.

jolt (jōlt) *v.* To shake about; bump into.

jovial (jō′vē-əl) *adj.* Merry; jolly.

jubilant (joo′bə-lənt) *adj.* Showing great joy.—**jubilantly** *adv.*

judicious (joo-dĭsh′əs) *adj.* Wise.—**judiciously** *adv.*

juncture (jŭngk′chər) *n.* A point in time.

justify (jŭs′tə-fī′) *v.* To defend.

K

kiln (kĭl, kĭln) *n.* An oven for baking or firing substances, especially pottery.

knoll (nōl) *n.* A small hill.

L

lacerate (lăs′ə-rāt) *v.* To tear.—**laceration** *n.*

lance (lăns, läns) *n.* A weapon with a long shaft and a pointed tip.

languid (lăng′gwĭd) *adj.* Without energy or enthusiasm.—**languidly** *adv.*

larceny (lär′sə-nē) *n.* Theft.

lash (lăsh) *v.* To tie securely.

launch (lônch, länch) *n.* A large, open motorboat.

lavish (lăv′ĭsh) *adj.* Generous.—**lavishly** *adv.*

lax (lăks) *adj.* Not strict; negligent.

lethal (lē′thəl) *adj.* Deadly.

level (lĕv′əl) *v.* To knock down.

liability (lī′ə-bĭl′ə-tē) *n.* A disadvantage.

lineage (lĭn′ē-ĭj) *n.* Family background.

linnet (lĭn′ĭt) *n.* A small songbird.

listless (lĭst′lĭs) *adj.* Showing no energy or interest.—**listlessly** *adv.*

lithe (līth) *adj.* Graceful.

loiter (loi′tər) *v.* To stand around idly or aimlessly.

lollop (lŏl′əp) *v.* To move in bounds or leaps.—**lolloping** *adj.*

loom (loom) *v.* To come into sight, as something fearful.—**loomed** *adj.*

lope (lōp) *v.* To move with an easy, bounding gait.

lucent (loo′sənt) *adj.* Glowing; luminous.

lumber (lŭm′bər) *v.* To walk with a heavy, awkward step.

luminous (loo′mə-nəs) *adj.* Able to glow in the dark.

lunge (lŭnj) *n.* A sudden forward movement.

lurch (lûrch) *v.* To stagger.

lurid (loor′ĭd) *adj.* Glowing or shining fiery red.

M

majestic (mə-jĕs′tĭk) *adj.* Grand; stately.

malevolence (mə-lĕv′ə-ləns) *n.* Ill will.

malice (măl′ĭs) *n.* Intention to harm another person.

mania (mā′nē-ə, mān′yə) *n.* Excessive fondness; craze.

manifest (măn′ə-fĕst′) *v.* To become evident.

martial (mär′shəl) *adj.* Eager to fight; warlike.

martyr (mär′tər) *n.* One who suffers or dies for something he or she believes in.

massive (măs′ĭv) *adj.* Huge.

mast (măst, mäst) *n.* A pole used to support the sails and rigging of a ship.

materialize (mə-tîr′ē-əl-īz′) *v.* To take shape.

materially (mə-tîr′ē-əl-ē) *adv.* Significantly.

mausoleum (mô′sə-lē′əm, mô′zə-) *n.* A large, grand tomb.

mawkish (mô′kĭsh) *adj.* Overly emotional.

maze (māz) *n.* **1.** A network of paths used in a laboratory to test animals. **2.** A puzzle; something that is confusing.

meander (mē-ăn′dər) *v.* To wander aimlessly.

megaphone (mĕg′ə-fōn′) *n.* A cone-shaped device to make the voice louder.

melancholy (mĕl′ən-kŏl′ē) *adj.* Sad; gloomy.

memorial (mə-môr′ē-əl, mə-mōr′-) *n.* Something, such as a monument or holiday, intended as a reminder of some person or event.

menagerie (mə-năj′ə-rē, mə-năzh′-) *n.* A zoo.

mesa (mā′sə) *n.* An elevation having steep sides and a flat top, usually found in the southwestern United States.

metabolism (mə-tăb′ə-lĭz′əm) *n.* The processes by which the body uses food or breaks it down into waste matter.

metropolis (mə-trŏp′ə-lĭs) *n.* A large city.

mettle (mĕt′l) *n.* Courage; worth.

microbe (mī′krōb′) *n.* A germ.

misjudge (mĭs-jŭj′) *v.* To judge wrongly.

mobility (mō-bĭl′ə-tē) *n.* Ability to move.

mockery (mŏk′ər-ē) *n.* Derision; ridicule.

moil (moil) *v.* To work hard.

molder (mōl′dər) *v.* To decay.—**moldering** *adj.*

molest (mə-lĕst′) *v.* To annoy.

monotonous (mə-nŏt′n-əs) *adj.* Lacking variety; dull because repetitious.

moony (mōō′nē) *adj.* Dreamy.

moor (moor) *n.* A stretch of open land, often swampy.

morality (mə-răl′ə-tē, mô-) *n.* Principles of right and wrong conduct.

mortal (môrt′l) *adj.* Subject to death.

mortgage (môr′gĭj) *v.* To pledge something valuable in return for a loan.

mosaic (mō-zā′ĭk) *n.* A picture or design made from small pieces of colored material such as stone or glass.

motivate (mō′tə-vāt′) *v.* To move to action.—**motivated** *adj.*

motive (mō′tĭv) *adj.* Causing motion.

mottle (mŏt′l) *v.* To mark with spots of various colors and shapes.—**mottled** *adj.*

mournful (môrn′fəl, mōrn′-) *adj.* Extremely sad.

mucilage (myōō′sə-lĭj) *n.* A type of glue.

musket (mŭs′kĭt) *n.* A shoulder gun used before the rifle was invented.

muster (mŭs′tər) *v.* To summon up; collect or gather.

myriad (mîr′ē-əd) *n.* A vast number.

N

network (nĕt′wôrk′) *n.* A structure made up of intersecting threads.

nominal (nŏm′ə-nəl) *adj.* Of minimal value.

nonchalance (nŏn′shə-läns′) *n.* A lack of concern.

notion (nō′shən) *n.* An idea.

nurture (nûr′chər) *v.* To rear; to care for.

O

obeisance (ō-bā′səns, ō-bē′-) *n.* An act of respect, such as bowing.

oblique (ō-blēk′, ə-) *adj.* At an angle; not straight.—**obliquely** *adv.*

obliterate (ə-blĭt′ə-rāt′) *v.* To remove completely; erase.—**obliterated** *adj.*

obscure (ŏb-skyoor′, əb-) *adj.* Unclear.

obstinate (ŏb′stə-nĭt) *adj.* Stubborn.

odious (ō′dē-əs) *adj.* Hateful.

ogre (ō′gər) *n.* A monster.

ointment (oint′mənt) *n.* A salve; something that soothes.

ominous (ŏm′ə-nəs) *adj.* Sinister; threatening.

omnivorous (ŏm-nĭv′ər-əs) *adj.* Eating every kind of food.

onyx (ŏn′ĭks) *n.* A semiprecious stone used in jewelry and other ornaments.

opaque (ō-pāk′) *adj.* Not permitting light to go through.

opportune (ŏp′ər-tōōn′, -tyōōn′) *adj.* Well-timed.

oppress (ə-prĕs′) *v.* To weigh down.—**oppressed** *adj.* Depressed or burdened.

option (ŏp′shən) *n.* A choice.

ordeal (ôr-dēl′) *n.* A difficult experience.

ornate (ôr-nāt′) *adj.* Very fancy.

ă pat/ā pay/âr care/ä father/b bib/ch church/d deed/ĕ pet/ē be/f fife/g gag/h hat/hw which/ĭ pit/ī pie/îr pier/j judge/k kick/ l lid, needle/m mum/n no, sudden/ng thing/ŏ pot/ō toe/ô paw, for/oi noise/ou out/ōō took/ōō boot/p pop/r roar/s sauce/ sh ship, dish/t tight/th thin, path/th this, bathe/ŭ cut/ûr urge/v valve/w with/y yes/z zebra, size/zh vision/ə about, item, edi- ble, gallop, circus/ä *Fr.* ami/œ *Fr.* feu, *Ger.* schön/ü *Fr.* tu, *Ger.* über/KH *Ger.* ich, *Scot.* loch/N *Fr.* bon.

P

pandemonium (păn'də-mō'nē-əm) *n.* Noisy confusion.

parasol (păr'ə-sôl', -sŏl') *n.* A small umbrella used for protection from the sun.

passel (păs'əl) *n.* A large number.

passionate (păsh'ən-ĭt) *adj.* Very affectionate.

passive (păs'ĭv) *adj.* Not participating.

patron (pā'trən) *n.* **1.** A customer. **2.** In ancient times, the god or goddess who protected a city.

patronize (pā'trə-nīz', păt'rə-) *v.* To be a regular customer.

peaked (pēkt, pē'-kĭd) *adj.* Pale.

peasant (pĕz'ənt) *n.* Someone who works the land; a country person of humble birth.

pedagogy (pĕd'ə-gō'jē, -gŏj'ē) *n.* Teaching.

pedestrian (pə-dĕs'trē-ən) *adj.* Walking.

pedigree (pĕd'ə-grē') *n.* **1.** Ancestry. **2.** A record of descent, particularly of purebred animals.

peer (pîr) *n.* An equal.

pelt (pĕlt) *v.* To run rapidly.

penance (pĕn'əns) *n.* Self-punishment for a sin or wrongdoing.

penetrate (pĕn'ə-trāt') *v.* To go through or into.

peninsula (pə-nĭn'syə-lə, -sə-lə) *n.* A land area almost completely surrounded by water.

perceive (pər-sēv') *v.* **1.** To become aware of. **2.** To understand. **3.** To notice or observe.

perceptible (pər-sĕp'tə-bəl) *adj.* Noticeable.

peril (pĕr'əl) *n.* Danger.—**perilous** *adj.*

perimeter (pə-rĭm'ə-tər) *n.* Limits; boundary.

periodic (pîr'ē-ŏd'ĭk) *adj.* At regular intervals—**periodically** *adv.*

perpendicular (pûr'pən-dĭk'yə-lər) *adj.* Upright; vertical.

perpetual (pər-pĕch'ōō-əl) *adj.* Lasting forever or for an unlimited time.

perplex (pər-plĕks') *v.* To confuse.

perplexed (pər-plĕkst') *adj.* Confused; puzzled.

persevere (pûr'sə-vîr') *v.* To continue in some line of action or thought despite obstacles.

persist (pər-sĭst', -zĭst') *v.* To continue to do something with great determination.

pervade (pər-vād') *v.* To spread through; extend all over.

perverted (pər-vûr'tĭd) *adj.* Misdirected; not used properly.

pestilence (pĕs'tə-ləns) *n.* A widely spread disease.

phantom (făn'təm) *n.* A ghost.

phenomenon (f ĭ-nŏm'ə-nŏn') *n.* An unusual happening.

philosophical (f ĭl'ə-sŏf'ĭ-kəl) *adj.* Wise—**philosophically** *adv.*

philter (f ĭl'tər) *n.* A magic potion or charm.

pilfer (pĭl'fər) *v.* To steal small amounts of money or objects of little value.

pillar (pĭl'ər) *n.* A column.

pillbox (pĭl'bŏks') *adj.* Shaped like a small, round box.

pine (pīn) *v.* To yearn for.

placid (plăs'ĭd) *adj.* Peaceful.

plague (plāg) *n.* A highly contagious, epidemic disease.

plaintive (plān'tĭv) *adj.* Sad.

pledge (plĕj) *n.* A token of a promise.

pliant (plī'ənt) *adj.* Easily bent; flexible.

plight (plīt) *n.* A difficult situation.

plowshare (plou'shâr') *n.* The cutting blade of a plow.

plump (plŭmp) *v.* To fall heavily.

poise (poiz) *v.* To balance or steady.—**poised** *adj.*

ponder (pŏn'dər) *v.* To think carefully about.

ponderous (pŏn'dər-əs) *adj.* **1.** Very heavy. **2.** Dull. —**ponderously** *adv.*

populous (pŏp'yə-ləs) *adj.* Having many people.

porcelain (pôrs'lĭn, pōrs'-, pōr'sə-lĭn) *n.* A hard, white, translucent earthenware, used for china, vases, and figurines.

potential (pə-tĕn'shəl) *adj.* Possible but not yet realized. *n.* An ability capable of development.

potter (pŏt'ər) *v. Chiefly British.* To putter; dawdle.

poultice (pōl'tĭs) *n.* A hot pack applied to a sore part of the body.

pounce (pouns) *v.* To spring on something.

prance (prăns, präns) *v.* To rise up on the hind legs and spring forward, as a horse.

precaution (prĭ-kô'shən) *n.* Care taken in advance, as a safeguard.

precedent (prĕs'ə-dənt) *n.* An act or decision used as an example in dealing with later cases.

precipice (prĕs'ə-pĭs) *n.* A steep cliff.

precipitous (prĭ-sĭp'ə-təs) *adj.* Steep.

preliminary (prĭ-lĭm'ə-nĕr'ē) *n.* Something that comes before the main action or business.

prelude (prĕl'yōōd', prē'lōōd') *n.* An introductory event.

premature (prē'mə-chŏŏr', -tŏŏr', -tyŏŏr') *adj.* Happening too early; too hasty.

premonition (prē'mə-nĭsh'ən, prĕm'ə-) *n.* A feeling that something bad will happen.

preoccupied (prē-ŏk'yə-pīd') *adj.* Already occupied or busy; engrossed.

preside (prĭ-zīd') *v.* To be in control.

presume (prĭ-zoom') *v.* To take for granted.

prevalent (prĕv'ə-lənt) *adj.* Widespread.

prig (prĭg) *n.* A smug, pompous person.

prim (prĭm) *adj.* Formal.—**primly** *adv.*

prime (prīm) *v.* To get a gun ready for firing.

priming (prīm'ĭng) *n.* Powder or other explosive material used to set off a charge in a gun.

primitive (prĭm'ə-tĭv) *adj.* Belonging to earliest times.

procure (prō-kyŏor', prə-) *v.* To get; obtain.

profess (prə-fĕs', prō-) *v.* To claim; declare.—**professing** *n.*

profusion (prə-fyoo'zhən, prō-) *n.* A large amount.

projection (prə-jĕk'shən) *n.* Something that sticks out.

prolific (prō-lĭf'ĭk) *adj.* Abundant.

prophecy (prŏf'ə-sē) *n.* A prediction.

prospector (prŏs'pĕk'tər) *n.* Someone who looks for oil or mineral deposits.

protrude (prō-trood') *v.* To stick out.

providence (prŏv'ə-dəns, -dĕns') *n.* **1.** The care and control exercised by God over the universe. **2. (P-)** God.

province (prŏv'ĭns) *n.* An area of duties and responsibilities.

provoke (prə-vōk') *v.* To stir up.—**provoking** *adj.*

prowess (prou'ĭs) *n.* Great ability or skill; strength.

pry (prī) *v.* To open something with difficulty.

pungent (pŭn'jənt) *adj.* Sharp-smelling.

puny (pyoo'nē) *adj.* Weak; undersized.

purgative (pûr'gə-tĭv) *n.* A laxative.

pyre (pīr) *n.* A funeral pile on which a dead body is burned.

Q

quack (kwăk) *adj.* Referring to someone or something that pretends to have power to cure disease.

quail (kwāl) *v.* To cower or cringe in fear.

quarters (kwôr'tərz) *n.* The place where one lives.

quell (kwĕl) *v.* To put down; quiet.

quench (kwĕnch) *v.* To put an end to.

quest (kwĕst) *n.* A search.

quiver (kwĭv'ər) *v.* To tremble.—**quivering** *adj.*

R

racy (rā'sē) *adj.* Daring.—**racily** *adv.*

radiant (rā'dē-ənt) *adj.* Bright; glowing.

radiate (rā'dē-āt') *v.* To send out rays of light or heat.

ramshackle (răm'shăk'əl) *adj.* Rickety; likely to fall apart.

rapture (răp'chər) *n.* A feeling of great joy.

ravenous (răv'ən-əs) *adj.* Extremely hungry.

recitation (rĕs'ə-tā'shən) *n.* Something that is told aloud from memory.

reckon (rĕk'ən) *v.* To guess.

recollect (rĕk'ə-lĕkt') *v.* To remember.

recommend (rĕk'ə-mĕnd') *v.* To advise.

recompense (rĕk'əm-pĕns') *v.* To reward.

redeem (rĭ-dēm') *v.* To recover.

redress (rĭ-drĕs') *v.* To make up for.

reek (rēk) *v.* To give off a strong smell.

reel (rēl) *v.* To sway; stagger.

refrain (rĭ-frān') *n.* A part of a poem or song that is regularly repeated. *v.* To hold back.

refuge (rĕf'yooj) *n.* Shelter.

refugee (rĕf'yoo-jē') *n.* A person who flees from danger to a safe place.

rehabilitation (rē'hə-bĭl'ə-tā'shən) *adj.* Concerned with using education or therapy to help someone.

reluctant (rĭ-lŭk'tənt) *adj.* Unwilling.—**reluctantly** *adv.*

reminiscent (rĕm'ə-nĭs'ənt) *adj.* Recalling some memory.

remote (rĭ-mōt') *adj.* Distant; aloof.

repast (rĭ-păst', -päst') *n.* A meal.

repentance (rĭ-pĕn'təns) *n.* Sorrow for wrongdoing.

repentant (rĭ-pĕn'tənt) *adj.* Showing remorse or sorrow for one's sins.

replenish (rĭ-plĕn'ĭsh) *v.* To fill again.

replica (rĕp'lə-kə) *n.* A copy.

reprimand (rĕp'rə-mănd', -mänd') *n.* A severe scolding.

reputed (rĭ-pyoo'tĭd) *adj.* Generally thought or considered.

ă pat/ā pay/âr care/ä father/b bib/ch church/d deed/ĕ pet/ē be/f fife/g gag/h hat/hw which/ĭ pit/ī pie/îr pier/j judge/k kick/ l lid, needle/m mum/n no, sudden/ng thing/ŏ pot/ō toe/ô paw, for/oi noise/ou out/oo took/oo boot/p pop/r roar/s sauce/ sh ship, dish/t tight/th thin, path/th this, bathe/ŭ cut/ûr urge/v valve/w with/y yes/z zebra, size/zh vision/ə about, item, edible, gallop, circus/ä *Fr.* ami/œ *Fr.* feu, *Ger.* schön/ü *Fr.* tu, *Ger.* über/кн *Ger.* ich, *Scot.* loch/N *Fr.* bon.

residential (rĕz'ə-dĕn'shəl) *adj.* Referring to the place where one lives.

resign (rĭ-zīn') *n.* To give over; consent.

resolute (rĕz'ə-lo͞ot') *adj.* Determined; unyielding.

resolution (rĕz'ə-lo͞o'shən) *n.* A decision or determination to do something.

resolve (rĭ-zŏlv') *v.* To make a decision.

resound (rĭ-zound') *v.* **1.** To echo back. **2.** To make a loud noise.

resourceful (rĭ-sôrs'fəl, rĭ-sōrs'-, rĭ-zôrs'-, rĕ-zōrs'-) *adj.* Clever in finding ways to handle problems.— **resourcefulness** *n.*

respite (rĕs'pĭt) *n.* An interval of rest.

restive (rĕs'tĭv) *adj.* Restless.

retort (rĭ-tôrt') *v.* To answer in a sharp or witty way.

revere (rĭ-vîr') *v.* To show deep respect toward someone or something.—**revered** *adj.*

reverence (rĕv'ər-əns) *v.* To honor.

ricochet (rĭk'ə-shā', -shĕt') *v.* To skip off a surface after striking it at an angle.

riled (rīld) *adj.* Annoyed; angered.

riotous (rī'ət-əs) *adj.* Abundant; lush.

rite (rīt) *n.* A ceremonial act.

ritual (rĭch'o͞o-əl) *n.* A ceremony.

rivulet (rĭv'yə-lĭt) *n.* A small stream.

roan (rōn) *adj.* Reddish brown speckled with white or gray.

robust (rō-bŭst', rō'bŭst) *adj.* Husky; healthy and strong.

rogue (rōg) *n.* A playful person; rascal.

roguish (rō'gĭsh) *adj.* Mischievous.

root (ro͞ot, ro͝ot) *v.* To dig in the earth with the snout.

rout (rout) *v.* To drive out.

rowdy (rou'dē) *adj.* Rough.

rude (ro͞od) *adj.* Crude; rough.

rudiment (ro͞o'də-mənt) *n.* A basic principle. (Often used in the plural.)

rummage (rŭm'ĭj) *v.* To search through a collection of objects.—**rummaging** *n.*

S

saffron (săf'rən) *adj.* Orange-yellow.

sagacious (sə-gā'shəs) *adj.* Wise.

sage (sāj) *n.* A wise person.

sanction (săngk'shən) *v.* To approve.

sanctuary (săngk'cho͞o-ĕr'ē) *n.* A safe place.

sanitarium (săn'ə-târ'ē-əm) *n.* A place where one may go to rest or to recover from an illness.

saucy (sô'sē) *adj.* Pert; bold.

saunter (sôn'tər) *v.* To walk slowly.

scabbard (skăb'ərd) *n.* A holder for a dagger or sword.

scepter (sĕp'tər) *n.* A staff a king or queen holds as a sign of authority.

schooner (sko͞o'nər) *n.* A kind of sailing ship having two or more masts.

scope (scōp) *n.* Reach.

scorch (skôrch) *v.* To burn.

score (skôr, skōr) *n.* A group of twenty.

scourge (skûrj) *v.* To whip.

scrawny (skrô'nē) *adj.* Skinny.

scroll (skrōl) *n.* A roll of paper or other writing material.

scuffle (skŭf'əl) *n.* A fight.

scurry (skûr'ē) *v.* To hurry. *n.* **scurry, scurrying.**

scurvy (skûr'vē) *adj.* Vile; contemptible.

scuttle (skŭt'l) *v.* To move hastily. *n.* A container for coal.

sear (sîr) *v.* To burn the surface of something.— **searing** *adj.*

sensuous (sĕn'sho͞o-əs) *adj.* Pleasing to the senses.

sentiment (sĕn'tə-mənt) *n.* A feeling; emotion.

sentimental (sĕn'tə-mĕnt'l) *adj.* Acting from feeling rather than from reason.

servitude (sûr'və-to͞od', -tyo͞od') *n.* Slavery.

shaft (shăft, shäft) *n.* A ray of light.

shamble (shăm'bəl) *v.* To shuffle; to walk in an unsteady manner.

sheepish (shēp'ĭsh) *adj.* Embarrassed.—**sheepishly** *adv.*

shiftless (shĭft'lĭs) *adj.* Lazy.

shoat (shōt) *n.* A young pig.

shorn (shôrn, shōrn) *adj.* Deprived.

shroud (shroud) *v.* To wrap in a burial garment.

shuttle (shŭt'l) *n.* A device used in weaving.

sidle (sīd'l) *v.* To move sideways cautiously or stealthily.

silhouette (sĭl'o͞o-ĕt') *v.* To outline.—**silhouetted** *adj.*

simultaneous (sī'məl-tā'nē-əs, sĭm'əl-) *adj.* Happening at the same time.—**simultaneously** *adv.*

sinister (sĭn'ĭ-stər) *adj.* Threatening.

skein (skān) *n.* A length of yarn wound in a coil.

skeptical (skĕp'tĭ-kəl) *adj.* Doubting; questioning.

skinflint (skĭn'flĭnt') *n.* A miser.

skirt (skûrt) *v.* To go around; avoid.

skitter (skĭt'ər) *v.* To move quickly over water.

skulk (skŭlk) *v.* To move in a quiet, fearful way.

slack (slăk) *adj.* **1.** Weak. **2.** Loose.

slacken (slăk'ən) *v.* To slow down.

slander (slăn'dər) *n.* Spoken statements damaging

to another person's character or reputation.

slither (slĭth'ər) *v.* To slide.

slobber (slŏb'ər) *v.* To drool.

sluice (slo͞os) *n.* An artificial channel for water.

smolder (smōl'dər) *v.* To burn without a flame.— **smoldering** *adj.*

snappish (snăp'ĭsh) *adj.* Irritable; apt to speak sharply.

snigger (snĭg'ər) *v.* To laugh in a sneaky way. Same as *snicker.*

sober (sō'bər) *adj.* Serious.

socket (sŏk'ĭt) *n.* An opening into which something can fit.

sodden (sŏd'n) *adj.* Thoroughly soaked.

solarium (sō-lâr'ē-əm) *n.* A glassed-in room which receives sunlight.

solder (sŏd'ər, sôd'-) *v.* To mend with solder, a metal alloy, which when melted can be used to connect metal parts.—**soldered** *adj.*

solemn (sŏl'əm) *adj.* Serious; grave.

souse (sous) *n.* Pickled pork.

sow (sō) *v.* To plant seeds.—**sower** *n.*

span (spăn) *v.* To stretch across.

spar (spär) *n.* A pole used to support a ship's sail.

spasm (spăz'əm) *n.* A fit.

specter (spĕk'tər) *n.* A ghost.

spindle (spĭnd'l) *v.* To send out thin threads.

spineless (spīn'lĭs) *adj.* Without courage; weak-willed.

splotch (splŏch) *n.* A stain or spot.

splutter (splŭt'ər) *v.* To speak in an excited, confused way.

spontaneous (spŏn-tā'nē-əs) *adj.* Not planned.

spouse (spous, spouz) *n.* A husband or wife.

sprint (sprĭnt) *v.* To run quickly.

spume (spyo͞om) *n.* Foam; froth.

spur (spûr) *v.* To urge a horse forward by using spurs. *n.* Pointed devices attached to a rider's boots.

squeamish (skwē'mĭsh) *adj.* Easily sickened or disgusted.

staccato (stə-kä'tō) *adj.* Abrupt and emphatic.

stark (stärk) *adj.* Rigid.

stately (stāt'lē) *adj.* Dignified.

steed (stēd) *n.* A high-spirited horse.

sterile (stĕr'əl) *adj.* Barren.—**sterility** *n.*

stevedore (stē'və-dôr, -dōr') *n.* Someone who loads or unloads a ship.

stigma (stĭg'mə) *n.* A mark of disgrace.

stipulate (stĭp'yə-lāt') *v.* To state the conditions of an agreement.—**stipulated** *adj.*

stolid (stŏl'ĭd) *adj.* Unemotional.

stratagem (străt'ə-jəm) *n.* A trick or scheme.

strategic (strə-tē'jĭk) *adj.* Important to the strategy, or plan of action.—**strategically** *adv.*

strive (strīv) *v.* To try hard; struggle.

stubble (stŭb'əl) *n.* The stumps of crops remaining after a harvest.

stucco (stŭk'ō) *n.* A covering used for building surfaces, made of cement and other materials.

stupendous (sto͞o-pĕn'dəs, styo͞o-) *adj.* Overwhelming.

stupor (sto͞o'pər, styo͞o'-) *n.* A confused state; daze.

subdue (səb-do͞o', -dyo͞o') *v.* To bring under control.

submerge (səb-mûrj') *v.* To put under water.— **submerged** *adj.*

subsequent (sŭb'sə-kwənt) *adj.* Succeeding.

subside (səb-sīd') *v.* To settle down.

subsist (səb-sĭst') *v.* To live.

succulent (sŭk'yə-lənt) *adj.* Juicy.

suet (so͞o'ĭt) *n.* Fatty tissue used in cooking.

sulky (sŭl'kē) *adj.* Slow-moving; sluggish.—**sulkily** *adv.*

sullen (sŭl'ən) *adj.* Gloomy; ill-humored.—**sullenly** *adv.*

sultry (sŭl'trē) *adj.* Hot and humid.

summerhouse (sŭm'ər-hous') *n.* A small open structure in a garden.

sumptuous (sŭmp'cho͞o-əs) *adj.* Extravagant; luxurious.

sunder (sŭn'dər) *v.* To sever or break something apart.

supple (sŭp'əl) *adj.* Flexible.

supplicate (sŭp'lĭ-kāt') *v.* To beg.—**supplication** *n.*

supposition (sŭp'ə-zĭsh'ən) *n.* Something thought to be true.

surfeit (sûr'fĭt) *v.* To overfeed.—**surfeited** *adj.*

surge (sûrj) *v.* **1.** To rise up or swell. **2.** To increase suddenly.

surly (sûr'lē) *adj.* Bad-tempered; rude.

ă pat/ā pay/âr care/ä father/b bib/ch church/d deed/ĕ pet/ē be/f fife/g gag/h hat/hw which/ĭ pit/ī pie/îr pier/j judge/k kick/ l lid, needle/m mum/n no, sudden/ng thing/ŏ pot/ō toe/ô paw, for/oi noise/ou out/o͝o took/o͞o boot/p pop/r roar/s sauce/ sh ship, dish/t tight/th thin, path/th this, bathe/ŭ cut/ûr urge/v valve/w with/y yes/z zebra, size/zh vision/ə about, item, edi- ble, gallop, circus/à *Fr.* ami/œ *Fr.* feu, *Ger.* schön/ü *Fr.* tu, *Ger.* über/кн *Ger.* ich, *Scot.* loch/N *Fr.* bon.

surmount (sər-mount′) *v.* **1.** To climb up and over. **2.** To be at the top of.

suspend (sə-spĕnd′) *v.* To hang.

sustain (sə-stān′) *v.* To support.—**sustained** *adj.*

swagger (swăg′ər) *v.* To walk in a bold, self-important manner.

T

tableau (tăb′lō′, tă-blō′) *n.* A striking scene.

tactful (tăkt′fəl) *adj.* Showing sensitivity to another's feelings.

talon (tăl′ən) *n.* The claw of a bird or other animal.

tantalize (tăn′tə-līz′) *v.* To tease by offering something and then withdrawing it.—**tantalizing** *adj.*

tarry (tăr′ē) *v.* To linger.

tart (tärt) *adj.* **1.** Sharp. **2.** Sarcastic.—**tartly** *adv.*

taunt (tônt) *v.* To make fun of.

taut (tôt) *adj.* Pulled tight.

tauten (tôt′n) *v.* To pull tight.—**tautened** *adj.*

tawny (tô′nē) *adj.* Tan; brownish-yellow.

teeter (tē′tər) *v.* To step or walk uncertainly.

terrarium (tə-râr′ē-əm) *n.* An enclosed container in which small plants or animals are kept.

terse (tûrs) *adj.* Brief; to the point.—**tersely** *adv.*

testy (tĕs′tē) *adj.* Touchy; irritable.—**testily** *adv.*

tether (tĕ*th*′ər) *v.* To confine an animal's movements to a limited area by tying it to a rope or chain.

thatch (thăch) *n.* A roof covering made of straw or leaves.

thong (thông, thŏng) *n.* A leather cord.

thresh (thrĕsh) *v.* To separate grain from straw.—**threshing** *adj.*

threshold (thrĕsh′ōld′, thrĕsh′hōld′) *n.* A doorway.

throng (thrŏng) *n.* A great number of people.

timorous (tĭm′ər-əs) *adj.* Timid.

toil (toil) *v.* To work hard.

topple (tŏp′əl) *v.* To fall over.

torrent (tôr′ənt, tŏr′-) *n.* **1.** A fast-moving stream. **2.** An abundant or violent flow.

torso (tôr′sō) *n.* A human body without the head or limbs.

totter (tŏt′ər) *v.* To move unsteadily.—**tottering** *adj.*

trace (trās) *n.* One of the chains that connect an animal to the wagon it is pulling.

trackless (trăk′lĭs) *adj.* Unmarked; without paths or trails.

tradition (trə-dĭsh′ən) *n.* A longstanding custom or practice.

train (trān) *n.* That part of a gown that trails on the ground.

trance (trăns) *n.* A dreamlike state.

tranquil (trăn′kwəl) *adj.* Calm.—**tranquilly** *adv.*

tranquillity (trăn-kwĭl′ə-tē) *n.* Peacefulness; serenity.

transaction (trăn-săk′shən, -zăk′shən) *n.* A business dealing.

transcend (trăn-sĕnd′) *v.* To rise above.

transfix (trăns-fĭks′) *v.* To make motionless.

transient (trăn′shənt, -zhənt, -zē-ənt) *adj.* Staying only briefly.

translucent (trăns-loo′sənt, trănz′-) *adj.* Allowing light to shine through but not allowing a clear view of anything beyond.

transparent (trăns-pâr′ənt, -păr′ənt) *adj.* Able to be seen through.

transplant (trăns-plănt′ -plänt′) *v.* To dig up and replant in another place.

transpose (trăns-pōz′) *v.* To change a piece of music from one key to another.

tremor (trĕm′ər) *n.* A trembling movement.

tremulous (trĕm′yə-ləs) *adj.* Trembling.

trespass (trĕs′pəs, -păs′) *n.* Violation of a law or duty.

trifle (trī′fəl) *v.* To treat lightly, as if unimportant.

trivial (trĭv′ē-əl) *adj.* Of little value or importance.

troll (trōl) *v.* To fish by dragging a line through water.

trough (trôf, trŏf) *n.* A long, narrow container that holds water or feed for animals.

turf (tûrf) *n.* Grass-covered soil.

turmoil (tûr′moil) *n.* Confusion.

turret (tûr′ĭt) *n.* A small tower.

tutor (too′tər, tyoo′-) *n.* A private teacher.

twine (twīn) *v.* To twist.

U

unanimous (yoo-năn′ə-məs) *adj.* Of one mind.

uncanny (ŭn′kăn′ē) *adj.* Strange.

uncommon (ŭn′kŏm′ən) *adj.* Unusual.—**uncommonly** *adv.*

understate (ŭn′dər-stāt′) *v.* To express in a restrained way.—**understated** *adj.*

unimpaired (ŭn′ĭm-pârd′) *adj.* Not damaged or lessened.

unique (yoo-nēk′) *adj.* **1.** Having no equal. **2.** One and only.

unutterable (ŭn′ŭt′ər-ə-bəl) *adj.* Not capable of being expressed or described.

upsurge (ŭp′sûrj′) *v.* To rise up.—**upsurgence** *n.*

urchin (ûr′chĭn) *n.* A mischievous youngster.

usurer (yōō′zhər-ər) *n.* Someone who lends money at a very high rate of interest.

V

vale (vāl) *n.* A valley.

vandalism (vănd′l-ĭz′əm) *n.* Intentional destruction of property, especially beautiful property.

vapor (vā′pər) *n.* A mist.

vault (vôlt) *n.* **1.** An arched structure. **2.** The sky.

veer (vîr) *v.* To change direction.—**veering** *adj.*

vehement (vē′ə-mənt) *adj.* Showing great force or feeling.—**vehemently** *adv.*

veneration (vĕn′ə-rā′shən) *n.* Great respect or reverence.

venison (vĕn′ə-sən, -zən) *n.* The flesh of deer used as food.

venom (vĕn′əm) *n.* **1.** Poison. **2.** Evil; malice.—**venomous** *adj.*

veranda (və-răn′də) *n.* A porch.

verdure (vûr′jər) *n.* Flourishing vegetation.

vermilion (vər-mĭl′yən) *adj.* Of a vivid-red color.

vestige (vĕs′tĭj) *n.* A trace of something that once existed.

vex (vĕks) *v.* To annoy.—**vexed** *adj.*

vexation (vĕk-sā′shən) *n.* Annoyance.

vicious (vĭsh′əs) *adj.* Dangerous; violent.

vigil (vĭj′əl) *n.* A period of watchfulness.

vigilance (vĭj′ə-ləns) *n.* Alertness.

villa (vĭl′ə) *n.* A country home.

vindictive (vĭn-dĭk′tĭv) *adj.* Revengeful.

virtually (vûr′chōō-ə-lē) *adv.* In effect; practically.

visceral (vĭs′ər-əl) *adj.* Very emotional.

vogue (vōg) *n.* Fashion.

vow (vou) *v.* To promise solemnly.

W

wager (wā′jər) *n.* A bet.

waggish (wăg′ĭsh) *adj.* Playful.

waistcoat (wĕs′kĭt, wāst′kōt) *n.* A vest.

wallow (wŏl′ō) *v.* To roll about.

wan (wŏn) *adj.* Weak; pale.—**wanly** *adv.*

warp (wôrp) *n.* The threads in a fabric that run lengthwise.

wary (wâr′ē) *adj.* Cautious.—**warily** *adv.*

wash (wŏsh, wôsh) *n.* The dry bed of a stream.

waver (wā′vər) *v.* To hesitate; be unsteady.—**wavering** *adj.*

wend (wĕnd) *v.* To go.

wharf (hwôrf) *n.* A place where ships are loaded and unloaded; dock.

wheel (hwēl) *v.* **1.** To turn around quickly. **2.** To fly in a circular path.

wheeze (hwēz) *n.* A whistling sound made when breathing is difficult.

whet (hwĕt) *v.* To stimulate or sharpen.

whimper (hwĭm′pər) *v.* To sob softly. *n.* A low whining sound.—**whimpering** *adj.*

whimsical (hwĭm′zĭ-kəl) *adj.* Unpredictable; odd.

whimsy (hwĭm′zē) *n.* Strange or fanciful humor.

wickerwork (wĭk′ər-wûrk′) *adj.* Made of wicker—twigs or sticks woven together for furniture or baskets.

wicket (wĭk′ĭt) *n.* A door or gate.

wily (wī′lē) *adj.* Sly; tricky.

wince (wĭns) *v.* To make a face as in pain or embarrassment.

winnow (wĭn′ō) *v.* To blow husks away from the grain.

wobbly (wŏb′lē) *adj.* Unsteady; shaky.

writhe (rī*th*) *v.* To twist or turn; squirm.

wrought (rôt) *adj.* Done.

ă pat/ā pay/âr care/ä father/b bib/ch church/d deed/ĕ pet/ē be/f fife/g gag/h hat/hw which/ĭ pit/ī pie/îr pier/j judge/k kick/ l lid, needle/m mum/n no, sudden/ng thing/ŏ pot/ō toe/ô paw, for/oi noise/ou out/ōō took/ōō boot/p pop/r roar/s sauce/ sh ship, dish/t tight/th thin, path/*th* this, bathe/ŭ cut/ûr urge/v valve/w with/y yes/z zebra, size/zh vision/ə about, item, edible, gallop, circus/á *Fr.* ami/œ *Fr.* feu, *Ger.* schön/ü *Fr.* tu, *Ger.* über/ĸʜ *Ger.* ich, *Scot.* loch/ɴ *Fr.* bon.

OUTLINE OF SKILLS

Page numbers in italics refer to entries in the Guide to Literary Terms and Techniques

READING/LITERARY SKILLS

WRITING

Writing About Literature

Creative Writing

Descriptive Writing

Narrative Writing

Expository Writing

SPEAKING AND ARTWORK

EXTENDING YOUR STUDY

INDEX OF CONTENTS BY TYPES

Poetry

INDEX OF FINE ART AND ILLUSTRATIONS

PHOTO CREDITS

INDEX OF AUTHORS AND TITLES

The page numbers in italics indicate where a brief biography of the author is located.

3
4
5
I 6
J 7